The Charlotte Armstrong Reader

The Charlotte

Armstrong Reader

COWARD-McCANN, Inc.
New York

Preface by ALICE CROMIE

Contents

Preface

by ALICE CROMIE

YEARS BACK in my first weeks of conducting "Crime on My Hands," a column of mystery reviews in the Chicago *Tribune*, my editor received a letter from Charlotte Armstrong saying that not only had she enjoyed my review of her current book, *A Little Less Than Kind*, but she had memorized it. I sat back confident that something of the sort would follow every time I could summon up a kind word for a piece of crime fiction, wholly unaware that the lady's grace was as rare and considerable as her talent. By the time this compliment fantasy had died from starvation, it was the season for another Armstrong novel and I had a twinge of worry that I might not like it. I was never quite such a dolt again; the only fretting to be done about Miss Armstrong was where to find a fresh superlative.

Charlotte Armstrong, queen of suspense, who kept the title in America although some British pretenders have made valiant tries for it, was born on May 2, 1905, in Vulcan, Michigan, the daughter of a mining engineer. At twelve she wrote her first play, cast it with neighborhood talent, retaining the starring role for herself, produced it in a barn, and raked in one solid nickel as profit. Thereafter she wrote for school publications wherever encountered and carefully bypassed journalism courses at Ferry Hall in Lake Forest, Illinois, the University of Wisconsin, and Barnard College, where she received an AB degree in 1925.

After graduation came a brief, quixotic whirl through the business world as she answered telephones in the classified advertising department of the New York *Times*, became a fashion reporter for *Breath of the Avenue*, a buyers' guide, and later had a try at working for a certified public accounting firm. The *New Yorker* published some of her poems. She married Jack Lewi in Chicago and for the next decade kept on writing "while the baby napped." The babies were Jeremy Brett Lewi, born in 1928, Jacquelin Lewi, 1935, and Peter Armstrong Lewi, 1937.

In 1939 her first play on Broadway, *The Happiest Days,* a tragedy about the generation gap, was produced under the direction of Marc Connelly and starred Uta Hagen. The days were short. Two years later a comedy, *Ring Around Elizabeth,* was also destined to flop in Manhattan, although perversely Philadelphia loved it. Luckily the thwarted playwright had a case of flu which gave her time to read all the mysteries available from the New Rochelle public library and to conclude that she could write one herself. It was *Lay On, MacDuff,* a propitious title, for Charlotte Armstrong was on her way at last, and no one since ever has cried, "Hold, enough!"

Her own autobiography, in an author's questionnaire, is short and snappily typed, with floating capitals and lost apostrophes, as if she couldn't wait to be done with it and get on to something more important. It concludes with a parenthetical afterthought: "(Sorry. I don't find myself very interesting this morning)." To which posterity can only say a fervent regretful "Damn!"

Happily for us, the elusive lady gives herself away in glimmerings and flashes, perceptions and insights, and the myriad delectations packed into her works. In *The Unsuspected,* she writes of Francis Moynihan: "He had just that crazy gleam, that funny high-sailing look, as if now he wasn't going to bother to use the ground. He'd get these restless streaks, as if something in his will, or something mysteriously lucky, or some fantastic kind of foresight, would signal to him. He'd scare everybody to death. Then it would come out all right." How better to describe the author at work? Or, again of Moynihan: "'Ask me something I can't answer,' he challenged, 'so I can fix up some answers.'" Wasn't she the one to dig up those splendid imponderables and then work out the ingenious explanations?

Her fiction world was often upper-middle-class suburbia with the outward look of Southern California, where she lived but where a swimming pool, as in *A Little Less Than Kind,* is not a status symbol or a convenience, but a likely spot for things that go dreadfully splash in the night, or where a matter of adultery, as in *The Turret Room,* makes no difference—even to a *grande dame*—"as long as you don't mention it." Where but in *A Dram of Poison* could be found such a wayward bus driver and jolly lot of helpful passengers? As Mr. Gibson ruminates: ". . . no man had ever had so delightful an experience as he had had this day of his suicide." And no reader either.

It was a day of infinite loss when Charlotte Armstrong died in Glendale, but it was not the end of the enjoyment she created. She had no great patience for the doom-minded. As her irrepressible characters said in *A Dram of Poison*, "What you don't take into account are the surprises. . . . Would your cave man understand the Red Cross? . . . Or the S.P.C.A., him and his saber-toothed playmates. Doom-schmoom. . . . Men might find something even better than common sense by tomorrow morning."

What we are finding now is that a Charlotte Armstrong novel of suspense is as bright, convincing, and utterly beguiling as if it were new-minted and she had never gone away.

The Unsuspected

Chapter One

ON A FEBRUARY MONDAY, in the afternoon, too late for lunch, too early for tea, the restaurant was nearly empty. A party of stout "girls" were quarreling over the check with high-pitched, playful cries. Two men at another table were eating very fast and swapping manly gossip.

A blond girl in a powder-blue suit was waiting in the lobby. She was a butter-and-eggs, sugar-and-cream kind of girl, with yellow hair, pink-and-white skin, round blue eyes. Her small nose, snubbed up at the end, might have been drawn by an illustrator of children's books. She was cute.

The man who came in very fast through the revolving door might have been roughly classified as tall, dark and handsome. He was muscular and a trifle too thin for his expensive suit. His face had a bleak and guarded expression. The girl in blue got up. They were not alike. You wouldn't have guessed from their meeting that they were blood relatives. But if you had watched them wisely you would have known them to be close in understanding, and that she was anxious about him.

She put her hand on his sleeve. "Let's get us a corner."

The man's face loosened a little. "How are you, Jane?"

"All right."

There were plenty of empty corners. They found a table against the partition that bounded the bar. "No uniform any more," she commented.

The man didn't answer. He looked across the big room with all the clean white tablecloths. It was very warm and dim and quiet, with soft music coming over the radio in the bar behind them. He looked down at five different kinds of spoons. His left hand massaged the familiar ache in his right forearm.

Jane said, "I had to see you. I was afraid you'd go up there."

"Up to Dedham, Connecticut? Why would I go up there?" He drew a breath. He didn't want to talk about it. He had hoped she wouldn't talk about it. He said, "She isn't even buried there."

"No," said Jane.

"She's dead."

"Yes."

"And that's that." She began to murmur something, but he said, "How've you been?"—warning her off.

"All right," said Jane again. She had picked up her purse and was holding it tightly with both hands. "Did Rosaleen write you often, Fran?"

"Of course she wrote." He moved his shoulders impatiently.

"What are you thinking?"

"I thought maybe," he said, "we could meet and have a bite without—"

Jane said, "You're the only one I can talk to."

"Then don't ask foolish questions," he said unhappily. "You know what I'm thinking. Naturally, I'm wondering why. Why?" He spread both hands flat on the table, as if he were going to push it aside and get up and leave. "If you know why, then you can tell me and get it over. Why did Rosaleen want to die so much that she had to hang herself?" He got it out brutally. It was what he was thinking.

Jane's pretty face began to look pinched, as if she were cold. Francis leaned back against the seat. "I want to understand it," he said more quietly. "And I'm prepared to understand it. Go ahead. And if you've got to go gently," he sighed, "I guess I can stand it."

"I've got to go slow," she said, a bit stubbornly. "Rosaleen wrote me a letter." She opened her bag and took out the letter. He could see Rosaleen's pretty handwriting, sloping back and running a little uphill.

"I don't want to read it, Jane."

"All right." She put the letter down on the tablecloth. "I don't want you to do anything but listen to me a few minutes. Fran, could you try . . . not to wince away so much?"

He didn't answer, but he relaxed a little. He knew she wouldn't talk about it just to hurt him. She began with care.

"Rosaleen must have written you about her job—about Luther Grandison, didn't she?"

"That's her boss."

"You know who he is?"

"Sure. I know. He was a director for the stage and the movies, wasn't he? The one who did all those wonderful melodramas years ago? Wrote a book of memoirs—famous guy."

"Yes," said Jane. "Well—" She picked up her fork and put it into the creamed chicken.

"So Rosaleen fell in love with her boss," said Francis.

Jane's fingers opened and the fork fell. "No, no, no! Lord, he's more than sixty! He's an ugly old man! He's not like that. That isn't it at all."

"What then?"

She didn't answer. She was looking at him as if she'd had a glimpse of the fantastic regions of his mind.

"Look, Janey, I said I was prepared to understand, but you don't seem to get it. I simply mean that it's been a long time and I realize what time can do. Rosaleen's been in the back of my life, the back of my mind—the back of my heart, if you want to put it that way— ever since I can remember. We were kids. We were cousins. Everybody paired us off in the old days. But time's gone by and we've been apart, and maybe she grew up and changed. What I'm trying to tell you is that if she did change and got mixed up emotionally—"

"But she hadn't changed," Jane said. "She hadn't changed at all."

Well then, he thought, the girl who had died still was Rosaleen, unchanged. Little and dark and tense and vivid. Her heels tapped quickly across a remembered room. The way she walked, the way she turned her head, the straight set of her shoulders, her pale skin, her black hair, her red dresses and her thin red mouth were alive again.

He forced his eyes to focus. "Then why?" he burst. "Then why did she do it?"

Jane put her hand on his fist. "No reason."

"No—"

"There simply wasn't anything," she said. "Now sit still, Fran. This is what I've got to tell you: First, there was something in this letter. I'll show you in a minute. Cousin Hilda had to go up there to Dedham and get—bring her—bring the body back. There wasn't anyone else to do it. Geoffrey was down in bed, sick. You were overseas. Buddy's gone. So of course I went too. All the time on the train Hilda kept saying she couldn't understand, she couldn't understand. That's what I thought you'd say. You know as well as we do how Rosaleen believed in everything. She was even—well, religious in a way, wouldn't you say? And not a bit afraid. She always stood right up to everything. She just couldn't have done it! That's what Cousin Hilda said. And I felt that too. There are some things you can't believe, even when they happen."

"Go on," he said tonelessly.

"When the train pulled in, I saw him out the window. This Luther Grandison. He was out there on the platform. I took one look, and he was kind of . . . stagy! Standing there, looking tragic, and people all around, watching him! Fran, it made me mad! I had the feeling somebody'd written the script. I—" Jane stopped.

He said gently, "What did you do?"

"I had a brainstorm. I told Cousin Hilda to pretend I hadn't come. And I went up to him after the services and asked for Rosaleen's job. I got it, Fran. I'm Grandison's secretary. He doesn't know I ever knew her. I'm Miss Moynihan."

He said, "Why?"

Jane said violently, "Because I hate him! I want you to listen. He talks on the air at four o'clock. He's a guest."

He had turned on the bench to look down on her. He seemed calm and detached. "So you hate Luther Grandison. What's it got to do with Rosaleen?"

Jane hesitated. "You know how she . . . did it, don't you? And you know she left a note? You know what it said?"

"Hilda put the clipping in her letter." His voice was flat.

"Didn't you think it was funny she didn't mention a name of any of us, even you?"

"I thought it sounded sick," said Francis. "And religious, maybe."

"You know she didn't sign it?" He moved his shoulders. "Fran, I found that note!"

"You found it?"

"I mean I found the text of it, in a book."

He kept looking at her, and his scalp seemed to lift and settle, his face changed. "Go on."

"It was copied out in her handwriting, but, Francis, it was copied. Out of an old book of trials in Scotland. One of those old cases. You know, he's kind of an authority on murder."

"Murder?" said Francis.

His voice was light and rather gentle. They were the only customers in the whole room now. The soft music from the bar was punctuated by the click of silver, off in a corner, where a busboy was sorting it away.

Francis was thinking. Murder. One person dead, that meant. He'd seen them die in quantities, seen the flames come up like an answer from the earth beneath. Yet when it was just one, alone, that was murder. There was something a little bit quaint and out of joint in the mixed values.

Jane said, "What shall I do?"

Francis picked up a spoon and balanced it on his finger. "You think Rosaleen was murdered?" He might have been asking, Do you think it's going to rain? "By whom?" he said.

"By Luther Grandison."

All he said, again, was, "Why?"

"Read the letter."

He took up the letter; his eyes raced through. Stuff about the weather, kidding stuff about Jane and Buddy. "Who is Tyl?" His voice was different; suddenly it had become crisp and demanding.

"Tyl's Mathilda. One of Grandison's wards. He has two—two girls. They lived there with him most of the time."

"Who's Althea?"

"That's the other one—the beautiful one. She's married to Oliver Keane now. Look."

Jane's finger pointed out the paragraph Rosaleen had written in her breezy style:

> The old spider makes out like money's too, too vulgar, but he had his reasons why he'd rather marry off Althea. Some day I'll tell you what makes me say that. It makes me mad. He's so smooth and philosophical, you tend to get fooled. The last thing on earth you'd imagine would be what I'm . . . imagining! Sorry, hon. Let it go until I see you.

But her pen had refused to leave the subject. The scrawl went angrily on:

> Nobody can tell me money's not like the blood in his veins! And if he's so wise, why doesn't he know that Tyl's heart is broken? Because it's broken, Jane, a real smash! And that's an awful thing to be in the same house with. She's going away, thank God. And Oliver's moving in.
> I think he does know it's broken! I don't think he cares! I think he

is perfectly selfish! I think— Sorry, I'm in a bad mood. I feel like
throwing things. Excuse it, please, and love.

YOUR ROSALEEN

"Well?" said Francis coolly.

Jane said eagerly, tumbling the story out, "Mathilda was the rich
one—very, very rich. Her parents both got killed in the same accident when she was a little girl. Her father lived just long enough to
turn her and all the money over to Grandison. And it was Mathilda
that Oliver Keane was engaged to. And only two days before their
wedding, he went and married the other one."

"Althea?"

"Yes, Althea Conover, and she's not rich at all. Of course, she's
gorgeous, and I guess poor Mathilda wasn't so hot. Althea's the
daughter of another friend. Grandy took her in."

"Grandy?"

"That's what the girls call him. Now, here's the thing, Fran. This
is the way Mathilda's money was fixed. She was to make her own
will at twenty-one, and she did. But she didn't get the money then.
She was to get control whenever she married! Don't you see?"

"No," said Francis.

"Grandy didn't want her to get married. So there must have been
something funny about the money."

He shook his head.

"I don't care," she insisted. "What if he'd done something he
shouldn't? What if Rosaleen did find out? She'd bring it right out in
the open. You know she would. She wouldn't have stopped to
think to be afraid. So, you see?"

"He killed her because she knew too much," said Francis, and
began to laugh. It was pretty rusty laughter.

Jane said, "I'll give up the job and go home, if you say so." Jane's
tea was cold. "Just the same," she said, "if Rosaleen felt like throwing things, that's not a suicidal mood."

Francis' face darkened. He looked at the date on the letter. "So a
man of over sixty took hold of a lively little dame like Rosaleen
Wright and hung her up by the neck? And she just quietly let him?
Come, Jane."

"It's a soundproof room."

"It is?" he said.

"He could have talked the noose around her neck," said Jane
bitterly. "The man can talk!" She looked at her watch.

"But hanging!" he burst out. "Why not poison? Why not—"

Jane broke open a hard roll. "If the note he got her to copy happens to talk about hanging, as it did, then maybe he thought it had better be hanging." She put butter on the roll and then put the roll down on her plate and pushed the plate away. She put her fingertips to her temples. "I'm not trying to believe this. If you really think I'm crazy, Fran, I wish you'd tell me so."

He said, "Honey, I don't know."

The waiter was getting nervous. Those two. They didn't eat. Now they weren't even talking. The man had looked kinda sad and tired when they came in, but now— Cripes, the guy was boiling. Whatever she told him, it sure made him mad. The waiter went over and got himself a drink of water, watching over the brim of the glass.

Jane whimpered, "I wish I hadn't said anything. Now I've got you upset, and what's the use?"

Francis turned his head and brought himself back. He'd been thinking, when they killed yours you killed them. That's the way it was in the war. But this was going to be different. He knew he had to get the anger swallowed under, and think about proof and stuff like that, think legal. Move slowly. Be sure. Put it in the department of the brain.

"Find out," he said aloud.

"The trouble is, I don't see how," said Jane. "Fran, I know there's something wrong. I know it as I know I've got a hole in the heel of my stocking, where it doesn't show. First I guessed and then I wondered, but the longer I'm up there in that house, the better I know it! I feel it! I smell it! And still I can't see what to do."

Francis beckoned and the waiter came sidling over. "Take this junk away and bring us sandwiches and coffee. Any kind."

"First you think, 'Go to the police,'" Jane was saying. "All right. With what will we go to the police? I've thought and thought—"

"Walk in," he murmured, "and say, 'I'm Miss Wright's fiancé and I don't think she committed suicide. I think she was murdered.'"

Jane nodded. "They'd say, 'Why?'"

"Naturally. So I say, 'Well, she didn't compose her own suicide note.'" He frowned.

"But they say," Jane took it up, "'Who did it?' And you say, 'Why, that nationally known figure, Mr. Luther Grandison, the famous director, the man who staged *Dead Men Do Talk* with Lillian Jellico in 1920.'" She looked at her wrist. "Oh, quick, we're missing it. Tell him to ask the bartender. The radio. I want you to hear Grandison."

"You know what he's going to say?"

"Of course I do. But I want you to hear."

Francis hailed a busboy, and Jane gave the message. Francis said, "Where were we? The police were laughing."

"Oh, they'd be laughing, all right," said Jane. "We say, 'We think he might have stolen some money from a ward of his, and his secretary found out and might have been threatening to expose him.' Then they laugh fit to die. They'd say, 'But Mr. Grandison made a lot of money in the theater before he retired. And in the movies. And his book.' They'd say, 'Prove it.'"

"Yeah," said Francis. His eyes had a kind of light behind them or deep within. "How are we going to prove it?"

"Well, there's a lawyer," said Jane wearily, "who comes up once in a while. He takes care of everything. Grandy doesn't. I write all the checks to pay the house bills. Grandy signs them without even looking. He won't talk about money. He won't look at figures. He pretends it's all so vulgar and distressing; says it affects his digestion. Says life should simply flow."

"Does he talk like that?"

"Oh, lordy, lordy, you have no idea how he talks."

"I've read his—"

Jane put up her hand. "Listen." The bartender had changed stations on the radio. Music was cut off. Instead, there was a voice. Jane's hand came down and her fingers fastened on his wrist. The place was quiet enough so that they could hear clearly. It was easy to hear and to understand that persuasive voice. If you began to listen, it caught you. It wove a musical snare for your attention, and then it spun a web of words to hold you, smooth words that came pouring without effort, pouring forth, delicately inflected, persuasive, fascinating.

"How many masks do we meet in a day?" the voice was saying. The cadences were full of regret and wonder, and a little relish. "How many ordinary human faces, two eyes, a nose and a mouth? The man on the bus, the clerk behind the counter, each has a secret. And there are some whose secret is not innocent, but who must wear their masks until they die. I call them The Unsuspected."

Jane's nails went into the flesh on Francis' wrist.

"I myself know such a man." This was Luther Grandison speaking. This was his voice. "Yes, I know a man who has committed that gravest and most interesting of all crimes, the crime of murder, and who never has been suspected at all. No, he lives, and has lived for years, wearing his mask, taken for one of us, ordinary, going about his daily business, and yet he did it! I say, he did it!" The voice fell. "I say I know. I had better add that the authorities also know. But alas, such knowing is not legal proof." The voice was so sorry. It was sorry about everything, but faintly pleased too.

"You see, with all our cleverness, we do not know how to tear the mask from his face. And, indeed, were I to give his name, he might use the law itself to punish me for what he would call libel. And yet"—in a thrilling whisper—"he did it!"

A beat of silence. Then the voice said softly, and it licked its chops with relish now, "Oh, they are among us. The Unsuspected! There's many a murder, not only unsolved but unheard of, unknown . . . unknown. You may be sure, men and women have gone to their graves, quietly assisted, with no fuss and no bother."

The voice died. It left its audience with that delicious little shudder that Luther Grandison knew how to give them. His famous trick of putting terror into the commonplace. It was like the little touches in his plays, the Grandison touches, in which he took the ordinary, and gave it just a little flip, and it was terrifying.

Jane opened her eyes. "That's Grandy. You see?"

Francis sat still with angry white face. "The Unsuspected," he murmured. "Has he got the crust to mean himself?"

Chapter Two

"Suppose I go to see this lawyer?" His voice was sharp and angry.

"You can't walk in there and say, 'Look, folks, I want to see all the dope on the Frazier fortune.'"

"The law could."

"The law won't!" she wailed. "He's unsuspected. And, Fran, if you try to stir up something that way, I can see what would happen. He'd be ever so gentle with you. But he'd treat you like a mu-

seum piece. He'd put you in his collection of psychopaths. By the
time he got through, everybody would be so sorry for the poor
young fiancé, unbalanced by grief."

"Like that, eh?" The rich purr of Grandy's voice hung remembered between them. "Well, let that go for a minute," snapped
Francis. "Start another way. How did he do it?"

"He's even got an alibi," said Jane despairingly. "Althea was with
him. I mean, she saw Rosaleen alive, and after that Grandy was
with her all the time, until they found—"

"Althea saw her?"

"Well, heard her speak, anyway."

Francis' eyes lit again. "What if we could show the alibi's a fake?"

"If we could! Fran, do you think a private detective—"

Francis let his lips go into something like a smile. "I think I'll attend to this myself," he said.

Jane moaned. She took hold of his hand, but he twisted it around
and patted hers reassuringly. "We're going to have to assume he
did it," he said in a moment. "Because if he really did, in fact, in
cold blood, then this Grandison is dangerous."

Jane agreed. "He's dangerous."

The waiter came with their new order. Francis bit into the sandwich. They were both hungry, suddenly.

"Could I get at those girls?" he asked her.

"Mathilda's drowned," said Jane, with her mouth full.

"She's what? How?"

Jane read his mind. "Oh, no, Grandy couldn't have had anything
to do with it. She started out for Bermuda and the ship went down
—oh, five weeks ago. They haven't heard a thing since."

"So she's drowned. That's the rich one?"

"Uh-huh."

"She was lost before this happened to Rosaleen?"

"Uh-huh."

"Who gets her dough?"

"He does."

"Grandison?"

"Yes, that's her will. Of course, they keep hoping Mathilda's still
alive. They can't do anything about the money yet."

"Meanwhile, he still controls it?"

"Of course."

Francis thought awhile. "How can I get to Althea?"

"What do you mean, get to her?"

"Talk to her. Get to know her. Well enough to ask a lot of interesting questions."

"You can't," said Jane. "There's no way." He looked at her. "Listen, Fran; in the first place, she's a bride. She and Oliver are still honeymooning. She sticks around their crowd, besides, and it's a closed crowd. Nobody could get in."

"Want to bet?"

"No, because I know. Grandy'd never bother with somebody just nice and ordinary and civilized and in between, like you, Fran. Somebody famous, maybe. Or somebody very humble. But not you. And, you see, if he didn't take you up, you'd never get to Althea."

"Is that so?" said Francis with a kind of mild surprise. "Could I get in there as a servant? I've never tried, but I don't doubt I could be a butler, for instance."

"No servants."

"No servants at all!"

"Not a one. He doesn't believe in them. He says they'd limit his complete freedom."

"No chauffeur, even?"

"Oh, no. He drives himself around in an old jalopy. He wears an old brown hat."

"I could be the gas man."

"Where would that get you?"

"Nowhere," he admitted. He drummed his fingers on the table.

"Fran," she said, "remember, I'm in there, after all."

"You lie low, Auntie Jane." He smiled. The absurdity of their relationship amused him once more. His father's baby sister, Jane was. His cute little Aunt Jane. "You keep your little old nose out of this. In fact, maybe you'd better not go back at all."

"Oh, don't worry. He thinks I'm a dumb blonde."

"Lots of people do, and they're so wrong," said Francis. "How am I going to get in there? Couldn't I pretend to be some famous character?"

"I doubt if you could hoax him. He's such a shrewd old—"

"Never mind. Would it be possible for you to lure Althea out to meet me?"

"Althea thinks the sun rises and sets with her Grandy," Jane warned him.

"How about this Oliver? What kind of guy is he?"

Jane wrinkled her nose. "Oh, he's all right. He's pleasant. He's the kind of man who understands women's hats."

"Lord."

"Of course, he thinks Grandy's practically God. They all do."

"Maybe Grandy does," said Francis grimly.

They both drank some coffee. He tried again. "Could I hire myself out to that lawyer, get into his office?"

"I don't know, Fran, I don't think you'd find anything. Surely he wouldn't let there be records."

Francis shook his head. "How did Rosaleen find out?"

Jane looked blank.

"Instinct tells me I've got to get to know Althea," he insisted.

"But, Fran, how could I lure her out? What could I say? 'Come and meet somebody who thinks your guardian is a stinker'? And if you hinted anything like that, she'd go straight back to Grandy—"

"Then you mustn't have anything to do with my meeting her," said Francis promptly. "I see. And yet I've got to get at her."

"You watch out for Althea. She's got silver eyes."

"Do you think," said Francis, and suddenly he looked very old, "that any woman, with or without silver eyes, is going to bother me?"

Jane drank some more coffee. Francis was looking down. She hated the drawn line of his cheek, the too-thin look of him. This wasn't the Francis she loved, who was sure of things, the one all other girls immediately assumed to be mysterious and exciting. He wasn't mysterious to her, not even now. She was his little old Aunt Jane, and she knew what ailed him was only sorrow, and that bitter anger he was holding leashed and ready. And God knew what he'd been through in the war, besides.

But Fran, bitter and old, missing that something wild and nimble in his spirit, that quicksilver quality. She thought, outraged, *He's only twenty-five.* She babbled out loud, unhappily, "I'm not belittling your fatal charm, darling. But it's not a good moment to establish yourself as Althea's boy friend."

"Let it go," said Francis irritably. Then, in a minute, he lifted his head. "Suppose I were Mathilda's boy friend?"

Jane felt a little shock. "They say—I mean, there wasn't anyone but Oliver."

"They're so wrong," said Francis softly. He kept his head up. She saw his nostrils quiver. "How old was Mathilda?"

"Twenty-two."

"That's fine. I think I'll be Mathilda's boy friend, all upset because she's drowned."

"But Fran—"

"When did she sail on this fatal ship?"

"In January."

"From New York? Alone?"

"Uh-huh."

"Then she met me in New York. I'm a new boy friend."

"But, Fran, she went off with a broken heart. You can't pretend—"

He wasn't listening. He went ahead. "Was she here in the city long before she sailed? How long, Jane?"

"Three days."

"All that time?" said Francis, in a pleased way. "And she was alone?"

"She was alone. Don't you see, it must have been that she ran away from the situation. There was that newly married pair moving in. Althea'd copped off her man. It must have been a hideous blow."

He didn't say anything. Jane, watching him, suddenly remembered the time he'd gone out and bet his allowance on a horse race, and won enough to buy his mother a wildly extravagant bracelet for Christmas. He had just that crazy gleam, that funny high-sailing look, as if now he wasn't going to bother to use the ground. He was going to take to the air. His spurning look. He'd get these reckless streaks, as if something in his will, or something mysteriously lucky, or some fantastic kind of foresight, would signal to him. He'd scare everybody to death. Then it would come out all right. This was the old Fran, the one she loved, with that leaping look.

"By gum, why didn't I marry the girl?" he asked, as if this were a reasonable question.

Her heart turned over. "Marry what girl?"

"Mathilda. Obviously, I married Mathilda."

"No! Fran!"

"Now, wait. Think about it. Be logical."

"Logical!" said Jane. "Oh, gosh! Logical!" She hung on to the table. "Now, just a min—"

"But that does it! She's the one with the money. See here, Jane, sooner or later won't they have to presume she's not coming back from her watery grave? Ah-ha, but when she married me, you know, she technically got control of her own money. So I'm the guy that'll be right there, asking bright, intelligent questions, when the books are opened."

Jane stuttered, "She w-willed it to Grandy."

"Never mind." He brushed her off. "I'll fix that. I'm an interested party. That's enough. That'll do it. And besides—look, honey. I go up there. Most natural thing in the world. My God, my bride! I'm all upset. I want to be with her nearest and dearest. Don't I? So I talk about her. So I talk. I talk to everybody. I talk to Althea. I'm a tragic figure. Althea's going to be powerful sorry for me." His eyebrows flew up. He looked full of the devil.

"But, Fran—"

"Don't say 'But, Fran.' Ask questions. Be helpful."

"No, no. Listen." Jane struck the table with her fist. "Don't underrate that man! Don't dare! Please don't try anything half-baked. He's too smart, too terribly smart! This isn't any parlor game. You can't just go and tell a plain lie and expect him to swallow it. You said it yourself. Assume he's guilty. Then he's bound to check. He'll be very wary."

"Let him check," said Francis coldly. "Let him be wary."

Jane closed her eyes. She heard his voice go on, now quick and excited.

"What you do is, you go back. Send me her handwriting. All you can find. Steal it. Send me pictures of her. Good ones."

"But, Fran—"

"Got to have them. Think about it."

"There's a roll," said Jane slowly, as if he had hypnotized her, "that Althea had in her camera. She had them developed last week and they all cried over the ones with Mathilda."

"Those are the ones I want."

"But, Fran—"

"Don't 'but.' "

"Fran, you're crazy!" She opened her eyes.

"Am I?" said Francis quietly. "O.K. The point is, I intend to get in there and find out what happened to Rosaleen. Because if anybody hurt her, he will get hurt. I don't mind what methods I use, or what trouble I take, or what lies I tell, or bribes I have to pay. If this is the way you get in and find out, then this is the way I go. You can't stop me. I don't think you want to, really. You might as well help, don't you think?"

"I'd h-help," she stammered. "But, Fran, Mathilda could not have—"

"You don't understand her psychology," he said whimsically.

"But, Fran!"

"But what?"

"But everything!" she wailed.

Francis leaned back. He was smiling. She thought, *He's lost ten years.* He looked like a man who contemplated moving heaven and earth with bright, interested eyes. "Ask me something I can't answer," he challenged, "so I can fix up some answers."

Chapter Three

THE APRIL MORNING was sunny, cool and clear. Down in her stateroom, the girl with the green eyes took a last look at herself in the mirror door. Her old tweed suit was, she thought, respectable enough. She was lucky to have found it, forgotten, in the Bermuda clothes closet. The black shoes weren't quite right, but they would have to do. She had no hat. The scarf she'd knotted around her head like a turban had blown away one day on deck. She wore her gold-brown hair very plain. It was clean and shining. For the first time in her life, she hadn't felt able to spend the money to have her hair done, so she had washed it herself, carefully. A good job, she thought. No gloves. Just this old brown-and-white summer bag. She picked it up.

Her luggage had already gone, such as it was. One nightgown, one toothbrush and a bag of very expensive Dutch chocolates rattling lonesomely in the clumsy suitcase. She'd spent half of what she had left for the chocolates; each one of them was just about worth its weight in gold. Well, but he loved them so. He must have them. It would make him so happy.

She smiled, and saw herself smile in the glass. Yes, she thought, she must remember to smile. Her face had grown thinner. It was bonier than ever now. Better smile. It wouldn't do to look woebegone or exhausted. She wasn't really, except for reasons that had nothing to do with what they would want to know. Not that they wouldn't love to know the real reasons.

She turned for a last look at her stocking seams. She felt very calm. She knew exactly how to behave. She opened the door of her stateroom and walked down the corridor.

An officer spoke to her. "They're waiting for you."

"Thank you."

Be a lady. Smile. Be pleasant. Be sweet and dull. She remembered her lessons.

The officer took her into the room where they were—several men and one girl. Their eyes licked at her.

The officer said, "This is Miss Mathilda Frazier."

She said quietly and in a friendly fashion, "How do you do?"

The cameras popped off like a quick lightning storm. They flashed one after another. Mathilda stood still, her lips curved pleasantly and a little shyly.

Grandy'd told her long ago, "Tyl, you're an heiress and, for various reasons deeply ingrained in the fundamentals of human nature, my dear, that fact makes what you do several times as interesting as what other girls do. Now, Althea, being penniless, doesn't have quite the same problem. Yet Althea, with her great beauty, has her own trouble."

She shook off the memory of Grandy, sitting in his favorite chair. Never mind Althea now. The point was, he'd taught her how to handle this. Dear Grandy, he'd taught her so much. Her heart felt warm when she thought of him.

The men of the press took an impression that she was well-bred, that she was shy. One or two of them approved of her ankles. It was the female among them who realized that, although her clothes were dull, this girl was beautifully made and essentially lovely. One of them suggested that she might like to tell her story in her own way.

"Never give them an emotion," Grandy used to say. "Look placid, dear. Placid as a milkmaid. That's the way."

"I was reading in my room when the ship caught fire," she began. "There was an alarm, of course. I took my coat and went up to my boat station. They lowered the boat almost immediately. It was all very orderly."

She stopped and smiled the shy little smile. But it was too brief, too bare. They began to question.

"Were you hurt, Miss Frazier?" someone said warmly.

"No, not at all."

"Did you see the fire?"

"No," she said. "I couldn't see anything."

"No smoke? No flames?"

"It must have been at the other side of the ship," she said in her clear, gentle voice.

"Were the passengers scared? Any panic?"

"Not that I saw," she answered. Better leave out about Doctor Phillips, praying so loud, arguing with the Lord under the stars. And how surprised he was when his prayer was so promptly and practically answered. He'd even, she remembered, seemed a little disappointed and thwarted, as if he'd had a lot of prayer in him yet, O Lord. "We were picked up in only two hours," she said.

"Who was in your lifeboat?"

"There were twelve of us passengers, and three crew members."

"Was it cold? Was the weather bad? Did you suffer?"

"It was quite warm," said Mathilda. "It was a lovely night."

One of the newsmen was a little redheaded fellow, a fidgeter. "O.K., so you got picked up."

"The S.S. *Blayne*," said one of them. Somebody sighed impatiently.

"How come they took you all the way to Africa?"

"I don't know," said Mathilda. *Never guess when you don't know.*

"Did you realize that no message came through from you?"

"We couldn't be sure," she said a little too quickly. *Be careful. Don't say too much.* She went on more slowly, with a little frown, as if she were taking pains. "Of course we tried. But they wouldn't use the ship's radio. And the port where we were taken was quite confused."

She looked straight at the female one. They would have no way to guess how she'd felt about it, how she hadn't really made much of an effort to get a message through. Mathilda knew now that it had been childish, that mood of not trying, that babyish, rebellious thought. *Let him think I died. Then he'll be sorry.* Her heart bounced, as it always did with the thought of Oliver or even at a hint that she was about to think of him. *Push it down.*

"What happened there?" somebody was asking.

"At the African port, you mean? Why, just waiting, really. You see, although we had to wait so long for a returning ship, we never knew but what we might be sailing the next morning. So we were busy waiting." *Watch it. Don't be colorful.*

"Where did you stay?"

"At a very nice little hotel." She saw it vividly—more vividly, almost, than she could see anything else in her memory. It was brilliant in the sun, that terrible aching sunlight that had poured over everything. And she could smell it. But she mustn't say so. Nor must she give them any hint of the brooding pain that filled all her days there under that brutal sun, the headache and the heartache all mingled together.

"But what did you do with yourselves?"

"Do?" she repeated slowly. *Take your time.*

"Yes, while you waited."

"We tried to be patient," she said gently. "Sometimes we played cards. There wasn't much to read."

Their faces were getting bleaker and bleaker. She knew they wanted adventure. And yet, she thought, honestly there hadn't been anything adventurous. Or if there had, she hadn't recognized it. Maybe someday, when she was old and looked back, details such as flies and headaches would have faded out; maybe it would look like an adventure then.

"Weren't there any interesting people?" asked the one who was a girl.

"Very nice people," said Mathilda primly. "There was Doctor Phillips and his wife. He is a clergyman. There were Mr. and Mrs. Stevens—"

"No men?"

"Oh, yes."

"Young men?"

"N-no," said Mathilda. "At least not younger than about forty." Mr. Boyleston had been forty. He had only one eye, but better not say so.

"No natives?"

"Of course there were natives," said Mathilda. "Although we didn't see very much of them."

Something eager was dying out of their faces. They were giving her up. All except the red-haired man, who still watched her face as if he were searching for signs.

"But finally you got a ship, huh?"

"Yes, finally we did," she said brightly. "It took us to Buenos Aires."

"That message gave the whole country a thrill. In fact, you made Page One."

Mathilda smiled politely and moistened her lips. *Was it thrilling to Oliver?* she wondered with the familiar sickening lurch of her heart.

"There was a chance to fly to Bermuda, and I took it," she said, "because I have a house there and people knew me." She glanced down at her suit. Better not go into the ragged crew they'd been.

"Did you have any money, Miss Frazier?"

"People were very kind," she said evasively. She kept smiling. *Don't boast.* Better not let them know that the mere rumor of her wealth had inspired enough kindness to bring them home.

"What do you plan to do now?"

"I must get home," she said. Was Oliver there? Was Althea there? Mustn't ask.

"To Dedham, you mean, of course? To Mr. Grandison's house? He broadcast a piece about you," said the female one chattily.

"'Tyl, dear, wherever you may be—' He had me bawling."

Mathilda's eyes stung. *Don't give them an emotion, even a good one.* She swallowed.

"I'll bet you're glad to be back," said the red-haired man, not perfunctorily, but as if he alone knew why.

"Yes, I am. Very glad indeed." Her green eyes met his steadily. *You can end any interview after a decent passage of time.*

"It must have been quite an adventure," said the female one a little flatly, as if she doubted it.

"Yes," said Mathilda. "I really think that's about all I can tell you. If you'll excuse me. Thank you for being so kind." *Always thank them.*

"Well, thank you." "Thanks a lot." They were through with her. They made as if to withdraw, all but the red-haired man, who drew closer.

"Why are you using your maiden name?" he said in a low, conversational tone.

Mathilda caught hold of her surprise and alarm and controlled it. Just her lashes flickered. "I beg your pardon?" she murmured. She took a step away. She was afraid, if he got too close, the emotional tension she was hiding so carefully would be palpable, like a magnetic field.

"He's waiting for you on the pier," said the red-haired man.

"Who?" She hadn't meant to ask. *Mustn't get involved.* This was the press. *Never converse. Recite.*

"Your husband," said the red-haired man.

Mathilda didn't move, didn't say anything. It took all her training to stand so still. The thought of Oliver broke through and flooded her whole mind. Could it be Oliver who was waiting at the pier?

By some miracle, restored to her? As if Althea had never so easily, so almost lazily, reached out and taken him away? Her heart pounded.

"All I'm asking is: Do you confirm it or deny?" said the red-haired man in a rapid mutter. "How about it, Mrs. Howard? Can I take that blush—"

Mathilda said, "If you'll excuse me, please." She looked full at him, although she couldn't see his face. She could feel her lips mechanically smiling.

"What goes on?" said the female one, abruptly popping up beside them.

The red-haired man was sending Mathilda a hurt, reproachful look, but she didn't see it. She said again, still smiling, "Won't you please excuse me now?"

"O.K.," said the red-haired man. "O.K." But he said it as if he were saying, "All right for you."

Mathilda went and sat quietly in a corner of the deck. "Such a nice, quiet girl," Mrs. Stevens had told the reporters. "Such a little lady. Why, not the least bit conscious of all that money. We have become very close friends," said Mrs. Stevens, with plenty of consciousness of all that money.

So the Stevenses came and fluttered around her, all talking at once, promising to look her up, never to forget her, begging her to promise them the same. Mathilda kept promising.

But the whole thing was back now in full force. Just as strong as if she'd never been shipwrecked and carried away to Africa, half the world away. She could see, bitterly, Oliver's face as it had been two days before their wedding day, when he had come in and been so strangely silent. She had babbled innocently along, happily, naïvely, all unwarned, unprepared, about who had sent what present, about such silly little things. And at last, when she'd stopped the chatter, puzzled, he'd said, "Tyl, are you happy?" And she'd been so startled. The whole thing had caught her in the throat. She'd finally answered in the extravagant language she never naturally used, simply because it meant too much; she couldn't answer him otherwise. She'd turned her back and cried, "Darling, of course, I'm just about out of my mind with happiness! Aren't you?"

He'd said, "Well, don't worry," in that flat blunt voice that wasn't like Oliver at all. And when, in surprise, she'd turned around, he'd been gone. Gone.

Nor had she, even then, understood anything. How dumb! How

could she have been so dumb? Stupid. Blind. Dumb. Did she crack wise? Oh, no, not she! Not dumb-bunny Mathilda, the ugly duckling with all the money.

Grandy'd had to take her aside into his study that night, with only one dim light, she remembered. Sitting beside her in the shadows, he'd told her in his gentlest voice, "Tyl, darling, I think this belated honesty of Oliver's is lucky for you. Oh, I realize that you won't see beyond the surface humiliation and it's true. Oliver ought to have told you more directly. Poor duckling. But this superficial blow to your pride is nothing, nothing. You must believe me. Someday you will know that this is right. Someday you will know that Oliver, however clumsily he's done it, hasn't really done you wrong."

Maybe. Maybe. Maybe. But Oliver was lost and there was a whole structure of dream and plan that tumbled down. And she had to learn all over again to be alone. And why did it have to be Althea? Damn her. Oh, damn her.

All her remembered life, Althea had been there with that power to take away. Never had Tyl had a glow, a hint of success, of happiness, that Althea hadn't somehow been able to dim it or put it out. Poor penniless Althea, who was so beautiful. Tyl ground her teeth.

"Nor must you blame Althea," Grandy'd said. "You must be charitable, my dear. She was in love."

"I know," she'd answered with a proud tolerance, biting back the cry, *But so was I! But so was I!* And still, in April, her heart was crying, *But so was I!*

"Won't it be wonderful to see all our friends?" sighed Mrs. Stevens. "Just think; any minute. Won't you come around to the other side, Miss Frazier, dear?"

Mathilda said desperately, "Won't you please excuse me?"

Chapter Four

MATHILDA'S LUGGAGE didn't keep her long. She seemed hardly to have begun to remember how to stand up on land, when they were finished with her. She was through customs, standing in another lightning storm of cameras, and a tall man had come up to her with a protective air.

Blinded, Mathilda couldn't quite see his face, but she heard a strange, kind voice saying close to her ear, "Grandy let me come." Her eyes filled with tears of relief. She felt a gush of emotion, a sense of coming home.

The red-haired newsman saw her falter and begin to cry; saw the tall man, with a kind swoop of his whole body that seemed to surround her and guard her, guide her quickly through the groups of people and put her into a cab, very neatly, very fast. The red-haired man ran his tongue around an upper molar. He might have been sneering.

Mathilda stumbled into the taxi. It took her a minute to find a handkerchief. The man beside her, with an odd effect of pure and scientific curiosity said, "Why is it they call Althea the beautiful one?"

"Because she is, of course," said Mathilda in honest surprise. Now she could see his face. It wasn't a face she had ever seen before. He was dark—dark hair, weathered skin. His eyes were dark, with heavy lashes. He had the kind of nose that suggests good humor, a nose not in the least chiseled or sharp, but boyish looking. His chin was firm. His face was thin, with no puffs of flesh. It was a formed face, the face of a man who had been, somehow, tested, although he was young. His eyebrows went up at an angle toward his temples. There was something gay about the way they flew when he smiled.

He spoke again before she had time to form a question. "Grandy would have come down. He wanted to. But he thought it would only complicate the publicity part."

Into her mind flitted the memory of the red-haired man and what he'd said. But the thought flitted out again. "Where are we going?"

"To a hotel. I have to pick up my stuff. And I want very much to talk to you."

He did have a nice smile. But it came over Mathilda, just the same, that all this was rather strange. Grandy's mere name had been enough for that moment on the pier. But now she drew a little away, shrinking back into her own corner of the taxicab.

"I want to talk to you quite seriously," he was continuing. She began to feel alarmed. He said lightly, "I'm afraid your Mr. Grandison has been up to some plain and fancy dirty work."

Mathilda took a deep breath. Her green eyes opened wider.

The man said, "I don't know where to start. I suppose it began with Jane—but of course you don't know Jane."

"I don't know you," said Mathilda coldly. "Will you please ask the man to take us to the station? I would like to go to Mr. Grandison's house by the first train."

He looked as if he hadn't quite taken in what she said. He sat still. If he'd been in a movie, you'd have assumed that the film had stuck. His eyes remained interested and alert. He made no move to redirect the cab driver.

"I haven't the faintest idea who you are," said Mathilda angrily, "and you may as well know that I will not listen to your opinions of Mr. Grandison. Since I've never seen you before in my life, I am perfectly sure you can't know Mr. Grandison anything like as well as I do. And you ought to know better than to think you can run him down to me."

He said nothing. Something about his pose collapsed just a little, as if a little air had gone out of a balloon. There was a small crumpling.

Mathilda was mad as hops. This was no newsman. She could let fly. She could be as vivid and as colorful with her emotion as she liked. She said, "Grandy has taken care of me since I was nine. He's been my father and my mother and my uncles and my aunts. He's taught me all I know and given me just about everything I've ever had of any value. All the things you can't buy. He's given me my home. He made it home for me. He's picked my schools. He's cared. He's spent thought and trouble on me. He's my family. And not because we have the same blood, either, but because he wanted to be, because he loved me and I love him. He is, in my considered opinion, the best and wisest man in the world, and anything he chooses to do is all right with me, and always will be. And if you won't tell the cab driver where to go, I will. Or I'll scream. Choose one!"

She saw, through her anger, with satisfaction that the man had really collapsed now. At least he had fallen back into his corner and was sitting there somberly, and it was as if he were locked inside a shell of very thick silence. He was saying nothing in seventeen different languages. He was stopped, gagged. He'd shut his mouth. *Well*, she thought, *he'd better*.

"Driver," said Mathilda.

The man got some words out painfully. "No, don't," he said. "We are to telephone."

"There are telephones everywhere," she said coldly. "Particularly in the Grand Central Station."

"Yes, but my—" He pulled himself together in order to speak at all. "Grandy sent me," he said. "Nobody's going to hurt you, you know. You don't really think so, do you?"

"Certainly not," said Mathilda with airy contempt.

"No train for an hour and a half," he said. He seemed rather indifferent suddenly. He looked out of the cab window, away from her. "If you like, I'll leave you after we telephone. You'll have to wait somewhere."

Mathilda sat back. She was still seething. She tried to remember exactly what he had said that had set off so much anger. But the phrase didn't come back to her accurately. She began to feel that she'd been too vehement. She had made a show of herself. She understood, now, that it had all been part of the home-coming emotion somehow.

His withdrawn silence smacked of reproach. After all, if Grandy had sent him— She cast about for some remark, something in the way of small talk, to indicate that the storm was over. She said chattily, "I hope you realize that I don't even know your name."

He did a strange thing. He put his hand up and covered his eyes, and sat very still and tense. She wondered if he had heard. "I don't know your name," she repeated.

"My name is Francis Howard," he said stiffly. He took his hand down and went back to looking out of the cab window. She could see his ear, the line of his cheek, not his eyes.

Howard. Mathilda's mind took what she at first thought was a capricious swoop, back to the interview with the press. Then she cried out, "Howard!"

He didn't look around, though he moved his head a trifle warily.

"That was funny!" Mathilda said. "There was one man who seemed to think— He said my husband— Why, that's what he called me! Mrs. Howard!"

"He did?" said Mr. Howard, in a bored, perfunctory way.

And he said no more. Mathilda stopped talking. Really, he was the limit. Certainly it was an odd thing to have been said and the coincidence was very odd. "Your husband is waiting for you, Mrs. Howard." Any normal human being, thought Mathilda indignantly, would want to know all about it, especially when it was the same name. He wouldn't just sit, looking indifferently away, out of the window.

The cab pulled up. A doorman helped them out, a bellhop came for her suitcase. She knew the place. Francis guided her into the lobby, into the elevator. Mathilda stood stiff and cold. The funny thing was that just as they walked into the elevator, as he gave the floor number to the boy, she caught a flash of his eye on her, and it was a look of both impatience and anger. Mathilda bit hard on her teeth. He had no business being angry with her, for the love of Mike! She marched down the corridor after the bellboy, holding her head haughtily.

They were admitted to a suite. Mathilda stood in the middle of the floor. She indicated the telephone. Francis was muttering to the bellboy about trains, bags. Without a word to her, he crossed to the telephone and asked for Grandy's number. He sat hunched over the phone, his right arm dangling. The call went through without much delay.

"Hello. . . . Jane?"

Mathilda thought, *Now, who is Jane?* It seemed to her that he'd mentioned a Jane before.

"Francis," said Francis. . . . "Yes, she's here." He looked around at Mathilda coldly, as if to say, "What, are you listening to a private conversation?" He said, as if he were speaking in code, "Is everybody well?" Then he said, with a hint of desperation, "Jane, can you get out? And I mean now?"

"Why, no," said Jane cheerfully from Connecticut, "of course not. He's right here, Mr. Howard. Here he is!"

Grandy's voice took her place. "My dear boy, is she really with you?"

"She's here," he said again, this time with a very odd inflection. He held out the phone to Mathilda. She took it, surprised, touched, excited, and suddenly ready to weep again.

"Oh, Grandy, darling!"

"Mathilda, little duck, are you all right? You're back? You're safe?"

"I'm fine," she quavered. "Oh, Grandy, I want to see you."

"Don't cry," said Grandy. "Don't cry. God bless us every one. What a darling you are to telephone. Are you happy?"

"Oh, Grandy!"

"Tell Francis to bring you home."

"I will, I will. I'm coming just as fast—"

"Strawberries and cream, Tyl," said Grandy. "You hurry, sweet-heart."

He hung up and she hung up, sobbing. Strawberries and cream was her special treat. How like him! How dear!

Mr. Howard was standing with his hands in his pockets, staring out the window.

"Grandy says you're to bring me home." She was willing to smile at him now.

He turned around. She thought, with a shock, *Something's hurt him. He's going to cry.*

He said in a low, vibrant voice that startled her with its passionate appeal, "Tyl, don't you remember?"

Chapter Five

"Remember what?"

He started to pull his hands out of his pockets and then thrust them deeper instead. "Never mind. Foolish question. Obviously, you don't. You can't or you—" He came one step nearer. "Tyl, what happened to you? Were you hurt, darling? You must have been . . . ill for part of the time. That's so, isn't it?" Everything in his manner begged her to say yes.

"No," said Mathilda. "That isn't so."

"But it must be so, and you've forgotten that too."

"I haven't forgotten anything!" she cried. "I wish you'd tell me! Who are you and what am I supposed to—"

"I'm your husband," he said sharply, almost angrily.

She backed away a little. In her mind was a vague idea of mis-taken identity. "Are you sure you know who I am?" she asked gently. "My name is Mathilda Frazier. I have no husband. I'm not married."

He moved away from her, and with his hands still in his pockets, almost as if he didn't dare to take them out, he sat down on a straight chair, keeping his feet close together. He looked like a man controlling himself at some cost.

"Sorry," he said. "Let's try to straighten this out, shall we?"

He smiled. Mathilda moved to another chair and sat down in it. Her knees felt a little shaky. It was just as well to sit down.

"Yes, please," she agreed.

They sat looking at each other.

"Do you remember," said Francis finally, in a quiet conversational tone, "when you left Grandy's house, that Sunday afternoon last January, to come to New York?"

Mathilda nodded. She thought, *But he knows Grandy. It can't be that he's mistaken me for someone else.*

"You came to this hotel," he was saying. "Do you remember that?"

"Yes," said Mathilda. "Yes, of course I did. Not this room."

"You were in Seven-o-five," he stated. The number seemed right to her. She could not have recollected it, but she recognized it. "You had some supper sent up," he went on. She nodded. "But a little later, about nine o'clock, you went down to the lobby."

"No," said Mathilda bluntly. Not at all. It was not so. She had crawled into bed to read. She hadn't been able to read or sleep either. She remembered getting up to look for aspirin, waiting for drowsiness that would not come, the desperate tricks she had tried to play on her own mind, the getting up at last to sit by the window, holding her head.

"So that's where it begins," the man was saying.

"Where what begins?"

"Your forgetting."

"But I— What is it you say I've forgotten?"

"You came downstairs about nine o'clock," he told her, "that Sunday evening. You were pretty distressed; you were feeling pretty sick about Oliver."

A thrill of dismay and excitement went through Mathilda. How did he know that?

"So you were restless and you came down to get something to read. It was a kind of excuse to get away from your room. You hated to go back. You drifted across the lobby toward the grillroom. That's when I saw you."

Mathilda said, "You couldn't have seen me. I didn't leave my room that Sunday night."

"Please," he begged. He closed his eyes. "You made me think of flying," he said in quite a different voice. "You made me think of the sky or a bird. You're like a Winged Victory in modern dress, but with better ankles. You've got such a tearing beauty, Tyl— you're windblown. It's in your bones, your long, lovely legs, the way you walk, your face, your nose. The molding of the upper part of your cheek, around the outside of your eye. I've dreamed about it. And how that dear old soul, your Luther Grandison, can be so blind as to call you his ugly duckling and never see the swan! Why, Tyl, don't you know you make Althea look like a lump of paste?"

Mathilda heard what he said; she heard the words. But her mind went spinning off into confusion. How could he say such things? How could such things be said at all? She tightened her fingers around her purse. She felt a little dizzy. She was used to people saying kind words about her looks. It was because she was so rich. She told herself that this, too, must be deliberate flattery, because she was so rich.

He opened his eyes, he smiled. His voice sank back as if it had begun to tire. "Maybe I'd better make it plain right away. I fell in love with you, Mathilda, but you didn't fall in love with me. I knew that. I still know it. If you only had, maybe you wouldn't have forgotten."

Mathilda took hold of herself. She dismissed the thought that someone must have gone mad. It wasn't helpful. She must think better than that. "Why are you trying to make me believe something I know is not so?" she asked quietly. "I do know, because I remember every minute of that time. There is nothing I've forgotten. I haven't been hurt or sick. I know exactly what happened to me in this hotel while I was here, and everything that has happened since. There is no gap." She straightened her shoulders. "I thought at first you might be honestly mistaken. You'd somehow or other got me mixed up with some other girl. But now I see you aren't mistaken, Mr. Howard. You're just lying. I'd like to know why."

He shut his eyes to hide a brief gleam that baffled her. He groaned. He took his hands out of his pockets and held his head for a moment. Then his hands fell, relaxed and open, and he said, "My poor Tyl. Don't—don't be upset."

But Mathilda was thinking hard. "What about Grandy?" she cried. "Grandy knows you! Does Grandy think—"

"Yes," he said. "I've been—well, I've been staying there."

Mathilda got up. She was furious. "So that's why, is it? You've wormed your way into Grandy's house! Are you trying to cheat him, some way? What was it you said? Something about dirty work? What are you trying to do to Grandy?"

"My dear—"

"Using my name! Using me!" she stormed. "You probably thought I was dead. Didn't you?"

"Perhaps I did," he murmured. He was sitting still, watching her anger almost as if it couldn't hurt him personally, but he was curious about it, examining it, studying it.

"You'd better tell me right away what you meant in the taxicab. About Grandy."

"I was being facetious," he said in a monotone.

"Oh, nonsense! Who's Jane?"

"Jane is Grandy's secretary."

"Where's Rosaleen?"

"Why, she's . . . not there any more," he said. "If you'll try to listen, I'll tell you what I meant in the taxicab." And she caught again that faint hint of antagonism as he looked up at her.

"If you please," said Mathilda grandly in her coldest voice, and she sat down stiffly.

"I was simply making small talk," said Francis. "I was going on to tell you how Grandy hijacked those strawberries."

"I don't believe you. Why did you all of a sudden act so collapsed? You crawled into the corner—"

"What you said," he murmured wearily.

"What?"

He made an effort. "You said, 'I don't know you.'" Mathilda was silent. "If you will try to accept this weird business that you and I remember the same period of time, the same place, entirely differently. If you will just for one brief second imagine me sitting there, with my wife, my lost girl, found again. Trying like the very devil not to break down and bawl. Thinking in my innocence that you understood, that we were putting off the real—greeting, shall I say? —until we could be alone. And then, without any warning whatsoever, you say—what you said. 'I don't know you. I haven't the faintest idea who you are.'"

Mathilda swallowed hard. "Have you been hurt or ill lately, Mr. Howard?"

He got up and went back to looking out the window with his back to her.

Mathilda said with malice, "My father left me a great deal of money."

He swung around. She controlled an impulse to cringe. But he was smiling. "Why, so did mine," he said pleasantly. "I'm nearly as rich as you are, sweetie pie." Astonishment crossed her face and he laughed. Then he came nearer and spoke very gently. "It was just love," he said. "I'm sorry you don't remember."

The bell rang. It was the porter, come to get the bags. He touched his cap. "How do, Mrs. Howard."

Shock sent Mathilda out of her chair. She crowded back against the desk. She was frightened now.

"Just a minute," said Francis. "Jimmy, will you do us a favor? Just tell Mrs. Howard when you last saw her."

"Why, lemme see, back in January. Last I saw her was Wednesday morning, right after the wedding. You gave me—"

"But I'm not married!"

The man looked distressed. "Honest, I never said anything. I never— I'd like to say I'm glad you got back safe, Mrs. Howard," the man stammered.

Mathilda turned away. Behind her, she knew Francis was giving him money. She heard him say, "Forget about this, Jimmy. Mrs. Howard's been ill."

She clenched her fists. So that would be his story. And she couldn't make a scene here, in front of a hotel servant. Or anywhere. She couldn't run to strangers or cry out that he lied. Not Mathilda Frazier. Not the long-lost heiress. No, never.

She must get home. Get to Grandy, who would know what to do. Just hold on to what she knew to be so, remember that he was lying, trying for some unknown reason to—to do what? Never mind now. Keep controlled. Get to Grandy as soon as she could.

But, she thought, *it's not the truth. That porter is lying too.*

She said, quite calmly, when the man had gone, "He was bribed."

Francis made no answer. She said, with more anger than she wished to show, "I dare say you forged a marriage certificate. Why don't you show me that?"

"Because the bride keeps the marriage certificate," he said slowly, "and I imagine you . . . lost it."

"No papers?" she sneered.

"Some," he said. "Look here, Tyl. Don't—hate me. Don't. I'm not trying— Please, can't we try to be a little bit friendly about this?"

He really did look upset and distressed, but she said coldly, "I think we'd better go to the station."

"Very well," he said.

She started toward the door. She stopped. "What papers?" she demanded. He shook his head. "I want to know how you managed to deceive Grandy!" she cried.

His face went black with emotion, suddenly. "Look here," he said roughly, "you hurt. You don't seem to know it, but I'll be damned if I see why I have to . . . be hurt. Either you listen to my entire story, let me tell you the whole thing, all that happened, all you've forgotten—which seems to me the fair thing for you to do, by the way—or we'll say no more about it. I'll see you to the train. And good-by. You can divorce me, get an annulment, do whatever you like. Ignore the whole thing. I'm not likely," he stated bitterly, "to want to marry anyone else for a while."

Mathilda hesitated. She thought, *I don't understand.* Her mind rebelled at its own confusion. It seemed to her that this man had been forcing her into confusion, and she wanted to fight back. She wanted to feel clear, to understand better. It was a way of fighting. She went back and sat down in her chair.

"Very well. Tell me," she said.

Chapter Six

"You WERE, as I said, standing near the grillroom. I saw you. I made up my mind to have a try at picking you up." He was speaking bitterly, bluntly and fast. "It worked. You were lonely and upset. You needed to talk to someone. We went into a corner of the bar and you did talk. You told me all about Oliver and Althea and what had happened to you. You were hurt, then; so hurt, my dear, so heartsore." His voice warmed, "I don't suppose you realized at all what was happening to me. I don't suppose you really saw me that Sunday night.

"I was someone to listen. A stranger, who wouldn't care, you thought, who wouldn't tell. Who'd listen and be sympathetic, and go away taking some of your trouble with him just by virtue of having listened. It didn't work out that way, because I fell in love, and I am a very persistent fellow and I would not go away. I'm afraid I hung around. We were together Monday. Had lunch. Roamed around. In the evening, we went back to our corner in the bar. This time, I talked. I told you I was in the Air Force, but I was being let out. I told you quite a bit. You listened. I wonder if you heard."

Mathilda closed her eyes, squeezed them tight. But when she opened them, he was still there, still talking.

"Tuesday," he said, "well, on Tuesday, in the morning, you said you'd marry me."

"Why?"

He took her up quickly. "Why you said you'd marry me, I . . . don't know. You never said you felt anything for me but just . . . comfortable in my presence. It was one of those half-cold-blooded things. I knew I was getting you on a rebound. And, Tyl, darling, I knew perfectly well that there was a little bit of a nasty human wish for revenge in your heart."

She frowned, but her heart had jumped in surprise.

"Oh, yes, that was obvious," he went on. "But I was going to get you on any terms at all. So I was pretty unscrupulous. Who am I to take a high moral tone? And you—honey, it was babyish, but I understood, still understand. It wasn't so much revenge on Oliver, the poor sap, but on Althea, the louse." He grinned.

"I—I see," said Mathilda dazedly. He leaned forward. His eyes searched her face. "No, no," she said. "No, I don't mean that I remember. It just sounds— It didn't happen, but you make it sound as if— I can see it might have."

He said, with an unfathomable expression in his dark eyes, "Thank you, Tyl." He went on, "At ten in the morning, Wednesday, we were married."

"It can't be done!" she gasped.

"It was done," he said calmly. "Are you thinking of all the red tape? It wasn't so bad. You already had your blood test. You had been all set to marry somebody else."

She winced.

"I had only to get a certificate from the medical officer. And they waive the waiting period, you know, for men in the service." He took something out of his pocket. "We got the license Tuesday. I do have a copy."

Tyl looked and saw "WHITE PLAINS, NEW YORK. MARY FRAZIER. JOHN FRANCIS HOWARD."

"That's not my name."

"It's your second name," he said gently. "Or so you told them. It was understood that you didn't want publicity. The newspapers would have had fun with all our haste."

She thought, *But why White Plains? Why not New York City?* She would have asked, but he was talking.

"Even now, it's been kept quiet, Tyl. Grandy and I agreed to that. Nobody knows except a very few. Oliver knows, of course, and Althea."

"Oh?"

Mathilda felt hysterical. It was so funny. What he was saying. Oliver, all this time—Oliver had thought her married to somebody else. So had Althea. Romance, tragedy, love and death, and Mathilda in the middle. All the while she'd been playing dull bridge with filthy cards, slapping at the flies, Althea had been believing this wild yarn. Mathilda put her thumb in her mouth and bit it. It was too funny, too terribly funny.

"And as a matter of fact, that porter was bribed. He was bribed not to say anything about us. My dear, you bribed him yourself. That's what he thought you—"

Mathilda said, "Could I have a drink of water?"

He got her the drink quickly. He was watching her as if he cared how she felt.

She said, "But I got on board my ship at noon on Wednesday."

"You remember that?" he murmured.

"Perfectly," she snapped. She was annoyed at a little demon of glee that kept thinking of Althea, outdramatized. She put the glass down, feeling calmer. "I was quite alone," she said.

"When we got back here after the wedding," he said, "there was a message that I had to report immediately. We figured that it would be better for you to go on, that I would go see what the hell, do what I could. I was optimistic. I said I'd fly down after you. I even thought I might make it as soon as you did." He paused.

"I won't go into how I felt. I thought, after all, I had you legally, and for the rest I had, more or less, planned to wait—if you understand me." He sent her a queer, tortured glance. "But now it looks as if I haven't got you at all."

She took up the glass and tilted it. "Is there more?"

"Some," he said. "There was Grandy. You hadn't told him."

"Why not?"

"I think you rather liked the idea of a dramatic *fait accompli*, for Althea's sake."

Mathilda squirmed. He was making her out a blind little fool, a hurt, silly child. Her face burned because, although it wasn't true, it had a strange possibility to it, an accusing possibility.

"Well," he went along easily, "you didn't know what to do. Finally, you sat down and wrote him a letter—the last thing you did before I took you to the pier." He had a letter in his hand.

"A letter to Grandy?" She felt proud of being so rational. "How does it happen he hasn't kept it?"

"Because of what it says!" cried Francis impatiently. "My God, Tyl, you forget! We thought you were drowned. The letter was . . . all I had."

She thought, *I can't catch him. He always wiggles out with a sentimental answer.* She unfolded the letter.

The letter was not only in her handwriting; it was in her words. The turn of the phrases. There were even some that referred to family matters, such as saying "a Julius," when you meant a myth. An old story about a man named Julius who never came. Nobody could have known how to use that word! The letter was signed with her own cryptic formula. "Y.L.U.D. Your Loving Ugly Duckling."

"You took that to Grandy?" she asked, and her voice trembled. "He believed it?"

"Yes," said Francis gently. "Yes, of course. But I didn't take it to him until late in February. You see, the news about your disappearance came while I was still at camp. I got out of there so fast the red tape is still bleeding where I cut it." He grinned.

Her heart jumped. The grin was more terrifying than anything else he'd said or done, somehow. She realized that this was a man of great force, very much alive, a strong man, a consequential human factor. And here he was, claiming to have let his life and affairs revolve around her. Nor could she imagine any reason for it.

"I was frantic. I couldn't find you. Look, Tyl," he said boyishly, "what else could I do? I had to go where Grandy was, because if by any miracle you did turn up, you'd let him know. And listen, my darling—"

"I have been listening," said Mathilda. She raised her head. "Have I heard it all?" She stood up. "I don't know how you managed that letter," she said steadily, "but it's all lies, just the same." *Fight him,* her instinct said. "And I would like to see," she said boldly, "if you please, the man who married us."

He had been watching her intently. Now, when she lashed out, he didn't flinch. Instead, his face softened. "Good," he said. "I'll have the bags sent over to the station. We may just have time."

A maid in the corridor called her "Mrs. Howard." Mathilda stammered something. The clerk downstairs leaned across to say in a warm undertone, "Welcome back, Mrs. Howard."

Francis led her across the lobby. He was looking down, smiling a little, a smile not exactly triumphant, but rather as if he hoped she wouldn't be angry that he was right.

"You're very thorough," she said stiffly. But she was scared.

"The headwaiter?" he asked. "Shall we find him? Or shall we go into the bar?"

"No," she said. "No more, not these. . . . It was a minister?"

"It was a minister."

"I want to see him."

"I'd better phone," he said, and left her. The lobby floor was billowing a little under her feet. She thought, *He couldn't bribe a minister or make him lie.*

Chapter Seven

WHEN GRANDY OPENED the door of his study to go forth, Jane could see from her desk down the long room to where Althea was languidly dusting the floor. Althea wore a blue denim coverall and her silver-blond hair was tied up in a blue scarf. She wore gloves—dainty ones, too—and now Jane saw her fold her hands around the handle of the dust mop and lean picturesquely on it. Althea dusting the living-room floor was something to watch, a picture. Althea made the most of her opportunities in Grandy's servantless house. She never missed an opportunity to be a picture.

And Grandy, thought Jane, with his dramatic sense. It was like living in the middle of a movie all the time, to be in this house with the pair of them. The way he opened the door of the study. Not merely so that he could go through it into the next room. No, there had to be a flourish, a significant sweep. He opened the door as if he were blowing a fanfare for himself.

"Mathilda is in New York," he chanted, "even now." He seemed to be tasting each word. "I spoke to her on the telephone." The way he said it, the warmth and wonder he could pour out with that voice of his, made you reflect what a miracle the telephone was, pay mental tribute to Alexander Graham Bell, realize the strides of modern civilization, all in a flash, and then go on to consider the infinite pathos of human affection, and, somehow or other, also the gallantry of the human spirit in the face of the infinite.

Althea said, "Was Francis with her?" She had a clear, high voice. She articulated well through her pretty, small mouth, with a precise, rather strong-minded effect.

Grandy put his ten fingertips together in pairs, tapped his mouth with the long triangle of his forefingers. "Oh, yes," he said, "and I think . . . spaghetti!" The lines around his eyes crinkled up shrewdly. "I shall begin my sauce. Yes, spaghetti will be exactly right. Both friendly and delicious, but not distracting."

Althea made a slow, wide circle with the mop. "They'll be here for dinner," she remarked. It wasn't a question. It wasn't a comment. It was as if the thought in her mind had got expressed accidentally.

"Flowers!" cried Grandy.

"Let Jane do the flowers," Althea said. "I'm just out of a sickbed. I decline to get my feet wet."

"The rain is only in your sulky little heart," said Grandy lightly.

Oliver, standing in the arch, asked suspiciously, "What rain? Whose heart?"

The minister's house was one of those city brownstones with a high stoop and a double-doored entry. The white lace curtains were spotless and crisp. The paint around the window frames was neat and newly done.

A servant opened the door. Her face broke into welcome. "Mr. Howard and your bride!" she said. "Oh, the doctor will be glad. I'll tell him."

She went briskly down the hall to tap on a door toward the back of the house. Francis was whispering in Mathilda's ear, saying that the servant had been a witness. To their wedding, he meant. Mathilda couldn't speak.

She felt the quiet of the house oppressing her. The very cleanliness, the spotless carpet, the shining wood of the stair banister, the faint smell of polish and soap, seemed inhuman and frightening. Somebody spoke from above.

A tiny elderly woman with soft, faded skin and faded blue eyes was standing on the stairs. "My dear," she said in a lady's voice, "we read in the papers that you were safe. How very kind and thoughtful of you to come."

The strange woman came all the way down into the hall and her hands touched Mathilda's. Her tiny hands were ice cold.

Francis said, apologetically, "She's been through a good deal, Mrs. White."

The woman's eyes narrowed. They looked at Francis very intently, very searchingly. They seemed to cling to his face, to pull away reluctantly at last. She whispered, "Poor child."

"She would like to see Doctor White," said Francis, and Mathilda had a strong sense that he was suffering.

"Of course," the woman murmured. They followed her in the track of the servant, who had vanished. This woman tapped, too, on the same door, and then she opened it. For a moment Mathilda could see only the outline of a man sitting behind a desk. He rose.

He said in a soft, powerful voice, "My dear Mrs. Howard—" He, too, came and touched both her hands.

Mathilda clutched. She was frightened. She found her fingers twined around his big hands as if she had been a child. She said, "I would like to talk to you by myself, please."

"Why, of course," he said with a certain tenderness. "Please, Hilda."

When they were alone, Mathilda said, "Doctor White, you aren't going to tell me that you performed any marriage . . . that I am the girl you married to—to Mr. Howard? Are you?"

His heavy brows lifted. "I am not likely to forget your face," he said. His eyes did not falter or change his odd look of sorrow. "You have a very beautiful face, my dear."

Mathilda was unbalanced a moment by such a strange and unexpected compliment to her appearance. Then she cried, "But I'm not the girl! If there was a girl! He's been trying to convince me, but I've never seen him before! I've never seen you! It isn't true! Please!"

He drew a book toward him and showed her the page. She saw the names again: John Francis Howard. Mary Frazier, written in her own hand. "No," she cried. She sank back in the chair and put her hands to her eyes.

"You are confused," said the minister in his soft, mellow voice. "That is a terrible feeling. I know. Won't you have faith that all will come clear to you in a while?"

She looked at him, startled. What was he trying to tell her? That she was mad?

"Try not to—dwell on it," he went on, with difficulty. "I don't think you can doubt your own senses."

"No," she said, stiffening. "I don't doubt them. And he can't make me. Nor can you."

"That's right," he said calmly. "Rest on what you remember, on your own best belief. My dear, if you are right and we are all . . . mistaken, for some terrible reason, then it must become clear sooner or later."

"But why?" she cried. "Why isn't it clear now? I'm not mistaken. I'm not sick. Why"—her voice rose hysterically—"why does everybody tell me this lie?"

He came around the desk and put his big hands on her shaking shoulders. "Remember this," he said at last: "I have known Francis before. I know that he has no wish to harm you, Mathilda. And you are not sick. Don't believe that for one second. Don't consider it." He walked away from her.

And the blood drained away from her heart in sudden panic because something about this man was familiar to her. He was a stranger, but some things about him she seemed to know.

"Come to see me again." He seemed distressed. He opened the door to the hall. The woman came and Mathilda felt herself being led away. The woman was talking softly about tea.

Mathilda was puzzled and angry and frightened, and comforted. She felt somewhere in this quiet house a secret, a secret to do with herself. She was comforted by a queer sense that if she knew she would understand. At the same time, she resented that there should be any secret.

"I won't drink tea here!" She flung it in the woman's face.

"Poor child," murmured Mrs. White.

When Francis and the doctor came belatedly through the door, she searched the minister's face for that sympathy. But his face had turned to stone. Even his eyes had changed. They no longer seemed to be seeing her. The sympathy and the mystery both were gone. He said, "I'm very sorry." But he was not. Not any more.

Mathilda thought to herself, *Don't make a scene. Don't cry. Get to Grandy. Grandy will know what to do.*

Chapter Eight

"DID YOU KNOW Rosaleen Wright?"

She was startled. They had been sitting side by side on the train, like strangers. She said, "Of course."

"Did you like her?"

"Of course," she said again. "We are good friends."

"Were," said Francis.

"What?"

"She's dead, you know."

"I . . . didn't know," said Mathilda finally. She was shocked clear out of her own circle of thoughts. "What happened to her?" she asked quietly, in a minute. "Was she ill?"

"She hanged herself," he said.

Mathilda wanted to scream. "Is this another of your lies?" she managed at last. She thought she had never been so buffeted and shaken up and confused and shocked by anyone in her life. This man seemed dedicated to the business of upsetting her.

"Why should I lie about that?" he snapped back angrily.

She shook her head. She held up her hand as if to beg for an interval between the shocks he kept dealing. Rosaleen, who was such a dear, such a comfort, so much her friend, the only one Althea had never bothered to take away. Rosaleen, whose steady friendship she'd known and kept and never flaunted, lest Althea stir herself to spoil it. Rosaleen, who was so steady and so strong, couldn't be gone, couldn't have been driven desperate, couldn't have been so shaken—

"I don't believe it!" she gasped.

"Don't believe what?" He was eager.

"That she'd do that."

"Now, don't you?" he said oddly.

"No."

"That's the story," he shrugged. "She hanged herself five days after you were reported lost. In Grandy's study. She stood on his desk and—"

"Oh, no!" she cried. "Never!"

"You knew her well?" His voice was warm. He must have leaned closer.

"But tell me," she gasped, "why did she? Why?"

"No reason."

"What do you mean?"

"I mean there wasn't any reason."

"But there must have been! I don't understand! What a dreadful thing!" Mathilda wrung her hands. "Oh, poor Grandy!"

"Poor Grandy indeed," he muttered.

Something in his voice touched off her anger again. She leaned forward and twisted to confront him. "There you go again. Now, why do you say that?"

He looked up innocently.

"You don't like Grandy. What is it? What are you trying to do? There's no use denying. I can tell."

"Just a minute," he said, "before you go all intuitional on me. Why do I say 'Poor Grandy, indeed'? Because it strikes me you feel sorry for the wrong person. Poor Rosaleen! Don't you think?" He closed his eyes. "You don't even try to imagine what I might be feeling. Can't you tell? You fly off the handle about Grandy. He's the one." He opened his eyes and met hers boldly, almost impudently. "Can't you see I'm jealous of that old man?"

Mathilda bit her lip. "Maybe," she said in a queer, high little voice, "you and I are just two other people."

He didn't smile. He reached into his pocket as if he'd thought of something. Mathilda brought her eyes to focus on what he held. She saw her own face, laughing.

Francis was murmuring, "Not that it caught you. Two dimensions wouldn't be enough. The beauty you've got is pretty near fourth dimension. It's motion. It's time. It's what I said, like flying."

Her throat felt dry again. What he said was babble. But this was a picture of herself that she had never seen. She thought, *The camera doesn't lie.* Then she thought, *It's a trick.*

But for the first time her imagination did encompass the impossible, and she thought, just fleetingly, *What if all that he says is true? Nonsense. You might forget, but you don't invent another way of passing the same time and paste it over the gap in your memory.* She must get to Grandy. She must not look at anything any more.

When the train got in, he took her quickly to a cab. Mathilda felt a little sick and dizzy. She'd had no time to be prepared. How could she face Oliver? How could she find a way to think of him, a way to live her life in his physical presence?

Oliver had always been around. Such a nice guy, such fun, always around, always willing to go swimming, to play a little tennis. Always ready to gossip or just chat. Oliver had no driving energy toward a purpose of his own. Nothing ever interfered with his availability. What he did for himself, work, if any, was always done unobtrusively, of second importance in his scheme of things. He was always around. One grew to depend on it.

Oh, she thought, he would be there now. Married to Althea. How to face Althea? How to hide this as she had always hidden Althea's power to hurt her? Ever since they were little girls, and Tyl's feet and eyes were too big for the rest of her, and she was unsure and shy, Althea, full of grace and pretty poise, had always been watching with her shining eyes. If Tyl had a friend or began an awkward progress toward something less lonely, Althea would manage to slip between and dazzle the friend away. Perhaps she never meant to do it. Perhaps she couldn't help it. No good. Tyl's heart wasn't ready for charity yet. How could she face them?

She was astonished to hear Francis say, "Take it easy, Tyl. He'll be feeling brotherly and a bit miffed. He thinks you're mine."

"Is Althea there?" she asked painfully.

He hesitated. Then he said, almost pityingly, "Why do you let Althea throw you? Don't you know she's envious of you? Always has been?" and while Mathilda gasped, he added savagely, "Althea's been tight in bed with la grippe, but she's up now."

Mathilda didn't understand that savage tone, she didn't understand him, but she felt softened toward him.

Grandy's portico. The big white front door.

Oliver said, "Well, Tyl!" He took her hand. He kissed her cheek. She felt nothing. The moment was blurred. There was Althea, standing back in the hall. She wore yellow. She was exquisite. Her oddly shining gray eyes weren't looking at Tyl at all.

A blond girl in a black wool frock who had the face of a baby doll smiled at her and went running down the long living room, calling, "Mr. Grandison!"

Tyl waited where she was for Grandy. She saw him coming— the arrogantly held gray head, the beak of a nose, the lively eyes behind the pince-nez, the unimpressive body with the fat little bulge of a tummy, the thin legs, the biggish, awkward feet.

She began to laugh and cry. He was purring. His beautiful voice that seemed not to need any breath came pouring out in endearments. Through her own tears, she could see in his black eyes the eternal spectator, who viewed with such lively interest and delight this dramatic and emotional moment in which he took part. He was just the same. She threw herself into his arms. She felt so safe. It was wonderful to feel so safe.

Chapter Nine

NEVER AFTERWARD was Mathilda able to put the finger of her memory on the moment that changed anything. It was like the tides on the beach. The sea would be coming up on the sand. Later, one was aware that it had begun to go down instead. But the moment of change escaped, couldn't be remembered, was not noticed at the time. So it was about Oliver.

There was a familiar hubbub. Grandy thought she was too thin. "My poor baby, your eyes are bigger than your face!"

Althea said, "That suit, Tyl!" with shocked disgust.

They introduced her to Jane Moynihan. Grandy had a visitor in his study who must be dismissed. He trotted off down the long room again. She saw Francis follow, saw him stop, halfway down, to speak to that pretty little girl named Jane. She saw Althea, watching.

Mathilda remembered later that she was able to turn easily and look Oliver square in the face, finding it the same friendly face, the same sandy eyebrows. Suddenly she could see the white walls of the African town in the sun. The waters of the oceans of the world were crisscrossed with the vanished tracks of the ships of men. She thought, *I've been away.*

He said, "Gosh, Tyl, you'll never know how I felt!"

She thought, *I'll never care.*

The tide had turned. It was going out. The strange thing was that it must have turned before this, and she hadn't known. But it was true; she didn't care any more how he felt, how he had felt or how he would feel tomorrow. The agony of caring was gone. Maybe she'd beaten it out of herself by caring so much and so hard. She felt very tired, as if all the sleep she'd lost over her emotions about him had accumulated in a reproachful cloud. It hadn't really been necessary.

Something must have gone out of her face, because Oliver could tell. She could see him persuading himself that he was, on the whole, relieved and glad. She saw right through. It was like watching the wheels go around in an insignificant toy. It was fascinating, but not important. Then the weariness lifted and Tyl felt free and lively. Her body felt light.

She said gaily, "Where are my things? Where do I go?"

"You're in the gray room." Althea was approaching with her mannequin's walk. "I'm afraid we took your old room, darling. Naturally, since it was always the nicest."

"Yes, I know," Tyl murmured. She was amused. It seemed to her that Althea was suddenly transparent too. Oliver picked up her suitcase. There was a little silence among the three of them, because Francis' two bags with his initials on them were there on the floor.

It came into Mathilda's head to tell them, then and there, and yet she didn't. She ought to have said, "I'm not married to Francis." But something was wrong with her mood. She couldn't have said it without giggling.

"Fran's been down in the guest house," Althea was saying.

"Oh, leave them," said Tyl carelessly. She was too much amused, too tickled, too giddy with inner mirth to tell them now. She ran upstairs. Her feet felt like flying. Althea came pelting after.

"Lord, Tyl, you are a skinny little rat."

Mathilda was burrowing into the gray room's clothes closet. She found a green wool dress. *In the eye of the beholder,* she thought. *In a pig's eye.*

"I've got good ankles," she said, muffled among the clothes. The knowledge that Althea couldn't hurt her made her dizzy.

Althea had sat down on the foot of the bed and her shining eyes that caught and reflected the light as if they had been metal, like silver buttons with black centers, were fixed on Tyl as if to read her very soul.

"What on earth happened to your hair?" she cried.

Althea's own hair was a soft silvery cloud of curls, cut short, swept up, every tendril blending charmingly with the whole effect. Mathilda shook her brown mane, which hung free to her shoulders. "I washed it myself," she said defiantly.

Althea's delicate eyebrows trembled with pitying comment. She touched the nape of her own neck with a polished finger tip. "I've been down with the grippe," she said, and sighed. "I've been miserable."

"Too bad." Tyl bit her lip. Laughter bubbled inside. She could hardly keep it under. *And I've been shipwrecked and rescued and half around the world,* she thought, *and it's eating you. Oh, it's eating you.*

Althea said, with grudging admiration, "You're a sly one." She sloped gracefully back on one elbow. "Where did you find this Francis of yours?"

Mathilda, in her slip, let her bare shoulders fall a little.

"A millionaire," complained Althea. Her voice verged on a whine. "Really, Tyl, you scarcely needed a millionaire. It doesn't seem just and fair. Look at Oliver and me, poor as church mice, both of us."

And it's eating you, thought Tyl. "I know what you mean," she said aloud, flippantly. "Maybe we ought to shuffle and deal again."

She saw, in the mirror, Althea's dainty body stiffen, saw the painted lashes draw down to narrow those gleaming eyes. *What ails me?* she wondered. She was treating Althea to a taste of sauce, as she had never dared before. She thought, *It's true. She is envious. She always has been.* She thought, *But I ought not to let her go on thinking I'm married. I mustn't be childish.*

She said aloud, "There's something you don't know about—"

"Is there, indeed?" said Althea acidly. "About true love, I suppose?"

Tyl picked up her own turquoise-handled hairbrush and made her mane fly. She thought, *Just for that, you can wait.* And again, suddenly, she wanted to laugh. Her mouth began to curve. She had to control it. The whole situation was so totally turned about. So ridiculously altered from what she had feared. For it wasn't Althea who had the husband Tyl had wanted. No. It was Althea who wanted the husband she thought Tyl had. Althea had her silver eyes on Francis.

Chapter Ten

INSIDE THE STUDY, the man named Press waited. He stood looking down at the floor.

"Now, as I said," purred Grandy, "I don't intend to repeat such a broadcast. They came around, you know, and I had to claim a good deal of poetic license. But you needn't worry. You are still unsuspected. As I said. And don't come here. I'll be in touch with you from time to time."

The man had a very round head and wide-spaced dark eyes. He looked up. The eyes had no hope in them.

"Don't you know," said Grandy ever so softly, "I rather enjoy playing God?"

The man named Press barely nodded. His eyes were still hopeless.

Outside, in the living room, Francis smiled politely at the blond secretary. "Had to tell her the yarn," he said, as if he were saying, "Hello, how are you?"

Jane's pretty baby face was a perfect mask. "Oh, no," she moaned.

"Something's going to bust any minute. Pray I get hold of Althea before it does. Who's in there?"

"That man Press. The same one."

"I'm going to tell Grandy the duckling's lost her memory."

"Why?" Her pleasant smile might have been sculped on.

"For time," he said. "To tempt him. Be ready to get out of here," he murmured, brushing by.

"Oh, Fran," moaned Jane.

Grandy's study door had a little whimsical knocker on the living-room side. It knocked back at you if the word was to come in. This was because the study had been completely soundproofed, so that Grandy's genius could work in quiet. Francis opened the door when the signal came.

"I thought you had company, sir," he said.

The visitor must have left by way of the kitchen. Grandy was sitting at his big light wood desk. He touched his pince-nez with his long-fingered, knot-knuckled hand. "No, no. Come in."

Francis walked across and sat down in the visitor's chair. He followed the precepts of good acting. He tried to think only of and within the frame of mind he was to seem to be in. He was a hurt, bewildered, rebuffed, humiliated and worried lover. At the same time, he mustn't miss anything he could glean from that face, that somewhat birdlike countenance, with its beak, its thin mouth, its black, brisk, bright and clever eyes.

"What is the matter?" asked Grandy, reacting promptly.

Francis looked up, surprised, looked down. "I don't know how to tell you," he mumbled. "I'm afraid I'm—" He rubbed his hand over his face, hoping it wasn't too theatrical a gesture.

Grandy stirred. He fitted a cigarette into his longish holder and slipped the holder into the side of his thin mouth. "Don't be tantalizing," he said. "What happened?"

Francis looked at him stupidly for a moment. "I don't know," he said at last, roughly. "Mathilda doesn't— She says—"

"D'ya mean she's . . . out of love?" Grandy inquired.

"She was never in!" he flung back. "No. Worse. She doesn't know me."

"What do you mean?" Grandy didn't show any shock, except that the gray hairs on his head seemed to rise quietly, and stand straighter, at attention.

"I don't know," insisted Francis, "I suppose it's—I don't know what it is. She just plain doesn't, or can't, or won't remember me."

"How very extraordinary," said Grandy in a moment.

Francis was able to watch, somehow, without looking at him directly. He kept his own eyes down, and yet he knew that the expression on that face was alert and tentative. It was more plain curiosity and excitement than anything else yet.

Francis said, "I'm sorry. It just hits me, now. What am I going to do? I don't understand things like that."

"Do you mean you believe she is the victim of amnesia?" purred Grandy.

"Must be," said Francis. "Or whatever you call it. I don't know, sir. I don't know anything about anything. All I know is, I went to find her, and there she was and she didn't know me. She says she hasn't been hurt, or sick, or anything like that. I don't know what to think. I'm not thinking."

The hell I'm not, thought Francis. He got up and walked over to stare out of the window. It was a good thing to do, he'd found, when you were trying to think while being watched.

What did it matter any more how desperate this throw was? He was close. He knew nearly enough. There was such a little way to go. And if Althea hadn't taken to her bed with a grippe and if Oliver, with his ridiculous fuss, hadn't made it so plain that Francis was not admissible to the sickroom; if he hadn't been thwarted, delayed—why, he might have been finished by now, and able to come out into the open and let things burst. And if that little mutton-headed heiress hadn't jumped down his throat at the first word about her precious guardian, if he'd had the least hope that she wouldn't go blabbing immediately, if he'd been able to talk to her, tell her what he was doing, how much he knew, explain, ask her to help—

He saw now how foolish he'd been to think he could explain to her. To think that any perfect stranger could shake her deep-rooted faith in a man she obviously loved and adored. He might have known. Althea was the same. Bright-eyed Althea was blinded by Grandy. He knew better than to try to approach her with such frank and open tactics.

He wondered why he'd been led to think that Mathilda might be more approachable. Just hope. Just wishful thinking. Well, he'd seen quickly enough that it wouldn't work. And he hadn't wanted things to burst.

There was Jane for one thing. He'd made a mistake to mention her name. He hoped Mathilda wouldn't begin to wonder about that. No, he couldn't have confessed the whole crazy device then and there, and risked Mathilda rushing to a phone and risked

Grandy finding out that Jane was . . . Jane. Not when Jane was here alone. Not when he had been too far away to stand between. Grandy was too smart. He could put two and two together too fast.

Well, it would burst now. Any minute. Unless, by this stubborn acting, he could muddle them enough. It was a nasty trick, a mean, cruel trick on the poor kid. Geoffrey had said so. Geoffrey hadn't wanted to go on with it. He'd been ready to balk. But when he saw how close it was, how sure Francis was now, and when he was reminded of Rosaleen—

Besides, sooner or later, the silly kid was going to be in danger herself. Blindly devoted to this evil old creature, she would never see what he was up to until too late. Wasn't it up to Francis, then, who knew all about it, to guard her, even from herself? Fancy thinking, maybe. A fine, high-minded excuse. There was some truth in it, although he didn't like it, didn't like any part of it.

But he had to make this desperate try. And at the back of his mind was the thought of the trap it set, the temptation. Grandy just might—just might pretend to be taken in long enough— After all, it would be very convenient for Grandy, in many ways, if there turned out to be something a little wrong with Mathilda's mind.

Grandy was being rather unnaturally silent. Francis turned around. He said, "What do you think? Ought I to fade out of the picture? Just to go away somewhere?"

Grandy was gnawing thoughtfully on his holder. His eyes were veiled. Francis thought, *He must be pretty sure I'm a fraud.*

Grandy said gently, "We certainly must do nothing at all in a hurry."

Francis felt a faint ripple of relief.

"She doesn't remember? She really doesn't remember?" Grandy crooned in his wondering way. "It's all gone out of her mind, you say? She feels she never saw you?"

Francis shook his head. He hoped he looked miserable.

"How very extraordinary," said Grandy again. "Poor duckling. Poor Tyl. You must have frightened her this morning. She's timid, you know, and shy, the little thing."

Francis thought, *Nonsense.* He'd fallen into the habit of checking this man's statements against his own evidence. It was very easy to let yourself go along with Grandy. You had to resist him. He thought, *I saw her spit fire. She's got plenty of guts. That yarn I told was well told. She might have gone to pieces. She isn't even little.*

She's a good-sized young woman. Even so, the picture of Tyl, little, forlorn, pitiable, lingered in his mind.

He said aloud, "I tried not to frighten her. I will do exactly what you say, sir. Believe me, whatever you want me to do for Tyl's sake will be done, sir. Anything. Divorce?"

Grandy flicked him with a glance. Then he began to speak in his mellow, rich, butter-smooth voice: "How curiously we are made. Is it possible? The needle writes in the wax. The needle of life writes in the wax of the brain, and the record is our memories. Does the needle lift from the wax and leave no record? Or does a fog come down? What can we say? Do you know, I think the miracle is not that we sometimes can forget, but that we remember so much, so well."

Francis thought, *And I've got to get the record out of Althea's brain and play it back.* He shook himself away from the hypnosis of Grandy's image. *What is this? Is the old bird nibbling?*

"I do think," murmured Grandy, and Francis braced himself for the verdict—"I do think, dear boy, the wisest thing—" The soundproof room had a dead atmosphere. Sound behaved queerly. Silence closed in fast here. Grandy let a little hunk of silence fall. "—wisest thing to do is wait," he said.

Francis sighed. He couldn't help it. He hoped it would pass in character.

"Yes," said Grandy. "Let time pass. Let us wait and see. We will not inundate her with proofs or with evidence."

O.K. We won't, thought Francis. *But will you be checking on me some more?* He knew there had been some checking. Jane had been sent; Oliver had gone. Maybe others. Would Grandy check the story further or was he already sure that the whole fantastic untruth that Francis was telling was untrue? Francis thought, *I'm not fooling him. Can't be. Why does he bide his time, then? Because he doesn't know my motive? He wants to find out? The one thing he can't know is that I care about Rosaleen.* He thought, *Never mind why. Time is what I want.* He hardened his heart. Mathilda would have to suffer.

"Yes, let her rest," said Grandy. "Let her realize that she is safe at home."

Francis stood up. Safety wasn't a thing for him to think about. "Right," he said.

Grandy called him back with a motion of the cigarette holder. "Your marriage, as I understand it, was merely . . . legal?"

Francis said, "That's quite true, sir."

"You will stay on . . . in the guest house?"

"Naturally," said Francis.

Chapter Eleven

GRANDY'S HOUSE stood on its own acre. It faced the westernmost street of the small city, a street that was almost like a country road, and its gardens spilled down a slope back of the house. Grandy said he had managed to have all the advantages of open country and yet escaped the need to do without city services. He claimed that his house was poised on the exact hairline of geographical wisdom. Grandy was full of theories about everything.

The house was not large. It was adapted to him. To the left of the hall ran his long living room, where he held court. On the south wall, a blister of glass was used for plants and porch furniture, and continued to the second story, where it became Grandy's exquisite and rather famous bathroom. His kitchen—another famous room— was directly at the back of the house. His study was not large—a one-story piece of the house tucked in between the kitchen and the living room. The dining room lay north.

He ran the entire establishment without servants. In the kitchen, he would preside over a collection of quaint copper pots, garlands of gourds, strings of onions, mixed in among all the latest gadgets in chromium and glass. He kept there a chef's hat which he wore seriously. Meals in his house were rituals in which the preparation of the food was just as important as the eating of it. He would bustle about and illuminate the proceedings with lectures in his fascinating voice. His lore, his stock of old wives' tales, was inexhaustible.

Mathilda came down in the green dress, and there he was in his cap, doing delicate last-minute things to the sauce. Oliver lounged against the wall. Francis was dusting glasses with a towel. Jane was setting the table.

Althea, on a high stool, was timing the spaghetti with Grandy's big round silver kitchen watch. She was still in her yellow gown— some soft silk with a wide skirt. She wore a lot of yellow. It was odd and striking on her. It gave a gold-and-silver effect and was arresting when black velvet would have been obvious.

Grandy came to embrace Mathilda. The big spoon waved back of her shoulder. He smelled of talcum and a little garlic. He beamed tenderly.

"Grandy," she murmured, close to his ear, "I need to talk to you. I have things to tell you." She knew it wasn't a good time, not with the sauce at the stage it was.

"I know," he crooned in her ear, "I know, dear, I know." Mathilda felt sure then that he did know. It didn't occur to her that he had been told, but just that he knew somehow. "After dinner," he murmured. "Let us be alone, eh?"

She was convinced that they must be alone while she told him. "Yes," she said eagerly, "alone."

He looked into her eyes. How anxious he was, how tender, how wise! Yes, he would know, of course. He sensed it already. She was quite safe. There was no hurry.

They trooped after Grandy, who carried the deep wooden bowl of spaghetti as if he held it on a cushion to show the king. But Grandy was the king too. There was candlelight. Mathilda at his left, then Oliver. Althea at the foot. Then Francis. Then Jane. Happy family. Mathilda felt gay. No hurry; and, meanwhile, it was all so terribly amusing.

There was Oliver, on her left. A mild man, married to dynamite, and he didn't know what to do, she could tell. He was a mild man, a little man, in spite of his size, a drifting kind of creature, willing to be available and kind. But he didn't know what to do about the flagrant behavior of his bride. He fluctuated between stern anger and the determination to put his foot down, and another mood, a conviction of weakness and the tired thought that it didn't really matter.

But Althea, in all her glamour, was down at the foot, being a young matron with such amusing reluctance. And Francis, beside her, was looking very gloomy, very much subdued. Mathilda was glad to see it. She felt it was only just that he should have to sit at the table with the ax hanging over his head.

At the same time, she felt a surge of violent curiosity about him. What was the man up to, this Francis Howard? What kind of man? Well-bred, you could tell at table. Really quite attractive, if you liked that dark type, that lean kind of face. "Fortune hunter." She remembered her formula. She looked at his clothes. They were in expensive good taste. But if money wasn't his motive, what could it be?

She thought; angrily, as she'd been taught to, *All that stuff about my beauty.* She thought, *If he thinks he isn't going to be caught out in his lies— If he thinks I won't find out what's at the bottom of them—* She caught a suffering look from his dark eyes, and she smiled a little cruelly.

Francis asked Jane for the bread. The little blond girl looked as if butter wouldn't melt in her mouth. Tyl's green eyes took stock of her.

Nobody had even mentioned Rosaleen. Rosaleen was gone, although she had sat on Grandy's right hand in her day.

But they began to ask Mathilda questions, and she left off her puzzling to tell the tidbits she'd saved for Grandy. About Mrs. Stevens' drinking spells. About Mr. Boyleston and his one eye at the bridge table. All at once it seemed funny and rather gay. Besides, it burned Althea up.

Down at his end, Grandy listened. And his black eyes were restless and shrewd. Once he said, "Poor Tyl," in the middle of the laughter and watched her face sadden obediently.

Francis saw it too. He thought, *Damn it, the kid looks intelligent. Can't she see what he does? He directs her. Plays on her feelings like an organ, the old vulture.* The beautiful bones of Mathilda's face haunted and reproached him. He was miserably tense and unhappy. He wished the dinner were over. He wished he didn't have to sit here, looking soulful, when what he would really like to do was to smash in that beaming hypocrite's beaming face and snatch Mathilda and shake some sense into her, and then take Jane and get out of here. Damn such a game!

Althea's little foot was in his way under the table. He brought his own foot to rest, touching hers, and let it stay. Damn such a game, but if you have to play it, play it!

When Mathilda had done, Grandy went to work and changed the mood. He brought sea mist into the room, gray, fast, lonely danger, salty death. He made them remember the coral bones of those lost at sea. He told one of his favorite ghost stories.

Tyl began to look less vivid. She sobered and shrank. The wild mood, the free feeling ebbed away. After all, she was only poor Tyl, plain little Tyl, with all that money, who could never trust anyone very much. She'd have made a lovely ghost, a sad little green-eyed ghost with a broken heart and seaweed in her lank brown hair. She might have come to haunt them. She shivered a little. She saw Francis looking at her with scorn.

Scorn! From that quarter! She straightened her back. She said adoringly, "Oh, Grandy, it's so good to hear you talk!"

Francis trod on Althea's toe. "In the guest house. After dinner. Will you?" Her silver eyes were both surprised and delighted.

Chapter Twelve

"I THINK they just stepped out, Mr. Keane," said Jane. Jane was the shy little outsider all the while, the one who made the obvious remarks and did the right thing.

Grandy looked at Mathilda, took the dish towel out of her motionless hands.

"Fine thing," Oliver said. He was trying to look very black. He seized on the state of Althea's health. "She had that cold. She oughtn't to be out."

Grandy said, "Poor Francis," gently, watching Mathilda.

She was wildly puzzled. Why was Grandy watching her so? What did it mean if Francis and Althea went out to the garden? Why "poor Francis"? Why Althea, anyway? She had a nightmarish feeling that the others knew what she did not know. She rejected it fiercely. Not so. It was she who knew and they who had been deceived. And the quicker she made it plain the better.

Grandy said, "Shall we—"

She thought he meant that they would talk now. "Yes, now," she said. But the doorbell rang.

"There now, answer the doorbell, Oliver. Please, dear boy. Who can it be?"

They went into the long room. Grandy took his chair by the fire. Tyl took her low chair at his feet. Jane, who had followed them, went a little aside, picked up a bit of knitting and put herself meekly into the corner of a sofa. It was just as if Grandy had composed the picture, directed the scene. Even the firelight flickered with just the proper effect. Luther Grandison at home. Curtain going up.

Oliver came in from the hall. "It's Tom Gahagen."

Gahagen was the chief of the detective bureau, a small, lean, nervous man with a tight dutiful mouth, but a friendly face. He listened with an air of waiting, while Grandy enlarged charmingly upon Mathilda's miraculous return from the sea. Then he said, clearing his throat naïvely, "As long as I'm here, Luther, there are a few questions. I thought it would be all right just to drop in and talk it over. Didn't want to make it formal, y'understand?"

Grandy nodded. "About poor Rosaleen?" Then he appeared struck to the heart by his own forgetfulness. He took Mathilda's hand. "My dear child, forgive me. You don't know—"

"Francis told me," Mathilda said.

"That's your husband?"

Mathilda's eyes widened. She heard Grandy say smoothly, "Yes, yes, her husband. . . . What did Francis tell you, duck?"

"Just that she—" Mathilda couldn't continue. She was shocked because Grandy had said Francis was her husband. She'd had it in her head all along that Grandy, somehow, knew better.

Gahagen said, "Very sad, the whole thing. Sorry to bring it back to mind, but there's a point we've just come across. Funny thing, too."

Jane's foot in the small black childish shoe rested on the floor, but only the heel touched and the ankle was tight. No one could see Jane's foot. Her face was calm and her eyes cast down, watching her work.

"You remember," Gahagen went on, turning to Grandy, "that day, along about early afternoon, some of the newsmen got in here?"

"Yes, yes."

"Took your picture?"

"Did they not?" sighed Grandy. "Yes."

Gahagen's eyes went to the mantel above their heads. "One of those shots was right here in front of this fireplace. That clock's electric, ain't it?"

"Yes, of course." Grandy's voice was sirup sliding out of a pitcher.

Gahagen said, "I'd like to have a look at your fuse box, Luther. Want to see what arrangement you've got in this house."

"Why, Tom?"

The detective slipped away from Grandy's bright and friendly gaze. He chose to explain all this to Mathilda. "You see," he told her, and she couldn't wrench her eyes from his plain, kind face, "the girl got up on Mr. Grandison's desk in there. You know his ceiling hook—the one he had put in for hanging special lights? She —er—used that, y'see, and stepped off the desk, like." Tyl felt sick. "Well, it isn't pleasant to think about, but she couldn't help it—kicking, y'know. Her leg got tangled in the lamp on his desk, pulled it over, wires came out of the bulb socket."

"So they did," said Grandy. He sounded politely puzzled.

"What we figure now," the detective said, "is that she must've blown a fuse. Blown a fuse when she kicked the lamp, see?"

"Is that possible?"

"Certainly. It's possible all right. Couple of bare wires, they're going to short-circuit. I'll tell you why we wondered. That electric clock up there was showing behind your shoulder in this picture, and it was all cuckoo. Gave the time wrong. It says twenty minutes after ten. And the picture was taken after two o'clock in the afternoon. We know that."

"The clock was wrong?"

"Lemme look at it, d'you mind?" The detective got up to examine the black, square modern-looking clock. "Yeah, see? This one is the old kind. It don't start itself."

Mathilda was near enough to Grandy to feel him suppress an impulse to speak. Oliver spoke up impatiently. "No, of course it doesn't. You have to start it after the current's been off. The new ones start themselves."

"Anybody cut the current off that morning?" asked Gahagen. "Was the master switch thrown at all, d'you know?"

Oliver said, "Not that I know of."

"Nor I," said Grandy. He edged forward in his chair. "I'm not sure that I follow you, Tom. What are you getting at?"

"Gives us the exact time," the detective said. "That is, if it does. Y'see, there was no power failure that day anywhere in town. We've already checked on that. So it must have been something right here in the house made the clock stop, see? Now I'd like to look at your circuits, eh? If this clock actually is hooked in on the same circuit as the study lamp, why—"

Again Grandy suppressed something. Tyl had a telepathic flash. Who'd told Gahagen about the clock and the circuits? The kind of clock it was, what circuit it was on? Because he wasn't wondering. He was checking.

"I don't understand," purred Grandy, "about the clock. But something's wrong with your thought, you see, Tom, because the lights worked."

"Yeah, we know." He nodded. "Lights were O.K. when we got here. So there's this question: Did anybody put in a new fuse?"

Oliver was looking blank.

"If so, who?" said Grandy softly. "Fuses don't replace themselves. I really—"

"They don't," said the detective. "If a fuse'd been blown, somebody knew it. Somebody replaced it. None of my men did." He waited, but no one spoke. "Well I don't suppose it's important. Still, I oughta— Where's your fuse box? Cellar?"

"Oliver, show him, do. . . . Jane, dear—"

Mathilda held on to Grandy's knee. The lights were going off and on all over the house. It was queer and frightening. Jane had gone to stand at the top of the cellar steps and call out which lights went off and when, while the two men below were playing with the fuses. Mathilda held on to Grandy's knee, which was steady. She had begun to cry a little.

Grandy was talking to her. He stroked her hair. ". . . nor will we ever know. Poor child. Poor, dark, tortured Rosaleen. She was so very tense. Tyl, you remember? Remember how her heels clicked, how quick and taut she was? Remember how she held her shoulders? Tight? Brittle, you see, Tyl. Strung too tight. Poor little one. No elasticity, no give, no play. And since she couldn't stretch or change, she broke."

"But why?" sobbed Tyl. "Oh, Grandy, what was wrong?"

"Not known," he said, like a bell tolling over Rosaleen's grave. "Not known. She didn't let us into her life, Tyl. You remember? She was with us and of us, but she was, herself, alone."

That's true, Tyl thought.

"I think it was in the air," he continued. "The house was waiting, days before. The storm in her was disturbing all of us, but we didn't know. Or we put it down to sorrow and suspense over you, my dear. But now I remember that morning. She was writing a letter for me, and the typewriter knew, Tyl. It was stumbling under her fingers, trying to tell me. I felt very restless. I didn't know why.

Althea was fussing with a new kind of bread. She was in the kitchen, I remember. I felt the need of homeliness. I wanted to smell the good kitchen smells. Instinctively, I left her, Tyl." He paused.

"And of course, since it was rather a fascinating thing Althea was trying to do—cinnamon and sugar and apples in the dough—I became enchanted with the process. I'm afraid we forgot about Rosaleen behind the study door. Alone in there. Oliver was with us. The three of us were happy as children." His beautiful voice was full of regret and woe. "But there is a fancy bread of which we shall not eat, we three."

She sobbed. "When—how did you—who?"

"It was Oliver who—" he told her gently. "Noontime. He opened the door to call, and there was that little husk, the mortal wrappings—"

Mathilda whimpered. She heard the men coming back, Oliver and Gahagen. Jane too. She wished they wouldn't yet. She wanted Grandy to say one thing more, something, anything to reconcile this tragedy, to heal it over, not to leave her heart aching.

"Well, it's on the study circuit, all right," said Gahagen mildly. He walked over and looked at the clock. "But you tell me nobody put any new fuse in?"

Grandy didn't repeat his denial. He sighed.

"Maybe somebody did and said nothing about it," suggested Gahagen.

"Possibly."

Oliver said, "But who? After all, we don't have servants, you know."

"Funny."

"Could the clock have been out of order?" offered Jane timidly. She was back in her corner. Her blue eyes were round and innocent, and wished to be helpful.

"It's running now," Gahagen said, frowning at it. "Who started it again after that morning?"

"By golly, I did!" cried Oliver.

"When?"

"Let me see. That night. I noticed it, set it and gave it a flip. Never crossed my mind till now."

"Don't sound like it was out of order. And it's on that circuit, all right. Kitchen, study, and this double plug, backed against the study wall. That's the fuse that went with the desk lamp when she kicked it over."

Grandy shook a puzzled head. He said wistfully, "I find mechanical contrivances very mysterious. Believe me, Tom, they are not always simply mechanical. They have their demons and their human failings. My car, for instance, has a great deal of fortitude, but a very bad temper. The oil burner is subject to moods, and the power lawn mower is absolutely willful."

Gahagen laughed. He said in a good-humored voice, "I don't want you to think we're snooping around after one of those unsuspected murders of yours, Luther."

"Oh, Lord," said Grandy humorously.

Jane turned her ankle over convulsively. Her heel clattered on the floor. She stopped knitting to look hard at the stitches.

"It's just that it was funny and we kinda wanted to check. Er—this Mr. Howard, he—er—wasn't here at that time, was he?"

"No," said Grandy. "No." His black eyes turned behind the glasses, slid sidewise in thought.

Gahagen frowned. "Have I got this straight, Luther? Now, when he came here, he was a stranger to you?"

"To me," said Grandy, "he was an utter stranger."

Oliver said, "Nobody knew him except Tyl." He said it with smiling implications.

Tyl opened her mouth to say, "But I didn't. I don't." She felt Grandy's hand on her shoulder. It said, *Be still.* She thought immediately, *No, no, of course, not now.* She leaned heavily against his knee.

"Where's Mrs. Keane?" asked Gahagen.

Grandy stepped smoothly in between Oliver and the answer. "She's gone out, I'm afraid. Unfortunately," he purred, "I scarcely know when to say she'll be in."

Oliver looked up, and then down. He pretended to be busy with a cigarette.

Grandy purred on, "But of course, in the morning— Suppose I ask her to drop in to see you at your office, Tom? Will that do?"

"Good idea," said Gahagen. "Yeah, do that. Couple of things I'd like to ask her. Maybe she changed the fuse."

"Oh, I doubt that," Oliver laughed.

"Well, if you'll ask her to stop by, that's fine. That'll—er—ahem." He cleared his throat.

It had all been between two clearings of his throat, like quotation marks.

When the detective had gone, Oliver said, "He was looking for fingerprints on that fuse. Now, why? What's the fuss about, do you know?"

"Dear me. Were there any fingerprints?" Grandy asked.

"No. Those milled edges won't take 'em. What is the meaning of all this?" Oliver looked alert. He wanted to hash it over. He liked to gossip.

Grandy looked up. "Eh? God bless us every one, I don't know, Ollie." Grandy sounded tired and sad. "Alas, I do not—I will never understand the ins and outs of electrical matters. I have not put my mind to them, don't you see?" There was something petulant in the statement, something childish, as if he were saying, "I could have if I'd wanted to. I did not choose to know."

"Althea couldn't change a fuse," said Oliver. Then his face rumpled up in the firelight. "Why didn't you call Althea, Grandy?" he asked uneasily.

Mathilda remembered with a start that Althea was only outside in the garden or in the guest house. Surely not far. She had no wrap. She had only slipped out for a moment. She couldn't have gone far. She looked at Grandy for his answer.

He said flatly, "It would have looked odd, I thought. I'm sorry, Oliver. After all, Althea out with Francis at this time—" He was looking at Tyl.

Yes, it was at least odd. Here sat Francis' bride, by his own reckoning, and only tonight was she returned from the sea. And where was Francis? Off somewhere with Oliver's bride. Or was Althea, as usual, after that which she had not? Or was Francis after Althea?

"You're damned right," growled Oliver, playing the he-man. His fingers did dramatic things with his cigarette. "It's plenty odd. Where the devil are they?"

Mathilda straightened her back. It was odd, but she ought not to feel annoyed just because she didn't understand. "Grandy," she begged, "can't we talk now? Alone, I mean. Please, darling, it's important."

Chapter Thirteen

DOWN IN THE GUEST HOUSE, Grandy's charming little cabin-style nook at the bottom of the garden, Althea was lying on the couch before the fire. Francis had put her there, put her feet up, touched a match to the kindling, set his stage. Now she was waiting. Her yellow skirt rippled off to the floor. The ruching at her neck made a deep square. She knew she was lovely. Her silver eyes still held the same expression of pleased and shrewd surprise. He knew he was nervous and too eager, and afraid to startle her with his need for haste.

"Althea." She moved her body in toward the back of the couch, folded in the cascade of her skirt with one quick gesture, making room for him to sit down. His face was above her. She let her lashes hide that pleased and wondering look. The ruching moved with her breathing. "Help me, will you?" Her darkened lashes lifted. "I've got a problem," he said. "Did you ever wonder," he went carefully, "why Rosaleen Wright did what she did?"

Althea looked disappointed. He groped for some way to interest her.

"I have an idea. I may have found out something—"

No flare. She was looking at him rather more coldly. To touch Althea, you touched what? Her vanity. Her jealousy.

"—about someone," he stumbled.

"Who?"

"Not Grandy," he lied quickly. He dared not make that mistake now. "Not Oliver," he added. He saw her mind scrambling behind the silver eyes. And in his need was able to follow it. She gave him the cue herself. "Someone else," he said lamely. There was only one person else, and her face was lighting up. "Help me," he begged. "I can't tell you more now. It would spoil what I want you to say."

"Me to say!"

"Listen." He took her hand. "Life is a needle. It writes on wax.

Your memory's got a record. And I want to play it back. Will you try, Althea?"

"My memory?"

"Only you," murmured Francis. "And that's a bit ironical, isn't it?" He gave her his self-mocking look. "It means a good deal to me," he confessed. "Something I've got to know."

He thought, *I'll mystify her. I'll give her romance. I'll give her drama.*

Althea raised her shoulders from the pillow. "I thought there was something queer between you and Tyl. I thought she didn't seem— you didn't seem— What is it? What did you find out?"

Francis turned his face away to keep it an enigma in the face of this.

"Maybe she didn't go to Africa," whispered Althea. It was venomous. "I thought the whole thing sounded phony. The little fraud! People with one eye and all that junk!"

Francis wondered what to do now, with this thrust of her imagination in the wrong direction. Use it. Use it, if he could.

He said, "It's the morning Rosaleen died. I want you to go back and remember. Everything. Whether the phone rang. Did you hear a sound? Did anyone come to the house?" He threw ideas at her. Mix her up. Never mind what she thought. Make her talk. There wasn't much time. She had to talk tonight, in this hour.

Althea said, "But that hasn't anything to do with—"

"You mean, she was drowned by then?" said Francis bitterly.

Althea's brows drew together. He got up and poked the fire. Let the woman think any wild thing, only let her tell him.

She said very meekly, "I don't understand. What is it you want me to do?" She tilted her head back to lengthen her long white throat.

He told himself, *Go easy. Forget that any minute somebody from the house may come down to see where we are. Pretend there's time. Make the most of this chance.* She was willing, for this moment, and she was thrown off the real track by her jealous wish that Mathilda be somehow damaged. But she wouldn't go deep enough or carefully enough unless he held her to the detail he wanted.

"Do you remember getting up that day?"

"Yes."

"Breakfast?"

"Yes."

"With whom?"

"Grandy, Oliver, Rosaleen."

"What did you have to eat?"

"Good heavens, Francis—"

"You can remember, if you try. I want you to try. Because of something later."

"Because of what?"

"I can't tell you until afterward," he evaded.

"But there isn't anything," she said.

He leaned down, took both her hands. "Althea, please."

"All right. Coffee, toast, marmalade. That's what we had for breakfast."

"Go ahead. Play the record for me. Then what?"

Althea closed her eyes. Her fingers tightened on his. "Breakfast," she murmured. "Then it was Oliver's turn to do the dishes. I did the downstairs. Rosaleen made beds. Grandy ordered on the phone. Rosaleen came down and went into the study with him. Is this what you want?"

"Go on. Little things."

"Oliver went downtown. He kissed me and went out by the front door. He had galoshes on. One of them flopped." She was smiling, exaggerating the details. Good, let her. "Let me see. I vacuumed. I had the radio going."

"What program?"

"News," she said.

"What station?" Radio gives times. His pulse was faster.

"Heavens, I don't know. But then the Phantom Chef came on. He talked about bread. I wanted some. I went out to the kitchen and got out his book—"

"Got out his book," droned Francis.

"Had a pencil," she went on dreamily. "Checked the recipe. Got out a bowl, flour in the canister on the table. I was looking in the icebox for what it took."

"Did the light go out?" He held his breath.

"Go out? Light? Oh, the icebox light? Yes, it was out."

"You didn't see it go out?"

"No, but it was out. How did you know?"

"Go on."

He'd broken the spell. Maybe a mistake.

"Grandy came out of the study," she said slowly, still puzzling over that accurate guess. "He was talking over his shoulder to Rosaleen. He couldn't hear."

"Why couldn't he hear?"

"The radio," she said impatiently. "I had it up loud."

"Radio in the living room?"

"Yes, the kitchen end. I turned it down. He said what he had to say, and she answered."

"You heard her voice?"

"Yes." His heart sank. "No," said Althea. "Why?"

Was she defensive? Be careful.

"It was her voice, I mean."

"What?"

"No, no, I'm wrong. Not then." He struck his forehead. "Of course not, because Grandy was there. Wait now. Rosaleen answered or you thought she answered."

"I thought she answered," said Althea carefully, "and she did answer, because Grandy said to her, 'That's it, dear.'"

"Then?"

"I went back."

"You were still at the radio?"

"Yes. I turned it up again." Her thoughts seemed to stick at something. Francis dared not interrupt her now. A log fell in the fire. Flames murmured over it. "Burn tenderly," said Althea.

"What—was that?"

"Burn tenderly." Althea smiled. "That's exactly what he said. It sounded so silly, blurted out loud without the context. He's pretty precious, anyhow. He can't do it the way Grandy can; although, of course, he tried to imitate."

"Who?"

"The man on the radio."

"Who said, 'Burn tenderly'?"

"The Phantom Chef. He did. That's the way he talks."

"He said 'Burn tenderly,'" said Francis gently. "Go on. Grandy had just, what?"

"Closed the study door." She shut her eyes again. "I said, 'I'm making bread.' I don't remember every word we said."

"Doesn't matter."

"I showed him the icebox light. He said it was the bulb. He'd fix it."

"Did he?"

"Fix it? Yes, I guess he did."

"Did he go down cellar?"

"To get the apples?"

"Yes."

"Yes, he got the apples. Oliver came home. We put the dough together."

Francis thought, *Don't let her see the trail. Don't let her see the point. Don't let her realize what she's told me.*

"Now!" he said breathlessly, and she tensed. "Did the phone ring?"

"No. No-o."

"Any bell?"

"No."

"Did you—was there a draft?"

"Draft?"

"Current of cold air."

"I don't think so."

"Someone came in the front door?"

"I don't know."

"Might have?"

"If it wasn't locked," she said.

No need to keep on with this any longer. He'd got what he wanted and covered it up enough.

"What is it?" she demanded. "What are you thinking?"

He shook his head. Althea said tartly, "And now you're going to be a little gentleman and tell no secrets."

Francis grinned at her. "That's right."

She settled back on the cushions. "Tell me something," she asked lazily. "Are you as much in love with Tyl as you . . . made out?"

He let his eyes look startled, and make a tiny negative sign. He felt he owed her that. He turned to the fire. He was thinking he'd have to send Jane in to New York tomorrow. That meant one night more. He was thinking he'd better remember to be dejected, not let excitement show. For the old man was keen.

What Althea was thinking, he neither knew nor cared. Her hand was warm in his, and from time to time he pressed it. He was thinking of Mathilda. A little while and he could explain to her and beg her pardon. He could explain why he'd had to go into that song and dance about love. Because the story made no sense without it. He'd explain. Then he was thinking of Rosaleen, of her gallant little figure that seemed to diminish with the days, as if she were traveling away from him toward a horizon beyond which she would someday vanish entirely. He was thinking that sometimes she seemed to be looking back at him. But when it was done, when he had finished his task, then she would turn her face away forever.

Chapter Fourteen

"GRANDY, can't we talk now? Alone, I mean. Please, darling. It's important." Mathilda hadn't seen them come in.

"What's important?" drawled Althea.

Oliver turned around to look at her, and his face flushed vividly with anger. Francis was a dark background, where the firelight and the lamplight barely touched him, as they stood there, just inside the room from the kitchen.

"Where have you been?" exploded Oliver. Her insolence set him off. The anger was genuine.

"Oh," said Althea, "talking."

"Talking about what?"

"Nothing worth repeating now," she said, and yawned daintily. "I do think I'll go up to bed," she said in the awkward silence. "After all, my first day out of it."

"Yes, do," said Grandy hastily. "Do, dear."

Jane got out of her chair. Mathilda thought she saw a glance pass between Jane and the white blur of Francis' face. "I think I'll say good night," said Jane primly. "Good night, Althea. Miss Frazier. Mr. Grandison, Mr. Keane." She murmured all their names politely.

All but one. She forgot to say good night to Francis. Mathilda thought it was odd. There was something in that forgetfulness that assumed he was different; either he didn't matter, or he would understand, or, thought Mathilda, he mattered most. Nobody else seemed to notice. Nobody else seemed to notice that she'd said "Miss Frazier."

"Good night," they said to Jane, raggedly.

Grandy said benignly, "Good night, child."

Jane showed them all her pretty smile and went away, withdrawing from the family, sweet, pretty and dutiful.

Althea stood where she was, looking strange, as if she'd been only half waked out of a hypnotic state or as if she were sleepwalking.

"Good night, Althea," said Francis. His voice had no caress or even much meaning.

"Good night," she murmured.

Oliver said, "Good night, all." He hadn't even a special word for Tyl, the returned one. He didn't even look at Francis. He was furious. His fury had a female quality. Oliver was in a tizzy.

"Now, Oliver," said Grandy with remarkable clumsiness.

Oliver bared his teeth as if to say "Keep out of this." He took his wife's arm to pull her along, but his hand slipped. The gesture was pitiful and ineffective.

"Oh, Oliver, don't grab at me," said Althea crossly.

"Very well," said Oliver. He was shrill. Tyl wanted to hide her eyes.

Althea swayed a little, standing there, looking down at Tyl. She wasn't very tall, but she looked tall at that moment, and slender, and mysteriously malicious. Tyl's heart contracted with a little fear.

Althea laughed softly. "Well, Tyl, you're back, aren't you? All the way back."

She bent her silver head and Grandy kissed her. She walked down the long room, vanishing into the dark at the far end. In a moment, Oliver snapped on the light in the hall and she was outlined in brilliance briefly. Then she was gone.

The three of them, by the fire, were silent until Francis threw his cigarette into the flames decisively.

"I'll go back to the guest house now," he said, with no emphasis at all. Tyl looked at him, but his face was turned away.

Grandy said softly, quickly, "Yes, yes, of course. For tonight."

Mathilda got up. She didn't know whether she wanted to run or fight it out now and smash that lie, this heroic suffering pose of his that lied so expertly. She looked at him with her anger and her suspicion and her resentment and her defiance in her eyes. But as he moved closer, she didn't shrink away. It came to her that she was not afraid of him. She would enjoy a good fight, a good, bold, hardhitting clash.

"Don't run," he said surprisingly. But when he stood over her very close, although he didn't touch her, she could tell that he wanted to, and not so much with love as with pity. "Good night, dear," said Francis. He sounded sad. They were not fighting words. The words were lonely.

Mathilda still stood there when he had gone. She couldn't understand. Couldn't understand. The only thing that explained him was the lie he told. If he really were in love— But he was not! He was a stranger.

"Grandy."

Grandy was all huddled in his chair. He looked shrunken up, his hand shaded his eyes.

She knelt down swiftly. "Grandy, what is it?"

"This house," he said. "Tyl, is it talking? Do you feel . . . something wrong?"

Her throat tightened. She cast a quick look behind her.

"I don't like it." Grandy rocked his shoulders. "Oh, no, I don't like it."

Tyl said, "Grandy, there's nothing. But there's something I've got to tell you."

He pulled himself up and smiled then. His hand came to cover hers warmly. "Darling, I know. I must lock the doors. Run up, sweet. I'll come. I'll tuck you in, eh?"

She nodded. She went upstairs slowly, grasping the banister too tightly. She could hear Grandy below, moving briskly, locking the doors. Whatever the mood had been, he'd thrown it off. And this was her home. Surely it was safe here. There could be nothing here to fear.

She went into the gray room and found the switch, but she didn't press it. She crossed quickly to the window in the dark. Was that a sound?

Outside, the night was not too deep for her to see a figure in the garden. Was it only this morning, she wondered, that she had first seen that figure, that man's shape? Only today?

The sounds were faint. She knelt and hid her head behind the curtain. She could see another figure, climbing down the trellis from the roof of the kitchen porch. Only she could see it, only from this room. Climbing down! Out of Rosaleen's old room to the porch roof, of course. That Jane! Her blond head caught a little light from the sky. The two figures met and shimmered in the dark and seemed to dissolve into shadows.

Tyl sat back on her heels. "My noblehearted lover!" she said. "My suffering bridegroom! Oh, brave good lonely soul!"

Chapter Fifteen

"Jane." Francis held her by the shoulders. He spoke in a low tone that wouldn't carry. His face was just a blur. "You've got to go to New York tomorrow." He shook her with his impatience. "Make it your day off. Disappear and leave a note. It doesn't matter if he doesn't like it. Get away early."

"What do you want me to do?"

"I've got it!" he croaked triumphantly. "I finally got Althea to talk about it. Listen, see if you don't get the point. We know the clock stopped at twenty after ten." He let go of her shoulders.

"Fran, I've got to tell you—"

"Not now. Wait. So the fuse blew at twenty after ten that morning. Now Althea says that Grandy came out of the study and was closing the door of it behind him at the very minute when the Phantom Chef fellow was on the air—the one who gives out recipes, you know, Jane. She remembers something he said. Jane, it gives us the time! Don't you see?"

"I see. I think I do."

"The fellow said 'Burn tenderly.' Remember that. Two words. Write them down. They take records of those programs. They must have taken a record of this one. Pray they have. You've got to go to the radio station and find out. Maybe they took a record there. Or if they didn't, sometimes the client does. Find out who pays for that program. See if they took a recording. Try the advertising agency. Try everywhere. Find that record, Jane. And then make them let you listen. Make up a yarn, anything. Don't you see? If you can listen, and time the thing, and spot the very minute when he said, 'Burn tenderly'—"

"Uh-huh," said Jane. "Uh-huh."

"That'll be the proof we're looking for. Proof! If the time is different from what I expect, then we're all wrong, and we'll know it. Jane, we can't be wrong. And if those words were said on the air that morning any time—even seconds—after twenty after ten, then we've got him! Got enough to go to the police. Because that would mean she was dead—" He drew away in the dark. "Oh, God, Jane, she kicked that lamp over while she was dying, and he stood there watching her!"

Jane said, in a minute, grimly, "That'll do it."

"Yes," he repeated wearily, "that'll do it."

"I'll go into town. I'll find out." She might have been taking her oath.

"Yes, you go in." He wished the night were over. He wished it were morning.

Jane said, "Fran, Gahagen was here."

"What?"

"Yes, and I—"

"What did he want?"

"He was asking all about the clock. He looked at the fuses too."

Francis groaned. "Did he say how the police came to be wondering about that?"

"No, he didn't say. But I think he knew, all right."

Francis groaned again. "The old man is keen. Damn! Why did this have to happen tonight?"

"How do you suppose Gahagen knew that you were the man on the telephone?"

"They could have traced the call. I couldn't help it. I had to check; had to know whether the police had found a blown fuse or noticed—"

"They never would have noticed," said Jane loyally. "You found the newspaper picture with the wrong time on the clock."

"But I wish Gahagen hadn't shown up tonight."

"Fran, what's the difference? We've got it now. All we have to do is check."

"Yes," he said.

They were whispering in the lee of a great mock orange. The night was still around them. Chilly. Francis shivered. His scalp crawled. He wished it were morning and Jane on her way.

"Fran, tell me." She clutched at his arm. "What about Mathilda? What happened?"

"Mathilda doesn't matter," he said desperately.

"But what did you tell Grandy? What did he say?"

"I told him she was balmy. He—I don't know. I imagine he's wondering, right now, what I'm up to."

"You don't think he believed you?"

"No, I don't think he believed me," said Francis bitterly. "I'm good, but I'm not that good. I think he doesn't understand and he's lying low. I hope he doesn't get his mind clear until tomorrow."

"Poor Mathilda," breathed Jane.

"Tough on her," he admitted. He could tell Jane. "But, honey, what could I do? Go on trying to tell her that old precious is what he is? And have her run to him with all we've got, so far? So he could block any move we'd try to make? Don't think he couldn't. Or could I bow out and say, 'That's right, ma'am. I'm lying. Must have had a brainstorm. So long.' And leave the job unfinished? When we were so close? I couldn't do a thing, Jane, but what I did. I felt like a heel."

"She must have been staggered."

"She's got a lot of fight; she can take it. She's got to! A few confusing days. Jane, how the old man's got those girls under his spell! Svengali business. I don't like it. He's had Mathilda thinking she's a poor little unattractive dumb bunny for years and years."

"She's not," said Jane dryly.

"She's certainly one of the most beautiful creatures—" said Francis irritably. "But no, she'll take his word for it! I don't think she knows, herself, what she is, or ever will know until she gets away from him."

"So if we get him, she'll be free."

"Yes," he said. "That's the only way I can look at it."

There was a slam of sound. Somebody had slammed the back door. They froze in the shadows and turned their faces furtively. Someone with a flashlight went around to the garage. The overhead doors rolled up. In a moment or two, they heard a car start. It was Oliver's. It plunged down the drive and they heard the gears clash, as if the hand that shifted was in a mood for bangs and clashes.

"Oliver?"

"But what—where's he going?"

"Hell for leather. I don't know." Francis took a step as if he would follow and see.

"He was simply furious with Althea. They must have had a fight."

"Quite a fight," said Francis.

The car's noises died away, leaving the night to its old chilly quiet. Jane shivered this time. "Better get back." She turned to look at the quiet house that had just erupted and spit out an angry man, and now lay biding its time, to explode again with some evil or other.

"Yes, you'd better," said Francis with sudden urgency. "Look here, we forgot something. Grandy may not know about the radio voice, but he does know one thing. I should have seen that. He knows the icebox light went out when the fuse blew. He knows, because Althea told him. That's what tipped him off, in the middle of the morning, that a fuse had been blown. He trotted right down cellar and fixed it. Now, she didn't see the light go out—"

"If it was out," said Jane. "And if it was really Rosaleen's death that put it out, Fran, haven't we got proof already? Can't we use that? Use it now, tonight?"

"No, because it might have been the bulb burning out, after all," said Francis wearily. "He'd wiggle out that way. Jane, I—"

"What's the matter?"

"God knows what he'll do!"

She trembled. "What?"

"I hate to ask you to lose sleep when you have so much to do tomorrow. Jane, watch Althea's door."

"Watch?"

"Because Oliver's gone," said Francis. "Oliver isn't there. She's alone. And Gahagen's tipped off Grandy. Get into the house, Jane. It's not—I don't think it's safe."

"You don't think he'd— Not Althea!"

"No?" said Francis. "Rosaleen was young and pretty, wasn't she?"

Jane said, "Oh, Fran!"

"If you see anyone," he told her, "flash your lights. I'll be around."

As one, they turned and almost ran into the darkness to the kitchen porch. He boosted her up the trellis. Mathilda's window was dimly lit. The house stood whitely over Francis. The night, he thought, was getting colder.

Chapter Sixteen

"Now," said Grandy, "now we're cozy." He sat in the big yellow chair, and Tyl put herself on the yellow ottoman at his feet. They were together in a little pool of light from the tall lamp over them. The room was warm. It had an expensive smell. She'd had time to get out of the green dress and into her own long warm robe of rose-colored wool. The soft fabric felt luxurious along her neck and arms.

"What's troubling you, duck? Now you shall tell me all about it."

"Just that Francis is a liar!" she burst out promptly. "A terrible liar, Grandy. I don't know the man! I never saw him before! The story about my having met him and got married to him—it's not true! Every bit of it is just made up. Because I remember exactly what I did in New York those three days. And he wasn't in it. So it's all a big elaborate lie!"

Grandy's black eyes narrowed.

Mathilda felt her temper rising. "Just about the biggest mess of lies I ever heard!" she cried. "Why, he had the bellhops and the hotel people all primed to say they knew about it. Even the minister, Grandy. And that letter to you! I never wrote any such letter. I couldn't have. Because it didn't happen. And that license business in the wrong name. It's just a fake! It must be!"

"Hush," he said.

"But you believe me? You do? Don't you?"

"Of course I believe you, Tyl," he said. "Of course, darling. Hush."

She sagged forward, put her arms on his knees and her head down. "But did you ever hear of such a thing? Why it's—" She wanted to cry.

"Extraordinary," said Grandy. "It's perfectly wild, Tyl."

"I know!" she cried. "I couldn't make a fuss! I had to get home! Grandy, what in the world can we do about it?"

"To think he fooled me," Grandy said sadly. "To think he fooled us all."

"Oh, darling, I suppose you couldn't help that," she soothed. "The letter was so well done. I know. But it's a fake, just the same. Grandy, what I can't understand is, what's he doing all this for? And what shall we do? You'll throw him out, won't you?"

Grandy said nothing.

"What do you think?" she cried.

"Oh, poor child," he said. "I was thinking what a dreadful day you've had. Poor darling, it's a wonder you didn't begin to think you were out of your mind."

"I pretty near did," she confessed.

"It was wicked."

"Yes, it was," she agreed, her eyes smarting with a rush of self-pity. "You don't know how confusing it was. I had to keep telling myself to hold everything and wait, because you'd fix him! And you will, won't you, Grandy?"

"Oh, yes, I'll fix him," said Grandy. She made a little satisfied sigh. "You see, duck, we did feel so dreadfully sad. And he seemed to feel the same. Quite as if he'd known you. I want you to understand—"

"Darling, I don't blame you."

"But I blame myself," said Grandy. "To think we pitied him and let him stay! Of course, he must have supposed you would never turn up."

"He thought I was dead. He thought I'd never come back to tell you he was lying." She nodded.

"We must ask ourselves," said Grandy, "what he wants here."

A car roared out the drive and off down the road. Grandy's pince-nez fell and dangled on the cord. "Dear me, what was that?"

"A car," said Mathilda impatiently. "Grandy, what is it about Althea? Why did they go off together?"

Grandy said, almost absent-mindedly, "You see, Tyl, Francis told me that you couldn't remember him."

She was amazed. "He told you? When?"

"As soon as you came. While you were upstairs."

"Before dinner?" her voice squeaked.

"Yes, right away."

"Then— Oh, Grandy, you guessed it was all a lie. You did know."

"Why, yes. I knew."

Mathilda sank back, puzzled, bothered.

"What I assumed was that his disappearing with Althea was a part of his act," said Grandy, shifting in the chair. "He was your poor, flouted, forgotten lover, and of course he had to be comforted. Althea's done a good deal of that sort of thing," he mused—"comforting Francis."

"I imagine," said Tyl faintly. She thought, *Althea would.* Faint color came to her face.

"Althea's impulse was to be kind," said Grandy, "and it was kind."

She thought, *But Althea's impulse isn't to be kind. That's not so.* She said, "Jane has impulses too. She climbed out her window just now to meet him in the garden."

"Eh?"

"Oh, yes, I saw them."

"Jane?"

Mathilda nodded. She thought, *How many women does he need*

to comfort him? Her cheeks were hot. "More part of his act," she said.

"But what's the act designed for, eh, Tyl?" Grandy looked both shrewd and stern. "I think we must know that. We must find out. Yes. You see, I told Francis we'd—er—wait."

"Wait?" Mathilda looked at him, surprised. "Wait?" she cried again, indignantly. Yet she wasn't as indignant as she might have been.

Grandy said, "Because I wonder what he's after, and I'd like to know. Yes. I'd like very much to know."

"So would I." Mathilda felt a little flustered, a little lost.

"You see, duck"—Grandy leaned toward her; his voice took on its old persuasive richness—"the thing's so delicate. We don't want it to be spread around. What fun the newspapers would have if you swear one thing and he continues to swear another. And to do with love and marriage. Oh, Tyl." She looked at him doubtfully. "And yet"—he changed his voice, watching her face—"I should adore to kick him out of here very fast and very hard in a spot where a kick would take the best effect, eh? Perhaps we will do just that. Yes, I think so." Then he said crossly, "What does the fellow want? Did he say anything at all, duck? Any little thing?"

She shook her head. "I haven't the slightest idea," she said. "At first I thought he must have wanted to get in here to get close to you. Because he wanted something from you, Grandy. But I—" She shook her head again. She remembered Francis had said he was jealous. "I don't think so any more. I just don't know."

"A very mysterious article, our Francis," mused Grandy. "Now, what could he want of me?"

Mathilda moved her hands, pulling her robe together nervously. Tomorrow they would kick him out like a dog, and he would deserve it. She lifted her chin. Serve him right. She said aloud, "Maybe you're right."

"Eh?"

"Maybe, if we waited, we could find out what he's after," she said weakly. She thought, *What am I saying this for?*

"Let us go slowly," said Grandy thoughtfully. She had a sensation of relief. They both relaxed, as if a decision had been taken. But Grandy had another thought. "Naturally, duck, you dislike him. I could see, at the table—"

"Naturally," she said.

"Therefore, if he annoys you in any way, if even his being here or anything he does—"

Mathilda tossed her head. She thought, *I won't let myself be annoyed.*

Grandy said, with sudden, almost boyish pleasure, "But isn't it the damnedest thing!" and Mathilda looked at his twinkling black eyes and she laughed.

"It certainly is," she agreed. "Oh, Grandy, I feel so much better now."

"Don't you let him make you think you've had amnesia," scolded Grandy fondly. "Don't you let him shake you, duck. Or undermine your confidence. No. He shan't do that. Not if I know it!"

Grandy kissed her. He went out. The door fell softly closed. She stood quite still a moment. *It's all right. It's all right. Of course, it's all right.* She slipped off the rosy robe. *Grandy believes me.* Mathilda brushed her teeth very thoroughly and vigorously. She put herself to bed with great decision and firmness. It was almost as if she had to prove she was firm and unshaken.

Grandy's beautiful bathroom, a bubble of glass and luxury, had been designed and built for him by one of his famous friends, an architect of the modern school. It had been installed for some four years. Before that, Grandy had for his own the bath between his room and the garden room, which bath now served the garden room alone. The connecting door to Grandy's room had been locked and forgotten.

So it was that Jane, sitting in the dark with her eye to the faintest crack at the edge of her own door, where she had just not quite closed it, saw Grandy come out of Mathilda's room, the gray room, cross the hall and pass Althea's door without a glance. She saw him go up toward the front of the house and enter his own place. She did not see him come out again, as indeed he did not, for she watched until dawn.

But Althea, gargling her throat, heard his tapping on the locked and bolted door.

"Grandy?"

"Slip the latch, chickabiddy. Are you decent?"

Althea slipped the latch. "I'm decent," she said sulkily.

He stood in the half-open door, looking at her with a worried frown. "Oliver?"

"Oh." Althea slashed at the rack with her towel. She had a white satin negligee pulled tight around her hips. The wide sleeves were embroidered in silver. "We had a fight. A regular knock-down, drag-out."

"I'm so sorry," said Grandy. "So sorry, dear."

"He'll get over it," she said. She looked angry to the point of tears.

"Was it because of Francis?"

"Such stupid nonsense!" cried Althea.

"He thought—"

"I don't know what he thought, but I can guess. Just because I wouldn't tell him what we were talking about."

"But why not, chicken?" Grandy moved in a little, all benevolence, all loving concern.

"I might have told him if he hadn't been so nasty." She sniffed. "Oliver gets on a high horse and he's just unbearable."

"Then it wasn't a secret?"

"I don't know," she said thoughtfully. A funny cruel little smile grew on her sulky face. "You know, Tyl's a sly one."

"Tyl?" Grandy showed his innocent surprise.

"Francis didn't tell me much," she said, "but he's all upset." She turned away to reach for her lotion. Grandy didn't move. "Such a lot of jealous nonsense!" she stormed. "So Oliver's gone off for the night, and let him! It'll do him good! After all, if Francis wanted me to talk to him, why shouldn't I? Francis isn't very happy."

"Why shouldn't you, indeed?" murmured Grandy mildly. "But you're upset now, chickabiddy, and you mustn't be. It spoils your pretty face."

Althea looked into the mirror.

"Better sleep," said Grandy gently. "Better try to sleep it all away."

"I know," she said. She turned to him repentantly. "Oh, Grandy, you're such a sweet—"

"I want you to sleep well," he said, petting her. One hand on her silver hair, he reached in his pocket with the other. "Some of your little pills, darling? They'll help you."

"Yes," she said. "Grandy, sometimes Oliver's so stupid."

"There," he said. "There. There are these little adjustments."

She took the pills childishly, a lot of them. He held the glass of water for her. She turned to dry her lips. "I hope I don't dream."

Grandy went around the sides of the glass with a towel slowly. He put the glass in her hand. Automatically, she set it in its place.

"Latch the door, chickabiddy. Sleep well." His beaked, beaming face, alight with loving-kindness, remained in the door a brief moment.

"You, too, Grandy," said Althea affectionately. She flicked the latch.

Grandy slept well enough. Jane's head ached where she rested it against her door. Francis, in the garden, was cold. Mathilda had dreams. Oliver, down at the country club, couldn't sleep at all. Althea slept and dreamed no more.

Chapter Seventeen

THE SUDDEN and unexpected death of Althea Conover Keane, caused by an overdose of sleeping tablets, was called an accident. Tom Gahagen was handling the case himself. He had them all together in Grandy's study, late that morning. All, that is, but Jane Moynihan, who had gone off to New York early. She had been on her train before Oliver came home. It was, of course, Oliver who came home in the morning and, finding it impossible to waken his wife by pounding on the locked bedroom door, had got in through a window finally, and found what there was of her.

Grandy sat behind his desk, and Mathilda's heart ached for him as, indeed, it also ached for poor white-faced Oliver, for poor Althea, for the dreary day, for herself, for everything. Grandy's hands shaded his face and he kept looking down at the polished wood, too desperately sad to raise his eyes, even to answer questions.

In this privacy, Gahagen at first said he assumed it was suicide. There was the fact that she had locked herself in, locked the hall door after Oliver when he had left her, about midnight. The connecting bathroom door to Grandy's room was bolted, and had been for years. She was securely locked in. She had wanted to be alone. The stuff she had taken was available there in her medicine cabinet. Althea had been fond of dosing herself. Locked in alone, obviously she took the stuff herself.

Added to this was her note. "Darling. Forgive me, please do," it read, and it was signed boldly with her big sprawling "Althea," of which the last two letters trailed off insolently, as if she assumed it wasn't necessary to be legible. Everyone would know.

A sad and cryptic little note, it was. Francis had found it on the floor, after Oliver had got in through the window and cried out and opened the door, and Grandy had rushed in to stand by the bed and look down at her. In all the confusion, Francis had seen the paper fluttering at Grandy's slippered feet, stirred, no doubt, by the breeze of his passing.

"Now, I'm mighty sorry," Gahagen said, "but I've got to ask you if anybody knows why she'd have wanted to do a thing like this?" The silence fell in a chunk, as it did here, in this unnaturally sound-proofed atmosphere. "What did she mean— 'Forgive me'?"

Tyl thought, *But that was what she always said.* She remembered Althea's easy, charming "Forgive me's." Something she, herself, could not say at all. The phrase sounded to Tyl, in her own mouth, pretentious and wrong. For Althea it had been so easy. "Forgive me for not telephoning yesterday." "Forgive me for splashing your dress." "Forgive me for not listening." Gahagen wouldn't know how trivial a matter could call out that phrase. She felt too heavy to make the effort to tell him so.

"Who's the note meant for?" he was insisting. "Who's 'darling'?" *Oh, anybody,* thought Tyl. *Everybody.*

Grandy answered as if he tolled a bell. "Surely she meant 'Forgive me for what I am about to do.' God help me, I was afraid."

"Afraid?"

"I don't like to say this now. Yet it's all I can think of. It obsesses me. I had a warning."

"What do you mean, Luther?"

"Premonition. The house felt wrong. She was not right. Not herself." Grandy took off his pince-nez and rubbed his nose. The homely gesture punctuated his talk. It was as if he'd made a homely gesture to reassure himself.

"Was it something she said, Luther?"

"No, nothing she said. Nothing she did. Nothing I can describe. It was . . . the lurking death wish that lies so secretly in the heart. . . . Oh, my house," groaned Grandy, "my poor tragic house." Tyl felt the world would come apart at the seams.

"Sorry, Luther," said Tom Gahagen. "You know I'm sorry. Got to ask a few questions, get it straightened out." He shifted uneasily.

Grandy said, "Don't mind me, Tom." Then, in tones of pure heart-break, "I am wondering, of course, what I ought to have done that I left undone."

"Aren't we all?" said Francis in a queer, harsh, angry voice. It was as if he'd been rude. Grandy's gentleness reproached him.

Oliver said monotonously, "We had a quarrel, a dumb, jealous quarrel. She'd been out in the guest house with Howard, and I didn't like it. So we said a lot of bitter, nasty stuff and I slammed out of here. She wouldn't tell me what they'd talked about, and I wanted to know. I thought it was my business. She said it wasn't."

The careful voice broke. "It couldn't have been over me that she did it. Because I didn't matter that much to Althea, and that's the truth."

It didn't sound like Oliver. He'd been shocked into honest humil-ity. Tyl could have wept for him.

Gahagen looked at Francis. "What were you and Mrs. Keane talking about so long?" he asked with cold precision.

Francis said, "She was in no suicidal mood."

"What d'you mean?"

"She was in no suicidal mood." He repeated his statement quietly. "I spent a good while last evening talking to her, and I would have known."

"What were you talking about?"

Francis shrugged. "As a matter of fact, I was telling her my troubles, and she was very kind," he said smoothly. "And she was not thinking about suicide."

Gahagen's glance passed from one young man to the other. His thought was transparent on his tight face. A triangle. Jealousy. Trouble. No way to get to the bottom of it.

Grandy said softly, "We can't be sure that note was not just a note she'd written some other time. Perhaps this was an accident. . . . Is that possible, Tom?"

Gahagen examined this soft suggestion and thought he under-stood it. Some tangle of emotions here that could not be publicly explained.

Mathilda spoke up at last. "Althea did use that phrase, 'Forgive me,' such a lot."

"She did. She did," murmured Grandy. "You're right, Tyl. So she did."

"You don't think it was a suicide note at all?" Gahagen sounded tentative, as if he might, in the end, take their word for it.

Grandy said, "Not necessarily. Quite possibly, it wasn't."

Francis said coldly—almost as if he knew, Tyl thought—"She didn't commit suicide, Mr. Gahagen."

"Then you think it was an accident?"

Francis didn't answer.

But Oliver's new and bitter voice said without drama, "I'd rather think so."

There was one of those silences.

"She was," said Francis firmly, insistently, even loudly, "in no more suicidal mood than Mathilda is right now."

Heads turned. What an odd thing to say! Gahagen's brows made puzzled motions.

"I'd like you all to look at Mathilda," said Francis easily. That is, his voice was easy; his arm, hanging over the back of the chair he sat in, was dangling with an effect of being relaxed. But there were two hard little lines near his mouth that Jane would have recognized.

"Why should we look at Mathilda?" purred Grandy. He had himself looked up at last. His black eyes were narrow behind his glasses. He looked wary and alert and as if he were listening hard, trying to hear more than Francis' quiet voice as it went on.

"Because I don't care for these suicidal rumors," said Francis. "I don't like premonitions after the fact. I want all of you to look very carefully at Mathilda, and if you see anything . . . ominous, then let us arrange to take very good care of her." Francis opened his hand, looked at the palm, turned it over, let it fall. "Since two pretty young girls have died in this house," he said, "I'd just as soon there wasn't any third one. So take a good look at Mathilda now. And if she's in a dangerous mood, let's have nurses in and watch her. Let's take no more chances."

There was silence—rather a strained silence. Tyl shook her head. "I don't understand."

"You want to live, don't you? You're not depressed? Not brooding? Not low? You feel well? You're young and looking forward? You've got something to live for?" Francis barked questions at her harshly, angrily. "You don't want to die?"

"Of course I don't want to die! I don't know what you're talking about!" She was so angry she stood up without knowing she had done so. With her head thrown back, her chin up, eyes bright, her breath drawn with indignation, her lovely figure taut and poised, she was most vividly alive.

"Now, Mrs. Howard—" Gahagen began soothingly.

Mathilda flashed around to face him. She would have said she was not Mrs. Howard, but Grandy was around his desk and beside her suddenly, and his hands on her shoulders were quieting and warning her. "There, duckling, there. Francis worries. Naturally. Naturally. You mustn't be angry." He turned to Gahagen. "I think he's made a point," he said. "We could not possibly say there was any mood at all. I can't condemn—" Grandy's voice broke a little. "I dare not damn Althea with a piece of imagined nonsense which may have been my own mood after all. And if we can't say for sure, Tom, ought we not to say it was an accident?"

"That—er—note—" began the detective.

"Such a strange little note," said Grandy. "So vague. So meaningless. I fancy she's written such a note to me or Oliver many a time. And as long as we do not know her reasons or even whether she had any, need we mention any note? To—to people? Frankly, Tom"—Grandy compressed his lips—"I don't want to hear them speculating. I don't want to hear their guesses. I don't want to know they're wondering why Althea wanted to die. For myself, I would rather believe Althea left us accidentally. I do earnestly believe that she loved and trusted us enough to wish to stay."

Francis put both hands over his face.

Tyl thought, *Francis is more upset than Oliver, even.* She thought, *Poor Althea, how could she make a mistake and die?* She thought, *Oh, my poor Grandy!* Pity and grief wheeled around, tumbled each other in her consciousness and yet hardly roused her. They were pale images of coming emotions, only their mental shadows.

But Francis' hands were hiding a black and deadly anger, full grown.

Chapter Eighteen

ALL AFTERNOON people came. Tyl was still encased in an aching paralysis that hadn't yet sharpened to pain. It didn't occur to her not to remain in the long room, not to stay there and bear it. She was there, and people came—Grandy's friends—and she stayed and watched and listened numbly.

Grandy was in his big chair. No tears, no sighs, no break in the rich gentleness of his voice. He made kind little inquiries of his friends about their daily affairs. Ever so gently, he kept his grief private. The assumption was that it lay too deep for tears. Tyl saw more than one turn away from him with a convulsed face. It was so beautiful a performance, such a touching thing.

Grandy's friends. Personalities, all of them. They would go to him and receive his gentle greeting, his sweet questions. Then they would go to Oliver, who was in the room, although he seemed not to know where he was exactly, and only stammered "Oh, hello," and "Thanks" and "Yes" or "No," stupidly. Then they would come to Tyl and Francis, who was there beside her, and they would congratulate her, weakly, on being alive. They muted their joy in her return in deference to the death in the house. It was as if they were all saying, "Too bad. He's lost his beauty, though of course he's got this one back. Too bad."

Althea would be a legend. The lovely girl with the silver eyes who died so young. *She'll never grow old,* Tyl thought, *but stay young and lovely in their memories. They will forgive her for everything. Well,* she thought, *I forgive her.*

Francis was introduced as Mathilda's husband. It didn't seem to matter. It was too hard to explain now. Too involved and fantastic. Let it go.

Francis was taking a good deal on himself. It was he who, when the emotional pressure got too high, knew how to break the fever. When Schmedlinova made a gliding run all the way down to Grandy, wailing like a Russian banshee, it was Francis who made a cynical aside and steadied Mathilda's jumping heart. It was Francis who sat at her elbow to say the right thing when she couldn't think of what to say at all. She found her eyes meeting his over people's heads. They seemed to have suddenly acquired a full code of signals that went easily between them. It was he who rescued Oliver from the poet who kept quoting, when Mathilda asked him to with her eyebrow. He took slobbering old Mrs. Campbell away before Mathilda screamed. It was his shoulder she found behind her when a sudden wave of fatigue sent her reeling backward. It was Francis who told her quite rudely, at six o'clock, to go upstairs and lie down. It was Francis who brought her a tray, who pulled the comforter over her feet, who dimmed the light. Lying on her bed, weary and numb, she supposed, with dull surprise, that Francis had been acting very like a husband.

When Jane got off the train at seven thirty, Gahagen's men were there to meet her. They took her to his office without telling her why. It was obvious that she hadn't known what had happened to Althea. She nearly fainted when they told her. In fact, Gahagen was alarmed and called the doctor. The girl was badly shocked. It was no fake, either. Gahagen was sorry that his duty had led him to distress her. After all, the poor little kid didn't know anything, had nothing to tell them, sat there twisting her hands, looked dazed and unhappy. Gahagen sent a man to run her up to Grandy's house.

Francis had taken so much on himself that it was only natural for him to meet her at the door and put his arm around her.

What they exchanged under their breaths was not much, because Grandy's voice said, "Is that Jane?" and people leaned around the arch to say that Grandy was asking for her. It was only natural that Francis should keep his arm around her and lead her to Grandy's throne.

It was a lovely scene. The yellow-haired child in the powder-blue suit with the little white collar kneeling there. Dear old Grandy bent over her so tenderly. And that tall, good-looking Howard man, standing there with Jane's little blue cap in his hand, that he'd picked up when it fell. The long room was quiet.

"I know," Grandy said. "I know, child. I know." His voice was soft and sympathetic, and it didn't change as it went on to ask, "What were you doing in the garden last night with Francis?"

Jane cut a sob or two. Francis, standing by, looked perfectly blank. He felt himself to be within the range of Grandy's eyes, although those eyes were kept on Jane. He struggled for blankness.

Jane took down the handkerchief, revealed her tousled face, all lumpy with weeping. "Oh, Mr. Grandison, I didn't know you knew. I'm sorry."

"Sorry about what, dear?" They were speaking low. The people in the room couldn't hear what they were saying. It all went for part of the tender little scene.

"He only had an hour," wept Jane. "It wasn't anybody's fault. I told him he shouldn't have come and tried to see me, but, seeing that he had, I couldn't just tell him to go away. So I thought it wouldn't really . . . disturb you."

Grandy said, "You're telling me it wasn't Francis?"

"Oh, no," said Jane. "Of course it wasn't. It was a—a boy I know. I'll never do it again, sir. I'm so sorry."

Grandy said, "But, my dear, I was not complaining. I was curious, y'know. Next time bring him indoors, child. We are not ogres."

Jane began to cry again, as if such kindness were too much to bear.

Francis said, "What's this about? Something to do with me?"

"Tyl thought she . . . saw you," Grandy said, with a curious little break of hesitation and doubt. His eyes turned. Not his head.

"Tyl did?" said Francis. He kept his face blank, turned his eyes, not his head. Too bad. Tough on Mathilda, but the kid would have to put up with this. It looked as if Jane had really fooled him. But at any rate, Tyl's evidence on what she knew or saw was tending to seem more and more unreliable.

Jane was getting to her feet. Francis took her arm. He said kindly, with just a trace of absent-mindedness, "Hadn't you better come along upstairs and wash your face or something?"

In her room they faced each other. "Well?"

She said, "I got it."

"What we thought?"

"Yes." She told him rapidly and rather mechanically. "I listened to it myself. Told them a wild story about a bet. I got a girl there to listen with me, as a witness. Got it cold, and it's what we want. The Phantom Chef said 'Burn tenderly' only once in that record, and he said it at ten thirty-five."

"Fifteen minutes." Francis struck his palm with his other fist.

"Yes," said Jane. There was no triumph.

"And Rosaleen hanging since the fuse blew at ten-twenty. That's proof."

"Yes," said Jane.

"Proof!" Francis was bitter and old again. "Jane, he's the devil. How can we fight the devil? That tongue of his, the power of it! He molds the thoughts in people's heads with his tongue, Jane. Their brains melt. He makes them think what he wants them to think. They're all his puppets. And he's the great director. Look at him now. He's killed twice, committed two murders, and everybody is down there weeping for him."

"Did he . . . kill Althea too?"

"Of course he killed Althea!" swore Francis.

"I couldn't tell Gahagen this alone, but now—"

"Oh, yes, we will now take our nice neat proof to the police," said Francis. "What proof?"

"The time, the radio, the record—all of it. . . . Fran, what's the matter?"

"I can swear Althea told me what she heard on the radio and when she heard it. But you realize . . . Althea isn't here any more."

"You mean we can't—oh, Fran—can't prove it?"

"If I had another witness—"

"Lie then," said Jane fiercely. "I'll say I heard her tell you."

"When?"

"Any time you say."

"You were in the house with them."

"Then you'll have to say she told you some other time."

"When?"

"Oh, I don't know."

"Not you, Jane. Not you, anyhow. It's too dangerous. Maybe you fooled them. All the more reason to keep you out of it now."

"But I'm not out. Why is it any more dangerous?"

"For God's sake, anything's dangerous, anything near him! It's dangerous for us to stand here and talk. It's dangerous to look side-wise at him. I stuck my neck out this morning. Maybe he'll chop my head off before dawn."

"Fran!"

"Why not? He must be on the track of why I'm hanging around here. He must know by now. He's too smart not to see my motive sticking out like a sore thumb. Oh, he's caught on. I hope he hasn't caught on to you. He's quick too. No sooner did he realize that the police knew a fuse had blown . . . Althea's snuffed out. Quick. Neat. No fuss, no bother. Althea was quietly assisted to her grave, all right. And no nasty little loose ends this time, either."

"But you think—you're sure he did it?"

"He did it." Francis dropped his hands. His voice was sick. "But I can't prove it. There's no proof at all. And if he knows now what I'm after, I expect he'll arrange to deal with me."

"You're different," said Jane sharply. "You're no girl."

"True," said Francis. "True. Just the same, if anything does go wrong—"

"Oh, Fran!" Jane shivered.

"Remember Grandy's back-door caller?"

"Do you mean Press, the garbage man?"

"Yes."

"Why?"

"Because," said Francis thoughtfully, "he comes to the back door. And I'm young and strong."

"I'll remember," said Jane. "But what are you going to do?"

"See here. No matter what happens, don't let anything make you admit you're . . . on my side. Mind that, Jane. Promise. Never mind, I've got a better idea. You go home. Resign. Nobody would blame you."

"But what are you going to do?"

"I'll try a bluff."

"What do you mean?"

"I'll insist I've got a witness to what Althea told me. I'll spread out the whole case against him. Pretend it's complete. Maybe I can bluff him. I've got to try. If I could only catch him off guard. Let him make one slip of that tongue! Don't you see, Jane, it could add just enough— You be in there and we—" He broke off.

"I'm not going home," said Jane. "You see, you need me."

"But how am I going to protect you? How can I protect Mathilda?"

"Mathilda?"

He was impatient. Couldn't she see Mathilda was in the most dreadful danger? Couldn't she realize, as he did so clearly, that some one of these days that proud head, those long lovely legs, the exciting green eyes, the whole lovely, bewildered girl, could die? If the old man took a notion—

"Yes, damn it, of course!" he cried. "Look, he's got to get rid of her someday. How am I going to be sure she's safe? She thinks the world of him. She'd do anything he asked, any time. Won't stop to think, because she's clinging to him now. Because she's got to believe in something! And, dear God, how can she believe in me? It's driving me"—he calmed down—"a bit wild," he confessed.

"But he wouldn't dare!"

"Jane, he's more dangerous than you know. He's what Rosaleen said. Perfectly selfish. There's nothing to make him hesitate."

"Can't we go to the police now?"

"Yes, try it. Maybe Gahagen will listen. I wish we had the cold proof. Jane, Grandy'll talk himself out of what we've got. My word's going to be less than enough, after the lies I've told. I don't see how Gahagen can listen."

Jane looked at his face and nearly wept.

"Unless— After all, he's guilty," said Francis. "And he's got guilt in his mind and a mixture of lies and truth to remember. He could slip. It's the only thing I can see to try. Attack. With all I've got. Bluff him down. So," he said rather softly, "I'll try . . . one more legal way."

"What do you mean?"

"Maybe you'll have to go outside the law to get the devil."

"Fran!"

"Sh-h."

Grandy was coming up the stairs. They slipped Jane's door tightly shut and stood without breathing.

If he was coming in here— If he were to find them whispering together—

Luther Grandison was near a violent death just then, as he walked placidly past the door where it was waiting and went into Mathilda's room instead.

Chapter Nineteen

Nor did he know that Francis went like a cat out Jane's window to the kitchen-porch roof and that he clung, tooth and nail, in the angle the house made there outside Mathilda's window or that he watched, one foot on the sill, cheek on the house wall, fingers wound in a vine. Grandy didn't know. Francis couldn't hear. Through the glass he tried to read across the dim room those thin, mobile lips through which the voice was pouring.

"Resting, darling?"

"I'm awake."

"Poor Tyl. Poor sweet Tyl."

"Oh, Grandy."

"Hush, don't cry." Grandy sat down, heavy and sad. "You're all right, Tyl?"

His anxiety pricked her like the tip of a knife he was trying out. "Of course," she said.

"Because it frightens me. I'm afraid."

"Don't be afraid, Grandy. I'm all right." She sat up. "You're thinking of what Francis said this morning?"

"I can't help thinking. There's that old, old, ancient rule of three. It frightens me."

Tyl's pulse began to pound in her throat.

"Make me a promise, sweetheart," Grandy said.

"Of course."

"Promise you'll come straight to me if you feel—if you have any feelings at all that you can't cope with or bear. Promise, Tyl?"

"Yes, Grandy."

"There's a pressure in my house. You can't see it, of course. You can't hear it. Five senses don't betray it to you, but you feel it all the same. I was afraid of it before. It's death, I think. Not our familiar death that comes on schedule for the old or the sick. This is Death, the fascinator. The Death that's like a dark lover. Don't you see, duck? If it got Althea, it was because it got her unaware. She didn't know. She hadn't been warned. There's an attraction, a dreadful pull. Have you never stood on the edge of a steep drop, Tyl, and felt the urge to go over?"

"Yes," she whispered. "Yes, Grandy."

"It's similar, similar. Pressure. Pull. What difference? Something wants you to go over and be done with everything. Francis was so right, duckling, to be afraid."

Tyl tightened her hands on the coverlet. She had been lying on top of the bed, still dressed. Now she sat up, tense, not resting her back against the headboard. The light was dim. Grandy's face was in darkness. His voice was vibrant. She could feel the vibrations in her breast.

"You mustn't worry about me," she said as stoutly as she could. "Please, Grandy. I do love you so. And I'm all right."

"Bless you."

"Grandy," she whispered, "if you're frightened, it scares me more than anything. Don't talk any more. Not about that."

She reached across. She thought he glanced at her, although she couldn't be sure, since his head didn't move in the dusk. Her fingers found the chain and she pulled on her light near the bed. "Let's talk about something else." She sent her voice high and gay. "Please, Grandy. Darling, I brought you a present and you haven't even seen it. I nearly forgot."

It took all the strength she had to be so gay. It took all the courage she could find to try to change the mood for him, as he had so often done for her.

"A present?" he said. His effort was obvious. But he understood and he would play. He would try to be cheerful. "A present for me!"

She slid off the bed and ran to her dresser. The bag of Dutch chocolates was in the drawer. Grandy took it in his hands. He bowed his head. For a dreadful moment she thought he was going to weep. But he did not. He opened the bag gleefully. He took a handful out and tossed them gaily on the bed. For her, he said. Their secret. Their childish secret hoard of goodies. He made a show of it. It should have been such fun.

But all the time she could hear the tears unshed behind his laughter, and when, at last, he kissed her gently on the cheek, and when he went away, clutching the bag of chocolates to his heart, Tyl threw herself on the bed and burst into tearing sobs.

Dear, dearest Grandy, he'd tried so hard, but it was enough to break your heart to see how hard he had to try.

Chapter Twenty

HER EARS MUFFLED by the sounds of her own weeping, it was a while before she heard the staccato tapping on the glass. Mathilda sat up, face wet, eyes red, hair tousled, frozen in the very image of distress, all rumpled by it. She saw him clinging there outside her window.

She knew who it was, and in a curious mood of suspended emotion she got off the bed and went calmly to open the window. Francis scrambled in. He gave her a quick look, enigmatic, and went immediately to lock the door to the hall. Tyl opened her mouth to protest. He hushed her.

"What was Grandy saying?"

She looked dumbly at him, the tears drying on her cheeks. For the moment, she couldn't remember what it was Grandy had been saying. Francis' face was serious, but his eyes hadn't that dark, reproachful, tortured look. On the contrary, they looked down at her with a warm light behind them, something simpler and more friendly than love.

He said, "I do wish you could trust me, Mathilda. I wish you could trust me a little bit, anyhow. I don't know what I'm going to do about you."

"You needn't do anything about me, thank you!" she said fiercely.

His hand on her arm invited her to sit down on the bed. He pulled the dressing-table bench over. They sat there, knee to knee. It seemed absurd, yet Mathilda had a feeling, half memory, that she owed him some courtesy. She sat where he had put her, and prepared to listen.

"You haven't believed very much of what I've told you," he asked her gently, "have you, Mathilda?"

"No."

"There's one thing maybe you could believe, if you'd try. I don't want anything bad to happen to you."

"Why does everybody think something bad might h-happen?" Her voice shook. "I'm all right."

He took her hands suddenly and eagerly. "What did he say? He was talking to you about something happening, was he?" She didn't answer. Francis released her hands, although she hadn't tried to pull away. "I wish you could believe me. This is the damnedest mess. I know. You've got good reasons not to trust me an inch. And yet—Mathilda, listen. I never did think there was any danger that you'd kill yourself. Can you believe that? I was only trying to fix it so nothing would happen to you."

She shook her head, couldn't understand.

He went on desperately, "Now I'm going to do one thing more . . . might help. I want to ask you—I want to beg you to make it a little easier."

"What do you think might happen to me?" she insisted. Her green eyes challenged.

His dark eyes wavered. Then they came back boldly. "You might as well know that much. I don't want you to be murdered."

"To be what?"

"Murdered, as Rosaleen was. Althea too." His voice was very low. Mathilda drew away, leaned back, away from him, watching his face. He was watching hers. It was a strange duel between them.

"Why do you think they were murdered?" she said at last. "Are

you a detective or what?" She was thinking, *This explains—* And
yet nothing was quite clear.

"I'm no detective," Francis said. "I'm just a blundering ass, tangled up in a mess here. And one girl died who might have lived if
I'd stayed out of it. I don't want you to be another."

"You have been lying," said Mathilda. She sat up straighter.
"You admit it now, don't you? All of that stuff in New York, all those
people—you lied. You fixed it."

He didn't answer. He kept watching her face.

"If you admit that," she said, "then I just might believe what you
say now."

Evading, he said, "Did you tell Grandy about it?"

"Certainly."

"About my lies?"

"Certainly."

"Did he believe you?"

"Of course he did!" She would have risen in her rage and gone
away, but he caught at her hand.

"Don't be angry. I asked a question. I just wanted the answer."

"Grandy knows I wouldn't— He knows it couldn't be true that
I— He knows—" she sputtered.

"Then why can't you tell me so, without getting so mad about it?"

"You won't admit you're lying!" she cried. "And I know you're
lying. Why won't you?"

"Is Grandy quite sure I was lying?"

Mathilda covered her face with both hands. "Please, go away.
Get out of my room. What do you want, anyway?"

He said grimly, "I want to fix it so you'll live, baby. I've got here
a will you made."

"A will?"

"Will. Last will and testament. I expect it's one of those things
you've forgotten. It was made in the three lost days." Francis' voice
and manner had changed. He was casual, glib. "Oh, it's legal, all
right. The whole thing is in your handwriting. Perfectly good last
will and testament. At least plenty good enough to raise an awful
stink if you should die."

"If I should—"

"My object is . . . that you don't die. I believe that if I show this
little paper in certain places, it will tend to lengthen your life." He
looked at her insolently. No, not insolently, but with a reckless look,
a gambling look.

She said, "Oh. Now I understand."

"You do?"

"It was the money." She laughed in his face. It pleased her to see his face sobering, losing some of that wild light. "Why I should have been confused by the lie you told about your wealth— What's one more lie to you? You thought I was dead. You thought I'd never come back! You worked out this whole scheme to chisel in."

"Muscle," he corrected. "Muscle in."

"You saw a chance to get your hands on the Frazier fortune! You're so good at forgeries. You really do lie very well."

Francis looked down at her white angry face. "I really don't know whether I can keep you from being murdered," he said with a curious, detached effect. "I'll try."

Mathilda sprang up. "I'm just beginning to wonder," she blazed, "if your scheme doesn't include my murder!"

They were eye to eye now in anger.

"In about a minute," said Francis, "I'm going to spank. I tell you you're in danger of your life. I know it. It makes no least difference to me what kind of liar you choose to call me. I'm some kinds of liar, but this kind I'm not. For some strange reason, I don't want you to die."

"Because you love me," sneered Mathilda.

"Unh-uh." It was a negative. It slipped out. It was an admission. She ought to seize upon it triumphantly. But she didn't. "Let's not worry about who loves whom," he went on gently, and he was smiling. "Let's forget that and go back and start over. Do you think you could listen to an idea?"

"What idea?"

"Sh-h, sh-h."

"What idea?" she repeated more quietly.

"I'll show this will to—show this around. Nobody then is going to murder you for your money except me. Right?"

"Right," she said.

"Now we'll protect you from me. Make another will, Mathilda, and hide it. Hide it from me, but tell a stranger where you hide it. The only thing is—promise don't tell—"

"Don't tell whom?"

"Don't tell anyone you know."

Mathilda drew her breath as slowly as she could. She shook herself down to calmness. "You are trying to make me afraid that someone wants to kill me. Why don't you tell me straight out who that person is?"

"Because," said Francis, "there are two Mathildas. One of them could not ever believe me. The other one knows already."

The silence closed in. Suddenly she found herself in Francis' arms. Her impulse was to let go, give up to the warmth there, put her face against him and let the tears through. But she struggled.

"Sorry," he said. He set her back on her own equilibrium. "I know what you're going through. Something about the way you take it breaks my heart." He spoke lightly. His eyes had that warm light. His eyebrows flew up with his smile. He half turned, as if to let her pull herself together. "Lookit! Chocolates!"

She watched him pick up a brightly wrapped candy, peel off the wrapper. She made herself remember that he was a liar. She said, "Your forgeries are so very clever, perhaps I'd better make a genuine will."

She went to her little gray desk, pulled out paper and pen. "To all whom it may concern," she wrote angrily, decisively. She put down the date in big firm figures and underlined it. "This is my will and it supersedes all others, including the one forged by a man who calls himself my husband. I am twenty-two years old, unmarried, perfectly sane. I don't know legal language, but I intend to make my meaning so clear—"

Standing behind her, Francis munched chocolates.

She wrote down that everything she had must belong to her beloved guardian, Luther Grandison. She finished it. She signed it.

Francis nodded. "Good," he said.

She looked up into his eyes. They didn't seem anything but clear and friendly. "If you'll just hide it," he said. "Please, Tyl. And tell a stranger. But only a stranger. What harm can that do? Call it a whim. Call it anything. Give me that little bit of trust or take it for a little bit of advice that can't hurt you."

She thought she could feel the warmth of his presence close above her. The moment crystallized, as some moments will, and for just that while she was aware of the whole setting—herself at the desk with the light falling on her hands, the paper under them, white against the rosy blotter, the green pen lying there. All the background was in her mind, as if she could see it too. The gray walls around them, the furniture, the bed with its yellow spread, its soft pale yellow silken quilt, the hollow in the pillow where her head had been.

And she heard the silence of the house beyond the room's walls. She was aware of the deserted gardens outside, below, and of the globe of the world turning through the dark toward dawn.

And in the core of the moment was the warmth of his presence, where he stood just behind her, looking down over her shoulder easily, not touching her and yet surrounding her as if there were a shield at her back.

She said, "All right. I'll hide it."

Where had her wrath gone? Where was the stubborn conflict and clash of wills? Mathilda tilted her head, looked up and back. She smiled.

He bent and kissed her warmly, heartily, like a brother, like a friend. An endearing kiss, it asked for nothing. It congratulated her.

Then he put a handful of chocolates in his pocket. "These are good," he said. "Good night." For the second, he hesitated, as if he wondered what to call her. Dear, or what? He touched her shoulder. "Thanks, pal," he said.

Then he put one long leg out the window absurdly, as if he were getting into a pair of trousers. His face grinned at her a last moment over the sill. She heard faint scrambling noises. He was gone.

She put the window down, stepped quickly back and away from it. She didn't want him to see her watching, if he should look back. Because, of course, she wasn't watching.

She had the new will in her hand. She folded it small. She looked about for a place. A little hanging shelf near the bed had some books in it. She took one down, a thin book of poetry—Lucile—in a cardboard case. She put her piece of paper inside, between the book and its case. It wasn't a very good hiding place, but it would do.

Mathilda undressed, got into bed. She told herself that when the light was out she would lie and think things through. She would start at the beginning and be clear about everything. She would try to organize the facts, make some sense out of what had been happening. She would try to understand with her brain, instead of feeling about in the confusion with a straining heart. Instead of drifting in and out of people's arms. She thought, *What a way to behave.* She must—must be clear.

But once the light was off and she lay snug under the yellow comforter, Mathilda fell immediately asleep.

In the morning, she was surprised to find that the door of her room had been locked all night. It wasn't her habit to lock her door.

It made her a little ashamed to think she'd forgotten. Because, of course, it was Francis who had locked it, and she'd simply forgotten.

Chapter Twenty-one

GRANDY PUSHED the button; the gadget operated. Francis opened the study door from the living room and came in. He crossed easily to the visitor's chair and sat down. Jane, at her little desk in the corner, kept the rhythm of her typing steady, but the sense of the line she had been typing dissolved into a jumble of meaningless letters, as if she'd suddenly begun to type in code.

Grandy had a cigarette in his holder. He pushed papers fretfully away and leaned on his folded hands. He inquired after Francis' health this morning.

Francis said, "I want to talk to you."

"By all means," said Grandy with some curiosity. . . . "Jane—"

"I'd like Jane to stay, if you don't mind."

"I don't mind." Grandy took the holder out of his mouth and fingered it delicately. He waited.

"Because," said Francis, "I'd like a disinterested person to hear what I am going to say."

"Would you like Jane to take notes?" said Grandy charmingly, obligingly. "She does shorthand very well."

Francis was not diverted. "I came to tell you that you are no longer unsuspected," he said quietly. "And murder's too much, you know, to excuse, even in one who has been so kind."

Grandy's interested expression remained unchanged, unless he looked even more interested. "Please do go on," he said in enchanted tones, as if this were the very thing he had needed to stimulate and excite him.

"When Rosaleen Wright hanged herself that winter morning," said Francis coolly, "she knocked over a lamp, uprooted some wires and blew a fuse."

"So Tom Gahagen was telling me," said Grandy amiably. One would think they approached a puzzle together.

"Your clock on the mantel just beyond that wall was stopped. The time was twenty minutes after ten."

Grandy shifted in his chair. "Yes, yes. All this we know. What's the significance?"

"Althea was in the kitchen that morning?"

"Yes. Certainly. Althea was in the kitchen."

"So were you, Mr. Grandison."

"So was I," he agreed benignly.

"You entered the kitchen," said Francis slowly, "by that door, from this room, at ten thirty-five."

"Whatever makes you think so?"

"You see what it means if that is true?"

Grandy's mouth flattened, expressing distaste. "Something very nasty," he said. "Very nasty." He cocked his head. "Do you follow him, Jane?"

Jane felt a trickle of perspiration down her back. "I don't—no, I don't, sir," she faltered. Her eyes were round as saucers and she looked frightened.

"Really a horrible idea," said Grandy thoughtfully. "That she hanged herself before my eyes, eh? While I watched?"

Francis shrugged.

"Oh, I see!" cried Grandy. "Dear me, I hanged her!"

"The odd part of it is," said Francis, "that you did, and I can prove it."

"That would be very odd indeed," said Grandy. "How?"

"Oh, not the icebox light." Francis tossed this at him. But Grandy's head did not tremble from its bright, interested pose. "Althea told me and one other person, who will remember what was said and so testify." Francis hesitated. "You see you killed Althea a trifle too late."

"So," said Grandy rather more heavily, "Althea too? My lovely girl, the one I've lost."

Jane let out a childish whimper. Grandy looked across at her. "My dear," he said tenderly, "can you bear to hear the rest of this? I'd like you to. Try not to feel. Just listen to the words."

Jane bent her head.

"Now," said Grandy, turning to Francis, his eyes glinting, "proceed, Mr. Howard."

Francis thought, *Jane's fooled him. He's acting for Jane.* He marshaled his attack.

"Althea turned the radio up, if you remember—or even if you don't"—Francis caught and controlled his temper—"at precisely the moment you entered the kitchen and closed that door. She was struck by a phrase said over the air. She remembered it clearly. That program was recorded at the time, Mr. Grandison. It gives away the exact minute. The minute you left this room. And that minute was ten thirty-five. Not earlier."

Grandy said, "My dear boy." He said it gently, with pity. "When did Althea tell you this?"

"The evening—the night she died."

"What a day and a night you've had since." Grandy spoke softly. "That is, if she really did—or even if you, for any reason, believe this story."

Francis found his throat unmanageable. The evil old bird was so full of pity. He was turning it, pretending to be seeing a point of view. He was not worried, not even looking worried. He was not reacting according to plan. The scene wasn't going right. A guilty man, accused, had no business to look so sorry for his accuser, so successfully sorry.

Grandy said, as if to be fair, "After all, you are nearly a stranger here. But even so, dear boy, what reason do you imagine I would have had for such a deed as that?" Then, almost gaily, "Come, Mr. Howard, I must have a motive."

"My wife's money," said Francis, "was and is your motive."

"Eh?"

"You played around with it. Rosaleen Wright found out."

"Oh, dear. Oh, dear." Grandy took off his pince-nez and rubbed his eyes. "Yes?" he said. The black eyes were brimming with mirthful tears. "But Mathilda isn't your wife at all, Mr. Howard. You see, we know that."

Francis heard Jane's gasp. *Oh, good girl, Jane.* He said aloud, coldly, "Would you be willing to let me or anyone examine the records of the Frazier fortune?"

"Certainly," said Grandy. "This does seem so silly. As for Althea's story, what occurs to me, Mr. Howard, is the thought that Althea told no story. I think you invented it."

"Two of us invented it?"

"That's not impossible," said Grandy smoothly. "Who is your—er—corroborator?"

"In view of my opinion of you," said Francis evenly, "I don't believe I care to say."

Grandy leaned back. "You don't mean it," he challenged. "You're not serious."

"I'm serious."

"Isn't it too bad," said Grandy in a moment, "that Althea isn't here to help us? Oh, I see! I see! That's why I'm supposed to have done her in? Well, really, that's not unsound. That's good thriller-level reasoning, Mr. Howard."

Francis bit on his cheek. "Also," he said, struggling to stay calm and seem confident, "there is Rosaleen's false suicide note. Cribbed out of an old book. What did you do? Ask her to copy it one day?"

Grandy's face fell. "Poor Rosaleen. Poor child," he crooned. "I didn't like to point out what she'd done. Poor sick little mind! Did we delve too much, I wonder, into old crimes and ancient madness?"

"Sick mind, my eye!" Francis shot up out of his chair. "And Althea was sick, too, wasn't she? Although nobody saw any signs of it but you. What will Mathilda be when her time comes? Or anybody else you decide to get rid of? Let me show you something now." He slammed the paper down on the desk, keeping his palm on it. "That's Mathilda's will. And I warn you, see to it that Mathilda doesn't die! Because, if she does, I don't think you'll care to have me and my lawyers going into financial history."

Grandy's eyes flickered. Francis held his breath, but the old man's hand was steady. He touched the paper. He read it. He took off his pince-nez and looked up.

"A forgery," he said softly. Brown eyes met black. Jane in her corner trembled.

"Do I see it all now?" mused Grandy, cocking his head. "Did you think she was lost at sea? Did you think you'd cut a piece of money with your fantastic story? I can understand so far, yes, indeed. But what are you up to now? Ah! Am I to pay you for suppressing your little ideas?"

Francis could have wrung his skinny neck. Might have done so, indeed, if Jane hadn't cried out.

"There now, you've frightened Jane," said Grandy in pouting reproach. There was no breaking there, no self-betrayal, no guilty squirm, no fear in this man. He was untouched, bland, confident, and the voice was sirup-smooth. Francis knew himself to be too angry to think, to have been outdone in self-control, and out-bluffed.

He turned and said stiffly to Jane, "I'm sorry if I frightened you." He said to Grandy, as quietly as he could, "I'll take my little ideas to Gahagen, then."

"Dear boy," said Grandy warmly, "if you believe all that nonsense, you most certainly should go to Gahagen or someone. Besides," he added ruefully, "although for my part, I only wish I could help you—I'm afraid you do need help rather badly—still, I did rather promise Tyl to kick you out the door."

Francis said, "Don't bother, Mr. Grandison." He left the room.

When he had gone, Jane thought, *For my life, for my life.* She twisted her hands, filled her china-blue eyes with horror. "Oh, Mr. Grandison, wasn't he awful?"

"Poor chap," said Grandy. "The fellow's a fraud, of course. My poor Tyl—"

"Oh, Mr. Grandison!" cried Jane, for her life. "Nobody's going to believe anything he says! He was just trying to make trouble!"

"And well he may make trouble," said Grandy. He put his hands to his forehead wearily. "Run, fetch me some coffee, my dear. That's a good girl. Yes, do."

"Oh, Mr. Grandison!" quavered Jane, still acting for her life. "I can't tell you how sorry I feel that you have to be bothered—"

She got out the door and stood trying to control a fit of nervous shaking.

Grandy drew over his desk phone, gave a number. "Press? . . . Ah, my dear fellow, there is something I'd like you to do for me. . . . Yes, I thought you would." Then his voice cracked like a whip, "This must be quick. Do you understand?"

"Whatever you say," said the man on the other end hopelessly.

Chapter Twenty-two

WHEN MATHILDA got down to the kitchen for her breakfast, there was only Oliver. He was sitting over a saucer full of cigarette butts.

"Where's everybody?" she asked.

"In with Grandy."

"Oh." Mathilda got herself coffee from the stove. She hoped it was good and strong. She had awakened in a cold sweat. She wondered if she was coming down with something. She felt numb and confused and as if a lowering cloud hung over the world, something black and terrifying, ominous, threatening, as if there was worse to come. Perhaps it was only that Althea was dead.

Oliver was lighting another cigarette. He glanced at her nervously as she sat down. "The funeral is this afternoon," he blurted out. "They've released the body. Grandy says get it over with."

Mathilda shivered. What could she say? Nothing to say. It was simply stupid to open your mouth and say, "I'm sorry." Oliver put out his cigarette and lit another. He didn't seem to know he was doing so.

"This accident stuff is all right for publication," he blurted, "but it wasn't any accident."

"What do you mean, Oliver?" Tyl put out her hand and touched his. She did feel sorry for him. There must be a way to let him know it.

"Because she must have eaten them! Eaten them!"

"Eaten what?"

"Those pills. By the handful."

"The sleeping dope?"

"Yes, because, listen, Tyl, Doctor Madison knows damn well how she used to love to take a lot of junk. He fixed her up with some extra-mild ones. He told me so, when I worried about it. He knew she'd take too many, too often. He said the effect was mostly psy-

chological, anyhow. Tyl, for her to die, she must have eaten a whole
bottle. So she must have wanted to die. Don't you see?"

"I can't believe—"

"You'd better believe it."

"Oliver, you didn't have any stronger pills in there, did you?"

"Never touch the junk. No. Nothing."

Mathilda shook her head. She could feel the cloud, that heavy,
depressing, shadowing bulk that seemed to exist in the back of her
consciousness, ready to come down and swallow her up in despair.
She was afraid. She drank more coffee hastily.

"I can't stop going over that fight we had." Oliver stared at her
with reddened eyes. "I can't stop."

"You mustn't do that," said Tyl. She, herself, felt that this was an
unsupported statement. If he had asked why not, she couldn't have
answered.

"I know," he said. "I know, but I can't stop. 'Burn tenderly.' What
does that mean to you?"

"What does what mean?"

" 'Burn tenderly.' "

"I don't know. I never heard such a thing."

"Wouldn't you guess it was love stuff? Wouldn't you think it came
out of some lousy poem? Or some fancy speech in the movies? 'My
heart burns tenderly.' "

"Maybe," she said.

"Yeah."

"What's the matter? Why are you worrying about that?"

Oliver put his head down, and for once his forelock fell over his
eyes without the self-conscious boyishness with which he had been
known to let it fall. "Althea wouldn't talk that night. Night before
last. Not at first. She just wouldn't talk to me at all. But then she
laughed and said that out loud. I don't think she meant to, but she
said, 'Burn tenderly.' Tyl, I thought she and Francis must have been
talking that way—you know, love stuff. Reading each other poems
or something. I was mad. I told her what I thought. I said that
proved it. She tried to tell me it was something some cook had said
on the radio."

"Cook?"

"Yeah. Do you believe it?"

"I don't . . . know."

"I asked her how she'd happened to remember some dumb thing
a cook said on the radio, especially at a time like that. She had a

story. She said it was because she turned the radio up in the middle of a program. She'd turned it down on account of Grandy coming in, and then she turned it up, and the guy said those two words just out of a clear silence. It sounded funny. She said she'd been telling Francis about it."

"Telling Francis?"

"Do you believe that?"

"It sounds crazy."

"That's what I thought."

"Why should she be telling Francis what some cook said on the radio?"

"Yeah, that's what I wondered. I think—I still think— Oh, I don't know what I think. Suppose she did carry on with him. Tyl, I'm sorry." His eyes looked desperate. He was lost in this anguish of new honesty.

"That's all right," she said weakly. "Oliver, don't keep beating yourself. She couldn't have been enough involved with Francis to kill herself. Anyhow, Althea wouldn't have killed herself for any such kind of thing. Do you know what I mean?"

Oliver nodded. He seemed to relax a little. "I know," he said. "She was . . . flirtatious, I guess you'd say. She liked to get men interested. That was what interested her. And it would have gone on all our lives."

"I expect it would," said Tyl sadly. It was true. Althea would never want what she had, but would always have watched with her silver eyes for her chance to step in and take what somebody else wanted. It was the act of taking away, the use of her power, that she had savored. Poor, restless, envious, uneasy Althea. Could she have seen herself and, with sudden clarity, known she must never grow old?

"Such a mess," groaned Oliver. "Everything gone wrong. From the minute we married. You got lost. Rosaleen did that . . . thing. Then Francis came, and she— He's very attractive."

"Yes," said Tyl.

"Now, this. I'm talking too much. I'm taking my troubles out on you. Tyl, you're swell. Sometimes I think I played a pretty dirty trick on you too. If I did, I hope you've forgiven me."

"Yes," she said with a shrinking feeling. "Don't talk about it."

"You know, Tyl, your money's a bad thing."

"I know," she whispered.

"I mean"—his eyes begged her to understand—"it works out a

way you probably don't realize. Althea was so beautiful, and there was your money, and I kept thinking, 'Am I fooling myself? Is it the money I care for?'"

"I suppose you would," she said painfully.

"It's easy to fool yourself. I've been fooling myself all my life. I don't know how to stop, either."

"Oliver, don't."

"So when Grandy said Althea would never have anything but love to make her happy—"

"Grandy?"

"You see, I didn't notice what was going on. I guess I just couldn't believe that Althea would—well, get interested in me that way. And of course, I didn't know the way you felt, either."

"The way I felt? What way, Oliver?"

"Oh, I mean the way it was. I'm the old-timer around here. You could be sure of me. I mean, you had to be so careful some ordinary fortune hunter didn't try to play up to you. Grandy told me you had a dread of that."

Mathilda hung on to the edge of the table. The cloud was coming down. It was going to get her. She felt sick with fear.

"He cleared that up," Oliver said. "He explained how your love for me was a gentle, friendly feeling, because you felt sure of me on that score. Not real love."

She thought she'd faint. She fought against it.

"Tyl—"

She managed to murmur something. "Everything's been awful this morning. I didn't sleep well." *But I did,* she thought. *I slept too hard and too long.*

"It's been awful. I know." Oliver brooded. "Dear old Grandy, of course, wanted us all to be happy. He was right, wasn't he, about you? I asked you right out that day—you made a wisecrack. I thought—I mean—"

"Don't stammer," she said sharply. "Grandy's always right. He knows me better than I know myself, almost."

She thought, *But I mustn't ever tell Grandy how wrong he was or what he did to me. It would break his heart if he knew. Besides, it's all over now, and it doesn't matter. He must have known it wouldn't last. Oh, Grandy must have known. And if I hadn't been so proud and wanted to run away and hide everything, he'd have drawn out the sting long ago. I was a fool. I should have trusted him.* She beat back her depression. She beat back fear.

Then she remembered the strange talk last night with Francis, about the will. The taste of fear rose in her throat. She thought, *What's the matter with me?*

She left Oliver and went toward the living room.

"Don't look like that!" Tyl cried. "Don't!" Jane was in there, crouching against the wall by the study door, like an animal stiff with fear. Tyl's hands went up to her eyes. She thought, *No, I can't stand it.*

"I'm awfully sorry," Jane said, straightening. "I don't know what's the matter with me."

"I'm sorry too," said Mathilda. "I don't know why I . . . screamed at you. I guess it's just nerves." She smiled faintly.

"I guess it's just nerves," Jane agreed. She smiled faintly back.

Tyl thought, watching Jane walk away, *I need another girl to talk to.* It didn't strike her that this was the first time Grandy hadn't seemed better than another girl to talk to.

Chapter Twenty-three

THERE WAS THE FUNERAL to face that afternoon. They made themselves sandwiches for lunch and snatched them in the kitchen. It was a queer, unsettled kind of meal, as if they were all just marking time, waiting time out until it should go by and bury Althea and release them to normal processes of grief and adjustment.

Francis wasn't there. The odd thing was that no one mentioned him. Grandy said nothing. Oliver was bound up in his inner struggle and seemed not to notice. It was not Jane's place, perhaps, to say anything about a missing guest. But Mathilda kept expecting him or at least expecting someone to say a word that would explain where he was, where he had gone, for how long. She did not ask any questions herself.

When they set out in the chauffeured car lent by a friend, there were the four of them—Grandy, Oliver, Jane and Mathilda. The four of them got in and settled themselves as if no one were missing. Francis wasn't there.

Mathilda thought perhaps he would meet them at the chapel. He would be among the others and he would come back with them when it was all over. Nobody asked any questions. It was a little strange that Grandy seemed not to have noticed at all. Mathilda's so-called husband was not where he ought to have been, even if he were only pretending. Not there, not by her side. Not there, as he had been yesterday. People would wonder.

Jane was quiet as a mouse. Jane didn't ask. Oliver didn't ask. Mathilda, herself, although the question was beginning to beat hard in her mind, didn't venture to ask. It would have been queer if she were the one to ask. She thought if she waited surely his absence would be explained. If she just waited.

The little chapel downtown in the small city was thronged with friends, the whole picturesque lot of them. Tyl sat beside Grandy and modeled herself after him in frozen calm. *Be a lady. Never betray an emotion.*

The ceremony was only an ordeal. She thought, if only Francis had come. If only he were on her other side, where he ought to be. But that wasn't true. He had no place—no real place and no real obligation. He only pretended. Oh, but why wasn't he there, pretending, now? She counted the scallops in the frieze. This was not the time to feel what you really felt about Althea, or remember her as she was, or try to understand her life and her death. *Don't cry. Count the folds in the curtains. One, two, three, four.*

When it was over, some few friends came back with them and there was tea. Francis wasn't there.

When people had thinned out, drifted off, finally gone, Oliver at last asked the question, "Say, where is Francis? Where's he been? He wasn't there at the chapel, was he?" Oliver's face turned to Mathilda for the answer.

Like throwing a ball, Mathilda thought. *Don't they know!*

"When he left us this morning, I believe he said he was going downtown." Grandy was mildly speculative. "Didn't he, Jane?"

Jane said, "Yes," faintly. "Yes, he did, Mr. Grandison."

"That is strange. . . . Tyl, do you know where Francis is?"

The ball had come back to her. "I don't know where he is," she said stiffly. "I don't know a thing about him. I never did. It's about time all of you knew he isn't my husband."

Jane knew already that Francis was a fraud. That could be seen in the steadiness of her eyes and heard in the murmur she made, which was only polite.

But Oliver was shocked right out of his chair. Mathilda had to tell him the details, and he wanted to hash them over and exclaim and wonder and go around and around over the puzzle of Francis. At the same time, she thought she could see a kind of inner gleam, a repressed sparkle in his eyes when he looked at her. Tyl felt herself getting angry. She answered him in a series of grudging short phrases. She didn't want Oliver's gossipy rehash. She didn't want to hear Oliver's ideas of why people behaved as they did. She didn't want to hear Oliver wondering what made Francis tick. She felt he wouldn't know.

She was sick and ashamed of the emotional background to Francis' story. She couldn't tell them that, of course. How she'd been in such a weeping, wailing, brokenhearted, upset state over Oliver. But without that part the whole story sounded trivial and cold. Here was a man who claimed she had married him. Why had she? Presumably because she had wanted to. And then she forgot. No background of emotional distress to explain how it all might have happened. Her upset and her silly baby thoughts of revenge. Ridiculously, she found herself defending Francis. Of course, it was a lie, but it had been a good lie.

"You don't understand," she cried.

"My God, do you?" cried Oliver, and she was too angry to answer.

Jane said perhaps he'd run away. She said it looking at Grandy as if they two had secrets about Francis.

Mathilda said in anger, "I'm going to bed." How had she got herself into such a temper?

Halfway up the stairs, a ring at the front door stopped her and sent her heart leaping. It was only someone to see Grandy. Might as well go up. But that voice? She stopped and looked down again. All she could see was the top of the man's red head. Francis had dark hair, not quite black. Francis hadn't come back at all; hadn't been seen all day.

Chapter Twenty-four

THE CELLAR WAS DRY. That, at least, was a blessing. He was alive and uninjured. More blessings to count. How long he would be able to count these or to count at all was very doubtful. Francis expected the worst. He expected that an attempt would be made to kill him. He expected it to succeed. He did not know how he could counter such an attempt, bound and tied as he was with strong harsh ropes, gagged as he was with old rags, trussed up like a chicken for the roasting, ridiculously helpless.

It was fantastic to be so helpless. Francis thought of the movies he had seen, of the many, many scenes in which a hero had been marched at the point of a hidden gun out of the cheerful streets to some lonely lair and been tied up. He thought that if he escaped to see another such movie, he would understand, he would sympathize, he would be more anxious. He would not wonder why the fellow went so quietly, nor would he be quite so confident that somehow, with his teeth, or his clever fingers, or by rolling about, the hero would get loose in time.

Francis couldn't see any way to get loose. The ropes were tight and firm. He could barely move his hands. His working fingers grasped at nothing but air or, if he rolled slightly, the bare cement floor of the cellar. The gag was tight too. No use rubbing his cheek against the rough cement. It only scratched and tore his skin. The gag wouldn't move. It was anchored tight. It was all he could do not to choke.

His ankles were bound together. He could not get up, would have had no balance, anyway. And there was nowhere to roll, no advantage to it. This part of the cellar was perfectly empty. The floor, the rough whitewashed walls, a little window high up, one naked light bulb, the wooden door to another room. Nothing else at all.

He had lost track of time. It was night. The little window admitted no daylight any more, although, for a while after he had been brought here, there had been some light, blocked by green bushes, coming dimly through the leaves and the dirt on the glass. Now there was only a black oblong, although some light must come from somewhere—enough to distinguish the white walls from the black window. Just enough for that.

Night would pass. Sooner or later, there would be that dim daylight. It was all he could look forward to, unless the woman should come down with food again. He didn't like to think of that woman. Mrs. Press, he supposed she was. Tall, very thin, emaciated, no more shape than a stick, and no more color. She was a caricature of a woman. A long-jawed face and hair tight back in a bun, all drab, pale gray tones. She looked like a slave, a drudge, one who had been kicked and beaten. She appeared to be perfectly obedient. But what he feared was that she was not obedient, because the eyes in that long, ugly face were neither sad nor dulled. The eyes were full of enthusiasm. He suspected that Mrs. Press would be, if not obedient, rather terrible. He hoped Mr. Press or somebody would be able to keep her in line.

Hope? Well, it sprang eternal, thought Francis. The ache in his arm, where the old wound was, beat with his heart. He began to wonder why he was still alive. He thought he could guess.

At midnight, although Francis didn't know it was only that, he heard them coming down the cellar stairs. Somewhere beyond the wooden door the stairs came down and there was a furnace and such other cellar furniture. Out there he heard their feet and heard their voices. Heard Press say, in his dull voice, "No trouble."

And he heard the rich warm voice of Luther Grandison, the famous voice, so full of sentiment, so beloved on the radio, heard it saying, "Good work, my dear fellow. You were very prompt, and I do appreciate it. Now, let us see."

The wooden door was unbarred from outside. It was opened. Someone turned on the light, and the unshaded bulb blinded him for a moment.

Francis thought, *He'll have to kill me now. He intends to kill me. Or he wouldn't let me see him. He wouldn't come openly.*

Grandy took off his pince-nez delicately. "Ah, yes," he said. "Can you remove that—er—impediment to his speech? I want to talk. You can control him, can't you?"

"Guess so," said Press. He moved indifferently to the business of ungagging his prisoner. He was a strong man, as Francis had discovered before—physically strong. He seemed to have no feeling about what had happened or might happen. Obviously, he carried out orders.

But there was a lean gray shadow behind him, a shadow with gleaming eyes. That woman. Francis knew himself to be afraid.

Press was loosening the gag. As it came off, Francis did choke. He coughed, retched, got control of his breath at last. He said nothing. What was the use, unless he shouted for help, and what was the use of shouting?

Grandy squatted down rather stiffly. After all, he was not young. His fingers fumbled about Francis' body. He was searching for something. He found it and stood again. He had the will in his hands—the will that was supposed to have been written out by Mathilda.

"I think we will just dispose of this," he said distastefully, and lit a match and burned it, holding the paper until the last possible moment, with perfectly steady fingers. Then he dropped the charred ash and stamped on it. The smell of burned paper seemed to fill the place.

Francis thought what a fool he had been. We are so vulnerable to plain, unadorned violence. We tend to think our enemies will play by the rules. We can't conceive of the rules being wiped out. We don't really, except on the battlefield, believe in the existence of ruthless, violent people. We believe them when we see them. He ought to have known better.

He said aloud, "There is a copy."

But Grandy smiled. It was said too late. A copy of a holograph will? Absurd, anyway.

Grandy said, "Now, please. I'll have the name of the person who heard Althea's evidence."

Francis made his mouth say pleasantly, "You will?"

"Oh, yes, I think so," said Grandy, in high spirits. The thin shadow that was Mrs. Press came a little closer. She had something long and sharp in her hand. It was metal. It caught light. Not a knife. An ice pick. Francis began to laugh painfully. It was nearly a giggle. Everything that was happening to him seemed so absurd. Such old stuff. And so effective. It was comical how effective it was, the threat of torture.

Press was leaning indifferently against the wall. Mrs. Press said, "Shall I?"

Grandy was watching Francis with cold speculation. "We'll see," he said.

"It won't be necessary," said Francis. "I'm no hero."

"Very sensible. Go on."

"There was no one," said Francis with perfect truth. "She told me about it down in the guest house that night. We were alone there."

"No second person?" said Grandy softly.

"No one at all."

Grandy lifted an eyebrow. "Mrs. Press," he said.

"No!" cried Francis, outraged. "Don't! I'm telling you the truth! There really isn't— I can't give you a name when there isn't any name."

"Just let us see," said Grandy, nodding. "Life follows bad literature so often, you know. Perhaps he is being a hero. I dare say he wishes to protect that witness."

"There wasn't any witness."

The woman got down on her knees. She put the point of the thing under his thumbnail.

"Who was it?"

"Nobody."

"Who was it?"

"Nobody. I was bluffing."

"What is your name?"

"Francis Howard."

"Not in the mood for the truth yet, Mrs. Press. Continue."

Francis ground his teeth. He mustn't tell his name, because of Jane. Because his name was Jane's name, too, and Grandy must not know. Jane would have the sense to leave his house now. Get out of that house. Jane was so much smarter than she looked. But Mathilda? What could he do for Mathilda? The pain was wicked.

"Sorry!" he gasped. "This is pretty futile! There wasn't anyone! Shall I invent a person?"

Grandy said, "Just one moment, Mrs. Press. . . . Now listen to me. I know your name is not Howard. I understand, now, the trick you played with that marriage license. I realize that you scoured the city and all suburban communities for a bona-fide license issued that day with the name Frazier on it. Finding one for a Mary Frazier was a great stroke of luck. Although you searched for it. You earned it. Of course, it follows that you simply assumed the other name on the license. You had to. I think your first name actually is Francis, all right. Not John. And your surname is not Howard.

"Let me make it plain that I know this because it has been independently checked. A newspaperman actually found the original bride and groom, and interviewed them. He came to me, quite puzzled. Just this evening. I appeared to be puzzled, too, and begged for time, but I was enlightened, you see? Now that you understand how much I know and guess, proceed, Mr. Howard."

Francis thought of his past life. He said, "My name is Shields." It wasn't. He hoped it would pass.

Grandy said, "Thank you. Now, about that witness."

"No witness," said Francis dully. "You can do this forever. I can't stop you." He closed his eyes and waited for the pain. He thought how futile torture really was. There was nothing certain about the results you got, after all. Innocent people would swear to guilt to escape it, as readily as guilty people would give up the truth. There is nothing solid in fear. Nothing a torturer can rely on. Bad evidence, in fact. It ought to be suspect. It almost could not be true. "Can't rely on it," he muttered.

He heard Mrs. Press breathing.

"That will do," said Grandy severely.

Francis felt the moisture form drops on his forehead and begin to roll away.

"I doubt if it matters," said Grandy thoughtfully. "You may have been bluffing. I think we've had enough of this sort of thing." He spoke as if it had all been in rather bad taste.

Mrs. Press said, "A couple of times more—"

"No more," said Grandy.

She obeyed.

Francis opened his eyes and looked curiously at Grandy. "Next?" he inquired.

"My dear boy," said Grandy, as if to say, "Really, need you ask?"

"Am I going to commit suicide? I warn you. I don't think that's altogether a good idea."

"Oh, I agree," said Grandy pleasantly. "It isn't a good idea at all. Jane gave me a thought, you know."

Francis absorbed the shock of her name, prayed it hadn't been noticed.

"Jane suggested to me this evening that perhaps, after your little failure this morning, you had given up your schemes. She wondered if you hadn't simply run away."

Francis tried to look flabbergasted. He thought, *Jane's all right. He's not onto her yet.* He tried to let his battered mouth form a sneer. "That's stupid," he said.

"Not at all," said Grandy brightly. "I think it's perfectly logical.

You see, first the scheme to get Mathilda's fortune was spoiled by the fact that Mathilda wasn't dead. The little will, all that careful preparation, wasted. Well, Althea's suicide, so soon after another death of the same kind in my house—of course, it suggested foul play. You would begin to wonder how you could turn that to account. Althea is dead. She can't deny whatever you choose to say she said." Grandy interrupted himself, so abruptly did he change the smooth spinning of a story into accusation. "You found that picture in the paper—the photograph of the clock?"

"Yes," said Francis.

"You pointed it out to Gahagen?"

"Yes."

"Well," said Grandy. "Well, well. Then, even before Althea died, you were scheming. Ah-ha! Perhaps you killed Althea."

Francis said, "I don't have the advantages of two bathrooms."

Grandy said, "Perhaps you put more powerful pills— Dear me, what an alliteration!"

"Planted them?" said Francis helpfully.

"Yes, indeed. You see, it's going to be quite an interesting story."

"I can see that it will be," conceded Francis.

"You have already disappeared. It did look so queer that you weren't at the funeral. It only remains—"

"To dispose of me?"

"Exactly."

Press spoke for the first time. "Look," he said. "Not here."

Francis wanted to whoop with laughter. Was the fellow aroused at last, thinking of his cellar floor?

"Oh, dear me, no. Certainly not here," Grandy reassured him. "My dear fellow, I shouldn't think of it."

"Whatever you say," said Press. He had a bitter, harsh voice. His eyes were without hope and yet smoldering. Francis thought, *He might help me. He's being compelled. None of this is his idea.*

But Press said, "I suppose I've got to do it for you. Only not here," and the flat resignation in his voice was not encouraging.

The woman made a movement. It was as clear as if she'd said it aloud. As if she'd said, "Let me. I'll enjoy it."

"Ah, well, in the eyes of the law we shall be equally responsible," said Grandy cheerfully. "And that, my dear Press, will be pleasant for you. We shall both be of the unsuspected, eh?" he chuckled. Press simply waited. "Is he perfectly secure here?" asked Grandy. They nodded. "Then I don't think we'll be in any hurry. I must get back. We must think it over, you know. Doubtless, something ingenious will occur to one of us." He turned to leave. His eyes went mockingly to Francis. "You don't ask for your bride?"

Press was putting the gag back into Francis' mouth. It obscured any expression there might have been on Francis' face and prevented him from making an answer.

"I'll take care of Mathilda," said Grandy smoothly, "when the time comes. Let me see—" He had no feeling, no sorrow. The soft regret that purred in his voice was only a habit, a trick in his throat. "You disappear. There will be Jane's story of what you said in my study. Then, of course, Mathilda's story of what you tried to do to her. The marriage hoax. She must tell that to everyone. She will tell it with great indignation. She will tell it so well. Oh, the wickedness of it! What a wicked, wicked fellow you are," crooned Grandy. "But you did not prevail. You were defeated. You ran away." Grandy nodded. "The girls will support me."

Then the wooden door opened, closed. The light went out. Feet traveled toward the steps. Francis listened, hoping it was three pairs of feet. He didn't like the woman.

Yes, he thought, the girls. Mathilda. What Mathilda would tell the police would be only the truth, all the truth she knew. And if Jane tried to tell the truth behind the truth, it would never prevail. Who was Jane to pull down Luther Grandison? She couldn't fight alone. There was no one to help her now.

Mathilda would help destroy herself. She didn't know any better. He understood. She couldn't believe. It was too much to ask of her. Grandy had her in his web, had always had her, and he would keep her and do what he wanted to do, whatever it might be. Spider and fly. Poor courageous little fly. She had courage. She could fight. On the wrong side, but still one could admire. Eyes closed in the dark, he could see her face.

He said under his breath, "Rosaleen, I tried. Listen, little one, I know what he did to you. I tried to punish him."

It seemed to him that Rosaleen forgave him, because he couldn't see her face. It seemed to him that, graciously, her little ghost moved on. He might himself be with her soon, wherever she was. He hoped Grandy's ingenious way would be quick, at least. His hand throbbed and throbbed. The pain was monstrous. It loomed so large in the silent dark.

And leave Mathilda to the mercy of Grandy who had no mercy. Francis thought what he would do if he were loose. And then he tried not to think of such matters. Because he couldn't see any way to get loose. The ropes were still tight and firm. He couldn't move his wrists to speak of. The wounded arm was very weak. The muscles weren't responding. His ankles were numb. Trying to move would rub his skin off, accomplish nothing. The gag was in as firmly as before. He couldn't make a sound. The pounding of his heels on the cement was only a dull thud, could never be heard by the world, if there still was a world up there beyond that black oblong in the wall. Still night. No dawn.

The whole situation was perfectly ridiculous. But ropes are ropes. They held. There was no miracle. Nothing happened during the night to loosen those bonds. When the light began to seep through the green leaves at last and touch the dirty glass, Francis was lying exactly as he had been lying, exactly as helpless, hopeless and lost.

Oh, there was a tiny flicker of hope left, but really it was not sensible. The people going about their business up there in the world would have no suspicion. His helplessness and his plight would be unsuspected. So what he'd tried to do would be of no avail. The best he could do at the time, but it hadn't been good enough. No, no hope. Put it out. And pray for Mathilda. Pray for her.

Chapter Twenty-five

ON FRIDAY MORNING, Grandy's house had fallen into a normal rhythm. Life was going on. It was the reflection of Grandy's own mood, of course. His house and the people in it were susceptible to his moods and always reflected them. And Grandy had taken an interest in breakfast that morning. Grandy had parceled out the household chores in his usual gay fashion. Even Oliver had reached a state of calm and had gone off on errands.

Jane, looking about twelve years old in blue-and-white-checked gingham, was swabbing the floor of Grandy's glittering bathroom. Mathilda herself, in a black skirt and a peasant blouse, was changing linen on the beds. Mirrors reflected them many times.

Mathilda had a prevision of how life, going on, would fill in and smooth over the place where Althea had been. How it would always fill in the empty places, flowing, smoothing, covering. Grandy's house was just the same. Although Althea was gone, Tyl had come back. Rosaleen was gone, but here was Jane. There would always be one girl or another reflected in the mirrors, changing the beds, mopping the floor. The changing of the beds would outlive them all. The little duties, the household chores, were immortal.

The enigma of Francis was gone too. Because everything was clear now about Francis. Grandy had said so. Grandy had explained his theories at the breakfast table. Jane had agreed. Oliver had agreed. Mathilda had . . . agreed.

She had a little headache this morning. She hadn't slept. She'd been listening in the night. She'd been waiting, in aimless tension, not knowing what she waited for. Briskly tucking in the sheets, Tyl realized that she still had the sensation of expectancy, of waiting for something, an anxiety that wouldn't rest, as if life could not take up, here and now, and go on, and fill in and cover over, with the inexorable wash of time. Although the whole house argued against her and she argued against herself.

Francis was gone. The enigma was explained as well as it ever would be explained. There would be no more to it. The tides of time would wash in every morning and blot and obliterate and smudge and wear down and blur. This day or two, so full of Francis, would recede, would decline in importance, would fade and blur and blend in with all other days of her life. It would be an incident, a queer happening. Once upon a time. Grandy would no doubt make one of his stories out of it. There might even be supernatural overtones before he got through. Mathilda shivered.

Jane wrung out the mop and stood it up in her pail. "I'll help with that," she said, smiling.

How pretty she is, Tyl thought. *I wish I could be just sweet and willing, like Jane.*

They took hold of opposite ends of a blanket. Something was communicated through the length of woolen fabric. Tyl was aware suddenly that Jane was not as she appeared, neither sweet nor willing, not placid at all. Jane was strung up tight. Together, they spread the blanket, tucked it in, folded the sheet back over it, drew up and smoothed the spread.

Tyl said, "Where did he go, Jane?"

Jane said, "He went to the police."

Mathilda sat down on the edge of the freshly made bed. She looked into Jane's eyes and saw the real girl, saw the hidden fear and sensed the hidden strength.

"Why?" she demanded.

Jane said, "He had things to tell them. If he had got to them, we'd know it. He didn't get there."

Mathilda blinked and groped back. "But you said he'd run away. You said— Grandy said—"

Jane said carefully, "He may have run away. He probably did." She was remote and closed off suddenly. Mathilda didn't want her to be closed off. She wanted to talk. She wanted to know. She wanted the real Jane.

"But you don't believe it," she whispered, "do you?"

"Do you?"

Something that seemed entirely outside of herself shook Mathilda's head for her, shook it in the negative sign. No, she thought, and she hadn't believed it at breakfast, either.

Jane leaned against the bed, bent a little closer. "Can I talk to you and be sure you won't . . . repeat it?"

Mathilda said, "Please."

Jane's doll face didn't belong to a doll any more. "He was in danger. He really was. He was getting too close. How am I going to make you understand?"

"I wish you could," wailed Mathilda. "Because I don't understand anything at all. What danger? What do you think happened to him?"

"I don't know," said Jane, "but something's got to be done. I—" She sat down on the other edge of the bed with her back to Mathilda and covered her face with her hands. "What have I been waiting for?" she said in tones of surprise.

"You're in love with him, aren't you?"

Jane shook her head. Her face was still hidden.

Mathilda said, "But I saw you. Out the window. There's something—"

"What difference does that make?" said Jane fiercely. "Never mind what Francis is to me. Or anybody. Or what he was to Rosaleen. You don't know, and you'll never know, and he's nothing at all to you. Just nothing. But if he's dead now, it'll be because you were so dumb."

"I?"

"I didn't mean that." Jane gulped, turned her face and tried to smile. "I'm worried just about sick."

"Why was I dumb? What do you mean?" Mathilda reached out to shake her.

"I mean he needed your help."

"Then why didn't he ask me or tell me? . . . Help for what?"

"He did. He tried. But you can't see things the way they are. Francis didn't blame you."

"What don't I see?"

"Listen," Jane said, "I was in New York the other day, tracking down something that absolutely proves—"

"Proves what?"

Jane said, "No, I can't tell you."

"Why not?"

"You— Nobody could tell you."

"What's the matter with me, that I can't be told? I'm listening, Jane. Please tell me."

Jane was watching her, searching her face, trying to read it.

Tyl said desperately, "You've got to tell me. I've got to understand, can't you see that? Jane, if you know what this is all about, please—" But Jane seemed to be withdrawing again. "What did you find in New York?" Mathilda begged. "What was it?"

"A record."

"A record?"

"The record they took of a radio program."

"Oh?"

"Yes, I timed it."

"Timed it?"

"It was a question of time. The time was ten thirty-five."

"What time?"

" 'Burn tenderly.' "

Mathilda said angrily and bluntly, "I don't understand a word you're saying. You're trying to confuse me. Start at the beginning, why don't you? What are you? Who is Francis?"

"I'm a secretary," said Jane. She shrugged.

"But what are you trying to do? You're in a plot, aren't you? Some kind of plot against—"

Jane lifted her chin.

Mathilda said, faltering, "It's against Grandy, isn't it?"

Jane said, "Do you know that if you repeat any of this conversation, my life won't be worth a nickel? It's worth about ten cents, as it is."

"Oh, nonsense!"

"Is it nonsense?" said Jane. "Where's Fran, then? Why didn't he get to the police station where he was going? What stopped him? Where is he now? Why doesn't he tell us, send some word? Telephone?"

"Because he—because the plot wouldn't work," answered Mathilda weakly.

Jane said bitterly, "You never had a thought in your life. Your mind's been formed for you. You're all wrong about everyone. You don't see straight. It's not your fault. I guess it's your misfortune. You couldn't see Oliver and Althea dancing like puppets on the ends of their strings, could you? You thought they acted for themselves. They didn't any more than you do. Nobody does in this house. Oh, Francis understood. You mustn't think he didn't understand. But he told you there was danger, didn't he?"

"He—"

"And there was danger, and there is danger. He was worried sick about you. You're so blind. And he knew what the danger was." Mathilda was trembling. She was angry and scared. But Jane went on as if to herself, "There's one thing for me to do. There's that man, and I know his name and where he works. And Francis wasn't any helpless girl, you see? So there would have to be a man. That's what he meant." Jane's blue eyes took in Mathilda with a strange, absent look. "You'll spill these beans, of course. My fault. I ought to have known better. Fran warned me. But you looked for a minute as if you'd . . . hear me. But you can't hear me. It isn't your fault."

Suddenly, Jane's voice quickened. "I am glad we talked. I was frozen up, too scared to move, just stuck, just letting things happen. Lord, you can't afford to wait! I guess it's worth any extra danger to get unstuck." Jane's face flamed with resolution. "I'd better get going." She came around the bed. She said, looking down, "Maybe it will work out all right for you sometime. I hope it will." She added gently, "Francis hoped it would, you know."

Jane went out of the room and down the hall to her own.

Chapter Twenty-six

MATHILDA FLED into the gray room. That which she had been trying not to think about had been spoken out—too plain for her to dodge it any more. She knew now the ridiculous reason, the preposterous—why, the utterly mad reason—for all Francis' lies. First, Francis was mixed up somehow with Rosaleen Wright.

All of a sudden she knew how. Rosaleen had never been one to talk about herself or to confide romantic details. Yet Mathilda had always known that somewhere in the back of Rosaleen's life there was a man she planned to marry someday. Tyl sat down to brood, to think back. She could remember only an impression. This man was an old playmate. A childhood friend, a relative, even—some kind of cousin. It was no flaming romance, but one of those comfortable things. She could remember no name.

Francis? Well, then, Francis thought Rosaleen hadn't killed herself. That was the whole thing. And Jane was in it, too, somehow or other. Certainly, Jane was in love with him. Of course she was. It was perfectly obvious that they were partners. Was Jane a kind of second-string sweetheart?

"Never mind," Jane had said. "He's nothing to you." *Nothing to me,* thought Mathilda, *and what am I to him? Someone to be used in his schemes?* She felt herself in a little glow of anger. Schemes against Grandy. Of all people in the world, dear, kind, lovable Grandy, who wouldn't hurt a fly, wouldn't even hurt your feelings if he could help it.

Surely she knew him best. All Grandy's ways, the splendid difference of the way he lived. An amateur of living, he called himself. Lover of life. Oh, he had taught them so much. He'd sent them to carefully chosen schools, but their real education had been in the summers with Grandy. And the world would be stale without him to teach them where its flavor lay.

Why, they wanted to make him out a monster. They wanted to say he was wicked, scheming, unfeeling. Grandy? Grandy, who didn't care about money or any of the stupid material things, who loved, above all, beauty and good food and good talk and ideas. Who believed in the love of these things.

The thought came like a stray. Grandy's fabulous bathroom had cost quite a penny. The love of some kinds of beauty was rather expensive. No, she wrenched at her thoughts. She was off the track. Love. Human love. Grandy believed in love. But he didn't know it when he saw it, said some cynical thing inside her head. He thought Oliver meant security to her. She rubbed her aching forehead.

Someone knocked softly at her door.

"Come in."

"Tyl, darling." And there he was.

Mathilda looked up, startled. There he stood, Grandy himself, his white hair ruffled, as it almost always was, his rather large feet turned out just a little, like the frog footman. His fat little tummy on his thin frame, his big-knuckled hands, his beak of a nose and his sharp black eyes watching her.

She saw him briefly, just in a flash, quite unadorned by her affection. She saw the man standing in her door. She knew he was alert and watchful, and she knew she was not sure, at that moment, of his love. Because she thought of a spider.

"Are you just sitting there?" he asked wonderingly. "Anything troubling?"

Mathilda swallowed. "Headache," she said.

"Ah, too bad." His sympathy was rich and easy for that voice of his. Her heart began to pound. She heard the voice for the first time as a musical instrument played by a mind.

"I won't bother you, sweet. Lie down, eh? There's just the one thing. Yesterday, Francis—"

"Yes?" Her voice shook more than she'd intended.

"Francis showed me a document," he said a little wearily and sadly, "that purported to be your will."

"I know," she said. Her shoulder ached where she pressed it into the back of the chair.

"You know, dear?"

"I mean, he showed it to me, Grandy," she said a bit impatiently. She turned all the way around in the chair and pulled her knees up the other way.

"Another forgery," he sighed.

"Yes."

The black eyes were watching. They were noting her downcast

eyes, the nervous interlacing of her fingers. They weren't missing anything. She felt like a bug on a pin. She wanted to squirm and hide, to get away. She bent her head and began to cry.

"Darling." He was very near.

Suddenly, she knew the safest place was nearer still. She wept against his shoulder. She could hide her face there.

"What is the trouble?"

She said, "Grandy, I don't know. The whole thing's so confusing."

He held her off a little, trying to see her eyes. But she kept them hidden.

"I thought you were confused last evening, sweetheart. Tyl, what are you trying to tell me?"

"The trouble is," she wailed, "I do—I did—somehow or other remember that minister, Grandy! It's as if I'd seen him before, in a fog or something!"

"Why didn't you tell me?" he said in a moment. "Poor child. And it's been bothering you all the while? You are shaken. That's it, isn't it? Now, you mustn't worry. You really must not."

She felt, in spite of his words, that he was vague. Could he be doubting her, after all? She got hold of her handkerchief and drew away, drying her eyes. "I'm sorry," she said. "It really doesn't mean anything. I really do know that none of what he said was true."

"Of course, you do," Grandy agreed. But his eyes filmed over somehow, and Mathilda had a wild, fantastic, fleeting impression that he was wondering what to do with this self-doubt of hers; not wondering how to dispel it, but how to use it some way.

"Duck, you do not remember writing out any such document as that will, do you?"

"Oh, no," she said. "Oh, no, I never did." He was standing there, looking a bit hurt. She thought she understood. She said, "Oh, Grandy, I'll make another one. I—"

She caught the tiny folding down of flesh at the corner of his eye, the merest trifle of satisfaction.

He said petulantly, "Tyl, you know I want to hear nothing about your money."

"I know," she breathed. But she did not know. She was not sure. The fear was in her veins again, running in a swift thrill from a sinking heart. She did not finish the sentence that had been interrupted. She did not go on to say, "I already have made another will, silly, so we needn't worry about the finest forgery in the world." She didn't say it.

Grandy moved across the room. For one awful second, she thought she had spoken and told him, and then forgotten her own words. She thought her memory had skipped a beat or at least that he'd read her mind. Because he crossed to the little bookshelf and took a book down.

"What a disgraceful collection," he murmured. "My dear, such unfit stuff in this room. I must find you something better."

She was beside him swiftly. "Oh, no. I love Lucile," she said, taking it gently out of his hands. "It's so stuffy and there's a Mathilda in it. And it puts me to sleep."

He chuckled.

"Oh, Grandy," she said. It was on the tip of her tongue to tell him how foolish she'd been, to confess and get it off her soul and be free, where she stood, with no disloyal fear on her conscience. She suffered a complete reaction. The pendulum had swung. Afraid of Grandy! Absurdity of all time! Impossible!

"Now you will tell me the real trouble," he purred, surprising her.

"It's Francis," she murmured.

She hadn't meant to turn her head away or to say that name. She held Lucile in her hands still.

"If anything has happened," she murmured again, "we'd feel so cheap."

"Darling, you are absolutely right!" cried Grandy. "Of course you are! We must take steps, eh?"

"Yes," she said in utter relief.

"Of course we must," said Grandy. "That's only decent, isn't it? For all his sins, Francis was a guest in this house. Yes, I think we must be sure he is not lying in a ditch somewhere. That's what you mean?"

"Oh, Grandy, darling," said Tyl, "you do understand everything!"

Jane's door closed with a little click. They saw Jane in the hall with her blue jacket on over the gingham dress and the little blue cap on her head. She looked quaint and young.

"May I go out for a little while, Mr. Grandison?" she said humbly. "Please, if you don't need me?"

"My dear, of course," he beamed. "Unless it is something I can do for you. I'll be downtown a little later."

"No, I don't think you can, sir," said Jane primly.

"Take the time you need, my dear," said Grandy kindly. "Oh—er—this business about Francis. Tyl thinks we must ask the police to search for him." Jane's face didn't change much. "In case, you know," said Grandy, "he is hurt or dead."

Jane said woodenly, "Of course."

Then she smiled her pretty smile. Her pretty lips formed their pretty thanks. Her feet tripped off. They heard her going down the stairs, not too fast.

But Mathilda knew she flew as one who from the fiend doth fly. She, herself, stood in a backwash of fear. Jane's fear.

Grandy went off to telephone. Mathilda felt disloyal. She felt guilty and soiled. She ought to have told Grandy about Jane. She fidgeted. She went downstairs. Grandy was in the study. The mailman was at the door. She went and opened the door and said, "Good morning." He put a sheaf of letters in her hands.

She said, "Will you do something for me, Mr. Myer? If anything should happen to me, will you look in a book of poetry called Lucile? It's on a shelf in my bedroom."

His mouth dropped open.

"And don't mention what I've said to anyone," she warned, and smiled and closed the door. He stood on the step outside for some time, but at last he went away.

She pulled at her fingers with nervous anxiety. Now she felt disloyal. And guilty. And soiled. But why? What was it now? She mustn't trust Francis. He'd said so himself. She shook her head angrily. She was only doing what he had suggested because she didn't trust him.

Besides, he isn't here, she thought, and she sat down and covered her eyes.

Chapter Twenty-seven

THE POLICE were going to check hospitals and all that, and send out a missing-person alarm, Grandy had told her comfortably. It meant that there would be an eye out for Francis for miles around. They would find him, he'd said confidently. Grandy had gone off in his ramshackle car, wearing his old brown hat jauntily.

But Mathilda, waiting alone in the long room downstairs, was not satisfied and far from confident. She wished Jane would come back, or that she knew where Jane was, so that she could go there. There were so many questions Jane could answer. Oliver was in the house, and Mathilda wished he'd go away. He was upstairs and any minute he would probably appear and perhaps he'd want to hash things over. She wished he wouldn't. She wished she weren't alone, but she wished it weren't Oliver who would probably come to keep her company. She wished—wished— She didn't know exactly what it was she wished or what she was waiting for. Vaguely, she was waiting for some word, some news. Did she expect them to find Francis in a hospital? Did she expect them to find him at all? What if they did?

She tried to think, tried to clarify. There were two opinions about the disappearance of Francis. One, that he had run away deliberately, having failed to do whatever he had been attempting to do here. Two, that he had been prevented by violence from getting to the police by someone who didn't want him to get to the police. And, of course, there was a third possibility, which took in all the normal suppositions, that he had been taken ill, he had been in an accident.

She realized that it was the normal kind of disappearance that the police would be able to check, and would be attempting to check now—sudden illness, accident, sudden death. They would also be covering the possibility that he had gone away voluntarily, in which case he wouldn't be hurt at all, but they would find him someday. Through their teletype system, his description, persistent vigilance.

But the possibility they would not cover, and, moreover, had no machinery for covering, was that he had met with malicious violence. For if he had been hidden away, they were not searching in the right kind of place or looking deep enough or close enough, she thought.

She was huddled in the corner of a sofa, as if the room were cold. If only Jane would come back. If only Oliver would come downstairs and not talk, but do something. If only the police would send somebody and start here. If only she could tell someone these thoughts, so that something would be done. She didn't think Grandy had made it clear. Grandy didn't suspect violence.

She began to shiver uncontrollably. She thought, *I'm freezing.* Jane's words came back to her, "Frozen up, just stuck, just letting things happen."

Mathilda uncurled herself and sat up. This was paralysis. She rejected it. She would not wait.

A little later, she was walking down Grandy's drive. The bus for downtown passed within two blocks of Grandy's house. This was one of the city conveniences of which he boasted. The nearest bus stop was obvious. Tyl had no choice to make. She knew this was the way Francis must have come yesterday morning.

She wore her short fur jacket and a little black hat. There was a strong spring breeze blowing her black skirt around her pretty legs. She stood there at the bus stop with her eager, forward-leaning look, and she had no trouble with the bus drivers. They were all glad to lean out as she hailed them, and listen to what she had to say. "Can you remember Thursday morning—yesterday morning? Can you remember if a tall man with dark hair and dark eyes, a youngish man, got on your bus that morning?"

"What time, about, miss?"

"I'm not sure. About ten, I think."

"Lots of people get on and off, miss."

"Oh, I know, but try to remember. He would be wearing a gray coat, I think."

"Not much to go on, miss. Lots of men—"

"Yes, yes, but try! It was at this stop. I'm sure of that. And yesterday morning. Just yesterday. His eyes were dark. His eyebrows— But I guess he wouldn't have been smiling."

"Sorry, miss. Don't think I can help you."

"How many drivers are there on this route?"

"Six, miss."

"Thank you."

She tried again with the next driver and the next. The fourth man sucked his lip and said, "What do you want to know for?"

"Oh, because he was going somewhere, and he never got there, and I've been wondering."

The driver said, "Maybe I got your man. A fellow that changed his mind."

"He . . . did?"

"Yeah, yesterday morning. Tall, you say?"

"Tall, dark."

"I wouldn't wanta say he was dark. I wouldn't have noticed. But there was a tall fellow in a gray coat waiting here, only he didn't get on."

"He didn't?"

"No. Just as I was pulling up, a fellow comes up behind him—friend of his, I guess. So he turns around and goes off with the other guy. Gets in his car, see? The other guy notices him and picks him up. Happens all the time. People getting a lift. That help you any?"

"He went off with a friend?" said Mathilda incredulously.

The bus driver thought she was a stunner. "Listen, miss, I only said he was a friend. How do I know? All I know is, this guy didn't get on my bus. He was waiting for the bus, see, but he don't get on, on account of this other guy?"

"Did you notice the other guy?"

"Gosh." The driver pushed at his cap. The passengers were shuffling in their seats. He couldn't chat any longer. "I dunno. Nothing special I can remember. But they got in this D.P.W. car."

"What's that?"

The door began to wheeze shut. "D.P.W.! Department of Public Works!" he shouted at her. The bus moved off.

D.P.W. D.P.W. Mathilda stood on the empty corner and looked around her. Houses here were set in fat lawns, far apart, well back from the street. Nobody was about or would have been.

Wait, there was someone across the street. A gardener doing some spring pruning. She ran across. She fetched up the outer side of the hedge and the man stopped his work.

"Please, were you working here yesterday?"

"Nah."

"Oh," she said, disappointed. She turned away.

"Whatsa matter, lady?"

"I only wondered if you'd seen a certain car," she said. "But if you weren't here—"

"I was over at Number Sixty-eight," he said, and spat.

"Where?"

"Over there." His thumb showed her the neighboring lawn. "I work there Thursdays. Here Fridays."

"Oh, then maybe you did see it! There was a car with D.P.W. on it. Yesterday morning."

"Yeah," he said, and spat again.

"You saw it!"

"Sure I saw it."

"Did two men get in?"

"Yeah." There was something curious and yet reserved in his

glance, as if he could tell her something if she had the wit to ask, but would not offer it.

"One of the men was waiting for the bus?"

"I couldn't say about that."

"It doesn't matter. I want to know where—which way did the car go?"

He pointed.

"That way?"

"Yeah."

"Did it go straight on? Did it turn?" She thought, *I'll never be able to do this. This is hopeless.*

"Turned left on Dabney Street," he told her surprisingly.

"Oh! Oh, thank you!" She started to run, stopped, looked back. "Was there anything—anything more you noticed?"

A curtain dropped in his interested eyes. "Nah, I didn't notice anything," he said.

But she thought, *He did. There was something about it, something queer.*

She thanked him again and walked briskly in the direction of the Dabney Street corner. Now what to do? Now, ought she to call the police? Tell them about that car? Surely they could trace all cars so marked. Those cars must belong to the city. She ran back again.

The gardener hadn't begun to clip yet. He was just standing there, looking after her.

"One thing more," she gasped. "It was a car from this town? I mean it was the D.P.W. here?"

"Sure," he said. "That's right." He pulled his disreputable hat down and began to work his clippers very fast, moving around a shrub with the deepest concentration on his task.

Mathilda started down the street again. At Dabney Street, she turned left, as had the car with Francis in it. That is, the car she thought Francis had been in. It seemed probable that he'd been in it. At least, it was possible. She walked a few paces, out of the gardener's sight at least. And then, at a loss, she stood still.

The pavement told her nothing. How could it? The houses here were a little less aloof, a little more chummy with the street, but still— A car passed yesterday morning. What remains to tell you that it has passed or where it went, which corners, after this, it turned, which way?

She felt very small and helpless. There was no use walking along Dabney Street. No use, she thought.

There was a little boy in leggings and jacket, sitting on his three-wheeled bike, watching her. He was part way up the walk of the first house around the corner. He was about three years old.

Mathilda started toward him. She would ask. She thought, *No, how silly! It's just a baby!* She stood irresolutely at the opening between hedges, the end of the walk where he was.

The door of the house beyond him opened suddenly and his mother appeared, rather suspiciously, as if she thought this strange young woman might have designs on her child. She hurried down the walk, wearing only her house dress, moving fast in the chilly spring air.

"Gigi . . ."

Gigi kept on looking at Tyl.

"Let me see your hands." He surrendered his dirty little paws. The woman began to put her fingers into the tiny pockets of his snowsuit. She looked over her shoulder at Tyl. "Was there anything you wanted?" she inquired with a polite grimace.

"I . . ." Tyl gulped. "I did want to find out something," she said, "but I don't know quite how to go about it. I was going to ask your little boy, but I'm afraid he's too little to remember."

"Remember what?"

"Just . . . whether a certain car went by yesterday morning."

"He wouldn't know," said the mother sternly.

"No, I guess he wouldn't," said Tyl. She turned away.

"You come right in and let me wash those hands," she heard the woman saying. "Where in the world . . . ! You didn't get into any *more* chocolate, did you?"

"Uhuh," said Gigi.

"You didn't pick anything up and put it in your mouth *today?*"

"Uhuh."

"You remember what Mommy told you? *Did* you?"

"Umum."

"He doesn't know," said the woman apologetically to Tyl, who still stood uncertainly on the sidewalk. "Lord, he'll pick up any old thing and it's *so* dangerous. Gigi, I *told* you to throw that paper *away.*"

The woman pulled something out of the little pocket and threw it on the ground.

Gigi bawled protest.

"You *cannot* have it! You *mustn't* keep dirty old things other people have thrown away. How *many* times . . . ?"

But Mathilda was at her elbow now, breathless, demanding. "When did he find the chocolate? Was it yesterday?"

"Yes, it was," the woman said in surprise.

"Oh, thank you!" cried Mathilda. "Thank you so much! That's just what I wanted to know!"

She swooped down and picked up the bit of bright metallic paper, gaudy enough to attract a child, bright enough to see in the grass. She flattened it out with eager fingers. There was the Dutch name hidden in the pattern. It was a wrapper from one of Grandy's chocolates!

Francis, in her room that night, had taken a handful. He'd put them in his pocket. No one on earth but Francis or Grandy could have dropped one of those candies. And there was a car that had turned on Dabney Street, that had picked up a man who had waited for a bus.

Francis! It was a trail! It was going to be a paper chase! Oh, clever Francis!

"Oh, thank you! Thank you so much!" Tyl flew back down the path. The woman stood in belated curiosity.

But Tyl went off down Dabney Street with the paper in her pocket and her fingers tight on it. Oh, clever Francis! But this showed he hadn't got into that car because he wanted to. Or why drop clues?

Chapter Twenty-eight

PERHAPS HE HAD TAKEN it out to eat it. Perhaps he had dropped it by accident. Perhaps somebody else, after all, had Dutch chocolates. But no, no, no. *At least*, she thought, *I've got to go on down Dabney Street and keep looking.*

She kept her eyes along the curb, remembering that Francis would have been the passenger, would have been sitting on this side. Still, it was yesterday. Other children on the street might have

found other candies, and how would she know? She thought of
Hansel and Gretel, of the birds that ate the crumbs and spoiled the
trail home.

She came to the next corner and stopped to think it out. A car
turning a corner keeps to the right. Francis sat on the right. She
went around the corner to the right, searching the inside curb.
Nothing. Then she thought that if the car turned left, he would be
on the outside. The middle of the intersection was no good. She
crossed over and searched along the curb near which Francis would
have been carried had the car turned left. Nothing.

Now what to do? She saw the search branching out hopelessly.
Now she had a choice of three, and each corner she would reach on
each of three routes would have, in turn, a choice of three. The
thing multiplied violently. It was impossible.

She went along Dabney Street, walking on down on the right
side, watching the curb. He had dropped a clue, hadn't he, after
they'd turned a corner? He wouldn't drop a clue at every cross
street. So, at every intersection she searched, after the turns. Six
blocks along, she saw a bit of burnished purple. Intact. Candy and
all. Another one! The car had turned right on Enderby Street. Oh,
clever Francis! Oh, clever Mathilda! She walked along jauntily,
happy and pleased and excited. She knew where to look now, for
sure.

She found a green wrapper twisted up, empty, on the brink of a
sewer. Her lip began to bleed where she'd bitten it, thinking how
near that clue had been to being lost. Head down, she plodded on.
She spotted a blue one from all the way across the road. She thought,
My eyes are good. They'll last as long as the candies do. She wondered how many there could have been in that handful. And how
many more corners—

She plodded on. Ten blocks on the same street. She stopped,
then, and went back in a panic. She'd missed it. Or it was gone. She
came along the same ten blocks again, almost despairing. Nothing.

On the eleventh corner there was a purple one shining under a
hedge. To the left, then. *Yes, Francis.* Eyes aching, she went on. The
trail had led her into a meaner part of town, a poorer part, at least.
A part where she'd never been. Not on foot. Not alone. Surely the
afternoon must be wearing along. This street seemed to have uneasy shadows. The trail had been so long. She looked at her watch.
No, it was not even two o'clock.

She stopped in her tracks. Her eye just caught it. She would have been by in another second. Inside the driveway, inside the straggly border of barberry bushes, there was a little heap of five or six candies all together. Bright and gay, like Christmas, they sparkled on the dull grass. Inside the drive. Inside the property line.

The house was a dirty white, an old frame house, respectable enough, closed looking. No sign of children here, no flowers, no outdoor life at all. A bleak porch, a tall door with old-fashioned hardware.

She made herself walk by, hiding as well as she could her sudden stop by pretending to search in her purse, as if she'd thought of something. She walked two doors beyond. Shrubs, just leafing out, hid her now. She stopped again. That was the house! In there. The thing to do was to call the police, of course. But would they come? Would they believe her? Would they be quick enough? Would they go into the house? Could she convince them there was enough to warrant going in?

She thought, *If I could only get closer.*

She dared not go to the door and ring and make an excuse. If Francis was in there, he would not, in any case, be sitting in the front parlor to be seen by a caller. He would not answer the door, either. That wouldn't be any good.

She turned slowly back and went, instead, up the walk to the neighbor house. There was a deep shrub border between the plots. She had an idea.

The lady of the house was at home.

"I beg your pardon," Tyl said with all the charm she could muster. "I want to ask you a strange kind of favor. You see, the other day my little boy and I were coming by, and he lost his ball. His favorite ball."

"Isn't that a shame," said the woman. She had a long flat jaw, and she pulled it far down, as if she were making a face. She meant well, Mathilda realized.

"Yes, it was too bad," she continued, "and I was just going by again, and I thought perhaps you'd let me look in among your shrubs there. I'll be very careful. I won't injure them; really I won't."

"Well, I guess you won't," the woman said rather grudgingly.

"Then you don't mind if I poke around in there a little? If I could find it, he'd be so happy. He's three," she babbled. "His name is Gigi. That's what I call him. I would be so grateful to you."

"Go ahead," said the woman harshly, as if she washed her hands of the whole thing.

"Oh, thank you."

"Don't mention it."

The door drew shut slowly. Tyl thought, *She'll go to a window. She's watching, remember.*

Slowly, she went across the narrow strip of lawn and peered on the ground along the edge of the border of mock orange and straggly overgrown lilac and shabby privet. She bent her head to appear to look at the ground, but her eyes were directed higher.

She looked up under her brows to inspect the shabby white frame house, so near, actually, in distance, although the fact of the shrubbery border set it apart from where she stood. There was only a driveway and then a narrow strip of ground with rhododendrons, and then the white house wall, the stone foundation.

Shades were drawn in the stingy bay of the front room on this side. The next window was high—on the stairs, probably. Two windows farther back would be the kitchen, and that would be dangerous.

She stepped within the shrub border, moving slowly, stirring leaves and sticks with her foot, but watching next door. She was disappointed. There really was no way to see in from this side. The bay was high and the shades were drawn close. She wouldn't dare to try to see into the kitchen, and besides, it was too high. The stair window would be no good at all without a ladder. In the stonework, however, below, there was a little window, down back of the rhododendrons.

She thought, *So my little boy's ball might have gone into the rhododendrons. Mightn't it? Do I dare?* She thought, *I must. They won't see me. Nobody sits on the stairs. The kitchen's too far back.*

She went stooping through the shrubs, crossed the invisible boundary line between the lots, moved quietly across the hard-surfaced driveway, kept her head down, kept her movements tentative, groping, wandering, but edging herself to that cellar window.

Francis was lying on his right side now. When Mrs. Press had brought him food, he had wiggled around. She had crouched over him, feeding him carelessly, not caring much whether he got the food in his mouth or on his vest. His mouth was stiff and sore. It was agony to try to eat, but he did try. He didn't speak to the woman. She didn't speak either. He felt about her as he might have felt about a sleeping dog. He didn't want to awaken her to being aware of him. He wanted her to feed him carelessly, as if it were only another chore. He didn't want that look back in her eye. So she had put the gag back in efficiently and gone away, and now he was lying on his right side, which was a change.

Press himself had not been down. If only Press could be reached. What if he knew that Grandy, too, was a murderer already? For Press was a murderer already and Grandy knew it. That much was clear to Francis now. Press was one of the unsuspected, perhaps the one the old man had in his mind that day on the radio. That was why he had to do what Grandy said.

But what if Press knew they were even? Would he obey then? If only Press could be told. But how, even if the man did come, could Francis explain all this, lying, as he was, speechless and gagged? The light was flickering.

What light? Daylight. That was the only light at all. Murky daylight from the dirty little window, and it flickered. He rolled his eyes. He saw a hand on the glass. Someone was crouching down outside the window, trying to see in. He lifted both heels from the cement floor and dropped them with a thud. He did it again. Again. The fingers curled. They tapped twice. He made the thud with his heels twice. He nearly choked, forgetting to breathe.

The fingers went away and came back. They expressed emotion, somehow. Whoever it was knew now. He could make out the shadows of arm movements. Fur. A woman.

The little window was nailed tightly shut.

Outside, Mathilda crouched behind the rhododendrons. She couldn't see clearly at all, only the barest glimpse of a bare floor where a little light fell. The window was too dirty. The place inside too dark.

But she had heard. She had signaled. She had been answered. The little window was locked tightly, nailed shut. She took off her shoe and struck the glass with the heel. It tinkled on the floor inside, so faint a sound she was sure it couldn't have been heard. She put her mouth up close to the opening, "Francis?"

Francis strained at the gag. His throat hurt with the need to answer. He tapped with his heels. It was all he could do.

"Francis? Can you hear?"

Tap again. Raise your ankles and let the heels fall.

"Can't you talk?"

Tap again. Tap twice.

"Tap twice for 'no,'" she whispered. "Once for 'yes.'"

He didn't tap at all.

"Can't you talk?"

He tapped twice for "no."

"But you're Francis?"

He tapped once for "yes."

"Thank God!" she said. "Are you hurt?"

"No."

"What shall I do?"

No taps. How could he answer?

"Can I get in?"

"No."

"I'd better go for help?"

"Yes."

"Are you in danger?"

"Yes." *Oh, Mathilda, so are you. Go away, quickly.* All he could do was tap once for "yes."

"I'll get help. I'll get the police."

"Yes!"

Tyl, he wanted to cry, *don't get Grandy. Of all people, keep away from him. Don't even tell him you've found me. Tyl, if you really do thank God, then hurry. Go to the police, the public authorities, to someone safe. Go away now, before that woman sees you. Go silently. Don't run yourself slam bang into danger. Don't run. Oh, Tyl, be careful. Take care of yourself.*

"I'll hurry," she said. He had an illusion that she'd heard him thinking. He raised his heels, tapped "yes."

"Don't worry," she said.

He couldn't answer that one. Worry! God, would he worry. Oh, clever Tyl. She'd followed the trail. She'd found it. But he couldn't talk, he couldn't warn her, he couldn't say— If only she would go now, silently, quickly, straight to the public authorities. If only he could have told her so.

There was hope now—too much hope. It was terrifying. Hope and fear. He was afraid for her. He almost wished she hadn't found him. He rolled his head on the floor painfully. He groaned beneath the gag. He almost wished for the peace of hopelessness.

Chapter Twenty-nine

MATHILDA WENT BACK through the shrubbery border. She stooped once, remembering, and pretended to pick up something, in case the woman next door should still be at a window somewhere.

Then she let herself move faster, went out onto the lawn and the street. She walked a little way. Then she began to run, gasping, heart pounding. Only get far enough away and then find a telephone. She was a little deaf and blind with excitement and haste. She didn't see or hear the rattling old car until it honked a surprised little squawk at her and pulled up at the curb. "Tyl! Tyl!" Her body didn't want to stop running. She had to will the brakes on.

"Tyl, what is the matter? Darling!"

And there was Grandy, tumbling out of his car, fumbling at his pince-nez to keep them on. Dear Grandy! He would know what to do! She'd forgotten everything but that she was in haste and Francis must be saved, and here was Grandy, to whom she had told all her troubles all her remembered life.

She threw herself upon him. Wept with relief. "Grandy, I found Francis! I found him! Something awful has happened!"

"Hush," he said. "Hush, Tyl. Now tell me quietly."

"Oh, Grandy, help me find a policeman! Somebody to get him out! Because he's in there! He's in there!"

"In where?"

"In that cellar! He's tied up! He can't talk! Oh Grandy, quick, let's get somebody!"

He held her, supporting her. "You say you've found Francis? Are you quite sure?"

"Of course, I'm sure! It is! Oh, Grandy, be quick!"

"But where, dear?"

"That house back there. The white one. Can you see? The first white one, with the reddish bush. That's where he is. In the cellar. I saw through the window. What shall we do?"

"Get the police," said Grandy promptly. "Tyl, darling, how did you— Look here. Are you sure?"

"I'm positive!"

"But did anyone see you?"

"I don't know. So hurry!"

"But how could you tell it was—"

"I broke the glass."

"Tyl, darling."

"Oh, hurry!" she sobbed. "Because he's in danger!"

He said, "Yes. This is bad business, isn't it?" Now he was matter-of-fact, no longer surprised. He sounded cool and brisk and capable. "Tyl, do you think you could take the car and go find a telephone? There's a drugstore a block down, or two blocks down—somewhere down there. You go call the police. Call headquarters. Ask for Gahagen himself. Can you manage?"

"Yes, I can," she said.

"While I go back and keep an eye on that house."

"Oh, yes!" she agreed gladly. "Oh, Grandy, that's right! Oh, yes, do! You stay and watch. Watch out for Francis."

"That's what I'll do," he said gently. "Go to the drugstore, duckling. Call from a booth. We can't have this all over town."

"Give me a nickel," she said resolutely.

He gave her a nickel. Watching her, he knew she would obey the suggestions. She would go to the drugstore. She would ask for Gahagen. It would all take time.

Mrs. Press opened the back door suspiciously. Then she let the door go wide, recognizing him.

"What have you got to put him in?" said Grandy briskly, without introduction.

"There's a trunk," she said.

"Get it."

"It's upstairs."

"Drag it down."

Recognizing emergency, she went without saying anything more. Grandy called a number on the telephone.

"Press?"—crisply. "Can you send a truck here in the next five minutes? Trouble. Police. Tell them to pick up a trunk." Sharply: "If you can't do it in five minutes, there's no use." Coldly: "You realize what will happen if you don't, this being your house?" Calmly: "Yes, I hoped you would. Tell them it's full of germs. Yes, germs. Typhoid. Anything."

Grandy hung up the phone. There was a loud bumping and crashing. He went into the stair hall and helped Mrs. Press with the big old empty turtleback trunk.

The two of them went down for Francis. Even with his limbs bound, even gagged and stiff and sore as he was, they had no easy time. Francis was sick at heart. This hurry, this wild anxiety of haste, could only mean that Tyl had made contact somewhere, somehow, and Grandy had found it out. So it was to be no good? No soap? Not even now, after she'd found him and thanked God? He would not see her face again, to thank her or to explain or just to see her face again?

He was damned if he wouldn't! The woman had great strength, and Grandy was not so weak an old man as he, perhaps, looked. They were desperate and in a hurry. They got him up the cellar steps, although all the way he bucked like a bronco. The scene in the hall was dreadful in its grim wordlessness. It was a voiceless battle of desperations. The yawning trunk was like a tomb, and the living man, in all his helplessness, refused to go.

But he fell. He fell out of their weakening grasp, and he had no arms. He struck his head. They folded him over, jammed him in, stuffed him down.

The woman, panting, said, "Better do it!"

Grandy screeched, "No time! No time!"

They shut the lid down. Grandy took the key and turned it in the lock. Together, they dragged again, tipped the bulky object over the front doorsill. Mrs. Press closed the door.

"With a knife," she gasped, "it wouldn't have taken long!"

Grandy said, "Blood?" He sneered at her stupidity. Then he warned her, "You don't know anything, when you're asked." He looked no more than a trifle worried now, a bit flustered. His frenzy was gone.

"I don't know anything," she said contemptuously. She watched him go back toward the kitchen. She heard the soft closing of the kitchen door.

The police car came wailing down the street to where Tyl stood, hopping with anxiety, on the drugstore corner. It barely stopped. It snatched her up. She showed them the way and told them as much as she could in the few brief noisy minutes it took them to swoop on, five blocks—the drugstore had been farther away than Grandy had said—down the street.

When the big, clumsy gray garbage truck came rumbling along, going in the opposite direction, the men on top, in their dusty boots and aprons and heavy gloves, looked wonderingly down. They leaned against the big trunk balanced there, the last of their load.

Chief Blake, who was driving himself, dodged by with a skillful twist and a brief snarl of his siren.

Chapter Thirty

THE CAR came to a skidding stop. One uniformed man went in a jogging run down the drive to the back of the house. Chief Blake and the other went up on the front porch. Tyl slid off Gahagen's lap, where she scarcely knew she'd been sitting, hit the ground with both feet. Grandy was nowhere to be seen.

"Got the right house?"

"Oh, yes! Yes!" She looked for him on all sides.

Then Grandy rose up out of the shrub border there by the driveway. He had old leaves in his hair. A smudge of earth streaked across his cheek. He came toward them. He was beaming.

"Lurking Luther never took his eye off!" His thin lips smiled out the silly words. "It is there as it was there!" He made a flat triumphant sweep with his palm. "Not a soul stirred. Not a soul saw me. I lay low, by gum, I did! What an afternoon, at my age! I had no idea how fascinating it is to put one's ear literally to the ground. Oh, cowboys! Oh, Indians!"

Gahagen grinned. "Your little girl's upset."

"But the marines are landing," said Grandy, "eh? Now, how do you do this, Tom? This is most fascinating. Beard 'em, don't you? Do we break down the door? I'd like to see that. I never believe it in the movies."

Mathilda's heart ached. She felt tired out, all of a sudden. Grandy could set a mood; he always did. But this mood struck her wrong. It jangled. It hurt.

"We try ringing the front doorbell first," said Gahagen. "Come on."

Chief Blake said, "How d'ya do, Mr. Grandison? What goes on here?"

"That's what we wonder," said Grandy, "and we do wonder, don't we?"

The chief was a big solid fellow, the type to be slow and sure—especially sure. "We'll find out," he promised.

A thin woman opened the door and stood looking hostilely at them. "Well?" Thin and drab and sour, she wasn't afraid of them or even particularly interested. "Well?" she snapped.

"We want to look in your cellar," said Blake, in all his huge simplicity.

"What for?"

"This young lady saw a man tied up down there."

The woman's eyes were not so drab as the rest of her. They examined Tyl with contempt and curiosity. "There's nobody in the cellar," she said. "I don't know what you're talking about."

"But there is!" began Tyl.

Grandy's hand warned her to keep calm, reminded her that they were among the officers of the law and all would proceed in due order.

"We'll take a look, if you don't mind," said Blake, and one felt that it would come to pass as he had said.

The woman surrendered to that certainty. "I guess I can't stop you," she said ungraciously.

The other uniformed man stood on guard where he was, there at the front door. The rest of them followed the woman into the house, down the dingy brown hall, past the doors to the sitting room, past a dining-room door. The cellar steps went down opposite here.

The woman opened the door and snapped on a light for them as if she said, "You fools!"

Tyl went down too.

There was a little furnace room, cluttered with old boxes, not neat. It smelled of stale wine and coal gas. Tyl looked up and saw the woman, standing above them with her hot, angry eyes fixed on Chief Blake's burly back.

There were two doors out of here, one to a laundry. Gahagen opened that and peered in, closed it again. They all turned to the second door. It was not locked. It led to a perfectly empty room.

"Any more rooms down here?" the chief said. His voice boomed.

"The cellar don't go under the hull house!" the woman called shrilly. "There's nobody down there! I told you!"

Mathilda stood in the empty little room and looked around at the stone walls. It was gloomy. Someone found the light. She blinked as the bare bulb sprang into glowing life.

"Where would the place be?" Chief Blake looked down at her. "Which side of the house, Miss Frazier, eh?"

"Mrs. Howard," said Grandy softly.

She felt her heart sink down—that sick, falling feeling. The taste of fear rose in her throat. Why did Grandy put that in? The fiction of her marriage? Why did he want them to think— She couldn't understand.

She moistened her lips. "It was right here," she said. Her voice was too thin. It piped up like a child's voice. "Here," she repeated, "because, don't you see, that's the window I broke?"

They all looked up. Sure enough. The window was broken.

"Now—uh—you say you saw him?" Chief Blake shifted around to face her—grill her, she thought.

"I couldn't see very well," she admitted, "but it was Francis, because he answered me."

"You talked to him, eh?"

"He couldn't talk, but—"

"But you say he answered. What do you mean by that, Miss—er—"

"He did. You see, he could make a kind of thudding noise somehow. Like a heavy tap on the floor. So—" She swallowed. It didn't even sound plausible to her. It sounded ridiculous, and yet it was true.

"It's true!" she cried aloud. "He did answer me! He pounded once for 'yes' and twice for 'no.' I asked if it was Francis!"

"Pounded, eh?" Chief Blake seemed to take what she said perfectly literally, and he looked about him.

Tom Gahagen said, "Maybe you weren't as smart as you thought you were, Luther. Could be, you were seen. Better search the whole place. . . . What d'ya say, Blake?"

"If the young lady's so sure—"

"I'm absolutely sure!" Mathilda told them desperately.

So the house was searched. She went along. She had to see it for herself. The cellar. They thumped the stone walls. They shifted the low pile of coal with a long shovel. Then the kitchen, cupboards, pantry. The dining room. She saw Gahagen lift the long tablecloth and look under. It struck her as absurd, as if a man like Francis were a child, hiding from them. They searched the sitting room. Not there. They looked thoroughly into the clothes closet in the hall.

The woman of the house stood by, against walls. She followed along and stood contemptuously back and watched. She was arrogant and sulky and sure.

"There's nobody here," she kept saying.

They went upstairs. Three bedrooms, more closets, a bath—a cubbyhole off the hall. No living thing. No dead thing, either. No person at all. They asked about the attic. There was a ladder to let down, and they let it down and a man went up. He came back sneezing.

"Nobody up there," he said.

And that was all there was to the house.

Chief Blake looked sidewise at Tyl's white face. "Try the garage."

The garage was cold and vacant. Just a tin shack. Nobody, nothing in it.

The men poked about the little back yard, lifted the slanting cellar doors with sudden energy and let them down again, slowly. There was nobody in the house or on the grounds except the woman, who stood on the porch now to watch in contemptuous silence.

"Well," said Gahagen. He let his shoulders fall helplessly. He looked at Mathilda. They all did.

"But I know he was here!" she said.

"He's not here now, miss," said one of the men.

"But he was. . . . Grandy!" she wailed for help.

"How long before you met Luther and sent him back to stand watch?" asked Gahagen sharply.

"Not long," she faltered. "A m-minute."

They shook their heads. They shrugged.

She wanted to scream.

"If you're through, I'd be obliged if you'd leave," the woman said, from the porch, her voice thin and dry with her contempt.

Tyl turned to her. "What happened?" she cried. "You know! . . . Mr. Gahagen, don't you see she must know? Why don't you make her tell?"

"Why, you—" The woman's eyes blazed. "Call me a liar?"

"Hush, hush," said Grandy. . . . "Tyl, darling, it's possible you were mistaken."

She moistened her lips. "No."

The woman said, "Now you seen what you seen, you better all get out of here." She went indoors contemptuously.

Grandy looked at Gahagen. "Perhaps Mathilda's overwrought—" His voice was gentle and sad.

"I'm not!" cried Tyl, knowing that the squeal of desperation in her tone denied her words. "I'm not." She tried to make it sound firm and sane.

"Oh, my dear"—in pity.

"Francis was here!"

"Hush."

Tyl thought, *I won't scream. I won't cry.* She said, "How could I have been mistaken? I told you about the candy."

"Candy? What candy was that, Miss Frazier—Mrs.—" Chief Blake would listen.

"Candy!" she cried. "That's how I trailed him! He dropped pieces of candy, like a paper chase. . . . They were some of your Dutch chocolates, Grandy. That's how I found the house. Did you think I went looking in every cellar window? Come out here to the front. I'll show you." Her voice rang with new confidence.

But on the dull grass, just emerging from its winter brown, there was no glittering little heap of candies now. There was nothing there. Nothing on the grass anywhere.

They stood and looked at the ground. Gahagen scraped with his sole, made a mark.

Grandy said softly, "Come home, Tyl."

"No."

"He isn't here, dear. You saw that."

"But he was!" she wailed. "Because I know he was! Grandy, you believe me, don't you?"

"There, there. Hush."

"This is the little girl that was on the ship?" Chief Blake was asking delicately.

She knew Grandy was nodding. She knew glances flew, now, above her head.

"She's been under a strain," Grandy said in his soothing way. His voice stroked and patted at the situation, stretching it here, pushing at lumps. He was going to cover over this indecency of the impossible. Everything would seem reasonable and able to be believed, after he had stroked the facts with his voice a while. "Dreadful strain," he was murmuring. "First that, and then Althea's death. Her own sister couldn't have been closer. And now, you see, her husband has gone off without leaving any word. It's no wonder. Poor child."

They were murmuring too. She could hear the hum of their consent and understanding.

"It's all been terribly confusing," Grandy said. "I can't even tell you all of it. But she really— It's no wonder if her senses begin to play her tricks. I think if you'd been through . . . stresses and the bewildering circumstances—" His voice murmured off, died in wordless sympathy.

Tyl felt frozen and trapped.

Her senses. Here it was again. She did not know what she knew she knew. Here was Grandy saying so! What Francis had said! She did not know what had happened. What she thought she saw, couldn't be trusted. What she thought she remembered, no one else remembered, and even inanimate things shifted and changed behind her back. Because her senses played her tricks? Did they, in fact? She didn't know, herself, at the moment. She wasn't sure any more.

Gahagen said cheerfully, "No harm done."

Blake said kindly, "Just as well to make sure. Say, that's all right."

"Never mind, little girl. We understand," their voices said.

She stood still in utter terror. What it meant, her mind didn't know. But her body was sick with fear.

A taxicab pulled up abruptly. A girl got out. The girl was Jane. She came to them quickly. She was decisive and demanding.

"What is it?" said Jane. "What are all of you doing here?"

Chapter Thirty-one

THE GROUP SHIFTED to let Jane in. There was a reluctance to say what they were doing here. No one volunteered.

"Ah, Jane, dear child," said Grandy. . . . "Gentlemen, this is my little secretary, from the house. . . . Look, dear, let us take Mathilda home in your cab."

"But wait a minute—"

"I thought Francis was in there," Mathilda said wearily. "I thought I'd found him."

The blond girl's eyes didn't flinch from hers. "That's strange," she said. "Because this is where Press lives."

"Press?" Grandy said it.

"Yeah, the name here is Press, all right," said Chief Blake.

"You mean Ernie Press?"

"Yeah."

"Why, I am acquainted with him," said Grandy. "Of course. Do you mean to tell me—"

Jane said crisply, "I'd like to know what this is about, please."

There was a shocked little silence, the result of her rudeness. Then Gahagen began to tell her.

Mathilda felt strength seeping back into her spine. Jane was no baby doll or child, either. Jane had force. Jane made sense. She listened eagerly. It was a different kind of sense from Grandy's, but sense. Something clear.

Tyl said, "Yes, and I did communicate, Jane. He did answer me."

"Let me tell you something," said Jane in her clear and surprisingly bold voice. "Francis warned me that if anything ever happened to him, I should look up this man named Press."

This was odd. Tyl felt the balance shift. She could tell that they were checked, turned back, made to think again.

"He works for the city," went on Jane. "The D.P.W."

"D.P.W.!" cried Mathilda. "Of course! Yes, yes! Francis got into his car. His car, Jane! It had D.P.W. on it. Ask the gardener."

Grandy bent forward, as if he drew a line across Tyl's eagerness to cancel it. "But of course Press works for the city," he purred. "Of course he does, child."

Jane paid him no heed. She went on, "I've been watching Mr. Press. He's been at his office down in the city yard. A little while ago he left suddenly. And very fast. He drove to the corner of Mercer Lane. That's about four blocks up and over." Jane pointed. "I followed him there."

"My dear Jane!" murmured Grandy with astonishment, and still she paid him no heed. Jane was a doll without any strings. Mathilda stood straighter.

"He spoke to the driver of a garbage truck," said Jane.

They all looked blank.

"The truck started up right away. It turned off. I followed Press again, until I found out he was only going back to his office. Then I thought I'd see what that truck did. Did it come here?"

"Eh?" said Grandy. He looked thunderstruck.

"Did it?" said Jane. "Because it turned this way." Her blue eyes were stern and clear. One would have to answer.

"Oh, me!" said Grandy. "I didn't see any garbage truck."

"Mr. Grandison was watching the house," Blake explained with his monumental patience, "the entire time, or practically so, between when Miss—er—the young lady says she saw—"

"Oh, he was!" said Jane with peculiar emphasis.

Tyl's pulse was racing. She thought she saw how everything could be reconciled. "No, no. Maybe he didn't see it!" she cried. "But it could have come along just the same. He might not have seen it. People don't. It's like a waiter. You don't see his face."

"Like the postman!" said Grandy quickly, almost as if he clutched at a straw. "Oh, my dear, can I be guilty of that stupidity? Chesterton's Invisible Man! You remember, Tom. You've read those things. The invisible people who come and go in the street and are not seen because you are so used to them. Now, I couldn't say —I really couldn't say whether I saw a garbage truck—"

"Suppose the dame in the house saw you, Luther," Gahagen offered. "She tips off her husband."

"Yes," said Grandy. He drawled out some doubt. "Ye-es."

"He sends a truck around."

"But, Tom—"

"Listen. He's the guy who knows exactly where those trucks are, all day, every day. They got a map and schedules. You'd be surprised. Say a lady loses her ring or a piece of good silver in the trash. Happens often. Why, he can stop the truck before they dump."

"Dump?" said Jane, her hand on her throat. "Dump?"

"Yeah, they dump down at the incinerator."

"Is that a fact?" said Grandy. "They do know, then, exactly where each truck—"

"Sure, it's a fact."

"Yeah, but what's the idea here?" said Blake. He slowed them down. He fixed on Jane. "You're saying, miss, that this man Press sends around a garbage truck to pick up a man?"

Jane swayed on her feet. "He sent a truck somewhere."

"And the man's gone," said Mathilda in a clear, bold voice. She stood by Jane. "He was helpless. He couldn't speak. He couldn't yell. He could have been carted away." Jane's shoulder leaned on hers. The girls were side by side. It was a lining up of forces.

"Now look here," said Grandy reasonably. Everyone turned to him. "I do understand that Press is in a position to—let us say— summon a garbage truck. I know that. I concede as much. In fact, I remember now that he had spoken of the system with which they run their noisome affairs. It's truly remarkable—truly—the things that go on in the background of our lives and we reck not of; we are unaware—"

Jane said, "What are you going to do?"

She said it to the others. Grandy went on smoothly, as if she had not done the unforgivable again and interrupted him, "I do not understand what it is you—er—imagine, Jane, my dear. How can a man's body be taken away on a garbage truck? You aren't saying that the men on the truck are all in cahoots? Now come. What had Francis done, ever, to the Department of Public Works?"

Jane said, "The incinerator." She lost all color. "The fires are so very hot!" Her face was dead white.

Tyl said, "They wouldn't— No! Where is the incinerator? . . . Jane, come on!"

"Wait."

"No."

"Girls, girls, you can't—"

Tyl cried out, "Somebody's got to—" Jane's hand was on her arm, gripping tightly. They were allied. They ran toward the taxi. Gahagen leaped after them.

Chief Blake said, hastily for him, apologetically, "Maybe we better run down there."

Chapter Thirty-two

THE TAXI DRIVER was delighted to be on official business and go as fast as he could go. Jane and Tyl and Gahagen rocked in the seat, bracing themselves. Jane's hand and Tyl's were welded together. There was no use trying to talk. Now and then, Jane made a little moaning sound. She didn't seem to know she was making a sound at all.

Tyl thought, *She must be in love.* Her own heart kept sinking all the time, over and over again. It would seem to swell and then fall, and the fear would come in waves. She thought, *Naturally, I don't want him to be hurt. I wouldn't want anyone to be hurt so terribly.* They rocked around the last corner and raced down a little hill to where the road led over a weighing platform and into the vast wasted-looking spaces around the city incinerator.

Jane said in Tyl's ear, "How was it that Grandy was supposed to be watching?"

Tyl said, "Because when I met him—"

"You told Grandy!"

"Of course. I—"

Jane's hand began to twist and pull. She was taking it away. She drew herself away. Tyl had the feeling that she'd been rejected. She was not included any more. The rest of this she would have to go through alone.

The taxi whizzed across the weighing platform. A man there shouted with surprise, came racing after them. They went up the ramp. The brakes screamed. They had come through the great doors and to a stop within the building. They were in a vast room—not really a room at all. The inside of this brick building was all hollow. It was nothing but a great space, enclosed by the high walls, roofed over and crossed with girders high above them, and with high windows, tilted like factory windows, some of them open, many feet up in the walls. This great space, on three sides, was empty. Echoing.

Clean. But in the faintly dusty air there hung a sourish, repulsive odor.

On the fourth side were the pits. Here was where the trucks came to dump the burnable stuff. Here was where they backed up to a wooden curb and shucked off their loads. The refuse fell into huge pits built into the floor. And beyond the pits, on the other side, a great partition went up to within perhaps twenty feet of the high roof. It crossed the whole side of the building like a high parapet, with the pits like a moat in front of it.

Above it ran a kind of track from which hung a big steel-jawed bucket that was working steadily, with sullen rumblings of sound. It came down, descended into the pit, nibbled and bit at the stuff in the pits and then went up, drooling, carrying its enormous mouthful over the partition, over the wall, to some mysterious fate beyond.

Tyl looked up. Like a demon tender of the fires of hell, a head, a face with a snout, was looking down with great flat eyes, inhuman and horrible.

The human man from the weighing platform came running up behind them. They heard the howling of the siren on the police car. Grandy and Blake and the rest.

Gahagen said, "Which trucks dumped here the last half hour?" He didn't know how to put the question.

The man said, "All the trucks been in and dumped for the last time. All through."

"All of them?"

"Yeah. They get through around now. They all been in. What's wrong?"

"We don't know," Gahagen said.

Grandy and the rest came puffing up. The man who worked here was surrounded suddenly by all these visitors.

Jane, looking sick, had edged toward the pits and was looking down over the rim. Her voice pierced the dusty, rumbling emptiness of the great bare place as if it cut through a fog. "There's a trunk down there!"

"Trunk?"

"What trunk?"

"Where?"

The line of men advanced cautiously, peered over, each with one foot out, one back, with identical bendings of necks, like a line of the chorus.

"Yeah."

"Trunk, all right."

"Well?"

The employee said, "Yeah, I asked about that. Said it was full of stuff hadn't been fumigated. Typhoid. People warned them."

"When did that come in?"

"Last truck. Number Five."

Above the voices went the rumbling of the crane. Jane looked up in horror. "Stop that thing! You've got to stop it!"

"Wait a minute," said the man who worked there. "Now, listen. What's the idea? What goes on here?"

Chief Blake said, pursuing orderly thought, "Any way of finding out where they picked up that trunk?"

"Sure. Call up the yards. Get hold of the men."

"There isn't time!" cried Jane. She ducked under Chief Blake's elbow and bobbed up in front of him. "You've got to stop that thing! Stop it right now! What are you waiting for?" Her fists beat on his big blue chest. "Don't you see, if he's down there—" She was losing control.

Grandy was peering into the pit distastefully. His face was pained. The big bucket went down again, gnawed at the nauseous heap, nuzzled at it, then slowly it rose toward the top of the wall.

"Listen, they gotta clean up the pits before they can quit," the man said stubbornly. "They don't stop just for anybody's fun, you know. The men down there firing, they wanna get through."

The fires, then, must be somewhere below, somewhere below the floor where they were, and beyond that wall, at the top of which still stood the man in the gas mask. His big glassined eyes were turned down and toward them.

Fire. Very hot fire. Very hot indeed, to burn what was down there in those pits, what went slowly up in the big steel bucket, hunk by hunk, mouthful after steady mouthful.

"What a place!" said Grandy. "What a scene! What a place!" His nostrils trembled. He peered over. His hand was on Mathilda's shoulder. She shrank away from the rim, and yet something drew her irresistibly. To lean closer. To look down. She could see the top of the trunk. It was a big, old-fashioned turtleback, a big box with a humped cover. It was half buried in the debris, tilted, top upward. She tried to imagine Francis, down there in the pit, bound and imprisoned, shut in a dark box, waiting to be destroyed. She knew that was what Jane thought and imagined. But it couldn't be. It couldn't be real. Such a thing could not happen, could not be happening.

The big, empty, smelly place, the rumbling crane feeding the hidden fires, the efficiency of destruction that was going on here—the whole thing made her want to close her senses against it, not to believe, not to watch; to turn and go; to run away and go to a clean sweet place and bathe and forget.

Jane was sobbing, "Oh, please, please, listen to me! You can't take the chance! You've got to be sure!"

Grandy swayed a little. "Jane," he said, "you think he's down there!" The thought seemed to make him ill. Tyl felt him going.

She screamed. Somebody grabbed at her and held her back. She screamed again and again. The demon on the wall threw up his hands and disappeared. Men milled around her and shouted. The fumbling faltered and stopped. The bucket hung half raised, and from its iron lips the gobs of garbage fell.

Down in the pit was Grandy. He lay on his back in the ruck, his thin arms and legs spread out, his face up. Was he dead? Had he fainted? She would have gone on screaming, but the man who was holding her put his hand roughly over her mouth to stop the noise.

Jane had crouched down, was almost kneeling, right at the edge. Her eyes had a glitter. She was watching hard. Gahagen was shouting hard. Somebody came running with a rope. Gahagen was making as if to loop it around his own waist.

But Grandy wasn't dead or even unconscious. As they watched in the new silence, he struggled up. He got part way out of the ruck. Then, on his knees, he began to move, slowly, with difficulty, crawling across the pit, wallowing in the refuse because he had to, to move at all.

They heard him say, "Wait. Not yet." He was wallowing toward the trunk. He was curiously like someone swimming. He reached the trunk and hung to it a moment as if he might otherwise sink and disappear. They saw him strain to lift the lid, lift it a trifle. Saw his white head bend to bring his eyes to a position to see within. They saw him let the lid fall, fumble a moment more as if to look again. Then he raised his arm.

They heard his voice come out of the pit, drawn out like a signal cry, humming and droning in the echoing silence, "Let . . . the ro-ope . . . do-own!"

The rope went down with a loop at the end of it. Gahagen lay on the floor, looking over, calling encouragement and instruction.

Jane was a frozen bundle huddled at the brink. Her hand was flat on the dirty floor. Tyl thought, *How can she bear to get her hand so dirty?*

Somebody called out from the big entranceway, and Oliver came running across the floor. He wound up, panting, "Cop told me! Where's Grandy? Tyl, what happened?"

Tyl thought, *No time for gossip.*

"He fell."

Oliver's eyes bulged with horror.

Grandy was dangling now. They were pulling him out. He was rising from the pit on the end of the rope. They hauled him over the edge and he crumpled into a heap on the floor. His lids went down wearily.

"Fainted."

"No wonder."

"Oh, by the way, gentlemen," said Grandy's velvet voice calmly, "there's nothing in the trunk but some pieces of plaster, I think, and some old rags."

"My God, Luther, you're game!" cried Gahagen. "Good man!"

"After all," said Grandy wryly, "I was in the neighborhood." He turned his head, eyes closed, a tired old man.

Somebody laughed. Somebody swore. Somebody must have given a signal then, because the rumbling whispered out of silence, began and grew.

Oliver was kneeling at Grandy's side. He was the image of devotion. "Get a doctor," he demanded. "Get an ambulance."

"Nonsense, my dear boy," said Grandy, but his lids were trembling. He looked very sick. He was filthy and contaminated—fastidious Grandy! An old man, after all. He lay on the dirty floor.

"This'll be the end of him!" cried Oliver in despair. "Call a doctor, one of you! Hurry, can't you see! Tyl, snap out of it."

Tyl stood looking on. She had not fallen on her knees. She felt unable to bend or to move at all. She contemplated the image of devotion. She saw the puppet working to swing attention and concern. She saw Grandy lying filthy on the floor and the people all beginning to swing, to center him.

The scene had nothing to do with her. She was alone, outside the circle and alone, suspended, lost. A puppet without strings would be as limp and lost. The bucket descended, to fall again at its work. She noticed that it had a weakness. She felt it was curiously repulsive that the great wicked thing with its greedy mouth was so weak at the neck. It had no neck, only cables. It fell weakly, and then it would nibble and chew and scrabble about, and gape and close and rise sternly, with the cable taut, to carry its load over the wall. Mathilda's eyes followed it.

Jane wasn't in the circle, either. That circle around Grandy, where invisible bands drew like elastic, where he was pulling them with the magnet of himself, and they were responding like iron filings.

Jane screamed. Jane got up from the crouching position and fastened on Blake's arm. "No, stop it! Don't let it start! You've got to look!"

"Look where, Miss?"

"In the trunk! In the trunk!"

"Mr. Grandison looked." The big arm rejected her.

"No, no, not Mr. Grandison! You can't trust him!"

"What do you mean, you can't trust—"

Oliver got up. "What the devil's the matter with you, Jane?" he asked severely.

"Francis is in that trunk! In a minute that thing is going to take it! Where does it take things? Where does it go?"

"The chutes. To the fires," somebody said.

"No!" Jane was nearly hysterical. "I tell you, you can't take his word! Any one man's word! You've got to stop that thing! Open the trunk! Let me see! Let me see inside!"

"Now, just a minute, miss. After all—"

"It's your duty!" she cried. Tears ran down her face. She was frantic.

Oliver said, "Slap her, somebody. Slap her in the face." His voice got shrill. "We've got to get Grandy out of here! He's a mess! Tyl!"

"Seems to me we've done our duty," Blake was answering. "Mr. Grandison saw what was inside the trunk. Now, miss—er—you don't know the trunk came from Press's house, do you? It could have come from anywhere in town. It's full of typhoid germs."

Tyl thought dully, *Grandy'll catch typhoid.* She was watching the bucket, on its way up now. It seemed to be working a little faster. The men who tended the fires wanted to get through and get home.

Jane said, "I know I can't make you believe he's lying. But he could be mistaken. You can't afford to take even that chance. Suppose he's mistaken? It's a man's life! Mathilda knows he was there in that house."

Tyl stirred. "Yes," she said dully. She thought, *If I can trust my own senses.*

The bucket was dropping down. Its cables were slack. It fell with that disgusting weakness at the neck. It fell, it nibbled, it crept quite near. Quite near the old turtleback trunk that lay half buried. The bucket's jaws were big enough to take it up—just about big enough. Perhaps next time.

". . . nobody in the cellar."

". . . girl musta made a mistake."

Blake said impatiently, "Now, look, miss. If I thought there was any danger—"

"I don't care what you think! I know there's danger!"

Oliver said, "What's this about, anyhow? I wish somebody would—"

Jane said, "Don't take the time to tell him."

Maddeningly, Blake began, "This young lady—"

"Stop that thing, I tell you!" Jane's voice was ugly with her terror. "Stop it!" She tore her throat with the cry.

Gahagen said, "Aren't you a little bit hysterical?"

Oliver said, "For God's sake, with Grandy maybe dying—"

Grandy was just lying there, pale and wan, filthy, done in, so weary and ill and pathetic.

Jane's eyes turned in her head to catch sight of the bucket going up. Not yet had it got the trunk into its jaws.

Mathilda was alone. She knew they were all gathered around Grandy, who lay so dramatically exhausted at their feet. She could hear voices talking, talking, and Jane arguing, reasoning, pleading. And the bucket was coming down again.

She heard Jane cry, "Somebody help me! . . . Mathilda, help me!"

One would have to answer such a cry.

But Grandy stirred, and she heard his voice, "Where's Tyl?" It carried through every other noise, that beloved voice, so rich and tender. "Where's my duckling?" he said. He called her to him. "Is she all right?" That was his anxious love. "Tyl, darling."

Mathilda's head turned. His hand was out, waiting for hers to slide within it. Appealing to her. Confident of her. His darling. Yes, of course, she was his darling.

She saw something on the floor. It was as if there was an explosion inside her head.

She gasped, put out her hand. "Oh, please . . . please." The words rose out of her throat to join Jane's. Then she thought, *Talk, words. Words won't do it. What's the use of talking?* For Jane had been talking; Jane was still begging them, weeping, pleading. But Grandy, lying on the floor with his eyes shut, was too strong.

Mathilda's body was taut now, and it felt strong and alive. Leaning a little forward, she said, quietly, aloud, "If Francis is down there, it's got to stop."

She flung up her arms. For a second she was poised in the air, a Winged Victory indeed. Then she had done it. She was falling, falling. She struck the soft, rotten, evil heap. She had leaped. She was down in the pit.

Above, men were shouting again.

Oh, yes, now the bucket would not come down. Mathilda smiled. She'd stopped it. She'd stopped it quickly the only way. In a moment or two, she struggled up and began to wade, as Grandy had done. She toiled and struggled. It was nightmarish, that journey through the evil muck. Her hand reached the trunk, touched its hard surfaces. Both hands now were at the lock.

From above, they saw what she was trying to do, and they saw her fail. They heard her when she called to them. Heard her cry when she said, "I can't! The trunk's locked! It's locked!"

"Locked?"

Gahagen looked at Blake, and he looked down where Grandy lay, rolled on his side now, peering over. Grandy's big, thick-knuckled hand on the curb, the rim of the pit, tightened, loosened.

Down in the pit, where the fumes rose and overpowered her, Mathilda fainted.

Chapter Thirty-three

MATHILDA WAS BATHED, scrubbed, scented and immaculate. She lay on the couch by the fire, wearing a coral-colored frock. Her legs were lovely in her best sheer prewar stockings. Her feet were comfortable in gold kid mules. Her hair had been washed and brushed until it shone. It was tied back with a coral ribbon. She looked very young and a little pale.

Jane was sitting on the little low-backed chair, the skirt of her brown dirndl spread around her. A bracelet slid on her arm where she propped up her chin. Oliver was back a little, with his face in shadow.

These three were silent, listening to what Tom Gahagen and Francis were saying, trying not to think about what had happened to Grandy. Grandy was dead.

It was not yet certain whether or not from natural causes, whether his arrogant spirit had arrogantly fled from the prospect of disgrace by some hocus-pocus of his own will and device, perhaps by poison, or whether an old man's heart had been unable to stand the various excitements and had literally broken.

Anyhow, he was dead. There would be no legal aftermath. No long-drawn-out, sensational trial. It was all over really. Except the chase after Press and his wife. They would be caught and explode into headlines. Yes, it was all over but the headlines. And they, too, would pass.

Francis was not only alive and well, but looking extremely handsome in a soft blue country-style shirt without any tie. Shaved. Shampooed. His hair looked crisp and still damp.

They were, perhaps, the cleanest group of people gathered anywhere at that given moment. Mathilda had the thought. But she didn't smile. Her whole heart ached. Pale and quiet, she lay, and although she listened, something inside kept weeping, not for the shell of Grandy, who lay somewhere in the town, but for the Grandy who had never lived at all, for the Grandy that never was, the one she'd loved.

With the one she'd loved went everything she'd known. All gone. She could not yet be sure what anyone was, what anything was like. She'd seen the world through Grandy's eyes. That world was gone. Even his chair they'd pushed away. The long room was his no more. It was a strange room in a strange house where she'd always been a stranger.

Gahagen said, "He never made as much money in the theater as people thought. You see what he did? The head of the firm that handled the estate for Frazier, he died. So Grandy got into disagreement with the juniors and took the business away. So there was nearly two years when the fortune was fluid, and Grandy was handling things himself, buying, selling, changing things around.

While he had everything confused, he must have managed to transfer a pretty big hunk of the stuff into his own name. Then he gave the business to a new firm. How would they know she'd been robbed? But I can't figure out how you ever got on the track of such a thing from the outside."

"Jane had a letter," said Francis. His dark eyes were somber and troubled. "It was little Rosaleen Wright who got on to it."

Mathilda's heart ached.

"I don't suppose we'll ever know exactly how," said Francis in that sad, patient way. "But she was here when Mathilda turned twenty-one and made her will. Maybe then—"

Mathilda said, "They did work on it a long time, the lawyer and Rosaleen. He wouldn't."

"Grandy wouldn't?" Somebody said the name she couldn't say.

"He said financial matters were too dull. He said it was a paper world." She turned her face to the inside of the couch.

"Maybe Rosaleen wondered why the records didn't go all the way back to your father's death," said Gahagen.

"She wouldn't have been fooled," said Jane suddenly. "There was something terribly honest about Rosaleen."

"You knew her well?" said Gahagen sympathetically.

"She was my cousin," Jane said. "We all grew up next door to each other."

"You never did think she killed herself?"

"No," said Jane. "And now I can imagine how he did it. I can imagine how he'd have asked her to write out that suicide note. He'd have made it seem plausible. He'd have—"

Mathilda closed her eyes.

Jane's voice was a knife.

"—maybe said to her, 'I'm experimenting, dear child.' There'd be that hook up in the ceiling. He'd have said he was trying to understand one of his old crimes. He could have got everything ready right under her eyes, because he'd have been talking, the way he talked, all the time."

Mathilda shuddered. The spell was broken. She could see now that he'd been a spellbinder. She could feel a shadow of the spell.

Oliver said, with a whine in his voice, "I wish you people had come to me. I could have helped you. Althea did tell me about that 'Burn tenderly' business. I was your missing witness, if you'd only known. I didn't know that you needed a witness. We just didn't get together."

Francis said gently, "None of you could be expected to see our point of view." He didn't say it reproachfully, but as if the fact had been troublesome, but not misunderstood.

Oliver said weakly, "I suppose that's so."

Gahagen turned curiously to Mathilda. "But you finally did see their point of view, Miss Tyl. What made you so sure, all of a sudden?"

She felt blank and dull, couldn't remember.

"Up to that point, you were pretty near ready to think you'd been seeing things, weren't you? I don't understand how you came to be sure enough to take a jump like that."

Mathilda said, slowly, "I don't know. Yes, I do, but I don't know how to explain it exactly."

"Don't try," said Francis quickly.

"Oh, yes," she said, "I'll try." She went on, groping. "You see, there were a lot of pieces. I'd heard all about the fuse blowing. Oliver gave me another piece. He told me how Althea had heard a man on the radio. Then Jane gave me another piece when she said she'd been checking up, and the man had said 'Burn tenderly' so late that morning. You see, I had all the pieces. They went together, just all of a sudden."

They sighed.

"But that wasn't all," Tyl said more vigorously. She felt better for being able to explain. "There was another handful of pieces. You see, I knew Francis had been down in the cellar." She was half sitting up now, her face was vivid. "And I was sure it was Francis, on account of the candy. Who else could have left that for me to see?"

"Who else but you could have seen it?" said Francis huskily.

"Well"—she shot him a green glance—"then Jane had her story about the man Mr. Press and the truck. I just suddenly saw that if Grandy wasn't"—she'd said the name—"wasn't a true link, if he was unreliable, then the impossibilities all cleared up. I just suddenly put the thing together and I saw that Francis had been there. He had gone; he must have gone somewhere, and Jane was on the track of how he could have gone. And then," she said, "I happened to look at Grandy, and I saw that piece of Dutch chocolate spilling out of his trousers pocket."

"The candy?"

"Yes." A little shiver ran down her slim body. "I didn't stop to think he might have had one of his own chocolates in his pocket. I just remembered that I'd seen them on the ground by that house, and that they'd disappeared. Who picked them up? If I wasn't crazy— Who knew enough to pick them up? Who knew what they meant? Only me, and Francis . . . and Grandy.

"So you see," she added quietly, "I understood that he wasn't reliable. I think I just . . . saw him."

"He was—" Gahagen shook his head. He had no adjective for what Grandy had been. "Then, when he unlocked that trunk under our noses to pretend to look inside! And he locked it again too. He didn't dare risk the thing falling open when the bucket picked it up. Of course, that finished him."

"You were quick to see that," Jane praised him.

Francis said, "I must say I'm glad I was out like a light most of that time. I'm just as pleased I didn't know about that bucket or where I was."

Jane said simply, "I nearly went crazy."

Mathilda, looking at the pulse in Francis' throat, thought, *So did I.*

"Well, that finished him," said Francis abruptly. "He might have pleaded bad eyesight. He just might have been able to pretend he couldn't distinguish me from a bunch of old rags in the bad light, eh? He'd have talked, and who's to say he might not have wriggled out of it, when and if you'd found my bones? But with that key in his pocket!"

"He fell in on purpose, to keep us from looking inside that trunk," said Gahagen. "It was a brilliant idea. Mr. Howard, here, might have been pretty well destroyed. We might not even have stopped the works to look again. I don't know. Can't say. Looking back, it seems impossible that we believed him at all. But, of course, we did believe him at the time."

Gahagen got up to go. Perhaps his tongue slipped. When he said "Good night," he called Mathilda "Mrs. Howard."

When he had gone, Francis moved restlessly about, poked at the fire.

Oliver came out of the shadows and took a nearer chair. "Doesn't he know you two aren't married?" he asked with bright interest.

Francis stood still, with the poker in his hand swinging like a pendulum. "I guess you realize now that Grandy deliberately rearranged your wedding," he said bluntly.

Whose wedding? What was he talking about? Tyl looked up. Met his eye. "Mine!" she gasped.

Oliver said, "Ours, dear."

Tyl let her head fall back again. She didn't know how revealing her face was. How its serenity and the simple curiosity with which she asked her question told them so much. "But why didn't he want Oliver and me to marry?" she wondered almost placidly.

"He didn't want you to marry, ever," said Francis angrily, "on account of the money. Didn't he teach you to think you'd never be loved except for the money? Didn't he make you believe you weren't personally very attractive? Didn't he play up Althea against you? Weren't you always the Ugly Duckling? And not a damn word of it true." He put the poker into its place with a banging of metal on metal. Mathilda felt surprised.

Oliver said uneasily, "He certainly tried—"

"Of course he was a pretty persuasive old bird," said Francis much more mildly.

Oliver's face was red. Of course, thought Mathilda. Oliver had let Grandy persuade him. He hadn't seen Mathilda or Althea either with his own eyes, but through Grandy's eyes. And now Oliver was ashamed. So now he was preparing to laugh it off. Oliver was about to be nonchalant. How well she knew all the silly expressions on his silly face.

"Mathilda doesn't care for me," said Oliver gaily. "Maybe I'll marry Jane."

"I don't think so," said Jane promptly. "My husband wouldn't like it."

Francis laughed and got up and put his arms around Jane. He put his chin down on her hair. "You're wonderful," he said. "Little old Jane." He kissed her. "Go to bed now. I want to talk to Mathilda."

When Jane had gone and Oliver had, rather awkwardly, gone, too, and they were alone, Francis' eyes were filled again with trouble. But Mathilda's green eyes were wide open now. The long room was a real room, after all. Those people were real. She could see.

She said, "I thought you were engaged to Rosaleen?"

"I was."

"But . . . you're married to Jane!"

He gasped. "I'm not married to Jane. Her husband happens to be in Hawaii at the moment. That's Buddy." He began to laugh. "It's ridiculous, but she's my little old Aunt Jane. My father's youngest sister, bringing up the rear of the family. Hasn't anyone told you? I'm Francis Moynihan."

"Oh." Mathilda played with her belt. She said, "I haven't seen things or people the way they are. It's hard to begin to see."

He said, "I know." He said, "But you'll be all right." He said, "You need to . . . look around now. Now that he's gone."

She turned her face away. Her heart—something—ached terribly.

He said, "I realize how you see me. I don't know how to explain to you or apologize. I dreamed up this thing before I knew you. In fact, I thought you were dead."

She murmured that she wasn't.

"I know," he said. He got up again and ran his fingers through his hair. He didn't seem to know how to go on.

She lifted her head. "But who is that Doctor White?"

He corrected her gently, "Doctor Wright. Rosaleen's father."

"Oh. Oh, then that's why— He walks like Rosaleen."

"Does he? Yes, I guess he does."

Francis looked unhappily into the fire. "What can I do now about this marriage business?" he blurted. "You see, I haven't told. Gahagen doesn't know. The papers will say I stumbled on something suspicious after I got here. I didn't want you dragged through all that—at least until I asked you what you wanted."

She said nothing. She thought, *Is it up to me?*

"Tyl, what can I do now to fix things? Would you like to get a— fake divorce? That might be better for you. Better than to confess all this ridiculous masquerade. What do you think?"

"Can we get a divorce if we're not really married?" she asked thoughtfully.

"Maybe we can fake something."

"Let's not fake any more," she murmured. "Do you think Doctor Wright would just quietly marry us—really, I mean?"

"Tyl—" He half crossed the rug to her, but he stopped.

Her green eyes were wide open and cool. "Then, you see, the divorce could follow."

"I see." He went back to poke at the fire. He ran his fingers through his hair. He took a turn on the hearth rug. Then he looked at her and his brows flew up. "It's a risk," he warned.

"Risk?" she repeated.

"Terrible risk."

She got up on her elbow and looked across at him with a curious intentness, as if she were, indeed, seeing him for the first time. "I don't think so," she said slowly.

He came quickly to her and sat on the edge of her couch. He

took her hands. "We'll do that, if it's what you think will be— Actually, it might be the sensible way. There's no risk, Mathilda."

"You don't mind?" she murmured.

He said with a twist of his mouth, "Why, I guess the rest of my life is yours. There's no one else I owe it to."

She shook her head, not satisfied.

His eyes lit, but he hid the light. "We'll do that, Tyl," he murmured. "Then . . . we'll see."

She nodded. He put his face down on her hands.

A Dram of Poison

Chapter One

THE TALL MAN switched on the light. "I won't be a minute," he said.

The shorter man looked around the room, which was a laboratory. He ambled over to gaze, without understanding, at some apparatus.

"It's here somewhere," said Paul Townsend, lifting and shifting papers on the desk, opening the left top drawer. "Letter I meant to mail. Simply forgot. Now where . . . ?" He was an extremely good-looking man, six feet high, in prime state at thirty-seven. His handsome face wore a little fussy frown.

"Take your time," said Mr. Gibson, who was older, in no hurry whatever, and who liked to browse. "What's all *this?*"

"Ah . . ." Paul Townsend found the letter. "Got it. That? That's poison."

"What have you done? Made a collection?" Mr. Gibson peered at a double rank of little square-bottomed bottles aligned to the fraction of an inch, neatly labeled, behind the glass doors of a cupboard.

"Lot of the stuff we use seems to be poisonous," Paul Townsend told him. "So best it's locked up." He came, dangling his letter between two fingers, and peered, too. "Sure is quite a collection," he said innocently.

"Looks like some gourmet's spice cupboard," said Mr. Gibson admiringly. "What are these good for?"

"Different things."

"I never heard of ninety per cent of them."

"Well . . ." said Paul Townsend in a forgiving way.

"Death and destruction," murmured Mr. Gibson, "in small packages." He put his forefinger on the glass door. (He fleetingly remembered having once been a little boy pushing his finger, just so, against the glass of a candy counter.) "Which would you advise?"

"What?" said Townsend, batting his long eyelashes.

Mr. Gibson smiled; delicate lines spread from his eye-corners like tiny peacocks' tails. "I'm taking a poetical view," he said whimsically, "of two dozen bottles of death. I don't think the way you do. Can't help it. Teach poetry, you know." He mocked himself good-humoredly and declaimed, "To cease upon the midnight with no pain . . ."

"Oh," said Townsend a little stupidly. "Well, if you mean what will knock you out quick and easy, take that one."

"That one?" Mr. Gibson made no sense of the polysyllabic word on the label to which his host now pointed. He couldn't think how it could possibly be pronounced by a human tongue. The number on the label was 333, which was simple and stuck in the brain. "What will it do?"

"Just kill you," said Paul Townsend. "No taste. No smell."

"No color," murmured the other.

"No pain."

"How do you know that?" Mr. Gibson had fine gray eyes and they were lit with intelligent curiosity.

Townsend blinked again. "Know what?"

"That there is no pain? Or no taste, for that matter? Fella's knocked out, as you say. You can't ask him, can you?"

"Well, I . . . understand there's just no time for pain," said Townsend a little uncomfortably. "Ready?"

"Quite a place," said Mr. Gibson, giving a last look around.

Townsend had his finger on the light switch. "Wait a minute . . ." He frowned. He was like a housewife with unexpected company. He saw deficiencies in his housekeeping. "I see something should have been put away. Maybe *it* wouldn't kill you, but . . . Now who left that out, I wonder? Would you mind turning away for a second?"

"Turning? Oh. Not at all." Mr. Gibson obligingly turned his back and stared at a cupboard full of beakers and tubes on the opposite wall. Its glass door made quite an efficient mirror, if you selected with your mind only the reflections, out of all you were seeing with your eyes. So Mr. Gibson idly watched Paul Townsend take a small tin of something from a table top, produce a key from a hiding place, put the tin inside the poison cupboard, relock the door, rehide the key. "O.K.," said Townsend. "Sorry, but I like to be absolutely careful."

Mr. Gibson said, "Of course," softly. It didn't occur to him to confess to his acquaintance that he now had a very good idea where the key was kept. This Townsend was a friendly chap who had happened to be eating a meal in the same off-campus restaurant and who had offered Mr. Gibson a ride home on this chilly January evening. No need to explain to the man. Mr. Gibson hated to embarrass him. And surely it did not matter.

He began to muse, instead, on poison. Why were there substances created of which men must not eat? Fire, water, air . . . all good for man . . . could yet, in quantity, in excess, or out of place, destroy him. Was it possible that poisons, too, had all their measures? Were they, in proper quantity, or place, or time, good, too? In minute quantity perhaps? Was it a question of discovering how much, or where, or when?

"What's that Number Three Thirty-three *good* for?" he asked as they left the building.

"Nobody knows yet," Townsend said amiably. "But it wouldn't be a bad way to die."

Mr. Gibson had no wish for death. He forgot about it and looked up at the moon. "It is a beauteous evening, calm and free . . ." he murmured.

"Nice night," agreed Townsend. "Little chilly, though. I'll drop you off now. Thanks for waiting. Then I'll get along home."

"Don't forget to mail your letter," said Mr. Gibson in friendly prose. "There's a box on my corner."

It was Mr. Gibson's birthday. Characteristically, he hadn't mentioned it. He was fifty-five years old.

He made his thanks and his good night and walked up one flight to his big and only room. He lit the lamp, took off his shoes, placed tobacco handy, selected his book. He was a bachelor.

It was quiet there. It was cozy in a masculine way. It was a little backwater and in it Kenneth Gibson was content. To himself, it seemed that his life had been spent in a series of little backwaters. He had never breasted the full turbulence of the center currents, but like a gentle, unresisting leaf had slipped along the edges of the stream, been caught and held in this or that small stopping place, slipped out, only to be carried into another and yet another, until he had sailed finally into this particular quiet reach where there was no storm but only the gentlest of ripples from time to time.

He had his niche of usefulness. He liked his work and liked his life. He had a feeling that it was soon over. If another ten or twenty years went by softly in the same pattern it would not seem long. He wasn't an aggressive or an ambition-pressured man.

Four weeks after his fifty-fifth birthday, Mr. Gibson went to a funeral. There he met a young woman named Rosemary James.

It was old Professor James who had given up the ghost. The college rallied to its own. He had been retired for some eight years, had fallen, indeed, into irascible irrationality. But he had once been the college's own and so he must have a well-patronized funeral. The word was given.

Other faculty members met his only daughter, Rosemary, for the first time that day. But Kenneth Gibson met her most significantly because of a quality he had that he, himself, thought of as a weakness. He had the gift, or the burden, of empathy.

To himself, it was a weak sensitivity. Oh, he had learned, in fifty-five years, to manage it pretty well. It had hurt him very much during the First World War.

Having been born in the first month of a new century he was, of course, eighteen years old in 1918. He had grown up in a very small town in Indiana, a backwater, with a father who owned a hardware store and was a cheerful tactless man, and a mother named Maureen (Grady) who was a little woman with a fanciful mind. He had gone from the village high school directly to the war, because it had seemed the fervently "right" thing to do at the time.

Young, compact of body and muscle, spruce and neat—for Kenneth Gibson from the beginning was one of those people who always look washed and orderly by some natural gift—even then, he had evidently had an affinity for paper and ink. He went through the war, in the fierce breeches and puttees of the day, as a clerk. Cheerful, willing, and meticulous, he had made a good one. But, although he marked paper with ink in some not unperilous places, he never actually got into a battle. So, when it was all over, nobody knew nor was anyone told that this lad was numb with horror. Nobody ever knew how his essentially fastidious soul had been lacerated by the secrets of slaughter he had come to know and had had to bear. Nobody, in those days, would have conceded the wounds in his mind to be either plausible or important. There were too many horrors experienced. He had only been able to imagine them.

Saying nothing, he dived for sanctuary and healing into books. He went to college. He escaped flaming with the youth of that time because he was older than, and a little out of step with, his classmates. Besides, he was busy healing his invisible wounds in his own way.

His father died the year he got his Master's. His mother was left in straitened circumstances, so Kenneth helped support her in her own place. He did not transport her, for he knew this would not be kind. But he took the burden. It never occurred to him, while he worked at his first meagerly paid teaching job, sent money to his mother, and even helped his younger sister Ethel on her way through college at the same time, that all this was any sacrifice. It simply seemed that his own life, as he saw it, had hit one of those backwaters. To clerk through the war was such, surely. To be a young teacher with family responsibilities was only another. He hewed to the line. He had to. No giddy young days for him.

In 1932 his mother, after an expensive illness, died, and he mourned her, but the depression was on the land and whoever had forborne to fire him from his job while his mother was alive, forbore no longer.

Ethel, eight years his junior, was out of school by this time, of course, and she was earning, and she helped him, for she too had a sense of responsibility and was reliable. He was deep in debt while he scrambled for odd jobs during those bad times.

When, at last, he got another modest teaching job he went into this backwater thankfully. It was a long grind to work off his debts, lean quiet years. But he did it. He learned to take a good deal of pleasure in seeing the old obligations melt slowly away as he satisfied them. When at last he was free and moderately prospering, the world was into the tense months after Munich.

He was thirty-seven by now, a bachelor. Of *course* a bachelor. He had never had enough to offer a woman of his own. Security. Prestige. Whatever. Before he got around to risking any personal alliance came 1941, and he went to war the second time.

Naturally, he clerked. Well-seasoned, perfectly at home with paper, he spent the war years in an office in a backwater—bearing this and indeed glad of it—for his soul could still wince. But never quite understanding what he was doing there that mattered at all.

He only knew that somebody thought it was his duty, which he, of course, did.

In 1945 he emerged from this and met his sister Ethel in New York and said goodbye. Ethel, his only kin, had never married either. (Was it something about the mother and father?) She was a grown woman—getting along herself, in fact—thirty-seven years old. Never a beauty, Ethel, but clever and industrious, and well established in a good job. Ethel did not need him. In fact, she frightened him a little, at that time, by her ease in the turbulent business world, her blunt courage, her perfect independence.

He admired her for it very much. But he said an affectionate, but not woeful, goodbye and came to California to a job in the English Department of a small liberal arts college in a little city that sprawled and spilled over a sunny valley. His permanent backwater.

Here, for ten years, without even a glimpse of his only kin, he taught about poetry—to football players, coeds, and all variety of young people—by a kind of moral supremacy. Kenneth Gibson was obviously no Bohemian wretch with wild eyes and rebellious ideas and, equally obviously, no silken aesthete looking down a haughty nose upon the bourgeoisie. He was, rather obviously, a nice decent well-contained little man, five feet eight, still taut and compact, by no means showing his age, although his fair hair had inconspicuous threads of white in it—a most respectable man, with fine gray eyes, with a nice mouth that often wore a touch of humor on it.

The young were rocked by the fact that *this* man actually took this stuff seriously. It behooved them to look into it themselves and see what it was worth, then.

So he did his work well, quite often succeeding in communicating his own conviction that poetry was not necessarily sissy . . . which was an achievement greater than he realized, poetry having the repute it has today.

He had his books, his acquaintances, his solitude, his work, his cozy room, and the beauty of trees, the magnificence of sky, the lift of the mountains on the horizon, and the music of men's ancient thoughts, to sustain his spirit. He had his life and he thought he foresaw how it would end. But then he met Rosemary James at her father's funeral.

Chapter Two

MR. GIBSON SAT DECOROUSLY with his colleagues in the gloomy little chapel and endured the cruel, but necessary, ceremony by a little trick he had of deliberately disengaging a lot of his attention. When it was over he realized, with a pang of outrage, that off at the side, behind the curtain in the "family room," Rosemary James had been sitting through it all alone. If he had known! He had never met the girl—poor thing—but if he had known, he would have churned up the community to find somebody—anybody—to be with her. Or he would have sat in there *himself*. He hated a funeral—anybody's funeral—and he found himself imagining her ordeal, and furious that it had *been*.

When he took her hand, beside the grave, he felt the vibration of her lonely anguish. He knew in the marrow of his bones that she was exhausted and in despair and had to have hope. Had to have something, however trivial, ahead of her. She could die without it.

So standing in the sunshine, on the sad turf, with the flowers heaped behind them, he said to her, "Your father must have many papers. I wonder if any of them should be published."

"I don't know," said Rosemary.

"I wonder," said Mr. Gibson. "Would you like me to go through them for you? We can't tell. There may be valuable things."

"Oh," she said, "I suppose there might. I wouldn't know." She seemed timid, poor thing.

"I'd be very glad to help if I can," he said gently.

"Thank you, Mr.—Gibson?"

"Then may I come over . . . perhaps tomorrow?"

"Please do," she said tremulously. "It's very good of you. Won't it be a trouble?"

"It will be a pleasure," he said. The word was deliberate. To speak of pleasure at the graveside was rough, was shocking. But she needed to have inserted into her imagination such a word.

She thanked him once more, stumblingly. A shy young woman,

too upset, too bewildered, to have any poise. Not a child, of course. In her late twenties probably. Slim . . . in fact a pitifully thin body, trembling now with strain and fatigue but standing up to it somehow. A white face. Frightened blue eyes, with little folds of skin at the upper outer edges that came down sadly. A lined white brow. Limp, lifeless brown hair. An unpainted mouth, pathetically trying to smile and yet not smile. Well, she could look forward now, if ever so little, to tomorrow.

"We'll see," said Mr. Gibson, and *he* smiled in full. "Who can tell?" he added cheerfully. "We might find some treasure."

Her eyes changed shape and he saw the flicker of wonder, of hope, and he was quite pleased with himself.

On his way home, he fumed. Poor thing! Looked as if a vampire bat had been drinking her blood. And perhaps he had. The arrogant angry old man whose brain had betrayed him and who lived out his final decade flubbing about helplessly hunting his own thoughts, which kept eluding him. Mr. Gibson was so very sorry for the girl. Poor, unattractive, tired, beaten creature—terrible ordeal shouldn't have *been* there all alone!

The Jameses lived on the first floor of an old house near the campus. The moment Mr. Gibson entered the hall, he received the news of poverty and decay and a sense of darkness. If this place had ever had any colors, they had now all faded down into a uniform muddiness that defeated light. Everything, although quite clean, was somehow stained. Everything was old. And there was a clutter that comes of never having guests and therefore never seeing one's home with a fresh eye.

Nevertheless, he perceived that Rosemary had smoothed her dull hair carefully, that her dress was fresh from the ironing board, and that she had a string of blue beads on. It was typical of Mr. Gibson that these observations did not make him want to smile. They made him want to weep.

She greeted him timidly and seriously. She took him with nervous dispatch directly to the old man's lair.

"Well," he said in flat astonishment.

The old flat-topped desk was heaped with pieces of paper, lying at mad angles to one another.

"It looks like a haystack," said Rosemary with a spirited aptness that surprised him.

"Sure does." He appreciated her phrase. Smiled over it. "And it's our job to find the needle. Now come, you sit here. We'll start in the middle of the top and dig our way straight down to the bare wood. O.K. with you?"

They sat down. Mr. Gibson began to spin out of his own substance an atmosphere of cheerful, purposeful, organized endeavor. Soon she was breathing less shallowly and her lips were parted. She was intelligent.

But after a while absolutely nothing could save the situation from tragedy but a sense of humor. The old professor had scratched on paper during many hours. But his handwriting was atrocious, and worse, what he had written, where it was decipherable, seemed to have no reasonable meaning.

Mr. Gibson, in automatic defense, began to force himself to see the funny side. "If that is a capital T, as it may be for all I know," said he in semicomical despair, "then the word can be 'Therefore.' What do you think? Of course, it might just as well be 'Somewhere.'"

"Or 'However'?" said Rosemary earnestly.

"'However' is a distinct runner-up," he drawled. "Or even 'Whomever.'"

"'Whatever'?"

"I have a psychic feeling there's an 'f' in it. How about 'Wherefore'? 'Wherefore art thou Romeo?' D'you know, Miss James, the word might even *be* 'Romeo.'" It was heavy work to be light about this.

"Oh, I don't think so," she said seriously. And then she looked startled. Then she giggled.

It was as if a phoenix had risen from some ashes. Her giggle was rather low-pitched and melodious. The tiny folds at the upper-outer corners of her eyes were built for laughter. It was their function. They were droll. The eyes themselves lost their dusty look and became a little shiny. Even her skin seemed to gain a tinge of color.

"I'll betcha we could make it read anything we like," said Mr. Gibson enthusiastically. "Do you know anything about the Bacon-Shakespeare ciphers?" She didn't. She listened while he told her some of the wild aspects of that affair.

After that, while she was still relaxed and amused, he said gently, "You know, I think we had best look at the bottom of the pile."

"Earlier, you mean?" She *was* intelligent.

"I think so, my dear."

"He . . . tried so hard." Her handkerchief came up.

"It was brave to keep trying," he said. "It really was. And we'll keep trying, too."

"There are mounds—" she said bravely, "of papers in the drawers. Some typewritten . . ."

"Hurray."

"But Mr. Gibson, it will take so much time . . ."

"Of course," he said gently. "I never expected to go through it all in an hour. Did you?"

"You mustn't get tired."

"Are you tired?" He thought she was.

"I wondered . . . Do you drink tea?"

"When I am offered any," he said.

She rose awkwardly and went to fetch the tea which had been her own bold idea. Mr. Gibson waited by himself staring soberly at the desk and all this waste of paper. He didn't think they were going to find any treasure. Also, he knew that he had, once again, been foolish and rash. He'd let an impulse lead him. When would he learn not to do these things? He had given hope where there was not much real chance. He had best softly kill the hope he'd raised. But he feared very much that it was too important to her.

While they drank tea and ate some thin store cookies . . . a tiny feast she'd made as dainty as she could . . . Mr. Gibson felt that he must pry.

"Do you own this house?" he asked her.

"Oh, no. We only rented this half."

"Will you stay on here?"

"I can't. It's too big. Too much for me."

He feared she meant too expensive. "Forgive me for asking, but is there money? Funds of any kind?"

"I can sell the furniture. And the car."

"Ah, a car?"

"It's ten years old." He saw that she swallowed. "But it must be worth something."

"Your father's income was . . . for his lifetime?"

"Yes."

"There is *nothing?*" he guessed sharply.

"Well . . . the furniture . . ." She stopped pretending that the furniture was of any value and met his eyes. "I will just have to get a job. I don't know just what . . ." She twisted the beads. "I hoped . . ." Her eyes went to the papers.

"Can you type?" he asked quickly. She shook her head. "Have you ever held a job, Miss James?"

"No, I . . . Dad needed me. When Mama died I was the only one left, you see."

It was easy for Mr. Gibson to understand perfectly what had happened to her. "Have you anyone who can advise you?" he asked. "Relatives?"

"Nobody."

"How old are you?" he asked her gently. "Since I am old enough to be your father, you mustn't mind if I ask these things."

"I am thirty-two. And it's late, isn't it? But I'll find something to do."

He thought she needed somewhere to rest, above everything. "Have you a friend? Is there some place you could go?"

"I'll have to find a place to live," she said evasively. He divined that there was no such friend. The difficult old man no doubt had driven all well-meaning people away. "The landlord wants me to be gone by the first of March," Rosemary said. "He wants to redecorate. It certainly needs it." She made a nervous grimace.

Mr. Gibson cursed the landlord silently. "You're in a predicament, aren't you?" he remarked cheerfully. "Let me snoop around and see what kinds of jobs there are. May I?"

Her eyes widened again. The flesh lifted. The look was wonder. She said, "I don't want to be any trouble . . ."

"That wouldn't be any trouble," he said gently. "I can send out feelers, you know. Perhaps easier than you could. 'Wanted: well-paying job for person with no business experience whatsoever.' Look here, my dear, it's not impossible! After all, babies are born and *they've* had no business experience and yet they eventually do get jobs." He'd coaxed a smile out of her. "Now, we may find something here, but I had better say this, Miss James. It is neither easy nor is it a quick thing to find a publisher. It's very slow, I'm afraid. Nor is there very much money for academic kinds of writing."

"Thank you so much for being so kind, Mr. Gibson. But you don't have to be."

She wasn't rejecting him. In the droop of her body was all her weakness and fatigue. But she was, nevertheless, sitting as straight as she *could*, and looking as competent as was possible. She was trying to free him.

But what she had just said was not true, alas. He did have to be kind. He did have to try to help her . . . and keep her going with tidbits of hope. He couldn't imagine how to do otherwise.

He said easily, "I'll tell you what. Suppose I come again . . . let's see . . . on Friday afternoon? We'll attack the typewritten stuff. Now don't you disturb it. Meantime, I'll snoop. And I did enjoy the tea," he told her.

She did not thank him all over again, for which he was grateful as he got out into the living air.

Mr. Gibson was troubled all during Thursday because he knew he was being weak and wouldn't let himself think about it.

When he went again on Friday (He had to! He'd promised) the typewritten pages in the professor's lower desk drawers turned out to be, for the most part, correspondence which on the professor's side became progressively more angry and less coherent as the nerve paths in his brain had begun to tangle and cross one another. Mr. Gibson pretended it was very interesting. It was. But as tragedy. Not treasure.

Nevertheless, Mr. Gibson strung out the task and kept calling. Oh, he knew exactly what he was doing. When he thought about it he did not approve at all. It was weak. He had entangled himself, and every visit wove another strand into the web. And he knew better. Nobody knew better than he that he ought to withdraw gracefully. She was no burden of his.

He could withdraw. In modern days, in the United States of America, no corpse lies on the street slain by destitution. There were charities and public institutions. There was social succor. Nor would Rosemary blame him if he slipped out of her affairs. She would only continue to be grateful for all he had done or tried to do so far.

But he was incapable of this kind of common sense. By now, he knew exactly how to make her smile. No organized charity could know *this*. It was a little ridiculous how much this weighed with him. As he knew. But he'd just gotten into the whole business too far. He had seen himself do it, but he had looked away. So had Rosemary seen it. She had even warned him. But now it was too late. He had constituted himself as the holder of the carrot of hope before this donkey's nose . . . without which she might stop, cease, or even die. . . .

Meantime, dealers came to look at the furniture and offer contemptuous minimums. The books were worth pitifully little in cash. One day a man said he'd give fifty dollars for the ancient car. By the time Rosemary conferred with Mr. Gibson and decided to accept it, he had withdrawn even this offer. Her possessions were without value.

Meantime, also, Mr. Gibson snooped for jobs in Rosemary's behalf. He discovered that there were indeed some which did not demand experience. They definitely required good health and some strength, instead. Rosemary did not have these qualifications, either. On the contrary, it was evident to Mr. Gibson that she was heading for a serious breakdown. He was able to see her rooms become even more neglected because she could do nothing about it. He guessed that she was able to keep her person neat only by a terrible effort, by a stubborn flickering of innate pride. Otherwise, she was limp with the inertia of physical and emotional exhaustion. And to call, to talk, to coax a little ease into her face, three times a week, this—although vital—was not really enough.

What was she to do? This began to obsess him. She had no funds, no strength. She seemed to eat . . . he wasn't sure how well. She'd have no place to eat, or sleep, soon, for the 1st of March loomed closer.

On the 25th of February he marched in and announced peremptorily that he had just paid the rent here for April. "You need the time. You *must* have it. All right. You owe me the money. That's nothing. I have owed money . . ."

She broke and cried until he was alarmed.

"Now, mouse," he said. "Please . . ." His throat ached with hers.

So she told him she was afraid her mind was going, as her father's had gone, because she was so weighted by a numbness and a languor. He, appalled, insisted upon bringing his own doctor to take a look at her.

The doctor scoffed. Old Professor James' trouble was not inheritable. This woman was frighteningly run-down. Underweight. Malnourished. Anemic. Nervously exhausted. *He* knew what she needed. Medicine, diet, and a long rest. He seemed to think he had solved everything.

Mr. Gibson chewed his lips.

"Say, where do you come in, Gibson?" the doctor asked amiably. "In loco parentis?"

Mr. Gibson said he guessed *so*. He bought the medicines. He gave her orders. He knew that this was not enough.

The same evening, one of his colleagues, casually encountered, nudged his ribs and said, "You're a sly one, Gibson. I hear you're shining up to old James' daughter these days. When's the wedding, hm?"

Chapter Three

ON THE ides of April, in the afternoon (for he always came after classes, by daylight), Rosemary was sitting in a mud-colored old armchair in her living room. Mr. Gibson could remark the fluff of dust accumulating along its seams. He thought to himself, It is impossible for anyone to be healthy in this dreadful place. I have got to get her out of here.

She had her hair pulled back today and tied in a hank at the back of her neck with a faded ribbon. This did not make her look girlish. She looked haggard.

She said, as primly as if she'd memorized it, "I feel so much better. The medicine is doing me good, I'm sure. And to know what the trouble is, that's been comforting." She dragged her eyelids up. "Mr. Gibson, I want you to go away . . . not come any more."

"Why?" he said with a pang.

"Because I am nobody of yours. You shouldn't worry about me. You weren't even a friend of ours."

Mr. Gibson did not misunderstand. "Surely, I am a friend now," he chided gently.

"You are," she admitted with a dry gasp, "and the only one. . . . But you *have* helped me. It is enough. Congratulate yourself. Please."

He got up and walked about. He admired her spunk. He approved of it. But he felt upset. "What will you do on the first of May?"

"If nothing else . . . I'll go on the county," she said.

"I see. You feel distressed about me? You don't want me to try to help you any more?"

She shook her head dumbly. She looked as if she had spent her very last ounce of energy.

"They tell me," mused Mr. Gibson aloud, looking at the horrible wallpaper, "that it is more blessed to give than to receive. But it does seem to me, in that case, *somebody* has to be willing to receive. And do it graciously," he added rather sternly. She winced as if he had slapped her. "Oh, I know it isn't easy," he assured her quickly.

Then he hesitated. But not for long.

The trouble was, his imagination had been working. He ought to have known that if a thing can be vividly imagined, it can be done. It probably will be done. He sat down and leaned forward earnestly.

"Rosemary, suppose there was something you could do for me?"

"Anything I could ever do for you," she choked, "I'd be bound to do."

"Good. Now let's take it for granted, shall we, that you are grateful and stop repeating that? It's a terrible bore for both of us. And I do not enjoy seeing you cry, you know. I don't enjoy it at all."

She squeezed her lids together.

"I am fifty-five years old," he said. Her damp lids opened in surprise. "I don't look it?" He smiled. "Well, as I always say, I've been pickled in poetry. I earn seven thousand a year. I wanted you to know these . . . er . . . statistics before I asked you to marry me."

She clapped both hands over her face and eyes.

"Listen a minute," he went on gently. "I've never married. I've never had a home made for me by a woman. Perhaps I have been missing something . . . in that alone. Now there's a skill you have, Rosemary. You know how to keep a house. You've done it for years. You can do it, and very nicely, I'm sure, once you feel strong again. So I was thinking . . ."

She did not move nor even look between her fingers.

"It might be a good bargain between us," he went on. "We *are* friends, whatever you say. I think we are not incompatible. We've had some pleasant hours, even in all this difficulty. We might make good companions. Can you look at it as if it were to be an experiment? A venture? Let us not say it's forever. Suppose we found we didn't enjoy being together? Why, in these days, you know, divorce is quite acceptable. Especially . . . Rosemary, are you a religious woman?"

"I don't know," she said pitifully behind her hands.

"Well, I thought," he continued, "if instead of a holy pledge . . .

we made a bargain . . ." He began to speak louder. "My dear, I am not in love with you," he stated bluntly. "I don't speak of love or romance. At my age, it would be a little silly. I neither expect romantic love nor intend to give it. I am thinking of an arrangement. I am trying to be frank. Will you let me know if you understand me?"

"I do," she said brokenly. "I understand what you mean. But it's no real bargain at all, Mr. Gibson. I am no use to anybody . . ."

"No, you are not, not at the moment," he agreed cheerfully. "I wouldn't expect you to do the wash next Monday, you know. But I am thinking, and please think seriously too. . . . Although there is one point I'd like to make quickly. I don't want to cheat you."

"Cheat me?" she said hoarsely.

"You are only thirty-two. Be frank with me."

She took her hands down. "How can I say I'd rather go on the county?" she said with sudden asperity.

"You could say it if it is so," he told her grinning. The air in the room lightened. Everything seemed gayer. "Did you ever have a hobby, Rosemary?" he asked her.

"A hobby? Yes, I . . . once or twice. I had a garden. For a while I . . . liked to try to paint." She looked dazed.

"Let me confess, then. I am presently enchanted by the idea of making you well again. Of getting you up, Rosemary, and yourself, again. As a matter of fact, it is exactly as if to do so was a hobby of mine. Now then. Now, *that's* honest." He settled back. "How I'd like to!" he said wistfully. "I really would. I'd like to put you in a bright pleasant place and feed you up and see you get fat and sassy. I can't think," he sighed, "of anything that would be more fun."

She put her hands over her face and rocked her body.

"No?" he said quietly. "If the idea repels you, why of course it's not feasible. But what will you do, Rosemary? What will become of you? Don't you see that I can't stop worrying? How can you stop me if I can't stop myself? I wish you would let me lend you money, at least." He fidgeted.

"I can cook, Mr. Gibson," she said in a low voice.

He said in a moment, "Then, I'm afraid you will have to begin to call me Kenneth."

She said, "Yes, Kenneth, I will."

They were married on the 20th of April by a justice of the peace. One of the witnesses was Paul Townsend.

This came about because, in the five-day flurry and excitement, when Mr. Gibson was house-hunting as hard as he could, he bumped into Paul Townsend, confided his problem, and Paul solved it.

"Say!" His handsome genial face lit up. "I've got just the place for you! It'd be perfect! My tenant left a week ago. The painters will be gone tomorrow. What a coincidence! Gibson, you're *in!*"

"Where am I in?"

"In my cottage on the lot adjoining my own place. A regular honeymoon cottage."

"Furnished?"

"Of course, furnished. It's a little far out."

"How far?"

"Thirty minutes on the bus. You don't drive a car?"

"Rosemary has a car of sorts. An old monster. Not even worth selling."

"Well, then! There's a garage for it. How does this sound? Living room, bedroom, bath, big den—lots of bookshelves in there—dinette, kitchen. There's a fireplace . . ."

"Bookshelves?" said Mr. Gibson. "Fireplace?"

"And a garden."

"Garden?" said Mr. Gibson in a trance.

"I'm a nut on gardening myself. You come and see."

Mr. Gibson went and saw, and succumbed.

The wedding took place at three in the afternoon in a drab office with no fanfare and not much odor of sanctity. The justice was a matter-of-fact type who mumbled drearily. No one was present except the necessary witnesses. Mr. Gibson had thought it best to ask none of his colleagues to watch him being married, in this manner, to this white-faced woman in her old blue suit who could scarcely stand up, whose gaunt finger shook so that he could scarcely force the ring over the knucklebone.

Then of course Rosemary had no people. And Mr. Gibson's only sister Ethel, although asked, for auld lang syne, could not come. She wrote that she supposed he would know what he was doing at his age, and she was happy for him if he was happy—that she would try to come to visit one day, perhaps during the summer, and then meet the bride. To whom she sent love.

It was an ugly dreary wedding. It made Mr. Gibson wince in his soul, but it was quick, soon over. He was able to take it as just necessary, like a disagreeable pill.

Chapter Four

PAUL TOWNSEND LIVED, together with his teen-age daughter
and his elderly mother-in-law, in a low stucco house of some size
on a fair piece of land. Beside his driveway lay the driveway per-
taining to the cottage. The cottage was built of brick and redwood
and upon it vines really did grow. Mr. Gibson's books and papers
(although still in boxes), and his neat day-bed, were already there
in the large square shelf-lined room off the living room, and the
lumbering old car that Professor James had bought years ago was
already standing in the neat little garage when Mr. Gibson brought
his bride home in a taxi. He opened the front door and led her in,
making no attempt at the threshold gesture. He sat her down in a
bright blue easy chair. She looked as if she were going to die.

But Mr. Gibson had his own ideas of healing and he plunged in,
heart and soul. He had wangled a week away from his classes. He
proposed to use it to settle. But the cottage had aroused in his own
breast some instincts he'd never known about. He also proposed to
make a home.

So, during that first hour, he bustled. He poured out his enthusi-
asms, all going forward. He made her look at color. Did she like the
primrose yellow in the draperies? (He thought privately that the
clean, fresh colors in this charming sun-drenched room would be
health-giving in themselves.) Where would he put his record
player? He wondered aloud, forcing her to consider the promise of
music. Then he officiated in the kitchen. He was not a bad cook,
himself, but he begged her advice. He did all he could to interest
and tempt her.

Rosemary could not eat any supper. She was not ready for a future. She was collapsing after an escape from the past. There would
be a hiatus. He feared she'd die of it.

So he insisted that she go at once to bed, in the soft-hued bedroom that would be hers alone. When he judged she was settled, he

brought her the medicine. He touched the dry straw of her sad hair. He said, "Rest now." Her head turned weakly.

He spent the evening unpacking books and listening . . . sometimes tiptoeing to her door to listen.

The next day she lay abed, unable to move, as good as dead. Only her eyes asked for mercy and patience.

Mr. Gibson had lots of patience. He was undaunted and took pains to make some very silly puns each time he brought her a snack to eat. He hooked up the record player and let music penetrate the whole little house. He believed in humor and in beauty and in color and in music and he mined the deepest faiths he had . . . for he *knew* he could heal her.

On the second morning, he went in to remove her breakfast tray and saw that she was lying against the pillow with her face turned to the window. Between the dainty white margins of the curtains there was visible a patch of ground planted with roses. On her face, for the first time in his knowledge of her, lay a look of peace.

"I used to love to sit on the ground with my hands in the dirt," she said to him. "There is something about earth on your hands . . ."

"Yes, there is. And something about light. And something about running water, too. Don't you think so?"

"Yes," she said stirring.

He thought this particular "yes" had a most positive sound to it. He went softly, however. He took care not to nag at her, not to bother.

On the third day Rosemary got up and dressed in a cotton frock. She began to make a brave effort to eat, as if she owed this to him. In the evening, he built a fire (for there is something about a fire, too) and he read to her. He read some poetry. It gave him such pleasure to realize that she was going to be the best pupil he had ever had. She listened so intently. It was lively to listen so. It was a spark of life which he would fan.

Once she said to him, during that evening, with a look of pain, "You are so sane." It made him wince to understand how eight years of her life had been spent alone with that which could not have been called sane. No wonder, he said to himself. No wonder it has nearly killed her.

Now his week off began to go leaping by. She helped dust some books. She couldn't, of course, dust many. Mr. Gibson had to go back to work on the Monday, so on Friday Mrs. Violette came in.

Mrs. Violette was produced for them by Paul Townsend. She was a cleaning woman; she worked for the Townsends in the afternoons. But she was a young person, very slim and quick, with shining black hair and skin of a soft peach color and a countenance of a smoothness and design that was foreign. At least there was something odd, and not plain American, about her looks—Near Eastern perhaps. One couldn't place her.

Mrs. Violette didn't concern herself with being placed. She was cool and detached, taciturn and competent. One knew that she could keep this little house clean with the back of one of her slim strong buff-colored hands. Mr. Gibson thought she would do admirably. She was not, thank heaven, some garrulous woe-loving old creature reduced to drudgery by adversities. She was fresh and self-respecting. She would be fine. Rosemary agreed, but wondered if it wouldn't cost too much.

"Until you are perfectly well," he told her, "Mrs. Violette is an economy. Now that's just sensible."

"At least *you* make it *sound* sensible," Rosemary said with a touch of life and opinion.

So Mr. Gibson went back to his classes on the Monday, convinced that Rosemary wasn't going to die.

He rode the buses. He wasn't much of a driver, for an automobile was a thing he had known, all his life, how to do without. So he left the ancient car in the garage until such time as Rosemary might wish to use it. She understood it, which was more than he did, and he rode his thirty minutes, brooding and half-smiling to himself over little schemes. For he was possessed by the joy of nurture which is closely akin, if not identical with, the deep joy of creation. He had never known this in his life before. It absolutely absorbed him.

Rosemary was eating well. She was stuffing herself to please him. (Ah, so it did!) When he came home, the little house would be shining from the administrations of Mrs. Violette, and Rosemary would recount to him how many eggs she'd had, how many glasses of milk, what toast. . . . And he'd say she'd be fat as a pig pretty soon and feel a sting behind his eyes.

One afternoon he came walking home, the two blocks from the bus stop, to see her sitting on the ground at the far side of the house, near the roses. He altered his course and stepped softly toward her on the grass. She looked up and her face was dirty where she had swiped an earthy hand across her nose. She was patting and combing the earth around one rose bush with her bare fingers.

This earth was dampish and richly dark. She told him it was in good tilth. Mr. Gibson squatted down to admire and, at the same time, to taste and turn and enjoy a word that was new to him. What a wonderful word! Tilth. He understood it immediately.

She said the roses needed mulching and he learned about mulch. She showed him how delicately she had pruned this one rose bush, how the buds must be left to grow outward. She seemed to understand what the plant needed. It seemed to him that she felt toward this one plant—all she could manage yet—much as he felt toward her, Rosemary. He didn't say so. When he helped her to her feet, it seemed to him that she sprang up rather lightly. It made him happy.

Then one Saturday morning, puttering in his room, he realized that, while he could hear Mrs. Violette in the kitchen, he missed another presence in the house. He looked out of all the windows and at last saw Rosemary sitting in the back-yard grass, in the sun, with a hairbrush in her hand. She was brushing her hair in slow rhythm and while he watched she did not cease to brush her hair. Something about the scene startled him. The rhythm, the sensuous rhythm, the ritual of it, the strangeness . . . Rosemary was a woman. She was a mystery. One day, when he had brought her to full life and health as he would do, why, he did not know with whom he would be living in this house! He did not know Rosemary, herself. . . .

Paul Townsend turned out to be an ideal landlord. He was genial and easy, but he did not intrude. One day, however, when three weeks had gone by and the Gibsons could be presumed settled in, Paul invited them to supper.

It was their first social event.

Rosemary wore her best dress. Mr. Gibson admired it aloud. It was a dullish blue, a pleasant enough dress. But he fussed a little. As soon as ever she felt just like it, he told her, she must buy at least two new dresses . . . maybe three. Rosemary quietly promised that she would. She accepted everything he urged upon her these days with no more weak spilling of grateful tears. In fact, she was full of grace in the matter of receiving.

They walked across the double driveway to Paul Townsend's house.

While not grand, this was certainly the home of a solvent man. Paul Townsend, a chemical engineer, owned the plant and laboratory down near the college, and it must return him if not a fortune at least a pleasant living.

He was a widower. Mr. Gibson had never known his wife, alive. Her picture was in this house many times. It was a little sad to see how young the pictures were. She did not look as if her daughter could be this tall Jean, fifteen, and in high school. A pleasant child, with a cropped and tousled dark head, fine white teeth in a ready smile, excellent company manners. Then there was Paul's mother-in-law, Mrs. Pyne, a cripple, poor soul, who inhabited a wheel chair.

Supper was not formal but nicely served and stiffly, politely eaten. Mr. Gibson watched Rosemary. Was she nervous about these people? Was it a strain? Was she strong enough?

The old lady asked kind commonplace questions, and told kind commonplace statistics about herself and the family. She had a thin, rather delicately boned face, and the tact not to mention her own disabilities. The young girl kept her place among her elders, served the meal, cleared the table afterward, and then excused herself to do her homework. Paul was a considerate host, full of good will and social anxiety.

But there are just so many commonplaces. Mr. Gibson set to work to dissolve the stiffness of this first meeting of Rosemary and her nearest neighbors. He was bound Rosemary was going to find it easy and pleasant to move into a world of friendly give and take. In fact, he talked a good deal for a while. At last, by prying and prodding for mutual interests, he discovered how to egg Paul on to talk about his garden. Rosemary began to listen and contribute. Mr. Gibson was eager to learn. Once Paul asked a silly punning question . . . whether Mr. Gibson had a sense of humus. Mr. Gibson was inspired to reply, "Not mulch." And Rosemary giggled. The old lady smiled indulgently and kept listening pleasantly as the session grew quite animated.

At ten o'clock they took their leave, for Mr. Gibson did not want Rosemary tired out. After the good nights and the kind parting phrases, they crossed the roofless porch at the front of Paul's house. They came down the five steps and crossed the double driveways in the soft chill air of night time. They went in at their own back door, skirting the shining new garbage cans, symbolic of a functioning house. They crossed the pale dim orderly kitchen and entered the living room, where a lamp had been left burning. The sense of home flowed into Mr. Gibson's heart.

"Wasn't that fun?" said he. "I thought *you* were having a good time."

Rosemary stood there, in the blue dress, slowly shrugging off the dark sweater from around her shoulders. She looked brooding and intense. "I have never known," she said vibrantly, "it was possible to have so good a time. I never, never, knew . . ."

It rather shocked him. He could think of nothing to reply. She tossed the sweater into her chair and sat down and looked up at him and smiled. "Read to me, Kenneth, please," she said coaxingly, "for just ten minutes? Until I simmer down?"

"If you drink your milk and eat your cookies."

"Yes, I will. Bring four."

So he fetched the nourishment. He opened a book. He read to her.

Afterward, she licked a cookie crumb from her forefinger. She thanked him with a drowsy smile. . . .

Kenneth Gibson went into his room, which had by now acquired the look of all the places he had ever lived for long, the mellow order, the masculine coziness. He went to bed a little bewildered. He was beginning not to understand her.

Chapter Five

ON THE 19th of May, Rosemary got up before him to make his breakfast. She had on a new cotton frock, for "around the house," she said. It was pink and a particularly springlike pink, somehow. She chattered away. She would like to try feeding the border with a new kind of fertilizer. Paul Townsend said it did wonders. Did he think $3.95 was too much to spend on it? And would he like roast lamb for dinner? Did he prefer mint sauce or a sweet mint jelly with his lamb? Wasn't the early sun on the little stone wall a lovely sight! Pale gold on the gray. Why was sunlight, in the morning, so crisp— and then, by noon, more like cloudy honey?

"Shadows?" he speculated. "Some day you should try to paint what you see, Rosemary."

She wasn't good enough, she said, although to *try* . . . At least, she announced, tossing her head, Mrs. Violette must wash and starch the kitchen curtains. They'd be nicer crisp to match the mornings. Didn't he think so?

Mr. Gibson sat there at the table, watching her and listening, and his eyes suddenly cleared. Scales fell. He saw Rosemary, not as she had been, or as he had been thinking of her, but as she *was*, this morning.

The crisp frock showed a figure that, while slim, certainly could not be called skinny any more. Neither was it bent and hollow with the posture of weakness. On the contrary, she sat quite upright and above her snug waist swelled a charming bosom, and the shoulder bones were covered with sweet flesh. Then her hair! Why, her hair was thick and shining and full of chestnut lights! Where had it come from? Whence *this* face? *This* face was not pasty white nor did the flesh droop in sad rumples. It was almost firm, and sun-gilded to a rosy-gold, and the lines in her forehead were a maturity (more interesting than the bare bold brow of youth could be). Her blue eyes were snapping with the range of her thoughts among her projects for this day. The odd little fold in the flesh at the corners was so characteristic, so significant of her fine good humor. Her whole face was so animated and . . . he didn't know what to call it but . . . Rosemaryish. And that low bubbly chuckle of hers was constantly in her throat.

His breast swelled. *Why, she is well!* he thought.

Mr. Gibson hid this for a secret temporarily while he smiled and patted all her plans on the back encouragingly . . . and said goodbye.

But he rode the bus with a joyful booming in his heart. *She is well again! Rosemary is alive and well!* He had as good as raised her from the dead.

All day long, the miracle rang in his heart. He would come back to it, back to it, and, every time, it boomed and rang like bells.

When he came home, to admire the lamb and watch her dainty hunger, and hear how the day had gone and was already only a foundation for tomorrow, he said firmly, "Tomorrow night, Rosemary, *we* are going to celebrate."

"Are we? Why?"

"Can you drive ten miles? Can the Ark go ten miles?"

"Why, sure it can," she said gaily. "I don't see why not."

"Then we are going out for dinner—to a restaurant I know. Out on the highway. Oh, you'll like it."

"But *why?*"

"To celebrate." He was mysterious.

"Celebrate *what*, Kenneth?"

"It's a secret," he said. "I may tell you tomorrow."

"What on earth are you talking about?"

"Never mind," he said shyly. He almost hated to share his very miracle—even with her.

In the evening of the next day (which was a Friday), the ancient car proceeded noisily out upon the highway, west of town. It rode high and old-fashioned, in a gait that was both stately and lumbering, like a stout matron who nevertheless has her dignity. Rosemary, in a new white dress with a splash of red roses on the bodice, with a big soft red wool scarf tied around the top of her, drove them without seeming to try too hard. *She is equal to this*, thought Mr. Gibson with pride, *because she is well. And there is no doubt about it.*

Mr. Gibson had gone so far as to reserve a table, for this little restaurant was very popular, both on account of its fine French cooking and its atmosphere, which was dim and smoky and smelled deliciously of sauces. It wasn't cheap either. But this was a celebration.

They drank a little wine. They ate hugely of one delectable dish after another, and Mr. Gibson teased by refusing to explain the reason for the reckless expense of this expedition. It was delightful to be together in the midst of the smoke and the savory smells and the soft buzz of other people's conversations. Mr. Gibson knew he was preening himself. He knew that Rosemary was, too. As if they were actors or masqueraders, and out of themselves and yet being themselves in a freer truer way. He couldn't help feeling on the suave side, and a bit of a gay dog. He enjoyed it. Rosemary looked as if she felt that she was rather lovely. And so she was, he decided.

At dessert time, they had a drop of brandy with their coffee. Then without warning these two people-of-the-world fell into a fit of childlike hilarity.

Just something he said, a turn of a phrase.

And Rosemary capped it.

And he extended it.

And they were off. The whole thing spiraled up. It got funnier and funnier. They were behaving like a pair of maniacs. Mr. Gibson laughed so hard he had to retreat behind his napkin. He felt himself aching. Rosemary had her hands to the red roses printed on her bodice as if she were aching too. They rocked together. Their heads bumped. *This* was an absolute riot. They shushed each other, faces red, eyes wet, and beaming, and daring each other.

People turned mildly worried faces to look at them, and *this* was the funniest thing they'd ever *seen*. And sent them off again. Nothing on earth had ever been so funny. But never could they explain *why* to anyone else. Which was extremely funny in *itself*.

Now people were smiling by contagion and staring with real curiosity. So they controlled themselves and made their mouths stiff and sipped brandy. Rosemary thought of one more word and *said* it and off they went, careening on laughter right off the earth to some other place.

It took quite a while to simmer down. But at last, just as suddenly, the little sadness fell. It was over. They mustn't try to start it up again. No. Force nothing. Sit, with the sweet contentment in their throats, the after-taste of laughter that lies so kindly on the very membranes like a salve.

"When will you tell me what we are celebrating?" asked Rosemary gravely.

"I'll tell you now." He lifted the last drop of his brandy. "We are celebrating you. Because you are well again."

Her eyes filled with tears. She didn't answer.

He said quietly, "Well, it's late. I suppose we should go."

"Yes." She fished the red wool thing from behind her. She seemed to be trembling. The waiter pulled the table away and they rose, moving slowly, as if still entranced, still sweetly remembering the food and the fun. He took the soft wide stole and held it, and she turned her back, and he folded it around her. He wanted to tuck it close around her throat, wanted her safe and warm. He couldn't help it that his hands were tender. Rosemary bent her head, and for one quick wonderful stunning moment she pressed the warm skin of her cheek caressingly upon the bare skin of his hand.

It was only a moment. It changed the whole world.

Mr. Gibson followed her to the little lobby and opened the door which the proprietor was helping to open (saying good night, say-

ing that a bit of a fog had come up, suggesting caution). Mr. Gibson
may have replied mechanically. He was absolutely stunned.

He had just discovered that he was in love with his wife Rosemary, twenty-three years his junior—but that didn't matter. Why,
he was crazy about her! Now he understood what they meant by
"in love." In love . . . in love . . . in love!

They stepped out into a place of strangest beauty—not like the
world at all. A heavy fog but oh, how beautiful!

Rosemary stepped back to rest a moment against him. Their two
bodies were all that was left of the old world and all that mattered.
Everywhere, veils fell. Across the road, the fields drowsed and
drowned.

"Would you rather I drove?" he asked her.

"No, no," she said. "I understand the poor old Ark. Oh, Kenneth,
isn't it beautiful!"

There was a vibration between them and he cherished it. It was
too dear and too new and much too beautiful to mention.

They got into the car. Rosemary started the noisy old engine,
and backed it out of the parking slot. Mr. Gibson strained to see,
and to guide her. But he hardly knew what he was seeing. She drove
slowly with full caution. The big old car went steadily. The world
was invisible ahead of them and vanished behind them. They were
nowhere, and yet here. Together and only ten miles from home.

Mr. Gibson didn't think behind nor too far, nor too clearly, ahead,
either. He only knew he was in love, and everything—everything
was piercingly different and beautiful.

The sudden headlights simply *became,* as if they'd just been
created. A car raced toward them, head on. He knew that Rosemary
took a sudden great pull on the steering wheel. That was all he
knew but a brutal noise, one flash of pain, and then from his senses
the world was gone, altogether.

Chapter Six

HE WAS trussed up, he was chained, like a dog in a kennel. He could not, even if he had had the ambition to try, get out of this bed and away from the contraptions that imprisoned him.

"Then, she *is* all right?" he said. "You've actually seen her?" He tried to bend his gaze and search *this* face, but the girl with the clipboard had seated herself and was too low. He could see the top of her head, but not the eyes.

"Well, no," he heard her voice saying, "I didn't actually see her. But I was up on her floor—trying to . . . you know . . . get information? And she's all right, Mr. Gibson. Honest. Everybody's told you."

"What do you mean by 'all right'?" he queried irritably. His leg up in this undignified shocking fashion, his torso constricted somehow, his senses obstructed, the whole shock and indignity of injury upon him . . . yet he himself was "all right" in hospital parlance. What did they mean, except that he wasn't in mortal danger? (Oh, was she?)

"Told me she was out for a while and shaken up quite a bit," said the uncultivated voice, "but that's all. Now please, Mr. Gibson . . ."

He rolled his head. It seemed to be all the freedom he had. But who, he thought with a flooding woe, is going to make Rosemary smile . . . ?

"Are you in pain?" the girl said not unsympathetically. "Maybe I could come back."

"I sure am in pain," he said. "Exactly. Right inside of it. I'm in some kind of cocoon made out of fuzz and fog . . ." (Fog? His heart winced.) He must have been given drugs. His tongue felt thickened but loosened, too. "I don't feel the pain, you see, but I know it is there, all around me. And it knows I know. What day is it? What time is it? Where am I?" he jested with his frightened lips.

"It's Saturday, the twentieth of May," she told him slowly and patiently. "It's nine twenty A.M. and you are in Andrews Memorial.

You were brought in last night, and honest, Mr. Gibson, *I'm* sorry but I *have* to get this information for the office . . ."

"I know," he said soberly.

He was afraid, sweating afraid, that they were all lying to him. It wasn't inconceivable. Battered and broken as he was, they might, in their wisdom, have decided to conspire and keep from him a sorrow. He opened his eyes as wide as he could and strained to lift his head and peer at this girl through the fuzz and the mist. "Sit a little higher. I can't see you," he demanded.

The girl elevated herself. She thought, Gee, he's got nice eyes. On a girl, they'd be gorgeous! Wouldn't it be, though? It's like me and my sisters all got the straight hair and the boys got the natural waves. . . . She lowered her gaze so as not to be caught with such thoughts.

"What are they *doing* to her?" Mr. Gibson said wildly.

"Why, they got her under sedation, I guess. Least I couldn't talk to her. Probably they want to watch her a few days . . ."

"That's right," he said excitedly. "Yes, that's what they must do. Keep her and watch her. You see, she hasn't been strong. She's had quite a time and this could set her back . . ."

The girl sighed and poised her pen. "I got your name and address. Now, lessee . . . When were you born, Mr. Gibson? Please, if you'll just let me get this blank filled out . . ."

"Sorry," he said. "January fifth, nineteen hundred. Which makes it entirely too easy to figure out how old I am. You don't even have to subtract, do you?"

The girl wrote "Yes" after "Married?" . . . "How long have you been married, Mr. Gibson?" she asked aloud.

"Five weeks."

"Oh, *really?*" Her voice became bright and interested. The next question on her blank was "Children?" She started to write a "No" and caught herself. "Is this your *first* wife?"

"My first . . . my only . . . Will you tell me one thing?" He fought to see her plain. "Is *she* in pain?"

"Look," the girl said, determined this time. "What can I *do*, Mr. Gibson? Honest to gosh, nobody's trying to kid you. They don't think she's even got a concussion. I'd know if there was anything bad. Believe me, I'd tell you."

He could see her face now, and it was kind and shiny and in earnest. "I believe you would," he said weakly. "Yes, thank you."

He was in a ward. There was no telephone. He was divided from

Rosemary. He was farther from her than if he'd been a thousand miles. He said, whimsical in helplessness, "Could I send her a postcard?"

The girl said, "Now. Probably *she'll* be able to come down here and see you . . . at least by tomorrow."

"They might let her leave before me?" said Mr. Gibson at once, in alarm.

"Well, I should think *so*. After all, *you* got to wait a while . . ."

"They mustn't let her." He couldn't bear to think of Rosemary alone. Mrs. Violette might be hired to stay, but Mrs. Violette was so remote and cool. . . . Paul Townsend would be kind, but he couldn't be with her. There was nobody, he thought in panic— Yes. Yes there *was!* Rosemary had no people, but he had a person. *He had a sister.*

"Could you send a telegram?" he asked abruptly.

"I guess I could see to it for you, or the nurse . . ."

"*You* do it. To Miss Ethel Gibson." He gave her the address. "Are you writing it down? Send this. 'Don't worry but car accident puts me in hospital. Rosemary O.K. but we need you. Can you possibly come.'"

"Love?" the girl asked, scribbling busily.

"Love, Ken."

"Twenty words."

"Never mind. Please send it. Will you do that for me? I don't know where there is any money . . ."

"I'll see about it," she soothed. "They can charge it on your bill. Now, do you feel better? Now will you tell me the answers to all this stuff?"

So he told her the answers.

"O.K.," she said at last. "I guess I got the whole story of your life. Now, don't worry, Mr. Gibson, I'll surely send the telegram."

"You're very good . . ."

"So long." She smiled. She liked him. He was kinda cute. Didn't look to be fifty-five, either. With the kind of skin he had—fair, and stuck to his cheekbones. A woman would have had to have her face lifted already. And him married only five weeks to his first wife. She thought it was cute, and a little bit amusing. "Don't worry so much about your bride," she said affectionately.

"I'll try not," he promised. But he had received the news of her amusement and thought he would not open himself for the amusement of strangers again.

When she had gone, he thought drunkenly: Story of my life. She hadn't got *any* of it. . . . Then his whole life's story went by him in a rush, and his heart throbbed hard for the disappointment and the postponement.

But he took hold of himself and called up patience. He would heal, painfully, in time. The pain was nothing. It could be endured. He was not reconciled to the time it would take, but he would endeavor to be.

If only Rosemary had not been set back too much! If only Ethel —good reliable sister Ethel—if she could come and keep . . . keep his house! He felt sure she would respond as he himself would have responded, of course, to such a telegram. Ethel might even fly. His sister, Ethel, was not as far away from him in time as was Rosemary, upstairs. Ethel would come and take care and, in time, all would be well again.

Meanwhile, Mr. Gibson saw that the man on his right lay stupidly inert with a tube running in a disgusting way through one nostril. The man on his right had his ear upon the pillow, under which was a magic disk that poured out a soap opera. The ward was full of men all waiting as best they could . . . and most in pain. Some of them might be in love, for all he knew.

Mr. Gibson lay remembering words, for words were good to help keep off the pain—that brute and wordless thing—and to pass the time.

. . . an ever-fixèd mark
That looks on tempests and is never shaken;
It is the star to every wandering bark
Whose worth's
Unknown . . .
Unknown . . .
Unknown . . .

He seemed to sleep.

Later in that shapeless day they brought him a wire: FLYING SOONEST. ETHEL.

Mr. Gibson sighed so deeply that it made his chest ache.

"And I almost forgot. Your wife sends love," the nurse said brightly.

"Does she?"

"She was pretty anxious to know how *you* were. Let me squinch this pillow over. Is that more comfortable?"

"I am comforted," he said quaintly. "Can you send her my love?"

"We sure can," the nurse said merrily. "I'll put it on the grapevine, right away."

People are good, thought Mr. Gibson, weak with satisfaction. People are really awfully good. Good nurse. Good sister Ethel. This misery would pass.

Chapter Seven

"GOOD TO COME," he said to her, the next morning. "So *very good* to come. So *glad* to see you."

"Think nothing of it, old dear," said Ethel, standing in her old familiar way, with the effect of being on both feet instead of settling her weight on one and using the other for balance, as most do. Ethel was a woman of some bulk. Although she wasn't fat, her waist was solid, her legs sturdy, her shoulders wide. She was wearing a tweedy suit of severe cut and a tailored blouse, but her short gray-threaded hair was uncovered and her square ringless hands were ungloved.

"Pretty state of affairs this is," she said in her hearty voice. She had bright brown eyes in a face that would launch no ships. (Ethel looked a good deal like their father had, he realized suddenly. Now that she was forty-seven.) "How do you feel?" she inquired.

"Don't ask me. You wouldn't want to hear about it. I want you to go to Rosemary . . ."

"I've been to Rosemary."

"You have?" He felt stunned.

"It's ten A.M. my lad," said Ethel. "And I got off that plane in the middle of the night and the milk-train or whatever I took landed me here at five A.M. I've met your landlord. I've seen your house. I've had a bath in it. And I got in to see Rosemary because *she* is in a semiprivate room, whereas all kinds of indecent things were going on in this ward, or so they implied." Ethel glanced at the man with the tube in his nostril and did not flinch.

Mr. Gibson gave out a weak "Oh," feeling somewhat flattened by her energy.

"Woke up your Mr. Townsend, I guess. Must say he was very amiable about it. When I identified myself, he let me in. Nothing to it."

"Paul's a good fellow . . ."

"Very charming," said Ethel dryly. "One of those dreamboats, eh? And a rich widower, too? My! Quite a little house you live in, Ken."

"Isn't it?"

"I put my things in what I judged to be Rosemary's room." Her wise glance understood everything.

"Yes," he said feebly. All at once, he could not imagine brisk, sensible, energetic Ethel in the little house, at all. He said impatiently—because she gave the effect of a gale blowing a sudden gust that disrupted a certain neatness and order of his thoughts— "Tell me, Ethel. How *is* Rosemary?"

"Not a scratch on her," said Ethel promptly. "She's a little unhappy. So sorry it happened. Worried about you. And so forth. I understand she was doing the driving."

"Yes, it's her car . . ." he began.

"Which car is pretty much of a mess, so Mr. Townsend tells me. I can't quite visualize . . ." Ethel frowned. "Usually it is the driver who gets the worst of it. Seems the other car hit yours right smack on the side where *you* were sitting."

"Other car . . ." Mr. Gibson winced.

"Two men in it. Neither one hurt, except superficially. *You* seem to have got the worst of it. Only a few bones broken, Ken? Sounds to me you are lucky to be alive to tell the tale."

"*I* can't tell the tale," he said testily. "*I* can't remember a thing about it."

"Just as well," said Ethel. "Spares you some interviews. It's going to be a kind of impasse, I'm afraid. Nobody will dare sue anybody."

"Sue?" He felt bewildered.

"You see, they were on the left in the fog, where they shouldn't have been. But Rosemary turned left, which was wrong of her. And the police smelled alcohol on both your breaths."

"A drop of brandy . . ." murmured Mr. Gibson sadly.

"The cops have literal minds."

"Rosemary." Mr. Gibson did not go on, discovering that all he wanted was to be saying her name.

"She's a nice girl, Ken," said his sister.

"Yes," he said relaxing.

Ethel grinned at him. Her eyes had such a wise look, kind and indulgent. "I gather that you have been up to some good deeds."

"Well . . ."

"She couldn't say enough, Rosemary couldn't. According to her she was broke and ill and down and out. I suppose this appealed to you."

Ethel was teasing but Mr. Gibson felt dead serious. "She was badly run-down. That's exactly why I wanted you . . ."

"Drastic, wasn't it?" Ethel cocked one brow.

"What was?"

"To *marry* her."

"It may seem so . . ." he said stiffly, on the defensive.

"She's on the young side, isn't she?" his sister said. "Let's see. You are fifty-five. Well, *she* thinks you are a saint on earth—and perhaps you are." She grinned affectionately.

"I haven't," said Mr. Gibson indignantly, "the slightest intention of being a saint on earth or anywhere else—"

Ethel laughed at him. "Soft-hearted old Ken. I needn't have worried. *You'd* never take up with a blonde, now, would you? It would be a poor thing, a waif or a stray . . ."

"I'd hardly say . . ." he began.

"She's obsessed with gratitude," said Ethel, wearing now a faint frown. "Devoted to you. Of course . . ." she resettled her weight, "as I gather, she took care of her father for some years?"

"Yes, some years. She certainly did."

"Deeply attached, then," said Ethel. "And you come along. I suppose she's transferred . . ."

Mr. Gibson moved his head inquiringly.

"Father-image," said Ethel.

He lowered his eyelids.

"She claims you saved her life and reason," Ethel went on. "I wouldn't be surprised, either. It would be just like you."

"In loco parentis?" said Mr. Gibson lightly.

"That's obvious enough," said Ethel carelessly, "to anyone who knows even the rudiments of psychology. Well, good luck to you both."

"She is a dear girl," said Mr. Gibson quietly.

"I'm sure she is," said Ethel in her indulgent way. "And you are rather a dear, yourself. Well, here I am. Got a month's leave of absence and all set to take over."

"So good," he murmured, feeling very tired.

"Your house is cute as a button, Ken, but it sure is a long haul on that bus. Give me three thousand miles on a nice safe airplane. Bus drivers are such a ruthless breed. The insensitive way they slam two tons of juggernaut through the innocent streets. Terrifies me."

"Terrifies *you!*" He rallied to tease and praise her. "Come now, not Ethel the intrepid! How are you, my dear?"

"A little fed up," she said frankly. "A little tired of the subway. In fact, Ken, I'm thinking I rather like your climate." She lifted her strong chin.

"Good," he said. "We'll make a native of you in six weeks."

"Well, we'll see. Now, what do you want? What can I bring you? What shall I do for you?"

His heart, which had shriveled a little, let go and expanded. "Be here," he begged. "Live in my house. Take care of Rosemary for me."

"Can do," said Ethel, and he relaxed against his sense of her strength. "Poor old boy," she said lovingly. "We are not—are we?— getting any younger. . . . Although you are the smart one."

"I?"

"To live as you do. Right out of the rat race. Letting the world go by. I think I'll resign from the fray myself. And acquire innocence."

"Innocence?"

"Dear old Ken," she said. "You and your poetry."

Late that very afternoon the hospital discharged Rosemary.

"After all," said Ethel cheerily, "there are so few beds and so many people so much worse off. And I am here to take care of Rosemary. If I had realized, I could have brought her clothing . . . but no matter. We'll take a taxi."

To Mr. Gibson her voice was patter . . . patter he scarcely heard. His attention was bent upon his wife Rosemary, upon the state of her body and her soul.

There she was, standing at the foot of his bed, wearing the white dress with the red flowers on it, and dirty and crumpled the dress was. She hugged around her the red stole. Her face was too pale for the strong red that wrapped her.

"Are you *sure* . . . ?" said he. *He* didn't think she looked well enough to go out of the hospital.

"I'm so sorry," burst Rosemary. "So sorry! Oh, Kenneth, I wish it had been me. I'd have done anything in the world rather than hurt you . . ." She was quivering with the need to say this.

"Oh, come now," said Mr. Gibson in some alarm. "We had an accident. Now, mouse . . . it's nothing to worry about." He thought, It's set her back, alas. "Here's Ethel come all this way," he soothed . . . "*Your* sister, Rosemary." (He had to give her something. He gave her Ethel.) "The two of you are going to have a fine time." He looked as bright and easy as he could. "I just have to lie here with my leg hung up like the Monday wash—until the bones take a notion to mend. But it *will* mend—"

He had coaxed no smile. Rosemary said, "I turned to the left, you see. I thought . . ."

"You are not to blame," said Ethel a little loudly and very firmly. "There *is* no blame."

"Of course not," cried Mr. Gibson, appalled at *this*. "Of course you are not to blame! What an idea! Now, Rosemary, don't think about it. Please. Just wipe it out of your mind. Be like me. *I* don't remember a thing about it, you know. Just whammo . . . and here I am." He smiled at her.

"Don't you?" she said a little pathetically. She moistened her lips. "How do you feel?"

"I feel ridiculous," he said crisply, "and pretty undignified, believe me." But he was powerless to reach behind that white-faced stare. He feared she was still shocked, still fighting against the fact of the accident, still trying to wish it away. "Take her home, Ethel," he begged. "Now Rosemary, I want you to do as Ethel says. I want you to rest."

"Yes. I will, Kenneth. I wasn't hurt at all."

"Good night, then," he said gently. "And Ethel, you take care of her." (He thought, Oh yes, she has been hurt. She has been set back. Oh, too bad!) He said aloud, "I want you to be well, Rosemary?"

"Yes," she said. "I will be well." Just as if it was something she'd do to please him.

Then she was gone.

Ethel shepherded her charge into the taxi and then made conversation. She was sorry for this stranger, her sister-in-law. (And *in-law*, she presumed, was exactly all.) However had this poor thing got herself into such a false and ridiculous position? Her brother, Ken, was such a dreamer, such an unrealistic soul. The whole affair was pitiful. Ethel set out to comfort Rosemary.

"You really shouldn't entertain this feeling of guilt," said Ethel kindly. "There *is* no such thing as guilt, you know."

"I don't feel that exactly . . ." said the sad mouth, the low voice of Rosemary. "I feel so *sorry*. I hate so to see him . . ."

"Of course you do," soothed Ethel. "He has done a great deal for you. I know. Just like him."

"Kenneth—" began his wife in a voice more resolute and shrill.

But Ethel cut in. "He's an old dear. But so vulnerable. Some people, of course, are like that. Charity does something for them. Expresses some need. Fills some deficiency."

Rosemary said, faintly breathless, "I love your brother very much. I think he's wonderful. I *hate*—"

Ethel looked at her and pitied her. "Naturally," she said. "We can only hate the ones we love, you know."

"But I don't hate *him*," said Rosemary. "I *couldn't. Possibly.*"

"Of course not," said Ethel. "That is the trouble. Of course, you 'couldn't possibly.' But you are still a young woman, Rosemary. That is just a fact and none of your fault. You really needn't feel guilty about it."

"But . . ."

"We understand," intoned Ethel. "We understand these things. Now. My dear, just try to relax. Just don't brood about the accident. Tell me, what are those incredible masses of flowers? Geraniums! I never saw such a sight. Now, I'm here to see that you rest and recover. Frankly, I am delighted. It makes a break for me that I have wanted for a long time. You see, I'm quite selfish, Rosemary. We all are."

"I suppose so," said Rosemary dispiritedly.

"You will soon feel strong and well . . ."

"Yes."

Ethel herself felt strong and well and pleased with the feel of the helm in her hand.

Mr. Gibson lay thinking about Rosemary. It had been a flat and almost stupid exchange between them. Lugubrious. Also conventional. Nothing like what he had wanted. But what else could it have been, here in the crowded ward, with the slack eyes of the man with the tube, the curious eyes of the man on the other side, both fixed on the spectacle of Rosemary. And Ethel, also there.

Mr. Gibson braced himself. Wait then. In no such public spot as this would he declare his love. Nor would he declare at all until he felt less unsure of himself than he felt today. What did he know about love, anyhow? He *could* have mistaken a fatherly joy for the other thing. Little enough he knew about that, either. Bachelor that he had been. (Innocent.) And of course another mistake was *quite* probable. Whatever *he* felt, Ethel could be right about Rosemary. Ethel was a shrewd and worldly woman, and her judgment deserved attention. He may have taken a gesture of loving gratitude in the wrong way entirely. *Of course* Rosemary was grateful to him. He squirmed at the thought of it. He had made her stop saying so. But that might have contributed to her—obsession, as Ethel called it. Well, he would have to be rid of *that*—be sure *that* wasn't warping and interfering. . . .

His heart was beating in slow rhythm, a kind of dirge-time.

> For should I but see thee a little moment,
> Straight is my voice hushed . . .

He felt very much aware of his broken self and the harsh truths of the hospital, the burn of the taut sheet upon his skin, the uncozy light. The scene in the restaurant was long long ago . . . the other side of the mist . . . far—and receding like a dream.

Certainly, *certainly*, the last thing he would do was upset Rosemary any more than she was upset, right now. He didn't want to upset her ever. To have one's adopted father . . . (Mr. Gibson's mind fled from finishing this thought. It was too abhorrent!) He had better swallow down what might be only some foolishness of his . . . at least for the time being. Ah, poor girl—to blame herself because she happened to be driving. But Ethel was sensible. Ethel's sound common sense would pull her out of *that. He* could not. He couldn't be there.

Mr. Gibson sighed and his ribs ached. Sometimes he felt pitiable, rather than ridiculous, to be so strapped and tied together as he was. So stopped . . . right in the midst of all he had been accomplishing. But he must endure. At least his sister Ethel had come. . . . God bless her!

Chapter Eight

DAYS BEGAN to take on shape and they went by. At first Ethel and Rosemary came together to see him every afternoon. It was not long before he ceased to look forward to this visiting hour. They spoke with such common-place cheer. They stood beside his bed and, all down the ward, others stood and spoke in the same way. Mr. Gibson felt as if he were in the zoo and human beings came here to make noises at the animals that communicated good will but little else. As if men in a hospital ward had lost their reason, their ideas, their imaginations. They were bodies healing, and nothing more.

During the second and third weeks, Ethel often came alone, saying that Rosemary was resting. And Ethel gave the cheerful trivial news. Mrs. Violette was a great expense, but they would keep her if Ken insisted. The weather was charming. Rosemary? Oh, Rosemary was being sensible, eating well, getting along fine. Mr. Gibson beat down a jealous sense that the two of them got on and the house ran too well without him. He wished he could get out of here. He didn't say so. He said he was getting along fine, too.

Paul Townsend dropped in once or twice, and spoke cheerful commonplaces. Shame this had to happen. Everyone well at home. Getting along fine.

Only when one or another of his fellow teachers came and the talk went—as it had gone so many years of his life—flitting through remembered books, did Mr. Gibson receive a sense of nourishment from the visitation.

One day, Rosemary came alone. Ethel had been speaking more and more seriously of staying on permanently. Today she had gone looking around for jobs. To Mr. Gibson's shock, Rosemary proposed to go job-hunting herself.

"After all," she said, and she was standing on both feet, much as Ethel did, "a substitute is going to finish off your year, Kenneth, and then it is summer. You are not the richest man in the world.

. . . You *shouldn't* work at anything *this* summer, after these injuries. . . . And in spite of the insurance, you know we can't recover all the cost of all of this." She looked very bleak for a moment. "But there is no reason why I can't help. I'm well now . . ."

She was *well* enough. She looked physically quite sound. He didn't know what made him fidget. He seemed to catch overtones of Ethel's briskness and practicality in Rosemary's voice . . . The new man in the right-hand bed was frankly listening to every word being said, and Mr. Gibson couldn't quite black out his own consciousness of this fact, either.

"A woman needn't be a parasite," said Rosemary, "unless, I suppose, she's married to some fabulous captain of industry who can afford a parasite . . ."

"Or *likes* them," he murmured. "Some men are old-fashioned." He revised his thought, sternly. "If you would enjoy a job," he told her, "*of course,* Rosemary. How . . . how is the garden?"

"All right, I guess."

"Have you tried to paint the little wall?" He was groping back after something far away, the other side of the fog.

"No," she said. "I haven't. I could never be a painter, Kenneth. Just a dabbler. Ethel says, you know, people go in for things like that in retreat from reality, and I'm afraid I haven't been aware enough of the . . . well, the economic world . . . the commercial world . . . the real world."

(Mr. Gibson thought to himself, Yes, this is Ethel. But it is good for her.)

"I guess I was more or less sheltered for too long," said Rosemary.

"We-ell . . ." he considered. "I dunno as I would call it *that.*" A prison is a shelter, he was thinking, in a way. *But* . . .

"I see now," she said vigorously. "There was something too dreamy and not quite tough enough about the way I let things go on. If I'd had more sense . . . if I had faced up to facts . . . I needn't have ever gotten into such a state as I was in . . ."

"As you *were,*" he said admiringly. "You sound like a very determined young woman now."

"I am." She smiled. The praise had pleased her. "There are jobs I could do, now."

"Yes." He knew. Jobs for rude health. First stepping-stones toward working experience. "Well," he sighed, "I never proposed to

keep you wrapped in what the British call cotton wool . . . forever."
He looked at the detestable ceiling.

> Curly-locks, curly-locks, wilt thou be mine?

he intoned . . .

> Thou shalt not wash dishes nor yet feed the swine,
> But sit on a cushion and sew a fine seam,
> And feed upon strawberries, sugar and cream.

He'd made her laugh. (If the laugh was a bit artificial, a bit strained, perhaps this was because the man in the next bed was wearing such a look of shocked contempt on his whiskery face.)

"What an unbalanced diet!" cried Rosemary, attempting to be gay.

"Much too rich and probably fattening," Mr. Gibson agreed, looking drowsy. Covertly he inspected her new briskness. Was it real? Was it Rosemary? Was he *wrong* to so dislike it?

"Do you need more books?" she said suddenly. "I wasn't sure . . ."

He squirmed his head. "It's an effort to hold a book, I find," he said miserably. "Maybe I have had too steady a diet of poetry. When 'life is real, life is earnest'—and there I go." His own smile felt somewhat artificial.

"Ethel has told me so much about you," said his wife. "How you always have helped people—"

"Oh, now . . ." he sputtered. He disliked this kind of pious judgment. Like everybody, he had only and ever tried to be comfortable.

"Just the same," said Rosemary resolutely, "Ethel and I are going to take care of *you*, for a change."

(Mr. Gibson didn't like the sound of this, one bit. But, he thought, perhaps she needed to get rid of the burden of gratitude and if this was her way, he would have to bear it.) So he told her, *willing* his eyes to twinkle, that he fancied this would be delightful.

After she had gone, he gave the back of his head to his curious neighbor, and mused on this meeting. Rosemary's vigor and resolution, he perceived, was a strain upon her. She was pressing herself to be something she had never been. But perhaps now needed to be? Well, if she needed to feel useful to him and this was her way, why, *he* must acquire the grace to receive.

He would just have to shuck off his sense of dismay, the illogical notion that he had *been* receiving, formerly, and now lost something precious. If Rosemary saw duty, why, *he* should understand this. *He* had seen duty and enjoyed the doing of it, often enough. He must obliterate this baseless feeling that something . . . some hidden thing . . . was very wrong within Rosemary. After all, he mused in sad whimsicality, if man cannot live by bread alone, neither can woman be satisfied by cream and strawberries.

He tried to keep from his old habit of quoting in his mind. Too many poems were about love. Maybe *all* of them. . . .

Mr. Gibson had a bit of a shock one day, when he discovered that some badly smashed bones in his thigh had grown back together somewhat awkwardly. Unless he wished to go through a series of attempts at bone-breaking and repairing that would be expensive (and no results guaranteed) he would be lame.

He said, to Ethel, to Rosemary, this was not important. It did not really matter if he limped a little.

But when he tried to walk, when he realized how he *must* limp, henceforth . . . it mattered some.

At last he went home. Ethel came to fetch him in a taxi. Rosemary kept the hearth: she met him at the cottage door. Still on crutches, Mr. Gibson swung himself into the living room, eager for the sense of home upon his heart.

It did not come. The colors looked a bit on the cute side. The furniture was obviously "furnished" furniture. What he remembered so fondly must have been totally subjective. Surely there were also subtle displacements. Chairs stood at other angles. He sat down, feeling pain.

Jeanie Townsend came to the door bearing flowers and greetings, and everyone had to pretend that the little house was not already bestrewn to capacity with flowers. But the child was welcome. She helped, with her presence and her good manners, this moment to go over all their heads and pass.

Then, her father ambled in after her, wearing his leisure clothes. The white T-shirt tight to his fine muscular torso set off the deep tan of his arms and neck. After the hospital ward, he was almost offensively healthy and powerful.

"Darn shame," said he, as he had already said twice before in the hospital, "a thing like this has to happen. Guess we never know, do we? Oh thanks, Rosie."

Rosemary was serving tea with trembling hands.

"I guess you'll be well taken care of, like me," grinned Paul, "by a regular flock of females." His big brown hands were startling upon a frail cup and saucer.

"Waited on hand and foot," said Mr. Gibson, accepting with his pale claw a slab of pound cake from Ethel. (She had always considered this a great delicacy, but Mr. Gibson rather enjoyed, although of course it wasn't *wise*, some frosting on a cake.)

"That reminds me," said Ethel, "speaking of waiting on . . . About Mrs. Violette, Ken. She *isn't* worth what she is costing."

"If both of you are going into trade," said Mr. Gibson mildly, "who is going to wait on me, hand-and-foot, then, pray tell?"

"But we aren't going yet," said Rosemary quickly. "Not until you are perfectly well again." She was sitting on the edge of a chair and her attitude was like that of a new servant in a new situation, too anxious to find her place, and to please. He longed to say to her, "Sit back, Rosemary. This is your house."

Ethel was speaking. "Even so, when we do go off to work, Ken . . . I *don't* like the idea of a foreigner left to her own devices. They all need supervision. They have little extravagances, you know. Things disappear from the icebox." Her somewhat craggy face was rather amused by human frailty.

Jeanie said, "We've had Mrs. Violette for more than a year. She keeps everything so clean . . ."

"Ah," said Ethel, "but there's only you, dear. Your poor grandmother—whereas, here . . . why, there is nothing to keeping a house like this. I've kept my apartment *and* held a job for years. And with two of us to share off . . . both grown and able-bodied. Be a cinch."

Paul said, "Rosie's fine, now."

Jeanie's eyes glistened. "I like Mrs. Violette," she said.

"A waste," said Ethel. "I *prefer* doing for myself."

Mr. Gibson, munching pound cake, knew with a pang that it would be impossible for him even to ask his sister Ethel how long she proposed to live in his house. After she had come so promptly, so generously, giving up all she had been doing for his and Rosemary's sake? He could not *ever* suggest that she had better go. Mrs. Violette would go, instead.

So the chairs would stand at angles that subtly annoyed him. The menu would include pound cake and certain other dishes. Rosemary wouldn't be mistress of her own house, not quite. Ethel would sleep in the second bed in Rosemary's room.

He was ashamed. He wrenched at his thoughts. How mean he was! How petty, selfish! (What a fool he was, too! Thirty-two from fifty-five leaves twenty-three, and no matter how many times he tried the arithmetic, he never got a better answer.) He had his place, his own bed he had made, cozy among his books.)

Ingrate! Here in this pleasant cottage, with two devoted women, both anxious to "take care" of him, why could he not count his blessings and give over, forever . . . wipe out and forget a foolish notion that he, Kenneth Gibson, was destined to love a woman and be loved, on any but the present terms? *Which were fine . . .* he shouted at himself inside his head. Admirable! His days would be sunny with kindness and good will and mutual gratitude.

Paul Townsend got up and stretched. He couldn't seem to help exuding excess health. He said he had to go, he'd left off in the middle of trimming his ivy. "And by the way, Rosie," he said with his warm smile, "if you really want some cuttings there are going to be millions of them."

Rosemary said, "Thanks so much, Paul, but I don't suppose I'll have the time . . ."

"Of course you'll have the time!" cried Mr. Gibson, shocked. "Don't let *me* be in the way . . ."

She only smiled and Paul said he'd save a few dozen in water anyhow, and Jeanie, who had been seen but not heard most of this time, as she got up to go, said sweetly, "I'm *awfully* glad you are home again, Mr. Gibson."

By the tail of his eye, Mr. Gibson perceived on Ethel's face a look he knew very well. It was the look she wore when she was *not* going to say what she was thinking. This was fleetingly disturbing. In just that moment, Mr. Gibson felt quite out of touch.

"Forgot," said Paul in the doorway. "Mama sends regards and all that. Say, why don't you hob—come on over and sit with her sometimes, Gibson? She'd love it."

"I may do so, some day," said Mr. Gibson as cordially as he could, and Rosemary let the Townsends out.

"They have been so nice," she said returning. "More tea, Kenneth?"

"No, thank you." Mr. Gibson dug about in his head for a topic to mention aloud. "Jeanie is a quiet one, isn't she? Nice child."

"I don't suppose she's especially quiet with her contemporaries," Ethel said. "Although she certainly does sit like a cat watching the mouse. . . . Deeply attached to her father. Unconsciously, of course, she's scared to death he might marry again."

"Why do you say that?" inquired Mr. Gibson.

"She's bound to be," said Ethel. "And of course, he will. That's inevitable. Man in his prime and a very attractive man to women, or so I imagine. And well off, too. I doubt if he can help himself. Some blonde will catch him." Ethel took up the last piece of pound cake. "I presume he is actually only waiting for the old lady to die. Although until he gets Jeanie launched off to school or into a romance of her own, he may sense there would be trouble from that quarter."

"Trouble?" said Rosemary politely.

"The inevitable jealousy," said Ethel. "A teen-ager, especially, can be so bitter against a step-parent."

"I don't know Jeanie very well," murmured Rosemary rather unhappily.

"They don't intend to be known, these teen-agers," Ethel said. "They like to think they are pretty deep." She hooted. They weren't too deep for her, the quality of its tone implied.

Mr. Gibson had known quantities of young people as they filtered through his classrooms. But the relationship, there, he reminded himself, was an arbitrary thing. They were supposed to respect him, on the surface at least. He had had many bright chattering sessions listening to the tumble of their inquiring thoughts. They'd show off to teacher. He would be the last to know them in a private or social capacity. He said rebelliously, nevertheless, "They *feel* deep."

"Don't we all?" said Ethel with one of her wise glances. "Shall I tell you whom I am sorry for?" she continued. "That's old Mrs. Pyne, poor soul."

"I don't feel as if I know her well enough to be sorry or otherwise," continued Mr. Gibson, for this was at least talk.

"Isn't it obvious?" said Ethel. "That to be old and ill and dependent upon, of all things, a son-in-law, is a pretty dismal fate? I see them wheel her out on that front porch of theirs every day and there she sits in the sun. Poor old thing. She must know, whether she lets herself admit it or not, that she is a nuisance. She must know it'll be a relief to all concerned when she dies. If ever I get old and helpless," said Ethel forcefully, "me for an institution. Remember that."

"I'll make a note of it," said Mr. Gibson with a touch of asperity. But he was doing anguished sums in his head. Take twenty years. Rosemary would be fifty-two, not many years older than Ethel was right now, and no one could be more the picture of strength than Ethel. But then he, Kenneth Gibson, would be seventy-five . . .

ancient, decrepit, possibly ill . . . possibly—oh, Lord forbid!—another Professor James. Then would Rosemary be waiting for *him* to die?

He said wearily, "I'm afraid I had better lie down for a while. I'm sorry."

They sprang to assist him to his own place, where, on his own couch, among his books—his long beloveds—he tried to rest and remember without pain the bleak, the stricken pity on Rosemary's face.

One of his legs simply was not the same length as the other one. He could never conquer that little lurch in his body. He was lame. Old. Done for. So he was.

Chapter Nine

LIFE IN THE COTTAGE fell quickly into a pattern. Some weeks later Mr. Gibson mused upon this. One should, he perceived, kick like a steer (if steers really do kick) in the first hour of any regime, because habit is so easily powerful and it is so soon too late.

Surely his sister Ethel had not meant to dominate. She was too fair and reasonable a person. But she had long been used to independence, to making decisions. He supposed he had been too physically weak (and too emotionally preoccupied) to notice what was happening. Of course Rosemary did not seem to think it her place to assert herself, for she was so abysmally grateful. Grateful to him. Grateful to Ethel.

However it had come about, the hours they kept were Ethel's hours. They ate on an early schedule, which made the mornings too short and too full of petty detail. Afternoons were consecrated to naps and too soon thereafter to the preparation of their early dinner. The menus reflected Ethel's preferences if only because she had them and both the Gibsons were too amiable and too flexible.

Evenings they spent *à trois*. These were long and dedicated to music, Ethel's choice—all severely classical, and sometimes listened to in learned solemnity. Or they conversed, about the music, Ethel leading. Ethel had many opinions and it was difficult not to listen and agree. Mr. Gibson hated arguments.

Then, Ethel liked a game of chess. Rosemary did not play. Once Mr. Gibson tried reading aloud for half an hour, but when Ethel capped the reading with a sharp and knowledgeable sketch of Mr. Browning as a Victorian lady's man, while he couldn't dispute the truth of all she said it yet made such a ridiculous picture in Mr. Gibson's mind that he put the book back upon the shelf with apologies to an old friend.

In fact he now lived with his sister Ethel.

Ethel in her long years in New York had got out of the habit of expecting social gatherings. Ethel reveled in being one of three. For her, this was a crowd. They had few callers. Paul Townsend, or Jeanie, dropped in once and again. Their visits were not especially stimulating. Paul was casual. Jeanie was all manners.

Mr. Gibson's old acquaintances did not drop in. He seemed divorced from the college completely, so far out in this little house, and all the work going on without him.

So he lived with Ethel, and Rosemary was there in the same house. For instance, it was, quite properly, his sister, Ethel, and not the comparatively new, the stranger female, who attended to what nursing Mr. Gibson needed, for she, of course, was better able to cope with certain physical indecencies. . . .

Mr. Gibson had begun to feel that he was in a soft but inescapable trap. He was unable to fight out of it. He didn't know that he ought to try. Rosemary deferred to Ethel in all things. Rosemary did not seem to want to be alone with him. He sometimes wondered whether anything was amiss with Rosemary. Oh, she was well and busy, willing and agreeable . . . but he and she seemed locked away from communication and he, covering his seething doubts, wore the same armor of perfect courtesy.

Mr. Gibson sat in the sunny living room one morning, which was where he tended to sit. He did not often sit out of doors, where Mrs. Pyne was to be seen a lonely figure in her wheel chair on the Townsends' porch. He had found he did not enjoy it. Perhaps the light was too cruel, and fell too harshly from the sky. Perhaps he had become used to a more cloistered effect and in physical weakness preferred it. At any rate, he sat indoors and thought to himself, this morning, that he had never met anything so grueling, so nearly maddening, as this adult atmosphere of mutual forebearance and perfect meaningless harmony.

While he pondered ways and means of rebellion, with only half a heart that ached obscurely but all the time, Mrs. Violette was dusting. (Both Ethel and Rosemary had asked him whether he minded, and he had said of course he did not mind.) He watched her swift coordinated motion with a little idle pleasure. There was no air of good will about Mrs. Violette particularly. She did her job, in her cool silent way, not caring whether he minded. She rather refreshed him. She was shifting the ornaments on the mantelpiece when she suddenly seemed to become aware of something behind her. She jerked her head around and with that abrupt movement the cloth in her hand flicked out at a small blue vase and it fell. It smashed.

"Oh dear," said Ethel, who had come in on quiet feet, "and that belongs to Mr. Townsend."

"We can find another," said Mr. Gibson automatically.

Mrs. Violette ducked down and began to pick up the pieces. He noted the easy crouch of the knee, the slim straight back.

Ethel said, "Such a lovely blue! Didn't I speak of that only yesterday?"

"I didn't mean to do it," spat Mrs. Violette with an astonishing burst of anger.

"Of course you didn't mean to do it," said Ethel soothingly. "You couldn't help it."

Mr. Gibson watching Mrs. Violette's face found himself beginning to blink. Why was she so furious?

Rosemary came, called from her bedroom by the noise, "Oh, too bad . . . I don't suppose it costs much, do you?"

Ethel said, "No, no, I've seen them in the dime store. It's not expensive."

"Please don't worry about it, Mrs. Violette," said Rosemary at once. "I just hope you haven't cut yourself."

"No ma'am," said Mrs. Violette, rising. She looked boldly at Ethel for a moment. "I'll pay for it," she said contemptuously. She walked across the room with the bits of pottery in her hand and disappeared into the kitchen.

"We can't let her pay for it," said Mr. Gibson, "when it was just an accident."

Ethel was smiling a peculiar smile. "She seems to know it was no accident," she said musingly. "How odd!"

"What do you mean, no accident?" said Mr. Gibson in surprise.

"She did it because she dislikes me, of course."

"Ethel . . . !"

"She does, you know. And I did admire the color of that vase in her hearing only yesterday. She dislikes me because *I* check up on her, which is more than either of you seem to do."

"But . . . what need . . . ?" he said bewildered.

"What need? Oh me," sighed Ethel seating herself. "I believe a servant could steal you blind and you'd never know, either of you."

Mr. Gibson felt like a Babe-in-the-Wood. Such a thought had never occurred to him.

"I don't think she'd steal," said Rosemary in a low voice, hesitantly. "Do you, Kenneth?"

"Of course not!" he exploded.

"Of course not," mocked Ethel. "No 'of course not' about it. These foreigners don't have the same ideas of honesty as you do. *She* wouldn't call it stealing . . . but you would, and so would I."

"What has she stolen?" said Rosemary, looking a bit flushed.

"She takes food," said Ethel, looking mysterious. "All foreigners take food. They don't think of it as property."

"She eats," said Rosemary. "That is true."

They were in conflict. Mr. Gibson held his guilty delighted breath.

"Nor any small loose-lying thing," Ethel went on, drawling. "Don't you ever take precautions, you dear sheltered people? Don't you believe in the fact of theft? I hate to think what would happen to you in less bucolic places. There is wickedness in this world."

"Really," said Mr. Gibson much annoyed. "I see no more reason to believe that Mrs. Violette would steal than to believe she broke that vase on purpose. And I was right here, Ethel. I *saw* what happened."

"You think you did," said Ethel, as to a very young child.

He felt shaken.

"It's the first thing she has broken," began Rosemary. "She's been quite remarkable . . ."

"Quite so," said Ethel with satisfaction. "Of course, it is the first thing. Don't you see she resents me, and has, since the moment I came? So she breaks something *I* liked. I am not *blaming* her. I merely understand."

Mr. Gibson had a faint sense of something fading out of his peripheral vision. "For heaven's sakes, Ethel," he sputtered. "Anyone can have an accident!"

"There is no such thing as an accident," said Ethel calmly. "Honestly, Ken, you *are* ignorant in some fields. Subconsciously she wanted to spite me. She likes to be let entirely alone the way *you* let her be. But, of course, *I* am not such an easy mark."

What on earth are you saying?" said Mr. Gibson in amazement. "Of course, there is such a thing as an accident. She turned to look because *you* startled her . . . and then her hand . . ."

"Oh no," said Ethel.

"Wait a minute." Mr. Gibson turned to see what might be on Rosemary's face but Rosemary was no longer in the room. She was gone. It was disconcerting.

Mr. Gibson turned back and said severely, "I don't agree with your suspicions, Ethel."

"Suspicions?" sighed Ethel, "or normal precautions? The fact is, old dear," she continued affectionately, "all of us can't live in a romantic, poetical and totally gentle world. Some of us have to face things as they are." Her bright eyes were direct and honest and he feared they were wise. "Face reality," she said.

"What reality?" he snapped.

"Facts," said Ethel. "Malice, resentment, self-interest—the necessities of the ego—all the real driving forces behind what people do. The conscious mind, old dear, is only the peak of the iceberg. You believe so easily in the pretty surfaces . . ."

"*I* do!"

"Yes, you," said Ethel kindly. "You don't know a tenth of what goes on, Ken. Your head's in the clouds. Always has been. Of course I love you *for* it. . . . But for every saint with his head in the clouds," sighed Ethel, "I suppose there has to be somebody to take the brunt of things as they really are."

"I see no reason," said Mr. Gibson with stubborn lips, "to mistrust Mrs. Violette."

"You wouldn't see a reason to mistrust anyone," said Ethel indulgently, "until the deep popped up and hit you in your nice fastidious nose. You have always sidestepped the nasty truths of this earth, brother dear. More power *to* you."

He stared at her.

"Oh, I'm sorry," she said, and she did look sorry, "I shouldn't say these things . . ."

"Why not?" he cried, "if you believe them."

But Ethel evaded and said, "You are a lot like Mama was, you know? I think you should have been the woman, Ken, and I should have been born the man."

"Tell me," he cried. "What are you saying?"

"You mustn't pay any attention. Your world of poetry and quixotic goodness and faith and all the rest is a pretty darned nice place. . . ."

"And *your* world?" he demanded. "I imagine you call *it* the real world," he said, goaded to some anger.

Ethel responded to the anger. "Mine?" She looked him in the eye. "It happens to be full of knives-in-the-back and all kinds of human meannesses. It cannot help but be. Men *are* animals, whether *you* like it or not."

"And you say," he groped back for something solid with which to challenge her, "that Mrs. Violette broke the blue vase deliberately?"

"Of course, she didn't consciously plan it," said Ethel. "You don't understand. But she did break it to displease me, just the same."

"I don't believe it," said Mr. Gibson.

"Don't then," said Ethel. "Stay as sweet as you are . . . that's in a song, isn't it?" She grinned at him and he knew her teasing was a form of apology. "You are a lamb, Ken, and everybody loves a lamb. I cannot help it if I am no lamb, you know. Now, I haven't upset you, have I?"

He thought he felt as upset as he had ever felt in his life. He scarcely knew why, but he was afraid for Rosemary. So he struggled up, and, using his cane, he limped into the kitchen.

Mrs. Violette was briskly washing the counter. Rosemary was there too, just staring out the window. He thought she looked rather lonely.

"Now, Mrs. Violette," he said, "please understand that *I* will pay for the vase. It wasn't your fault."

Mrs. Violette shrugged and said nothing.

Rosemary said in a brisk voice, "Mrs. Violette tells me she has to leave us, Kenneth. She's going away with her husband, next week."

"Is that so?" he said unhappily.

"Yeah, we're taking off to the mountains," said Mrs. Violette. "He's going after a new job for the both of us. If we get it, we'll stay on up there."

"On a ranch," said Rosemary. "How nice that will be!" She sounded rather desperately cheerful. "But we'll miss you, Mrs. Violette."

Mrs. Violette made no response. She didn't care whether she'd be missed. She wasn't even angry at Ethel any more, for all Mr. Gibson could see.

"Ought we to try to get somebody else?" said he across to Rosemary worriedly.

"No," she said. "No. I'm able. Ethel and I can manage beautifully." He couldn't read her eyes *at all*.

"But if one day," he said, "Ethel were to go and live on her own, then . . ."

"Oh, she mustn't do that!" cried Rosemary. "That would be a shame! Your only sister, Kenneth, and so good to come . . ." He saw her hands on the round wood of the kitchen chair. The knuckles were blue-white. "Such a fine person," Rosemary said. "So wise and so good."

Mr. Gibson felt alarmed. Something *was* wrong with Rosemary. She was a stranger and far away and how could he tell what was the matter when she seemed shut up against him . . . when her eyes seemed to search his so . . . could it be? . . . fearfully. Ethel was right, he conceded. There must be a good deal going on that he missed. He felt lost. What anxiety, what stress could there be, to so inhabit Rosemary's eyes? "Yes," he said absently. "Of course she is."

Meanwhile, Mrs. Violette scrubbed vigorously at the sink there in the small room. Ethel came in and said jauntily, "Lunch, dears? I'll start the vegetables."

Out in the yard, Paul Townsend was working near the low stone wall. He was on vacation. School was out; Jeanie was around and about; Mrs. Pyne sat on the porch. There was no privacy.

Chapter Ten

MR. GIBSON RETIRED to the privacy of his own skull where he made plans.

This mysterious distress in Rosemary was intolerable. Therefore, first, he would find out what troubled her. Then, he would see to it that whatever it was troubled her no more. He felt much better, as soon as this course became plain and imperative.

He was determined, however, that he would not seek this information from Ethel, although, curiously, he was quite sure Ethel would know all about it, for he conceded that Ethel *was* wise and much more alert than he. But no. He would find out what bothered Rosemary in the simplest possible way. He would ask her. But he would do it in private.

Very well, then. This very evening he would struggle out of the hypnosis of routine. When Ethel announced bedtime, as she was so often the one to do (and night falling, and no company coming, the world still) he would not let her "tuck him in," which habit she retained although he no longer needed anyone's help in getting to bed. He would tell Ethel to go to bed herself, but he would ask Rosemary to stay. He would say to Ethel, "Ethel, I want to talk to Rosemary alone. Do you mind?"

She couldn't say she minded. Why should she mind? It would be so simple. Even as he told himself these things Mr. Gibson received a preview in his imagination. He saw Ethel's smile . . . the wise indulgent and rather amused expression she would wear, as she would nod, as she would say, "Of course I don't mind," and he knew he shrank from the prospect.

She would wear the same look that girl in the hospital had worn. Why was it so "cute" or even a little bit funny that he was fond of his wife? Come now, it was ridiculous to be this sensitive. Well, he would *act*, then. And when they were alone, how could he reach out to Rosemary, and reachieve her confidence?

He hobbled back into the living room after lunch, busy turning in his mind what words he could say, how gentle he would be, but how insistent. This was the hour of his siesta, but today he did not go at once into his study-bedroom to close the blinds and lie quietly upon the bed for the accustomed period. Today, he stood looking out the east window, across the driveways, seeing, but not noticing, Paul Townsend's bare torso bending and moving there at the edge of his back lawn in some gardening activity—to which he passionately devoted his vacation days.

He could hear, but did not pay attention to, the women's voices in the kitchen. He knew Mrs. Violette was ironing, that Rosemary and Ethel were clearing away the dishes, all in the routine.

He stood in the midst of routine, plotting how he would break it, when he heard Rosemary's voice go suddenly high and full of passion and protest. He heard only the emotion, not the sense of what she said.

Then the kitchen door banged. He saw Paul Townsend straighten and lift his head. He saw Rosemary come stumbling, slowly and distractedly, into as much of the scene as he could see.

Saw Paul drop his long-handled weeder and go quickly toward her.

Saw his head bending solicitously.

Saw that Rosemary was violently weeping.

Saw Paul lift his arms.

Saw her sag, as if it were impossible not to do so, into their embrace.

Mr. Gibson wrenched his head and turned away. He could see nothing. The living room was dark, dark as night, to his light-struck eyes. He must have made some sound, for he heard Ethel say, "What's the matter?" He knew she was there in the room and he knew that she went to look briefly out of the window behind him before he felt her strong hand under his elbow.

She guided him into his own place . . . for he felt so stricken he needed guidance. But after a moment or two Mr. Gibson's sight cleared and he was quite calm and extraordinarily free. He sat down in his leather chair and laid his cane on the floor carefully. "What did you say to make her cry like that?" he asked quietly.

Ethel clamped her mouth tight for a moment. "Never mind, dear. Never mind," she said rather softly. "It's just that Rosemary insists upon misunderstanding some perfectly simple remark of mine. She thinks I meant to reproach her . . . as if I would. Of course she's emotional . . ." Ethel touched his knee, "just now. Ah Ken. I'm sorry we saw what we saw. I don't think it meant very much. Not yet."

"Yet?" he said shrewdly.

His sister drew a sigh from her shoesoles. "Ken, I am sorry to say so, but you were so foolish . . ."

"Was I? But what I wanted to do . . ." he organized his thought painfully (he cast out the phrase "in the first place") "was to make her well," he finished.

"So you have, I'm sure," said Ethel, with kind eyes. "But did you never look ahead to afterward? Didn't you realize that Rosemary, *well*, would not be the same girl?"

"I know."

"She is young. At least, comparatively . . ."

"I know. I knew that."

"When she was so ill," said Ethel, "she felt old. But she is not old. Nor does she feel old any more."

Mr. Gibson resented the kindergarten simplicity of this. "I *know*," he repeated.

"But the foolish thing, my poor Ken . . . was to bring her here— next door to such a man. A man who even shares a hobby with her! You have practically arranged for this to happen, you know."

Mr. Gibson couldn't assimilate his new thoughts. Thoughts like this had come nowhere near his mind before. Rosemary and Paul! He said, "Then they . . . they . . . ?"

"They've been friendly. Now, Ken, Rosemary is a good girl and devoted to you. But she is younger . . ."

(I *know*, screamed Mr. Gibson inside his head.)

"And he is just the right age for her and a most attractive man. I think I could have prophesied," Ethel said sadly.

Mr. Gibson sat still and contemplated folly. Folly to rent *this* little house? *He* could never have prophesied. Ideas like *this* had not entered his mind.

"Like all handsome men," Ethel went on, "he is a little bit spoiled, I suppose. Careless. He wouldn't have the self-discipline *not* to be charming. He can't help exuding that physical magnetism. Poor Rosemary. You mustn't blame her, either. There is no blame. She'd have no way of knowing how she would be drawn. The body dictates. These things are beyond one's control really. My dear, you ought to move away at once."

But Mr. Gibson contemplated his crime.

He had cheated her after all. He had given lip-service to his foreboding of this. (Yes, he *had* prophesied! Now he remembered . . . although too easily, selfishly, and in such foolish delight, he had forgotten all about it.) Of course, he could not blame Rosemary.

"I don't blame her," he said aloud.

"There is no such thing as blame," said Ethel gently. "Once you understand. She simply could not have helped herself."

"She must be . . ." He could imagine Rosemary's pain. "But does Paul . . ."

"Frankly," said Ethel, as if she had been being anything else, "I don't know how much he is attracted to Rosemary. She's not beautiful, of course, but very nice-looking and quite a lady. She is also so *near*. Propinquity is such a force."

Rather drearily Mr. Gibson supposed to himself that it was. *He* had no doubt that Paul was attracted to her.

"From his point of view," said Ethel looking shrewd, "there will be, as I say, the difficulty about the daughter. Oh, I've seen Jeanie watching Rosemary."

So had Mr. Gibson, now that he thought of it. Jeanie was so quiet, sat so still in a room, watching everyone.

"There's the old lady, too," Ethel went on. "Paul's in no position to dash gaily into . . . well, let's call it romance. . . . Move away, Ken. Rosemary is essentially loyal. It may not be too late."

"Yes, it is," said he. He had remembered something. He had been puzzled at the time. Rosemary, standing in the living room, saying with such brooding fervor ". . . never known it was possible to have so good a time. . . ." And the occasion—had it not been the first evening she and Paul Townsend had ever spent in each other's company? Wisps, he supposed, of attraction spinning between them, even then. Oh, how inevitable it had been! He saw himself—old—and now lame.

"If you want to keep her," Ethel said, "I know you are *very* fond of her. And Rosemary is *deeply* . . ."

"I'm fond of her," he said grimly, cutting off the detestable word "grateful" before it could offend his ears once more. "But I have no intention of . . . how shall I put it? . . . collecting for services rendered."

"You are very wise," said Ethel.

"Especially," he said rather primly, "since we discussed the possibility of divorce before the wedding."

"Ah then . . ." Ethel sighed and her face brightened. "I am very glad. Then she knows she can be free if that seems best? Well . . . this puts a different light on the matter. You and I could make do," she added thoughtfully.

"Yes," he said.

"It's not a bad life. We'd have our work. We'd be rather cozy, out of the fray. One should plan one's old age, Ken. And neither of us with chick nor child. Perhaps we ought to stick together."

"Perhaps," he agreed.

"Not *here*, of course."

"No."

"If Rosemary and Paul Townsend were to marry . . ."

"No," he said conquering the shudder that threatened to destroy his poise completely, "certainly not here."

"I wouldn't be precipitous, however," Ethel warned. "If Paul is not . . . That is, if the thing's one-sided. Rosemary might need us."

"She needs to be rid of her obligations," he said harshly. "Or how can she know surely . . . ?"

"You are so right," said Ethel warmly. "And when you are generous and Rosemary is honorable, as I'm sure she is, why, there's no problem."

(He knew there was a little problem all his own. But he'd take care of that.)

"She'll come to you, one day," said Ethel, "when she finds the courage. I can't tell you how relieved I am, old dear, to know that you went into this with your eyes open. I've been a little bit afraid for you. A late-blooming romance can be so devastating to a born bachelor. Now then, can you sleep a little?"

"I think so," lied Mr. Gibson valiantly.

He lay on the top of his bed. He couldn't bear to imagine, from Rosemary's point of view, her dilemma. He tried to contemplate his old age.

But on another level, his plan beat in his mind. First find out what troubles Rosemary. Then, see to it that it troubles her no more.

What is love? he thought at last with a sick descending and a thud of certainty. What is hers for *me*? Not my physical magnetism, heaven knows. A lame old crock. A limping horror. The fact is, I *have* her love, as much as I am going to get. She's fond of me. But my love for her must set her free.

He lay there half an hour or more before he remembered, with a tiny crash of dismay in his brain, that Paul Townsend was a practicing Catholic, and Mr. Gibson was not so sure that divorce would be enough.

Chapter Eleven

THREE DAYS WENT BY. Rosemary did not come to him. She had recovered herself. She was just the same.

He did not press her to come, or to tell him anything. He began to be afraid that she never would.

Next door, Paul Townsend worked in his garden, carelessly healthy and happy and strong and visible. Old Mrs. Pyne sat on the porch. Young Jeanie flitted in and out. The cottage ran on, exempt from life and change, in that spurious harmony.

Mr. Gibson spent much time alone with a book open. He contemplated his innocence.

Ethel was right. He did not know one-tenth of what went on. He was ignorant in most fields. Modern psychological theories were to him just theories, to play games with. He'd *believed* in the poetry. Honor. Courage. Sacrifice. Old-fashioned words. Labels, for nothing? Oh, long ago, he had hidden himself in books, in words, but not the harsh words of fact. Poetry! Why? Because he was too thin-skinned and not brave enough to bear realities. He had not faced facts. He did not even know what they were. He must lean on Ethel, until he learned more.

He had been strangely innocent, now he saw. . . . Socially innocent. He had derived a good deal of innocent pleasure from the fact that students and teachers spoke to him on the campus paths, or in a corridor, or sometimes even on a street of the town. A nod, a greeting, a murmur of his name, had secured to him his identity. (I am not lost in eternity. I am Mr. Gibson of the English Department and there are those who know it.)

But he had had enough of people in the course of a day. His captive audiences, his classes, had permitted him the exercise of his voice. Then there were office hours during which he sometimes talked to students with kindness, with optimism for them, and only the most meager precautions against their guile and their flattery and their showing off had been enough. So he had felt a fullness in his days, and a shy trust in the near little world; and his privacy, his solitude, had seemed natural and pleasant and not limited. Actually he had lived a most narrow, a most sheltered, a most innocent life. He knew very little about "reality."

This must be how he had come to do, at the age of fifty-five, so stupid, so wicked, so foolish a thing. He had married a sick defenseless dependent trusting Rosemary. On the ridiculous premise that it would be an "arrangement." He now looked back upon the joyful early days with pity for his own blithe ignorance. The facts of flesh. The facts of propinquity. He had ignored all facts in a cloud of romantic nonsense. Yes, the romantic sentimental silly notion that he would be a healer! What ego! Then, worse, how could he have thought, ever, for one moment, that this quixotic marriage could turn into a love match? *That* had been impossible from the beginning, and set forth in plain arithmetic. Thirty-two from fifty-five leaves twenty-three and ever would.

He was her father . . . emotionally. He was help, kindness, protection, and she loved him for all this, as he knew. What frightened him now was the possibility that Rosemary might go on with her bargain, until he was ancient, and never tell even herself how she wished that he would die. Rosemary might undertake to endure. She *had* endured eight years with the old professor.

She would not want to hurt him. Why, she had felt almost distracted with grief there in the hospital when she had blamed herself for so trivial a thing as his broken bones.

She would neither hurt him nor break her obligations. She would freeze in loyalty and cheat herself. It was possible she did not know (or let herself know) why she had gone so naturally into Paul's arms.

The more he thought about Paul and his virtues, which were many, the more Mr. Gibson felt sure that Ethel was right. Rosemary had fallen, or was going to fall, in love with *him*, who could not possibly represent her father, but was of her own generation, virile, charming, good and kind. She could not help it.

He perceived that Rosemary had better never know a thing about *his* foolishness, for what would be the good if she knew? Pity did not interest Mr. Gibson in the least. He wanted none of it. So he banished his love, exiled it forever from his heart. He would think no more about *that*.

He retreated deliberately. He seemed to absorb himself in reading and writing. He tried not to notice . . . which might help him not to care . . . where Rosemary was or what she was doing. If he felt depressed, he told himself this was nobody's fault but his own and it would pass.

One day he found a stanza:

> The gentle word, the generous intent
> The decent things that men can do or say
> All these to gladden her I freely spent
> But could not touch her when she turned away.

He shut up the book. Catullus was *also* a fool. That was the only meaning of it. And a whiner, too. Mr. Gibson resolved to be no whiner. He read no more poetry.

His depression did not pass. It deepened. Night and day he lived with it and forgot how it felt to be without it. He began to assume that this was what one got used to, as one grew old.

But a change was coming. The day was coming upon which the women were going, as Mr. Gibson had once put it, into trade. They were going on the same morning, and Mr. Gibson, in his misery, did not bewail the coincidence, for he no longer yearned to be alone with Rosemary.

Ethel, accomplished secretary that she was, had gotten herself a plum of a job that let her off at four in the afternoons. This, she explained with satisfaction, would permit her to be the cook at dinner time.

Rosemary's hours were a little longer. She was going to assist the proprietor of a small dress shop, helping with the stock at first and looking forward to becoming a saleslady. It was an excellent beginning.

In further coincidence, the same day would see the last of Mrs. Violette. Mr. Gibson was going to be alone.

On the eve of this day, the three of them sat in the living room according to habit. Music was playing low from the radio for a cultural background. Rosemary was basting white collar and cuffs upon a navy-blue dress against tomorrow. Ethel was knitting, a thing she did with uncanny skill. (Hours and hours she had sat knitting before her radio, listening to music, to political speeches, to educational programs. She preferred a radio to a record player. She'd never had a record player.) Mr. Gibson was turning the pages of a book sometimes two at a time. His face was calm and benign. The scene was domestic and harmonious, but his sense of it was not . . . for this was the end of his experiment. And now all fell to dust. Rosemary was not only well, she was about to go forth and earn. She needed nothing he could give her, but much that he could not. So now he would let her go . . . he agreed in his heart . . . the sooner the better.

Imagination had painted his future before him. He could see himself and his sister Ethel, mutually helpful and devoted, in some smallish apartment near the college, at work by day until they faltered, and every evening Ethel knitting, the radio on. He said to himself that he could make-do. He had done with much less than a devoted sister at his side. He really did not know why he should feel so disheartened, so desperately unhappy about it.

"It all ought to work out very nicely," said Ethel, "although I do dread the bus ride. To be at the mercy of those buses, thirty minutes each way. A waste, really. Mightn't it be wise to move a little nearer in to town?"

Rosemary's hands and head jerked. "Move?" she murmured.

"After all," said Ethel, "this *is* pleasant of course, but when you are working, Rosemary, you won't have the daylight hours . . . Did you prick your finger, dear?"

Rosemary said quietly, "No, Ethel. I did not."

"Ah . . . well." Ethel smiled indulgently. "We ought to think of Ken, too. Will it be wise for him to ride the buses in the fall—with that leg?"

"I hadn't thought . . ." said Rosemary in a rush, and her face came up.

"I should think I could ride on a bus," said Mr. Gibson, "without . . ." His voice caught, because he could see very plainly the red smear of Rosemary's blood on the white of the collar in her hands.

"You did run that needle into your finger, dear," said Ethel chidingly. "Just look at the stain. On your business clothes, too . . ."

"It will wash," said Rosemary faintly, and rose; and, walking stiffly, she bore her work toward the kitchen.

Mr. Gibson wondered what it meant. "I suppose," he said, staring at the cold grate and feeling frozen, "she pricked her finger and stained the collar because she doesn't want to go to business tomorrow."

He waited timidly for Ethel to agree.

But Ethel smiled. "I don't think so," she said, "for why should she tell a lie about that?" (Mr. Gibson faced it. Rosemary had lied.) "It happened, of course," said Ethel lowering her voice, "when I spoke of leaving *here*."

"Leaving—?"

"Leaving *him*, I imagine," said Ethel, sotto. "How she gives herself away!"

He heard her sigh, but inside himself he was collapsing and shrinking with distaste. Given that nothing is what it seems; even so, he couldn't guess what it really was. In the old poems, man was captain of his soul, and he, so steeped in them, would never learn. How could he learn? He was old. His heart sank. Mr. Gibson felt solid, felt treason, too—he couldn't help it—and he hated it. He turned his eyes back into the book and did not look up as Rosemary returned.

"Did you use cold water?" Ethel fussed.

"Of course," said Rosemary softly. "It's nothing." She was taking up her needle, as Mr. Gibson could see through his temple somehow out of the side of his averted face. Did Rosemary know why she had run a needle into her flesh? It made him sad to think, Not necessarily.

"Now, Ken, you will be all right tomorrow?" his sister asked fussily. "Mrs. Violette will be in to finish up your shirts, you know, and she *could* stay and fix your lunch."

"No, no," he said. He didn't want Mrs. Violette. He looked forward to being alone.

"You do feel all right?" said Rosemary timidly anxious. "Nothing's bothering you, Kenneth, is it? You don't look as well as you did, somehow. Do you think so, Ethel?"

"I wonder if I'm not missing my work," he said resettling his shoulders. "I'm used to working . . ."

Rosemary's head bent over her sewing. He wrenched his gaze from her hair.

"You mustn't give me a thought," he said. "In the first place, I have lived alone a matter of nearly half a century, in my day . . . and secondly, the Townsends are right next door, and Paul is around." He despised himself for throwing out Paul's name.

"That's so," said Ethel. "Their new cleaning woman won't be in 'til Friday, and of course Mrs. Violette will be gone. Paul, unless he can shift the load onto Jeanie, is going to be stuck right here with old Mrs. Pyne." She seemed to take a faint malicious satisfaction from this.

"Paul is very good to the old lady," said Mr. Gibson (for jealousy he *would* not descend to, generous and just he *would* be). "I think it's extraordinary."

Rosemary looked up with a flashing smile. "I think so too," she said warmly.

Mr. Gibson turned a page, which was ridiculous. He had not even *seemed* to read it.

"I've wondered," said Ethel with that shrewd little frown of hers. "Are you sure that this property isn't Mrs. Pyne's property? I suppose Paul is her heir."

Rosemary said, smiling, "Sometimes you sound terribly cynical, Ethel."

"Not at all. I am only a realist," said Ethel smugly. "At least I like to think I can face a fact."

"But can't a man be simply good and kind?" Rosemary inquired. "*Really?*"

Mr. Gibson's heart seemed to swoon.

"And also good-looking?" said Ethel with a grin. "I suppose it's possible. Perhaps he *is* as good as he is beautiful." She cocked her head and counted stitches.

"But Paul has a prosperous business, hasn't he, Kenneth?" insisted Rosemary. "He makes money."

"He is a chemical engineer," said Mr. Gibson. "Yes . . ." (All of a sudden he saw Paul's laboratory like a vision before him and a row of bottles in a cupboard. The vision flickered and went away.)

"So he doesn't *need* Mrs. Pyne's money—if she has any," said Rosemary. "I just don't think he's mercenary."

"Nor do I," said Mr. Gibson, valiantly.

Ethel said, "Of course he isn't, as far as he knows. Lots of people never admit the most basic facts. However, almost everyone will do an awful lot for material advantage. . . . Oh, we can kid ourselves, can't we, that it's for some fancy other reason. But whether you eat, whether you're comfortable, whether you feel secure, counts. Indeed it does. And all the time."

"I suppose it does," said Rosemary flushing. She bent over her handiwork. She seemed defeated.

Mr. Gibson found himself fearing what might be in her mind. Rosemary had come to him for material comfort, for security. . . . Oh, she could not have helped herself—but she knew this now. And so did he. He had urged it. He had meant it to be so.

"Naturally it counts," he said aloud gently. "Quite naturally so. . . ." He turned a page.

Ethel said with a little snort, "What do you think a baby yells for? He yells to be warm and fed, and *that is all*. Let me turn to the weather. I wonder if it will be hot tomorrow."

Mr. Gibson thought to himself. To be warm. To be fed, for *me* to be comfortable. . . . Is that what's in the iceberg? All of our icebergs? Do none of us know *why* we do anything? Because we won't admit that we are animals? Ah, but what are we here for, then? Are we compelled, always, and every time? In all this fluid busyness, has each of us his private doom?

He disliked the idea. He tried to face it. Ethel faced it. *She* was strong enough. He wouldn't hide from a fact either . . . not any more. Was it *this* fact that depressed him so? He seized upon it.

On the air they were talking about a bomb test, with pious hope that the terrible power would never be unleashed against fellow men.

Ethel listened and Ethel said, "Of course they'll unleash it."

"The bomb?" Rosemary was startled.

"Do you think they won't?"

"I . . . hope they won't," said Rosemary with wide eyes.

Ethel shook her graying head. "Be sure they will."

"How can you . . . ?" Rosemary gasped.

"It's just a question of noticing," said Ethel, "that human beings *are* what they *are*. And believe me, a weapon in the hand is as good as thrown. Don't you know—in cold fact—that *anything* could cause it to fall? Human beings are so primitive . . . essentially. They don't mean to be. You can't call it their fault, but their nature. For which none of us are to blame. But they get angry; once angry, they begin to call the other side a monster. There seems no reason why it is not fine and honorable and brave and good to slaughter a monster. They do *not* wait and try to understand or to reason differences away. They simply do not. And even if they were to try—human reason is so pitifully new and such a minor factor. . . . People will always *act* from the blood and the animal residue."

"How do you face a fact like that?" asked Mr. Gibson quietly.

"The bomb falling?" she said, misunderstanding. "As far as I am concerned, I'll stay put and be blown up with the world I know. I don't even want to survive. Don't tell me you do!" She looked as if he could not possibly be so childish, could he?

"No," said Mr. Gibson thoughtfully. "No . . . not especially. But then, I am old."

Doom, he thought. Well, then, we are doomed. He wasn't thinking about the bomb.

"I don't see," said Rosemary to Ethel, "how you have the courage to think the way you do."

"Courage," said Ethel, "is about the only useful trait. The best we can do is hang onto our nerves and try to understand."

What good is it to understand, thought Mr. Gibson, if we are doomed anyhow? "Then all our pretty intellectual toys . . ." he said, seeing the words he had lived by go sliding into limbo.

" 'Toys' is good," said Ethel appreciatively. "Enjoy your poetry while you may, Ken. When or if anyone survives," she shrugged, "be sure there won't be much time for poetry. Now, it hasn't fallen yet," she nodded as if to reassure them, "and *I'd* like to live out my allotted time just as you would. We have a built-in wish to survive that operates, this side of catastrophe." She smiled. "So let us hope," she said.

"You have no children," said Rosemary in a low voice.

"Neither have you, and let us thank God," said Ethel.

But Mr. Gibson thought, It is true. We are doomed. And the doom is in the iceberg, the undersea part of it. None of us have ever known why we do what we do. We only have the illusion of knowing, the illusion of choice. We are *really* at the mercy of dark things, unknown propulsions. We are blind dupes. That's what Ethel means by reality. Oh yes, and it is true. Mrs. Violette *had* to break the vase. Paul *must* marry someone. Rosemary *must* fall in love with Paul. And I made a fool of myself. But I *had* to. It wasn't my fault. My choices were all made by the genes I got from my mother. Ethel took more from Pa and so is different . . . but she is clear-headed, she at least can *see*.

My whole life has been an illusion. Everyone's life is an illusion. We are at the mercy of what's unknown and cannot be known either. One day we will blow it all up, knock the earth off its orbit, possibly, as surely as Rosemary will go to Paul, as I will send her. . . .

He sunk his head upon his breast, Paul, who was a widower, a chemist, a Catholic . . . Paul was doomed, too. Doomed to be happy and make Rosemary happy, for a little while, before the world blew up.

While he, Kenneth Gibson, would live with his sister and grow older . . . limp out fifteen or twenty years. *Not so!*

There was one rebellious act he could think of. Just one. He received a tremendous heartening lift of his spirits. A little spunk—he could escape.

And he could remember the number on the bottle.

He slept a little toward morning. When he woke he knew this was the day. He would be alone.

Chapter Twelve

THE MORNING was bustle. Rosemary, neat and excited, in the navy frock with the white, went first away.

Mr. Gibson followed her to the door. He was wearing his robe of small-figured silk, and in it, he felt the same small neat and decent man he had ever been. He did not know how white and ill he looked.

"Goodbye," she said. "Oh, please, Kenneth, take care . . . ! You worry me. I almost wish . . ."

"No, no, you must not worry." His eyes devoured her. "Goodbye, Rosemary. You must remember . . . this was what I wanted for you."

"To see me well?" she asked, "and able? Is that what you mean?"

He didn't answer. He was looking at her face very carefully, since it would be the last time he would see it. He was so *very* fond of her. She *was* his, in a way.

"Is that *all?*" she said suddenly.

Mr. Gibson tried to remember what he had just said. "By no means," he answered steadily. "I want you to be happy, too." He smiled.

"Yes, well . . . I . . ." Her eyes fled and came back. "What can I do to make *you* happier?" she cried. "I'm so—I love you, Kenneth. You know that, don't you?"

It was odd that in this last moment they seemed closer, as he recognized her old familiar passion of gratitude. "I know," he told her gently, "dear girl. I am as happy as I can be," he said with reassuring accents.

Rosemary shook herself and jerked away. He watched her, so straight, so lithe, so healthy—so youthful—down the drive.

Paul Townsend was on the porch sniffing the morning. He waved, but Rosemary didn't see him there. Mr. Gibson was just as glad.

Her loyal nature would doom her to endure.

Ethel went next. "Ken, when you walk to market, pick up a head of lettuce, too? There's a good man."

"I will," he promised.

"And pay Mrs. Violette off . . ."

"Yes."

"And I'll be back, four-ish . . ."

"Yes, Ethel. Goodbye, dear. Good luck. You have been—perfectly fine."

"Pish tush," said Ethel. "Of course. Well, I'm off."

Mr. Gibson closed the door.

He went into the living room and sat down. Mrs. Violette was ironing. He would not, of course, kill himself until she had gone.

He was a fastidious and thoughtful man. (He could not help it.) There would be no mess about this. Nothing distressing for anyone to clean up. Nothing horrible. He knew where he would go and what he would take. It was quick and surely neat. He would be found lying in full decorum on his bed, in all peace. They would think, for a while, that he slept. The shock would thus be graduated and as gentle as he could make it.

But he must leave a letter. The letter must be just so. It must set everything as free as could be.

His blood felt cold. He must try not to be sentimental. This was a choice he was making, icy and clear. He didn't fear the dying. He tried to look beyond.

He had no insurance to be affected by a suicide. Rosemary would have his few bonds, his bank account. Yes, a letter to that effect, too. She'd be all right. Paul would stand by. (She would be free.) Ethel of course was self-sufficient. Ethel would help Rosemary to understand—what he chose they should understand. There was absolutely nothing to worry about.

Except the bomb which would blow up their world one day, but this he could not help.

Everyone's doom was his own.

Mr. Gibson sat in a dream.

At twelve o'clock he was dressed and ready to go downtown, and Mrs. Violette was finished. So he paid her.

"Mr. Gibson, could I have this old string?" she asked him, and showed him what she had fished from the kitchen wastebasket.

"Of course," he said. "Do you need any more?"

"I got a lot of stuff to tie up," she admitted. "We're going to take 'most everything in the back of the truck."

"How about this?" He gave her a ball of mustard-colored twine.

"That's *Miss* Gibson's." Mrs. Violette's small but ripe-lipped mouth made a hiss of the appellation.

"Well?" he bridled. "Surely I may present you with a bit of string."

Mrs. Violette said, "I don't like to take *her* stuff. Never mind, anyhow. I got to go to the bank and I can pick some up . . ."

"Take it," he said urgently. "I'd like you to take this."

"Well, then . . ." Mrs. Violette seemed to understand his need. She began to wind twine upon her spread fingers.

"No, take it all," he said. "Please do."

"I don't like to take more than I'll use."

"I know that," he told her. This was, he fancied, a rather silly, very trivial rebellion. He just wanted something to be as it used to be. He wanted to feel—generous. (Or . . . for all he knew, he wanted, in some ridiculous revenge, to do his sister Ethel out of the price of a ball of twine.)

Mrs. Violette took the whole ball. "I'm sorry to leave you and Mrs. Gibson," said she.

"I'm sorry if my sister has upset you," he said tiredly.

"Me and Joe are going up to the mountains," said Mrs. Violette. He perceived that this was an answer. "And I got to be ready by five o'clock . . ." She stopped speaking and looked at him. He had the strange conviction that she knew what he proposed to do.

"That's all right," he said soothingly.

Mrs. Violette's face lit in a rare smile. "Well, then, goodbye," she said. "They say that means 'God be with you.'"

"Goodbye," said Mr. Gibson rather fondly.

She went out the kitchen door with the ball of twine in her pocket. Now he was all alone.

At 12:10 o'clock he left the cottage and walked . . . doing quite well without his cane, although he lurched when he came down upon the shortened leg and could not help it . . . went two blocks west, crossed the boulevard there and caught a bus for downtown. Paul Townsend he had left safe at home behind him, working away in his herb garden this morning. So Mr. Gibson knew how to get what he wanted.

He did not see the people on the bus. He did not notice the familiar scenery as the vehicle proceeded on the boulevard, then went threading around residential corners until it came upon a business street and thicker traffic. Mr. Gibson, in a mood both bitter and dangerously sweet, was composing a letter.

There was a temptation to be pathetic, and he must resist it. He must make Rosemary understand the cold choice. He must in no way seem to reproach her . . . A difficult letter. What words would do *this?*

He came out of his absorption in time to get off the bus on a downtown corner. This little city had grown, like all California towns, as a wild weed grows. It had left the college here, and in its own park, close to the town's old center . . . and had sent tentacles romping out into valleys and lowlands on all sides. But Mr. Gibson would not go there, to the college—to walk on a campus path and be spoken to by name . . . not again. They would not miss him very much, he thought. Some younger man would come in. . . .

Paul Townsend's place of business was a block and a half in the opposite direction, and Mr. Gibson turned his uneven steps that way. He began to imagine his next moves . . . and, as he did so, he realized that he ought to have brought a container. He stopped in at a delicatessen and purchased the first small bottle he saw on the shelf. It happened to be a two-ounce bottle of imported olive oil, and quite expensive.

"I am Kenneth Gibson. Mr. Townsend's neighbor. He asked me to stop by and fetch a letter out of his desk," said Mr. Gibson with cool nerves.

"Oh yes. Can I get it for you, Mr. Gibson?"

"He told me exactly where to put my hand on it . . . if you don't mind . . ."

"Not at all," the girl said. "This way, Mr. Gibson." She knew who he was . . . Mr. Gibson of the English Department . . . a trustworthy man. "In here," she said with a smile, and ushered him into the laboratory.

He did not look at the cupboards but went to Paul's desk and opened the left top drawer and took, at random, an old letter out of a pile. "This seems to be the one."

"Good," she said.

"Er . . ." Mr. Gibson looked distressed and embarrassed. "Is there by any chance a . . . er . . . men's room . . . ?"

"Oh yes," she said becoming at once crisp and remote. "Right over there, sir." She indicated a door.

"Thank you."

As he had calculated, she left for the outer regions.

He went into the small washroom and turned the cap upon the bottle of olive oil and gravely poured the contents away into the sink.

He came out. Now the laboratory was his alone. He found the key with no trouble. He took down No. 333. His hands were steady as he poured its liquid content into his own container. It was a delicate task, from one small opening into another, but he was cold and clearheaded. He scarcely spilled a drop.

He did not take it all. As he put No. 333 back in place he thought the depletion of the supply would not be noticed for some time. He made no attempt to wipe off fingerprints or anything of that sort. He had elected not to take the whole bottle from the cupboard away with him, only because he needed time. Time to get home. Time to write his letter. He did not want the fact of some missing poison noted too soon and the girl asked and his name given and he interrupted.

Mr. Gibson put the poison he had stolen into the green paper bag, relocked the cupboard, hid the key, left the premises. He thought he might have made a cool and successful thief: he might as well have been a thief all his life for all the difference. . . .

He stood on the downtown corner, waiting for a bus, feeling absolutely numb for the moment. Just as one came, just as he got on, he thought he heard his name spoken. But he wasn't certain, didn't really care whether anyone had called his name or not. . . . So he moved on and sat down by a window.

> I have a tree, a graft of love
> That in my heart has taken root
> Sad are the buds and blooms thereof
> And bitter sorrow is its fruit—

Oh, stop! Stop this senseless jingling of old words. Villon was long dead.

Looking blindly out, the thought crossed his veering mind capriciously that perhaps he'd had, just now, a supernatural warning. But he knew what he was doing. Death. Well? He was simply going to step out of his doom. To him it seemed not an unintelligent thing to do. A *just* God would understand.

How could he put this in a letter? ". . . Very tired . . ." he would write. No. No. It was possible that he would have to lie. What matter if he did or did not lie? ". . . I am not as well as I appear. I have known for a long time . . ." Should he hint that he had begun to doubt his sanity? Yes, *that* . . . Rosemary should understand. And perhaps he *was* insane. In fact, he did not and could not know himself, *really,* why he was doing this deed. Not even this could he know. Doom. In the iceberg of his subconscious the motive lay and worked.

Mr. Gibson, sunk in icy gloom, saw nothing out the windows, nothing inside the bus which went its doomed way on the streets of the town carrying all the doomed people. If he could have done anything for Rosemary, or for any living soul . . . he might have stayed. But all, all were doomed, and to help each other or even to love each other was only another illusion.

Some sense of time and space prodded him to notice the stop that would let him off at the corner where the market was. So he got up and, filled with such pain that he was nearly blinded, he went toward the door. As he stepped off, he thought he heard his name called again.

Angels? Well, if he was about to damn himself through eternity, then he was going to do so. All his life he had done all the duty he had been given to see, made his apparent choices, and if he still had an illusion of choice, this deed appeared to him to be as much his duty as his pleasure . . . and he would do it.

And one duty besides . . . a promise to keep . . . the marketing he had said he would do for Ethel. *Then* he would come (with what relief) to the end of his duties.

So Mr. Gibson went into the big market and took a wheeled basket and pushed it along the aisles. He selected lettuce, he took cocoa, he took a loaf of thin-sliced white bread . . . he took cheese (the kind Ethel preferred). And he took tea for Rosemary. (It might comfort her.)

He stood at the check stand, dumb and lost in utter helplessness, while the girl fingered the buttons and rang the prices. He lifted the big brown bag in his arms. He walked two blocks east, and one north. . . .

The roses at the far side of the cottage were not blooming now.

Old Mrs. Pyne was sitting in her wheel chair on the Townsends' porch. She waved cheerily at him.

Mr. Gibson staggered his course to bring himself near enough to speak to her. (He could ask her. He could inquire about Paul and what the Church might say about marriages and divorcées. . . . But why? He didn't *want* to divorce Rosemary and be, for God knew how many years, her and her husband's friend. No, he didn't *want* that loophole into life. He would rather pretend it wasn't there. Kid himself, he thought bitterly, that the deed would be done for Rosemary's sake.)

He said, "Hello . . ." weakly.

"Goodness!" said the old lady leaning forward, "isn't that too heavy for you, Mr. Gibson?"

"Not too heavy." (But it was. It *was* heavy, his bag of food and death.) "How are you, Mrs. Pyne?" He smiled falsely.

"I'm all right," she said. "Isn't this a glorious day?" Her voice took on a special and almost shocking vigor. "It's so marvelous to be able to sit out in the sun."

"Yes," he said. "Yes . . . well . . ."

He stumbled across the double driveways. He heard Paul's voice calling, "Hi! How goes it?" Mr. Gibson pretended not to hear.

Marvelous to be able to sit in the sun? It was! Yes, it was! He unlocked his door and went in, beginning to know that, quite possibly, he could not do what he had planned to do. So in a night and a morning of acute depression—he had only made a fool of himself once more. He, Kenneth Gibson, was not cut out to be a suicide. No. *He* was fated to set Rosemary free and be her and her husband's good friend for his natural life and limp on in time and bear all. It was not his doom to die today. He couldn't change his doom. Doom is not doom if there is any way out of it. *And he was doomed* . . . to go on being the neat, decent, too thin-skinned little man he had been born to be.

Because it was marvelous to be able to sit in the sun! And this was enough to keep a man alive!

Mr. Gibson began to feel a bit hysterical. No, no, he *would* do it! One second of resolution—that was all he needed. Surely he could manage to lift hand to mouth—one quick gesture—without thought . . .

But if he waited to write a letter. No, no! His whole decision was running away, running out of him. But couldn't the doomed of God ask a little kindness of the devil? Quick, then! Or suffer the tragi-comedy out, be a spectator in his own skull and watch his own acts with what bitter amusement could be salvaged.

He was in the kitchen. He did not have—he did not even want—that kind of courage. Not any more.

He put the big brown bag on the counter. He took out the head of lettuce, the piece of cheese, loaf of bread, the box of tea, and, heavy at the bottom of the bag, the can of cocoa. And now he groped for the bottle of death. He would do it *at once!*

The big bag was absolutely empty.

Yes, quickly.

His hand met nothing.

His death would be a mystery: death always was. Where—?

But surely he had put the small *green* paper bag, twisted up around the little bottle, into the market basket, and the checker girl would have put it in with his purchases. She hadn't. It wasn't here.

Where was it? The terrible quick poison he had gone so far to steal?

He searched his jacket pockets. *Not there!*

Had he dreamed the whole thing? No, surely he remembered pouring the olive oil into the sink far too vividly to have done it in a dream. He had lost it? But the poison was *now* in a bottle labeled "olive oil." Nobody would have any way of knowing it *was* poison! Colorless, odorless, instant . . .

What had he done?

Oh, what wicked error had he made this time?

Where had he left a bottle of poison that looked so innocent? In what public place where innocent people came and went?

The shock nearly caused him to fall down. Then his blood raced and cried *no no no* in perfect revulsion.

Well, it was the end of him. The end of Kenneth Gibson. The end of all respect for him, forever. But *somebody else* was going to get the poison and die of it unless he could prevent this.

The lightning change of all his purposes sent him stumbling to the telephone. He dialed. He said, "Police." His voice did not sound like his own. Every bit of any kind of courage he had, stiffened his spine. Face it. All right. *No nonsense, now.* A sickness seemed to fall off him.

The front door of the cottage opened. His wife Rosemary was standing there.

"I came," she said, intent upon herself and her own thoughts, "because I have got to talk to you. I can't—be such a rabbit—" Her face changed. "Kenneth, what's the matter?"

He had held up his hand for her to be silent. He thrust away every thought but one.

"Police? This is Kenneth Gibson. I have mislaid a small bottle filled with deadly poison." He articulated very clearly and spoke forcefully. "The bottle is labeled olive oil. It is roughly a pyramid, about five inches high, and it's inside a green paper bag. Nobody is going to know that it is poison. Can you do anything? Can you find it? Can you put out a warning?"

Rosemary shrank back against the door.

"I stole it. From a laboratory. . . . Can't give you the name of the stuff. It is odorless, tasteless . . . fatal. . . . Yes, sir. I took a Number Five bus at the corner of Main and Cabrillo at about a quarter after one o'clock. Got off at Lambert and the Boulevard . . . must have been one forty-five. I was in the market there possibly ten or fifteen minutes. It's just after two o'clock now. . . . Yes. Walked to my house . . . and just now discovered I haven't got it. . . . No, I am absolutely sure. . . . *I* put it in the olive-oil bottle. . . . Brand? King somebody-or-other. . . . Yes, I did that. . . . Why? Because I was going to use it myself," he told the barking questioner on the line. "I intended to kill myself."

Rosemary whimpered. He did not look at her.

"Yes, I know it may kill somebody else. That's why I'm calling. . . ." The voice raged in a controlled way. "Yes, I am criminal," said Mr. Gibson. "Anything you say. Find it. Please, do all you can to find it."

He gave his name again. His address. His phone number.

He put the phone upon the cradle.

"Why?" said Rosemary.

He had thought never to see her again.

"Kenneth, I didn't. I didn't. Forgive me. I *didn't—*"

He scarcely heard what she said. He spoke harshly. "Go back to your shop. Know nothing about this. Don't get into it. Leave me. I may have caused someone to die. I may be a murderer. No good to you now. Leave me." He willed her to vanish.

Rosemary shoved herself away from the slab of the door, and stood on her feet. She said, "No. I will not leave you. It isn't going to happen. Nobody will be poisoned. We will go and find it."

He made a gesture of despair. "Oh no, mouse, no use to dream . . ."

"That's *wrong*," said Rosemary. "*That's untrue*. We *can* find the poison. *I* can—and *I will*. And you'll come too. Paul will help us!" she cried and whirled and opened the door. "Come . . ." she said imperiously.

"All right," said Mr. Gibson. "We can try, I suppose."

He walked out into the sunshine. He was very cold. He was as good as dead. He was so ruined a man—by this stroke of fate or whatever it was—it seemed to him that he had most unfortunately survived himself.

Rosemary ran, calling, "Paul! Paul!"

Paul bobbed up from behind a hedge. "What's up?" he said cheerfully.

"Help us. Kenneth had some poison. . . . He's left it someplace. We have to find it."

"Poison! What's this!"

"Your car. Please. *Please*, Paul. It's in a bottle labeled olive oil. Anybody might get it. He's left it at the market. Or on a bus. We have to go there."

Paul tossed her some keys. "Get out the car," he said. His hand clenched around Mr. Gibson's forearm. "What's she talking . . . ?"

"It is Number Three Thirty-three," Mr. Gibson said perfectly distinctly, "I went downtown and stole it from your cupboard."

"What in *hell*—!"

"I was going to kill myself," said Mr. Gibson without apology. "Now I may kill somebody else."

Paul stepped back and withdrew his hand as if from contamination. He turned and yelled at Rosemary. "Did you call the police?"

She was vanishing into Paul's garage. "Yes! Yes! Hurry! Hurry!" she shouted.

Paul said, "Got to tell Mama—get a shirt—" He leaped up on his porch. "Don't go without me," he yelled back over his shoulder. Mr. Gibson stood still. Rosemary was in the garage trying to start a strange car.

But the quiet neighborhood was still quiet. This crisis was like a dagger plunged into flesh that did not yet feel any wound. He, the cause, stood still and could smell lavender and feel the weight of the sun's heat. He experienced a moment out of time. He might as well have killed himself, for he knew he was lost. But also he was being born again. He closed his eyes and turned his face to the caress of the light.

Then Paul's De Soto came bucking and plunging backward. It stopped and Rosemary swung the door and leaned out. "Get in."

Mr. Gibson went meekly, and climbed into the front seat as she shoved over. She seemed to be quite sure that Paul was coming to do the driving.

Paul came in an instant, buttoning a blue shirt over his naked chest. He shoved long legs under the wheel. "Where to, Rosie?"

"The market," she said decisively.

Mr. Gibson sat in the middle. He might as well have been a wax dummy.

"I called Jeanie to come home," Paul said, speaking as if his teeth were ready to chatter. "She's at her music lesson. Mama will be all right alone for half an hour. I'd just helped her to lie down. Didn't tell *her* why. Couldn't leave her with a shock. . . . What got into him?" said Paul angrily.

"I must have been crazy," said Mr. Gibson quietly. It was the easiest thing to say. He was beyond horror and beyond pain.

"Pray it's in the market," said Rosemary, "and they've found it. Paul, do you know what it is? It *is* poison?"

"It's dangerous stuff, all right. As I told him— How did he get *at* it?" Paul demanded with that anger.

The ghost of Mr. Gibson explained, and Paul grimaced as if he had to hold his teeth clenched. There seemed a convention that Mr. Gibson could speak and be heard and yet not be considered quite solidly there. Paul was perspiring. The car went jerkily. It was only three blocks to the market. "What are you doing home, Rosie?" Paul said in a nervous explosion.

"I wanted to talk to him. Alone. I didn't *like*— This is the first day Ethel's been . . ." They had turned the corner. "Look! A police car!"

If Mr. Gibson felt a twinge: it felt like simple wonder. What, he wondered, was going to happen next?

He tried to push at this wonder and make himself feel alive. What was he doing plunging around the streets—? Who was he? Who were these people, young, busy, pushing people . . . Rosemary thrusting both legs out of the car to the pavement of the market's parking lot and Paul yanking on the brake and tumbling out the other side.

Mr. Gibson sat for a moment, abandoned and strangely exposed, for both front doors of Paul's car were flapping open. When he felt a stirring somewhere at the bottom of his being it was still remarkably simple. It was curiosity.

So he slid under the wheel and got, as nimbly as he could, out of the car. He limped rapidly after them into the market.

Chapter Thirteen

"Sure I know him," the little checker girl was saying.

She had black tangled hair, enormous dark eyes, and wore huge gold buttons in her ears. "I always thought he was *nice,* you know what I mean? Sure, I saw him. *That's* him, isn't it? But I didn't see no green paper bag. It *wasn't* in with his groceries. He didn't *have* no green paper bag. See . . ." She moved closer to the tall policeman and looked up at him almost yearningly. "We aren't busy so close to lunch. We never are. So I seen him come in. Right in that door. He didn't look good. He looked like he was sick or something. I seen his bare hands. If he had it, then he musta had it in his pocket. Did you look in his pockets?"

"Did you look in your pockets?" Rosemary flashed around and seemed to bear down upon him. (She wasn't anybody he knew.) Then the policeman seemed to be searching him while Mr. Gibson stood helpless as a dummy or a small child whose elders don't trust the accuracy of his reports.

The checker girl said, almost weeping, "Why'd he want to do a thing like that? Gee, I thought he was *nice.* . . . I mean some customers aren't so nice, you know, but *he* was nice." She used the past tense as if he had died. Nobody answered her.

"And listen," she sobbed. "I didn't put no green paper bag in with anybody else's stuff, either. Only been three or four people through my stand. It isn't *here.* Probably he never had no poison." She peeked at Mr. Gibson fearfully.

"If it isn't here," said Rosemary, tensely, "it must be on the bus."

"Wa-ait a minute," the policeman said. "Now—" His eyes were cold. They fixed upon Mr. Gibson as if he were an object and an obstacle. (One could tell that he was used to obstacles.) "You are positive that you had this green paper bag with this poison in it when you got on the bus?"

"Yes, I am positive," said Mr. Gibson with perfect composure.

"And when you got home?"

"It wasn't there."

"You were emotionally upset?" the policeman said. "You think you forgot it on the bus, then?"

"I 'forgot' it," said Mr. Gibson, "because, I suppose, subconsciously I did not really want . . ." The words were coming out of him as from a parrot.

Rosemary took his arm rather roughly. "Do you *want* a stranger to die?" she cried at him.

The knife went in. "No," said he. "No. No."

"Well, then!" said Rosemary with a curious air of triumph. "You see, it *isn't* true!"

Paul said, "Wait a minute. What are the police doing?"

The policeman said, "They are after the bus, all right. And we are broadcasting. I'll search this building thoroughly, now, just in case . . ."

"What do you think the chances . . . ?"

The policeman shrugged. He didn't think much of them. He was a sad man. He'd seen a lot of trouble. He did his best and let it go at that. "Whoever might find a bottle—looks like it's olive oil—might throw it away," said he. "Might take it home—use it. Who can say what people are going to do?"

Ethel can, thought Mr. Gibson, and for a moment feared he might whinny this forth nervously.

"Can't *we* find the bus?" Rosemary was urging.

"Gee, Rosie, I dunno," said Paul. "Are you sure he shouldn't be seeing a doctor . . ." Paul jittered.

Rosemary said, "Hurry, hurry . . ."

The checker girl said, "Oh gosh, I hope you find it! I hope nothing bad is going to happen!" She peered at Mr. Gibson from her eye corners. "Look, you're all right now, aren't you?" She seemed to care.

Mr. Gibson couldn't answer. What was it to be "all right," he wondered, with a shadowy sadness.

Then they were back in the car, as before.

"Number Five. That is the bus that goes on out the boulevard?" asked Rosemary.

"Yes."

"But how will we know which one? Did you notice any number on it?"

"No."

"But the police could get the number of the right bus, couldn't they? Since they know the time you caught it downtown, the time you got off at the market."

"Maybe."

"Then, maybe they have caught it already. They *must* have. It's two fifteen."

Rosemary was babbling! It was vocalized worry. Mr. Gibson was answering in monosyllables. Paul was driving the car. He wasn't driving it very well. The car jerked and jittered. The man was nervous. Mr. Gibson—so curiously removed from self by his ruination (which was complete)—found his senses able to perceive. He felt a resurgence of an old power. He was no longer cut off. Paul, he realized, shrank from him as evil. Paul was almost superstitiously afraid of a man who had intended to kill himself.

Mr. Gibson wondered if he ought to try to explain. The trouble was . . . he could not now remember how it had gone, all his reasoning. He thought it odd to be sitting in the middle with the two of them so bent on preserving him from the doom of becoming a murderer. Doom . . . ah yes, that was the word. Now he remembered. . . .

"I was going to write a letter," he said out loud. "I was going to explain . . . At least, I—"

"Well, *don't!*" said Rosemary vehemently. "Not now. Just don't *talk* about it. Whatever you thought, whatever it was, whatever it *is*. Now, we have to find that terrible stuff and stop it from hurting anyone. Afterward," she said grimly, "you can talk about it if you want to. Paul, can you drive faster?"

"Listen," said Paul, nervous and sweating. "I'd just as soon not wreck us, you know . . ."

Rosemary said, "I know. I know," and she pounded with her small female fists the side of Paul's car. "But I *am* to blame for *this*," said Rosemary.

Mr. Gibson tried to protest but she turned and looked fiercely into his eyes. "And *you* are to blame. *We* are to blame. That has to be true. I'll prove it to you. I'm tired," she cried. "I am so tired—"

Paul said, "Don't talk, Rosie. He must have been crazy. Let it go and say he was crazy."

But Mr. Gibson had a strange feeling of solidity. He thought, Yes, of course, I am to blame.

The boulevard was a divided street. In the weedy center space there lay old streetcar tracks, now superseded by the bus line. The boulevard was lined with little low apartment buildings, arranged in the charming California style, around grassy courts, and in a gay variety of colors . . . pink ones, yellow ones, green ones . . . all sparkling clean and bright in the light of this fine day. Like big beads on the pretty chain, there came from time to time the shopping centers. A huge food market, with banks of red and yellow and orange fruit along the sidewalk, its bulk like a mother hen beside its chicks—the drugstore, laundromats.

After ten minutes of going, the boulevard lost its center strip and became just a street curving off through residential patches into a long valley, where houses became smaller and shabbier and more countrified as the city frayed about the edges. Mr. Gibson, sitting in the middle, looked at all this scenery as if he had come upon a new planet.

They passed one bus going their way, and, after a while, another. Neither could be the right one.

It was Paul Townsend, now, who was doing the talking. "Number Five turns around at the junction, I think. Let's see. If you got off about one forty-five, then *it* would get to the end of its line around two forty or a bit after. We might meet the right bus, coming *back*. What is it now? Two thirty."

"I can't tell the right bus," Mr. Gibson said.

"The police can. Watch the other side of the street . . ."

Mr. Gibson's brain, although feebly, was turning over. "Whoever found the bottle," said he with detached composure, "may have gotten off the bus at any stop along the way."

"Yes, but—" Paul's eye flirted nervously toward him. Paul wanted to worry out loud, but not this much.

"In fact, once the bus has turned around to come back—that means that every person who was on it while *I* was on it, *must not* be on it any more."

"Maybe whoever found it turned it over to the driver. Maybe they have like a lost and found department . . ."

"Maybe," said Mr. Gibson stoically.

"Who's going to take and eat food that he just *found?*" said Paul. "Especially if it looks as if it has been opened. Did you break a seal?"

"No seal. It was a question of turning the cap . . ."

"How full was the bottle?"

"Full enough."

"It wouldn't pour quite like olive oil."

"It's oily enough," said Mr. Gibson. "The bottle will smell of olive oil."

"Listen—" said Paul, "even if we don't find it . . . don't forget the police are putting the alarm on the air. That's what he said."

"Not everyone," said Mr. Gibson, "listens constantly to the radio."

Rosemary said, "And we should face the facts, shouldn't we?" She turned her head and looked fiercely at him as before. Her eyes were such a fierce blue. Mr. Gibson realized that inside the body of Rosemary—behind the face of Rosemary—within all the graces of Rosemary, which graces he loved—there was somebody else. A fierce angry determined spirit he had never met and never known. This spirit said boldly, "If anyone dies of that poison, you'll go to jail, I suppose?"

"I suppose," he said and felt indifferent.

"In any case, you'll lose your position?"

"Yes."

"People will know . . ."

The people in the market, the people on the bus, the police, the neighbors, the public. Yes, thought Mr. Gibson, everyone will know. . . .

"But if nobody dies and we find the poison," said Rosemary, "*everything else we can bear.* Isn't that a *fact?*"

Mr. Gibson put his hand up to shield his eyes. It *was* a fact, as far as he could tell.

"Keep your chin up," said Paul nervously. "Who knows? What time is it? Ten of three—the bus has turned around."

"Look!" said Rosemary. "Look . . . up ahead! There it is! There it is!"

Chapter Fourteen

THERE WERE in fact, two buses. One wide yellow vehicle was pulled up on the shoulder of the road. A black-and-white police car nosed against it from behind. Beside it stood a group of three, two policemen and the bus driver.

The other bus had stopped a few yards ahead and a group of people—ten or a dozen—were climbing on. These people seemed, all of them, to be looking back with crooked necks toward the policemen.

Paul made a wild U-turn. His car stuttered and bounced and stopped behind the police car. The time was 2:54. Mr. Gibson found himself limping after his companions over lumpy sod through tall dust-plastered weeds that grew between the road and a patched wire fence. It was an unexpected setting for a crisis. Most crises, thought Mr. Gibson, take place in unexpected settings.

"I'm Mrs. Gibson," he heard Rosemary cry. "It was my husband. Did you find it? Is it *here?* The poison?"

Not one of the three men opened his mouth. So Mr. Gibson knew that they had not found it.

"Who are those people getting on that other bus?" cried Rosemary against their silence. "What's happening?"

"Passengers," said one of the policemen. "They don't—none of them—know anything. We're letting them go about their business." He swung around. "You the man left this poison someplace in the olive oil bottle?" He had selected Mr. Gibson instead of Paul . . . and Mr. Gibson nodded.

"Well, we can't find it on this bus."

"Which seat did you sit in?" snapped the second policeman.

Mr. Gibson shook his head.

"How big was the package?"

Mr. Gibson showed them mutely, using his hands.

"In a *paper* bag?"

Mr. Gibson nodded. This policeman, a young one, gave him a disgusted look, sucked air into the corner of his mouth, and swung up through the open door of the bus. He didn't like any part of this situation. His partner, an older man, with a thicker mask on, helped Rosemary up by her elbow. Paul went, too. Four of them ducked and bobbed, searching in there, where the policemen must already have searched.

Mr. Gibson stood in the dusty weeds. This was the bus? He had ridden this bus? He had no recollection of any details at all. Now, here he was, standing in the sun, on the dusty earth, with a field spreading away from him . . . and he, his own survivor.

The bus driver, a lean man in his thirties with a long and rather surprisingly pale face, stood in the weeds, too, hands deep in trouser pockets, watching him. "So you would your own quietus make? Hey?" said the bus driver softly.

Mr. Gibson was immeasurably startled. "I botched it," said he pettishly.

The bus driver poked out his lips and seemed to be touching his tongue up over his teeth. He moved back far enough to lean in at the door of the bus. "This man sat halfway back on the right side, near the window, alone," he bawled.

The four inside responded by gathering together on the right side of the bus. The driver came forward far enough to lean on the high yellow bus wall.

"You botched it, all right," he said to Mr. Gibson. "Hamlet made a mess of it, too. Hey? Going to try again?" He had sandy lashes.

"I doubt it," snapped Mr. Gibson. "I'll take what's coming to me." He pulled back his shoulders.

"Gibson, hey? Teach at the college, don't you?" the man said. "What do you teach?"

"Poetry."

"Poetry! Hah!" The man grinned. "There's a million poems about death, I guess."

"And about love, too," said Mr. Gibson with frozen-feeling lips. This was the oddest, the most unexpected conversation he had ever gotten into.

"Sure—love and death," the bus driver said, "and God and man —and all the real stuff."

"Real?" Mr. Gibson blinked.

"You think it *ain't?*" the bus driver said. "Don't gimme that."

The younger policeman came out of the bus. "Nope," he said. "No soap. We'll look again in a few minutes."

"Yeah?" said the driver. "Whassa matter? Don't you trust yourselves?"

"Eyes can do funny tricks," the policeman said stiffly.

"O.K. by me. I don't mind being out of service. Nice day." The bus driver looked at Mr. Gibson again with contemplative eyes.

Rosemary jumped down out of the bus. "What can we do?"

Paul behind her, took her arm. "Better go home, Rosie," he murmured. "The broadcast is the only hope, now. Nothing *we* can do but wait."

"You remember him?" cried Rosemary to the bus driver.

"Sure do, ma'am."

"Did you see the paper bag?"

"Might have," said the bus driver, narrowing his eyes. "Seems to me I get the impression he shifted a little package to his other hand when he put his fare in. It's just an impression but I *got* it. Might mean something."

"Did you see it in his hand when he got off?"

"No, ma'am. People getting off have their backs to me."

"Did you see who took the seat he'd been sitting in . . . ?"

"No, ma'am. Lessee. He got off at Lambert? Well, I had a little poker game with a green Pontiac there—where he got off. This Pontiac and me was outbluffing each other, so I paid no attention. . . ."

"Was the bus full?"

"No, ma'am. Not at that hour."

"Do you *understand?*" said Rosemary. "It's a deadly poison. In the wrong bottle. Do you *understand* that?"

The bus driver said sweetly, "I understand."

"Did you notice *anyone* getting off with a green paper bag?"

"I can't see their hands when they're getting off, ma'am," he reminded her patiently.

Rosemary clasped her own hands and looked off across the field.

Paul said, "Somebody picked it up and took it and there's no way of finding out who. . . . The broadcast warning will either reach him or it won't."

The two cops were listening quietly. The older one shifted his weight.

"Maybe," said Rosemary. "Maybe there *is* something we can do. You were there," she said to the bus driver. "Did you recognize *anybody else* who was on the bus then?"

"Hey?" said the bus driver, wrinkling his brow.

"Anyone else we could find and ask? Somebody who was also there and might have noticed?"

"Wait a minute." The driver seemed to bristle up. "This stuff's poison, hey?"

Paul said, "Damned dangerous," and looked angry. "He took it from my lab. He knew what it was. He should never . . . Oh, come home, Rosie."

"A stranger," said Rosemary, still addressing the bus driver, "trusting in a label. Some stranger to us, who doesn't want to die. People do trust labels. . . ."

"Yes," he said, "they got a right to. And there was my blonde."

"Blonde?"

"Yeah, and while *she* wouldn't . . . I don't *think*. . . . Nobody," said the bus driver forcefully, heaving himself away from his leaning position, "is going to poison my blonde!" He grew taller. "Is that your car?"

"Who is this blonde?" the young policeman said moving in.

"I don't know her name."

"Where does she live?"

"I don't know where she lives."

"She was *on* the bus?"

"Yeh, she was on the bus."

"If you don't know her . . . how come . . . ?"

"She doesn't know that she's my blonde—not yet. One of these days . . . Aw, I was biding my time. Now look," the bus driver said, "I'm *going*. One thing I *do* know and that's the stop she gets off at. *I* can find her. And nobody's going to poison my blonde."

He set off toward Paul's car.

"Oh yes! Paul," Rosemary cried, "Kenneth, come on! We'll all go, find her. *She* might have noticed . . . Hurry, come on!"

The whole group was streaming toward Paul's car.

The older policeman said, "Wait . . . I can call in, you know. I can get a prowl car there in seconds . . ."

"Where?" said the driver. "When I don't know where myself? All I got is the stop. Corner of Allen and the Boulevard. What can *you* do with that? Thanks, anyway, but I guess I got to go find her myself. I'll know her when I see her, see?"

"What about this bus?"

"Life and death," said the driver, with his hand on Paul's car. "Let them fire me." Paul was right behind him. "Give me the keys," the driver said.

"My car . . . I'll drive." Paul looked as if he were suffering. His mouth was grim.

"You are an amateur," said the bus driver, and took the keys out of Paul's hand.

Mr. Gibson knew only that Rosemary's hands were pulling and hustling him. He and she got into the back seat. Paul got in beside the bus driver.

"Good luck," said the older policeman, rather kindly. "Call in, now." The younger one was chewing grass.

The bus driver was moving levers. Paul's car surged backward, slipped out into traffic. It seemed to respond with pleasure to a master's hand. "I can make better time, that's all," the bus driver said. "Driving's my business. Every business has its skills."

"That's all right," Paul murmured.

They were sailing back toward town.

Chapter Fifteen

"My NAME's Lee Coffey," said the bus driver suddenly.

Paul straightened up with an effect of relaxing, of feeling better. "I'm Paul Townsend," he said in something nearer his normal amiable voice. "A neighbor of the Gibsons'."

"I see. And the lady is Mrs. Gibson."

"Rosie," said Paul, "this is Lee Coffey—"

"Her name is Rosemary," Mr. Gibson heard himself saying loudly. "My name is Kenneth Gibson. I am the man . . ."

"How do, Mrs. Rosemary?" the bus driver said over his shoulder. "Say, Mr. Kenneth Gibson, what *was* it that was coming to you . . . you'd rather take poison?"

Mr. Gibson tried to swallow with a dry mouth.

Paul said quickly, "No, no, don't talk about it. It was a temporary . . . He didn't even know what he was doing. He must have been crazy. He's all right now."

"What puts him all right, all of a sudden?" the bus driver said.

"Why, he knows . . . he has friends. He's got everything to live for."

"Candy?" said the bus driver.

"I don't know what you mean."

"I never could get that," said the bus driver, sliding the car skillfully to a strategic position in the center lane. "How come—now you take a suicide sitting on a ledge up high, see . . . ? People trying to talk him out of it, offer the same as lollypops. Everybody's his friend, they tell him. Come home, the dog needs him. Or he can have beer. He can have chocolate. . . . Seems to me if a man gets to the point of taking his life he's got more serious things in his mind. It's no time for candy, is it?"

"You are wrong," said Mr. Gibson forcefully.

"That so?"

"There is one moment when a lollypop is enough, either way."

"I see," said the bus driver. "Yeah. . . . Well, *you'd* know. That's very interesting."

The car moved. It was not speeding. But no second was lost by indecision or by fumbling. Mr. Gibson found himself admiring this with peculiar pleasure.

"If you *want* to talk about it . . ." the bus driver said, and Paul said again, "No, no . . ."

Mr. Gibson answered truthfully. "I'd like to talk to *you* about it. Not just now, I guess." He felt expanded and relaxed in contact with a mind that interested him. A mind that cheerfully pried off a certain lid . . . a lid that had been stifling and muffling and shutting up that which is interesting.

He looked sideways at Rosemary, and her eyes were visited by the ghost of a smile. "Tell me about your blonde, Mr. Coffey," she said almost brightly.

"Look at me, rushing to the rescue," the bus driver said, "of a blonde who doesn't know she's mine. I'll tell you a little bit. I see her nearly every day. Watch for her, now. I'm getting to know her. I'm thinking of getting up the nerve to speak to her. Never have. Doesn't matter. I already know that I like her a lot. So how can I let her get the poison? Will this offend her, Mrs. Gibson?"

"Rosemary," said Rosemary gravely. "No, it won't offend her, Mr. Coffey. It won't offend her at all."

"Call me Lee," said the bus driver. "These are unusual circumstances. Listen, Rosemary, she is a beautiful blonde."

"You are a very interesting man," said Rosemary.

"That's possible," said Lee Coffey thoughtfully.

It was Paul who came in with an ordinary question. "Have you been a bus driver long?"

"Ten years. Since I got out of the Army. Because I like to think."

"Like to think?" Paul repeated after him, seeming to find this shockingly obscure.

"Ruminate. Ruminate," said the bus driver. "That's why I like a useful but not creative job. You start pushing and trying to a purpose . . . or even just trying to make a million dollars . . . it warps your thinking. *My* thinking, anyhow. The kind I like."

Paul said, impatient with bewilderment, "How can you possibly find this girl, this blonde, whoever she is . . . ?"

"He'll find her," said Rosemary with parted lips. "Don't you think so, Kenneth?"

"I do," said Mr. Gibson. "I think so." He felt astonished. The car slipped up to a red light and stopped smoothly.

"Mr. Coffey—Lee?" Suddenly Rosemary took in a great breath and threw herself on her knees in the tonneau. "Please help me? Tell me something?"

"Sure if I can . . ."

"You are an expert driver. I can see that you are. Will you tell me . . . I believe you will *know*. I can believe *you*."

"What's the trouble?" said the bus driver, sending them swiftly off the mark as the light changed.

Mr. Gibson sat astonished while Rosemary knelt and poured out words toward this bus driver's ear.

"It is a foggy night," she said. "I am driving. I am trying to be careful. I know . . . to the best of my knowledge . . . that I am on the right side of the road."

"Go ahead," said the bus driver encouragingly.

"I also think I know that there is a deep ditch to my right. I think we have come that far . . . you see?"

"Yeah . . . yeah . . ."

"All of a sudden there is a car coming head on . . . and *he* is on his *left* side of the road. I have to do something quick."

"Can't deny that," said Lee Coffey cheerfully.

"I turned *left*," said Rosemary intensely. "You see, I thought . . ." She buried her head on her arm.

"So what happened?" asked the driver.

"He turned to his right, so we collided. Please tell me. *You* tell me if I was wrong."

The bus driver turned the situation over in his mind. Meanwhile, they glided upon the boulevard, having already reached the spot where the divided street began. The scenery floated by.

"You had three choices," the man said calmly in a moment. "You could turn right, supposed to be proper . . . and take a chance on the ditch. Pretty sure to be dangerous. You could stay where you were because you are legal . . . and take the chance the other fella's going to correct himself and turn off in time. That takes cold nerve and an awful lot of stubborn righteousness. Or, you can turn

left as you did and figure to get around him on the *clear* side . . .
even though it's the *wrong* side . . . of the road. Hey?"

"It seemed clear . . ."

"Was it?"

"Well, yes, actually it *was* clear. You see, I thought . . . I thought
he might be confused and think he was on his right side. I didn't
know he'd turn off. How could I know that?"

"You did no wrong," Lee Coffey said gravely. "You tried for a
solution. Who can do more? Makes sense to me."

Rosemary's breath shuddered in. "But the result was that the car
hit us on our right, and—Kenneth was hurt. . . . *Only* Kenneth was
hurt. Not me. Tell me, please . . . did I mean to put him between
me and that other car? Did I choose to hurt him rather than myself? Is *that* why I turned to the left, *really?*"

"You just told me why you turned left, didn't you?" Lee Coffey
said.

"I thought I was trying to save us both. But, you see . . . there
was no ditch. I was mistaken about that. We hadn't come to the
place where the ditch began to be there, along the right side of the
road."

"Fog," said the bus driver. "O.K. You *were* on the right?"

"Yes."

"He, the other fella, *was* on his left?"

"Yes."

"And you thought there was this ditch?"

"I think I thought—but Ethel—says, there's no such thing as an
accident. As if—as if . . . subconsciously I *made* happen what I
wanted to happen . . ."

"No such thing as an accident!" cried the bus driver. "Where has
this Ethel been living?"

"Wait," said Rosemary, warningly. "She's . . . very wise. She's
not stupid . . . and she's good . . ."

"She is, eh? Well, I'll tell *you* something. Nobody's that wise.
There happen to be plenty of accidents."

"But *are* they? *Really?*"

"The subconscious, hey?" said the bus driver. "Well, I see what
she's getting at, all right. Sure. Some people are accident-prone
. . . this is a thing that's been discovered. It's like some people take
to getting sick because they'd rather . . . Certainly. But not so, in
your case."

"Not—?" Rosemary trembled.

"*How* so?" demanded the bus driver. "What did your subconscious *do?* Explain it to me. Did it go up in the ether someplace and have a conference with the other fella's subconscious? He didn't have any accident either if Ethel is right. Hey? So did your subconscious say to the other subconscious, 'Look here, old chap, I'm fixing to have an accident. Is this O.K. with you? How about right now?' So the other subconscious says, 'Fine, fine. Well met. Me, too. *I* was fixing to have an accident, myself . . . and now is as good a time as any. So here's how we'll work it . . .' Aaah . . ." The bus driver gave an effect of spitting over the side. "Explain to me how these two subconsciouses met, there and then, if not *accidentally?* Or if you're going to say . . . well, only one of them *meant* to do it . . . Now you got to admit the *other one* anyhow had an accident. So which one of you did . . . or didn't? You or him? Hey?"

Rosemary said nothing. She knelt as if in prayer.

"Certainly," Coffey continued, "there'd be no accidents if you could know everything. But who can know everything? You can anticipate just so much. You cannot—now I don't care—you *cannot* always guess when who is going to do what, where. Neither you nor your subconscious, either! It's too much! There's too damned much going *on* in this universe. So there's going to happen what we call accidents. You see what I mean?"

"Yes," said Rosemary. "Yes, I do." She sighed deep.

"Those who skin out of having accidents are the ones who take care, who look ahead and so forth. But on top of that they better have some very snappy reflexes. See? And even they don't always skin out of all the things they meet—"

"Rosemary," said Mr. Gibson sternly. "Ethel never said this thing to you. She couldn't have told you that you deliberately hurt me."

"Not deliberately. No—but she thinks I *must* have meant to, because I *did,*" Rosemary sobbed. "She keeps saying she doesn't 'blame' me. She keeps saying she 'understands.' Oh, Kenneth, I'm sorry—I wouldn't say a word against Ethel but this . . . this has been . . ."

Paul said angrily, "I told you you shouldn't pay any attention to Ethel."

"Easier said than done," said the bus driver . . . bluntly, accurately, and astonishingly.

"Doom," murmured Mr. Gibson, recovering from a stunned sensation. "Yes—doom—well. . . ."

"Now, the subconscious," said the bus driver, throwing out one hand as if he had been lecturing all along and was starting a new paragraph. "It's down there and it operates all right, *something* like they say. There's a little more to it. For instance, *why* would you want to hurt him?"

"Because—" said Rosemary indistinctly. "But it isn't *true.*" She wiggled back up upon the seat.

"I'd say you had an accident," Lee Coffey told her. "For the love of Pete, Mike, and Maria . . . I don't see the point of this Ethel!"

Rosemary was crying.

Mr. Gibson began to feel quite angry for Rosemary's sake. "Ethel isn't infallible, mouse," he said indignantly. He felt a surge of malicious mischief, too. "I've heard Ethel say, for instance, that bus drivers are perfectly ruthless brutes. Now, obviously . . ."

"What!" Lee Coffey raised his head. "Let me tell you, for your information, *nobody's* got more ruth than us bus drivers. Ruth's our business. It's a job, takes a mighty responsible party and no joking. You got to drive in whatever weather, whatever traffic, and *on* schedule, and what you meet you meet with your mind on safety first. Listen, we got more ruth than any twenty-five private drivers in this world." He was sputtering. "We *can't* take chances. We aren't *free* to. Passengers, pedestrians, school kids, nuts, drunks . . . we got to look out for everybody in the world. We got to handle it, and if we *do* have an accident, believe me, it *is* an accident. What's this Ethel talking? Who *is* this Ethel?"

"My sister," said Mr. Gibson, tossed in the storm of this outburst, yet somehow wanting to laugh out loud, which seemed unsuitable.

"Some sister," said the bus driver gloomily.

"She came to . . . take care of us . . . after the accident . . ."

"I must confess," said Paul, his syllables falling rapidly, "that we don't . . . Mama and Jeanie and I . . . we just don't care too much for Ethel. She seems so cold and superior . . ."

"My sister Ethel!" said Mr. Gibson.

"Ruthless. Hey?" muttered the bus driver. "Every last one of us, hey? The whole category? 'Ay, in the catalogue ye go for men . . .'"

"You are fond of Shakespeare?" asked Mr. Gibson.

"Sure, I am. Not only his language hits the spot: his music does, too. *You* like Shakespeare, don't you?"

"I like Shakespeare very much," said Mr. Gibson with his hair rising on his head in delighted astonishment. "Do you like Browning?" he asked with strange urgency.

"Some of it. Quite a lot of it. Of course you got to get onto his system."

"He was kind of a lady's man."

"The ladies were the ones who had the time to—you know—ruminate, in a refined way," said Lee Coffey, "or they used to before they started being riveters and tycoons."

"Just so," said Mr. Gibson almost comfortably.

Rosemary was not weeping any more. She sat with her shoulder to his. "Did you ever hear Ethel speak of a blonde?" she said demurely.

"What'd she say?" demanded the bus driver.

But Paul Townsend was fidgeting. "Look, I don't like to keep worrying," he said plaintively, "but where *is* this blonde? She *might* have the poison herself, you know. She might be in danger. She might be dead. I don't see how you can talk about Shakespeare and Browning!"

The bus driver said calmly, "She must live within four or five blocks of this next corner. What time is it?"

"Three twenty. Three twenty-two in fact."

"Yeah, well—not many take olive oil for a snack between meals."

"Oh, that's *true!*" cried Rosemary, clapping her hands. "We have more time than we thought."

"Maybe," said Mr. Gibson hopefully but he thought, within, where a twinge—the pain of life—was creeping. But there are accidents. He felt a sweet sense of expansion, and a piercing alarm, all together.

Accidents are possible.

Chapter Sixteen

THERE WAS a light at the corner of Allen Street and the Boulevard. Lee Coffey turned right on Allen. Nobody said a word. Paul's car mooched down the first block: the driver seemed to be testing the very air for the scent. The car crossed one intersection. Then, in the middle of the second block on Allen, it stopped.

Lee Coffey analyzed the situation aloud. He held his head down; his eyes were roving; he spoke like a conspirator. *"Her* place will be on this side of Allen. Or around a corner from this side. She waits for the light on this side of Allen . . . see? If she had to cross, she'd cross at the Boulevard, see what I mean?"

Mr. Gibson, on the edge of the seat, nodded solemnly. At the same time he felt a little childish pleasure, as if this were a game.

"Now," said Lee, "the first block was all duplexes. Five- and six-room places. But these are private houses, old enough and big enough for taking in roomers." He was right. This second block was an old block. The houses stood up off the ground. There roofs were up in the tree-tops and the trees were high—conditions not always present in the bursting newness of a California town. "I don't think she's got a lot of dough," he went on, "and I do think she lives by herself. If she had a family, somebody would have a car." This was true in California, U.S.A. "And they'd work it so she wouldn't have to take the bus as much as she does. I get a pretty good idea who rides with me, you know."

"But what can we do," said Paul, "when you don't know her name?"

"What are we going to do, Lee?" asked Rosemary confidently, eagerly. She was on the edge of the seat too.

"This is what we are going to do. We ring doorbells. We take one block at a time. Each of you ask for a blond young lady, not very tall, who is some kind of nurse. Why I say that . . . I've seen her wear white stockings. And, while lots of jobs will take a white uniform, there ain't a female on earth wears white stockings unless she has to. Now, if you find her, or any news of her, give a yell, make a noise to the rest of us. Ask if they've seen her walking by, and if so, which way she turns. But *don't* tell why you're asking." His eye caught Mr. Gibson's wince. "Because it would take too long," the bus driver said. "O.K.?"

This all seemed very logical and clear to everyone. All four of them tumbled out and were deployed. Rosemary ran back along the sidewalk to start at the beginning of the block. Paul went striding far to the left to begin at the end. Lee Coffey started where he was, his nostrils seeming to quiver. He had some reason, Mr. Gibson guessed, to suspect *this* spot, a certain house. A reason he could not or would not explain. Lee Coffey was to work to the left.

Mr. Gibson took the next door and would work to the right and meet Rosemary.

He limped up the front walk of the house assigned to him and rang the bell. Nobody answered it; nobody seemed to be at home. Mr. Gibson stood on the strange stoop and rang and rang in a dream. (He was Mr. Gibson of the English Department. No. He was crazy. No, but he was a criminal. Or he was a man in a desperate plight who had friends to fight fate for him. How could he let them down? or let them know that they were doomed? Mr. Gibson, half dead, half born, was not sure about anything.)

He had just pulled himself together to abandon here and proceed to ring another when he heard a shrill whistle, looked, and saw Lee Coffey beckoning with huge gestures of his long arms.

Mr. Gibson's heart leaped up. He was pleased that Lee Coffey should be the one of the four of them to find the scent. He was pleased with the magic of it. It was almost enough to make you dream a man *could* put intelligence and intuition against odds and make progress. Which was romantic and naïve, but he *liked* it. As he limped leftward, Rosemary was running to catch up with him and he saw Paul hurrying back.

They flocked up upon the gray porch of a neat gray frame house that made one think of New England. There was even a lilac bush . . . an exotic and difficult plant here in the West—growing beside the porch railing. In the door stood a small blond girl at whom Lee Coffey looked down with hidden eyes.

She was wearing a long wrapper of blue cotton. Her hair was tousled, as if it had just left a pillow. Her face was broad at the eyes and curved quickly into a small chin. It was an attractive little face, not conventionally pretty. The skin was smooth and fine. The mouth was serious. The gray eyes were serene. The only thing "blonde" about her, in Ethel's sense, was the color of her hair.

"And here she is," said Lee, like the Little Bear in the story.

"What is it, please?" the girl said in a self-assured voice. She wasn't a person easily surprised, one could tell. For a slim little girl, she seemed very strong.

Lee blurted, "We aren't here to accuse you, ma'am. But did you find a bottle of olive oil on a bus today? And did you bring it home?"

"No, I didn't," said the blonde quietly.

The atmosphere of excited triumphant hope swirled and began to die down.

"Did you see," said Rosemary doggedly, "my husband . . . this man . . ." she put her hand on Mr. Gibson, "on the bus?"

"No, I didn't," said the blonde. Her eyes traveled from face to face. "Something is wrong? I remember you," she said, coming to Lee Coffey. "Aren't you the driver?" Her eyes were very clear and steady.

"Yes, ma'am." Mr. Gibson found himself waiting for Lee to tell whose blonde she was, but his sandy lashes were discreet.

She wrinkled her fair brow. "Will one of you please tell me what's the matter?"

Rosemary was the one of them who told her. When she was a quarter of the way into the exposition, the small blonde, by gestures only, brought them all inside the house. As if trouble as bad as this better not stand where the breeze might blow and communicate it. So they all sat down in the parlor, on edges of stiff sofas and chairs, while Rosemary went on.

This small blond female had an air of calm and precision about her. She listened without making noises of alarm or even appreciation. But you knew she did appreciate and was alarmed.

"Then Lee . . . Mr. Coffey, here . . . remembered *you*," finished Rosemary, "and so we came. Hoping you had it. Or had seen something."

"I wouldn't have taken it, I'm sorry, even if I'd seen it. It wouldn't have occurred to me." The blonde's immaculate ringless hands clasped her knee. "I didn't see anything of a paper bag or a bottle." This serene little person had never been in danger from the missing poison.

But now there was no way to continue. They had come to an end. Magic had found the bus driver's blonde, but not the poison. It was not here.

Mr. Gibson squirmed. He found himself incorrigibly on the side of the magic. "You must tell us your name," he said impulsively. He wanted the bus driver to learn her name.

She said her name was Virginia Severson. It suited her. She looked very virginal, and clean, calm, cool in a Scandinavian sort of way. Rosemary rallied and told her all their names. Once again, the civilized ceremony of mutual introduction seemed to relax Paul Townsend. He was charming.

But all this was only delay. The stiff, shabby, spotless parlor seemed airless and stagnant.

Miss Severson said, "I sat pretty well forward in the bus. You must have been sitting behind me." Her grave eyes examined Mr. Gibson. "I'm sorry." She turned her face to Lee Coffey. "You were clever to find me," she said.

"One day," said Lee, "I saw you breathing through a lilac . . ."

"Are you from the East, too?" she said warmly, "that you noticed a lilac?"

"I'll tell you another time," said the bus driver softly, "how come I noticed the lilac."

The blond girl let her lashes down. "I wish I could have helped you," she murmured.

Paul twitched. "Say, if the police have been broadcasting a warning all this time, maybe we should call . . . ?"

"Call," said Rosemary with her hands clenched.

Virginia Severson showed Paul the telephone. Mr. Gibson surrendered himself to his chair; hope faded. All the magic belonged to the bus driver. The poison was still lost, still threatening.

The girl came back, biting her lips. "I am a nurse, you know," she said to them. "This . . . well, it shocks me."

"A man has his reasons," said Lee Coffey, gently. "It's easy to say he was crazy. It's also lazy."

Virginia Severson tilted her head and shot him a glance that was suddenly alert. "His reasons aren't the question, right now, are they?" she said. "I meant unlabeled poison, Mr. Coffey. Floating around. That's *shocking!* I'm trained to be careful with drugs."

"We'd like to find it, Miss Severson. We'd mighty like to find it," he drawled. His intent gaze was challenging.

"Of course, you would," she said. "*I* would, too." She seemed to feel the force of his challenge. "Let me try to think . . ." she said soberly and sat down, pulling the long blue wrapper around her pretty feet.

Paul came back and spoke reluctantly to Rosemary's yearning face. "Nothing." He looked nervous and defeated. "Not a word. It's three thirty. Where *is* that stuff?"

"It's somewhere," said Rosemary with a little gasp. "*Somewhere!*"

Mr. Gibson found himself pushing his imagination, too, trying to picture the bottle in the green bag . . . *somewhere*. But where?

"Rosie, this is too tough," said Paul. "I don't think we're accomplishing anything."

"Yes, we are. Be quiet," said Lee Coffey reverently, "Virginia is thinking." The nurse smiled at him. She had a lovely smile, and the bus driver let his face look fond.

"Lee . . ." said Rosemary, her voice ready to break, "Miss . . . Virginia. It's no time for . . ."

"We're not," said the bus driver quickly.

Mr. Gibson understood perfectly. But Paul Townsend didn't. His tall frame remained in the archway and his handsome face wore a lost expression as if to say, But what are you all talking about? Virginia had understood too, Mr. Gibson guessed, as her lids went down again. And Virginia *agreed*.

How remarkably quickly, thought Mr. Gibson, things *can* be communicated. Lee Coffey has told this girl he's long noticed her, has liked her looks, likes her now, and expects a good deal of her. And she has told him she is . . . not offended. She would even like to deserve his good opinion. She already knows this is an interesting man. Yet both of them resolve that they will not pursue this enchantment . . . that, first, they will help me if they can. A bus driver, he thought. A blonde. His eyes stung suddenly.

Nobody spoke. Until the little nurse said, at last, in her quiet unexcited voice, "There was somebody *I* know, on the bus. Would that help?"

"Oh yes, it might," cried Rosemary, jumping up. "Oh yes! Oh, good for you!"

"You see?" said Lee Coffey.

"Mrs. Boatright was on that bus," the nurse told them, getting to her feet. "Mrs. Boatright. I remember now, wondering how three or four cars could all be unavailable, at once. She had a heap of packages, too. On the bus. It seemed strange. She's so very wealthy . . . at least her husband is. She lives in a huge place on the hill. I'm sure it was she. I once met her at Red Cross headquarters."

"Walter Boatright . . ." Lee Coffey sprang up and dove into the hallway and came back with the phone book.

"But I'm afraid *she'd* have an unlisted number," Virginia said. "In fact, I know she has."

"*Know* what the number *is?*" The bus driver lowered the book.

"No. Sorry."

"Do you know the house?"

"Yes, but not the street number, either."

"Can't we go there?" Rosemary cried. And Paul half groaned and the bus driver looked at his blonde.

"You all start," Virginia said. She was already at a plain white door the far side of the room. "Don't wait. I'll catch you at the car."

Lee Coffey grinned and glanced at his watch, and then took Mr. Gibson by one wing. "Is she a blonde?" he murmured, almost carrying Mr. Gibson down the porch steps past the lilac bush. "Do you blame me?"

"She's a lovely blonde," said Mr. Gibson, overwhelmed. "This is so good of you."

"And all for money, too," said Rosemary tartly. "All for material advantage." Mr. Gibson looked at his wife, who had his other arm. Her blue eyes were bright.

"Listen, we got our teeth in it now," said Lee with enormous gusto.

"We're going to find it," said Rosemary.

Mr. Gibson could almost believe this.

Chapter Seventeen

THEY STUFFED HIM into the tonneau and Rosemary sprang in, too. She shoved over, and Lee Coffey, using nothing but an air of expectancy, stuffed Paul Townsend in at the other side of Rosemary. Then he slipped into the driver's seat and turned the key. The motor caught. The door of the house opened. Virginia skipped down the walk, wearing a brown jumper over a white blouse, brown pumps on her bare feet; her blond hair was neat and shining. The bus driver grinned and let the car move just as she slipped in beside him. He had not waited even one-tenth of a second. She had not failed him either.

Paul said admiringly, "That was a quick change!"

Nobody paid any attention to him. It would have been better not to have commented.

As the car moved, the little nurse began to describe the location of the house they were seeking, and Lee sent them spinning around the block, across the Boulevard, and on north. They were heading for a swelling slope in the northwest section of the town where lawns grew wider and houses larger as they stood higher on the hill. Mrs. Boatright's house, she said, would be close to the top, on a short street, where there were only three or four houses, and hers had vast lawns behind a wall.

"The higher the fewer, I guess," said Paul.

Virginia turned to look back. "Is there an antidote to this poison, Mr. Townsend?" she said in a professional kind of way.

"Paul," he suggested.

She smiled at him. "What ought to be done . . . in case . . . ?"

"I'm afraid I don't know of any antidote," Paul confessed, sliding forward in the seat, the other side of Rosemary. "Of course I'm no doctor. All we understand, in our business, is what the danger is. We're trained to be careful, too."

"How did he ever get hold of it?" the nurse frowned.

Paul told her. As Mr. Gibson listened, he began to know that Paul Townsend was projecting himself somehow and being quite skillfully charming to this most attractive little person. Mr. Gibson found himself curiously affronted.

He looked at Rosemary, dear Rosemary, who sat still between them with her hands clenched . . . whose resolution was their strength, who had begun this fight and fired them all from her own spirit and collected these valiant lieutenants.

He said, "What a fighter you are, Rosemary!"

"I am a rabbit," she said bitterly. "I was always a rabbit. I should have begun to fight long, long ago."

Paul turned and covered her tense hands with one of his. "Now, now, Rosie . . . try to take it easy. You'll make yourself sick. Worry doesn't help any, does it, Virginia?"

The nurse did not answer. The bus driver said, "She's getting a lot of mileage out of her worry. Hey, Rosemary?"

"Yes, thank you," said Rosemary, rather forlornly, collapsing a little from her rigidity. Paul took his hand away. "I'm worrying now," she said, "trying to imagine a wealthy woman picking up a strange package on a public bus. I don't suppose she would."

"She might," said the nurse brightly. "By mistake, you see? Suppose she gathered it up with the other packages she was carrying. I didn't see her get off. I got off first. But who can say? And suppose she had things to eat in her own packages? She might dump them all in the kitchen. And she surely has servants. Her cook, for instance, wouldn't *know*. Her cook might think Mrs. Boatright had meant to bring home some olive oil."

"A *little* bottle?" said Rosemary pathetically. "A very *small* quantity? What time is it?"

"Three thirty-seven," Paul told her.

"It's still early, anyhow," said Rosemary, with a desperate smile. But Mr. Gibson thought, It's late. He thought of time gone by. Time enough for someone to have died already and very mysteriously, too. So that the news of the result might not yet have caught up with the cause. This fight might already have been lost, for all they knew.

"The Boatright kids are in their teens," said the nurse thoughtfully. "They certainly wouldn't be fed their supper this early."

"Olive oil?" said Rosemary. "What would a cook *do* with it?"

The nurse said, "Salad? Oh . . . to moisten a sandwich filling . . . possibly for a snack . . ."

"Don't *say* that!" said Paul.

The nurse said, "I guess I'm helping her worry."

". . . Resembles thought," muttered the bus driver.

But Mr. Gibson was appalled. A child! Oh, if a child were to get the poison! He said aloud, "All of you ought to leave me. You are very good to trouble yourselves—"

"No trouble," said Virginia. Mr. Gibson discovered that he believed her. "I believe you," he said to her in surprise and she smiled.

"Don't worry," Paul began.

"Stop saying that," said Rosemary quietly. "It doesn't help, Paul."

"I told you, Rosie," he said rather crossly, "you ought to have talked to him, laid things on the line . . ."

"You did. You told me. You were right," said Rosemary, looking straight ahead. "Yes, Paul." Her hands twitched.

"You musta seen something brewing, Rosemary," the bus driver said sympathetically, not quite understanding. He hadn't the background. "A man doesn't decide in a day."

(But I did, mused Mr. Gibson, wonderingly. In a night. I seemed to.)

"Have you been ill, Mr. Gibson?" the nurse asked, "or taking drugs for pain? I see you limping."

Mr. Gibson was bewildered. (His heart hurt. He wasn't dead at all.) "A broken bone or two," he murmured. "Just an accident." Rosemary turned her face to look at his. He looked away.

"I only wondered," said Virginia gently. "There *are* illnesses that can be very depressing. And some drugs, too."

Mr. Gibson, gazing at a curb whizzing by, thought *Doom*, yes. Here comes doom, again.

"I was depressed," he said without spirit. "That's a name for it."

"If you had only seen a doctor," the nurse scolded him delicately, with her soft regret. "So often a doctor can help these depressed feelings."

"By a little tinkering in the machinery?" said Mr. Gibson rather bitterly.

"They do know how to help sometimes," the nurse said, rather mechanically. She seemed to be tasting, perhaps diagnosing this answer.

"You go for this psychosomatic stuff?" inquired the bus driver abruptly.

"Don't you?" she said.

"Long ago," he declaimed, "long ago *I* threw a whole bunch of arbitrary distinctions outa my head. Either—or. Body or mind. Matter or spirit. Hah! *Now* it turns out matter is *less* solid than spirit, far as I can figure what they're talking. Nothing's any more ungross than the human body. Or a chair, either. Zillions of cells— atoms and subdivisions of same—whizzing around, and . . . *they* made outa what? Waves. Rhythms. Time itself, for all we know. Caution to the jaybirds," he concluded.

Virginia laughed out loud, delightedly.

But Mr. Gibson was on his way down for the second time. *Doom*, he said to himself, and aloud, "I suppose I was ill. At least that's a name for what I was."

"*Now*," said Virginia. "Look, we are so ignorant."

"Yes, we are ignorant," said Rosemary gladly.

"Anybody who knows anything at all about medical science—or any other, I guess—only *begins* to know how ignorant we are," said Virginia. She looked brightly back at Mr. Gibson. She expected him to be glad.

"Where there's life there's hope, you mean?" said Paul. He seemed to think he was joining in.

The nurse frowned. Her small chin was almost resting upon the back of the front seat as she sat twisted around to talk to them. "I meant we know enough to know there's an *awful* lot more to be found out. We do know just a little bit about how to find it. Don't you *see*, Mr. Gibson? There are people looking for ways to help all the time and they've found some. I've seen. Nobody knows what they *might* find out by tomorrow morning. You should have asked for help," she chided.

"So should I," said Rosemary not very loudly.

Mr. Gibson didn't reply. He was busy perceiving something odd. It was hard to fit into the structure of doom. That was what was odd about it. Say the individual is depressed because of his internal chemistry, call it his machinery. *Even so.* He is not *quite* doomed . . . not if his fellow men, men who hold their minds open because they humbly know their ignorance . . . not if these have discovered even *some* helpful things to do for him. And this was strange, a strange weakness—wasn't it?—in the huge hard jaws of doom.

"That's funny," he said aloud.

Nobody asked him what he meant and he did not tell. The car slid up a tree-lined street and all the passengers were silent for a block.

Then Paul fidgeted. "I should have called home. I wonder if Jeanie got back . . . and Mama's O.K."

"It must be nearly four o'clock," said Rosemary. "Ethel will be home." She lifted her head; it was almost as if she tossed it haughtily.

Ethel! Gibson felt shocked. What would Ethel say? He couldn't even imagine. Absolutely nothing that had happened since eleven o'clock this morning had made Ethel's kind of sense.

"*I* don't think he was ill," the bus driver blurted. "*I* think he was shook."

Virginia tilted her head to look at him respectfully.

"To his foundations," said the bus driver.

"But everybody loved him," said Rosemary, and raised her clenched hands like a desperate prayer.

"Why sure, everybody thought a hell of a lot of Gibson," said Paul indignantly, as if Mr. Gibson had offended unpardonably.

"Everybody?" said the bus driver ruminatively. "Now, let's not promise candy."

"Candy?" said the nurse with curiosity.

"He had *something* on his mind; it wasn't hardly just missing the brotherly love of his fellow man," said Lee. "Hey? And look, honeybunch," he said to his blonde, "we are now on Hathaway Drive, so where's this mansion?"

"It's the white Colonial," said Virginia.

Rosemary said, "Maybe the poison is here."

Mr. Gibson was a chip in a current. He got out of the car with all the rest of them.

They had pulled up within the wall, in the wide spot where the drive curved before the pillared entrance. The wide and spanking-white façade looked down upon them, and all the exquisite ruffles of the dainty window curtains announced that here money, and many hired hands, made order.

Now Virginia took the lead. She rang the bell. A maidservant opened the door. "Is Mrs. Boatright here? We must see her quickly. It's very important." Virginia's crisp grave manner was impressive.

The maid said, "Come in, please," looking as unsurprised as she was able. She left them standing on the oriental rug of the wide foyer. To their left was a huge room. A pair of saddle oxfords hung over the arm of a gray-and-yellow couch, which shoes wiggled, being attached to a pair of young feet. There must be a girl, flat on her back on the sofa. She was talking. There was no one else in there. She must be talking on the telephone.

A boy, about sixteen years old, came in a jumping gallop down the broad stairs. "Oh, hi!" said he, and romped off to their right, where there was another room, and a lot of books and a piano. The boy snatched up a horn and they heard some melancholy toots receding.

Then Mrs. Walter Boatright, in person, sailed out of a white door under the stairs. She was about five and a half feet tall and about two and a half feet wide. Every ounce under the beige-cotton-and-white-lace was firm. She had short white hair, nicely waved, and a thin nose made a prow for the well-fleshed face. Her eyes were blue (although not so blue as Rosemary's) and they were simply interested. "Yes? Oh, Miss Severson. How do you do?"

Virginia gave a little start at being called her own name, but she omitted any more preliminaries. "I saw you on a bus, today, ma'am . . ."

"I'm so sorry," cut in Mrs. Boatright, her words mechanical, while her eyes still inquired and expected. "Had I seen *you*, my dear . . ."

The little nurse brushed this aside. "Please. Did you pick up a small green paper bag by mistake?"

"I doubt it," said Mrs. Boatright, accepting the abrupt manner as urgency without showing a ripple in her poise. "Now shall we just see?" She turned. Her bulk moved with surprising ease and grace. "Mona."

Mona turned out to be the maid.

"Ask Geraldine if I brought in a small green paper bag."

"Yes, Mrs. Boatright."

"What is in the bag?" inquired the lady of the house of her callers.

Virginia told her.

Mrs. Boatright compressed her lips. "Yes, I see. This is serious," said she. "Dell." The girl on the phone bobbed up, using the muscles at her waist, and said, "Hold on a sec, Christy. Yes, Ma?"

"Put up the phone," said Mrs. Boatright. "We'll need it. Get Tom. Tell him to search his car carefully for a small green paper bag with a bottle in it."

"Yes, Ma. . . . Call you back, Christy. Bye now."

"My son picked me up at the bus stop," said Mrs. Boatright in explanation, meanwhile sailing toward the phone.

The girl, Dell, who was perhaps eighteen, went across before them in a gait like dancing. Her eyes were curious but smiling.

A woman in a blue uniform came out of the white door. "No ma'am," said she. "No green paper bag in the kitchen at all."

"Thank you, Geraldine," said Mrs. Boatright and then into the phone, "The police, if you please?" She said to the five of them, who all stood speechless watching her operate, "Which of you is Mr. Gibson?"

Mr. Gibson felt himself being pointed out from all sides. He stood in a dream, not miserable enough, but rather guiltily fascinated.

"Police?" said Mrs. Boatright. "Has the poison in the olive oil been located yet? . . . Thank you." Mrs. Boatright put the phone up and wasted no more time than she had words. "Not yet," she said. "Yes, you *were* on the bus with me. Now, what can I do?"

"It's been a chain," said Rosemary, quivering between disappointment and hope. "The driver remembered *her*. *She* remembered *you*."

"And I," said Mrs. Boatright (who had not yet said "Oh dear" or "How terrible") "remember Theo Marsh." She nodded and held them in order with a kind of invisible gavel. "But, first, let's be *sure*."

"Not a thing in my car, Ma," said the boy, Tom, reappearing. He looked at the group with curiosity but did not ask questions. "Who . . . ?"

"Marsh?"

"Where . . . ?"

Mrs. Boatright rapped the air for order. "The only way to reach Theo Marsh that I know of," said she, "is to drive out there. He has no phone in his studio. The man isolates himself to work." She saw their ignorance. "He is the painter, of course."

"Where is this studio?" asked Lee and added, "madame?"

"Can I describe it to the police, I wonder?" Mrs. Boatright gathered her brows.

"Can't we *go?*" said Rosemary. "We've already been so far. It's better than waiting . . ."

"Might be quicker," Lee said, "surer."

Mrs. Boatright said, "As a matter of fact, it might be wiser. Theo Marsh might, just whimsically, lie low and refuse to admit a policeman. But he knows me." One felt nobody could lie low, if Mrs. Boatright chose otherwise. "Now," the lady turned lightly on her heel, "both Cadillacs are at the garage and won't be available 'til six o'clock. Walter was forced to take Dell's car. It seems, Tom, we must use yours."

The boy looked as dashed as if his mother had proposed removing his trousers to lend them to a tramp.

"We have a car, madame," the bus driver said, his sandy lashes somehow admiring her, "and there's still half a tank of gas in her."

"And an excellent driver," Virginia said.

"Very well," said Mrs. Boatright. "Mona, bring me my tan jacket, please, and my bag." She made another of her swift turns. "Meantime, Tom, search the house for a bottle of olive oil in a green paper bag. By no means touch the contents. It is poison. Geraldine, serve dinner at six-thirty; I may be late. Dell . . ." (The girl was back.) "Call your father. Say I am called away. At seven, if I am not here, call Mr. Coster of the Board of Education and say I am unavoidably detained. Call Mrs. Peters and tell her I may not have the lists for her until tomorrow. Apologize." She took her jacket from the hands of the maid who had hopped to do as she was bidden. "Let's go," said Mrs. Walter Boatright. She sailed out of her front door and the five of them straggled along in her wake.

The bus driver got under the wheel and tucked his blonde beside him and Paul got into the right front seat.

Mrs. Boatright let Rosemary go first into the tonneau while she turned and said to her son, "Keep Dell off the phone. I may call."

"Gosh, Ma, give me something easy," the boy said.

His mother flipped her hand farewell and she got in and Mr. Gibson, last, beside her.

"Where to?" said the bus driver respectfully.

"Go out the Boulevard," said Mrs. Boatright, "all the way to the end of the bus line. Theo Marsh has a studio in the country. Quite a hideaway. But I believe I know the turn. If not, we can inquire at the junction."

The car was moving already.

"I don't just remember anybody who looked like a *painter*," Lee said, "getting off the end of the line. You mean, a fine-art-type painter?"

"If he got off sooner," said Mrs. Boatright, "we cannot know where he was heading, and there is no use wondering about it. We must go on what we know."

"Sure thing," said Lee. "That's abso-tootly right."

"Very rustic, that studio," Mrs. Boatright continued. "The man's a fine painter, yes. But I'm just afraid . . ."

"Afraid?" Rosemary's voice sounded tired. Mr. Gibson couldn't see her now. Not with Mrs. Boatright in the middle.

"If Theo Marsh, of all people, found a bottle of olive oil on a bus . . . I assume it *was* imported?"

"Yes," said Mr. Gibson.

"*He* would accept it joyously, as a gift from the gods, and he, and that model of his, would add it to some feast or other with no hesitation. What a loss it would be!" said Mrs. Boatright. "A fine artist! We can't spare *them*."

"What time is it?" asked Rosemary tensely.

"Only four o'clock . . . just about one minute after," Paul told them. "Too early for supper."

"Alas," said Mrs. Boatright, "I imagine Theo Marsh will eat when he is hungry. I doubt if the man has names for meals."

"Is it very far?" asked Rosemary pathetically.

"Thirty minutes," promised Lee Coffey. "Do *I* know that boulevard!"

The car picked up its heels and scooted rapidly down curving streets.

"Now what's all this," said Mrs. Boatright severely, "about suicide?"

Mr. Gibson put his hand over his eyes.

"Ever since Ethel came," said Rosemary passionately. "Ever since *she* came! I don't know what she's done to him. I was too upset by what she did to me."

"You are his wife, my dear?"

"Yes, I am," said Rosemary as defiantly as if somebody else had claimed the title.

"And our driver is the driver of the bus, is he not?" Mrs. Boatright was proceeding with order, ignoring outbursts. "And the other gentleman?"

"I am their neighbor," said Paul. "Townsend is my name."

"And our friend," said Rosemary with a forced sweetness as if she were struggling to keep polite and calm.

"And Miss Severson was a passenger?" Mrs. Boatright sailed right on. "Does anyone remember the tale of the Golden Goose?"

"Hey!" said the bus driver. "Sure, I remember. Everybody who takes ahold has to tag along. That's pretty good, Mrs. Boatright."

"But who is Ethel?" Mrs. Boatright had come around a curve and would have all clear.

"Ethel," said Rosemary in a desperately even tone, "is Kenneth's sister, a good woman, a fine person, who came here to help and to take care of us, after we had an accident . . ." Her voice rose. "I shouldn't have said what I did. But I can't—I cannot be grateful any more. It's no time to be grateful. It just doesn't count any more." The strain was telling and Rosemary began to cry. "This terrible trouble and it's getting late and I'd so *hate* it to be an artist . . . way out in the country and no help nearby . . ."

Mr. Gibson, too, could see, ahead of them, a rustic studio strewn with bodies.

"There wouldn't be much help," said Paul miserably. "That stuff works fast."

"Now, we'll see, when we get there," said Mrs. Boatright, "and not before. Mr. Coffey is making the best possible time. We are doing the best possible thing."

"It's so long . . ." wept Rosemary.

So Mrs. Boatright, who was in equal parts mother *and* commanding officer, took Rosemary to her bosom and began to stroke her hair. Mr. Gibson felt a tremendous relief. He blessed Mrs. Boatright. The three heads in the front seat were still, facing forward.

"Gratitude," said the bus driver suddenly, "is for the birds. There's all kinds of ins and outs to this, Mrs. Boatright, and we don't know the half of them. But this Ethel—see, Mrs. Boatright?—she puts it into Rosemary's head that Rosemary meant to get him smashed up in an auto accident, which is why he is limping, did you notice? Well, this Ethel, she's got poor Rosemary feeling guilty as hell because she was driving at the time, although it was a pure and simple accident . . . but this Ethel she's the kind who knows better than you do what your real motives were, see? And Rosemary thinks she shouldn't get mad at Ethel, because this Ethel shows up to help and all and besides this Ethel is her sister-in-law and I don't guess Rosemary *likes* squabbling with the relatives. Some people thrive on that. Hey? Some people make a career out of it."

"I see. I see," said Mrs. Boatright, stopping his flow. "Had you seen much of this sister-in-law before?"

"Never," wailed Rosemary.

"Let her cry," said Virginia. "Cry hard, Rosemary."

Paul squirmed. "Look . . . she can't take much more of this . . ."

"It's high time she bawled her head off," the nurse said fiercely. "And Mr. Gibson, too."

But Mr. Gibson sat, dry-eyed and amazed.

"I'm sorry . . ." sobbed Rosemary. "It isn't really Ethel, herself. I know that. But it's her ideas. It's the way she thinks. And what can you do? I know I'm a rabbit but, even if you aren't a rabbit, how can you fight that kind of thing? I've told myself . . . I've told her . . . I couldn't have meant it. But the idea is, *I* wouldn't know if I had! I'd be the *last* to know! And how can you argue with somebody who just turns everything you say *around?* Who just makes you feel as if every time you opened your mouth you were giving some horrible inner beastly self away? If you insist, *she* thinks Aha, you protest too much! So you *must* really mean the exact *opposite.* If you talk loud, because you feel so strongly that you're right . . . why, a loud voice means you must be trying to sell yourself a lie. It's maddening," said Rosemary. "You can't *know* anything. You can't trust yourself, at all."

Doomed, said Mr. Gibson in his throat or his mind. Nobody seemed to hear him.

"What I'd like to know," said Lee Coffey angrily, "is who gives this Ethel her license to read minds. Hey? *I'd* give Rosemary a fifty-fifty chance to know, as well as Ethel, what Rosemary means by what she says."

"No, you *can't*," wept Rosemary. "You're the *last*. That's the paralyzing thing!"

The nurse said some angry syllable under her breath. The driver's head agreed savagely.

"Gratitude," said Mrs. Boatright, rhythmically stroking Rosemary's hair with one plump jeweled hand, "lasts on, for a time, after the deed that caused it. But it's like a fire, don't you think so? It's lit, it burns, it's warm. But it needs fuel. It doesn't last forever unless it's fed."

Mrs. Boatright was making a speech. She had a clear voice and she knew how to breathe and she could be rather eloquent. Even Rosemary stopped her weeping noises to listen.

"No one should be the prisoner of stale gratitude—to change and also *mix* the metaphor," declaimed Mrs. Boatright. "I think of the children in this world, enslaved by parents trading on gratitude for old deeds that should have been done for love only in the first place. I think of parents who have become, in fact, whining nuisances that flesh-and-blood rightfully resents and yet blood, that is thicker than water, scourges itself for resenting. I shudder at so much unhappiness. Gratitude can be a dreadful thing when it becomes a debt—you see?—and there is guilt and reluctance. But if, by continued feeding, faith is created, and mutual respect is accumulated and confidence grows, in love, in friendship, then gratitude turns into something better. And something durable." She paused and one expected the pattering of ladies' hands over the luncheon tables. Here was only the rushing sound of the car, and Rosemary saying, "I know . . ." in a choking voice.

"If parents, for instance," said Mrs. Boatright, wistfully, in a more private kind of voice, "could only grow up to be their children's friends . . . Have you children, my dear?"

Paul said hastily, almost in alarm, "They've only been married . . . less than three months . . ."

There was a silence, deep . . . except for the sounds of the car's progress.

Lee Coffey said in a moment, "Is that so? I didn't know that."

"A bride and a groom," said Virginia slowly, her voice caressing the words sadly.

The news was sinking into the fabric of all their speculations, dyeing everything to different colors. Mr. Gibson felt like crying out, No, you don't understand. It was only a silly, unrealistic arrangement. And I am fifty-five. She is thirty-two. It leaves twenty-three.

He cried out nothing.

Mrs. Boatright turned and said to him, "Rosemary finds your sister difficult. Rosemary has been unhappy. But Rosemary wasn't the one who stole the poison, was she?"

"No," he said. "No."

"Then what was the matter with *you?*" she asked.

He couldn't answer.

Paul turned around. "You certainly raised the devil," he said. "You might have been a little bit thoughtful of Rosie at least. *And* Ethel. And *me*, for that matter. If you'd thought of others and not yourself . . ."

"He does think of others," said Rosemary faintly.

"Not today, he didn't," said Paul, "and what he did was a sin." He jerked his head to look forward. The back of his neck was righteous and furious.

"'Oh . . . that the Everlasting had not fixed His canon 'gainst self-slaughter . . .'" crooned the bus driver. "That's what you mean, hey?"

"You know what I mean."

"Yes, but that's *our* culture," said the bus driver. "You take Japan . . ."

"*You* take Japan," said Paul, sulkily.

Mrs. Boatright, who had a way of going back and clearing up one thing at a time, said, "I serve with the Red Cross, the Board of Education, the Society for the Encouragement of the U.N., the Council for Juvenile Welfare, the American Women for Political Housecleaning, and the church, of course, and I work in these groups. But not for 'others.' Isn't this *my* world? And while I am here, *my* business?" She conquered her oratorical impulses. "There is a weakness about that word 'others,'" she said privately, "and I never have liked it."

"It's not definitive," snapped Virginia. "Show me one patient. *An* other."

"The odds ain't good," said Lee Coffey ruminatively. "Couple of billion 'others'; only one of you. You *can't* take an interest, except pretty vague and slightly phony, in the whole caboodle of 'em."

"Quite so," said Mrs. Boatright genially. "You can only start from where you are."

"Although once you get into this business," said Virginia softly, "you are led on."

"One thing comes after another," agreed the bus driver, and the nurse looked at him, with that quick alert tilt of her head again.

"Do you get paid, Mrs. Boatright?" said Rosemary, straightening up suddenly.

"Of course not." Mrs. Boatright was scandalized.

"You see? She's just a parasite," said Rosemary, half hysterically.

"Hey!" crowed Lee Coffey. "That sounds like good old Ethel to me. Ethel says any dame whose old man has got dough is just a parasite? I'll betcha she does. So she never met a high-powered executive like Mrs. B. I'm telling you, this Ethel has got everything bass-ackward. Hey, what was it she said about blondes? You never did tell me."

"Blondes," said Rosemary clearly, "are predatory nitwits."

"Are-ent they, though?" said Lee to his nurse fondly. "Aren't they just? *All* of 'em. This means you, too, honeybunch. You and your definitive, your patient." He chuckled. "Oh boy, you know, that's Ethel's trouble, right there? She starts out with 'some,' slides into 'many,' and don't notice herself skidding right off the rails into 'all.'"

"Ethel's a pain in the neck," said Paul grumpily. "I told you, Rosie, the day she sent you into a fit—"

"Ethel," put in Mrs. Boatright thoughtfully, "is beginning to sound like a scapegoat."

Mr. Gibson stirred himself and said rather sharply, "Yes. And you are all so very kind to be pro-me; I can't think why. . . . But I'd like to get this straight, please. *I* stole the poison. *I* meant to die. *I* stupidly, criminally, left it on the bus. *I* am responsible, guilty, wrong, and totally to blame." He *knew* this to be true.

"Yes," said the bus driver in a moment, thoughtfully, "when you come right down to it, *sure* you are."

But Mr. Gibson was thinking dizzily . . . Yes, but if I am to blame, there was freedom. I could have done otherwise. Without freedom, there is no blame. And vice versa. His brain swam. I don't know, he thought, I thought I knew but I don't know.

"Not a lot of use in blame, though," the bus driver was saying. "It shouldn't linger. You shouldn't blow on *them* ashes, hey, Mrs. B.?"

"Make a note of an error," said that matron briskly, "for future reference . . . but file it. Now, Rosemary, powder your nose and put on some lipstick and brace up. Theo Marsh may very well be lost in some masterpiece with the thought of nourishment far, far from his mind. It would be quite like him."

"I haven't got a lipstick," wailed Rosemary.

"Use mine," said Virginia warmly.

"Put a good face on it, girls," said the bus driver tolerantly. "A man, he takes a shave . . ."

Mr. Gibson saw Paul Townsend rubbing his jaw.

The whole thing struck him. The six of them, this heterogeneous crew, hurtling out into the country on a guess and a prayer, and conversing so fantastically.

Mr. Gibson heard a rusty chuckle coming out of him. "You know," he said, "this is remarkable?"

Not a one of them agreed. He felt all their eyes, Lee's in the rear-vision mirror, Virginia's and Paul's turning back, Mrs. Boatright's at his side, Rosemary peering around her. All the eyes said, What do you mean? Not at all!

"Are we getting there?" said Rosemary.

"We are," said Mrs. Boatright.

When they passed the place where the yellow bus had been left, on the road's shoulder, it was gone. Lee said, "Hey, I wonder am I fired?" No one could tell him, and since he had sounded merely, and rather merrily, curious to know, no one tried to console him, either.

After a while Mrs. Boatright said, "It's a dirt road. Going off to the right a few yards beyond the junction. The house is wood, stained brown, and it sits on a knoll."

"I can *see* a house like that," said Virginia. "Look. Is that it? Up there?"

Chapter Eighteen

THE LOW STRUCTURE on the high knoll looked not only rustic but abandoned. The front wall was blank. Weeds grew up to the doorstep. On a narrow terrace of old brick, overrun by wild grass, a few dilapidated redwood outdoor chairs sat at careless angles, their cushions faded and torn. A cat leaped out of one of these and fled into the wilderness.

No sound, no sign of life came from this building.

Mrs. Boatright rapped smartly.

Without sound, the door swung inward. They could see directly into a huge room and the north and opposite wall was glass, so that this space was flooded with clear and steady light. The first thing Mr. Gibson saw was a body.

The body was that of a female in a long flaring skirt of royal blue *and nothing else*. It was lying on a headless couch. As he blinked his dazzled eyes, it sat up. The naked torso writhed. It was alive.

A man's living voice said, "What have we here? Mary Anne Boatright! Well! Is this a club?"

The torso was pulling on a loose white T-shirt, slightly ragged at the shoulder seams. It went strangely with the rich silk of the skirt and the skirt's gold-embroidered hem.

"This is important," said Mrs. Boatright, "or I wouldn't disturb you, Theo."

"I should hope it is," said the voice. "It better be. Never mind. I'm tired. I just decided. Put your shirt on, Lavinia."

"I did, already," said the girl or woman on the couch who was sitting there like a lump, now. She turned her bare feet until they rested pigeon-toed, one over the other. Her eyes were huge and dark and placid as a cow's.

Mr. Gibson tore his gaze away from her to see this man.

"Theodore Marsh," said Mrs. Boatright formally, but rapidly. "This is Mrs. Gibson, Miss Severson, Mr. Gibson, Mr. Townsend, Mr. Coffey."

"You don't look like a club," said the painter. "What are you? I've surely seen several of you before, somewhere."

He was tall and skinny as a scarecrow. He wore tweed trousers, a pink shirt, and a black vest. His hair was pure white and it looked as if it had never been brushed but remained in a state of nature, like fur. His face was wizened and shrewd, his hands knobby. He must have been seventy.

He was full of energy. He moved, flippety-flop, all angles, beckoning them in. He had yellow teeth, all but three, which were too white to match the rest, and obviously false. His grin made one think of an ear of corn peculiarly both white and golden. He certainly had not been poisoned.

"Did you find a bottle of olive oil?" Rosemary attacked in a rush.

"Not I. Sit," he said. "Explain."

Mr. Gibson sat down, feeling weak and breathless. The nurse

and the bus driver sat down, side by side. Paul remained standing, for his manners. His eyes avoided the sight of the model's bare feet.

Mrs. Boatright, standing, her corsets firm, told the painter the story succinctly and efficiently. Rosemary, by her side, punctuated all she said with wordless gestures of anxiety.

Theo Marsh subdued his energy long enough to listen quickly, somehow. He got the situation into his mind, whole and fast.

"Yes, I was on a bus. Took it in front of the public library late this morning. You the driver? I did not study your face."

"Few do." Lee shrugged.

"Can you help us?" interrupted Rosemary impatiently. "Did you see a green paper bag, Mr. Marsh? Or did you see who took it?"

The artist took his gaze off the bus driver and put it upon Rosemary. He leaned his head sharply to the right as if to see how she would look upside down. "I may have seen it," he said calmly. "I see a lot. I'll tell you, in a minute. Let me get the pictures back."

Mrs. Boatright took a throne. At least she deposited her weight upon a chair so regally that it might as well have been one.

"You, with the worries and the graceful backbone," the painter said, "sit down. And don't wiggle. I despise wiggling women. I must not be distracted, mind."

Rosemary sat down in the only remaining place, on the couch beside the model. She sat . . . and her spine *was* graceful . . . as still as a mouse.

(Mouse, thought Mr. Gibson. Oh, how have we come here, you and I, who surely meant no harm?)

Six of them, plus the model Lavinia, all stared solemnly at Theo Marsh. He enjoyed this. *He* didn't seat himself. He moved, flippety-flop, all elbows and angles, up and down.

"G-green," stammered Mr. Gibson.

"Green?" the painter sneered. "Look out the window."

Mr. Gibson looked, blinked, said, "Yes?"

"There are at least thirty-five different and distinct greens framed there. I know. I counted. I put them on canvas. So tell me, what color was the bag?"

"It was a kind of . . ." said Mr. Gibson feebly. "—well, green-ish . . ."

"They have eyes and see not," mourned the painter. "All right." He began to act like a machine gun, shooting words.

"Pine green?"

"No."

"Yellow green? Chartreuse? You've heard of that?"

"No. It wasn't—"

"Grass green?"

"No."

"Kelly green?"

"Theo," said Mrs. Boatright warningly.

"Am I showing off, Mary Anne?" The painter grinned.

"Yes," said Mrs. Boatright.

"Well then, truce to that." The painter shrugged. "Well then, gray green?"

"Y-yes," said Mr. Gibson, struggling. "Palish, dullish . . ."

"In other words, paper-bag green," said the painter, amiably. "Of course." He rambled to the left and stopped still and looked blind. "I sat on the left side of the bus," he said dreamily. "For the first ten minutes I examined a hat. What blossoms! Watermelon shade. Nine petals, which is *un*likely. Well, to proceed. I saw you . . . the man there with the good eyes. That can't tell one green from another."

"Me?" squeaked Mr. Gibson.

"A man of sorrows, thought I," the painter continued. "Oh yes, you did have in your left hand a gray-green paper bag."

Mr. Gibson began to tremble.

"I watched you a while. How I envied you your youth and your sorrow! I said to myself, this man is really living!"

Mr. Gibson thought one of them must have gone mad!

The artist's eyes slid under half-drawn lids. "I saw you put the paper bag down on the seat." The eyes were nearly closed now, and yet watched. "You took a small black-covered notebook out of your pocket . . ."

"I . . . did?"

"You produced a gold ball-point pen, about five inches long, and you wrote—brooded—wrote . . ."

"I did!" Mr. Gibson began to feel all his pockets.

"Then you got to brooding so bad you forgot to write. I lost interest. Nothing more to see, you know. Besides, I discovered an ear without a lobe, two seats ahead of me."

Rosemary had jumped up. She stood over Mr. Gibson as he drew his little pocket notebook out and flipped the pages. Yes, pen marks. He looked at what he had written on the bus. "Rosemary . . . Rosemary . . . Rosemary." Nothing but her name three times. That was all.

"Trying . . . a letter to you," he stammered, and looked up.

Rosemary's eyes were enigmatic . . . perhaps sad. She shook her head slightly, walked slowly back to the couch and sat down. Lavinia changed her feet, and put the top one underneath.

"I saw *you*, Mary Anne," the painter said, "and pretended not. I lay low. Forgive me, but I didn't want to be snared and exhibited."

"I saw *you*, you know," said Mrs. Boatright calmly, "or we wouldn't be here. Had nowhere to exhibit you, profitably, at the moment."

"You lay low?" The painter sighed. "Ships in the night. I am a vain man, amn't I? Well, let's see. Let's *see*."

"The paper bag?" pressed Rosemary.

"Quiet, now," the painter's eyes roved. "Ah yes, the heart-shaped face. Saw *you*."

"Me?" said Virginia.

"On the right side, well forward?"

"Yes."

"Where you could turn those gentle eyes where you liked," said the painter, mischievously.

Virginia's face turned a deep soft pink. Lee Coffey's ears stood up.

"I didn't try to see whether *he* was looking sly at you. Perhaps in the mirror?" said the painter and swung to the driver. "*Were* you?"

"Me!" exploded Lee, and then softly, "Me?"

"Theo," said Mrs. Boatright severely, "you are showing off again. And behaving like a bad little boy."

"I don't care to have her embarrassed," said the bus driver stiffly. "Get on to the subject, the poison."

The painter flapped both hands. "Don't mind me," he said irritably. "I see things. I can't help it." (The bus driver picked up the nurse's hand in his, although neither of them seemed aware of this or looked at each other.) The painter clasped his hands behind him and arched his thin ribcase and teetered on his toes. "There was that ear . . ."

"*Whose* ear?" demanded Rosemary fiercely.

"Can't say. All I noticed *was* the ear. We could advertise. Wait a minute . . . Didn't Mary Anne say your name is *Gibson?*"

"Yes."

"Then somebody spoke to you."

"Did they? Why, yes," said Mr. Gibson. "Yes, that's true. Somebody said my name, twice. Once while I waited. Once, just as I was getting off. *Somebody knew me.*" He was suddenly excited.

"Who, Kenneth? Who?"

He shook his head. "I . . . don't know," he said with shame. "I paid no attention."

"He was sunk," said the painter nodding vigorously, looking like a turkeycock, his wattles shaking. "He was *sunk*. I noticed that."

"Did you notice who spoke to him?" Rosemary demanded.

The painter looked dashed. "Darned if I did," he said with chagrin. "I'm so eye-minded. Oh, I heard. But I made no picture of the speaker. I did not connect. However . . ." He paused in vanity until all of them were waiting on him. "I believe I did see somebody pick up the paper bag."

"Who?"

"Who?"

"Who?"

They exploded like popcorn.

"A young woman. A mere girl. A very handsome young female," the painter said. "I was looking at her face. But I do believe she picked up that greenish paper bag and carried it off the bus. Yes."

"When?"

"After he got off, just after. I was driven back to the ear by default."

"Who was she?"

The painter shrugged. "I'd know her," he said, "but I'd have to see her. Names, labels, mean nothing to me."

"Where did she get off?"

"Oh, not many blocks after . . ." Distance meant nothing to him, either.

"Was she dark?" said Paul Townsend, tensely.

"I suppose you mean . . . to put it crudely . . . was her hair of a darkish color? Yes."

"Jeanie!" cried Paul. "Oh Lord, oh God, it could have been Jeanie. Where's your telephone?"

"No telephone," said Mrs. Boatright. "Who is Jeanie?"

Paul had moved into the center somehow. He was tall and angry. He glared at everyone. He was a raging lion.

"But Paul," said Rosemary, "what makes you think it could be Jeanie?"

"Because she went to her music lesson, just about *then*. Her teacher is out on the Boulevard. She *could* have got on as he got off. *She* knew him. *She* would have spoken. She *might* have taken his empty seat. Jeanie!" Paul's handsome face contorted.

"Who is Jeanie?" the painter wanted to know.

"My daughter!" yelled Paul. "My daughter!"

"But if Jeanie saw *him* . . ." Rosemary frowned and concentrated.

"How could she know where he'd been sitting? How could she know it was him," said Paul, losing control of his grammar in his agitation, "who left the poison? Maybe she . . . Oh, no!" Paul groaned. "Jeanie's got sense. Jeanie's a darned sensible kid. You all know that," he appealed pitifully. "But I got to call home. If anything's happened to Mama! Oh no, oh Lord . . . I've got to get to a phone. She was *pretty*, you say?"

The painter said, "She was lovely." His eyes were watching. "Not quite the same thing."

"Jeanie is lovely. That's sure. I'm getting out of here." Paul was beside himself. "Listen, Mama likes her supper early. Jeanie will be fixing Mama's supper too soon now. It's getting on to five o'clock. I got to call. If Mama were to get that poison, what would I do?"

"Mama?" Mrs. Boatright raised her brows at the Gibsons.

"His mother-in-law," said Rosemary rather awesomely. "An old lady . . . a crippled old lady . . ."

"She may be old but she's lived long enough to know something," raved Paul, as upset as anyone had ever seen him. "She's raised my Jeanie—raised *me*, if you want to know the truth. She's a wonderful old lady, God love her. . . . The whole house depends on her. I could *never* have gone on without her, when Frances died . . . Listen, I'm very sorry but I have to get going and it's my . . . well, my car."

"Mr. Marsh," said Rosemary, springing up, "could it possibly be his daughter?"

"Could be," said Theo Marsh. "No resemblance."

"Jeanie looks like her dead mother," cried Paul. "Not a bit like me. Listen, I'll take you all back into town, but you'll have to come *now*."

"I'll drive," said Lee Coffey with instant sympathy. "You're kinda upset and I'm faster. I suppose this is possible?" he said to the rest of them.

"Is there a phone at the junction?" cried Paul.

"Yes, a phone," said Virginia, her hand still in Lee's hand.

"Oh yes," said Theo Marsh, "at the gas station. *Up*, Lavinia." The model stood up in her weird garb. The rest of them were streaming to the door.

"Wait for us," said the painter.

"Are *you* coming?" said the bus driver curiously.

"Certainly, *I'm* coming. If you think I'm not going to be on hand to see how this works out! I'm not a man who misses much. Snap it up, Lavinia. We dump her at the junction. Her father runs the gas station."

Mr. Gibson had time to marvel at this, as they streaked for the car.

Lee, Virginia, and Paul were in the front, as before. In the back, Mrs. Boatright's broad beam occupied the center solidly. On her left, Theo Marsh held Lavinia on his lap, and on the right, Mr. Gibson held his wife, Rosemary. He felt tumbled and breathless, but fallen into a warm and lovely place, in the lee of Mrs. Boatright's good and warm and solid flesh, with Rosemary's physical being pressing upon his thighs and his arm holding her.

The car flew down the hill. It stopped. Everybody swayed. Paul was out and at the telephone. Lavinia kicked the long blue skirt about with her bare feet and got out clumsily. Mr. Gibson heard her say, "Hi, Paw."

"I suggest you get some pants on," a man's voice said without passion, "and take over the pumps, Lavinia. Mother's been announcing dinner the last five minutes and I'm famished."

Mr. Gibson heard Paul shouting that the line was busy. That something terrible could have happened.

Theo Marsh bellowed back, "Look here, you at the telephone. Let Lavinia get on the telephone. She's absolutely reliable. I guarantee that." He was leaning over the side waving his long skinny arms.

"No nerves, Lavinia," said the unseen father complacently. "What's up?"

"Let *her* keep calling," bawled the artist. "While we get there."

"I'll tell them," said Lavinia. "Don't touch any olive oil and youse guys is on the way."

"No nerves, no diction," said the sad voice of the gas station man, with a shudder, unseen by but nevertheless divined by Mr. Gibson.

"Yes, do it." Paul was hoarse. "I can't stand here." He beat the telephone number out three times. (Lavinia got it the first time.) Then Paul climbed back into the car.

"All right, Lee," said Virginia to the bus driver.

"Off we go," howled the painter in joy. "So long, Lavinia. Good girl," he told them. "She understands one hell of a lot about art."

"She does?" said Rosemary breathlessly. The car lurched and Mr. Gibson hung on to her.

Rosemary leaned to see around Mrs. Boatright. "Of course, as an artist, Mr. Marsh," she said in suspiciously sweet tones, "you live way out here to retreat from reality."

"The hell I retreat from reality," said the artist angrily. "Who told you that?" Mrs. Boatright contrived to shrink her bosom back against her backbone, somewhat, as they talked across her. "*I* see more reality in half a minute than any one of you can see in a day," raved the artist. "*I* don't even drive a car. I . . ."

"Because of your eyesight?" piped up Mr. Gibson promptly.

"Right," said Theo grumpily. "Good for you, Gibson, if it was Gibson speaking." The artist retreated into silence. Mr. Gibson felt as if he had just won a thrust.

"Hey?" said the bus driver over his shoulder. "What's this?"

"He sees too much," explained Mr. Gibson. "An ear, for instance. He'd be in the ditch."

"I bet he would." Rosemary actually chuckled in her old Rosemaryish way. Mr. Gibson was exhilarated. He pressed his cheek secretly against her sleeve, not wishing to laugh. After all, he was still a criminal. But with mirth rumbling inside of him, just the same.

"Pretty keen, this Gibson," said the bus driver to the blonde. "Mighty lively corpse he makes, hey?"

Paul said tensely, "Drive the car."

Virginia said soothingly, "He is. He will."

"Don't worry, Paul," said Rosemary, rather gaily. "Jeanie is a sensible girl."

"I know that." Paul turned and swept them with a harassed look. He put both palms swiftly over his hair, not quite holding his head, but smoothing it on, as he turned to yearn ahead once more.

"I've got the rest of you sorted out, but who *is* Paul?" asked the painter, reducing his volume. "*He* wasn't on the bus."

"He's a neighbor of theirs," said Mrs. Boatright. "This is his car. We ought to have called the police, you know."

The painter said under his breath to the back seat, "I doubt very much it was *his* daughter who took the green paper bag. *She* was distinguished. Whereas he . . ." The painter made an unspellable noise. It meant Big Deal!

"Paul," said Rosemary rather drowsily, "is as good as he is beautiful."

"And perishing *dull*," said Marsh. "Am I right?"

Rosemary's arm came around Mr. Gibson's neck, to hang on, of course, for they were speeding. "Well, he *is* conventional," she said softly. "He's nice, but . . . everybody can't be interesting, like *you*." She leaned from Mr. Gibson's breast to peer at the painter.

"Oh ho, *I'm* interesting all right," said Theo Marsh.

Mr. Gibson felt furiously jealous. This conceited ass was seventy if he was a day.

"And deeply interested, too. Same thing, you realize. Say, what's-your-name-Gibson . . . why did you plan to kill yourself in the first place?" asked Theo Marsh. "No money?"

"Money!" shrieked Rosemary.

"Why not?" said the artist. "Money is something *I* take care to have about me. Believe me. I'm a shrewd moneymaker. Am I not, Mary Anne?"

"A leech and a bloodsucker," said Mrs. Boatright calmly.

"Well, money is a serious matter," said Theo with a pout, as if nobody would talk seriously. "So naturally, I wondered. Is he broke?"

"No," said Rosemary shortly.

"In some kind of way," said Lee Coffey, with his keen ears stretched backward, "he was broke . . ."

"I assume," said Theo Marsh loftily, "that *something* bothers him. Want to know what, that's all."

"He won't say," said Mrs. Boatright, "but perhaps he can't . . ."

"Yes, he can," said Theo Marsh. "He's articulate. And I'm listening. It interests me."

"Oh, it does?" said Mr. Gibson spitefully. He felt Rosemary's body tensing.

"Shall I guess?" said she, in a brave voice that was full of fear. "He married me ten weeks ago . . . to s-save me. He *likes* to help waifs and strays, you see. It's his hobby. But when I got well . . . there he was, still stuck with me."

"What!" cried Mr. Gibson, outraged. He grabbed her with both arms as if she might fall with his agitation. "No. No!"

"Well, then?" she trembled. "I don't know why you wanted to do it, Kenneth. I only guess . . . it's something Ethel put in your head." She leaned forward, far away from him, and put her hands on the front seat and laid her face on her forearm. "I'm afraid—it's something about me." And Mr. Gibson's heart ached terribly.

"We don't know," said Lee mournfully, over his shoulder. "Nope, we still don't know what it was that shook him."

Virginia said, "I should think you might tell us. We've been so close. Please tell us." Her little face was a moon setting on the horizon of the back of the seat. Her hand came up and touched Rosemary's hair compassionately. "It would be good for you to tell us."

Mrs. Boatright said with massive confidence, "He will, in a minute."

Paul said, "You can take a short cut up Appleby Place."

"I'm way ahead of you," said Lee, "and Lavinia's had them on the phone by now."

"Lavinia!" spat Paul. "That girl with no clothes!" He evidently couldn't imagine being *both* naked and reliable.

Marsh said airily in his high incisive voice, "I guess Gibson likes his secret reason; hugs it to his bosom. Won't show it to us. Oh, no, we might spoil his fun."

"Don't *talk* like that!" cried Rosemary, straightening up. "You sound like Ethel."

So everybody talked at once, telling the painter who Ethel was.

"An amateur," the painter groaned. He had one foot up against the seat ahead. His socks were yellow. "How I loathe and despise these amateurs! These leaping amateurs! *Amateur* critics." He uttered a long keen. "Amateur psychologists are among the worst. Skim a lot of stuff out of an abbreviated article in a twenty-five-cent magazine . . . and then they know. So they treat their friends and neighbors out of their profundity. They put their big fat clumsy hands in where the daintiest probe can't safely go, and they rip and they tear. Nothing so cruel as an amateur, doing good. I'd like to strangle the lot of them."

Mr. Gibson stirred. "No," he said. "No, now I want you to be fair to Ethel. I'll have to try to make you understand. It's just that . . . perhaps Ethel made me see it . . . but it's the doom." There. He had told them.

"Doom?" said Mrs. Boatright encouragingly.

He would have to explain. "We aren't free," he said earnestly. "We are simply doomed. It . . . well, it just suddenly hit me very hard. To realize . . . I mean to believe and begin to apply—the fact that choice is only an illusion. That we are at the mercy of things *in ourselves* that we cannot even know. That we are not able to help ourselves or each other . . ."

They were all silent, so he pressed on.

"We are dupes, puppets. What each of us will do can be predicted. Just as the bomb . . . for instance . . . is bound to fall, human nature being what it . . ."

"Baloney," groaned the painter. "The old sad baloney! Predict *me*—Gibson. I dare you! You mean to say you got yourself believing that old-fashioned drivel?" he sputtered out.

But Rosemary said, "Yes, I see. Yes, I know. Me, too."

Then everybody else in the car, except Paul, seemed to be talking at once.

The bus driver's voice emerged on top. "Lookit!" he shouted. "You cannot, *from where you sit*, predict! I told you. Accidents! There's the whole big fat mixed-up universe . . ."

"What if *I* can't predict?" said Mr. Gibson, somewhat spiritedly defending his position. "An expert . . ."

"No, no. We are *all* ignorant," cried the nurse. "But it's the experts who *know* that. They know we're guessing. They know we're guessing better and better, because *they're* trying to check up on the guesses. You *have* to believe that, Mr. Gibson."

Mr. Gibson was suddenly touched. His heart quivered as if something had reached in and touched it.

Mrs. Boatright cleared her throat. "Organized human effort," she began.

"This is *not* the PTA, Mary Anne," the artist said severely. "This is one simple intelligent male. Give me a crack at him." He had come so far forward to peer at Mr. Gibson that he seemed to be crouching, angular as a cricket, on air. "Listen, Gibson. Take a cave man."

"Yes," said Mr. Gibson, helplessly, with a kind of melting feeling. "I'm taking one."

"Did he foresee his descendants flying over the North Pole to get from here to Europe tomorrow?"

"Of course not."

"So . . . how can *you* be as narrow-minded as a cave man?"

"Narrow?"

"Certainly. You extrapolate a future on what's known now. You extend the old lines. What you don't take into account are the surprises."

"Hey!" said the bus driver. "Hey! Hey!"

"Every big jump is a surprise, a revelation," lectured the artist, "and a tangent off the old. Penicillin. Atom splitting. Who guessed they were coming?"

"Exactly," cried Virginia. "Or the wheel? Or television? How do we know what's coming next?" She was all excited. "Maybe some whole vast opening up in a direction we've hardly thought of . . ."

"Good girl," said Theo Marsh. "Have you ever done any modeling?"

"Of the spirit, too," boomed Mrs. Boatright. "Of the mind. Men *have* developed ideals undreamed in antiquity. You simply cannot deny it. Would your cave man understand the Red Cross?"

"Or the S.P.C.A.," said the bus driver, "him and his saber-toothed playmates. Doom—schmoom. Also, if you *gotta,* you very often do. Take a jump, I mean. I'm talking about the bomb . . ."

"So the bomb might not fall," said Rosemary. She lifted her clasped hands in a kind of ecstasy, "because men might find something even better than common sense by tomorrow morning. Who knows? Not Ethel! Ethel is too—"

"Too rigid, I expect," said the painter. "Death is too rigid. Rigor is mortis. Keep your eyes open. You'll be surprised!" This was his credo. Mr. Gibson found himself stretching the physical muscles around his eyes.

"It's gonna fall if you sit on your fanny and expect it," the bus driver said, "that's for sure. But everybody isn't just sitting around, telling themselves *they* are so smart *they* can see their fate coming. Lookit, we'll know the latest news today, when we look backward from fifty years. Not before. The present views with alarm. It worries. It should. But these trends sneak up like a mist that you don't notice."

"Righto!" shouted the artist. "*You* don't even see what's already around you in your own home town."

"People can, too, help each other," said Rosemary. She was sitting on his lap yet turned in facing him. "And I'm the living *proof.* You helped me because you *wanted* to, Kenneth. There *wasn't* any other reason."

"The ayes have it," the painter said. (Perhaps he said "eyes.") "You are overruled, Gibson. You haven't got a leg to die on. You can't logically kill yourself on that silly old premise." He drew back upon the seat and crossed his legs complacently.

The bus driver said dubiously, "However, logic . . ."

The nurse suddenly put her forehead against his arm.

Mrs. Boatright said firmly, "If you see that you were wrong, now you *must* admit it. That is the *only* way to progress."

And then they waited.

Mr. Gibson's churning mind settled, sad and slow as a feather. "But in my error," he said quietly, "I may have caused a death."

Paul said uncontrollably, "If anything happened to Mama or Jeanie, I'll never forgive you."

"Don't say 'never,'" said Virginia, raising her head and speaking gently.

"It ain't scientific to say 'never,' hey?" said the bus driver, and leaned and kissed her ear.

The car shot off the boulevard upon a short cut.

Everyone was silent. The excitement was over. The poison was still lost. They hadn't found it.

And if in error there was learning and if in blame there was responsibility and if in ignorance there was hope—and if in life there are surprises—and if in doom there were these cracks—still, they had not put their hands upon a little bottle full of death, and innocently labeled olive oil. And *it* was no illusion.

Chapter Nineteen

Mr. Gibson sat holding his wife in his lap, and this was bitter-sweet. "Rosemary," he said softly in a moment, almost whispering, "why did you say you hadn't run the needle into your finger . . . when you had?"

"Why do I *think* I said it?" But her face softened and she discarded the bitterness. "I just didn't care to have Ethel know . . ." Her breath was on his forehead.

"Know what, mouse?"

"How much," said Rosemary. She drew a little away to look down into his eyes. "I loved our cottage," she said. "My—sentiments. She hasn't any sympathy with sentiment. I suppose it was sentimental, but I didn't want to go away."

Mr. Gibson squeezed his own eyes shut.

"But *you* went away, Kenneth. Ever since the accident," she whispered into his hair. "What did Ethel say to you?" He hid his face against where her heart was beating. "I thought maybe you agreed," she said, "with *her* that I tried to be rid of my bargain. You would have been kind to me, even so. I couldn't tell."

"That was an accident," he murmured. "Mouse, I told you . . ."

"I told *you* things . . . you didn't seem to believe," she said. "She *is* your sister, you *do* respect her. I thought you believed her, and you *said* you couldn't remember—I was afraid. . . . She had me so confused."

Paul said loudly, "Turn right, here. That's it. The third drive-way." Paul, who was single-minded now. Paul, who said "Don't worry" when everyone did. But who urged them to worry when they seemed not to. Paul—who was so young—under whose genial good manners lurked a rather sulky boy.

"Ethel will be there now, I guess," said Rosemary, sucking in breath.

She moved, increasing the distance between them. The car stopped. Mr. Gibson opened his eyes. He saw the little cottage's roof on his left with its vines. It looked like home. But home was not for him . . . not any more. He had been confused and in hope-less confusion, he sadly surmised, he had doomed himself.

He limped badly, getting up on Paul's front terrace.

Jeanie Townsend, alive and strong, opened the door and cried eagerly, "Oh, did you find it?"

"She's not the one," croaked Theo Marsh. "I didn't think so."

Paul grabbed her in both his arms. "I was so scared, baby," he panted. "I thought maybe you'd got on the same bus . . . I thought maybe you had that poison."

"Oh, for Heaven's sakes, Daddy!" Jeanie wiggled indignantly to get away from him. "How dumb do you think I am?"

"How's Mama?" Paul let her go and rushed past her.

Obviously, there was no poison here.

Jeanie looked at the crew of them . . . half a dozen suddenly drooping people on the doorstep. "Won't you come in?" she snapped, the polite child struggling with the angry one.

"Did Lavinia call?" asked Lee Coffey. "Hey, Jeanie?" He had exactly the same air with the young girl as he had with the elders.

"Somebody called. "Was that Lavinia? We knew already. It was on the radio." Jeanie tossed her cropped head. She had on a red skirt and white blouse and a little red latticework on her bare feet for shoes. "When I went down to the mailbox—oh, a long time ago—I heard it on Miss Gibson's radio. So I turned on ours." She looked very haughty as if of course she would know what was going on in the world.

Mr. Gibson looked at Rosemary and she at him. "Then Ethel knows," he murmured. He could not see an inch into the future. Rosemary moved until their shoulders touched.

"Well, I guess she mightn't know it was *you*," said Jeanie, backing inward, "because it didn't give your name on the radio. Grandma guessed that part of it."

"And you didn't run over and tell this Ethel or hash it out with her, neighborly? Hey?" asked the bus driver curiously.

"No," said Jeanie. She looked a little troubled about this but she didn't rationalize an excuse. Obviously she hadn't felt like hashing things out with Ethel Gibson. "Aren't you all coming in?"

They all came in.

Paul was in the living room and down on his knees beside old Mrs. Pyne's chair, and his handsome head was bowed. It was a strange position for him . . . theatrical, corny.

Mrs. Pyne was saying, as to a child, "But Paul, dear, you needn't have had a moment's worry about Jeanie or me . . ."

Paul said, "You'll never know . . ." He sounded like a big ham.

Jeanie's eyes flashed. "What makes you think I'd eat any old food I found lying around or feed it to Grandma? Don't you think I know better? Honestly, Daddy!"

But Paul knelt there.

Now Mrs. Pyne smiled around at them all, and her smile plucked out Mr. Gibson. "I'm so glad to see you," said the old lady. "I've been praying for you constantly since last I saw you."

Mr. Gibson moved toward her and took her frail dry hand. It had strength in it. He wanted to thank her for her prayers, but it seemed awkward, like applauding in church. She was a perfect stranger to him, anyhow, now that he saw her as the core of this house.

"Say, excuse me," said Theo Marsh, in a businesslike way, "are you interested in modeling?" Mrs. Pyne looked astonished.

"My name is Helen Pyne," said the old lady with spunk in her voice. "Who are you, sir?"

"Theodore Marsh, a humble painter." This Theo was part clown. He made a leg. "Always looking for good faces."

"Humble, hey?" murmured the bus driver comically. "I'm Lee Coffey. I drive the bus."

"I'm Virginia Severson. I was a passenger."

"I am Mrs. Walter Boatright," said that lady, as if this sufficed. She stood, like the speaker of the evening, thoughtfully organizing her notes in her mind.

But it was Rosemary who burst out to Theo Marsh . . . "If it wasn't Jeanie you saw . . . then we don't know . . ."

"It wasn't Jeanie," said the artist. He had cocked his head as if to see Mrs. Pyne upside down. Mr. Gibson suffered an enlargement. He, too, saw the old lady's face, the sweetness around the eyes, the firmness of her dainty chin. Mrs. Pyne was not only more beautiful, she was even prettier than Jeanie.

"Then who? Then who?" Rosemary implored.

"I have great confidence in the police department," said Mrs. Boatright decisively, and took a throne. Rosemary stared at her and ran for the telephone.

Paul came out of his trance or prayer or whatever it was. "How did you know so much about what was going on?" he asked his mother-in-law adoringly.

"I knew it was bad, of course," the old lady said soberly, "when I heard Rosemary call. When Jean turned on the radio, I knew at once who had left the bottle on the bus. I had just seen such trouble in his face, you know. Although there was nothing I could do."

"Mrs. Pyne," said Mr. Gibson impulsively, "what you said made it impossible. I don't think I would have done it. But, of course, by then the trouble was different. I had already lost the poison."

"And haven't found it," she said sadly.

"No." He met her eyes. He accepted his guilt and her mercy.

"We must all pray," said Mrs. Pyne.

"Trouble?" said the bus driver. His eyes slewed around to Virginia. "Trouble and logic . . . how do they jibe? I don't think we got to the bot—"

Virginia seemed to shush him.

Rosemary wailed on the phone, "Nothing? Nothing at all?" She hung it up. She walked back toward them. "Nothing. No news of it at all," she said and twisted her hands.

"No news is good news," said Paul.

But they all looked around at each other.

"A dead end, hey?" said the bus driver. "Ring around a rosy and no place to go from here." Fumes of energy boiled out of him and curled back with no place to go.

"Think!" said Virginia fiercely. "*I'm* trying to think. *Think*, Mrs. Boatright." The little nurse shut her eyes.

Mrs. Boatright shut her eyes but her lips moved. Mr. Gibson realized that Mrs. Walter Boatright was importuning a superior in heaven, on his account.

But they had come to an end. There was no place else to go.

He had rocked to his own feet now. It was time he took over. He said vigorously, "You have all done so much. You have done wonders. You must all go about your business, now, with my grat—my love," he said loudly. "It's on God's knees . . . I guess, after all." (Was this the same as doom, he wondered?) "Rosemary and I must go across to Ethel." This was his duty.

"Yes," Rosemary agreed somberly.

"Ethel's hard by *here?*" said Theo Marsh with a wicked gleam in his eye.

"Theo," said Mrs. Boatright warningly.

Paul Townsend was himself again, and host in this house. "How about a drink first?" he said cordially. "I think we need one. Don't worry, Gibson . . ." He stopped himself cold.

"Wurra, wurra," said the bus driver. "Each for his own. That's what makes the mare go." He took a gloomy bite of his thumbnail.

Paul said, "I guess I dragged you all here for nothing." He looked boyishly penitent.

"A little drink won't do me any harm," said Lee. "Virginia would like one, too."

Theo Marsh perched like a restless bird on the edge of a table. "Thirsty as the desert in August, myself," he admitted. "What's to do now?" He cracked a knuckle.

Mrs. Boatright said, "We don't seem to have any clear course of procedure." She assembled her will. "I will call home and have a car sent, to take any of you wherever you wish. But first I would enjoy a rather weak drink, Paul. Thank you. Meantime, we may think of something." Mrs. Boatright was not accustomed to being beaten by circumstance.

Jeanie said, "I'll help you tend bar, Dad." And the bus driver began to tell Mrs. Pyne the saga of their search.

It was curiously like a party, and a party of loosened tongues, at that, well past the polite preliminaries. Mr. Gibson sat beside Rosemary on a sofa and tried to remember that he was a criminal. Some-body, somewhere, could be dead, or now dying, by his hand.

Young Jeanie seemed to have caught on to the wide-open atmos-phere. Holding the tray, she said to the Gibsons, "I'm sorry I got so mad, but Dad should have trusted me. My goodness, most of the time he leans on me too much."

"He's so fond of you, dear," said Rosemary, "and of your grand-mother, too."

"He's absolutely tied to Grandma's apron strings," said Jeanie im-patiently. "I *wish* he'd get married."

"*Do* you?" said Rosemary sharply.

"Of course, we both do. Don't we, Grandma?"

"Wish Paul would marry?" Mrs. Pyne sighed. "We've not been very successful matchmakers."

"Look, I'm happy," said Paul, passing drinks.

Rosemary leaned forward and said deliberately, "But Mrs. Pyne, wouldn't Jeanie be terribly jealous of a stepmother? Isn't a teen-age daughter bound to be?"

"Subconsciously?" said Virginia, her clean-cut little mouth form-ing the word with distaste.

Mr. Gibson felt very queer. He kept his face a blank. He had a conviction that Lee Coffey, Theo Marsh, all of them, could see right through his skin.

"Here comes Ethel, hey?" said Lee. "Oh boy, this Ethel—"

"Jeanie," said Mrs. Pyne gently, "is *truly* fond of Paul."

"Honestly!" burst Jeanie. "How can she think that about *me?* She doesn't even know me. And I know the facts of life! I've been try-ing to marry Dad off for four years now. Pretty consciously," she flared.

"Ethel though," said the bus driver comfortably, "*she* knows bet-ter. Hey, Rosemary?" He winked.

"I don't think she knows much about teen-agers," said Jeanie. "We're a pretty bright bunch."

"Quite so," said Mrs. Boatright. "One should make a practice of listening to young people. Go on, my dear."

"We've even heard of Oedipus," Jeanie rushed on—flashing Mrs. Boatright a look of fierce response. "We're not stupid. I ask you, what's going to happen to Dad when I go off? And I'm *going*, some day."

"And I," said Mrs. Pyne, nodding calmly.

"If he hasn't got *somebody*, he's going to be just lost," said Jeanie. "He's an awful comfort-loving man."

Paul said, "These women . . . they nag me . . ." He lifted his glass. His eyes were suddenly inscrutable.

Mr. Gibson sipped his own drink, in automatic imitation. It was cold and tasteless, and then suddenly delicious.

"Well, of course," said Rosemary wickedly, "Ethel has her own ideas about crippled old ladies, too, Mrs. Pyne."

Paul looked very angry.

Mrs. Pyne lifted her hand, as if to forestall his anger and she smiled. "Poor Ethel," she said. "Well, she must live as best she can and think what will comfort her, I suppose. Never married. No children. Such a limited experience of life."

Mr. Gibson murmured his astonishment. "Ethel? Limited?" He had never thought of this.

"I don't think she has many connections with real people," said Mrs. Pyne. "That is to say, individuals. Or how could she judge them in such lumps?"

"She doesn't look—can't see," said Theo Marsh.

"They're a wild and wonderful lot," said the bus driver, patting Virginia's hand, "if you take them one by one. And that's the way I like them." Virginia blushed and shushed him.

"Still," said Mr. Gibson, clearing his throat, "Ethel has had quite a successful business career. She has faced up to facts all her life." (His tongue felt loose. He was almost enjoying this party.) "Whereas I," he went on, "am the one who has had the limited existence. A little poetry. Some academic backwaters. Even in the war, I . . ."

"How can you read poetry and not notice the universe?" said Lee indignantly. "You know who is limited? Fella who reads nothing but the newspaper, watches nothing but his own p's and q's, plus TV in the evening, works for nothing but money, buys nothing with the money but a car or a steak, does what he *thinks* the neighbors do and don't notice the universe. Actually," he sank back and slipped his fingers on his glass, "I never met anybody like that, myself."

"You read about him in the newspaper," said Theo Marsh.

"What war, Mr. Gibson?" asked Virginia.

"Oh . . . both wars. I was too old for Korea . . ."

"Oh yes," said Rosemary with charming sarcasm. "He has had so little experience. Only two wars, you see. Then there was the depression, the years when he took care of his mother, when he paid for Ethel's education. And that was weak and drifting of him, wasn't it? The years he has taught . . . who counts those? Ethel doesn't. I don't see why not," she added in a low voice. "Or why, when a man has led a useful life for fifty-five years and is kind and generous and good . . . why Ethel seems to assume he is so naïve and so . . ."

"Innocent?" supplied Mr. Gibson, his eyes crinkling. (He was having a *lovely* time.)

"*Back*waters?" snapped Theo Marsh. "What d'ya mean? What does she think life is made of? Your name in the metropolitan newspapers? Café society?"

"No, no. Facts," said Mr. Gibson. "Mean-ness. People who run knives in your back. Egos and burglars . . ."

"Please." The painter stopped him with a loud groaning. "Why is everything loathsome and unpleasant called a fact? Thought fact was another name for truth. And evil truths may be . . . but truth does not *equal* evil. I'll tell you, you can't paint a decent picture without the truth in it."

"Or write a decent poem, either," said the bus driver, "or teach a decent lesson. Or earn an honest penny. You know, I think he *is* innocent." He looked around belligerently.

"I think he's a dear," said Virginia warmly.

Mrs. Boatright was nodding judiciously. "Theo," said she, "I believe the Tuesday Club would listen to you on this subject . . ."

"For a hundred and fifty lousy bucks?" said Theo. "Bah! Those cheapskates!"

Mr. Gibson tried very hard not to be having so much fun. Here, beside Rosemary, in this clean and comfortable and charming room where the dainty gentlewoman in her wheel chair was their true hostess, where all these lively people spoke their minds . . . No, no—he *must* remember that he had to face the music.

Sometimes, however, he thought with a boom of pleasure that would not be denied, there *is* music. That's the funny thing! This group of people, the way they talked to him, the way they argued with him, contradicted him, tried to buck him up, liked him and worried for him, and fought with him against fate, and gave him of their own faiths . . . this touched him and made music in his heart. He thought no man had ever had so delightful an experience as he had had this day of his suicide.

But such pleasure was only stolen. He must go. He must face whatever would come, nor would it be music, altogether.

Chapter Twenty

He started to rise.

"Wait a minute," said the bus driver. "Listen, kids . . ."

"Yes, Lee?" said Mrs. Boatright alertly.

"We got our hair down, all of us. Hey? Let's not skim the surface here. Don't go, Gibson. Yet. I want to know the answer to one question that's been worrying me. Rosemary . . ."

"Yes, Lee?"

Mr. Gibson sat down. He trembled. This bus driver *was* a shrewd man, in his own way.

"Now, this Ethel, she decides your subconscious wants to get rid of him. That's right, isn't it? Tell me, what reason did she decide your subconscious had for this?"

Rosemary flushed.

"She'd figured *out* a reason?"

"Yes," said Rosemary. "Of course she had." Her fingers turned her glass. "These marriages never work, you know," said Rosemary almost dreamily. "Kenneth is twenty-three years older than I. Isn't that terrible! Ethel thinks that subconsciously . . ." she went on very quiet and yet defiant and brave, "I *must* wish I had a younger mate."

"Like who? Hey?" said the bus driver, his eyes lively, his sandy lashes alert. The painter sat up. Mrs. Boatright looked suddenly very bland and supercalm.

"Like Paul," said Rosemary.

"Now we're getting to the bottom," said the bus driver with satisfaction.

"Aha!" said the painter.

"Oh now, look, Rosie," said Paul, crimson. "Now you know . . ."

"I *thought* I knew," said Rosemary, and smiled at him.

"If our hair is down," said Jeanie bluntly, "all right. I'll tell you something. *She* is too *old*—for Daddy."

Mr. Gibson felt a wave of shock ripple through him. Rosemary! Too old!

"He likes them rather plump, about five years older, and two inches shorter, than me," said Jeanie impudently, "as far as I can figure on the basis of experiments, so far."

"Now you . . . just be quiet, please," said Paul, much embarrassed. "I'm sorry, Rosie, but after all you *are* his wife. I certainly . . ."

"Don't be sorry," said Rosemary gently. Her face became very serene as she lifted it. "You've been kind, Paul. You've tried to comfort me. You've told me not to worry. But I am too old for you, of course. Just as you are . . . forgive me, dear Paul . . . just a bit too dull for my taste. You see, *I* like a seasoned man."

"Good for you," said Theo Marsh complacently. "Intelligent woman."

"Ethel just can't seem to believe," said Rosemary, calm and sad, "anything so simple. The fact is, I *married* the man I love."

Mr. Gibson, looking at his glass, could see her fingers, slim and fair, upon her own.

"However," said Mr. Gibson out of a trance, able to speak quite coolly, although somewhat jerkily, "it is still possible that, as Ethel says, I am, for Rosemary, a father-image."

Rosemary looked at him with mild astonishment. "Not *my* father," she said calmly. "*My* father, since the day I was born, was mean and didactic and unjust and petty and spoiled and childish. I don't like to sound disloyal, but that's the truth. Kenneth isn't *anything* like *my* father," she explained graciously to them all.

"It is a little ridiculous, though," said Mr. Gibson chattily. (This was the strangest party!) "I am fifty-five years old, you see. For *me* to be so deep in love, for the first time in my life, is quite . . . comical. Somehow. It makes everybody smile."

"Smile?" said Virginia. "But of course! It's *nice!* It's pleasant to see."

"I should have said . . . snicker," revised Mr. Gibson.

"Who," growled the bus driver, "does it make snicker?"

"Not at all," said the artist. "*I* was in love last winter. If anyone had snickered at me, I'd have spit in their eye." He would have. Everyone believed this.

"How come this Ethel put the Indian sign on the both of you?" asked the bus driver. "How come she shook you? Anybody can see you two are in love." He was a gentle ruthless man.

"I was a rabbit," said Rosemary. "I should have spit in her eye." She was sitting very straight. "I am to blame."

Mr. Gibson felt exhausted and also very peaceful. "I, too," he said. "But I am old, lame, unsure . . . and extremely stupid. I permitted her to upset me. My fault. My blame." He wanted to cry. He drank thirstily.

"Whereas, our Paul," said the painter, "is as handsome as the hero in a slick magazine. And as good as he is beautiful. No offense. No offense. Sex, I presume?" He crossed his yellow socks and tried to look innocent. "According to lethal Ethel?"

"Lethal Ethel, that's *good,*" said the bus driver angrily. "That's *apt,* that is."

Virginia said, "Surely people *know* when they're in love . . ." and bit her lips.

Rosemary leaned back with a little smile gentle on her face. "Do you know something? There is a fact they never take account of— in a magazine story or the movies either . . . that *I* ever saw. Why is it you . . . want to be where someone is? Why?" She looked at Virginia. "It *can't* be just because he's good-looking. (Although Kenneth *is,* very.) It certainly can't be just because somebody is *young.* To me," she continued to the lamp beside the sofa, "the most important thing of all is how much fun you have together, and I don't mean sex. Although—" Rosemary gulped and went on. "Do you understand me? I mean—just enjoying each other's company. We had such good times . . . as I had never known. We laughed," said Rosemary. She leaned forward with sudden vehemence. "Why don't people talk about *that* as if it were attractive? It is. It's powerfully attractive. I think it's the most powerful attraction of all."

"The most permanent," said Mrs. Pyne, softly.

"Absolutely," said Mrs. Boatright. "Or the race could not endure. *All* beloved wives, for instance, are not size twelve." She rocked a little indignantly on her great haunches.

"Hm," said the artist, "my fourth wife now . . . I had a most delightful companionship with that one, all around the clock. And although her ankles were *not* perfect, she is the one I mourn . . . it's a fact." He looked mildly astonished.

"I . . . agree," breathed Virginia. The bus driver slid his eyes under his lashes.

Mr. Gibson, with joy shooting in his veins . . . and shame and sorrow, too, but with an iron resolve that the rest of this was his own private business however much he loved— Yes, he did!—all of them . . . took Rosemary's hand and got to his feet. He said with a simplicity that achieved privacy with one stroke, "Thank you all very much for everything you have done and said. But we must go now."

To Mrs. Pyne he said, "If you will pray for us—that the poison be found . . ."

"I will," she vowed.

Paul said shyly, nervously, "Sure hope it works out O.K."

Jeanie said, "Oh, we all hope so!"

Mrs. Boatright said, "The police may still find it. Mustn't underestimate the organization."

The painter said, "It could be on a dump heap, right now and you will *never* know . . . *never* hear . . . You realize?"

The nurse said, "Oh, please . . . be happy." Her whole cool responsible little person was dissolving in sentimental tears.

The bus driver said earnestly, "Lots of good books been written in jail; I mean to say, 'Stone walls do not . . .'"

"I'll remember that, Lee," said Mr. Gibson affectionately. For this man was the one who had set the fashion, the one who had decreed, in the beginning, that there would be no candy. He offered none now, really.

Mr. Gibson slipped one arm around Rosemary's waist and guided her out of the house.

They left seven people.

"He's a darling," sobbed Virginia. "She's a dear. . . . Can't we save them? *Think*, everybody!"

Then the seven were silent in that room—silent and sad and still fighting.

Mr. Gibson and his wife, Rosemary, walked rather slowly and quite silently along the terrace to its end and down the steps and across the double driveway. It was a quarter of six o'clock. A sweet evening coming. They passed the shining garbage cans. Beyond the steps to the kitchen there grew a shrub, and Mr. Gibson pulled his wife gently to the far side of this friendly green mass where no window overlooked them.

He took her in his arms and she came close. He kissed her gently and then again, less so. Her head came upon his shoulder.

"You do remember the restaurant, Kenneth?"

"I do. I do."

"How we laughed! I thought after you were hurt, that you couldn't, didn't remember."

But remembered woe was far away. She only sighed.

"I remember the fog, too," he murmured. "We said it was beautiful."

"We didn't—altogether—mean the fog?"

"No." He kissed her, once more, most tenderly. "It's an old-fashioned plot, mouse. Isn't it? A misunderstanding. But then, I am an old-fashioned man."

"I love you so," said Rosemary. "No matter what—don't leave me."

"No matter what," he promised. He was a criminal. He might leave her, although not "really." There was bitter. There was sweet.

In a few minutes, he turned her gently, and they began to go up the steps to the kitchen door.

Chapter Twenty-one

ETHEL GIBSON returned to the cottage shortly after four o'clock that afternoon. She frowned to find the doors unlocked, the place wide open, and empty. Very careless of her brother! Still, he might be over at the Townsends', just across the driveways. Ethel did not feel in a mood to join him, if so. She had arranged her day in her mind and did not like to break her plan with idle and unexpected sociability.

She put off her summer suit-jacket and marched into the kitchen. What disarray! Really, order was essential in so small a house. Ethel did not like living in this cottage; an apartment would be so much less labor. She thought they would be moving elsewhere before very long. Now she compressed her lips. Lettuce limpening on the open counter. Bread not neatly in the bread box. Cocoa, tea, should be on the shelves. Cheese ought to be refrigerated. A green paper bag. Now what was this? A tiny bottle of olive oil. Imported! *Much* too expensive!

She shook her head and proceeded to clear the things away, properly washed the lettuce and put it in the crisping bin, the cheese in the icebox, threw the paper bag into the kitchen wastebasket, placed cans and bottles in the cupboard.

She stepped into the living room long enough to switch on the radio. Music was a habit with her. She paid no attention to it but felt its absence.

She then walked back to her (and Rosemary's) bedroom, drew off her business clothes and hung them, put on a cotton dress. Ethel then threw herself down upon the bed to relax. Music came distantly. When there were voices, she did not listen. She never listened to commercials. Her mind ran over the first day at this office. This job would serve. She already felt that she had some clues to the hidden springs of the boss's character. She foresaw an orderly, courageous, and useful life in this quiet town. Excellent for her health. She dozed.

She was wakened at a quarter after five by the telephone. The house was still empty.

"Yes?"

"This is the Townsend Laboratories calling," said a female voice. "Is Mr. Kenneth Gibson there?"

"No, he is not." Ethel was crisp.

"Where is he, do you know?"

"No, I do not. I daresay he will be here at dinner time."

"When?" The voice faded feebly.

"At a quarter of six."

"Oh. Well, will you be sure to have him call this number?"

Ethel took down the number.

"It's important," said the voice, fading again as if in some mysterious agitation.

"I'll tell him," said Ethel, soothingly.

Ethel hung up. She was slightly annoyed.

Inconsiderate! Consideration was the first rule in such a ménage as this. Rosemary should have returned, must soon. Where could Ken be? She couldn't imagine. Yes, she could. Probably he was lost in a book at the branch library.

Dinner at a quarter of six.

She would start dinner.

They knew the dinner hour.

The radio still played. She felt a bit martyred in this mysterious loneliness and she turned it off, feeding a grievance.

She went into the kitchen and began to prepare their dinner. It would be very simple. Ethel approved of a spaghetti dinner, inexpensive and nourishing and easy to put together—these packaged brands. She dumped the boughten sauce out into a pan. Thought better of this. One ought to doctor up a boughten sauce, she knew. Ethel chopped an onion fine and put it into the sauce. She was not a sensitive cook. She had eaten what restaurants put before her, for so many years. Food was food. It was either cheap or it was expensive. Still, she realized that she ought to have sautéed the onions. Perhaps in the olive oil? What did Ken mean it for, anyway? The bottle didn't hold enough for a salad dressing. Ethel did not like it in a dressing, having made do with cheap vegetable oils for so long. Surely not for fruit! No, he must have fancied the taste of olive oil in the spaghetti sauce. Perhaps it was some fancy of Rosemary's.

She grimaced but took the bottle down and turned the cap. Oh, well . . . she dumped it into the saucepan. She hoped it would not taste too much. She washed out the bottle and set it upside down to drain. King Roberto stood on his head. Ethel filled a large pot with water for the pasta.

She began to cut up fruit for salad. She doubted the lettuce would be crisp at all. Five thirty-four and nobody home *yet*.

Ethel began to set the table in the dining alcove of the living room. From here she could see the driveways and she heard and saw Paul's car come in and a great load of people begin to get hastily out of it. Ethel averted her eyes. It was beneath her to spy on the neighbors. A party, she presumed. The word "party" meant something lightweight to her, timewasting, profitless chitchat. (Nobody ever asked Ethel to parties.)

Now the table was set. The water at a boil. The sauce ready enough. She turned it low. She mixed the salad.

When the clock said twenty of six, Ethel felt injured. She threw the pasta into the boiling water, and went into the living room and sat down with her back to the mantel to watch the clock on the opposite wall.

She would knit for nine minutes.

Then dinner would be ready. And they *should* remember and be considerate. *She* was always considerate.

At eleven minutes of six she marched to the kitchen.

She heard their feet.

"Where on earth have you been?" said Ethel heartily. "I see you're together . . ."

"Yes," said Mr. Gibson, "we are together." He was a little surprised to see the same old Ethel, standing on both feet in her accustomed way, vigorous and sure of herself.

"Dinner is *exactly* ready," said Ethel. "Now, you just have time to wash. There is nothing for you to do, Rosemary. I've done it all. Now, get to the table while I drain this and mix in the sauce. Shoo!" said Ethel, indulgently.

Meekly, they crossed the kitchen. But they kissed in the hall.

"Doesn't know . . ." said Mr. Gibson wonderingly.

"No, she doesn't seem to. They aren't broadcasting your name . . ."

"Well, we must tell—"

"Yes . . ."

"Not easy."

"No." The sweet was so very sweet.

"Everybody ready?" hallooed Ethel.

Mr. Gibson let Rosemary go and he went into his own place. It already looked antique to him, a former way of life. Could he have books in a cell, he wondered? Alas, he couldn't have Rosemary. Face reality. Face wicked folly. Face love. Face it, that you are beloved.

He washed, musing, perceiving that Ethel was right. Or somewhat right. He had *not* seen clearly his own motives. He *had* rationalized. He had plastered a black philosophy in the mind over a quivering wound in the heart. Although it was not really that simple, either. Still, worms *might* have eaten him. . . . Well, he knew a little more now. He knew he had been too suggestible, too quick to abandon his own faiths. He ought to have trusted himself better.

Ethel made us both doubt ourselves, he mused, gave us that terrible feeling that one *cannot* trust oneself, no use to try. Such doubt as this, in quantity, judiciously used, might be a tonic and a medicine. But oh, too much, swallowed blindly at a bad time, had shaken him to his foundations.

It was dangerous stuff.

He met Rosemary in the hall. Their hands touched. They went across the living room to the dining alcove.

"Sit ye doon," said Ethel with ponderous good will and forbearance. "You naughty children." Her eyes were wise and speculating. She'd soon "know" where they had been.

They sat them down. Ethel spooned portions of spaghetti from the steaming mass in the wooden bowl. "Confess," she said. "What have you been up to?"

"There was a little mixup," said Mr. Gibson. He stared at the spaghetti, not feeling any appetite.

Rosemary nervously took up her fork. "We'll tell you about it, as best we can," she began. Dear Rosemary, brave enough to try to help him tell.

"I suppose you've had a talk?" said Ethel, giving them one of her looks. "Now, my dears, it is not my business and I do not pry. It is your privilege to have your little secrets—"

Rosemary put the fork down abruptly.

"Any decision that will affect me," said Ethel kindly, "I'm sure you will tell me about."

"Yes," said Rosemary steadily.

Mr. Gibson saw, in Ethel's eyes, himself, the lamb, the soft-hearted, the unworldly, the born bachelor, wifeless, living on into old age with his devoted spinster sister. Doomed to this. It was not true.

"We are very much in love, Ethel," he said quietly and firmly, "Rosemary and I."

Ethel's eyeballs swiveled and a blank look came down. But her mouth twitched in tiny disbelief, and the veiled eyes wondered. She did not speak.

But Rosemary spoke. "Just what was said—"

"What . . . ?"

"Just what was said. That's what is *meant,* Ethel."

"I'm so very glad," said Ethel in a false-sounding flutter. "But don't let dinner get cold . . ."

She didn't believe them. Her face remained blank but Mr. Gibson had an image of her thoughts, writhing and scrambling to detect some "real" meaning behind what he had said . . . until they writhed like . . . like a bowl of spaghetti. He couldn't stomach the stuff. However, he had better eat her dinner or offend her. He turned his fork.

Ethel's fork thrust into her spaghetti.

Suddenly, people were shouting. Startled, they all looked toward the window.

Six people steamed off Paul's porch and came roaring across the driveway.

"Gibson! Hey! Hey!" the bus driver was shouting.

Mr. Gibson skipped to the front door nimbly, limp and all. He was terribly, amazingly, glad to see them. Life throbbed in the house suddenly when in trooped Lee Coffey with Virginia on the end of his arm. Then Theo Marsh—flippety-flop—his seamed face beaming, and young Jeanie, ducking lithely under his waving limbs.

And then Paul, holding the door for the looming up of Mrs. Boatright, who came in like an ocean liner.

"*We found it!*" they all shouted.

"Everything's under control," yelped Lee, who was waving a sheet of paper. "The marines have landed! We did it, after all!" He pounded Mr. Gibson on the back rather violently. "*No* sting! O grave, where is thy . . . !" he babbled.

"*Tell us,*" screamed Rosemary, over the noise, "*one* of you—"

"This Jeanie child," roared Theo Marsh, "this Jeanie is so sound and intelligent that *I* am lying in the dust at her feet. Fool! Fool, that I am! My life! My work!" He snatched the paper from the bus driver.

"But what—?"

The nurse said, "Well, *tell* them!" Then *she* told them. "It was Jeanie who asked Theo to *draw* the face he'd seen."

"And he drew it *so well,*" cried Jeanie aglow, "that Grandma recognized her!"

The paper was thrust under Mr. Gibson's nose. A few pencil lines —a face, a beauty.

"Mama said it was Mrs. Violette," yelled Paul, "and I couldn't believe her. *I* never thought she was so darned lovely."

"Have eyes . . . and see not," droned the artist. His hair stood on end. He held the drawing in both hands and moved it softly to and fro. "Has she ever done any modeling?" he crooned. "These exquisite nostrils!"

"But what—" gasped Mr. Gibson, "what's *happened!*"

"Virginia called up her house," explained Lee excitedly. "This Violette or whatever. And it *was* this Violette. Some sister or other was there and this sister says, Yes, she *had* it!"

"This sister ha—?"

"Mrs. Violette *had* it!" boomed Paul. "She's gone to the mountains. She took it with her! But Mrs. Boatright called the police . . ."

Lee said, "And *she's* buddies with the high brass. *She* told *them* what to do, all right." He spanked Mrs. Boatright on the shoulders. "Hey, Mary Anne?"

"They will stop her car," said Mrs. Boatright calmly, "or truck, as I believe it is. We secured the license number. An all-points-bulletin. The organization is quite capable." Mrs. Boatright was beaming like Santa Claus, for all her calm.

"So you *see!*" gasped Virginia. "She's not going to use it en route. How *could* she? So you are saved!"

Ethel stood there.

"Furthermore," said Mrs. Boatright, looking around as if this were a committee, "I see no reason, at all, since there has been no catastrophe, for *any* further proceeding. Justice will not be served by publicity or by punishment. Mr. Gibson is not going to kill himself. Nor will he ever do such a thing as he did. I do believe that I convinced Chief Miller . . . If not, I will."

"You did already," cried Lee. "You beat it into him, Mary Anne. Believe me, you were superb! So All's Well that Ends Well! Hey? Hey?"

"Hey?" joined Theo.

Rosemary made a little whimpering sound of relief and staggered and drooped into a chair.

"Is there any brandy?" said the nurse anxiously, observing this collapse with a professional eye.

Ethel stood there. She had no idea what was happening. She understood nothing. "Brandy in the kitchen," she said mechanically, "left-hand cupboard, over the sink . . ." Her face went into a kind of social simper. She expected to be introduced to them all.

But the nurse ran toward the kitchen with the bus driver on the end of her arm.

The telephone rang and Mrs. Boatright rolled in her swift smooth way to answer it.

It was Theo Marsh who turned, elbows out, chin forward, eyes malicious, and said loudly, "So this is Ethel? Lethal Ethel?"

"Really," said Ethel, turning a dull red, "who *are* these people!"

Mr. Gibson, trembling in every limb, had fallen into a chair himself. He realized that Ethel was completely at a loss. She was not on the same level as the rest of them. She couldn't understand their swift communications. She'd been insulted besides . . . But he could not speak, for he was saved who had been doomed, and he tingled and was dumb.

Rosemary said weakly, "We were just going to tell you—just a min—" She gasped to silence.

There was a silence as they all understood this with surprise. Ethel did not *know?*

Mrs. Boatright spoke into the phone, "Yes, he is here. . . . But may I take a message—? The Laboratory? *Oh,* I see. But it *has* been found, you know, and no harm done at all. . . . Oh, you did? . . .

No, you couldn't have known at that time. . . . I see. . . . Oh no,
it was never loose upon the public. That was just an error. . . ."
She went on murmuring.

Out in the kitchen the nurse found the brandy with dispatch, but
then Lee, with enterprise, embraced her. They stood in a clinch. A
green paper bag lay on top of the other trash in the kitchen wastebasket. The bottle, with King Roberto's picture on it, stood upside
down on the counter. But they whispered, and they were not looking at the scenery.

In the living room, Theo bared his particolored teeth at Ethel.
(Mrs. Boatright was too busy on the phone to restrain him, for now
she was calling to have a car sent.) So Theo said, "Ethel herself?
The dead-end kid? The doom preacher? The amateur psychiatrist?"

Ethel looked as if she would choke.

"I cannot see," she cried, hoarse with rage, "why a perfect freak
of a strange old man is permitted to come in here and call me
names! Until somebody in this room makes sense, I intend to eat
my dinner, which—" her voice rose to a scream—"*is getting cold!*"

Ethel never could bear an interruption in her schedule, or any
surprises. She went to the table and sat down with a plop and
plunged her fork blindly into the congealing mass of the spaghetti.
Theo Marsh drifted after her. He leaned on the wall and watched—
his head cocked.

But to Mr. Gibson, in the chair, in the living room, his senses were
returning. His eyes were clearing. He had assimilated the news, the
wonderful surprise. He was saved. He was free. He loved and
was loved and nobody was going to die of the poison, and prayers
are really answered for all a human being dares to *know*, and he
looked about with relish to receive the sense of home—his dear—
his earthly home.

And his breath stopped.

"Rosemary!" he cried. "What is *that?* On the mantel?"

"What, darling?" Rosemary, who had risen, restless with joy,
moved, drunken with relief. "This?" She took a ball of mustard-
colored string up in her hand. "There's money here," she said wonderingly, "where the blue vase used to stand."

So Mr. Gibson, his wits working as fast as ever they had in his
life, quickened with terror, plunged like a quarterback between Paul
and Jeanie past the body of Theo Marsh to seize the loaded fork
from the hand of his sister, Ethel.

"Mrs. Violette was *here!*" he shouted.

"Really, Ken, I couldn't say," said Ethel huffily. "But you left every door in this house unlocked and we could have been robbed . . ." She was livid with anger.

"Olive oil!" he shouted. "A bottle of olive oil! *Where is it?*"

"In the sauce," said Ethel. "I presumed you meant it for the sauce." Her brows were at the top of their possible ascent. "Have you gone mad?" she inquired frigidly.

At this moment the nurse and the bus driver came on loud quick feet. "What's *this!*" Virginia said. She had a glass of brandy in one hand and a small empty glass bottle in the other, which bottle she shook at them.

"And this! *Hey!*" puffed Lee Coffey, showing them the green paper bag.

"It's *here*," said Mr. Gibson. "Don't touch it, Ethel! It is a deadly poison!"

"Poison?" she said recoiling.

Mr. Gibson scraped spaghetti off all three plates into the bowl and then he took up the bowl in a grim clutch. "It must have been Mrs. Violette who spoke to me," he told them. "She did have to go to the bank. I remember she said so. She took the bus, down and back. She spoke the second time when she *saw* me leave it in the seat. *She knew it was mine.* She brought it back with the string!"

"She is so very honest . . ." said Rosemary awesomely.

"That's *it?*" cried Theo. "You *got* the poison, *there?*"

"It's here. And it's been here all afternoon," said Mr. Gibson, and he took the bowl tenderly with him and sat down and held it on his lap and bowed his head.

"We must inform the police," said Mrs. Boatright briskly—but with deep pleasure.

"We are all heroes," said the bus driver.

But Jeanie Townsend, girl heroine, stood with all the other heroes, and frowned. "But why doesn't Miss Gibson *know* about the poisoned olive oil?" she asked. "I heard them telling all about it . . . on *her* radio. *This* one, right here."

"I . . . don't under—what poison?" said Ethel, rising, tottering. "I don't understand. Olive oil?"

Paul began, "He stole it from my lab . . ."

"The laboratory called earlier," said Mrs. Boatright sharply. "They were just on the line. They had discovered their loss. The

police had not got to them then. But surely, they *must* have told you
about your brother who had the *only* opportunity—"

"I—took a message," said Ethel thickly. "Nobody mentioned . . .
poison? Did Ken have poison?" Her eyes rolled.

"He was going to do himself in," said the bus driver chattily. "But
he thinks better of it now."

"Do himself . . . *what?* Please . . ."

"He thinks better of it now," said Rosemary shakily. "Oh, darling,
have we really found it?"

"Right here," said Mr. Gibson. "I've *got* it." He tightened his tight
fingers. Rosemary looked angelic, suddenly, as if she would now
fly up to the ceiling on great white wings.

"Je-ust a minute," said Theo Marsh. He looked at Lee Coffey.
"What have we here?" he inquired. "Hoist?"

"Hoist! Hoist!" croaked the bus driver. "I see what you mean.
With her own petard." He flung out one arm.

"Uh-*huh*," said Theo. "We better analyze this. Now, Ethel . . ."
He rounded upon her. "You know, of course, that we are all impelled by subconscious forces. Primitive and low. Hey?" (He had
picked up the bus driver's "hey.")

Ethel looked absolutely stupid.

"You say you didn't 'hear' the warning? Hah-hah-hah." The artist
gave forth a mirthless sound. "But the subconscious hears all things,
my dear. Now, *you* know that. Then the laboratory phoned. But
told you *nothing?* Nor did you ask?"

"Likely story, all right," said Lee cheerfully. "Where was *your*
subconscious . . . hey? All God's chillun got sub—"

"Her subconscious was putting two and two together," said Theo,
shouting him down. "Therefore it is *obvious*, is it not, Ethel? *You
wished to kill your brother and his wife. You must have.*"

Ethel stared at him.

"Because you nearly *did* kill them, you know," said Theo. "There
is a deadly poison in that sauce. Don't try to tell us you never
'meant' to do it." He put his thumbs in the armholes of his vest. He
looked like the sheriff in a Western.

"I . . ." croaked Ethel, "I had no warning . . . I don't understand.
. . . Please." Her wits seemed to return. "You mean we would have
become ill?"

"You would have become dead," said the bus driver.

Her eyes popped, staring.

"Failing this," said Theo, "you then obviously *wished to kill yourself.*" Theo veered to the bus driver. "Say, how does that come in?"

"We'll figure something," said the driver enthusiastically. "*We'll* tell her what her motive was."

"Sex?" said Theo, brightening.

Mr. Gibson was speechless.

Rosemary said indignantly, "It *doesn't* come in. *Stop it*, both of you."

"Subconsciously," began the artist, his bright malicious glance examining his victim.

"Theo," said Mrs. Boatright.

"Lee," said Virginia in exactly the same tone. The bus driver's shoulders dropped, his arms turned outward in a gesture of apology and relaxation. But he was grinning.

Mr. Gibson, however, watched his wife. Adoringly. (My darling, he thought, is truly kind and compassionate of heart. And if this is innocent, how sweet it is, this innocence, how lovely!) For Rosemary stood beside Ethel, furiously defending her.

"Ethel just does not *hear words* when she turns on music. She has *trained* herself *not* to. She really *wouldn't* have heard the warning. She is *not* trying to kill anybody. She *didn't* mean to. She *couldn't* have. It would have been an *accident*. And *you know it*," she defied the artist, "and don't be so *mean*, now."

"Rosemary," said Ethel brokenly, reaching for her. "I don't understand this . . . honestly. I certainly wouldn't want to hurt you or anyone . . . honestly—"

"Of course not," said Rosemary, caressing her as one would comfort a frightened child. "Don't you pay any attention to these cutups. Now, I believe you'd never mean to, Ethel."

Mr. Gibson thought dizzily, Rosemary and I must try to help poor Ethel . . . poor, brave, unlucky Ethel, faithless, cheated of love. He seemed to himself to pass out for a moment or two. Everybody seemed to be telling Ethel the whole sequence, and he could not bear it. He revived to find himself still sitting in the chair with the bowl of poisoned food tight in his hands. He looked about him.

Now Ethel sat alone.

Mrs. Walter Boatright was on the phone telling the police department exactly what it was to do now. (It would do as she said. He had no doubt.)

The little nurse, finding nobody interested in the brandy, had slipped to the floor beside Ethel's chair and sat there thoughtfully sipping it herself.

The bus driver and the painter were wringing each other by the hand, the artist literally hopping up and down in intellectual delight and still muttering, "Hoist! Hoist!"

"Judge not! Hey?" said the bus driver. "The biter bit. A bitter bite."

Jeanie had run for the door in a streak, a moment ago (now he recalled), yelling, "I'll tell Grandma." And Paul, who had been hugging her, in his joy, now hugged Rosemary. (Anybody. Any soft huggable body. Mr. Gibson understood perfectly.)

He hugged the bowl and thought, Now who could predict such a scene as this? He felt delighted.

But he did not contemplate it long. Hanging onto the bowl, he plunged into the celebration, himself, in person.

A police car had slipped into the drive; now a cop got out.

He was young, and not too sure what he'd been sent here for. He approached the door of the cottage. Before he could ring, it was swinging in before him with a tremendous welcoming verve, pulled by a small, compact man with dancing eyes. This man had a slight, brown-haired, merry-eyed woman tucked under his other arm. She was smiling too, and she helped balance, between them, what looked to be a wooden bowl full of spaghetti. These two stepped back in unison, like a pair of dancers, bowing him inward.

In the small foyer, a big handsome gent was crooning into the telephone. "It's O.K., dear. It really *is!* Everything is wonderful and I'll be home soon." (The cop had no way of knowing he was talking to his mother-in-law.)

In the living room, a wiry old gentleman in a pink shirt whistling tunelessly through his teeth, and with his thin legs prancing, was enthusiastically steering the majestic bulk of a beige-and-white-clad matron in the waltz. She stepped lightly.

Another man, in a leather jacket, crouched for the purpose of kissing the not unwilling lips of a cool little Nordic blonde who was sitting on the floor. From a tiny glass in her limp hand, something trickled on the back of his neck. He wasn't minding.

The cop's eye assessed all this. He was here, he supposed, to ask questions. "I dunno much about this," he confessed, looking at the plain-faced, middle-aged woman who sat in the midst of all the hilarity, stricken and still, staring at the carpet (as if she'd been shook, all right, he thought). "Is she the one," he said aside with pity, "who got careless with some poison?"

The man at the door hesitated. Then he said, "No, it was I. But mercifully . . . Come in. Come in," said Mr. Gibson cordially. *"I'm all right now."*

The Turret Room

Chapter One

HIS FEET were lumps of pain. The foot he had once broken ached a little deeper than the other, which put an accent on the rhythm, LEFT right LEFT right, but there was not enough difference to make him limp. In fact, he was striding along pretty good, pretty good, but he knew that he had better not break his stride or he might not get going again. His head was light. He fancied that he was riding on a wheel. Well, it had been too much, it had been too far, it had been a stupid thing to do, to walk all the way, but he could not stop, now.

The last time he had stopped, when was that, about four miles ago, the other edge of town, to put on his clean white orderly's coat in the gas station, to shave, to wash his face and hands, to comb his hair, he had been tempted to take a bus, but he had known, even then, that he could get himself going about once more, and that would be all. And no bus came nearer than half a mile to the big house on the knoll.

He guessed it was afternoon, the third day he had been walking. The first day had been so fine. On the morning of the second day, he had been pretty stiff, pretty sore, but he'd walked that off and been pleased with himself. *This* day had been bad, all the way. Psyche and soma, he thought. I'm trying to fool myself into aches and pains, because some of me wants to give up. I'm getting there. And I'm getting scared.

It was a nice street he was on. He had always thought so. It was the older part of the little town. There were big trees. All the houses were big houses. Nobody walked. There were no children playing in the yards. There must be children, he thought, but each child has his own little paradise around at the back. If there are any children . . .

He was getting there, but his heart was too tired to beat any faster when he turned in at the drive where the old iron gates stood open, as they always had, as he remembered. He dared not stop, but just as he made the turn he lifted his right arm and sent the little canvas carrying-bag sailing into the juniper bushes.

He had his pride. He had walked some seventy-odd miles in two days and a little more than half a day, LEFT right LEFT right, all the way, and he was going to make it, but he would not even seem to suggest that he stay. He was hot and he was very tired, but he had washed, and put on the only clean garment that he had. He would do now what he had to do, partly because he was afraid to do it, and then he would take the bus back up North, and begin the new life.

There it was, the house with the tower. It wasn't much of a tower. It was too low, nothing but a rounded turret, half embedded, half protruding, but it had the little slitty windows that you see in pictures of castles. The tower was stone, and the house was stucco, gray, the color of stone. But the roof was red tile and the ground floor went sloping over the ground horizontally, with shutters on the windows. The main part had been built (he seemed to know) by Wendy's great-grandfather and the wing at the right added on by her grandfather. One of them, probably the first one, had planted the tree.

It was a rubber tree, or some such thing, and it had sure grown, he thought. Sure grown. It stood smack in the middle of the big arched window at the front of the house, and it spread, it snubbed against the tower, it spread its upper limbs over the tower, it had shed huge leathery leaves on the tiles, on the ground, all around. So it stood, like a huge plume, an outburst of natural laughter, ignoring the façade of the house.

Harold Page put his leaden feet down, one after the other, until he came up to the big wooden door with its ornate iron hinges. He lifted his leaden arm and his wooden finger found the bell.

Before he had to ring again, the big door was opened by a girl and she wasn't Wendy. She wasn't anyone he had ever seen before. She didn't look as if she belonged here. She was a pretty girl, about twenty-four or twenty-five, he thought, and she was wearing black capris, neat and tight but not too tight, and a pale pink tailored blouse. Her hair was a pale yellow, smooth, and drawn back, held by a pale pink band, and her gray eyes immediately winced with alarm.

"You're . . . not from the hospital!" she said to him.

He could hardly lift his tongue. He could hardly think. He was feeling a bitter disappointment. He was thinking, They don't live here anymore. His voice came out in tired gasps. "That's right. The Whitmans? They . . . live here?"

The girl said, "Well, *of course. Yes.* What *is* it?" Her neat flat black slippers took a step backward upon the dark brown tile, and Harold stumbled forward. The cool and faintly stale air of the house hit him; he almost fell.

"Walked . . . all the way," he mumbled. "So hot . . . Excuse me."

The girl said, "You'd better come in. It's always cool in here."

I know, he thought. I know. She seemed to shepherd him across the narrow foyer to the arch and the two steps down into the big room that was just exactly as he had remembered it. He slid his feet cautiously on the slippery tile steps, until they hit the carpet, and there he stood. The ceiling was still very high, the walls still looked like yellow stone, the velvets on the big chairs were the same, some gold, some a faded rose. And the turret wall still invaded the room's huge rectangle, with the stairs still winding up around its gentle curve. The floor of this room was below the level of the ground outside the huge window, and there was the tree, seen from within, overpowering, its great bare trunk rising from a knot of gnarled roots, its leaves pushing at the upper window within the peak of the Spanish arch of the glass, shutting the house away from the sky and turning its ancient, expensive austerity in upon itself.

It was very cool in here.

But now this modern-looking girl said urgently, "Did anything happen?" Just as he had brought himself to ask, "Is Mr. Whitman here?"

He couldn't talk over her, he hadn't the energy. In fact, he wasn't sure how much longer he could even stand. But she let him speak.

"Or Mrs. Whitman? Or old Mrs. Whitman?" Any of them, he was thinking, but I had better not ask for Wendy.

"Well, none of them are here just now," she said, in a different voice, a careful voice. "I'm Edith Thompson. I'm a kind of poor relation. Hey, you'd better sit down."

He guessed he had better, before he fell down, so he staggered as far as the first big chair and fell into it. Now his back was to the window and the tree. The girl came, treading lightly and softly, moving with easy grace, around him and the chair, to face him.

"Excuse me," he apologized. "My legs just don't . . . want to hold me up." The light was falling coolly and steadily upon her and he thought he could guess something. "You must be related to Mrs. Whitman. Myra, I mean." His voice sounded draggy and dreary. He was glad of this respite, though. She would let him wait, and by the time anybody came, he would be feeling much better.

But the girl said, crinkling up her eyes so that her small straight nose seemed to sharpen with suspicion, "Why do you say that?"

"You have the same color hair. I thought . . . maybe . . . You look a little bit like her . . ." He was rambling.

The girl took her breath in, and smiled. "Do I?" she said in a friendly fashion. "No, I'm related to old Mrs. Whitman." She sat down on the ottoman.

"Granny?" he muttered. He couldn't pay attention. He was beginning to drift. The deadness of the air, the softness of the chair, this hiatus between the end of the journey and its objective. . . . He had better pull himself together. So he said, as briskly as he could, "Excuse me. It's not very polite to fall apart like this. But it sure was a long long walk and today was the worst. Turned so hot. Will they be back soon? Please?"

The girl just looked at him. He seemed to be able to see her mind turning around to remember the first words she had said to him. "From the *hospital!*" she exclaimed. "You don't mean you've walked all the way from *that* hospital? You *are* Harold Page, aren't you?"

"Didn't I say? I'm sorry." (Surely, he had said.) "I don't know what's the matter with me," he continued truthfully.

"Would you like a glass of water?" She was half up; her whole impulse was to be kind.

"Oh, I sure would," he sighed, "if it's not . . . too much . . . trouble . . ." His lips were feeling thick, now, and his mouth very dry. He heard her say something about Mrs. Beck lying down, she would get it, he must rest a minute, and he mumbled something. Then she was gone and he was all alone, and he shivered.

Almost two years since he had been here. Very bad years. Or very good, who could say? He had learned a lot. He was twenty-one years old, now—not such a boy, not such an ignorant innocent. He was right to have come, although he shouldn't have walked. He hadn't arrived in very good condition. But he was here and he would wait. Harold bent over and with exquisite pleasure, took his shoes off. He leaned back deep into the chair and closed his dry and stinging eyelids. In a little while, surely, the coolness would get through the skin, where it was making him shiver, and in toward his bones.

She didn't make any noise, returning, but he felt her presence, opened his eyes and struggled more erect to take the glass, and the paper napkin upon which she was holding it, into both his hands. He drank thirstily and thanked her with all his heart.

She smiled, just a trifle falsely, and sat down on the ottoman again. Her eyes seemed solemn, and he had revived enough to feel a little awkward with a stranger. He put the glass on the table and played with the paper napkin. It was white, with a name printed in mahogany brown script across one corner. THE WHITMANS. "I used to be so impressed, you know," he said shyly. "Just think, people who had their name printed on their paper napkins."

She said, with faint impatience, "Everybody does. Tell me, why did you *walk?* You said, all the way? But that must be about seventy-five miles!"

"Not counting up and down, either." He smiled at her. "Oh, I was kind of lured into it, I guess. I started out, walking to the bus. But it was so great, you know, walking and looking around. I thought, why should I settle for a stinky bus? I had it in my mind to hitchhike, maybe. By the time I was out on the highway I found out that's not so easy anymore. Anyhow, I got to thinking, they might ask me where I'd come from. . . . Maybe they'd be scared."

He hadn't really tried to hitch a ride. Walking was a wonderful way to get to thinking, alone and free.

"You were released from there on Monday?" the girl was saying, in her brisk tone.

He hesitated. He really was too tired to explain the whole thing. "Well . . . I didn't start walking until Tuesday morning," he told her. "I have a room in the town. School doesn't start for a while yet. I wanted to find out . . . Maybe you can tell me. Where is the baby?"

He didn't know whether he was a coward or not, to ask *her*. She wasn't answering. Her eyes opened very wide and she looked perfectly astonished. "But don't you *know!*"

How would I know? he thought. Who would tell me? And why don't you know that I wouldn't know? Don't you know that I was cast out and thrown away? But he spoke patiently. "I've written letters. Nobody answered. I *said* that I was leaving the hospital, on Monday. I was afraid they might have moved away."

"Didn't Myra tell you?" the girl said, with strange urgency. She was watching him, most intently.

"Do you mean *she* wrote to me?" He couldn't understand the question. "I didn't get *any* letters," he explained. The girl frowned, and he went on, still patient. "I've got no folks and my buddies aren't the writing kind. All I had were a couple of legal notices. One, that the divorce was final. I guess that gave me the nerve . . ." His voice was going dreary again. He thought he knew what the trouble was. "You can tell me," he said gently, "if the baby died."

The girl sat straight with a jolt. "Oh, no, no, no! He's all right. Oh, I'm sorry. I was thinking of something else. He's in a special school, that's all. The Patterson School for deaf children. It's about forty miles north of here on the coast road—"

"I know where that is," he cut in joyously. "I see. That's *good*."

"You did know that he was born deaf?" The girl's voice was careful. It promised kindness, but not too much kindness. She was paying attention, that was the thing. She was really listening.

"Oh, yes. Oh, yes. They let me hold him, once." He could remember the feel of the little soft light body. "I was the one who noticed. It's a thing about the formation of the ear. My father had it and my brother, who died. But not Mom or me. I told Wendy about the risk, but she said she didn't care."

No, Wendy didn't care in those days. Wendy, so wild and wonderful, didn't care for anything.

"And I believed her," he murmured, and glanced up, somberly.

"They'll teach him to talk, you know," the girl said heartily, as if to raise his spirits. "And they may even be able to invent some kind of hearing aid."

"That's wonderful, isn't it?" But he kept somber. "Wendy must be . . ." He looked behind him, and up the long curve of the stairs, to where the wrought iron of the stair-rail continued across the balcony of the second story. "I suppose Wendy is living—near him?"

She said, "No," throwing the syllable away, and the corner of her mouth twitched.

Their eyes met and there was a telepathic flash. He knew that he and she were the same kind of people. She, too, would suppose that a mother would wish to be near her child. She must have been brought up to assume this, as Harold had been. His family hadn't been rich, as the Whitmans were, but it had been a family; it had assumed such things. Over and above his personal loss, it was too bad that he was the only one left now, from such a family, because four people, who looked out for each other without having to think about it, made something better than just four people. He was convinced that this girl knew what he was thinking and agreed with him.

But she plunged into more questions. (The baby was all right. It wasn't that, then. Yet, something was bothering her.) "You didn't walk night and day, did you? Have you got any money? Where did you sleep?"

"I haven't much money right now," he answered. "Enough for snacks. That's all right. I thought Mr. Whitman might lend me a part of the bus fare back, since I have some expectations. Not that I came to ask *them* for anything, except where the baby is. I feel . . . I felt very strongly that I ought to know that."

What he was saying came back oddly to his own ears. It was true enough, but not enough of the truth.

"I wish you had telephoned," she said, and bit her lips.

"Yes, but the truth is, I came myself—" he struggled to express the whole truth—"because I'm still . . . and I don't want to be, but I *am still* . . . afraid of these people."

And that's as close as I can get, he thought. I have to speak to them and hear them answer. I have to look at them and meet their eyes.

"Where did you spend last night?" she was demanding.

"Last night? I slept on a lawn swing. The house looked empty. There was a big dog, but he was friendly. In fact, he kept me company. I was glad to have him." He thought it was small talk. He smiled.

"Where was this?" She wasn't smiling.

"A little town . . ." He couldn't remember the name.

"Did anybody see you? Did you talk with anyone? Last night? Or this morning?"

He moved his head, wonderingly. "I started early, this morning, because I was cold. What's the matter?"

Now he knew that she had been gathering toward a resolution. Her face changed. She sprang up on her good lithe legs. "You shouldn't have come here and you've got to leave," she said decisively. She was a brisk crisp kind of girl, with lots of energy. "Right

now. You had better get on a bus as quick as you can and get out
of this town. *I'll* give you some money."

He twisted in the chair to watch her. She ran to the stairs, which
began at the edge of the big window, and swiftly up the first short
flight to the landing, which made a curving balcony upon the curving wall. She opened the wooden door, ornately carved to make a
decoration here, into the turret room. It was a bedroom, he knew
that, used for a guest room, for overflow or unimportant guests. It
was halfway up and halfway down, and it was round, which is a
very unhandy shape, he remembered someone saying. It had a tiny
bathroom, put in as an afterthought, which cut up the space grotesquely, built as square as could be against the rounding outer
wall, in which the windows were too small for so large a room. He
had glanced in, he remembered, when one of the maids had been
cleaning one morning. He remembered the strange green gloom
where the eastern light came feebly through the leaves of the big
tree.

He was shivering again. He stood up, slowly, and as his weight
came upon his feet he knew that the left one was a normally tired
foot, but the right one, which had once been broken, was more seriously damaged. He limped toward the stairs.

The girl flashed out of the turret room and stood above him on
the balcony, a flat black purse in both hands. She began to rum-
mage in it. "Oh nuts! I should have cashed a traveler's check yesterday. Never mind. There's some change, at least. Or I could meet
you . . . No, that's too risky."

She seemed to be talking to herself. He said, "What's wrong?"

She took a step to look straight down into his face. "*You* weren't
in this house last night." She announced this.

Of course not, he thought. Of course not. "No," he said.

"Then I don't see why you should walk right into it, now."

She started down but he stopped her. "Now, wait. I've come all
this way—"

"To find out where the baby is? Well, I've told you."

Standing on his left foot, feeling dizzy, Harold began to shake his
head. "That wasn't all."

"You don't know a thing about it, do you?" the girl said softly,
with compassion in her voice. "I didn't think you would. Oh please,
just get away."

"From what?" he said severely.

She took a deep breath and made a grimace. "Well, you've walked right in. Listen, you are supposed to be one of those berserk ex-husbands." She was still on the stairs, looking down. "The police are looking for you," she said, as if it broke her heart to tell him so.

Harold steadied himself. "Why?"

She ran down and came close to him. She put her hand on his arm and he had to struggle not to lean, not to fall. Her gray eyes were very clear and sad, but her voice was still brisk. "Because somebody got in here last night and beat up Myra Whitman, your ex . . . step . . . whatever-she-was mother-in-law. And she is in a coma in the hospital, *here*. That's where I thought you'd come from, at first. That's where they all *are*. And Cousin Ted is fit to be tied. He is even . . ." She sucked in her breath. Her hand was strong, now, on his arm. He must be leaning. "I don't see how you ever got through," she said, in a worried tone. "Maybe that coat. Why are you wearing a white coat?" She was trying to lead him to the chair.

"My orderly's coat," he said. "To be clean." He moved out of her grasp, stumbling. He put up his hands and caught hold of the iron balusters. With his back to her, trying to understand the full import of the situation and already understanding it too well, he asked her, "Why do they think *I* beat up Myra?"

She answered with a quiet respect, very clearly, "Because you beat up Wendy once. Because you've been in a mental hospital. Because you wrote that you were leaving there on Monday. Because the divorce is final and you didn't want the divorce. You just . . . fit the pattern, I suppose."

He didn't look around. "Is that all?"

This time she did not answer.

So he turned. He made himself able to stand up. "Where is Wendy?"

"She . . . she still lives here."

"I see." He swayed. "So it's going to happen all over again."

She caught his arm again and held it, strongly. With her other hand she touched his neck, under the ear. "Are you feverish?"

"I don't know. What did Wendy say?"

"Wendy said she saw you running down the drive last night."

Well, there it was. It was so wrong as to be somehow right. He almost laughed.

After a while, he was in the chair again and the girl was on the ottoman, watching him anxiously. He had the sense that she had gone to look out the front door, that nobody was coming, that they were here, in this cool and somehow sunken room, safe and alone, for a little while more. Before it happened to him, all over again.

He said calmly, speculatively, "Why does she tell these lies? Why do they always believe her? I understand myself much better now. I had to learn. But I don't understand these people."

"What did they do to you? I've always wondered." Her face was close to his, her skin was very fair. Something about her eyelids kept a secret. "I learned some time ago to watch out for Wendy. Tell me?"

He might as well tell her while there was time. "I didn't ever beat up Wendy. Ever. It's true I didn't want the divorce, because I wanted to make a family." (A family that would be a family, as he understood a family should be.) "Out of Wendy and me and the baby," he went on. "Of course, I was in the service then. I couldn't send much money." (But he would have worked. He would have made a family and a home.) "But when they wanted me to, well, stand still for Wendy to sue me. . . . You know how it's done. The man has to play that he's guilty. I said, No, I *wasn't*. And I *wouldn't*. So that's when I had to watch her bruise her own arms and claw her own face—because when I tried to stop her, that was worse. Well, so she got the divorce and the baby, too. There wasn't a way . . . not a way in the world. How could I call Wendy Whitman a liar, with her folks behind her? *I* had no folks. I was nineteen years old. She wouldn't have had to do that. She wanted to be rid of me, she could have been. Without telling such a lie and taking everything . . . you know . . . everything away from me." There was no whine in his voice, he was just telling her.

The girl said, "And you *saw* her?"

"In a dream, you wonder?" He sat up straighter. "Well, you see, I have *been* analyzed. Oh, I've had hypnosis, drugs. They tried the whole works on me. Oh, they tried, in the worst way, to find some part of me that 'knew' I'd done it. But there wasn't any. I was a strange case, I guess. I'd actually been frustrated. And here I go again."

He smiled at the perfection of the wrongness of it. He smiled at the girl, who was looking troubled. "At least I'll know better, this time, than to hold it all in," he told her, "until I'm fighting like a wildcat whenever anybody looks cross-eyed at me. That's how I broke my foot, back in camp, after she started the divorce. And I fought the doctors and the nurses, too. They finally sent me to psychiatry."

"And to that hospital, for all this time?" she said delicately.

He knew she wanted to believe him. "Would you like to call them?" he said, gently. "Then you'd *know* that I was discharged as a patient months ago. As soon as they got it out of me what had happened, and that it was true. I cried for about a week, but I stopped hitting people. But, see, my foot's no good for the army. I had nowhere and nobody. There was just this old great-uncle, who died. I had a notice—"

"There's no time, now," she interrupted.

But he wanted to tell her a little more. "I'm going to *be* a doctor, I hope. They let me work there. I got fascinated. Now I want the training. Dr. Wesley says I can do it. I'm starting school . . . I mean, I *was*."

He looked around. The good dream faded. No, first, it was going to happen to him all over again.

She was tugging at his arm to get him to his feet. "Oh, hurry, please, before they come. Just go away."

"Is there any use in that?" he asked her delicately, not wishing to offend. He felt dizzy standing, and his head was very light.

"Please believe me. You can't be found in this house. Or in this town, even. Maybe it doesn't have to happen to you all over again."

"How come you believe what I say, miss?" Harold had begun to wonder.

"Edie," she said, fiercely. "I'm Edie. Oh, listen, I lived here myself when I was a teen-ager and *I* knew little Wendy."

He wasn't taking it in. "I'm glad if you do believe me, but I can't see why." Isn't she a member of this family, he was thinking.

"Then I'll tell you something," said Edie. "I came here for a couple of weeks between jobs, just for my own sake to . . . to see . . ."

There was that telepathic flash again. "To see," said Harold slowly, "whether you could, somehow, for your own sake . . . now, manage to stand up to them? Or even—forgive them?"

"I suppose that's it," she said impatiently, but with friendliness, too. "That's something like it. Do you know that you are burning? How are you going to make it to the bus? I wish I had a car."

"I'll have to stand up to them," he said remotely.

"No, not now. I'll tell you what." She was turning him and guiding him. "Both maids are away. There's only Mrs. Beck, and she's busy. Nobody will go into the turret room but me. Please, wait in there. Will you, please? Just let me pave the way for you. Let me break it to them gently that you've come."

"Why?" he said, stubborn, knowing that she hadn't told him everything.

"All right." She took the challenge. "Because Cousin Ted has cast himself in the role of the heroic defender of his womenfolk and he's got a loaded gun in his pocket and he is stupid enough to shoot you. Is there any sense in that?"

He blinked at her. "Well, not for *me*," he said, half-humorously. He knew she believed what she had said. He was inclined to believe it too.

So he went up the stone stairs in his stocking feet, one hand on the rail, her strong hand under his other arm. He was very dizzy. He said, "But I don't know why *you* believe me."

"Myra's had her hair dyed red, for a year."

"What?"

"Don't argue," Edie said. "You don't feel well enough to figure that out. You don't feel well enough to be shot at, either." She turned him into the turret room and shut the door behind them.

Chapter Two

THERE was one thing about the turret room. Once you had closed the small, but heavy, wooden door, you felt sheltered. The door was thick, the walls were thick. The room was cool. Between the ceiling and the beating California sun, there was an attic, a tiled roof, and the heavy shadow of the tree.

Edie Thompson made the boy stretch out on the double bed. She found some aspirin in the medicine cabinet and made him take it. There was a flowered quilt, kept folded at the foot of the bed. She pulled it over his ankles for the sake of the sense of shelter it would add. All the while, she spoke soothingly. She would talk to the Whitmans. She would fend for him. She would try to make them see that they were mistaken, or at least that they might be mistaken, before the sight of him could shock them into doing something foolish. It made more sense, she said. And he needed rest.

He rested quietly. He was a good-looking boy. Naturally, thought Edie. Wendy would never have taken up with anyone who wasn't. He was medium tall, on the slim side, brown-haired, brown-eyed, and his face was saved from prettiness by some rugged carving of his long thin nose. But a boy, very young—maybe a country boy. Just an ordinary nice kid, a little naïve. One without defenses, who had suffered in a way that the tougher kind of young male animal, the city kids, the gang kids (whom Edie knew), might not. She had worked with some of *them,* the very young ones. Of course, he was running a fever. Maybe that made him seem in need. Gave him his air of helplessness. She wanted to help him.

Edie was a social worker and she knew better than to call her judgment infallible or her belief the guarantee of truth. But after all, she had been conducting interviews, for a year and a half now, in the grubbiest sections of a great city, and she thought her chances were fair to spot a phony, a loony, or a criminal. Edie was a girl with firm opinions, and a good deal of self-confidence these days. She was energetic and sometimes impatient with people who were not. This was a bit of handicap in her profession. Sometimes Edie was not altogether sure that she had chosen the right profession, but its practice had given her some skills. A kind of intuition, for instance, based on experience.

If this boy was what the newspapers call "berserk," she would be very much surprised. She thought he was, if anything, too innocently sentimental. She could not sense in him the devious cleverness he would have to have to toss out that mention of Myra's coloring—*if* he had quarreled with a redheaded Myra here, last night. "Berserk" people were not clever. It was a contradiction. Of course, he might have two personalities. It could be Jekyll lying there, weary and gentle and sad. Hyde could have burst in last night. She didn't believe that. She believed what he had told her—all of it.

The fact was, she didn't believe *Wendy.*

Edie had moved to one of the narrow windows and was looking down at the driveway and the gates. They would be back soon. Then she must be the go-between. That was it. Be a buffer. Try to steady the situation. There was a certain amount of hysteria in it. Assumptions had been made. The Whitmans were perfectly con-

vinced that Harold Page had done it. Edie must try to crack open
their minds and insert enough doubt so that the poor kid might not
be hurt too much. Not again.

There was that. She thought, *If* what he says is true (and I believe
him), then he is tender to unjust suspicions. For him it opens an
old wound, it hurts more. Oh, there was some physical danger. If
the boy had been greeted by Cousin Ted in that gentleman's present agitated state, Edie thought it quite possible that Cousin Ted
would have shot, at least *at* him. But there are worse wounds than
a bullet makes.

Edie leaned on the wall and felt power curling her fingers. She
was the go-between. She knew both sides. She had lived here herself and knew the regime. She had been brought up in a frugal
household, however, by parents both loving and high-minded, and
she had seen the seamy side besides, in her work. It seemed to Edie
that the duty fell upon her with a click of fitness, and she accepted
it, not without joy. It was a joy for which she had thirsted, and had
not found yet. Maybe her new job . . . with a heavier load, more
cases. Maybe. Meanwhile, she believed in Harold Page, and her joy
was the joy of battle. She would fight for him.

Edie had a dim notion that somewhere along the line she was
merrily rationalizing. But didn't everyone? She believed him when
he said that Wendy had cheated and lied. That much was easy. Did
she believe that he had walked so far?

Yes, she believed that too. For one thing, it was too fantastic not
to be true. Truth was the most fantastic thing in the world. Sometimes she thought that people knocked themselves out, split their
human brains, trying to make order in a world that was *really* and
incorrigibly fantastic. He said he had walked seventy-five miles. It
was possible. Human beings *could* walk, the motorcar notwith-
standing. And there was his fatigue, his limp . . . *his shoes!*

She saw a car turn into the drive and after it, another, and yet
another. *Three* carloads of people arriving? Fantastic— But what
about his shoes?

She went swiftly to the door. The boy did not stir. Edie shut him
in, alone, and ran down the lower flight of the stairs. The dusty
empty pathetic shoes were near the chair. Edie made a swipe across
the carpet with her foot and swept them under the chair as the
outer door opened, and she heard Cousin Ted's voice.

He had a high voice with an irritating nasal quality. "I want to
talk to Charles, Mother, and these other people."

"All right, Ted. All right. All right," said old Mrs. Whitman. She entered and the house became her house, the kingdom was her kingdom.

She was a spry little woman of seventy-five, dressed elegantly, if uncomfortably for the hot day, in a gray silk suit, a costume complete with small flowered hat, with gloves, with neat gray shoes. She came nimbly down into the big room and did not greet, but waited to be greeted.

"Hi, Granny," said Edie, feeling her heart give a great guilty leap. "How is Myra?"

Granny began to chatter in her clear, light, well-articulated manner. "Oh, mercy! Oh, my! I am very sorry that I went." She proceeded to the sofa and seated herself with good control, without, in any way, collapsing. "Myra is just lying there, looking a perfect fright, by the way. I can't help thinking it was rude to go and stare at her. Especially since her mouth is open." The old lady began to remove her gloves, and Edie, watching her, felt the same old bewilderment. She never had been able to tell whether Granny meant to be funny, meant to be tart, or simply meant what she said.

"But what does the doctor say?" she asked.

"Oh, *he* is very calm about the whole thing, the doctor is. They are making tests. Maybe they'll operate. Maybe, mind you. Or, as far as I can understand it, maybe Myra will simply open her eyes and come to." Granny removed her hat.

"Then she can tell us what happened, I suppose," said Edie with a sense of solution.

"You can suppose all you like, Edie, my dear," said Granny, "but it seems that a blow on the head joggles the cells or whatever is *in* there . . ."

"Oh?"

"And if Myra doesn't remember, that will seem odd, don't you think?" said old Mrs. Whitman, putting her white head to one side. She had blue eyes that somehow never seemed connected with what Granny was saying. The eyes kept moving, as if something very wary hid inside and did not much care what was being said or done, but watched out for itself. "Suppose one were minding one's own business and woke up in a hospital, two or three days later, people having been staring . . ."

But Edie had caught sight of the water glass, in the corner of her eye. It seemed to shine like a star. Without thought, her mind occupied with dismay at the idea that Myra might never remember, and guilt for her own equivocal position, Edie moved out of the range of Granny's eyes, snatched up the glass from which Harold Page had drunk, and slipped away to the far end of the high mantelpiece, where she tucked the glass behind an ornament.

"I do hope," Granny was saying, "that it never happens to me. Where are you? Where is Mrs. Beck? I want a cup of tea. Ted had to go and see those grubby people and haul me about with him. I don't know what possessed me. I had presumed that I had reached a stage of life . . . Edie?"

"I'm here," said Edie. Her heart was racing. I have got to get over this panicking, she thought. What I propose to do, I had better do well. And soon. I had better consider how I am going to talk to Granny.

". . . when I need not be troubled," Granny rippled on, "by any miserable notions of duty. For pity's sake, doesn't one reach a point when one has *done* it? *Iced* tea, I think."

Edie said, soothingly, "Mrs. Beck is lying down. She had such a bad night—"

"So did we all," Granny cut in. "Ambulance, commotion, police. It was quite stimulating."

And again, Edie was not sure whether this was supposed to be sarcastic or just fact.

This old lady was not really Edie's grandmother. She was her great-aunt. Edie had fallen into the way of calling her Granny (Wendy did) when she had lived here, seven or eight years ago. At that time Granny had been Authority, whimsical and powerful, and naturally resented. Now Edith Thompson was a person who had been in the world, and Lila Whitman had no real authority over her. But somehow, she was just as powerful and just as whimsical as ever.

Edie sat down on the edge of the sofa, beside her, and said earnestly, "Granny, did you hear *anything* last night, when it happened?"

Granny's dainty claw fumbled with the tiny box she wore on her breast. "I never hear anything at night, Edie, for the simple reason that I cannot sleep upon my hearing aid. One of these days I'll wake up and find I've been hit on the head by some madman . . . or whatever he did to poor Myra."

"They think," Edie began to recapitulate, "there was some kind of struggle and she fell. . . ."

But Granny had half risen from the sofa. She seemed to be staring across the room.

"What?" gasped Edie. (What have I forgotten? What does she see? Does she know he is here?)

But the old lady sank back. "Oh, mercy! I suppose it *is* a mercy, they left no X to mark the spot." Myra had struck her head, the theory was, on the hard tile of the hearth.

Edie began to think that the old lady might be enjoying herself. "Do you *believe* it was Harold Page?" she said, a trifle angrily.

"Of course it was," said Granny. "Oh, he has been such a nuisance! I could have told Wendy, in the beginning. She didn't ask me. Well, I keep quiet, you know."

No, you don't, thought Edie.

"One may as well," Granny ran on. "One might better. Wendy never listens. Few do. Few do."

"Granny, will you please listen to me for a minute?"

But old Mrs. Whitman had no intention of listening very much. She was off. "There was Wendy," she explained, "all of sixteen long years old but barely. And 'everybody' was getting married."

Oh surely, thought Edie, listening hard, that is sarcasm. A form of—what? Humor?

"By 'everybody,'" Granny continued, "we must understand, first, her father (to Myra, of course) and second, one girl in Wendy's class who had eloped, which exploit was regarded with a certain enviable awe. So Wendy picked up this soldier. Of all things! Ted ought to have had it annulled right away. But Ted indulges Wendy scandalously, if you ask me. Which he does not. Since Genevieve died, he has had some notion that Wendy *cannot* be crossed. To him, it is like speaking ill of the dead." Granny sighed. "I don't suppose," she said and her blue eyes wagged in their sockets, "that my son has ever been the most brilliant boy in the world. Not that it matters."

Edie opened her mouth but before she could speak, Granny smoothed at her skirt briskly and said, "We have plenty of money."

I never will understand her, thought Edie. "How can you be so sure that it was Harold Page?" she said, coldly.

"Oh, for pity's sake, *of course* it was Harold Page. Wendy saw him." Granny continued to brush her skirt.

"Couldn't Wendy ever be mistaken? Like any other human being?" said Edie, rather hotly. "Even so, she doesn't say she saw him inside the house. The police didn't find any fingerprints."

"Oh, Edie," said Granny, not bothering to lift her eyelids, "don't be so retarded. Nobody leaves fingerprints anymore. Passé. Passé."

And there it was again, the puzzle. Was the old lady being funny?

"And obviously," said Granny, "he *was* inside the house, because, if not, he couldn't have done it."

Mrs. Beck, the housekeeper, from where she was standing, just within the dining room, could hear the voices in the big room. Neither voice was the one she always listened for. She smoothed her clean white silk uniform and stepped forward. It was time she made an appearance.

She said, politely, "Do you need me, Mrs. Whitman? How is Miss Myra, ma'am?"

The old lady turned her frosty head and spoke in the way she had that was always so cool, and a little bit nasty. "She'll be all right—sooner or later and more or less, that is. May I have some iced tea, please, Mrs. Beck?"

At least she always says "please," Mrs. Beck thought, with satisfaction. "Yes, ma'am," she said in the humble, but cool, way she had long ago adopted. "Miss Edith?"

The cousin, or whatever she was, who was here for the fortnight, said, "No, thank you." Then the girl's gaze flicked toward the stairs. "Wait. Yes, I will, thank you."

Mrs. Beck looked toward the stairs, herself. "Is Miss Wendy here?" she cooed. She never could help that change in her voice.

"No, no," said the old lady. "What's his name—Ronnie Mungo—came and fetched her at the hospital. Otherwise she wouldn't have gone, I imagine."

Mrs. Beck said nothing. Let the old lady be aware that Wendy didn't care for Myra. Anyone could know that.

"He carried her off to the country club for lunch. Why not? With plenty of lemon."

Mrs. Beck made the submissive duck of her head that she had long ago adopted. Go make the iced tea, then. Mrs. Beck had some powdered tea. Good enough, with water from the tap. She went through the long dining room and turned the corner to the kitchen.

Mrs. Beck was fifty years old. She was tall and there wasn't much flesh on her big bones. She had been in this house a long time. It was her kingdom. She had come when the first Mrs. Theodore Whitman was still alive, Miss Genevieve, who had died before the year was out. After that, it hadn't taken long to shake the house into the pattern that Mrs. Beck desired. She and the old lady had an unwritten compact. The old lady got whatever she wanted, and Mrs. Beck ran the house. When Miss Myra had come along, Mrs. Beck had been leery of *her,* for a while, and taken protective measures. But it had turned out that Miss Myra, the second wife, the one whose age fell between the old lady and little Wendy, had known better than to try to interfere in any way. She had never tried to run the house. She had never tried to run anybody. She had kept herself to herself and minded her own business—until last night.

Mrs. Beck knew how Myra was. She had called the hospital, herself, and inquired. Myra was in a coma. Mrs. Beck turned on the water with a twist of her strong wrist to let it run cold.

In the big room Edie was saying, "Granny, when I was eighteen you wouldn't let *me* have a date with Ronnie Mungo."

She hadn't meant to say that, but it was an old sore point, and now that Edie was grown and out from under authority she could discuss it, couldn't she? She could find out for sure. The old lady's face, however, showed no concern, no ruffling, not even the memory.

"I wouldn't?" she said placidly. "Why was that, I wonder? Well, Wendy will marry him, I suppose—or so she said on Sunday. Now that she's legally free. And they will go and travel about and be gay with their money, which will suit them very well."

She doesn't care, thought Edie. She simply does not care. "Tell me this," Edie said, wishing she could take hold of the narrow, elegant shoulders and shake—hard, "Why on earth would Harold Page get into this house and fight with *Myra?*"

"Myra," said Granny, with a thoughtful air, "can be *very* annoying, in her quiet little way . . ."

Edie was tired of trying to guess whether this was in fun or not. "Would you answer me?"

"For pity's sake," said Granny, "what is Harold Page to you, child? Or he to Hecuba? A madman needn't have a reason."

"It's pretty passé to say 'madman,' Granny."

"I beg your pardon."

"Mad? *Just* mad?" If this is a quarrel, thought Edie, then let's have it.

"But of course he is," said the old lady carelessly. "He must be mad to do such a thing. Myra may be annoying at times, but one shouldn't knock her on the head. One can always manage to be *more* annoying, or something of the sort. That is, if one is sane."

Edie strangled incredulous laughter. "He did it because he is mad? He must be mad because he did it?" she asked.

"Well?"

"But that's circular!" Edie threw out her hands. Maybe Granny was simply rather stupid. Maybe that was the answer to the riddle of Granny.

The old lady was as slippery as water. She said tartly, "Nothing of the sort. Or, if so, what about it? It happens to be what happened *and* what usually does."

Edie swallowed.

"Still . . ." said Granny, "I wish her mouth had *not* been open." Her own old lips came tight together and seemed to knead each other.

Chapter Three

EDITH THOMPSON was an orphan. She had come here, badly shaken by the sudden death of both her parents, when she had just turned seventeen years old. She had been given board and room, here. She had gone to high school in this town. Wendy was not at public school, but attended Miss Somebody-or-other's. Public school, however, was good enough for Edith Thompson.

She had not made many friends in high school. Girls who lived as frugally as she had lived were shy of the Whitman ménage. Girls who lived as the Whitmans lived were few and not very friendly. Boys were much the same. In this house, Edie had been a poor relation, taken in physically but in no other way. Her cousin Wendy had been eleven, and twelve, and never her companion. On the contrary! Edie had been miserable and lonely. But after she had won through the period of lonely mourning, her native energy had seethed. She would get away. *She* would get away.

At eighteen, then, she had quietly enrolled herself in a college, far away, back East, and paid her first semester's tuition from her own small hoard. And bought her ticket. When the time came, she had quietly packed her clothing and gone. It was true that old Mrs. Whitman had then given her a check which rebuilt the little emergency fund, but Edie had worked and scrounged the first year, won a scholarship the next year, and after that it had been easier. When she took her first full-time job, she had sent the money back, with a letter that tried to say how valuable the security had been to her. She'd had a letter in reply that had said almost nothing.

Edie had prepared herself for social work because that had been her parents' field, and she had been taught to think that it was important and fulfilling. She had now served her apprenticeship and was going into a "better" job. Sometimes Edie suspected that she'd been kicked upstairs. She didn't have her father's patience, but a temper of her own. It was hard for her to resign herself to things-as-they-are. Edie tended to try to push things, and people, around to change, to progress, to *do* something about something. Well, the new job paid more and there would at least be more of a kind of responsibility. Whether it was the right kind for her, Edie did not yet know.

There was a two weeks' interval of leisure, however, and she had written.

Edie wasn't sure just why. The Whitmans were her only relatives. That served for a surface reason. But there is such a thing as wishing to knit up the several threads of your past, especially in a period of transition. She had wanted to come again, on a different basis. She had wanted to see, with older eyes, the scenes of her youth. To taste, with a more mellow palate, that which had been once so bitter. She had written and Granny had answered "Do come," and added, "if you like," seasoning cordiality with a touch of indifference.

When Edie had arrived, late on Sunday last, it was just as if she had never gone away at all, or at least as if she had not been doing anything in the meantime. The Whitmans made no effort to entertain her. They seemed to assume that they were taking her in, giving her board and room because she was poor and she needed these, just as they had before.

They did not ask about her work. When she told them what it was, Granny had said, "Edie, you do remind me of your mother. Going around the world, doing good. A nosy busybodying and presumptuous kind of career that never attracted anyone else in the family. I can't imagine why it ever attracted her."

She fell in love with my father, Edie had answered, but not aloud. She felt that Granny could not imagine *that*.

Edie took note of what had happened here in the meantime. Genevieve gone; Myra, instead. But Myra had made no effort to form an independent judgment of Edith Thompson. Courteous and aloof, she treated Edie like a poor relation. Myra was a small-boned, sleek little person, not as young as she used to be but much younger than her husband. She moved quietly from one social engagement to another and spent the Whitman money with shrewd good taste. One day, Edie guessed, when Granny was gone, Myra would enter into her kingdom.

Wendy—to whom so much seemed to have happened in the meantime, marriage, childbirth, divorce, and now an engagement to marry again—Wendy was still in no way a companion. She went in and out. She went by. She scarcely seemed to notice her cousin Edie. Of course, she was only just nineteen years old and naturally intent upon her own affairs. Wendy was going to marry Ronnie Mungo.

And that was that.

After the first day, Edie had shrugged her shoulders and sallied forth to sample the climate and observe the customs of the natives in southern California. She had prowled the bright little town, gone to the bright beach, ferreted out a concert to which she had gone, alone, on Wednesday night. And come back into the middle of the commotion, just as the ambulance was pulling away.

She had tried to be steady and helpful. But Wendy, up in her room, did not need her. She had Mrs. Beck. Granny refused to budge from the center of things. Nobody could put her to bed, with assorted comforts. Edie had tried to help with breakfast this morning, but Mrs. Beck was there in the kitchen and not in need of her.

When the Whitmans had gone off to the hospital, late this morning, Edie had stayed behind. She did not belong to this household. She did not need them, either, and she was fully resolved not to stay the whole two weeks, where she had no place.

But now she had made herself a place, indeed—right in the middle. She had hidden Harold Page in the turret room and she had promised to do something to help him. She had better get on with it. But how?

There was no reasoning with Granny.

Edie had seen three cars turn in at the gates. She knew that there were people around and about. Even so, she was startled when the front door burst open and three men marched in.

Cousin Ted came first. He was in his fifties, a dapper man of middle height, with a torso too bulky for the rest of him. He seemed to dwindle toward the floor and his very small feet. Dark-rimmed glasses rode on his smooth pink face and his hair, still dark, was like a cap that he wore pushed well back from his high rounded forehead. He was in a state of dramatic excitement, as if this were his kingdom and he were in command.

He rushed to the foot of the stairs and made an ushering sweep of his arm. "Start up there, please. My daughter's room and one other."

"Yes, sir," said the second man.

Edie was on her feet, her heart in her throat. The second man was a perfect stranger, stocky in a blue suit, obedient to Cousin Ted. He put his wide black shoes on the treads. Edie's feet in their black slippers whirled her to the newel post. "What is he *doing*, Cousin Ted?" Edie sagged, inside, as the blue back simply crossed the balcony above and went on up.

"He is closing and fastening all the shutters on this house," said Cousin Ted, giving her a fierce and hostile glance.

"Mercy!" said Granny. "Isn't that going to be rather dismal, Ted?"

"Oh, Mother . . ." Cousin Ted had a way of saying this, on the puff of a sigh, whenever his mother deflated him.

"Good afternoon, Charles," piped Granny.

The third man had come in less precipitously than the others. He stood beside the big window with his hands in his pockets, looking at nothing. He was a heavy man with a strong-featured face and cold blue eyes. He made a perfunctory murmur of names. "Mrs. Whitman. Miss Edith."

"Mr. Tyler," said Edie. She had met him last night.

She was thinking of Harold Page. If they were to burst in on him now, with no warning to either side. *No!* Edie rounded the newel post and began to slip up the stairs herself. "Cousin Ted," she said, "there *are* no shutters on the turret room."

"I am very well aware of that, Edie, since this happens to be the house where I was born." Cousin Ted was testy.

Charles Tyler had stepped close to the glass and was looking out and upward to the right. Edie was not sure that she wasn't going to faint, poised there on the fourth step, because if Harold Page, for any reason, happened to be standing in the window on that side . . . But Tyler said, without much interest, "Tree looks like a way to get in, all right."

"I know that, too," snapped Cousin Ted. "That's why one of the guards is going to watch that tree."

"Guards?" gasped Edie. "Do you mean—policemen?"

"No, no," said Cousin Ted, who, in the role of the forceful man, was managing to be extremely cross. "I've hired professionals who will do as *I* say. One for each corner, at the back of the house. The solarium is vulnerable. So is the kitchen and the cellar door. But nobody will break in here a second time."

This proclamation rang on the air. Cousin Ted pulled in his chin and, for a moment, looked fat and satisfied.

Edie said, "But I thought . . . Nobody *broke* in. You didn't think so last night, sir?" She was speaking to Charles Tyler, who was the Chief of Police in this town.

He tilted his face to look at her. "Myra may have let him in. After all, she knew him."

"She should have known better," chirped Granny. "*I* wouldn't have let him in."

"Don't be alarmed," Tyler said to her with a kind of professional comforting, "I have prowl cars in the whole area. They'll find him."

Cousin Ted seemed to take offense. "And how a prowl car is going to find an escaped madman who is more likely to be hiding in the shrubbery than walking along the street . . ."

Tyler's cold eye brushed over him. "We know our business."

Mrs. Beck came in with a tray upon which she carried two tall glasses with lemon slices perched upon their rims. There was a hospitable shuffle and murmur, below, to which Edie paid no attention, because she could see the man in the blue suit, the guard or whoever he was, starting down. She herself had reached the balcony and now she put her back against the door to the turret room. If necessary, she would say, "Don't come in here. I have something to tell you, first." But what would she say, next?

Cousin Ted called out, "Conrad? You didn't forget the window at the end of the hall?"

"No, sir," the man called downward. "We can have pretty tight security, I'd say, Mr. Whitman." He was descending. "Where now?" He paused just one step above where Edie stood. He had his hand on the banister and his coat fell open.

Edie said, in quick desperation, loudly, "Mr. Tyler, this man is wearing a gun. Is that all right?"

"Certainly he has a gun," said Cousin Ted furiously. "How else can he protect us?"

"And Cousin Ted has a gun *too*," cried Edie. "What if they shoot the wrong person? *I* think it's terribly dangerous."

Granny made one of her remarks that was either silly panic or brave comedy. "I shall turn off my hearing aid. I cannot *abide* the noise of guns." Then she took the tea.

But Tyler had lifted his heavy head. "You've got three qualified men for this job, Conrad?"

"Yes, sir." The man in the blue suit was intent upon proving his answer. He came down the one step, he crossed the balcony, where Edie was shrinking against her door, he thumped his wide feet on the lower treads. The wood of the door at her back was solid and opaque and she let it hold her up.

Tyler and the man exchanged a few low sentences, with the effect of using an inside language, unintelligible to the ordinary public. Then Tyler turned on Cousin Ted, who stood there, goggling. "You'd better not carry a gun, Ted." The Chief's choice of words was milder than his tone.

"I tell you, Charles, if this escaped madman shows himself on my property, I have the right . . ."

Tyler said, brushing him off again, "Not you. Trained people. Put it away."

So Edie thought she saw her solution. Trained people, of course. It was Charles Tyler to whom she must appeal, just as soon as Cousin Ted, who really was a stupid man, had put away his gun. Or perhaps she could manage to speak to Mr. Tyler alone, and that would be even better. She perceived that Mrs. Beck was standing, stranded, with the other glass of iced tea on the tray. Edie did not want to move away from the turret room door. Not yet. So she said, "Put it on the table, please, Mrs. Beck?"

Cousin Ted had bounced back and was protesting. "Now, look here, Charles, I am not an athlete. And I do not care to leave a loaded gun where this madman might get hold of it. I won't take that risk."

Tyler said, wearily, "Leave it empty."

Up on the balcony, Edie closed her eyes. A stupid man is a very dangerous man, she thought. How can Cousin Ted *be* so stupid? She began to feel helplessly angry.

The guard said, "Where now, Mr. Whitman?"

"Oh. Yes. Mrs. Beck, take this man with you, please. I want him to close and lock whatever can be closed and locked. And don't forget the cellar." Cousin Ted, inflated again, gave orders.

The tall housekeeper disappeared from Edie's view, and the guard followed her. Edie heard her say, "This is the cellar door." The only cellar to the house was beneath the turret. The door to the stairs, leading down, was well around the curve of the turret wall.

Edie was not only angry, she was beginning to realize what was happening here; she was frightened. But her anger spoke. She took three steps to the balcony rail and called down. "Cousin Ted, don't you know that he didn't 'escape'?"

"He's out! He's loose!"

"He was discharged."

"That's what I said. He's *out!* We know that."

Edie began to shake her head and she started down, to do battle with unreason. Granny's voice caught her and stopped her feet.

"Mercy! You're not thinking that he might have gotten *in*," said Granny. "You mean while we were all away? Oh mercy!"

So the steam went out of Edie's anger.

"But I was here," she said, "and so was Mrs. Beck." Was she sounding nervous?

Granny was twisting around to peer at the housekeeper. "You didn't hear anything? In the shrubbery?"

Mrs. Beck said, "No, ma'am. Of course, I would only hear something at the back. Oh, I did hear the front doorbell. Miss Edith must have answered it."

Now was the time for Edie to say flatly, "Yes. It was Harold Page. I let him in. He's in my room." But she seemed to have lied, already. It was *not* the time for the truth. She set her legs to moving and sauntered down the remaining stairs. "Bell? Oh yes, just somebody . . . wanted something."

Cousin Ted turned with a shuffle of his small feet. "Get along," he snapped, over his shoulder. "Take him along, please."

So the housekeeper made a pointing gesture and the guard, who had evidently been down cellar, now closed the cellar door, turned the key in its lock, made an "after you" kind of gesture and followed her to the dining room.

Cousin Ted now came to Edie. He stood close and spoke low and his brown eyes behind his glasses were suspicious. "Edie, did you talk to the press?" he breathed at her.

"No, Cousin Ted, I did not," she said indignantly.

"For Wendy's sake, for all our sakes," he went on in the same ridiculously portentous manner, "we do not want scare headlines."

Edie shook her shoulders. "Mr. Tyler," she said boldly, "there *will* be headlines, if Cousin Ted shoots *anybody*."

Tyler's voice had a weary authority. "She's right, Ted. Come on, now. Put the toy away."

"Actually, Ted," said Granny, "I don't believe you have fired a gun since you've had bifocals."

"Oh, Mother . . ."

Edie breathed in deeply. He was deflated. He took the very small handgun out of his jacket pocket and trotted reluctantly toward the big carved chest that stood under the balcony. He was going to put it away. Edie simply could not tell whether his mother had deliberately deflated him, as a means of control, or had done nothing at all but utter a stray thought that had crossed her mind.

Edie's hope was not in them. She turned to Tyler. "Could I please speak to you, sir?"

"Go ahead." He did not budge.

"About Harold Page. Could I speak to you, alone?"

Charles Tyler took her in, with cold eyes. He knew who she was. A grand-niece. A social worker. He'd met social workers. He supposed they were earnest decent people; he didn't care for their bleeding hearts. This was a young one. He knew right away that she was going to defend the accused. And nuts to that.

"You know this man?" he said coldly. Her throat moved; her eyes winced. She didn't know the man. "You were here last night when this happened?" She'd been at some concert; she hadn't been here, last night, when it happened.

"Go ahead," he invited grimly. She didn't know anything.

Long ago, Charles Tyler had figured out a clear direction for himself. It was his business to apprehend a lawbreaker. What society then chose to do with same was not his business. Sometimes he felt like whoever it was that had to push some boulder up a hill forever. Or a housekeeper sweeping the dust with an old broom and watching the dust settle back again. They kept letting these kooks out. He'd pick them up and put them in and then they'd soon be out again. Look at this one, this kookie Harold Page. They'd had him in. By what kind of guess and gamble they'd let *him* loose, Charles Tyler did not know. Long ago, he had stopped trying to figure out the "whys" of this world. He was supposed to keep law and order.

A man who got into a house that wasn't his, and beat up a woman, was a criminal. Whatever else he might be was not Charles Tyler's concern. He told himself all this quite often.

"I know," said the girl, "you want to pick him up." She smiled nervously.

Tyler didn't smile and didn't even answer. Good for her, he thought, if she knows that much.

"What will happen to him if you do?" she went on.

A blast of rage happened invisibly within Charles Tyler.

Ted Whitman, busily taking the ammunition out of his little gun, turned around to face them and puffed himself up. "Oh, he'll be put away, *at least*. Myra *Whitman* . . ."

That did it, for Tyler. How he wished to hell his sister had never mixed herself up with this bunch! She'd married the Whitman name, the house on the hill, the status and the money—and in the bargain had taken that spoiled kid, the stepdaughter, *and* her kookie ex. And now she was lying in the hospital. Why? *No* reason. And all her brother could do was sweep up this kook, not because his violence was senseless but because it was against the law. Put him in, again. And not because she was Myra *Whitman*.

"Myra *Tyler* Whitman," he said between his teeth. He gave Edie a glance like a knife to cut her head off. She'd be of the school that pleaded for the poor criminal who "hadn't known what he was doing." Charles Tyler didn't care whether he knew. Charles Tyler cared whether he had done it.

"I don't think you need to worry, Edith," he said bitterly. "When I pick him up, he'll tell me everything he knows about what happened to my sister." If it takes a month, he was thinking. Oh, he'd sweep this one back into the dustbin. But *good*. He turned his back and gazed gloomily at the big tree.

Edie Thompson took a step backward. Dismayed. The Chief of Police had been coldly angry last night, but he had been giving orders, very busy, and the anger had seemed no more than natural, and well-controlled for what it was. It had blended with the confusion and everyone's consternation. But she *couldn't* talk to him, not now. She didn't dare. She thought he was in the clutches of a deep personal rage, an outrage. Whoever was suspected of having hurt his sister was going to be in for a very rough time. He had the power. And a suspect like Harold Page, so fitted to the crime, and so defenseless . . . No, she couldn't talk to the big policeman, now. And maybe never.

Not *she.* Edie knew that, somehow, the man was closed against her in particular. She sensed that. Couldn't think why. But it was paralyzing.

The big man turned again, his face fallen into an impassive gloom. "I'll get along now, Ted. I'll have a couple of men check the grounds, Mrs. Whitman."

He nodded, and started for the foyer.

Granny called after him, "Charles, you are very kind."

And Edie let him go. She went over to the table beyond the sofa where Mrs. Beck had put her tea. She sipped and found it hard to swallow. She didn't know what she was going to do.

She didn't follow Tyler out, to catch him in the driveway, to beg his objectivity as she confessed. She was afraid.

Wait. Think. Maybe . . . Edie now saw her project stretching out in time beyond her anticipation. Maybe—keep the boy hidden and safe while time worked and they *all* cooled off?

But how could she do that?

How could she do otherwise?

Chapter Four

THE GUARD came back from the dining room-kitchen wing of the house, and Cousin Ted prepared to usher him to the east wing. This was the newer part of the house, in which Granny had her large and comfortable quarters and Ted and Myra the master bedroom, and Ted, his study.

Granny was stirring. "If he is going into my room," she announced, getting up in her spry way, "then so am I. I want him to look under the bed, quite thoroughly. I don't care for this idea that someone may be lurking. You have given me a very unpleasant picture, Ted, and I don't think it was very kind of you."

"Oh, Mother . . ."

Edie almost echoed him. It was a "Granny" speech, and unfathomable. She took a strong swallow of the cold tea. If they would only leave her alone in this room, *now*.

In fact, this room was often deserted. Perhaps because of the stairs, and the turret, this room was a kind of overgrown passageway. Nobody lived in it. Granny was in the habit of keeping to her own place where she had surrounded herself with an elegant clutter. Ted and Myra tended to use the solarium, incongruously so named, for it looked northerly, down the other side of the knoll and off to the sea. Wendy lived upstairs. That was her nest. It was usually some unhappy house guest, like Edie, who sat uncomfortably in this big cold place and wished she could find a book to read. There were no books in this room. There was no clutter, either. Sometimes there was a gathering here, before dinner, when there were dinner guests. The family did not gather here. In fact, the family did not gather.

So Edie had hopes that they would all vanish and she would have her chance. Maybe she could get the boy *out*—immediately.

But Cousin Ted was not vanishing, yet. He dawdled and turned back. He went trotting to the big carved chest and, while Edie watched him in dismay, he yanked open the top drawer and took out his beloved gun.

"Cousin Ted?" she croaked.

He turned and glared. He was going to reload. "If *I* see Harold Page, I do not intend to be helpless. I may not be as incompetent with a weapon as people think. Well?"

Well, she couldn't stop him. She said meekly, "I only wanted to ask you if you would please cash a check for me."

"Oh, Edie," on the puff of a sigh. "Not now."

"Then may I please borrow Myra's car?" (If Edie had a car, maybe she could get the boy into the car, somehow.)

"I am very sorry, Edie, but that car is quite new and Myra hates other people to drive it."

(Myra's in the hospital, thought Edie. She won't know. She *can't* care. I need a car.) "Then Wendy's?" she said. "Do you know where her keys are?" (Wendy was off with Ronnie Mungo. Wendy didn't need a car.)

"No, I surely do not," said Cousin Ted, and then virtuously, "You must take that up with Wendy herself. Where do you want to go? I'm off to the hospital again in a few minutes. Drop you? If it's convenient."

He put the gun into his pocket. Edie said quietly, "Thank you, but it's not that important."

He started across the room to the east wing but something must have pinked him. He said to her, "How you can think of your own little concerns at all! Don't you realize what a terrible thing has occurred? Don't you understand that we are in great danger until this vicious madman is recaptured?"

Edie thought she could spit at him. "So is the whole population, too," she cried.

"What? What?"

"If *we* are," she raged, "if there *is* a vicious madman loose, then there *should* be scare headlines."

Cousin Ted raised his brows. "I will not be hounded by newspaper people. Really."

They stared at each other. It was Cousin Ted who said it. "Aren't you being rather stupid?" he said.

Somebody was shaking him by his shoulder, so he woke out of what was not quite sleep. It was that girl who wasn't Wendy. She was talking to him in a low angry voice; he could tell that she was not angry at him. She wanted him to sit up, put on his shoes, go somewhere with her. So he turned his legs, he pushed his torso, he sat on the edge of the bed with his feet to the floor, trying to banish those dizzying dreams or visions, those disconnected pictures, trying to see where he was and what was going on.

"It's the only chance," Edie was saying. "Right now. Quickly. Hurry. Before there is a guard out there. I'm going with you. I'll walk you out of here. If the police see the two of us walking together they won't think it's you. We can get out the front door right now. If you'll hurry . . ."

She went springing across the round room to her dresser; she seemed to be putting things into her purse. She had left his shoes on the floor, right under his eyes.

Harold looked down at four objects. Two shoes, two feet in gray socks. He closed his eyes and stretched up his brows and opened his eyes again. This was the turret room, that's right. The furniture looked as if it had been tossed in here, because it could not stand snug to the round. The strange tall narrow windows had blinds on them, against the glass, but there were no curtains. The glass was too far within the thickness of the wall. A crazy place.

He could hear her going on, in that low and furious voice, "No way to make them listen to anything. They are *impossible*. The only thing to do is get you away from here. Could you hurry?"

He looked down at his shoes and his feet. He reached for one of the shoes, but his hand fell. It wasn't necessary to try. He looked at the four objects. Two shoes, the same size. His left foot, looking a little larger. The right foot, outsized and impossible.

She said, close to his ear, "What's the matter?"

His hand swung, trying to point. "I can't . . ."

Her hand came down on his shoulder.

"I can't," he said. "My broken foot. I'll never . . ."

He felt her urgency die. Her hand began to press him back and he let it. He lay back. "I see," she said softly. "All right."

"I'm sorry. I just can't." He was very sorry that he couldn't do what she wanted him to do and put his shoes on.

She was like a nurse, now, or maybe his mother. She was helping him lift his legs back to the bed. She was pulling up the cover. She touched his forehead with a corner of the sheet, to wipe the perspiration away. "Never mind," she said. "How do you feel?"

"Oh, I'm better," he told her. "Much better. I feel a little woozy but I'm much, much better."

"Are you hungry? Are you thirsty?"

"I'm fine."

She sat down on the edge of the bed. This was a cool and quiet crazy place. They were lost in there—out of the world. But a sound came. The thin high ringing of a telephone bell, far far away.

"That's the telephone," she said quickly, as if she thought it might have frightened him. He lay looking at her profile, at the head held tensely on the twist of her neck. He could see the strain. He remembered her name, now. He was sorry to see her so strained and worried.

"You had better tell them where I am," he said calmly. "This isn't your trouble. You don't want to be in the middle, Edie."

Her head turned and she looked at him as if she marveled. Then, she smiled. "Oh, I'm not in the *middle*. I'm on your side."

He smiled up at her. He could see everything very clearly now, at least in his mind. "Just the same . . ."

"All right." She sighed. "But rest. Will you rest, a little while? Will you promise me? Don't make any noise? Don't stand too close to the windows? Then, I'll promise you that if I have to tell them, I'll give you warning first. Is that all right? A deal?"

"Deal. Only don't . . ."

"No, no, I won't," she said. "*I* won't be in too much trouble. I want to telephone somebody who'll come and help us both. Okay?"

"All right."

She touched him, giving him a comforting pat. She got up and went over to the dresser and took the band off her hair and began to brush it. Harold lay watching her with pleasure.

When Edie came out upon the balcony, Cousin Ted was there below with the guard, who was looking out the big window at the tree. "I see what you mean," he was saying. "That's quite a tree, ain't it? Pushing on the house, just about."

"It was planted by my grandfather," said Cousin Ted, importantly.

"A family tree? Right?" The guard, grinning at his own pleasantry, glanced up at Edie. "Don't worry about a thing, miss," he said cheerily. "Conrad's will take care of it."

Cousin Ted did not care for so much cheeriness. "Night and day, remember," he snapped. "I'm paying for it."

"Oh, sure thing, Mr. Whitman," Conrad said. "I'm coming around to take night duty myself. I'll place the men now. Don't worry."

He knew he was dismissed and he saluted. Conrad had a little agency. He often supplied the guards at a wedding reception. He had done that for Mr. Whitman's wedding to his second wife. He was pleased with this job. He could charge a lot. (Night and day.) He was glad he was on the right side of Mr. Whitman. He went up to the foyer. He was gone.

Edie knew, as if he'd said so, that the guard was glad to be on the right side of Mr. Whitman.

Cousin Ted was patting his pockets, as if to check whether he had everything.

Edie ran down to him. "Cousin Ted, before you go, please—listen to me? It wasn't Harold Page who got in here."

"Oh ho," said Cousin Ted with an idiotic expression of joyous secrecy. "Indeed it was."

"Why?" cried Edie. "Because Wendy says she saw him? Cousin Ted, will you *think* about that, for just one minute? She saw him from her upstairs window—running, so she says. *Down* the drive. But she didn't do a thing about it. Wendy went to bed. *You* had to come home and find Myra . . ."

"She simply didn't realize at the time," said Cousin Ted. "Now— please tell Mrs. Beck—will you, Edie?—that I won't be home for dinner. I intend to stay with Myra as long as they will let me, which will be, I suppose, nine-ish. You'll be safe here without me, now."

"He was not here last night," said Edie loudly, spacing the words, insultingly.

"Who? What?"

"Harold Page. There's *no* reason to think so, except—"

"You don't know what you are talking about," said Cousin Ted with relish. "Charles Tyler just called me. They've found his bag. Oh, yes. Some small canvas affair. His name is on it. They found it in the shrubbery, down at our gates. So you may as well stop talking nonsense, Edith. He was here, all right. But this is a fortress now. He can't get in again. Not alive."

His thin mouth was looking viciously satisfied. He left the house.

Up in the turret room, Harold got off the bed, took off his sweat-soaked, wrinkled white jacket. He hung it over the back of a chair. It might dry. He would have warning. He would rather not look too messy when he faced them. He limped toward the bathroom. Oh wow, his right foot was puffed up, pretty bad. Maybe he could soak it. Soma, he thought.

When he was in the cramped little bathroom, he was facing one of the windows, breast high, and he felt surprised to see the world out there, and the sun shining. It was kind of a shock to him. He blinked and stared and then his gaze came downward and he saw a man, standing a few yards from the corner of the house where the dining room was. He was just a man in a gray suit but—no, he wasn't, either. He kept moving, a little back and a little forth, and he kept looking around. He was a guard!

Harold's head cleared. It was as if the veils and mists, through which all things had looked so dreamlike, melted away. Now he remembered, she had said there were guards, the girl had said so. Now that everything was clear and hard, Harold had the instinct to hide. He was in danger. There were guards down there and they were guarding. What? They were guarding the house against Harold Page. But Harold Page was *in* the house. It was kind of a joke on them, but it wasn't funny. Guns, she had said. He thought, I sure as hell better get out of here.

He went back to the round room and stole across to the opposite window, the one where the green leaves were pressing high on the window glass. He leaned cautiously into the embrasure. He couldn't see to his right, through so many leaves. He looked downward, to his left, and there was the big window and he could see into it and there was Wendy.

She was right down there, standing the way she always had stood, on her two feet at once and her feet apart. She was talking to somebody. There was another figure standing behind her. But Harold didn't look at it.

He looked a long time—about twenty seconds. He drew back and crossed the room and put himself down on the bed, on his back. He had expected to feel funny. He hadn't thought it would hit him quite so hard. He felt as if he'd been socked in the stomach. He had to understand this, now, and live through every bit of the pain. He had to let it hurt him. He'd learned this. He lay on his back with his wrist across his mouth.

Chapter Five

SCHEMES WERE racing through Edie's mind. She was standing beside the big carved chest, where the telephone was. Ought she to call the doctor at the Mental Hospital, this Dr. Wesley, the one who knew and had counseled Harold? He could help. He could say, for one thing, that Harold was not a madman, and for another, that he had not escaped. Surely he would be concerned, and would understand why Edie could not throw the boy to these wolves without trying everything else, first. He would understand what terrible damage might be done by a repetition of the same kind of injustice that had hurt the boy so much once before. He would be on Harold's side.

Or would it be best to call a lawyer, here? What lawyer? Or would it be best to call a cab, and just get Harold Page out of this house, maybe with the driver's help? Just face the guard down, and go. She could cash traveler's checks. Where could she go? With a boy who needed a doctor. To what doctor?

She was still standing beside the telephone when Wendy and Ronnie Mungo came in.

"What in the world is going on?" demanded Wendy, stopping by the window. "Daddy's got armed men around the house? How stupid!"

There she stood and Edie could feel herself pulling together with one clear purpose, to fight this enemy. She said, dryly, "Why? Aren't you afraid of the famous madman? Hi, Ronnie."

The man saluted. Wendy said, contemptuously, "Afraid of Harold? One word from me and he'd cry salt tears."

Wendy was nineteen now. She was pretty. Her hair was dark with certain reddish lights in it, and it was abundant, and it swirled prettily around her golden face, in which her eyes were the color of tea-in-a-cup without any cream. She was just a fraction of an inch shorter than Edie, but she wore very high heels on her very tiny feet. She wore bright colors. She wore, now, a yellow dress with green buttons down the front and a green scarf tucked in at the neckline. The dress was cotton and had cost as much as all of Edie's summer dresses put together. Wendy's figure was an hour-glass. Edie's was the straighter, the daintier—yet Wendy made Edie feel faded and diminished. Poor.

Wendy was moody and the mood, for now, was pouting. She kept her back to Ronnie when she spoke. "Ronnie? Six-thirty?"

It crossed Edie's mind that Wendy's peers had never liked her, either, that she could remember.

"I take it we are going through with this dinner party?" said Ronnie Mungo in his pleasant tenor. He was as tall and elegantly made as ever, although not so young as when Edie (aged eighteen) had thought of him as an "older man." He had a well-practiced smile; he seemed as friendly as a puppy, in spite of his practiced manner of speaking, which took care to take nothing very seriously.

"It's supposed to be given *for* us," said Wendy sulkily.

"Well, fine."

Wendy threw her green purse on the sofa and herself after it. She was not pleased with life at the moment.

Ronnie came to lean on the back of a chair and take the cover off a candy box. His blue gaze slipped to Edie, who was standing her ground, who was not, this time, taking herself off with some small excuse to leave them together. He winked at her. "Our little flower," he said in a pseudo-confidence, "is drooping. . . ."

"Oh, shut up," said Wendy, who was drooping sulkily where she sat.

Edie looked away from the man's face, the one she had studied curiously, whenever the two of them had gone by, in these last few days. It was time to study Wendy.

Edie could feel herself hardening, feel herself gearing for battle. She knew exactly why she had, so soon and so easily, believed in Harold Page.

The time little Wendy, who had half a dozen cashmere sweaters, had taken Edie's one best one, and worn it, and torn it, and sworn she had never touched it. The time little Wendy had told her grandmother something. Edie was sure of it! . . . Because Wendy had wanted to go to Palm Springs for the weekend with her parents, but could not have gone unless they took Edie, too, to look after her. The very one-and-only weekend Edie had been supposed to have a date with Ronnie Mungo. And (get on, quickly) the time little Wendy had said she saw Edie in the solarium, on the morning that the parakeet had escaped from its cage and been destroyed by the cat. Time after time. Incident after incident.

Two kinds. The times when Wendy lied because she wanted something, and the times when Wendy lied because she did not want to be punished for something she had done.

So Edie knew that Wendy was the enemy. Not Granny. Not Cousin Ted. Under the pressure of shock, after what had happened to Myra, they were merely being larger than themselves, Granny more maddeningly frivolous (or whatever you could call it) and Cousin Ted actively stupid instead of just bumbling about.

But it was Wendy who had put Harold Page into this affair, where he did not belong. He had nothing whatever to do with it, and Wendy knew that. Otherwise, why wasn't *she* afraid of him? There was a coincidence, of course. Harold had written to say that he was leaving the hospital on Monday. So Wendy had seized upon that, and the pattern that he fit so cozily, when she had lied last night.

Edie was hardening and at the same time flaming. Oh, Wendy was a liar, although she took care to lie only as often as it was wise to lie and continue to be believed. Edie did not doubt that she had lied to get her divorce and nearly wrecked the boy, that time. *This* time, she was not going to get away with it. By a saving coincidence, her cousin Edie happened to be here. Edie had not allowed the boy to walk into the trap and she would smash the lie and destroy the trap before she would give him up. But she had better not flame. Better be cool, be careful.

She said coolly, the latent anger almost hidden, "Myra is still in a coma, since you ask."

Wendy did not move an eyelash. Ronnie Mungo responded pleasantly. "She'll come out of it, won't she?"

Edie went nearer him. Let Wendy brood, *if* she was brooding. "I guess so, Ron. Myra was in this room when you brought Wendy home last night? Did she say anything special?"

Ronnie tucked the candy into his cheek. "Myra? We-ell, we had a sparkling exchange, you know?" He sat on the arm of a chair and let his rump fall into the seat, so that his legs dangled. "Let me see. Myra said 'Good night.' And I replied. 'Good night,' I said." He grinned at her. Irreverence was his specialty. But Edie thought his bright eyes wondered what she could be wondering. Or did they guess?

"What did she say to you, Wendy?"

"Who? Nothing. I didn't listen." Wendy shifted and sat on her foot. "If Myra is going to be groggy all the rest of the summer," she said sullenly, "that's going to put the frost on a big wedding."

Ronnie said to Edie, as if this were an aside, one grownup to another, "This is the bother, you see?"

Is it? thought Edie. Is this *really* what's bothering her today? Are *her* moods swinging wider than ever? Is *she* larger than herself by the shock? More unreliable than her already unreliable self? She said aloud, "Myra can hardly help being what you call 'groggy.'"

"Oh, Cousin Edie," said Wendy, thrashing around, "that's not the point. I don't see why we need Myra at the wedding. She's not my real mother."

"She's a reasonable facsimile," said Edie, idly. She was thinking, No, Myra is not. Myra, to you, is nothing. Who is anything, to you? Are we going to find out?

Wendy said crossly, "Look, I'm trying to think."

You think, thought Edie. You just think, little cousin. Because somebody hurt Myra last night. The police found "signs of a struggle." And if it wasn't Harold Page, who was it then?

Ronnie Mungo listened to the silence shrewdly for a moment. Then he said, "I'm not so crazy about waiting at the altar in a white jacket while the bride comes down the aisle, like doom in lace. It's possible to have a 'little' wedding. Wait, I've got it. The word is 'quiet'?"

Wendy swiveled her dark head and sent him a long stare.

"Or," he said, shifting his long legs to lie stretched out in the chair, "maybe you want to call the whole thing off? Another day, another bridegroom? In which case, we better not make an announcement at this party. Or even go."

He sounded as if he didn't care. Maybe, to get along with Wendy, you had to seem to care even less than she. Edie sat down, to listen.

"I wanted the whole show." Wendy pouted. "The cake and the flowers. And eight bridesmaids."

"And the veil?" said Edie, her anger slipping. "Which, I presume, you missed, the first time around."

"Edie, will you kindly . . ." Wendy sounded exasperated, but only as if with a fly. "*She* never got married at all, Ron. And what are you, Edie . . . twenty-five?"

"Withering on the vine," drawled Edie. She settled into the chair.

Wendy got up and crossed to the solarium doors and stood there with her back to them.

Ron said in a moment, casually, "So you're a social worker now? Get a bang out of that, do you, Cousin Edie?"

"In a way," said Edie slowly. She was trying to cool down.

"Doing good, eh? I don't understand that sort of thing, believe me." He was playing with his key case, tossing and catching it.

Edie said sweetly, "I believe you." He was an attractive man, to women. He must be, thought Edie. He's been married twice already. Why did his wives divorce him? Something dark moved in her blood as she wondered.

But Wendy turned around and came waspishly back into the conversation. "Why are you trying to understand *her*? It's me you're going to marry."

"Oh? Then it's on?" said Ron, lightly.

Wendy was full of storm. "If we're not going to have a big wedding, what is there to wait for?"

"Okay," he said. "How about tomorrow?"

Edie could see Wendy's face changing and she gasped, "Wendy, you can't."

"I most certainly can," said Wendy coldly. "The divorce is final. I'm of age, now. I will get my mother's trust money when I marry. And I have spelled it out and spelled it out and I'm not going to spell it out anymore. Because I *can* . . . if I want to."

She went prancing across the carpet on her tiny feet, like a child in a tantrum.

Edie said, frowning, puzzled, "With Myra in the hospital—"

"So much the better," snapped Wendy. "*She* doesn't particularly want me to marry Ronnie."

Does she not? thought Edie. Does she not, indeed? And when was it that you spelled it out so many times?

Ron got up and moved toward Wendy. His pleasant voice, with its constant undernote of mockery, might have been designed to tease. "Ah now, naturally, I am not good enough *for* you. But the old folks *will* be reconciled, in the end." He was reaching for her. But Wendy stepped away.

"Tomorrow?" she said coldly.

"Well, no," he answered, quickly serious. "As a matter of fact, we can't get the red tape cut that soon."

"But we can get our blood tests tomorrow."

"True."

"Can we get on a plane to Paris? I mean *soon*. After the whatever-it-is . . . the three days?"

"Should be possible. I'll see."

"All right, Ronnie."

Edie sat marveling at this exchange, so cold, so coldly decisive. She began to think that Granny was right. These two would suit each other very well.

Now Wendy was softened and she kissed the man's cheek lightly. "Go away, now. Be back by six-thirty and we'll go to this party."

"Have to take one of those bodyguards along?" he said, with a mock shudder.

"Of course not," said Wendy. "How would Harold know where I was? Anyway, maybe they've caught him by now and put him back where he belongs."

"I won't worry about it if you don't, sunshine," Ronnie said. "So long, Cousin Edie. Do good, now."

Edie said thoughtfully, "I'll try."

When he had gone, Wendy seemed to think herself alone. She didn't look at Edie. She went prancing toward the door to the long dining room and sent her high voice calling, "Becky? Beck-*yyy*? Come here, will you?" She didn't wait for an answer, but turned.

Edie said, with the deadliest calm she could manage, "Wendy, when you marry Ronnie Mungo, what are you going to do with the baby?"

"The what?" said Wendy.

"Your child. Your son."

There may have been a flush under the golden skin of the pretty face. But Wendy said flatly, "He is deaf as a stone. How could I do anything with him? Somebody will have to take care."

"What does Ronnie say, about the baby?"

Wendy was staring at her. "Not a word. We don't discuss it." Then she whirled to turn her back. "Didn't she *hear* me!"

"What," said Edie, in the same deadly tone, "is your idea of marriage, I wonder?"

Now Wendy turned again and she was smiling lopsidedly, lips closed, one end of the mouth tucked up into the flesh of the cheek. "It depends on the one you marry."

"I remember Ronnie from a long time ago," said Edie, feeling blind.

"I'll *bet* you do," her cousin said.

"He was a pretty spectacular playboy, way back then. When I was eighteen, I cried all night. Maybe you remember? *Somebody* had told your grandmother *something*."

"Way-back-then?" said Wendy, insultingly. She wasn't going to admit anything.

"How old is he now? And how many wives?"

"He's thirty-four," said Wendy. Her temper flared. "And who cares how many wives. He hasn't got one *now*. What in the world is your idea of marriage? You should try it sometime." She seemed to dance impatiently. "Oh, where is that old idiot? I want her to press my yellow dress. Money is the thing, you know, Edie. Too bad you'll have to wait for yours, until Granny dies."

Edie was lost. "Ronnie Mungo has money, you mean?"

"I'll have money, is what I mean," said Wendy. "Of my own."

Edie was stumped, really stumped. Money would have been the last thing to cross Edie's mind. Mrs. Beck came bustling and Wendy said, "Oh, there you are, Becky. You come on up."

Mrs. Beck's long-jawed face was looking perfectly foolish with devotion. "Yes, lamb. Yes, love."

"I'm going to the party," said Wendy, on the stairs.

"It will do you good. Do you good, lamb," said Mrs. Beck, drawn upward behind her.

Edie sat still, where she was. She had not missed, of course, the obvious fact that Mrs. Beck was Wendy's slave. She remembered mentioning something like that, and how Granny had said, in Granny's way, "Oh, Mrs. Beck's been raising Wendy. After all, if *she* was willing, why should I?"

But this was not to the point, really. The point was, how could

Edie protect a country boy—rather a pathetically unlucky boy, a boy who was not in the best physical condition to defend himself— from these terrible people? In particular, from Wendy Whitman, who had lied, would lie, being possessed, as far as Edie could tell, of no scruples at all. Which of the household could she approach, to ask for mercy and understanding, or even a mind open to the reestablishment of justice? And, if none, what could she do for Harold Page?

Mrs. Beck came swiftly down, a yellow dinner dress over her arm. Wendy's in a yellow mood today, she was thinking. Ah, yellow suits her. She reached the bottom of the stairs and was starting for the kitchen regions, when Miss Edith called her name.

"Yes, Miss Edith?" Mrs. Beck had very little time for Edie.

"Mr. Whitman asked me to tell you that he won't be here for dinner."

Good, thought Mrs. Beck. "I see," she said aloud. "Thank you. Miss Wendy won't be here either." She was counting in her mind; that left the old lady and this Edith. This Edith spoke again.

"Mrs. Beck, you were in the house last night when it happened? You didn't hear anything at all?"

"My room is at the back," said Mrs. Beck. "I don't hear." (Let her believe that.)

"What about the doorbell?" Edie said, quick to remember.

"I don't," said Mrs. Beck, frowning judiciously, "recollect hearing the doorbell. Of course, I woke up, later on . . ." Now, it occurred to her that she might find out something. She tossed the dress over one shoulder and began to move around the room, straightening this and that. "I am behind in the work," she sighed, "with the maids away." Selma was having a bout with the flu and Angie was on vacation. Mrs. Beck was not sorry that they happened to be away.

"Miss Myra *is* going to be all right?" she said. "Don't they say?"

"They say so." Edie was standing. With pants on, at this hour! Mrs. Beck could not approve. Then Edie said, "Do you believe it was Harold Page?"

"Why, Miss Wendy saw him." Mrs. Beck swooped upon a bit of white, tucked between the cushions and the arm of a big chair. It was a paper napkin. She began to pleat it in her hands.

"So she says." Edie was speaking with a nervous air of suspicion. "Of course, Miss Myra will be able to tell us the truth very soon. It may have been some other—madman."

Mrs. Beck knew that her eyes were turning. She let out a sigh. "I'm very upset about Miss Myra. To think . . . in the hospital!" She clicked her tongue. "I wish I could go see her for myself."

"Why not?" said Edie.

"There's only two for dinner. I wonder if I could take the evening . . ."

"Mr. Whitman's going to be at the hospital until the evening visiting hours are over."

(Ah!) Mrs. Beck said, "Oh, I see." She started toward the kitchen again. Had to press the dress. And think about this.

But Edie had something else on her mind. "Mrs. Beck, were you here when there was that other trouble? When Harold Page was supposed to have beaten Wendy?"

(Supposed to have?) Mrs. Beck felt like letting out a piece of her mind. "Oh, she had to be rid of *him,* Miss Edith. Had to be rid of *him.* He was not for her. She ran away, for the fun of it, you know. So young. But I couldn't approve."

Maybe she shouldn't have said that. It wasn't supposed to be for her to approve. Mrs. Beck's kingdom was in secret.

"You do approve of Ronnie Mungo?" the girl was saying.

"That's different." Mrs. Beck was glad to be telling the truth. "Mr. Mungo is a man-of-the-world. And I'll be with her, you know. He's promised me. Why, we'll travel. Do her good to get away from here." Yes, away from the old lady, and the silly man, the clever stepmother, the gloomy old house. And the town, too.

"Why," Edie was asking, "didn't Wendy 'get away' to college? Or take a job?"

A job! Mrs. Beck felt shocked. But how ridiculous! "What would *she* take a job for, Miss Edith? That's not for *her.* She needs to be gay and enjoy herself, the pretty thing. Oh, I understand her. Poor little motherless child." (My child.) "Oh, she has suffered."

"She has?" Miss Edith was not believing. "How do you feel," the girl said angrily, "about the poor little motherless, fatherless baby?"

Mrs. Beck knew how she felt and she said it. "Oh, now that was *very* hard on Wendy. To bear a child that wasn't *right.* Oh, poor lamb! So hard! But we've put that behind."

She began to stroke the fabric of the dress. She was talking too much. Well, she had a lot on her mind. She said, "Pretty, isn't it? Does need pressing. I must hurry." So much to do. So much to think about.

Edie said, loudly, "*I* don't believe Harold Page was here last night at all."

Mrs. Beck stopped in her tracks. She turned and made her mouth humble and her voice gentle to correct. "Why, he must have done it, Miss Edith. Poor crazy person. I'm sure he didn't know what he was doing." She thought of another point to make. "Miss Myra might have brought it on herself, you know. Not knowing how to handle him." Mrs. Beck would have known how to handle him.

"We'll find out," Edie said, "when Miss Myra wakes up."

Mrs. Beck was glad to hear Wendy screaming down the stairs. "Becky! I can't find my gold slippers."

Her gold slippers? Oh, yes, on the shelf. Mrs. Beck could put her hand on them. "I'll find them, lamb," she called upward. "As soon as I can, love. Don't you worry."

She said to Miss Edith, sternly, "Excuse me."

Now then, through the long dining room, into the big square kitchen, pull down the ironing board. So much to do. Sometimes Mrs. Beck thought that she, and she alone, had to handle the whole world and all the people in it.

Edie sat down in a chair feeling frightened and small. Wendy would lie; Mrs. Beck would back her up, whatever Wendy chose to say. The woman had made Edie's skin crawl. No hope there. Still, nothing was any worse, or any better either, since Wendy had gone upstairs. Not really. Was it? Why did Edie have the feeling that she herself had just done something she ought not to have done, something dangerous? Why was she feeling frightened?

Chapter Six

AT A QUARTER OF MIDNIGHT, the prisoner came out of the turret room with his hair combed neatly, and his white coat on. He came down the stairs on his stockinged feet and told Edie that he was going to give himself up, now.

She sat up on the sofa and began to try to talk him out of it.

The big room was dim; there was only one lamp burning. The house was very quiet. It was safe enough to talk here, safer than the turret room, perhaps, the guard being where he was. Granny slept without her hearing aid. Cousin Ted had retired long ago and was asleep in his bedroom, beyond the study, far at the end of the east wing. Mrs. Beck's room was away at the back. She might not have come in yet, but even if she had, she would not hear soft voices.

No one could see in. The doors to the solarium were closed. A night light burned in the foyer; Wendy was still out. But the only window in the foyer was well around the wall. Velvet draperies were drawn across the big window and they were heavy. They did not cover the highest part where the glass went up into an arch, but the tree obscured that section. Black leaves made a pattern against the silver night. No one's angle of sight could come through there and strike down to where they were.

Edie was sitting up on the sofa wearing a short nightgown with its matching peignoir. She had her slippers on her feet although they were covered by the big, soft, puffy, flowered quilt. She had thought she would sleep down here. (If there was such a thing as sleep.) If anyone ordered her to her room, she would simply go. So it was safe enough. It had seemed safer to be more or less on guard, outside that door.

She had stolen some food for Harold Page at dinner-time. After he had eaten, he had fallen asleep. Edie had held some hope for darkness, but the moon was up, too soon, too bright.

There was little hope, anyhow. Edie had spotted the positions of the guards and they had been well placed. The man on the dining room corner could see, along two sides of the house, both the kitchen door and the outside cellar door, at the base of the turret. The guard on the corner of Cousin Ted's study could see the whole back terrace; there was no way to slip out of the solarium and across that bare expanse to the shrubbery, unseen. The guard near the big tree could see the front door and the driveway turnaround. That took care of doors. As for windows, there was no sliding down the turret wall, no getting out by using the tree, and on the other windows, no shutter could wag and wag unseen. To be caught *getting out of a window* would be madness. These men had guns.

Someone far more intelligent than Cousin Ted had placed those guards to keep Harold Page out of this house. They were equally well placed to keep him in.

She had not attempted to walk him out boldly, by daylight. She was sure that the guard would query a shoeless man, and the boy's weakness and illness would be too obvious. No such exit could seem casual. So she did not dream of trying to walk him out by this moonlight, either. He must stay until morning. It was safer and there were other ways to help him.

But her prisoner was restless.

She said to him now, "Dr. Wesley will call me back in the morning. They promised me. I left *my* name. And please let me try again with Mr. Tyler? In the morning? It would be better if I could get to him. He's the Chief of Police, and even if he felt like torturing a confession out of you, he wouldn't do that. I mean, it isn't done. He scared me this afternoon. I shouldn't have let him scare me. I do think I might get him to listen. Are you cold?"

The boy leaned on the back of the sofa and was shuddering.

"*I'm* scared," he said gravely, "but the one who scares me . . ."

She read his mind. "Wendy's at a party," she said, a little bitterly. "She'll be a while, but please go back. Please wait?"

His head shook a slow negative.

She said, "I wish you hadn't left your bag outside, you know. *That's* made things worse." She was feeling a little annoyed, because she wanted to save him so much more than he seemed to want to be saved.

"I want to get it over with, *before* Wendy comes," he said. "I feel, you know . . . somehow or other . . . I'll never, never . . . She can always beat me."

No, she can't, thought Edie. Not this time.

"Oh, come on. Cheer up," she pleaded. "Please. We've gone this far." He wasn't agreeing. He was leaning on his elbows, with his hands clasped lightly. He had good hands. His young face was grave. "Were you in love with her, Harold?" Edie asked.

"Oh, yes."

"Wendy can be very attractive."

"I know," he said. He smiled at her. He wasn't jittery. He didn't seem to be afraid. He was chilled, and feverish. "I came up here on leave with a few of the fellows that time," he began. "We hung around the beach. And here came Wendy Whitman and she chose me. Well, I suppose I believed in chemistry or love at first sight or something corny." He didn't sound bitter about it. He was just remembering. "I really did believe that it was so. Just two days, and then we were tearing down to the border in Wendy's car and she drives like a racer. Oh Lord-ee, it was wonderful! We got into Mexico. We lied about our ages. We got married. We found this motel. I thought to myself, Boy, now you have got everything in the whole world. You have got it all.'"

His hands were quiet. Edie thought, Oh the poor kid, why did he have to meet Wendy Whitman? *Ever?*

"But my leave wasn't lasting forever," he said, shifting to lean sideways, "so we came back here."

"Was the family upset?" Edie tried to imagine. *This* boy openly in this house.

"They didn't seem to be, not too much," he told her. "They seemed a little bit stiff toward me but I thought that was only natural. Nobody chewed me out."

"Cousin Ted and Myra weren't married yet, were they?"

"No, but they were engaged. Myra was here all the time. They were fussing about *their* wedding. Listen, I was so doggoned silly happy, I didn't really notice anything. I had to go back to camp the next day, and I went. On a big fat pink cloud. Next leave I could get, it was the same. I didn't see them much. Talk to them much. Notice much. Wendy was going to come and live near the Post. We were making plans"—his eyes flicked to her face—"that is, when we bothered. But she put that off and put it off and those plans . . . just died. It seemed to get to be too late. Actually, after Wendy got pregnant . . ."

Now his eyes were blind. "Yes?" she prodded.

"She was moody," he said, quietly. "Mustn't touch. Then I saw I was . . . I was like a piece of furniture that somebody had left around the house. They'd act as if 'Oh, yes, that's Harold, isn't it?' And they'd walk around me. As if they didn't see me or hear me unless I got in the way. And it kept getting worse."

His face seemed to be drawn fine with the memory of that incomprehensible misery. But he drew himself up a little. "You see, Wendy didn't like being pregnant. She hated that. She gloomed around. Or she'd snap at me or get in a temper over nothing. Well, I tried to be patient and all that stuff. It was a mystery to me."

Edie's heart hurt. Oh you poor kid, she was thinking, you've been taken. You've been cheated. You're too innocent.

"When the baby was born," he was going on, "they didn't even —I called *them* and then they told me. So I came, as soon as I could get a pass. That's when they let me hold him, that once." He brooded a moment. "And when I finally left this town, when it was all over but the proceedings, I went, sitting in the back of some truck, and I was crying and swearing. I thought I'd *never* be back. Well. But I have a son, and whatever *they* think, I hold myself responsible."

Edie was pierced; this seemed to her so comical and so sad.

She thought, Somebody has to tell him. She said as gently as she could, "Harold, I don't know whether you've ever thought of this . . ."

But he straightened, and he grinned down at her.

"Sure I've thought of it, and so has everybody else. It's the first thing *to* think of. Sounds just as if she needed a husband in a hurry? But he's *my* baby, all right."

Oh no, you are wrong, she was thinking. They fooled you and it was wicked.

"If that was the truth of it," the boy went on, "I could have figured it, you know. Not that I wouldn't have been plenty burned, but I'd see they had some kind of a reason."

"Are you sure of the birth date?" Edie pressed. "You say they didn't call you."

"That was because I didn't matter." He looked down at her somberly. "The ears? Hereditary in my family? I guess you forgot."

"I guess I did," she murmured. Her face felt hot. He wasn't as innocent as she had assumed and nobody was. She had been innocent to assume . . .

"So how is it to be understood?" he asked her, and she had a funny feeling that, in this moment, he was older than she. "Do you know?"

"There's probably nothing to understand," said Edie hotly, "except that Wendy is spoiled rotten and always has been. Or"—she began to struggle with her own ideas—"not so much spoiled as . . . I don't know. But they shut themselves up here. In a tower. They have their own version of the world and other people. Other people don't count much. They don't even care about each other, *very* much, but they still are the only ones who count at all. And you can't change them. It used to infuriate me. Genevieve, Wendy's mother, was alive then, and she was a silly woman. You know, I work with real people, who pay attention, at least sometimes. But the Whitmans . . . Well, I know exactly what you mean about being made to feel as if you were some old box in this house, to be stumbled over.

"Wendy . . ." She paused to say this carefully. "I'll tell you one thing. Their idea of Wendy is set, like concrete. No matter what she does, she is their pretty, sensitive little Wendy, then, and now, and forever more. Their idea of me is set, too. I am unfortunate and have to be fed. It got so . . . I had to get away. I couldn't grow. I was going to lose my sense of being anything."

He was listening gravely. He seemed to be understanding what she could not quite express. This is a nice boy, thought Edie, and her anger rose.

"The truth is," she cried, "Wendy always did get away with murder!"

"*Ssh.*" His eyes had winced.

"Did you hear something?" she whispered.

"I don't know. I guess not." He had lowered his head. "Look, Edie, I'm going out there now and surrender to the guard in front. It's the best thing and the best time."

"Don't. Don't," she cried. "*I'm* scared."

He seemed sorry to hear this. "Ah, no. Why?"

"How do I know he won't shoot you down?" she chattered. She did not want him to give up. She did not want him to be beaten. By Wendy.

"Would you like to go first, then?" he suggested. "I guess he wouldn't shoot *you* down . . . not in that outfit." He was smiling.

"I don't want you to do it at all," she insisted. "Not yet. Maybe there'll be a better way. If your Dr. Wesley would only come. He'd stand up to them. At least, he wouldn't let them hurt you."

"It wouldn't matter if they hurt me," Harold said.

"Yes, it would." She saw that he swayed. "Do you feel dizzy still?" She reached up to touch his forehead. It felt dry and hot, but not as hot as it had been. He was shivering.

"I guess you don't see why," he said.

"Come. Sit," she pleaded. "You shouldn't be chilled. Tell me." She thought, I am doing wrong not to get him to a doctor. But oh, not a prison doctor.

He moved around the sofa, limping, and sat down beside her. As she held up the quilt to let him sit, and tucked it back over his lower body, she thought, I could hide him, right where he is, if anybody comes. I don't want him to go out there and have the guards whistling and shouting and calling the police. I don't want him pushed around. Or headlines in the papers, "berserk ex-husband." He's had enough.

"It's bad," he said seriously. "Listen, I said I was scared of Wendy. But that's not quite it. Oh listen, Edie"—she felt him trembling— "I loved her. I was crazy about her. And she hurt me worse than anybody ever . . . The thing is, now I'd like to hurt her. Oh, I sure would. So, see, she's still there between me and . . . and being all straightened around. I hate her and I love her, so much . . . I don't think I'd dare to meet her, even. I would like to beat her, Edie, until she notices that I'm alive. And that's the truth that I'm afraid of."

"I know it's hard. I know," cried Edie instantly. "But don't let her—"

"Look, I'm not a vegetable," he burst, "and she's telling a lie again, and it makes me plenty mad. But I don't *want* to hit her, either. So you see, I'd better go."

To Edie, in the moment, the whole situation became even more explosively dangerous than she had, until now, believed it to be. She knew she ought never to have hidden Harold Page in the turret room. She ought to have made him go away, the moment she had realized who he was. Perhaps she ought never to have interfered at all, but called the police herself. Been the good citizen. Washed her hands. No one would have blamed her. She seemed, instead, to have made herself judge and jury, although she was prejudiced, and had insufficient evidence, and took risks. The fact that the boy was aware of his present impulse toward violence did not deny that it was there.

Edie didn't yet believe that he had beaten anyone, nor did she quite believe that he ever would. But there had been violence in this house, and now she could feel the threat of future violence to be hanging most dangerously over it. Everyone seemed to have been swinging far out, along an exaggeration of his own tendencies. Something was going to crash; something would be smashed and hurt.

"You don't have to meet Wendy," she said to him. "I won't let you meet her. I only want to get you completely out of all this miserable . . ."

The still air seemed to eddy. "*Don't* come in, if you don't want to." Wendy's living voice rang with hostility.

The boy turned his whole body; a look of terror was on his face. His hand clawed at the back of the sofa and slipped. With a complete swinging out of her own emotions, at the first sound of Wendy's voice, Edie pushed at him. He slid to his knees on the floor.

His head burrowed into the sofa seat, as she pushed it down. She had time to whisper ruthlessly, "Don't let *me* be caught like this." This was her wits in service to the surging of her will. Use anything, use his pity, to make him hide, so that Edie Thompson could snatch, from Wendy Whitman, her prey.

She took the edge of the quilt in her right hand and swung her arm. The lightweight quilt billowed and settled. He was hidden. She could feel the weight of his arm over her folded knees. She folded her own body, in order to scrunch down and rest her head below the top of the sofa-back.

She heard Ronnie Mungo's mocking voice. "Don't know when I've heard a more gracious invitation."

She heard the front door thud shut. She heard Wendy's golden heels, tapping on the tile. She heard her own blood in her ears.

It was warm and safe, where Harold was hidden. He had a wonderful sense of comfort and safety. He knew that he was in a place where he did not have to do anything at all. He also knew where he was, the way Dr. Wesley would say it.

"Why can't we?" Wendy's mood was stubborn. "That's what you haven't explained."

Edie kept her head low. She couldn't see them. But they were in the room.

Ron said, "It may be a hell of a long drive, but not that long. If we start out now, we arrive too damn early in the morning." His patience was on the edge of indifference. "And excuse me, my sunshine, but getting married in the first faint dawn—"

"Oh, stop clowning," Wendy snapped.

"Why rush into this, then?" His voice became mild and colorless. "It wouldn't 'look well,' would it?"

"Another day, another bride?" Wendy was sharp.

"I didn't say that. If you want a rough translation, why offend your wealthy grandmother? She isn't willing *all* the money to your cousin, is she?"

Neither of them spoke, for a moment, and Edie was forced to breathe. Then Wendy said, "But Ronnie . . ." in such a tone as to make Edie swallow hard. If there was going to be any canoodling, all of Edie's essentially puritanical soul writhed at the thought of eavesdropping.

"Hey," she croaked, "I'm sorry, but I'm here."

She heard a harsh rustling and then Wendy's furious face was looking down at her. "What are you doing there?"

"I was trying to sleep. Excuse it, please." Edie tried to be flip.

Ron spoke, behind her. "What *have* we here, an honest woman? Didn't care to listen in on two such turtle doves?" Was he laughing? Edie rolled her eyes up and saw his face, upside down. "What's the matter, Edie, honey? Scared of the bogeyman?"

"Well, you can just get yourself up and trot yourself to your bed." Wendy was giving orders.

"No," said Edie, faintly.

"NO!" It was a shriek.

So Edie unfolded her body enough to sit higher, keeping a tight clutch on the quilt. She felt very steady and not much afraid. You never heard that word before, she thought, did you, little cousin? To herself she said, with resolution and despair, No, I will not expose him and humiliate him and give him up, until I absolutely have to. I will probably have to. But not this minute. Or the next.

The telephone rang.

Edie said, clearly and sharply, "But if I get up and go to my room, then I'll crack my door and listen to everything you say or do and take down notes." It was childish, but Wendy was childish. Edie was ready to fight with Wendy, childishly, physically, any way that seemed necessary. She thought, Even if I lose, Ron wouldn't hurt him. She thought, This can't last many more seconds, but I'll make it last as long as I can. She found herself nourishing a little hope that Ronnie Mungo would see, would help, if Wendy went into a real tantrum.

The phone rang again. "She's got a nice little blackmailing technique there," drawled Ron, sounding amused. "*I'm* taking notes, sunshine. Go on, answer the phone."

As the phone rang for the third time, the ring choked off.

Edie was blinking with surprise. She wiggled her stiff body even higher and twisted to see where they were. Wendy had gone to the phone and stood with the instrument in her hand, although evidently too angry to speak into it. Ron was sauntering toward a chair, and as Edie twisted far enough around to see him plain, he grinned at her and perched on the chair arm. Does he know? she thought. And if so, is he helping me?

"By the way," he said, as benign as an old gentleman of Victoria's day, "you look very pretty."

Edie felt terrified. "I'm sorry," she murmured.

"Not I." His smile crinkled.

Did he think he was pleasing her? Her hands still tight on the quilt, Edie bowed her head. "Don't tease me," she begged, and thought to herself, But he is teasing Wendy, of course.

Oh, Lord, get us out of this? Her knees had shifted. She wondered briefly whether the boy was there. He was completely hidden. It was as if he existed only in her imagination.

Wendy said into the phone, "Yes? . . . Oh yes, Doctor."

Doctor! Well, there it goes, thought Edie. It must be Dr. Wesley, calling back, too soon. She would have to move; she would have to speak to him. She had a prevision of the quilt, rising uncannily, and then falling away from the boy, and people screaming.

Wendy said, "Oh yes, this is her stepdaughter . . . No, I think he's . . ." She took the instrument from her ear and said to Edie, "Where is Daddy?"

Edie said, "Asleep, I imagine. He said he'd take his phone off."

Question and answer were commonplace. They were spoken in an intermission, commonplace, outside of fear, outside of rage, outside of stratagem, outside of war.

Wendy purred into the phone. "He is asleep. Must I disturb him? . . . Oh, I see . . . Yes, I will . . . Thank you, Doctor."

She hung up and hugged her short white wrap. Her yellow skirt fluttered. Edie had a sudden hope.

"Anything . . . ?" she cried.

"Myra's scheduled for surgery at *six* A.M. instead of seven. He just wanted to let us know." Wendy was sullen.

Ron said, "Want me to wake your father?"

"Oh, why?" said Wendy. "No use to go down there now."

"Was she conscious?" said Edie. "Did she speak?" This was her hope. Maybe the whole thing was over!

"How can she speak," said Wendy, furiously, "until they fix whatever's the matter with her? Edie, if you don't begin to mind your own business, and not everybody else's, I'll tell Daddy to throw you out. And he will, too."

"I don't doubt it," murmured Edie, scrunching down.

"Go to *bed*."

"Don't you tell me what to do, Wendy, please." Another prevision: Wendy peeling the quilt away and the boy, exposed, cowering. Helpless. Crying salt tears. No.

But Ron, who was back of her head and unseen now, said, "Why don't *you* go to bed, Wendy, and sleep that off?" His voice was flat.

"Sleep what off?"

"Whatever foul mood you're in. I'm not driving to Mexico with *it*, I'll tell you. Matter of fact, *I'm* going to bed."

Edie could see the tea-colored eyes narrowing. "Alone?" said Wendy, nastily.

Ron said, "It could be." Unperturbed.

He must be going. Wendy was being drawn away. Edie found that her head could turn. They were close to the steps to the foyer. Her hands relaxed on the quilt, and dared to lift it, just a little. If he was there, could he breathe? He was there. Her fingers touched his cheek. He was breathing, quietly. She could feel his breath on her hand. She pressed two fingers into his cheek, and tried to send a silent message. Be still. Wait.

And strained to hear what they were saying.

"Well? Are we getting our blood tests tomorrow, or are we not?" Stormy.

"Just in case, eh?" Ron's voice was its normal faintly mocking drawl. "Why not, then?"

"So, in three days? Or never?" Wendy seemed to be threatening. There was a brief silence.

Then Ron said, "Or sooner? You can drive to Mexico by daylight, you know. In a sunnier frame of mind. Tomorrow?"

"If you are here early. And I mean early." Still threatening.

"And if not?"

Edie could hear no answer.

"Then never, eh?" he said, with light acceptance. "Right. I'll sleep on it." His voice became louder. "Good night, Cousin Edie. I'm sorry if I teased you."

"Sleep well," said Wendy grimly.

He was gone and Edie was trembling. Who would help her, now, to cope with Wendy? The guard, she thought. I can always call for him. But maybe . . . Maybe. "Good night, Wendy," she said on a yawn, with good hope.

Let Wendy go up to her own nest. Let the boy go back to his safe prison. Let everything hold, simply hold, the way things were.

Chapter Seven

RONNIE MUNGO's headlights illuminated the figure of Mrs. Beck, just as she was turning into the path that led around the house. She knew who it was; Wendy was in, then. She tried to walk a little faster.

The moon was up. The flagstone path was clear. The night air was pleasantly cool and her dark coat was comfortable. She said, "Good evening," to the first guard. To the second guard, at the dining room corner where she must turn, she said something about a double feature being much too long. She noted, with satisfaction, the relaxed friendliness of their responses. Evidently, there had been no excitement here. They had seen no madman.

She took from her handbag the back door key and the paper napkin which she meant to destroy. She had chosen to bring it with her, all the way home, because across the corner was printed the Whitman name. She had every right to have it. And all was well, now.

Charles Tyler said to his wife, "Could be, he suicided. That's where the 'berserk' ones are usually headed." Heading for oblivion, he was thinking. *They* don't believe in heaven or in hell. What do they care how many innocent souls get hurt on their way? People who jump off buildings, and never mind what decent citizen is minding his business on the street below. Or what cop has to risk his life, either. People who turn on the gas and blow out the wall, and never mind who might be living his inoffensive life on the other side of the wall. Kooks. Augh . . . He stretched in anger.

There used to be the good old days in crime, he mused. Criminals who went professionally about *their* business, with understandable motives. They wanted money that they hadn't earned in the common market. So, they'd have a project. Took intelligence, of a kind. But not so much anymore. Now it was the kooks, infesting the world. And breeding like maggots. Violence for violence's sake.

For no gain, *all* loss. Sometimes he sure felt he'd like to give *them* violence, but he knew that was old-fashioned and useless. He could be as sorry for some poor kook as anybody else—but if one of them broke the law, then he broke the law. If that wasn't clear, then Charles Tyler didn't know where he was.

"Guess I'm getting old," he mumbled.

His wife patted him. She herself had never liked his sister Myra, a cold and greedy little package if Josie Tyler had ever seen one. It didn't matter what Josie felt, but she suspected it mattered that Charles had never much liked his sister, either. He'd be feeling guilty for it now.

Josie said, "You'll get him."

"Whatever that'll mean," he grumbled.

"That means you'll get him, because you are good, and you will," said Josie loyally, and thought, Poor Charles. Poor Charles. "Go to sleep," she soothed.

Two police cars kept circling the neighborhood of the Whitman house, using spotlights on the shrubbery.

Inside, old Mrs. Whitman was asleep and snoring, daintily. Her son, Ted, was having a dream.

In the big room, Wendy Whitman was raging at her cousin.

"What do you mean by hanging around down here? Were you going to say a few well-chosen words against this marriage? Or maybe you thought you'd wait, for Ronnie to see how 'pretty' you look, in bed! Too old for me, is he? But just right for *you*? Is *that* it? You keep away from Ronnie Mungo."

Edie sat up and wiggled cautiously out from under the quilt. Her feet hit the floor and she stood up and moved toward the fireplace. Wendy turned and Wendy followed. Edie knew, now, that if only the boy kept quiet he was safe. It would cross nobody's mind that he could possibly be where he was. But she was afraid that Wendy might snatch at the quilt, Wendy might even launch herself at Edie, to scratch and bite. Wendy was in a towering rage.

"I'd be very glad to let Ronnie Mungo alone," Edie said, rather primly.

"*I'm* going to marry him," cried Wendy. She wasn't pretty, now. She was quite frighteningly ugly. "Nobody's going to stop me."

Berserk? thought Edie. She remembered that she could always yell for the guard to come. She thought she would prod, she would attack, she would go on the offensive. Wendy was in a fit state to say too much.

"Tomorrow?" drawled Edie. "What *is* the big hurry?"

"Cousin Edie, remember what I said. . . ." Was Wendy struggling to control herself?

"So Myra tried to stop you last night?" said Edie. "What well-chosen words did she say? And what did you do about it?"

Wendy was visibly trembling. But she suddenly wrenched her body around as if she spun on the tip of one toe, and ran for the stairs. "Who listens to Myra?" she said, gutturally. "Or you? Or anybody so stupid?"

Wendy was going to run upstairs to her own room and it was best that she go. Yet, in the moment, Edie felt that she had failed and that she must try again. She had forgotten where the boy was. But she remembered the boy.

"Wendy." She stepped close to the stairs and looked up. "If you are running off tomorrow, won't you at least, before you go, admit that you might not have seen Harold Page?"

"Oh, what's the matter with you now?" wailed Wendy.

"Don't you know there isn't really any other evidence against him?" Then Edie could have eaten her words. What was she doing, trying to reason? With this enemy?

Wendy said, brutally contemptuous, "I'll say I saw him do it, then. I'll leave a note."

"Never mind. Go to bed." Edie bent her head. She dared not look behind her at the sofa. She had made another bad mistake. She ought to have let her cousin go.

She heard Wendy say, "Don't you tell me what to do."

Wendy had turned and was coming down.

"Let's skip the whole thing," said Edie, trying to smile. "I don't understand you."

"I'll say what I want." Wendy's voice was loud and it became louder. "And I'll do what I want. What"—now she was screaming —"can't you understand about *that?*"

Edie took care to back away toward the fireplace. She was terrified, now. But she said, valiantly, "You don't care what you do to somebody else?"

"Ha, neither do you! You're the dopiest— If you weren't so busy fooling yourself, you'd know that *nobody* does." Wendy was not quite screaming but her voice was very loud. "Nobody gives one damn about anybody else, not really. Or ever has."

It seemed to tear out of her as if this were the truth, as Wendy saw it, and Edie gasped. "Look, that is . . . just not so," she said, with a pang that was almost pity.

"It *is* so." Wendy was screaming, again. Her face was flushed. Her neck was ugly. "It is *so*. Don't try to sell me your stupid ideas! They're lies!" Her head went back and the neck looked almost deformed. "Don't you think I know," said Wendy gutturally, almost strangling herself, "that Ronnie Mungo was *your* dream boat, when you were young? And you came back, looking for him. Hah!"

But Edie could not take this in. She was pierced now by alarm and enlightenment. "I wish I could help you."

She said it and did not think she would be heard but Wendy shouted, "You—do—not! Just remember! Ron is not for you. He's mine. Oh, I'm so *tired*—"

"What the devil," said Cousin Ted, irritably, "is the matter out here?"

Edie whirled. There he was, in his bathrobe, a brocaded garment with a satin sash. His back hair stood up. She whirled again. Wendy had backed up against the lower balusters and seemed to be plastered there. Edie didn't know what to do. She went sidling toward the sofa. She didn't know anything better to do than to slip into her corner, and hide her feet, and feel the presence of the boy. Her brain seemed to stop; the last image that faded from its screen was the remembered sight of the gun in Ted's pale hand.

When Mrs. Beck heard that raving, she bit her lips and began to trot. Just as she was, having just come in at the kitchen door, she hurried through the rooms.

She saw Wendy backed against the stair railing and her father crossing the carpet, sliding his feet, approaching her as he might approach a thornbush.

Wendy said, "Oh, go away . . . *everybody*. . . ."

Mrs. Beck heard the hysterical note. This would not do.

Her father said, "Sweetheart . . . Now, sweetheart . . . What's the trouble?" But he couldn't do anything with her, and he knew it. So did Mrs. Beck know it.

Wendy put her head back and shrieked. "Just . . . please . . . *everybody* . . . I don't *care*. . . ."

No, no, thought Mrs. Beck. Can't have *this*. She was in the big room now, and she put her purse and the paper napkin out of her hands, upon the top of the chest. She said to Mr. Whitman, who looked goggle-eyed in his helplessness, "I'll take her."

Wendy twisted and ducked away from her hand.

"Not a thing to worry you, my lamb," said Mrs. Beck softly.

The girl's bright eyes blazed. "I am not your lamb. I am *nobody's* lamb."

But Mrs. Beck could handle her. She summoned up her powers and began to do so.

Edie, twisted to look over the back of the sofa, could see the housekeeper's black back, in that coat, but she could not see Wendy now, nor what Mrs. Beck was doing, with her right hand raised. She heard the housekeeper begin to croon, "Who was the prettiest girl at the party? Who was the prettiest one?"

A sound came out of the girl; perhaps Wendy said 'No' but it was very weak.

"Come, love, Becky will take you up to bed and make you cozy and she'll fix some chocolate."

Now, Edie could tell that Mrs. Beck was touching Wendy's nape, stroking it softly with bare fingers. Wendy seemed to be almost falling. Suddenly, the housekeeper knelt on the floor. Edie could see Wendy's head hanging. Her hair had fallen over her brow. "Let Becky take your shoes, lamb? It was the shoes. Nasty shoes. Pinched you, didn't they?"

And Edie thought, appalled, She's talking to a child—a child of three!

Wendy answered, like a spoiled child of three, "I hate them." She kicked off one shoe. It slid on the carpet. Mrs. Beck made crooning noises and gently removed the other shoe. "We'll throw them away. That's what we'll do." She gathered up the other one.

"Throw them away," said Wendy. "I don't *want* them anymore." She was turning, docilely, as Mrs. Beck, now standing, was gently pressing her to turn.

"Come, lamb, come, love. Up we'll go, now."

They went up the stairs. Wendy went up in her stockinged feet, quietly, docilely, and Mrs. Beck went up beside her, touching her, stroking her. Edie had time to think, in wonder, Who is enslaved to whom?

Then Cousin Ted sighed, deeply. He walked in a small circle, sighing, "Oh, dear. Oh, dear." Then he glared at Edie. "*Why* do you cause such trouble in this house?"

Her mouth opened, and closed.

"What are you *doing* there, anyway?" he said, beginning to bluster. "It's after midnight. Go to your room."

"Yes, sir," said Edie meekly. She did not move.

"And try," the man blustered, "to be a little more considerate of your cousin, and all of us, in this very difficult . . ." He spotted the quilt and turned down his mouth as if he had tasted something rotten. "What is *this?*"

There was a loud knocking, somewhere. Edie's heart had leaped once, lurched, and leaped again.

"Oh, what now?" said Cousin Ted crossly, and he went trotting to the two steps, up them, across the foyer. Somebody was knocking loudly on the door.

Edie slipped all the way under the quilt herself, with one arm over the boy's shoulders, and breathed, "A little longer. We can't give up now. . . ."

He did not even move.

He didn't care too much, for himself, if it was now or later. He knew very well that he would be found. The floor was hard against his knees. He was perspiring. He noticed his discomfort. But it didn't matter, either.

He was thinking that once you had learned to suspect yourself, you did that first. Psyche and soma. Once you found out that your emotions could make you sick, you got into the habit. You blamed *them.* Like his foot. Plain old soma, but here he had walked on it, much too long and far, telling himself more than half of the way that it was mostly in his mind. Yes. He supposed that once you'd found out how some unknown part of you could make you do or feel what you didn't know you wanted to do, or feel—and it could just take you over—once you'd learned how to watch out for that, then you tended to blame *it* first, every time. Was that why he hadn't suspected? Kept blaming himself?

He was trying to figure out why it was that he had never thought, in all this time, that Wendy might have forces loose in her, and taking over, that *she* couldn't control. But now he could look back. Nobody had helped her. He hadn't helped her. He hadn't even known about such things in those days. Nobody had helped her at all. Not then. Not since?

He shuddered, then he tried not to shudder because of Edie, who was so scared and trying so hard to be kind to him. He realized that it would be better for Edie if he were not found now, here, where he was. For himself, it didn't matter. He would have to face up to it all, before long. To it all.

The guard was the same man who had been in the house during the afternoon. "I heard some screaming?" His air apologized.

"Ah." Cousin Ted was trying to recover the role of the master. "Shows you were alert. Good. But that was my daughter, poor little girl—very upset. Sensitive child. Her stepmother in the hospital and this wild man running loose. No sign of him?"

Edie, arranged against the arm of the sofa, half covered by the quilt again and ready to scream herself, thought, *I won't.* She beat down her need to scream. No, I will not. I will not turn this boy over to such a fool as Cousin Ted. And his gun.

She was suddenly brave and bold. Boldness was the safe way. "Cousin Ted?"

"What? What?" Cousin Ted wanted everything smooth now, so that he could go to bed.

"Would you please ask him to search my room? Because I'm afraid . . ."

"Nonsense," said Ted, with his usual confusion.

"Which is your room, miss?" the guard said, sounding happy to have something to do.

So she pointed, and the guard went cautiously up the lower flight, his gun drawn, with Cousin Ted, fussing and jittering, on his heels. The guard turned up the light in the turret room and both men went in.

Edie peeled back the quilt to let the boy breathe a moment's cooler air. "Don't move," she whispered. "*Sssh* . . . another minute, now. They . . ."

He turned his head and his face was flushed but composed. He whispered, "My shoes."

She swung the quilt back to cover him, knowing that he had remembered what she had forgotten, and wondering at the steadiness of his nerves.

Mrs. Beck came hurrying down the whole flight of stairs, glancing in at the open door of the turret room on her way, but only briefly. She said to Edie, too absorbed in what she was doing to be surprised that Edie was there, "She's fine, now. It was just a little nerve-storm. Best leave her to herself, Miss Edith. I know what she needs. I understand her."

Mrs. Beck sailed off to the kitchen. Wendy was quiet, now.

Looking at nothing. She was often so, after an outburst. Trancelike. And a good thing, too. Mrs. Beck would take care not to stir her up again tonight. But all was well. Mrs. Beck had come in good time. She took milk from the icebox, thinking, I've always been lucky.

Edie, waiting for what would come next, felt weary. But almost calm. They would find Harold's shoes, no doubt. But they would not find Harold. Not in the turret room, of course, and not where he was, either. There was something to be said for the set of their minds. They were so sure they were keeping him out.

The guard came down first and spoke to reassure her. "Nobody up there now, miss. I guess, though—"

But now Cousin Ted bounced out of her room, waving the shoes. "Look! Look!" He was beaming. "Edie, how was it that you didn't see these? No wonder you were frightened." He made no more sense than usual.

"Best to let Chief Tyler have those, sir," said the guard respectfully. And added, "They were under your bed, miss."

Edie was looking terrified enough, she felt sure.

"And here's proof!" Cousin Ted brandished the shoes, delighted with himself. "Oh, I'll keep them safe. And Charles shall have them, in the morning. He did get in by the tree. Well! I always thought so. I *said* so, don't you remember?"

The guard mumbled a "Yes, sir," although he remembered nothing of the sort.

"Now, you . . . you will keep your eyes open *and* your gun ready," Ted was admonishing.

The guard said stolidly, "Sure will, Mr. Whitman." He saluted and went up to the foyer. Cold air crept in from the wagging front door and touched Edie's cheek again.

Cousin Ted circled happily. "Well, I'm certainly glad that I had the foresight . . . Imagine, by the tree?" He stopped to look at her.

Was he going to ask her, again, how it had been possible that she hadn't seen those shoes? "The doctor phoned." Edie spoke quickly.

Ted was diverted. "Oh? Oh, dear . . ."

"Myra is in for surgery at six A.M. But Wendy said they don't think it is necessary for you to come down now."

That diverted him. He said earnestly, goggle-eyed, "They would know. They are the experts. I *am* exhausted. I'll simply go down very early. Yes, that's wise. Oh, dear . . ."

His eyes darted this way and that. He wanted in the worst way to get back to his bed.

Edie said, as kindly and as warmly as she could, "You've had so much to worry you."

"Yes, I have," he said nobly. "Some rest, yes. You, too. Good night."

Edie watched him go. You get to be a liar in this house, she thought. You get to handling people.

She breathed long and free for a moment before she peeled the quilt away. The boy lifted himself up, stiffly. His face was flushed. Heat radiated from his body. The skin around his eyes looked bruised blue.

"Are you all right?" breathed Edie. "Oh, listen . . . never blame yourself for being afraid of Wendy."

"I know. I could hear. I'll . . . just go out and speak to the guard . . ." His foot failed him as he put weight on it. He managed to twist and fall, sitting . . . "in a minute."

She said, "I think you had better not. My room is safer than ever. Now, they have searched it."

"I can't hide like this anymore."

"I know it's not a very honest position," she babbled, "but we were lured into it, you might say, and now—"

"I can't, Edie."

"You'll have to, Harold," she said, severely.

He looked at her gravely, waiting to hear why.

"Because of the baby," she said. "Surely, you see that *you'll* have to get him away from Wendy, and them, and bring him up yourself?"

This was clear to her now. Very clear. Like a beacon. She wasn't analyzing, she just knew, that in all the hullabaloo, this was the guiding light. The true consideration. The justification and the far sight.

She watched his face as it softened to delight. "If I could . . ." She had touched a deep dream, a hope hidden.

"You don't dare not try," she said flatly. "So come on. And quickly."

He went with her up to the turret room. Edie turned off the light at the door, fearing too many shadows on a blind. She closed the door behind them and helped him, in the darkness, until the bed creaked under his weight. Edie sank to the floor beside him. She heard his throat clear to speak and she hushed him.

So he whispered, "Do you think it was Wendy? Do you think she had a . . . quarrel with Myra?"

"I know it," she whispered back. "I *have* known it. Oh, how do you know things? Tensions. Little looks. *I* was wondering . . . oh, long before you came. And I think Mrs. Beck knows it, too. Don't you?"

"But why"—he was gasping—"why don't the Whitmans begin to wonder?"

They were avoiding the mention of what might be wrong with Wendy, that ought to have been noticed.

"Oh, because their version suits them and they never change. Not if they can help it." Edie felt grim about this. "But—I don't see how to *prove* she did it, do you?"

"No."

"Well, she's not going to get away with blaming you," Edie whispered fiercely. "It's too much. I won't have it." She was as good as saying to him, it's not your business anymore. And it was not. It was Edie's business, because there was a child, and Edie knew these people.

"That woman is bad for Wendy. Oh, she is bad," Harold mourned.

"I know." Edie was not ready to think of Wendy as a victim, of society or circumstance. "But I've known girls . . ." So-called "underprivileged" girls, Edie remembered, who had been physically and even mentally stunted by an environment. ". . . living in a world Wendy's never even heard of," she went on indignantly, "and doing better. Wendy's like a newborn. She always *has* been, Harold. Just as if she never did find out that other people can feel at all. Not that she doesn't care. She doesn't *know. I'm* afraid of her."

(But I'll beat her, Edie thought. Although not physically, I *will* beat her, this time.)

"You'll absolutely have to take that baby and you keep him and love him and teach him," she went on. "The courts are tough, though. It won't be easy. You have too many counts against you, already."

She could sense that he stiffened. "Berserk, and all, you mean?"

"And prejudice," she raced on, "in favor of the mother."

"I guess some men . . ." He was whispering on breath that moved both in and out. "I can't help it, about my baby . . . I do care."

Edie believed him. She didn't call it innocence or naïveté, but a kind of normal decency. A kind that could get you hurt, however.

"I've seen some women," she said, truthfully, "who don't care at all. Wendy doesn't want him."

"What *does* Wendy want?" She heard him murmuring, "I wish I . . . ever knew."

"Ssh. Listen to me. What if Myra, after the operation tomorrow, is able to say that it was Wendy? Then, you'll never be arrested for this trouble. There won't be that on your record, too. And neither will Wendy qualify to keep the baby anymore. Everything will be easier. So shouldn't we wait, and leave things as they are, a little while longer?"

Edie was arguing with somebody. She wasn't sure with whom. "I don't want the police to put you through some miserable inquisition, now," she went on. "You're not feeling well. It isn't fair. It isn't—wise, either."

"For the baby?"

(Yes, for the baby. For you, too. *I* care, thought Edie. Something, here, is all mixed up with what I *really* care about.)

"The only thing . . . you ought to see a doctor." Edie had begun to see that she was arguing with herself, and her conscience was stirring.

"Oh, that's nothing." He dismissed the state of his health.

"I know I'm busybodying," she burst out. "I just can't help it." She waited for him to dispute her arguments.

But he did not. "I understand about him being deaf, you know," the boy was whispering. He seemed far away, in a dream. "My father was a—you know—useful man and we loved him and my brother. . . . It's nothing so terrible."

"I know."

"And I could take care of him."

"Yes." She groped to touch him and as she did, he went sagging down upon the pillow. "We must be quiet," she breathed.

"Yes."

Edie thought, Well, I won. Did I win? But I will win. And all I said is true.

She was wild to help him, now. She felt so fond of him, and such pity. And such partisanship. She thought he deserved his child and the poor little child deserved this father.

And Wendy deserved to be beaten.

She got to her feet, wondering what was to be done, now, except wait for morning. She thought of the quilt, left behind them. She didn't want somebody helpfully bringing it to this door. She whispered her purpose to the boy and left him.

Everything seemed quiet in the Whitman house. There was no

sound from upstairs, where Wendy had her nest. Edie flew down
the lower flight, feeling lighter and freer, now that the boy was safe
in the turret room. She wondered, briefly, about making another
phone call, in the middle of the night, very urgently, to that Doctor
Wesley. No. But she had glimpsed something there, on the chest
where the phone was.

She went to look closer. It was a paper napkin. One that belonged to the house. There was the name on the corner, in that reddish brown. The Whitmans. She picked it up, to make sure, and a
pin pricked her finger. Pins? Edie took the thing over to the end of
the sofa into the lamplight. The paper napkin had been folded and
pinned. Had someone been making a boat? Or a hat, for a child?
What child?

She heard Mrs. Beck coming.

Edie put her hand down and the thing it held slipped between
the soft folds of her peignoir. Mrs. Beck was coming from the
kitchen, carrying a cup of chocolate. In order not to spill it, Mrs.
Beck was staring at it, steadily. The housekeeper came, placing her
feet carefully, straight into the big room and then on a curve to the
stairs, and then she went—up, across the balcony, up the higher
flight. She had not turned her eyes, even once. She had not spoken.
She had not even seemed to notice Edie there.

Edie embraced the big puff of the quilt in both arms. She would
wrap herself in it and sleep on a chair, on the floor, somewhere inside of her door where she could guard and yet be hidden. She was
terrified.

Edie had heard of tunnel vision. That woman had a tunnel *mind*,
she was thinking. She scampered up to hide, not understanding
why, after such hairbreadth escapes, she was so frightened, now.

Wendy, in her ivory bed, would not, of course, *drink* the chocolate. Mrs. Beck knew that. Mrs. Beck would pretend to be hurt.
After all Becky's trouble? No? Good night, then. Very hurt. But, of
course, not really, because Wendy had to hurt *her* sometimes. Mrs.
Beck understood that very well.

Conrad, on guard, stood in the moonlight and looked up at the
tree. Sure, it could be done. He could do it himself. Swing hand-
over-hand along that one big branch and you'd come right to the
window. Your feet would hit the sill, just right, with enough spring
left in your knees, and then you could take ahold. He could see

where. A casement window. Say it was open? Easy as pie. Or even if it wasn't open. Then, would this nut have taken off his shoes? Might. Some of these lunatics were pretty sly, or thought they were. The guard looked behind him at the darkest thicket. No wind. If a leaf moved, you'd know it, on a night like this.

Harold Page did not move. He lay quietly, living the whole thing—with a difference—over again.

It had been a bloody night in the small seaside city. Cars had moved, unluckily. A drunk had run head-on into a carload of merry widows. A man had had a flat and stopped too close to a curve. A sports car had glanced off his rear and rolled over into the path of a bus. Sirens had haunted the distances.

At the hospital, speakers had called out doctors' names. People had run in the corridors. But now, late, the town settled.

Myra Whitman did not move.

As if she had been hit on the head, Edith Thompson fell a thousand miles into sleep, on the floor of the turret room.

The guards on the outside of the Whitman house shuffled their feet; they yawned.

The moon moved and went down; the sun came up.

Chapter Eight

MRS. BECK was never tired. She was up and bathed and attired in a spotless fresh uniform, ready for what the day would bring. It had brought nothing, yet. Well, too early, she supposed. She crossed the big room to open the draperies, noting that there was dust in here. Well, Angie would be back on Saturday, which was tomorrow, and maybe Selma, too, so Mrs. Beck would give it a lick and a promise later on. *Maybe,* she thought.

She peered out to see whether the guard was there, wondering about breakfast for three of them. She would wait for orders. Probably there would be no such orders.

Mr. Whitman said, behind her, "At his post, is he?"

"Oh yes, sir. He is there." Mrs. Beck turned her head and gasped. Mr. Whitman had a gun in his right hand. He was fully dressed for the day, in his dapper fashion, and his small feet in their shining shoes trotted firmly.

"Oh, this," he said. "I'll scarcely need it at the hospital, mad as he is." Mr. Whitman was making for the chest under the balcony, to put the little gun away.

Mrs. Beck said, agreeably, "No, sir. I'll have your breakfast, sir. Coffee is made but I hadn't expected . . . You are early, sir."

As he lifted his hand, Mrs. Beck caught a glimpse of motion and saw Wendy coming down the stairs. She was in her blue pajamas and her short peach-colored quilted robe. Mr. Whitman was saying, "No, no. No breakfast. They may have Mrs. Whitman on the operating table right now. I must get on. It wouldn't do. After all, there *is* a coffee shop." Now he looked up and saw Wendy on the balcony.

He shut the top drawer and looked at his wrist.

"Has my watch *stopped?*"

"Ronnie's coming," Wendy said.

"This early!" Her father goggled.

"Maybe."

Mrs. Beck, listening carefully, widened her lower lip and felt her chin flatten. She willed Wendy to look at her. Wendy glanced at her and said, "I don't want too much, Becky, but I want it now."

"I'll fix breakfast right away, Miss Wendy," said Mrs. Beck, in soft submission. She went around Mr. Whitman and into the dining room. She went no farther.

"I don't understand," Mr. Whitman was saying. "Oh. You are coming to the hospital?" (Mrs. Beck rolled her eyes, he would never learn.)

Wendy said bluntly, "What for?"

"Oh. I thought perhaps you were going to stand by . . . Of course, it isn't necessary, sweetheart. If it would upset you. Well . . ."

(Mrs. Beck could almost hear the slow turn of his brain.)

"But why is Ronnie coming so early?" he exclaimed.

(Mrs. Beck listened hard for this answer.)

"Maybe we'll get our blood tested." Then Wendy added impatiently, "so that we can get a marriage license, Daddy."

"But there's no hurry about that, surely. Myra won't be out of the hospital, at the very best, for some time yet."

"I know. But we could have a 'little' wedding or a 'quiet' wedding. Or something."

(Mrs. Beck jerked up her chin. Oh no, she thought. Oh no, you don't!)

Mr. Whitman was talking. "Sweetheart, mind you—I have *not* said that you *may not* marry Ronnie Mungo."

"That's good. Because I'm of age, now. And you can't say it." It was sullen and there was latent anger and Mrs. Beck took a step.

"But I *must* say," Mr. Whitman was going on, "that both Myra and I were very much surprised by your announcement and we feel that this man, while he is of good family and has money—"

(Oh no, groaned Mrs. Beck to herself, he will never learn how to handle her. He will always make a mess of it.) She was not at all surprised to hear Wendy's jeering voice cut in, "*Had* money."

"No, no, but as Myra says, he *is* older, he has had so much experience . . ."

"Myra," said Wendy mockingly, "should be careful what she says."

Mrs. Beck stepped briskly into the big room.

"Now, please." Mr. Whitman was turning around, walking in a little circle in the way he had of doing when he didn't know *what* to do. "Let us not . . . I haven't the time," he said.

Wendy said, "I'm not asking for any of your time."

"Well . . . tell Ronnie that I want to talk to him." Mr. Whitman was starting for the foyer.

"Why should he talk to you?" Wendy called after him. "*I* don't even have to talk to you."

She was spoiling to quarrel with somebody and Mrs. Beck guessed who would do. She walked farther into the room, smiling and nodding.

Mr. Whitman saw her and was relieved. "Now I must go," he said fussily (as if it mattered where he went or when). "Now I must be off. Now, I *am* late. I hope you won't do anything too . . ." His eyes were asking Mrs. Beck to take care.

"That's all right, sir," she said to him reassuringly.

He went away, reassured. Leaving things to her. Where they belonged.

Wendy stood lacing her fingers and looking at them. Mrs. Beck said, "Honey lamb . . ."

But she wouldn't look. She went skipping to the telephone. "If Ronnie is going to be here, he won't be *there*."

Mrs. Beck went after her. "There is no hurry," she crooned. "There really is *no* hurry. I told you—"

"Oh, be quiet!" Wendy tossed her head and her eyes flashed defiance. "He should have left—"

Then the phone rang, under her hand.

Mrs. Beck took three steps backwards, folded her hands, and waited quietly.

In the hospital, when they had found her, they had made some gestures, in the interest of opening the way for a miracle. But they had expected none, and none came. Myra was not to be resurrected. In the midst of this activity, however, a nurse had discovered the little scrap of torn pliofilm and now came grave and secret conferences among the staff. It was not until almost six in the morning that Dr. Sturdevant, Myra's physician, asked whether the family had been notified.

It turned out to be his duty to notify them. Someone else would call the police.

By the time the good doctor reached a telephone, he had missed Theodore Whitman, the daughter told him. Mr. Whitman was on his way to the hospital now. So the doctor told Wendy that he had some very sad news, that Mrs. Whitman had died during the night, that he knew this must be a great shock—

Wendy cut in on him. "Well, thank you, I guess," she said in a voice that was both tense and forlorn.

When she hung up, he let it go. He went down to the lobby to wait for the husband.

Wendy hung up and looked at Mrs. Beck and the housekeeper looked deep into the brilliant eyes to see what might be stirring. She said softly, "I told you." She thought she could read in the eyes that Wendy had not taken her meaning, until now. Ah, Mrs. Beck had thought not. But now, surely, Wendy would see that all was well and there was no need to do anything precipitously.

Edith Thompson startled them by calling down from the balcony, "Was that for me?"

Wendy said "No" sharply and turned her back. "It was nothing."

"Was it the hospital?"

"Miss Wendy said it was nothing, Miss Edith," said Mrs. Beck reprovingly.

Edie came running down the stairs. "How could it be nothing?" she challenged.

"A wrong number is nothing," said Mrs. Beck, haughtily. Then she said to Wendy, "Come, lamb. Have your breakfast?"

Wendy did not want to come. "I was going to make a phone call."

Mrs. Beck did not want to go. "Miss Edith?" She suggested where Edie should go. "Will you have breakfast?"

"Oh, Becky," said Wendy, almost gaily, "don't *fuss!*"

So their eyes met and one of Wendy's brows flew up and Mrs. Beck thought, *That's all right.* Still she did not want to leave these two together. Everything had to be watched, everything. And listened to. So the housekeeper drew apart, but she did not go.

The one sound that penetrated to the turret room was the shrilling of the telephone. Edie had been sure it was Dr. Wesley, calling back. She had been ready. Dressed in her cheap green-and-white cotton check, and the little green flat slippers she had found, for two dollars, and wore so proudly, she had been brushing her hair.

The boy sat in a chair because, he said, to lie on the bed too long was tiresome. His foot was better. Edie thought he seemed listless, but his fever was, at least, no worse. He was patiently waiting.

Edie herself felt bold and strong this morning because, by her watch, Myra was already being prepared for the surgery that was going to make her able to tell the saving truth. It was a question of waiting patiently. Edie knew that it might be hours yet. She must smuggle him some food.

They were talking. They had developed a muted way of speaking that was better than a whisper.

"I've got it figured out, you know," said Edie. "That is, *if* you said in your letter that you might come here."

"I said I wanted to see the baby. I said I *could* come."

"That's a part of it, then. But listen. You were notified that the divorce was final? Then, Wendy must have been notified at the same time. All right—that's why she announced her engagement on Sunday."

Edie stopped the motion of the hairbrush. Was it?

"She's hell-bent to marry Ronnie Mungo," Edie kept on, aloud.

"I don't understand her. Or him, either. She—told me that money was the thing."

"Money?" The boy straightened and he looked as bewildered as she had felt by such a thing.

Edie began to pull the brush slowly through her blond mane. As soon as Wendy was free to marry, Wendy had announced her engagement. That was on Sunday. On Sunday evening, her cousin Edith Thompson had arrived. Had Wendy, perhaps, wanted Ronnie Mungo openly committed to her before Edie appeared? No, surely that couldn't have been a factor.

But it was true that Ronnie Mungo had been what Wendy so sneeringly called Edie's "dream boat" ever since the day that he had chosen her, out of a bevy of young girls, giggling and squealing at the tennis matches. The day he had taken her into the clubhouse for what? A lemonade! Memory made her squirm. He had asked her for a date, Ronnie Mungo, the rich, the charming, the older man. But nothing had ever come of it. She had been forced to break the date. (Wendy had seen to that.) He had seemed to take this lightly, had never called her again. Edie had wept more than one night. As Wendy knew. But Wendy couldn't have been afraid . . .

The boy was saying, "Something bugging you, Edie?"

He was leaning back and for the first time she saw him as he must have been before Wendy Whitman had chosen him to destroy. Nice-looking, easygoing, physically attractive, full of good humor, cheerful and slangy. Aware no doubt of the counter-moral world that boys know, in which to go to bed and walk away was the thing to do and as often as possible. But a boy who, for all of that, had taken his marriage seriously and no doubt more seriously than he had seemed to take it.

Now, Edie guessed, what appeared to be his naïveté was candor. Having had to pick up the pieces of himself, he had put them back together differently. He had been trained out of the normal ways that the young have, of covering their feelings over with such thick layers of currently fashionable slang phrases that the sentiments often sounded like their own opposites. She knew how kids talked. It was a part of her job to probe through to the loneliness, the panic, or even the human yearning to be good, that they hid from the whole world, and often from themselves. But this boy had been probed and in the process stripped.

"What's up?" he said now.

She smiled at him. "Personal tangent. Where was I? Oh yes.

About Ronnie Mungo. Wendy hasn't been dating him very long. The family was surprised at the engagement. Nobody said a word against it, of course, because what Wendy wants, little Wendy gets. But now I'm pretty sure that Myra must have been the exception. Well, if she did say a few 'well-chosen words' on Wednesday night, Wendy is perfectly capable of flying into a fit. She's not used to being denied. So they fought, and Myra fell, and out she conked. It had nothing to do with you at all."

"I guess not," he said quietly.

"But, now hear this. Wendy or Mrs. Beck or both of them knew what was in your letter. So they used it. They simply fitted you in. They didn't care what happened to you. They wanted Charles Tyler to waste his time and keep away from Wendy. Because *he* was furious."

It made Edie furious. It made her sick. The callous ruthlessness.

"And then, you see, you walked right in," she said.

"I wonder why I came?"

Edie's mouth opened.

"I said it was to find out about the baby. And it was. Truly. Partly. I also thought that since I was going to school, and going for a . . . well, a career, I guess you'd say . . . I ought to face them first and face them down. By 'them,' I guess I was meaning Wendy. I wanted to show her that I was still alive, and okay, and going places. But it isn't any use, you know, Edie. I would just like to get out of here, now."

She understood him. "Sure, and *I* guess *I* came," she told him, "to show them that I was somebody, all by myself. But they are not impressed." She whacked at her head. "Why should I care so much whether they notice me or not? That's what I'm wondering, now."

"It sure looks like you're the last to know why you do what you do."

She looked at him sharply. He was slumped in the chair, not necessarily directing his remark at anyone.

All right, Edie admitted to herself. Wendy almost got it right. I came to lay a ghost. Here I am, being courted . . . by two men, in fact . . . Simon Carr. Good, kind, gentle, long-suffering, and very like my father. The other one, Tony Lynch, is poor, but lively, and is not going to be poor forever. He couldn't care less about the poor, as such. Although he is absent-mindedly moderately generous. So what is my problem? I won't know until I lay the ghost of Ronnie Mungo, and all that phantom fun, the rich and easygoing good times, the glamour and the leisure I never got to try and never will. With Tony, I'll work until he makes it, and *then* what will I do with myself? It'll be late, for glamour. With Simon, I'll work until I die. Will it have a meaning? I don't know. I don't know. How dear to my heart is . . . anything? I don't seem to be in love. But was I? Once? With Ronnie Mungo?

When the phone rang, she had thought at once, There's Dr. Wesley. She had waited for Harold to move, lest he be seen through the opening door. Then she had rushed forth.

When they said the call had not been for her, Edie believed them. The thing to do was to wait, as quietly as could be, until her call did come. She had intended to go meekly to her breakfast and watch her chance to steal a meal for Harold Page. But there was Wendy, looking very pretty, tousled as she was, standing with her hand on the telephone. *I am expecting an important call,* thought Edie with a stab of irrational anger. She said, "Are you feeling better now?"

Wendy's head snapped around on the neck as if she'd been severely shocked. "What do you *mean,* better now?"

"Better than you did last night?" said Edie, with mild surprise at so violent a reaction.

"Oh, *why!*" Wendy cast Edie out of her attention and picked up the instrument.

"Because," said Edie, moving closer, insisting upon attention, "I'd like to ask you, now that you are calmer, whether you are really going to stick to that lie about Harold Page."

"Oh," burst Wendy, "*what* lie?" She pushed her hair out of her eyes. "I wish you'd stop nagging and nagging at me. Will you please?"

Edie heard the housekeeper say, in a warning tone, "Miss Edith . . ."

But she moved around to be able to see Wendy's face. Wendy was dialing. "You may cause trouble," Edie said, "but you'll never *prove* he did it. And if you tell that lie in a courtroom, there is a law—"

"Oh, *law!*" Wendy whipped around to turn her back.

"No law for you?" said Edie, in cold fury. "Then why should you be afraid to tell the truth? Nothing can touch *you,* can it?"

"That's *right,* Cousin Edie," said Wendy looking over her shoulder, with her mouth tucked up at the corner. Then she ducked her head and her hair fell forward.

Edie heard the housekeeper, behind her. "I think . . ."

Wendy tossed her head high. "He doesn't answer. He must be on his way." She was smiling.

"All you are thinking about," said Edie, "is marrying Ronnie Mungo—come hell or high water?"

"Right, *again*." Wendy's brow flew up. She was triumphant. She stretched like a cat.

"And you won't even listen to me?"

"Miss Edith, I don't think . . ."

"Why should I listen to you?" said Wendy cheerfully. "Why is this any of your business?"

"Why is what any of whose business?" said Granny, briskly. "Good morning."

There she was, dressed as Lila Whitman would be dressed even at this hour, quite elegantly, in blue. She had tiny blue earrings on, very tiny "morning" earrings. Her small person was tidy and perfumed.

The group of three broke open. Wendy danced away. Mrs. Beck moved toward the dining room, with a submissive duck of her head. Edie said to Granny, "You're very early."

"*Too* early," Granny agreed. "For the simple reason that I went to bed too early, and enough is enough. What are you talking about so early?" Her blue eyes darted from one girl to the other. Wendy was mum. She scarcely seemed to have heard the question.

"Why," drawled Edie, "about Wendy eloping with Ronnie Mungo today."

"Don't *you* love to cause trouble!" cried Wendy, throwing her head back but keeping her eyes almost closed. It was as if there was something here she did not want to see. Edie glanced behind her and saw the tall white figure of the housekeeper seeming especially tall, especially rigid.

"Really, Wendy," said Granny in her own lofty manner, "what are you thinking of? With Myra in the hospital, being cut up this very minute, or so Ted tells me," Granny was in full flow, "it is very bad taste to run away and marry anybody. As for Ronnie Mungo, what is *he* thinking of? I wonder."

Wendy laughed. Her eyes flashed open. She was filled with reckless elation. "Oh, he's been lying awake, all night, thinking about the money."

"Whose money?" said Granny, suspiciously.

"*My* money. I looked it up, Granny." Wendy was insolent. "My mother's money. You can't do anything. Nobody can. Not now."

Granny's eyes, for once, steadied and she gazed coldly at her granddaughter. "We shall see," she said.

"Yes, won't we?" Wendy taunted her.

"My poor child," said Granny, and Edie was surprised to hear the genuine pity in her voice, a condescending pity from one who felt herself superior—yet pity. "I have no intention," said Granny grandly, "of wasting my energies trying to make *you* see what *I* see. Especially at this hour, and without my coffee." Pity had vanished.

"Coffee is ready, Mrs. Whitman," said Mrs. Beck obsequiously. "Miss Edith."

As Granny started to cross the room, Mrs. Beck said to her, in a different voice, in an aside, "Better let me handle her."

Granny stopped and slowly turned her elegant head. Her whole small elegant self proclaimed that this was her kingdom. Mrs. Beck had overstepped. Granny said, with a faint fastidious lifting of her pink lip, "I think you will find, Mrs. Beck, that, on the whole, everyone tends to go to hell in her own way, and there is no use bothering about it." Then Granny, stepping rather high, walked proudly out of the room.

Mrs. Beck went swiftly to Wendy and touched the girl's nape but Wendy twisted away. Staring, fascinated, Edie stood still until she realized that the housekeeper was sending *her* a steady stare, was watching Edie watch, was making a cold and hostile suggestion. Go away.

Edie said, "Excuse me." She started for the dining room, to snatch at the opportunity she could see. Then she thought of something else. "Wendy, if Ron is coming for you then you won't need your car?"

"Why?" said Wendy, sullenly.

"May I borrow it, please?"

"No," said Wendy.

"Why not?"

"Because I don't happen to feel like lending you my car, Cousin Edie."

Edie could tell that Wendy was simply being difficult, for no reason to do with Edie or the car, but just to be difficult. It was intolerable.

"So that is the law?" said Edie in silky fury. "If you don't feel like it, then you don't do it? And vice versa?"

"Well, bully for you," said Wendy. "Right, three times in one day!" She darted around Mrs. Beck to the bottom of the stairs. "I feel like getting dressed," she said airily.

Mrs. Beck came striding toward Edie and she said, with her brows drawn together in a kind of aching sweetness, her voice purring, "Miss Edith, wouldn't it be best if you didn't argue? The automobile, after all, is Miss Wendy's property."

Edie said sweetly, "Of course. She may do as she likes . . . with the automobile."

She went swinging furiously through the dining room, the pantry, into the big kitchen, to the breakfast room that was only partly partitioned off. Granny was sitting there, very stiff and upright in her chair.

"May I bring you some coffee?" Edie tried to swallow down the signs of her anger.

"Not at all," said Granny. "We hire a servant."

So Edie, behind her back, filled a cup and found a sweet roll to put on the saucer. It was all she dared to take. She put the meager breakfast well to the back of a shelf in the pantry, to be smuggled up to Harold Page as her chance arose.

She was thinking, Money? Wendy *is* marrying for money. Her own money, which she gets when she marries. But she didn't get it when she married Harold Page, having been too young at that time. Didn't she know that she was too young, as stipulated in the will? Was money the meaning of *that* marriage—to Wendy?

As Edie poured coffee for herself, Granny said, "As long as I have exactly what I require for my comfort, Mrs. Beck may run this house. But not *unless*. Will you go and tell her, please, Edie, that I wish my breakfast served at once, and I wish my toast well buttered?"

And Edie thought, This matters. *This* matters. Not only that she be served, but *who* serves her. She thought, How terrible!

In the big room, Mrs. Beck said, "You mustn't run away today, lamb."

Wendy, who had been motionless on the third stair, backed from the banister to the wall and then circled downward. She avoided the woman and danced free in the room. "What do you mean, I *mustn't?* It's if I *can*, Becky. If Ron gets here in time. And I get *away*. Before they find out . . ."

"That Myra is dead?" said Mrs. Beck softly. She took a tiny step. "Why, I told you. I said there wasn't any hurry. And there isn't.

Not now, lamb. Oh, I knew that you were worried. Lamb, I knew. But nothing is going to happen. They'll blame the madman. So you needn't run away and miss"—Mrs. Beck was near enough to touch her now—"all the pretty clothes," she crooned, "and the presents and the parties and the flowers and the champagne . . ."

Wendy pushed her hair back with a nervous hand. Mrs. Beck could tell by the change in her eyes that someone was there. Edie called out, "Excuse me, Mrs. Beck? Mrs. Whitman would like her breakfast served and her toast buttered."

"Yes, miss," said Mrs. Beck. "Right away." Her mouth contorted. "*I'll butter it,*" she growled in her throat when Edie was gone. She bent to the girl. "Come, lamb, think about your lovely wedding and the whole town to see you in your beautiful gown. And then when you go to Paris, or some happy place, Becky will be along to take care of you and fix your hair. And always take care of you."

Wendy, still under the woman's touch, went slowly to the sofa and put one knee on it. Then she collapsed, she let herself fall on the sofa face down. She lay quiet.

Mrs. Beck moved around behind the sofa, and looked down. The mop of hair was over the brow. The breathing was quiet. The hand she could see was relaxed and limp, where it lay. Mrs. Beck nodded and went swiftly, almost on tiptoe, away.

She'd have to butter up the old lady, for now. It wouldn't do to have a run-in with *her.* Not yet, thought Mrs. Beck with satisfaction. But one of these days.

As for Wendy, poor little lamb, she would be all right. This was all too much for her, so hard . . . But Mrs. Beck could take care of her. And always would. And always, always would. Mrs. Beck would run the wedding.

She passed Edie in the pantry. This Edith was a nuisance, but she didn't count for much else, surely.

Edie was carrying the cup of coffee and she fixed her gaze on it, so as not to spill. She had good balance and her legs were lithe to obey her so that she walked fast. She sped through the big empty room. (Wendy must have gone, she thought, on upstairs to dress.) She was halfway, when the turret room door began to open, and by some peripheral sense, Edie knew it. She stopped and looked up.

"Go back!" she warned, low in her throat. "Don't be seen!"

But he stepped out upon the balcony. Oh, dangerous! "Was it Dr. Wesley on the phone?" he said.

"Oh, no, no, not yet. Oh, listen, be careful." Edie gazed on the coffee and hurried. It sloshed a little as she went up the stairs.

"He *will* call," she said to him, earnestly, as they met on the balcony. "This is for you. Oh, please . . ."

The cup and saucer went from her hands to his and the liquid sloshed over the rim. "I'm nervous, Harold," Edie said, surprising herself. "I don't know . . . I just sense . . . Come. Eat. Aren't you hungry?"

He lurched on his bad foot, turning, going back into the turret room. Without looking behind, Edie closed the door.

Down in the big room, Wendy was lifted up, on the sofa, like a lizard supported by its forefeet. Strands of hair fell over her eyes, but not so many that she had not seen.

Chapter Nine

THE OLD LADY was demanding, very demanding, picky and choosy about every single thing. But Mrs. Beck was humble and strong to endure. Finally the meal was over and the old lady was left with her extra cup of coffee and the morning newspaper, which she seemed to enjoy. She habitually read every line on the society pages, and never made a comment.

Mrs. Beck felt free, at last, to scurry back into the big room.

Wendy was lying on her face, on the sofa.

"Now, lamb," crooned Mrs. Beck, "you see? Wasn't Becky right, lamb? Now, you should come and take your breakfast. And make our fine Mr. Ronnie Mungo wait a little bit?"

Wendy lifted up like a lizard, and said hoarsely, "*What* did you tell me last night?"

"I said there was no need to worry. Didn't I say that, lamb?"

Wendy got to her knees. "What . . . did you do?"

Poor lamb. Afraid? "*Sssh*," Mrs. Beck gave warning. "Oh, I . . . You see my white uniform?" She had been very clever, very resourceful, and it was pleasant to explain. "And I made me a little nurse's cap, out of a white paper napkin." She hadn't been able to find that napkin, this morning, in this room. No matter. It belonged in the house. "Nobody stopped me," she crooned. "They won't know. They'll blame the madman."

She had been very very careful. She had had to wait a long time, in the hospital, for a safe chance. But she had taken care to arrive after Mr. Whitman would have left. She had hidden her dark coat and had felt forced to go check on it, every now and then, to be sure that no one had put it helpfully elsewhere. She had walked in the corridors, testing her disguise. Carefully. No one had questioned her. But it had taken a long time for her chance to come. Not easy, to have been so patient and careful.

But around midnight, there had been a lot of excitement. By that time, the corridors were quite dim, and when everyone was suddenly so busy, then Mrs. Beck had slipped along and into Miss Myra's room.

It had been too bad, in a way. Miss Myra had not looked as if she would ever say anything. But if she did, then a long dream died and Mrs. Beck knew how to save it, surely and carefully, and put an end to worry. It was simple, although chancy for a short time, of course. They had left Myra's door propped open and Mrs. Beck had not dared to close it all the way. But she had dared to put the thing over Myra's head and step into a shadow and wait. That was all it took. She had been a *little* nervous, waiting—and afterwards, tearing at it with her nails, to split it and get it off. But she had done it. Quick and easy, once she had wisely waited for her chance.

Then she had found her coat and walked four blocks to a bus, shredding the pliofilm bag as she went and getting rid of pieces. No one had questioned her. Noticed her, even. How smoothly she had done it! No one could possibly know.

"Even if they figure out what happened to her, they'll just blame the madman," she soothed. (Why not?)

But Wendy jumped up and whispered hoarsely to her face, "You are a fool! You are stupid!"

"Sssh. No, no. You forget. Myra could have wakened up and said it was you, lamb. We didn't want that."

"Stupid old fool!" wailed Wendy.

Mrs. Beck sighed inwardly and began her pursuit. She took tiny steps. She crept nearer. "Ah, now . . . Ah, now . . ." But Wendy stopped her own tiny steps away, and tipped her head suddenly to gaze at Mrs. Beck with those brilliant frightened eyes. Defiant?

Mrs. Beck thought she had better let her have it. Good and strong. "You think Myra wouldn't have told? But oh, my lamb, remember, it wasn't as if she had just fallen. Oh, she fell. But then you were on her, like a wildcat, and banging her head and crying and carrying on . . . I saw it. I heard it."

Let the girl remember how Becky had taken her out of that. "Your daddy would have to do something about you," she added softly, "if I told them."

The girl bent, as if her spine snapped. "She shouldn't have said that I was bad."

Mrs. Beck was nodding, approvingly.

"And put on that act about an 'old friend she was so fond of'"— Wendy was mocking viciously—"and not wanting *him* to get mixed up with *me*. The hypocrite!"

"*Ssh. Sssh.* I know. Her and Mr. Mungo." Mrs. Beck licked her lips. "*I* told you that, when she first came."

And so she had. She did it to turn the girl against Miss Myra. In those days, Mrs. Beck had been afraid of Myra. So, a nasty secret, to be kept "for Daddy's sake." But Wendy blocked from ever being won over to Myra, no matter what blandishments the strange woman in the house might have tried. (In Mrs. Beck's domain.) It had been a way to handle Wendy, all right. *Then.* But Mrs. Beck took fleeting note of the fact that Wendy had grown. "For Daddy's sake" would never work. Not now.

"She shouldn't have said," Wendy whimpered, "that I was lost and I was impossible."

"Now, lamb, don't get yourself excited. It's all over. There is no need. Becky's got you out of the whole thing. Nobody will know." Mrs. Beck put out her hand, but Wendy ducked and skipped away. "I'm getting myself out of it," she said. "I'm going with Ronnie. As soon as he comes. As fast as I can. Today."

Mrs. Beck had overstepped, somehow. She knew it at once. She sucked her lip. She said quietly, "Where?"

"To Mexico. And then to Paris. And then around the whole world—anywhere, away from here. Away from this whole mess. And away from you, too."

Well, Wendy had to hurt her sometimes, but only in unimportant ways. This would not do. Mrs. Beck said, "Mr. Mungo promised me—"

"I don't care what he promised. *I* don't want you anymore."

All was not well—anymore. *Nothing* was well. My life, thought Mrs. Beck. My whole life! "Oh, but you can't leave me here, Miss Wendy, lamb! I'm not going to be stuck here with the old lady."

"I'm going to dress." The girl ducked around her and ran to the stairs. So? She would do what *she* wanted, when *she* wanted? So *she* thought? You little fool, thought Mrs. Beck. *I live your life.*

"You may as well not bother," she said coldly. She wasn't crooning. Wendy stopped and looked. "When they find out, they'll make you see the doctors. When they find out," said Mrs. Beck, taking tiny steps, approaching, "that it was you who knocked your stepmother down and beat her head on the hearth, like a crazy girl."

But Wendy leaned over the banister and sent down a ferocious whisper. "Then, they'll find out that it was *you* who did something to her in the hospital—so that she died."

Mrs. Beck took a tiny step backwards. Wendy turned like a tiger and came sneaking down and around the newel post.

"They won't—notice," said Mrs. Beck. "It was her head—"

"Yes, they will notice." Wendy was approaching. Mrs. Beck stepped back once more. "You are an ignorant old woman. Besides, *I* can always tell them, can't I?"

"Come, lamb," said Mrs. Beck. She licked her lips. The lamb was a sudden lion. "Ah now, come, love. We'll have to put it on the madman, the both of us. What's the harm in that?" she wheedled.

"You're a fool! What you don't know . . . Harold is right here in this house. So how could he be in the hospital last night? You don't know everything."

"I don't believe you," said Mrs. Beck. (But she was startled.) "In this house!"

"That's right and you'll be in for it, but *I'm* not going to be, Becky."

"I don't believe it," said Mrs. Beck again.

"Don't, then," the girl said. "I don't care. But they'll know whatever it was that happened in the hospital. And *I'm* not going to be in the mess you're in."

They knew, in the hospital, what had happened. Charles Tyler was there and he knew. Murder. Someone, with malice aforethought, had got in here and killed his sister Myra. Not in sudden passion, but carefully, by patient plan.

Tyler ran a small department. He was himself the head of Homicide. He could leave the meticulous examination of the hospital room to his expert and the routine questioning of everyone on the floor to a plainclothesman, the sharpest detective that he had. By phone, he mobilized his uniformed men to beat the bushes all over town.

A kook could have some lucid moments. Or hours. It had to be the one who had beat her up in the first place. Or if not, Charles Tyler would know the reason why. Get that kook! *Get* him! Flush him out of the bushes. Get him to *me!*

Ted Whitman he had left, temporarily, to the doctor, who was comforting him with pills and platitudes. Somebody would have to drive the poor wretch home. Tyler, Tyler supposed. He had to go there anyhow.

Mrs. Beck's eyes were turning sideways, slyly. "What if they do know, at the hospital, how it was done? The madman still did it. He got in here afterwards. That's easy."

"No, it's not," said Wendy. "How could he get in here, during the night, with the guards all around? You're stupid!"

But Mrs. Beck had thought of something. "No. The guard on the front was *inside*, one little while. I saw him. I remember. So that's what we can say. That's when somebody . . . Miss Edie must have let him in."

"Oh, she . . . did . . . that!" spat Wendy.

"Well, then, *she's* in for it," said Mrs. Beck, feeling briefly encouraged. "We'll put it on her and the madman. I'll tell you what to say, lamb. Don't you worry. Becky will always be nearby."

Mrs. Beck was thinking, Let her take some tranquilizers. Let her play she's upset, "for Myra's sake." Put her to bed, and I'll watch. Mrs. Beck was trying to believe that all was well, but it was not. She had made a stupid mistake just now. She needn't have said a word. There was no use appealing to Wendy, "for Becky's sake." Wendy had grown out of all that sort of thing. Mrs. Beck had to get Wendy in hand. Then she could deal with the rest of it.

Wendy was looking at her under lazy eyelids. "Becky, I—don't like this much."

"No." Mrs. Beck had to agree. With the madman in the house, everything was touchy and chancy. That Edith could be a real nuisance. It was very upsetting.

"But you know," said Wendy, "we *could*. I saw where Daddy put his gun."

Mrs. Beck was startled. She looked suspiciously at the girl. What did she mean? Did she mean what Mrs. Beck thought she meant? Well? The housekeeper checked over the house, in her mind, rapidly. The old lady should be safe in the breakfast room for a good while, yet. Mr. Whitman was gone. Where was that Edith? She said, slowly, "We would be afraid . . . just women . . . of a madman *in* the house."

Wendy turned on her toe and glided to the big carved chest. She opened the top drawer, reached in, and her hand came out with the little gun. "It's loaded. He didn't bother."

Oh, now wait, thought Mrs. Beck, in a fluster. Now, wait. . . . She hurried to Wendy, who held out the weapon. Wendy's hand was shaking.

It came to Mrs. Beck that this "mess" could be mutual, and perfectly so, even as they both got out of it. In her mind basked the long dream. Wendy, in possession of her own fortune, and Mrs. Beck, alone, to groom her and advise her. And that Ronnie Mungo (whose fortune had diminished and who was therefore vulnerable) to be their gigolo. Until, if *he* got to be too much of a nuisance, Mrs. Beck could always break up the marriage. She had done it before. Then, she might find a nobleman for Wendy, perhaps. Whatever turned up, that seemed desirable. The dream was long. And glorious.

But Wendy must be brought to hand, *now*. Mrs. Beck must make their positions clear, if she wished to partake of the full glory of the dream. She thought she saw the way. What about a kind of stalemate?

She said, "It won't make any difference, which of us . . . Remember? That's the law." If Wendy knew that, there was one thing.

"I know. I know that." The girl's hand shook. "But I'm too n-nervous." The gun was about to fall and Mrs. Beck snatched it. Her hand was not shaking.

Still, she did not quite know how this was to be done. It wasn't a bad idea, thought Mrs. Beck, all by itself—to get rid of the madman. Since then they could say whatever they liked about him, and a dead madman would please everybody and relax all nervous vigilance. If, at the same time, she could entangle Wendy consciously in a conspiracy to kill . . . Mrs. Beck did not put it quite that baldly to herself. It wasn't a bad idea, she thought, because Wendy was an excellent liar, providing she was lying "for Wendy's sake." Mrs.

Beck, who was already a murderess, saw nothing to lose. But one must be careful, of course.

The housekeeper backed away to look up at the turret room. "What about that Edith? If he's with her . . ." How could it be done, in that event, at all?

Wendy said, throatily, "Oh, he's not up there. He's in the cellar."

"How do you know?" snapped Mrs. Beck. She walked around to where the cellar door was cut in the turret wall. The key was in the lock. "It's locked," she said.

"I know. I locked it."

"*You* did?" Mrs. Beck looked at her sharply, but Wendy was swaying a little, as if she were exhausted by all these problems.

"I thought I heard something," Wendy said drearily. "I just cracked the door. I don't think he saw me."

Mrs. Beck did not quite believe her. She tended to doubt that the man was in the house at all. Maybe Wendy was having hallucinations. (This was possible.) She held the gun in her left hand and turned the key with her right. She felt the girl's breath. She felt (and she shivered) Wendy's fingers on the back of her neck.

"Becky, it's silly to be afraid of him, isn't it?"

Mrs. Beck was more than physically touched. Why, Wendy was scared—and just a baby, really! Mrs. Beck had to look out for them both. She felt the girl's fingers as an appeal. For just a moment, she almost believed in love. "I don't know, lamb," she murmured.

Wendy said, "But he didn't do anything, really—did he? *I* knocked Myra down. *You* killed her. *Didn't* you, Becky?"

Love fled. Mrs. Beck twisted her neck and gazed into the brilliant, reckless, threatening, hate-filled eyes.

"Unless we put it on the madman," Wendy said, "how are we going to get out of it?"

"This will be the both of us," said the housekeeper, sourly.

"I know."

(Wendy was willing? She didn't beware of putting herself in the worst of the mess, too? But *was* there any madman to do it to? Mrs. Beck felt confused.)

"There isn't much time," Wendy was saying softly. "Ron should be almost here. Of course, I couldn't run away with him today, could I? I mean, if . . ."

Mrs. Beck felt suddenly fierce and righteous. She firmed her hand on the doorknob. "If the madman is in our cellar," she said, "he has *no business* there." She yanked open the door. The only thing in her mind was, I'll have to see. I'll have to see.

Then she felt the force on her back, the flat hand pushing, violently. She tried, too late, to catch her footing, but the cellar stairs were steep and went almost directly down. She felt the first shock, as her shoulder hit the stone of a step, and the second, as her arm bent wrong. And then, in pain, she tumbled on. She felt no shock at all, from the hard stone floor.

In the big room, Wendy turned the key and put it in her pocket and went dancing away from the closed and silent cellar door. Screaming at the top of her lungs.

When Edie popped out of the turret room, Wendy was standing down there, still in her robe, with her hands to her head, screaming and screaming. One couldn't hear another thing in the world!

"What's the *matter?*" Edie shouted.

Whether or not Wendy heard, she answered, in a lesser scream, "Somebody! Somebody in the tree! The *tree!*"

Edie ran down the lower flight and looked out and up, at the tree. She was frightened. She felt as if her hair were turning white and her scalp knew it. But the tree stood, as it always had—huge, grotesquely near—an uncanny tree.

Now, she heard Granny. "Oh, mercy! Oh, my heart!"

So Edie turned and raced across to the old lady, who was tottering near the dining room door. Granny was frightened, too.

Edie said to Wendy crossly, "There is nobody in the tree. For heaven's sakes!"

Wendy was still, suddenly, with her arms tight at her sides, looking as if she had almost been frightened to death, thought Edie.

Now, Granny was babbling piteously. "The tree? Don't let me see him. I do not wish to see him." She was holding her thin-boned delicate hand over her eyes.

Edie guided her to a chair and sat her down. Then she ran to the place near the bottom of the stairs where the cord hung, grasped it, and made the velvet slide. The room darkened. Almost all of the tree vanished from sight. Only a leafy portion hung motionlessly above the velvet, against the sky.

"Wendy, what is the matter with you?" blazed Edie. "Nobody's there. Couldn't be. The guard's right outside. And he's going to be in here any minute, thinking somebody's been *murdered!*"

Wendy was very pale and she stared. Her whole body was shaking. "I'm sorry," she stammered. "I'm nervous."

Granny said, "You have certainly made *me* nervous."

"But I thought . . . There was a shadow. Like a big . . . a s-spider. Look, I'm just shaking."

She certainly was. But Edie could feel no sympathy. "Go find Mrs. Beck," she said rudely. "She'll comfort you. *I'd* better go tell the guard it was all in your mind."

Edie ran up to the foyer and out the front door. (Ah, but the air was good!) The guard already had his gun drawn and was coming around the corner. Edie breathed in deep and sighed out, and began to explain.

Granny was saying, in a voice like tin, clanking, "You are very inconsiderate, Wendy, to have nerves at your age. And I don't think you are in any condition . . . Where are you?"

"Here." Wendy's voice was faint and feeble. She was somewhere back, near the cellar door.

". . . in any condition to make any decisions whatsoever. I shall sit here and not budge. If this Mungo boy appears, I intend to speak to him. Perhaps you will not elope today."

"Won't I?" Wendy sounded distrait. "Oh. Well . . . There isn't any . . . hurry." She was drifting across to the stairs. "But I'll dress," she said with sudden firmness. Then her voice cracked, shrilly, "In case, you know?"

Wendy ran up the stairs as fast as she could run. She flew into her room and shut the door. She began to snatch and assemble the elements of a costume, but in a moment she dropped everything, fell on the bed, face down, and put her hands over her ears, although—from the whole house beyond her door—no sound could reach her.

When Edie came in and saw no Wendy, but only Granny in her chair, she ran in a panic up to the turret room and fearfully slipped within. The boy was alone, standing at the side of the eastern window, looking downward. He turned and came to her, quickly.

"Just Wendy, having a fit of some kind," Edie panted.

"I heard you, outside." He put his hand under her elbow. "You didn't tell the guard about me?"

She shook her head. "I promised you . . ."

He neither praised nor reproached her. His hand was hot and dry and strong. "You all right?"

She nodded. She asked him, silently, to wait, and silently he nodded that he would. So Edie left him, thinking that he was the coolest, sanest single person in this terrible house. Imprisoned here.

Harold was feeling sane enough—but hot and weak and sad, and he sure wished he could get out of this.

Edie pulled herself together and sauntered down to the big room. Oh, this staircase and the door to the turret room, suspended half-way, in full view . . . the last possible exit. But hold. Hold on. The good news could come soon.

She said to Granny, trying to make light of Wendy's hysteria, "What was *that* all about?"

The old lady stopped the kneading motion of her thin pink lips and spoke sharply. "I do not know. I certainly do wish that they would catch this madman and be rid of him. It is simply too nerve-wracking." The phone rang. "Answer that, Edie, please. I cannot budge."

Chapter Ten

AT THE FIRST NOTE of Cousin Ted's voice, Edie thought, with a wonderful surge of relief, He knows! It's all over. Myra has told them who did it. But when the voice went on, in that tone of fren-zied grief, Edie felt stunned. She seemed to be making the proper responses, of shock, of sorrow, of concern for him. When he choked and hung up, she went to Granny, still feeling numb, but duty bound to break the news.

Granny said she assumed the news was bad and what was it?

"Myra has died." Edie softened her voice as best she could but she had no softer words.

The old lady's brows went up. She began to fumble with the little box on her breast, as if to suspect it. "What's that?"

"Oh, Granny, she was already dead when Cousin Ted got there."

"On the operating table?" asked Granny loudly and calmly.

"No, no. In her bed. Cousin Ted said they tried everything. But . . . I am so sorry. For her. For everyone."

"Then she was murdered," said Granny, in the same bold voice. "*My* son's wife."

"What did you say?" Edie had been thinking—if anything—that Myra could never speak, would never tell, and for this she had been so stunned and sorry. Now she took it further.

"Murdered!" said Granny vehemently. "And in this house. Right there." She pointed. "Right there. It may be in the newspapers." The old lady balled her dainty fist and struck the chair arm. "Oh, what is to be *done* about this madman! Call Charles Tyler at once."

"Mr. Tyler is with Cousin Ted. They are coming here. I don't know what to . . ." Edie straightened from where she was bent over Granny. She looked up at the turret room. Her heart felt like a small hard stone. Myra was dead of her injuries. Harold Page was wanted for murder now.

At the hospital, Cousin Ted mopped his eyes pitifully. "I simply couldn't go on."

"Just as well," said Charles Tyler. "They'll hear *how* it happened, soon enough." He, who had questions to ask, didn't mind the advantage of a bit held back.

"That's what *I* thought," said Cousin Ted, expanding with anybody's approval, "much better to break it in stages. My mother, you know . . . my poor mother. And Wendy . . . so sensitive. I should sue, Charles, I think. Really. In a hospital? If people are not safe in a hospital . . ."

Tyler said, "I'd better get you on home. I have work to do. We'll go now." He was in charge.

What to do? thought Edie. She could think of absolutely nothing that she could do.

"I must have a yellow pill." Granny was fumbling with a tiny silver pillbox. Her voice had faltered from that bold calm. She was nearly whimpering. "I am all thumbs this morning. Open my box, Edie. I can't open my box."

Edie took the tiny thing in her hands, but her fingers were cold and stiff. "I can't, either," she admitted.

"I don't," said Granny, stiffening and summoning up some strength for her voice, "I don't *propose* to carry on about this. Ted will, of course. It is expected of him."

Edie felt as if she had been slapped in the face. This was so monstrously cynical. Or was it?

"And Wendy will carry on when *she* hears," said Granny, grimly.

"I ought to tell her." Edie winced at the thought.

"Oh, *ought*," said Granny. "A little peace. A little minute." The blue eyes were darting to and fro. "Myra was a cold woman. I never wished her any *harm*. It is very cold in here, Edie. This was always a cold room. Perhaps it is the tree. Fetch me my white wool shawl— somebody? Where is Mrs. Beck? I have some yellow pills on my dressing table, I do believe."

The old lady was trying to struggle to her feet. Edie caught hold of her arm to help her, as the phone rang. They stood a moment. It rang again.

"I shall have to cancel my luncheon on Saturday," said Granny. "If that is for me, I *cannot* speak now."

She seemed to have her balance, so Edie went to the phone. "Mrs. Beck?" she called in the direction of the dining room and kitchen. There was no response. The phone kept ringing. Edie picked it up.

"Miss Edith Thompson, please?"

"Yes, this is she . . ."

"Dr. Wesley calling."

"Please hold on, just one second." Edie put her hand over the mouthpiece. "It's for me, Granny." (At last. At the wrong time. But at last.)

"I cannot speak on the telephone now," said Granny regally. "I must have a pill and my white shawl. I don't know why it should be so cold in August." She was proceeding, walking slowly but fairly steadily, toward the east wing, mumbling to herself. "Weather is not what it used to be. Seasons are all confused. Myra was young and I am old."

When she was gone, Edie let her breath out. "Hello? Dr. Wesley?"

"I believe you asked me to call you?" said a man's voice.

"Yes, sir, I did. I am related to the Whitman family. This is about Harold Page."

"Oh, yes?"

"Dr. Wesley, I may have to speak fast." Edie looked on all sides while she talked. Mrs. Beck would appear any moment, surely. Or Wendy might come downstairs.

"A terrible thing has happened. Someone got in here, at the Whitman house, on Wednesday night, and injured Mrs. Whitman who was taken to a hospital in a coma and has now died." Edie felt proud of that sentence. It was pretty good. It told a lot. "All of them here," she hurried on, "think it was Harold Page, and the police want him."

"Harold left *us* on Monday . . ."

"I know. But he didn't do it. He *is* here now. I have him hidden."

"I beg your pardon? *Hidden,* did you say?"

"That's what I said." Edie was forced to swallow.

"You are speaking from the Whitman *house?* He is *there,* you said? They don't know it?"

"No, they don't know." Her sentences were sounding sillier. She didn't know how to frame another.

"I am wondering," the voice said suavely, "why you called *me?*"

"Well, could you come down, sir, and help me? Help *him?* He didn't do it."

"My dear Miss Thompson," the doctor said, "surely you can tell the police that he didn't do it. In what way . . . why should *I* come?"

"Why because, although it isn't true, his ex-wife is swearing that she *saw* him that night."

"I should think that it's a matter for the police, really."

"Yes, but surely *you* must see how it is the same thing, all over again."

"The boy is all right, you know."

"But to go through . . ."

"I see. *I* see." The voice was enlightened. "You think that he will be damaged emotionally; perhaps you are thinking 'psychologically'? But Harold is perfectly well, you know."

"He *isn't* well, physically. He has a fever."

"Then he ought to see a physician."

"Yes, sir, I know that."

Edie wanted to grind her teeth. She began to think there was such a thing as being *too* sane. She couldn't seem to reach this man with any of her own sense of tragedy and peril.

"I think," he was saying now, "that you mean to be kind. But Harold Page is as able as any of us to meet whatever his environment presents, and he ought not to have special privilege. He is not a cripple, Miss Thompson, and he need not lean or depend."

"Yes, I realize . . ."

"So we mustn't treat him like a cripple, must we? Don't you agree?"

"Yes, but isn't there anything?"

"I doubt that there is any wise thing that I can do. You say he is unjustly suspected of a murder? The police will surely investigate, will they not?"

"Yes, well . . ."

"I would say that you ought to *call* the police, at once. To have hidden him is—unacceptable behavior and I, frankly, am rather surprised that Harold allowed it. He knows he must face reality." The doctor suddenly stopped sounding stuffy. "Turn him in, my dear," he said. "Trust the authorities. Secrets and stratagems are pretty romantic."

Edie said coolly, "Thank you very much for your advice."

She hung up. She thought, I'll get the guard. No, I'll tell Harold. No, *first*, I'll get the guard. No, I promised. She seemed to hear the front doorbell clear its throat. She sped up to the foyer to throw the door open. She would fling herself upon Charles Tyler.

Ronnie Mungo said cheerfully, "Good morning."

Edie stepped backward and let him in. "You are so wrong," she said into his smiling face. "This is going to be one of the worst mornings I ever saw."

"What's up?" He looked alert.

"Oh, listen . . ." Well, fling herself upon anybody. "Could *you* do anything?" she cried.

Ron took her by the arm and helped her down the two steps. He glanced around and saw that they were quite alone. "How can I say," he answered in his lighthearted way, "until I know what the matter is?"

Edie pulled away from his hand. "No. No use. Wendy will lie and lie and lie . . ." She sunk her teeth hard into her forefinger.

Ron said, unperturbed, "What about? And where is she?"

"She's dressing, I guess. To run off to Mexico with you. Or so *she* imagines." Edie didn't care what she said anymore. She couldn't think what to do.

"Imagines?" he drawled.

"Myra is dead." She threw it at him.

"Oh, oh," said Ron softly. "Well, that does put the frost on. Too bad. I was fond of Myra—in a way." The pleasant smile-wrinkles framed, she saw, a pair of foxy eyes. "Were you?" he asked, obviously wondering why *she* should be this much upset.

"You don't know the half of it," Edie burst out. "Harold Page is in my room."

"What? You don't mean the 'madman'?" He wasn't taking it seriously yet. He was putting quotes around the noun.

"Only he isn't. He didn't *do* it. He wasn't *here* that night. He hasn't done one single thing that's wrong. I've had him hidden in my room since yesterday."

Ron took her by the shoulders with firm hands. He was looking down at her with a stern expression. "For God's sake! Why?"

"Because I couldn't get him out," she cried. "Cousin Ted has had us bottled up. And now Harold's own doctor tells me what a fool I am. So *you* needn't bother."

"I wasn't going to," Ron said. He smiled at her, now, but she sensed that wheels whirred in his head.

Edie began to mimic the doctor's voice. "Harold Page is 'as well able as any of us to meet what his environment presents.' So, the poor kid, sick with a fever, walks right into a murder charge. Oh, I've done well!"

"Murder?" There was an edge to the pleasant voice now. A shock?

"Well, of course, murder!" she cried. "He is supposed to have knocked Myra down and broken her head and now she is dead of it."

Edie was feeling as isolated as if she lived in an iceberg, all by herself. Was she the only one in the world who cared what happened to Harold Page? "And I have to go and tell him." She hid her face.

In a moment she heard Ron's voice, close to her ear. "You mean to say this chap is innocent?"

"Yes. Yes. Yes. Even of being mad. But it won't *matter*." She turned her back.

"You're sounding pretty upset, Cousin Edie."

"Oh, *I've* been a romantic idiot," she wept. "I haven't 'faced reality.' And now the jig is up. The bubble's burst. The end has come."

She had no handkerchief. She mopped her face with her sleeve. Then Ron was putting his handkerchief into her hand. "But look," he said with a certain comical stubbornness, "if he didn't *do* it, then he *didn't* do it? Did he?"

He had almost made her laugh.

"Maybe I don't get all this," Ron said.

You don't, she thought, but you may as well have it. Her heart jumped as she said quietly, "Are you wondering who did?"

Her vision had been mopped clear and she looked directly at him. What kind of a man was this, anyway? If she had laid the ghost, killed the dream she had once built up around him, then she did not know him at all. She did not know why he had come, so early in the morning, to run away with Wendy because Wendy insisted. A man who had had two wives already—could he have built a romantic dream around Wendy, aged nineteen? Or was it Wendy's money?

He said, "Oh, come on now, Cousin Edie, I know Wendy takes a bit of handling. Are you calling her a murderess?"

Had he read her mind or had he thought of this before? No matter. No difference. Edie said, "All right. I can't prove it. But Myra is just as dead."

She turned her back on him and walked away, trying to compose herself and make ready to go up to the turret room and tell Harold Page what was up. Poor Myra, she thought. I haven't spared her a minute, to mourn her.

But she hadn't known Myra, either.

"I don't see," said Ron, "what you thought you were going to do with him."

She turned around and he was looking a little angry, which was odd.

"Get him away, of course," she cried. "Out of this house and out of this town. Where the Chief of Police is the victim's *brother*, and that's a darling situation, too." She was going to cry again. She sank into a chair and huddled there, using his handkerchief.

"Edie, maybe *you* had better calm down."

She had to agree with that. Oh yes. Be calm. Don't care, that meant. Stop caring. "What does it matter," she raved, "if *I* rant and rave like Wendy? Anybody might as well. I couldn't help him. I can't, now. Oh, the world has moved and left *me* far behind. I was trying to be . . . I don't know what . . . to do good, I guess. But it was only busybodying."

She realized that he was crouching beside her, that he seemed about to pet her and comfort her. That would be intolerable. Edie pulled herself straight and took one hard swipe at her eyes with the handkerchief. "Okay," she said sternly. "So much for me. Oh, he'll be all right. That is, if they don't shoot him on sight. That is, if they have enough pity to get him to a doctor before they beat him with sticks, or something. *Maybe* he won't suffer too much. *Maybe* he won't get sent back, as a homicidal maniac. Somebody else might believe him. It *may* come out that Wendy drove him there in the first place, with her lies, and doesn't mind if she does it again. Justice *may* prevail. If it doesn't, then Wendy will just get away with murder. Two of them. Myra. And Harold Page—to all intents and purposes. That's wrong, *I* think. Flat wrong, plain and simple. That is, if anything is simple anymore."

Ron stirred and said, "Er . . . could I do anything?"

"What could you do?" Edie flashed. "I forgot. You came to carry Wendy off and marry her."

"Could be," he drawled, "I suddenly don't feel like marrying Wendy Whitman."

"Just because she's insane?" Edie then became ashamed of herself. She got out of the chair. Jumped into her familiar skin. "I'm very sorry, Ron," she said in her normal voice. "Pay no attention to that, please? I don't know what to *do*, you see. There's nothing I can do about this."

But she found herself feeling a little better. It was dead-end, frustration alley. You snarled and you bit. But after a while, when you were sane again, you just hit the wall. She could not help Harold Page.

So she had been insulting a stranger, this Ronnie Mungo whom she did not know, because a dream or two had died—but *he* had not dreamed them. She said again, "I'm sorry. I shouldn't insult you. You have nothing to do with it."

He was looking at her thoughtfully. There seemed to be a tiny worry line on his brow. "I'm sorry, too," he said, "because it looks to me as if *you've* had a little too much to do with it. Aren't you going to be in a bad spot?"

"Oh—" Edie dismissed that.

"Look, I guess I see why you did all this. But I don't think Tyler is going to take it kindly. Matter of fact, I think it's against the law."

She shook her head sadly.

"Not going down too well with the old lady, either. Is it?"

"No," said Edie, who didn't care about that.

"Do you know what I think? I think we had better get him out of here."

Chapter Eleven

"WHAT?" Edie didn't trust her ears.

"Right now." (He meant it?)

"How could . . ."

"I have a car out there."

"There's a guard out there," she said, bewildered.

"Then get him in here."

"How?"

"Call him in. Tell him a story. Tell him you're hearing sinister noises, somewhere inside the house. Get him out of *this* room, and the way is clear."

"Would he come?" Her heart beat faster.

"What's he there for?" Ron held his head tilted. He was grinning at her. His eyes were reckless.

"Then you'd take Harold?" She couldn't believe it.

"Certainly. Whisk him out of town. That's what you would like. That would take you off the spot."

She said, in confusion, "I want *him* back where he'll have somebody on his side, *some* chance." But that was wrong. Dr. Wesley wasn't on Harold's side. Oh nonsense, of course he was—although not romantically.

"There's going to be one hell of an uproar if he's caught in *your* room," said Ron rapidly. "You're going to land right in the soup. Harboring a wanted man."

"He's not a murderer."

"I believe you. So—get him out. Chicken?"

"Are you doing this for me?" She couldn't imagine why he was doing it.

"For auld lang syne," Ron said lightly.

"There wasn't any."

"Then for the auld lang syne that never was," he said. "You're pretty cute, Edie."

"Don't tease me."

"For kicks, then," he said impatiently. "Call it that. Shall we *do* it?"

Now, she saw a thousand reasons why they couldn't do it. "Cousin Ted and Mr. Tyler are on their way—"

"They're not here, *yet.*"

"But will he go?" She started for the stairs.

"Well," said Ron with a great shrug, "if he won't go . . . that's gratitude for you."

"Is there *time?*"

He came over to her and spoke rapidly, making a plan. "You call the guard. Right now. I'll lure him where we want him. You put your pseudo-madman in the back of my car. Make him lie low, on the floor. I'll nip out and drive off. Why not?"

She thought, Does he think it's a game? Then she thought, Yet why not? The way things are is so bad, so dangerous, so wrong. What way could be any worse than the way things are?

Ron said, "Aw, come on, Edie. Just as I'm finding out that do-gooding can be fun."

She couldn't help but smile. "Where shall I say, though?" She ran up to the foyer. She was thinking of Granny, Mrs. Beck, Wendy. "There are people all over the house." East wing, west wing, upstairs. "I'll have to say I'm hearing noises in the cellar."

"Cellar. Fine. That'll do. Quick, now."

Edie knew they had not thought this through. But there wasn't time to think it through. There was only just time enough to do it. Surely, it would be better to get Harold Page out of the house. How could that be doubted, whether you could produce your reasons in an orderly row or not?

She was out in the air again, in the bright morning. The guard saw her at once and turned toward her. She ran to him; he was still Conrad, the one she knew. "Oh, could you please?" Edie made herself breathless, which wasn't difficult. "There *is* somebody in the house, I think. There's something making noises. Now, we're all scared."

"*Inside!*" But he was moving. He would come. "Where, miss?"

"In the cellar. Something *down* there . . ."

"I'll take a look." He followed her.

They hurried across the tile of the foyer and down into the room, so darkened by the drawn draperies. Coming in from the sunshine, the guard was blinking.

"It seems to be a kind of rustling," Edie was improvising.

"How could he get in there?" the guard muttered. "I locked the outside cellar door myself." He was bristling now. He stopped short, as Ron met him. "Sir?" He blinked.

"Better check, don't you think?" said Ron, in a low voice, as if not to frighten the intruder. "*You'll* know how to handle it."

"Yeah. Sure," the guard said. "I can handle it."

He walked and Ron, beside him, became a kind of guide. They were going around the curve of the wall. At the cellar door, they would be invisible from the stairs. The stairs would be invisible to them. Edie was poised to ascend.

Then she heard Granny's voice. "Who is that man? Young man?"

Edie looked and there sat Granny, in a chair near the door to the east wing, wrapped in her white shawl, looking as if she had been sitting there for hours.

"Oh, Granny, go away!" wailed Edie.

Ronnie Mungo had said much the same, although more tactfully. "Mrs. Whitman, maybe you had best not be out here just now."

But Granny, trotting into the big room, with her shawl wrapped around her snugly, had gone on talking to herself. ". . . help remembering how one lies down in one's coffin. I do not believe that this is the time to . . . I believe that I would rather sit . . . How do you do?"

Then she had sat down, established herself. "Ronnie Mungo, is it not?" the old lady had said. And then, "There has been a death in the family."

When Edie, poised on the first step, wailed in disappointment, the guard took it for female fright. "It's all right, ladies," he said to her and Granny, too. "I can handle it." He said to Ron, "Could be a rat, you know. Something of the sort. This is the cellar door, right?"

Ron said, in a voice too loud, "Get him out."

Edie knew that he spoke to her. All right, she thought, do it anyway. In spite of Granny. She won't know what is happening soon enough to stop it. Edie ran up to the balcony. No, no, she thought. If Granny sees him, she will cry out, and the guard will look. He might even shoot.

The guard was not looking, now. He had taken Ron's words as addressed to himself. "Listen," he said, "if he is down there, I'll get him out, all right."

Granny shrilled, "Get whom? You are in *my* house."

"Get the madman, ma'am." Conrad accepted her authority.

Granny's voice began to tremble. "In the tree?" she quavered.
"The tree? I have never really been comfortable with that tree. . . ."
She was remembering the fright that Wendy had given her. Her
thin hand came to cover her eyes. Edie saw Ron swing to the old
lady. He was going to stand over her, distract her, keep *her* from
looking. She heard him say, "The tree?" Too loud. To Edie?

Well, of course. *The Tree!* Edie nodded understanding. The draperies had been drawn. Lucky! Harold could swing out of the turret
room by the route of the tree limb. Could do, in reverse, what they
were all so sure he had done, were afraid that he might do. The
guard, at least, could not see any part of the big window from where
he was, near the cellar door.

But the guard was not near the cellar door. Edie heard his call
and looked down. He was directly below her, looking up. "Where is
the key to the cellar door, miss?"

Ron said, "I'll find it. Can you hear him, down there, now?"

Ron veered away from Granny to shepherd the guard back around
the curve of the wall. Edie, on her toes on the balcony, her hand
sweating on the knob of the door to the turret room, heard a sound
she was not making. Latch click?

Ron had reappeared below and was gazing up. Everything was
frozen—except the front door of the Whitman house, which was
swinging open.

Edie said, in a false bright voice, with the ridiculous inflections of
some ancient stage-piece, "Here come Cousin Ted and Mr. Tyler
now!"

"Find the key," called Ronnie Mungo. "If you can. Maybe you
can. The tree?"

Nobody noticed that he had not said "key" a second time. Except Edie, who thought, Nothing could be worse than it is—so why
not? They'll be distracted, too. This is better.

"If I can," she promised gaily.

Cousin Ted was entering slowly, as became a man bent under a
great sorrow. Before he and Charles Tyler had come down into the
big room, Edie had turned the knob and slipped from their sight.

She had to explain to Harold very quickly. She had to get him to
move, to go, to understand—very quickly.

He had heard the phone ring, a couple of times, but Edie hadn't
come. He had heard her speaking to the guard again, just now. Outside. He hadn't caught it all. He'd heard the word "cellar" so he

knew she hadn't been mentioning where he was. He was alerted, though. Something was up. So when she came, on such a wave of urgency, he was ready to listen closely.

"The guard's inside. Everybody's there. You've got to get out, by this window. By the limb of the tree. Slide down the trunk. Can you do it, Harold? There's a red car, parked near the front door. Scrunch down and don't let the other guard see you. Get into the back seat and lie on the floor. Quickly. Right away. Ronnie Mungo's going to drive off with you. You have got to get out."

He was making a kind of token hesitation. He was going to do it. He'd be glad to. Right away. But she added, "Myra is dead. Now, they think you murdered her. I know you didn't. Do this for me?"

It shook him. It really shook him up. He turned, under her pushing hands, and by the strength of his own first impulse. Then he was crouching in the narrow embrasure. His bad foot held him well enough. The window was slightly open. He pulled it open all the way. There was no guard below. Not far above his head was the limb of the tree, in easy reach. He glanced at the big window below. The draperies were closed. He wondered if Wendy was standing the other side of them. If he thought *once more* of Wendy, he couldn't do it. And he wanted to get out.

The limb of the tree was very thick. He must cup his hands well over the top of it. It wouldn't do to fall. He would break his foot again, or a leg. If his arms didn't feel so heavy, in themselves, if he wasn't feeling so rotten, lousy, altogether, it would be a piece of cake. But he could *do* it.

The girl was saying behind him, "Quick. Quick. Quick."

So there was no time to think whether he should.

Ted Whitman reached the floor of the big room just as his mother screamed, a tiny, dainty "Oh," but a scream, even so.

"What?" said Ted. "What?"

Mungo was there and he said, "There's someone in the cellar." Old Mrs. Whitman, from her chair, was hanging to his sleeve.

Charles Tyler pushed past, saying with relish, "That so?"

And the old lady said in a shrill quaver, "Now, Teddy, don't *you* get killed. Let somebody else go."

"Oh, Mother . . ." said Ted.

Edie, cracking the door of the turret room, heard Cousin Ted saying, "Myra . . . Mother, did they tell you?"

And Ron say to him sharply, "The cellar, sir. The cellar." So Cousin Ted was turned and directed toward the cellar door.

"Now is the time," said Ronnie loudly, "to be a brave girl."

Edie was past being brave. Harold was already launching himself upon the tree. She could not help him. She might, by helping Ronnie get away. She started down.

The guard said from around the curve, "No key, sir."

Tyler said, "Where *is* the key?"

She saw that Ron was gazing high above her head. She knew that the glass was bare, high in the pointed arch. She knew that the leaves of the big tree would be shaking, there.

No one else must look. No one else must see. What could they do with Cousin Ted, who hadn't gone far enough, who wasn't out of the way yet. *He* might see.

"Cousin Ted, you must have a key to the cellar door," Edie sang out.

So Cousin Ted began to pull his key case out of his pocket. "What? Key? To the cellar? Why yes. Naturally, I have a key."

So he went, in almost his normal gait, around the curve to where the other two men were standing. From there, none of them could see the window or the shaking of the tree.

Edie found herself clinging to the newel post, not daring to look behind and above her.

Granny, grasping Ronnie's sleeve with a tight little hand, was bridling and babbling. "I am neither brave *nor* a girl, young man, but it is kind of you. What *I* shall do is sit. I can't help thinking that if one were to die in any sudden public way, one's limbs . . ."

The tree limb shook. The eastern sun was shifting southerly. Edie could see the shadows. Leaves were dancing on the carpet, over there. Over there.

". . . may be tumbled about and one's clothing disarranged . . ." Granny went on and on . . . "and one might look perfectly vulgar and unable to do a thing about it. And after a long life, during which one has struggled to behave with decorum, at least . . ."

Edie let go of the newel post and raced to Ron's side, where he was trying to disengage the old woman's clutch upon his sleeve. Edie must take over here. Ron had to get out of the house too. And into his car, in order to drive away. Quickly.

She could see the group of three now, around the curved wall, near the cellar door. The guard said, "I guess you gimme the wrong one, Mr. Whitman."

Cousin Ted said, "What? Oh, dear . . ."

And Tyler said, "Get *on* with it."

Granny tightened her fingers and said, "Ronnie Mungo? There was something I was going to say to you. But this is *not* the time . . ."

"No, no," said Edie. "Let *me* . . ." She put her hand on Granny's little claw and began to work, to loosen those fingers.

"When I was young," said Granny, "there were so many strong young men. Where are they now?"

"*Sssh*, Granny . . . let me . . ."

Tyler said, warning, "Stand away, Ted."

The guard must have found a key that worked and he must have turned it. Ted stumbled backward.

And the tree shook. The shadows danced on one bright patch of carpet. The leaves were dancing against the high glass. A twig scratched? It scratched on Edie's ear like a scream.

But the two men, Tyler and the guard, had their guns out and they stood concentrated and waiting upon the exact right second to open the cellar door. It's going to work, thought Edie. It'll be all right. We'll *do* it.

Ronnie Mungo moved his arm abruptly and tore the sleeve of his jacket out of the old lady's grasp. Edie was bent to take over here, to stand by the old lady. He was turned toward the window. He could go, now. Ron's left arm came up and his hand fell upon her shoulder.

She knew it fell, signifying doom. She looked behind her. Wendy was coming down the stairs. She was wearing a summer suit in peacock blue, with a turtlenecked white blouse. Her head was bare. She was lugging her small white train case. She was stepping to the balcony. Her tiny pretty feet twinkled in bright blue.

Edie could feel the old lady's hand like a nest of trembling wire, she could feel Ron's hand heavy and warm and ominous on her shoulder. The shadowed leaves made a dancing pattern, all around the three of them, that Wendy could not help but see.

Oh, Wendy, let him go.

But Wendy, staring downward, had seen the dancing shadows. Slowly, she turned her head. "There is somebody in the tree," she said promptly, loudly, but with an air of perfect calm, and no hysterics whatsoever.

"What? What's that, sweetheart?" Cousin Ted stepped back still farther. Now he could see.

"He is getting out, Daddy," said Wendy, in that same matter-of-fact manner. "By the tree. See?"

Tyler came quickly to Ted's side. "Stand still."

Now, Charles Tyler could see.

Granny said, "Is it the wind?" Granny had seen.

The guard, with his gun drawn, came to where he could see.

See the leaves shake, unnaturally, in no wind, and shake one last time and then seem to be trembling to stillness.

Edie was between them all and the window without knowing how. "No," she was saying.

She heard her cousin Wendy say, in a note of exasperation, "Why is it that you never believe a word I say?"

Then, Wendy ran down to the cord, yanked it and the draperies opened.

Harold Page, in his white coat, with no shoes on, was pasted against the base of the huge trunk, not clinging but limply leaning. As they watched, his foot went from under him, his body began to slide. Slowly he slid and he crumpled. He melted into a silent heap on the ground.

Chapter Twelve

HAROLD HADN'T blacked out completely. He had known when the men picked him up, not gently, and when they had half walked him back into the Whitman house. So he hadn't got away. Psyche or soma, he thought drowsily. Probably I really wanted the attention. (The phrase was a bit of an inside joke, back in the hospital.)

He was drooping forward in a soft chair, his head hanging, his eyes half-closed. He should be *paying* attention, listening to their voices, watching their faces. Wasn't that what he had come for, to get for himself what sense he could of the truth about these people? Break some false old images? The trouble was, he had found out enough already. (Oh, Wendy . . .) So you broke an image that's been bugging you. And it bugs you plenty—although differently.

The room was quiet now. There had been a lot of loud talk and confusion in here until the big man, Myra's brother, had roared for order. Now, there was order. Myra's brother was talking on the telephone, giving instructions, asking for people to do things. "And I want a patrol car at the Whitman gates, and fast. I've got a couple of Conrad's men on them, now. No newsmen in here. No exceptions. *I'll* give out a story, when I'm ready. And lay on that ambulance. This kook is supposed to be feverish and I'm taking no chances."

Harold remembered that Myra was dead. And the whole thing over to her brother? Tough for him, Harold thought, and noticed that he wasn't afraid for himself. Funny. He'd been afraid. He'd been furious, too. Now, he felt neither. Myra was dead, and that was a terrible thing and there would have to be consequences. He was in the path of the consequences. They were going to happen to *him*, and he understood that.

But Harold wasn't feeling much. Just . . . like a little tugging, like a whole lot of little arrows being drawn out of his very skin, all pointing across the room, over there, where Wendy was sitting close to that Mungo fellow, sitting quietly, as if she, too, were in a trance, much like his. (Oh, Wendy . . .)

He heard Edie speak up. "Please, Mr. Tyler, if you would only . . ."

She was sitting on the ottoman at his knees, bright-eyed, watching intently for a chance to fight for him. She was on Harold's side; he guessed he knew most of her reasons. Some sad, he thought. This was a sad house, altogether.

Tyler's deep voice spoke behind his head. "Just be quiet."

Ted Whitman said, "Charles, *I* think you ought to—"

Tyler barked, "I'm in charge, here."

Oh, he was. He had made them all sit down and be quiet. If Harold turned his head a bit he would be able to see Granny, in a chair the other side of the fireplace. He had looked at her once, but she wouldn't meet his eyes. She never had, he mused. Harold couldn't remember either of his own grandmothers. He had tried, in the days of his marriage, to be very polite and respectful to old Mrs. Whitman, but he had never quite been able to follow what she was saying. The old lady had always confused him and made him feel

uncomfortable. Wendy had no respect. Wendy used to laugh and
brush her off.

(Oh, Wendy . . .)

Then there was Mr. Whitman, who always seemed to be very
very busy and never getting anything actually done. Wendy had
either wheedled something out of him or brushed him off, too. Harold had a freakish flash of concern for Mr. Whitman. Myra would
have kept his fortune for him. His mother couldn't live forever. But
Myra . . . being dead . . . Funny, he used to be afraid of them all.

Edie said to Mr. Tyler, "If you arrest Harold Page, I don't think
you realize the damage you'll be doing."

But Charles Tyler knew exactly what he was doing. He had come
here, in Ted Whitman's car, part the kindly brother-in-law and
joint mourner. He now awaited the arrival of assistance, because he
was the Chief of Police with a job to do. There was a little more to
the apprehension of a criminal than the physical matter of putting
him in one place rather than another. Tyler knew evidence when he
saw it, testimony when he heard it. It was up to him to "get" the
murderer and that was exactly what he was going to do. This little
twerp from out of town, this social worker, wasn't going to tell him
how to do it.

He said, "Harold Page is under arrest, right now."

"But I told you. He wasn't here on Wednesday."

Tyler hadn't told *her* anything yet, but he remembered all she
had told him. Crazy. Not that crazy things didn't happen. On the
contrary, they often did. It was a crazy thing, for instance, that his
sister was dead, the way she was.

But he had what it took, right now, to arrest the kook at least for
attacking Myra on Wednesday night. "Seen running from the scene."
He'd get what it took to put him on the scene of the actual murder.
And it wouldn't be "crazy."

Tyler moved to where he could look down on the kook. Clean
enough looking kid, which didn't mean a thing. Noticed with anger
what he was wearing. Noticed what he was not wearing. Noticed
the gray socks.

"You tell me he walked seventy-five miles?" said Tyler blandly.
Disbelief was deep enough to sound polite.

"Ridiculous!" piped Ted.

"Nobody would do such a thing," pronounced old Mrs. Whitman,
"not even a madman!"

They were gnats in Tyler's ears. He paid no heed.

It wasn't too wise for him to touch this kid, but he wanted to see the eyes. He put his palm on the boy's forehead and shoved the head back. The eyes were a little sad and cloudy.

"That's right? You *walked* seventy-five miles, did you?" Tyler was loud, as to a foreigner.

The boy's eyes brightened and widened as if with an impulse to smile and then saddened. He said, "Yes, sir."

He didn't try to explain. He *can't* explain, thought Tyler, who didn't want an explanation, anyhow. It would only be kookie. The question was, *Had* he walked? He limped. The Chief had seen that.

"You can prove you walked? You can prove you were someplace else on Wednesday night? Eh?"

The boy blinked. He seemed to search his memory. "I don't think so," he said. "There was only this dog . . ."

"Dog!" Tyler exploded.

"He slept on a lawn swing," Edie was saying rapidly. "A vacant house. Somebody may have seen him."

Tyler shut her up with one look. He supposed he'd have to waste somebody's time, someday, to go wherever this lawn swing was supposed to be, see if there *was* a lawn swing. Interview a dog? Augh. . . .

He looked down at the boy, who bore his gaze, not seeming to be too nervous. Kooks often were not, especially when they ought to be.

Tyler could hear the Whitman girl murmuring, across the room, "Can't we go now? To Mexico?"

And Ronnie Mungo's quick, "No, no."

Go to Mexico? thought Tyler with an inner snort. That was a Whitman for you. This kid, Wendy, was a witness; she couldn't go. As for Mungo—well, Mungo was no kook. Tyler had some questions for Mungo. There were things Tyler knew about Mungo, and there were some things he was going to want to know. He would find out, all right. But not now.

Now, think about the evidence against Harold Page. Also, about the testimony in his favor. Here was this girl social worker. Was she some kind of kook, too? "You say you've had him hidden, in this house, since yesterday afternoon at about two o'clock?"

"Yes, sir." She didn't explain, either.

The Whitman twitter began. Ted said, "Impossible!" The old lady said, "Preposterous!"

But, although unlikely, it was not impossible. Tyler had heard of cases. He himself had known one attic case, where a woman had hidden a deformed child from her second husband, in the same house, some eleven years. The Whitmans might not have known that Harold Page was in their house for one night.

They didn't know much, in his opinion.

The old lady was a relic. Oh, she was smart, in her way. She kept her status. It had not diminished. People tended to kowtow. She had both social and economic power in the town. She watched over the Whitman money, or watched her hired hands watch it. But she didn't know anything about the world at the bottom of the hill, and never had, he reflected. As for Ted, there was a joke in the town. The Estate managers were said to pay one man a handsome salary to do one thing only—keep Ted Whitman's fingers out of any and all pies. Ted was an idiot.

And Myra had to marry *him!* Well, Myra had been, her brother supposed, ready to settle for this. Myra had run around . . . and in circles . . . for quite some time. She'd had it, on romance, Tyler supposed. If that was what it could be called.

She was dead, now. Murdered. *His* case.

He focused on this Edith Thompson. He'd like to be rid of her nuisance quality right now. "You tell me why," he snapped. "Why would you hide this man in your room? You in love with him?" A somewhat kookie reason, but existent.

Her face was pale and she started to get to her feet. "It was because I didn't believe—"

"Sit down," he snapped and it was as if he had shoved her.

She didn't *believe!* Oh, deliver me from kooks. And fools. And bleeding hearts.

Wendy Whitman popped up from her spot on the sofa, like a jack-in-the-box with its spring released. "She let him in! She hid him! He could have killed somebody!" the girl wailed.

Tyler glanced at the boy and the boy's face was as bare as bone, and pure pain.

Ted was trotting after his daughter, who circled the floor behind the sofa like a distressed animal. "Criminal! Absolutely criminal! Now, sweetheart . . ."

The old lady was leaning forward. "You, guard!" She spoke to Conrad, who stood back of Harold's chair. "You are paid to keep your eye on him. On the madman, remember!"

The guard said, "Yes, ma'am."

And Charles Tyler felt like sweeping the whole pack of Whitmans out of his way with one brush of his arm.

Deliver me, not only from kooks and fools, but spoiled brats, useless idiots, and rich old women.

The guard, Conrad, spoke up. "Excuse me, Chief Tyler, but I guess you remember?—I was in here, going through every room, yesterday afternoon? Before we put the guards on?"

And Tyler turned to him with some relief. This was his language.

"You weren't in *my* room," spoke up Edie Thompson, speaking the language, too, and with spirit.

Edie was feeling better, now that Harold Page was in the open. It was not her nature to hide in corners. She was more or less the happy warrior, now—fighting openly, although she could think of nothing else to do but dispute every word that was, to her *knowledge,* not true. Her truth wasn't going to sound true. Her reasons hadn't sounded very reasonable. Nobody wanted to believe that she had done what she had done, and she couldn't blame them.

The guard gave her a nod that agreed, and went on: "I was going to say, I searched that room, up there (That's your room, miss?) around midnight, and he wasn't in it then. She knows and Mr. Whitman, he can tell you, too. We . . ."

Edie opened her mouth to answer the look on Charles Tyler's face, to "explain" the truth about where Harold Page had been, around midnight, but before she could phrase a sentence that would have the slightest chance of sounding true or reasonable at all, Cousin Ted cut in.

"Of course he wasn't there. Now, this is what really happened, Charles." He was up and balanced on his tiny feet, his face flushed with victorious understanding. Cousin Ted had it all figured out.

Tyler listened in moody silence; he was more or less just waiting. But things could come out.

"He got in here," said Cousin Ted, "on Wednesday night, by way of the tree. We know that. After he fought with my poor Myra, he ran away. We know that, because Wendy saw him. Very well." Ted was in ecstasy of logic. "Now, the house was searched on Thursday, yesterday, and he was *not* here. So it is obvious that Edie for some reasons of her own (which I, for one, simply cannot imagine) is *only* trying to give him an alibi. But the *point*"—Ted let out what was almost a crow—"the point is, Charles—the madman was not getting out just now. He was getting *in*. *Again!* That, alone, is against the law. Arrest him!"

Cousin Ted was really a ridiculous man. There he stood with his arm thrown out dramatically, in his own eyes the hero who had solved everything.

Tyler said, wearily, "I *have* arrested him. Waiting on the ambulance."

But Harold's eyes were slowly widening. So was Edie's mouth. "Wait a minute. What did he *say?*" There was a thing that Cousin Ted had said, that played back with a surprise in it.

Tyler seemed to suffer a playback of an idea.

He strode to Harold, took hold of the white coat, gathering it close to Harold's throat. "This coat you're wearing," said Tyler. "That's how you could sneak into the hospital last night? Where my sister was lying in a coma, helpless, and you put the thing over her head? Where did you get this coat?"

Harold said, "My own."

"Absurd! Absurd!" Cousin Ted was almost dancing, behind them.

"Neck—look—neck—" choked Harold.

Tyler let go and seemed to fling the boy backward. Mistake to touch. He knew that. Better not. He said, bitterly, "I suppose there's no getting any sense out of him."

But Edie was up and in battle array. She cried out sharply to the big angry man, "Why don't you *look* inside his neckband?"

"What's that?"

"How do *you* know he doesn't make sense?" she howled.

His anger and hers met head-on. With a dark look on his face, Tyler turned again, and yanked Harold's torso forward, then the white coat backward. He read from the inside of the neckband— HAROLD PAGE. He tossed the boy against the chair.

"Nobody told *me* she was killed in the hospital," cried Edie.

("In the hospital!" someone echoed. Ronnie?)

"If that's so," Edie went on triumphantly, "then he happens to have an alibi. And what are you going to do about that?"

"Happens to wear a white coat?" Tyler said.

"Happens to have worked as an orderly in a hospital. Which happens to use white coats, *too*. What a coincidence!" She threw this in his teeth.

The clash was strange, this time, because it melted into a kind of joining. He and she were, at least, clashing in the same terms.

Charles Tyler believed in coincidences, all right. He was the one who knew all about them. He kept a little working scale in his mind. One coincidence? Par for the course. A mere maybe. Two coincidences? Suspect. Watch it. Three coincidences? *No.* Almost always, significantly connected. A real freak, if not. So, putting the white coat on this scale, it was a mild "maybe."

"Maybe," he said sourly. He thought, But he's in town, and there's the second one.

Then Wendy Whitman, who had been shifting, moving, not quite pacing but flitting, as it were, back and forth, burst in. "I don't know what you people are talking about! Didn't you hear her *say* she let him in? And hid him! *She* didn't care if he murdered us or not. She doesn't even *belong* in this house."

"Thank God!" flashed Edie.

And Tyler was startled by the antagonism between the two of them, the blond girl and the dark one, the poor girl and the rich one (whichever was which). It burned like a naked flame. Tyler's mind said, Ah! What's all this? His mind was also tucking away something about this social worker. In his experience, *they* were not fire-spitting types. They were trained out of it. They were trained, he often thought, out of every emotion known to man but one—which they called "compassion" and which consisted of having *no* human feelings of their very ego-own.

Maybe he had this social worker wrong. She *was* a young one. He looked at the kook, this Harold Page. These females wouldn't be fighting over *him,* surely. What the devil was that skinned look on the kook's face?

Harold could feel his ears grow, so hard was he listening. Wendy was behind his field of vision, somewhere in this big room. He couldn't see her. He heard the antagonism, yes. But more. *He* could hear the fear. But Wendy was not afraid of him, as he alone could know. What was she afraid of, then? Phantoms, maybe? Or punishment? He wished he could know. He wished he could look at her and talk to her. He felt so funny—as if his thumbs were pricking.

Scared? thought Tyler. What scared him, just now?

He sent a piercing gaze to Edie. "What is your relationship with this man, Edith?" he said coldly. "Why are you so bound and determined to get him out of this?"

"Because he doesn't belong in it. He is *not* that nice convenient figure, the 'berserk ex-husband.'"

Insult me, thought Tyler. Good. Get worked up, and tell me something. "You intended," he went on, "to smuggle him out and never mention a wanted man to the authorities?"

"*You* were the authority, yesterday," she said. "That's why I stopped and thought better of mentioning it." Then, her face broke and she smiled at him. "I made a mistake, I think."

Tyler said nothing. Flattery would get her nowhere.

At least, thought Edie, she had his attention and that was good. She was standing up, now, and he hadn't told her to sit down. She went on as vehemently as she could. "But I'll tell you and swear to this. Harold Page certainly did not get into Myra's hospital room last night because he was here, with guards all around, and I myself was with him, nearly all night long."

Granny said, "All night long! Disgraceful!"

Edie flashed around to look at her. "Then *you* believe me, Granny?"

"I do not," said Granny, loftily, "*care* to believe you, Edith."

Edith chewed on her lip and faced Tyler. Did something stir behind his cold gray look? "My word should be as good as *that*, at least," she said.

"Back it up," he said coldly.

"Well, Dr. Wesley knows." Edie thought, How strange to have to *prove* it!

"Who is he and how does he know what?"

"He is Harold's doctor." She saw the flaw. "Well, I *told* him on the telephone—but earlier this morning. And Ronnie Mungo knows."

Ronnie Mungo, long ago, had retreated to the outer fringes where he had remained an interested spectator. As soon as the draperies had opened, in fact, Ronnie had abandoned the cause as if he had never joined it. He had been sitting beside Wendy, when Wendy had been sitting, but merely beside her. Now he sat alone on the sofa, with his pleasant smile, his air of having better manners than to interfere in any way, masking him completely.

Tyler challenged, "You go along with that? Mungo? You knew Harold Page was hidden in this house?"

"Let me put it this way," said Ron, with an easy air, yet as if he wished to be scrupulously truthful. "I *believed* that he was here, when the lady said so." He was neatly and pleasantly being on both sides at once. Then he added, "I believe it now, don't you?"

Before Tyler could speak, Wendy, hanging over the back of the sofa, with her hair down over her face, said as if she were cursing, "He *was* here. He *was* here. How long are you going to *talk* about it? How long are you going to *talk?*" She seemed to be cracking with something.

Scared? Tyler wondered.

Down in the round cellar at the base of the tower, it was almost dark. The tiny slits of windows, at ground level, were filthy and shrubs grew close. It was chilly, down there within the circling stone. Sound did not penetrate that stone or down so deep. Nor could a small whimper, near the floor, escape as far as an ear, upstairs.

In the big room, Ronnie Mungo hushed Wendy, with a touch of annoyance. "Be a little quiet, toots."

"Can't we get out?" She sounded as if she must get out or die.

"No, no. Not now."

"Never?" said Wendy, like a child who had learned a new word recently, but did not like the taste of it. She pushed herself away from the sofa and went to the stairs, where she dragged up two steps. She sat down on the fourth step and put both her hands on the iron balusters. She peered through, between two of them, as if she were in a prison cell, looking out.

Tyler watched her, thinking, Well, *this* one's a kook, for sure. He knew Wendy by reputation. He had daughters. Wendy was willful and wild, unsatisfactory as a friend. None of the young people who swam in the currents, down in the town, busy with their lives, could be bothered to put up with her.

What a bunch! he thought, looking around the room. The old lady was glaring at her granddaughter with a curled lip. Ted had frozen between flutters. There was neither repose nor purpose in him. And Myra took this every day? What a crew!

He turned his mind sternly to Ronnie Mungo. Sticking in Tyler's craw was the query: Why in hell did *Mungo* go for that rescue bit with this Edith-social-worker-person?

Oh, he would find out, once he got his witnesses where he could go to work on them, one by one, with all the skill and patience that he possessed. Where the devil was that ambulance and the others?

Tyler told Conrad to watch it and went up into the foyer and outside. Air was good. He breathed deep and tried to track the notion about Mungo that was stirring somewhere in his head. What if Mungo would rather the Page kid didn't have an alibi? Pretty vague. Pretty fancy. But—something like that.

Chapter Thirteen

A POLICE CAR raced up the drive and pulled up at his very feet, with a flourish. Ah! Another one, down at the gates. Ah, more like it!

"Where's the ambulance?" he demanded.

"Dunno, sir."

"Check on it. Must be some foul-up."

"You got the kook in there, Chief? We'll take him in."

"Nope," said Tyler. "Trouble enough, without 'police brutality.'"

His men grinned, showing appreciation.

"Roust up that ambulance and you . . . sit here. Just sit on it."

"Yes, sir."

"It's a snake pit," he told them. "One of those."

They were using the com. Tyler stepped back toward the house. Stood, gazing over the town. His town.

He had a snake pit up here, all right. One of those damn cases with plenty of meat for columnists and commentators. He foresaw the chewing-over, the speculation, the theories and the counter-theories, spun out, like Ted Whitman's, on shaky premises. The shakier the more fun. All the "logical" trappings of the whodunit, a gamboling of brains. And the hearts bleeding for Harold Page. They always bled for the accused. Not for Myra, who was dead. No fun in that. The accused might turn out innocent. Myra would not turn up alive.

He had to apprehend her murderer.

And what if the kook's alibi stood up? Guaranteed, by the very guards appointed to frustrate him? Then, somebody else was the murderer.

Tyler already had an alternate in mind, although it was, as yet, pure speculation. Mungo. Once upon a time, as Charles Tyler had known, Mungo and Myra had been pretty cozy. What if she had made some kind of threat, trying to stop Mungo from getting married to the kid with the money? Mungo was trapped, all right. Tyler had heard it on the grapevine. He'd gone through money like he had his own mint, and he had paid off two very expensive wives in his day. Never earned a nickel, either. A sporting type, this Mungo. Traveler, sailor, tennis player. Tyler thought that one could begin to feel a little less spry on a tennis court as one grew older.

Suppose rich boy is against the wall and here is little rich girl, spoiling to get her hands on her mama's money and Mungo wants, in the worst way, to help her do just that? In the worst way? Bad enough to kill?

Would Myra risk the threat, though, when to make it good she would expose herself, too, and what would Ted Whitman do then, poor schmoe? Tyler didn't know, but guessed, that Ted would put his head back in the sand as fast as he could. The old lady was a different proposition. She might boot out Mungo, and Myra, too. Myra would have been taking a risk. Had she been torchy enough for Mungo, still? Jealous? Women had their motives and Tyler was the first to admit that he didn't always understand them. He knew some that seemed to exist. He had a glimpse, now, and his mind said, Ah! Myra wouldn't be crazy about finding herself Ronnie Mungo's *stepmother*. It rang authentically female.

But in spite of the ring of this, he was really reaching and he knew it. Wishful, even? Maybe so. He resented this Mungo, but he knew that he did. So Tyler's mind came heavily over to the other side. Not likely *Mungo*, prowling the hospital, when eight out of ten pairs of female eyes would have noticed him. Why was that? Tyler didn't know. But he knew it was so.

Well, he thought, get back in and maybe stir up a little more and keep listening. He'd get down statements later on. But before a story crystallizes, you can often catch on to a whole lot of loose ends, handy for pulling when you need them. The crystallizing process, as he well knew, was a smoothing-out process. What didn't fit got cast aside. Truth got tailored. Maybe he could get hold of a little more of the raw stuff.

The cop came to tell him that the ambulance had gone to the *hospital!* And, oh, the cop knew that Tyler wasn't going to see anything funny *about* it, and the whole department, in fact, quivered in anticipation of his blast. For such a foul-up!

But Tyler, with his cold look, said, "Get on to the ambulance. Tell them, no noise. And when they get here, if they ever do, hold them. Just let me know."

He turned to go in—a man who recognized pressure when he had it, and who now thought he might as well use what pressure had come into his hand.

Let them squirm.

The big room was silent, now that Granny was off the phone. The moment Tyler had left them, she'd been on it, ordering her doctor to her side, immediately, and if he was with another patient, then let another doctor tend to that patient. She was Lila Whitman. Now she was at the far end of the sofa, in another chair, and Ronnie Mungo was hovering in attendance.

Edith was trying to seize on silence to organize herself and think how to be more effective. But the silence was a distraction. She wished Wendy wouldn't sit on the stairs and stare, like an animal in a cage. Granny hadn't gone near her. Her own father hadn't gone near her. Where the dickens is Mrs. Beck, all this time? she thought.

Harold could barely sense where Wendy was—his mate, his love, his hate, his enemy—and he none of these to her. There was nothing he could do anymore, with her, to her, for her, or against her. All lines between them had been cut long ago. He put his heavy head back, to wait on fate. When had they been divorced? he wondered. What and who had put them asunder when they were young? Something had worked on Wendy while he'd had to be away. He could swear to that, now. Where was Mrs. Beck, by the way?

Charles Tyler stood at the top of the two steps and thought, Well, there they are. The whole crew! Or was there someone missing?

Granny, at sight of him, began severely. "This is making me very very nervous, Charles. I have called Dr. Brewster and I shall take his advice when he comes. I cannot see why I should be required to endure this sort of thing, or why you do not simply remove him. That mad person."

Ted, as if she'd touched one of his buttons, began to chime, "You had better take him away, Charles. That murdering monster! Or I don't promise . . ." Which was ridiculous. Ted, playing that he was on the verge of vengeful violence, when he couldn't, at the moment, seem to struggle out of his chair.

Tyler said, "Sit still. Be a couple of minutes." He came to stand behind the "murdering monster," making a muttered request to Conrad, who at once went briskly to the foyer where he would know exactly when the ambulance came.

The boy was sitting quietly, his fine hands relaxed. Young hands, corrected Tyler. Most young hands look fine.

Edie said to Tyler quietly, "He had no reason on earth to do anything to Myra."

(She was thinking, And you know he didn't do it.)

But now Ted bounced up. "She is talking about motive, Charles," he explained. (And Edie saw humor flash in Tyler's eyes.) "That's very simple." Ted puffed up. "He killed her so that Myra wouldn't tell."

"Tell what?" said Edie flatly.

"Why, that he had attacked her!"

"Why had he attacked her?"

"Because. He want to kill her, of course." Cousin Ted left his mouth open and panted softly. "What?"

Edie couldn't help it. She laughed. She looked up at Tyler and said, "Excuse me. I'm sorry. But if *that* doesn't go round and round . . ."

The Chief of Police said, broodingly, "No. It often happens pretty much that way. People trying to cover up bad with worse. They fool themselves that this will fix it."

Edie knew that her whole face reacted to accept his correction and to agree with him. Hadn't she listened, time and again, to people of all ages telling long sequences of "good" reasons for doing wrong? Being sucked on downward, spiraling down and down, and ever explaining that they swam with purpose, ever intending to come to a turning place, when all of the past wrongs would be covered up, at last, and they could rise up again.

"Looking for the turning-around place," she said, aloud.

Then her heart gave a bit of a happy jump because the big policeman knew what she meant, respected her phrase, and accepted her as one who also knew these things. We are getting on, she thought, if we are beginning to communicate. She had begun to think of his eyes as intelligent, not cold.

But now Wendy was blown off the stairs as if she had been picked up by the wind. She was down on the carpet, whirling like a leaf in a storm. It was as if her long cramped immobility had exploded with an accumulation of the need to move. It seemed she would dance away into the dining room. But she did not go. She whirled back and wound up slap against the back of the sofa, where she clung.

Tyler eyed her warily. Harold shut his eyes tight. Granny said tartly, "Now, Wendy . . . Now, I was *afraid* . . . This is *just* the sort of thing, Charles . . . It's too much for a sensitive child. Not to mention *me*. Where *is* Mrs. Beck?" Granny was on her feet. "We pay the woman. Take him away, Charles. Do. You know as well as I do that Harold Page needs no motive."

"Oh, *he* doesn't need a thing," said Edie, with hot eyes. "Not even the opportunity."

She looked to Tyler to resume communication, but she seemed to have lost him. "The prison ward is the place for him," said Tyler. He seemed to be watching Ronnie Mungo, who had scrambled up and was now beside Wendy with an arm around her. Wendy was suddenly as still as stone again.

Edie thought, This policeman has to understand, and he will. I believe he will. She rose and went closer to Tyler. "No, it isn't the place for him, sir. Especially not for him. I wish you'd let me tell you . . ."

"We don't abuse a prisoner," Tyler said.

"I don't mean that. I am thinking of his child."

"You are fond of the child, are you?" His eyes pierced.

"I've never seen the child."

"What is your motive, then?" Tyler sounded patient. "I wouldn't mind understanding your motive."

"But they are making him the scapegoat. They did that once before. He came because he cares for the child. Surely, the child has to be thought of. I am concerned, because, don't you see, that if you . . ."

Wendy called out, like her old self, rude, ruthless, "Listen to her! Carrying on about the child. The child! What a hypocrite! What did she care, when she hid the madman in our house? *She* decided he wasn't dangerous. Well, *we* thought he was dangerous and it's *our* house. What kind of big old concern is that?"

Oh, Wendy was slippery. Wendy could make sense. The antagonism was raw—but there was reason in what she said.

"Certainly," said Cousin Ted.

Chapter Fourteen

Mrs. Beck was pretty sure that her upper right arm was broken or perhaps her shoulder, by the feel of it. Her face felt bashed in on one side and she didn't want to touch it with her one usable hand. Her legs, however, seemed to work and on them she had crawled slowly up the steep and narrow stone stairs, not thinking of anything but the pain and how to get relief from the pain. Now, she sat in a heap on the tiny landing, not much more than a top step, just inside the door. The door was ajar, just slightly. She could smell the smells of the house, the upper living house and she could hear living voices. Knock? she was thinking. Thrust? Be enough to sag upon the door. It would open. She would be in the light. But—wait. Might as well be careful.

Harold had found a little vigor for his voice. "Wendy is right, Edie. Let it go, now. Don't you be in any more trouble."

Tyler snapped, "This a confession?"

"No, sir," said Harold, "but there will be due process. I can afford a lawyer, this time."

"Due process!" said Granny. "The impudence! Well, we shall have *our* lawyers." She started to walk, as if to the phone again.

Wendy bent over as if her spine snapped and was draped over the sofa-back, her hair hanging to brush the cushions. Ron reached to try to lift her upright and Granny said, with a fastidious flutter of her dainty nostrils, "Do put that child down somewhere, Mr. Mungo, and keep her calm. Wendy, my advice is simply that you must rise above this whole sickening vulgar business until the doctor comes."

And Mrs. Beck, biting on pain, thought, Wait a minute. Wendy was there, was she? And *how* was she? This was very important. Mrs. Beck knew very well that she and Wendy—never mind a broken bone or two—might still be in the same boat. And did they have the madman?

Granny said, "Ingratitude! We took Edith in, Charles, when my niece died. For two years in this house, she had everything she could possibly want. She chose to leave."

And Ted began to echo and embellish. "Ungrateful! Resentful, too! Always did resent our Wendy. Envy, you know. Why, all this is nothing in the world but—"

"But *what?*" howled Edie. She had begun to shake. All right, admitted that she had been foolish. Led deeper and deeper, after a first step she ought never to have taken. It seemed months ago that she had thought to be, for an hour perhaps, the gentle go-between, wise for both sides. But just the same, she would take no more of the Whitman brand of nonsense. "Nothing in the world but what?" she shouted, being human and humanly enraged, because she had tried to be grateful for their "everything" and she had failed. "Spite?" cried Edie. "Do you think I am making up his alibi just to annoy you? Or do you think I brought him into this house hoping that he *would* kill you all off?"

Tyler was looking at her. Nothing in his look condemned her for being human, but he was the judge, just the same. He was sane. And Edie felt ashamed. Even Cousin Ted could say a true thing. Edie did resent them. Resented Wendy. She had meant no harm, but she had taken risks. Tears swam into her eyes. "If I had let *him* run the risk of being shot on Thursday—at least there wouldn't have been a scapegoat." (And now she was shaking because that was true. And would Myra, then, have died?)

"A scapegoat for whom?" said Myra's brother.

Mrs. Beck licked her dusty lip. That Edith—carrying on. Well, Mrs. Beck could hold against the pain for another minute. She had better. She didn't know the smart thing to do. She didn't know, for instance, why they weren't looking for her. Something funny . . . Now she could hear the old woman, very close.

"Charles, if it were not for you, I would call the *police*. In fact, I think if you cannot control this situation you ought to resign."

She must be at the telephone. Mrs. Beck's thigh ached, where the stone edge of a step pressed into it. Her whole torso was aching. Her head whirled.

"As it is," Granny picked up the phone, "I *shall* call my lawyer." She was dialing the operator. "Edith, you know," she said haughtily to Tyler, "was brought up to believe that all poor people are saints and angels, but anyone with means must be a villain. That's why she's on his side. It's psychological." Granny was being gentle with the ignorant.

Edie put all of her fingers into her hair. "Poor people come in all kinds, Granny," she said, shakily.

"Certainly they do," snapped Mrs. Whitman, with her own superb illogic, "but *you* don't *know* that."

Then she was grandly commanding the operator to reach her lawyer for her. The operator began to be extremely tiresome, seeming to think she needed the number. Ronnie Mungo came to help.

Harold was thinking about wealth. At the moment, he had very little cash. About a dollar and a half, he thought. He'd had enough saved from his meager salary to pay a week's advance on the room in the boardinghouse. Enough left to get him down here, and back, on the bus. He hadn't saved any money by walking. It had cost him more, having to eat so many times. He wondered if money would have made any difference, in those days.

"The Will isn't through probate yet," he said aloud. "I borrowed on it, though, for my tuition."

"What's that?" Tyler said, in a moment.

"My great-uncle's will. He was quite wealthy." Harold looked up, because there was a peculiar silence. Everything was stopped. "You can check," said Harold.

To Edie, it was very funny. It was hysterical. "Everybody change sides," she sang out blithely. "I'll be against him, and all of you can be *for* him."

"That," said Tyler severely, "will do—from you."

"I should think so," said Granny grimly.

Ronnie Mungo, having gone to her aid, was on the phone for her. He rolled an eye across the room, turned his back, began to speak, conveying Granny's orders. Granny left him to do it and huffed her way back to the far chair. "Edith," she said, "I shall change my Will. Don't *imagine* that I won't!"

Ronnie Mungo kicked at the cellar door and it closed with a sharp click. Mrs. Beck made a little yelp. It was no louder than a mouse-squeak. Then, she sagged in darkness.

Cousin Ted was snatching at his chance to be forceful. "Edith," he said, "I suggest that you pack your things."

"Yes, indeed," said Granny, and Ted swelled with her approval. (He had said the right thing.)

"Very well," said Edie calmly, "but I can't leave town. Can I, Mr. Tyler?"

"No," he said. But his attention wasn't on her. He wasn't following the family clash. He had the feeling that something else was going on here, and he was missing it. His eyes slid to watch Mungo as he came slouching toward Granny, the courteous male, having done her telephoning for her. Oh, quite the little helper around here. But "not involved." You bet not, thought Tyler. So what has got him shaking in his boots, all of a sudden?

Edie was saying, "I'll have to stay to make a statement. I believe that Wendy fought with Myra, Wednesday night."

Granny burst furiously, "Now, she *cannot* say that, Charles. Shut her up, if you please? At once!"

(Not I, thought Tyler.)

"They fought, I think," said Edie, steadily, "over Wendy's engagement to Ronnie Mungo."

Mungo was leaning on the wall now, behind Granny. He looked as if he would like to crawl through it.

"Back that up, Edith," said Tyler sternly, even as his mind said Ah!

"Mrs. Beck could back that up for you," said Edie. "Where is she?"

That was when Wendy toppled over. Just as she was, where Ron had left her, huddled on the sofa, with her arms still tight around her knees, she fell sideways and lay in the knot. "I don't know where Becky is. I don't want to hear anymore. I wish you would get this over." She uncurled convulsively and lay on her face with her wrists against her ears and her fingers clawed, stiffly. "I want Becky," she whimpered.

Mrs. Beck, lying on her side on the tiny platform, legs trailing down, her neck bent where her head was against the lowest board of the cellar door, could hear very clearly. For some reason, sound came through the low slot, the natural crack at the bottom of the door, and was reflected directly into her ear.

Now, though her head swam, her nostrils flared, scenting hope, scenting power. But she couldn't move, not yet. Couldn't reach up and turn the doorknob. Couldn't twist and raise until her good hand and arm could do that. In physical weakness, she must wait. And listen. Carefully.

Tyler said to Edie, "Do you accuse Wendy of getting into the hospital last night? Of putting a pliofilm bag over my sister's head until she died? Of watching her die? Of waiting—to take the bag off, afterwards?"

His words were brutal and Edie winced away from them. Like *that?* No passionate half-accident? (Oh, did the damaged brain know what was happening? Did the body struggle? The blind unconscious organism's will to live?) She gasped. "No, I don't, sir. I didn't know . . . it was . . . like that. I don't know."

"Or," said Tyler, "do you think it was Mungo did *that?*"

Chapter Fifteen

MUNGO KEPT his hands in his pockets but swayed forward from the support of the wall. "If that's what is on your mind," he said, "check it. I took Wendy to a party with twenty people there. At Sandy Waltham's. We left when they can tell you and arrived here when the guard, over there, can say. You check it. Find out there wasn't time." He sounded bold and angry.

"And after you left here?" said Tyler, without apparent emotion.

"I went directly to the Broken Drum, where I am known. Got a little drunk and a fellow went home with me. We kicked life around until the sun was up. Ask him. Paul Milliman."

"I'll do that," said Tyler.

"And I got here this morning," Mungo went on, "when, Edith can tell you. And the guard, too."

Tyler said, "Thank you very much." And saw Mungo flush a little. He sure overdid *that,* Tyler thought.

Well—the Chief thought he'd gotten about as much as he would get, here. He'd start the check on Mungo. Might be late. The criminal has the advantage of knowing what to cover up before the police can know it. This Mungo was no kook. The Chief realized that it would be a pleasure to "get" him.

He glanced at Conrad, who nodded. So the ambulance was out there. Tyler said, "Okay. We'll take Page now."

He had forgotten about Edie for a moment.

Edie said, "You are taking Wendy, too, of course."

And Tyler sighed invisibly.

"She has been accused. As much as he has. Or wasn't it against the law for *her* to knock Myra down? Is Wendy immune?"

Might as well be, the Chief thought. Don't fight it, little social worker. I can't take her on your belief. You weren't here.

"Well, I can tell you," said Edie, hotly, "that she has always been a liar, that she faked a beating, and said Harold did it, to get her divorce. In fact, she's not exactly normal. She doesn't give one damn about her own baby. Or much else. She's unstable enough to have hallucinations, just about. And rages! Don't you believe me? Shall I *put* her into a tantrum? Right here and now? It's not very difficult."

The Whitmans were stricken dumb.

Harold Page was the one who stopped her with his sudden cry. "Ah, don't! Don't, Edie. Please? Don't hit her. You've hated her long enough."

He was so impelled that he started to get up, to go to Wendy, but the guard leaped and put a quick strong arm in his way.

Tyler watched Edie go up to the big window and stand there with her back to the room. He thought, Honey, you are probably right, which is nothing to be ashamed of, in my book. But who *killed* Myra? You don't know.

Granny had found breath and said, "I would advise *nobody* to listen to that insanely ungrateful girl. And until this trash is out of my house, *I* shall not listen at all." She then, with a flourish, turned off her hearing aid.

Tyler said glumly, "I'm in charge here." And then to Conrad, "Just hold everything." And he went into the foyer to open the front door and call his people himself. He'd get one of them to pass along instructions for the checking up on Ronnie Mungo. He was thinking sadly, How weak is reason, against the very root of force. He couldn't condemn Edith Thompson for a touch of human passion.

In the big room, Conrad hung over Harold.

Harold knew he couldn't get to her, but might he dare speak? The old lady was very stiff and blank of face. Couldn't hear. Ted Whitman, in a comical way, looked deaf, too. Mungo was leaning on the wall, kind of out of it. Edie was by the window. The big Chief was gone.

"Ah, Wendy . . ." He said it. The crying of his heart was in the timbre of his voice. "I wish you could have talked to me, whatever it is. I wish I could have listened, in those days. But I thought . . . I was young. I thought you had everything."

No one stirred.

"What was it that you wanted?" he asked, in another moment. No answer.

"Why did you ever marry me?" If he could only reach her, this one last chance.

She rolled her dark head, suddenly. "I forget," said Wendy drearily.

"Now you want to marry him? So much?" "Hell-bent," Edie had said. Harold was breaking his heart to understand.

"I don't know," said Wendy faintly.

"I wish I could have figured out what it was you really wanted. I wish you could have come away with me, and lived in an apartment." He did wish that. He did wish she could have got away from here.

"That was not for me," she said. "Not for me."

But why not for her? he wondered. "Did you feel . . . so bad," he asked her, "about the baby's ears?"

"No," said Wendy. "Not for me, that's all. Not for me." It was so dreary. She sounded as if she had always been defeated.

"Wendy, do you love . . . ?" He was thinking about sermons that said you must love or perish. He didn't know how to finish.

"I don't know what you mean," she said, wiggling. "Don't *talk*." Then she raised up. "*Anywhere*," she burst. "I wish . . ." But she didn't say what she wished so fervently.

Harold said, gently, "If I could do it all over again, I would. I wish I could." He wasn't asking for the future. He waited to know whether she understood his basic apology for not having been what she wanted. "Do you know that?"

In a moment, Wendy's head fell and turned slowly to bury one ear. Her hand came up and covered the other. Harold guessed it didn't matter whether she knew. She didn't care. It was an answer of sorts. "I'm truly sorry," he murmured. The strong arm, that had been something to lean against, now seemed to be helping him sink back. He wanted to say thanks but he didn't, couldn't. Love and let go.

Edie stared out the window. She had hated Wendy. She had let her temper go, just now, and that wasn't any good either. Anger and hate. The destroyers. She heard, in Harold's voice, what was right. To try to understand, to forgive, to go on loving. (Oh, poor kid!) Well, that's fine, she thought. That's right and good, I guess. BUT. ALSO. MEANWHILE. She rebelled, fiercely.

She looked up into the tree and thought that there was a huge and flaming BUT, and a hard ALSO, and an urgent MEANWHILE. It was a good and useful idea to learn to dissipate the destructive emotions that ate on one's own insides. The boy had learned to do it, in order to save himself.

BUT, was it enough, just to save yourself from that? When long before you could "save" somebody like Wendy, you had to fight what she *did?* Didn't you? MEANWHILE, she mustn't be allowed to go on, ruthlessly lying and destroying. Oh yes, try to understand her. ALSO try to stop her. If you could stop her, without hating her, so much the better. But she had to be stopped, just the same. My father was wrong, in part, she thought. Or I'm not like him. No, I am not like him. I thought I was. She turned.

Tyler was coming in. The ambulance men were behind him—two in white coats—to take Harold away. Harold agreed. He was even now trying to get to his feet. Poor kid! Chewed up in this house, and spat out, and never mind his pain? His injuries?

Edie thought, But here is a wrong. And it is Wendy's doing, this wrong. It's her false witness that is forcing them to take him as a suspect. Why doesn't my witness count? Can't I stop it?

It seemed she hadn't. So it was dead-end, frustration alley. The police would take the scapegoat off to a prison ward, for another black mark on him and another martyrdom. Harold would survive. But would he ever get his child?

Edie had been in on custody cases. She could hear a judge saying, "In view of the fact that he is a young man, alone—in view, also, of his psychiatric history *and* his police record."

"Your Honor, he was acquitted."

"I am aware of that. Even so, in view of the circumstances and position of the mother's family, and this child's affliction—all things taken together—for the best good of the child . . ."

But the Whitmans would *not* be for the best good of the child.

So, you kicked and screamed a little, but then your wits began to work like rats, hunting and searching for some way to *stop* them.

Granny said, suddenly and imperiously, from her frozen face that looked blind because she could not hear, "Will someone be kind enough to bring me a glass of cold water?"

And Edie was up on her toes.

"Mr. Tyler." Her tone turned him. "There is a glass on the mantelpiece. When he came, yesterday, he was very hot and tired. That glass has my fingerprints and Harold's on it. When did we put them there? Have you seen him offered anything? Don't you think you ought to take along the evidence that proves his alibi?"

A kind of fading took place on Tyler's face. He followed her gesture and found the drinking glass. He teased it out of concealment, gingerly. The boys from the ambulance, and one of the cops from the car, were on the foyer steps. "Hold it a minute," Tyler said to them. (He hadn't for some time, seemingly, doubted that the Page kid had this nutty alibi.)

"All right," he said to Conrad savagely. "Now, you run me down, right now, exactly who was in and out of here last night."

"I was on," Conrad said eagerly, "from midnight."

"Charles!" Ted yelped. "Surely . . ." You are my brother-in-law, the sentence finished, unsaid.

"Sit down," roared Tyler and blasted Ted back into the chair. He looked around. Ted settled. The old lady sitting still, deaf as a post. *She* hadn't done it. Mungo, against the wall, keeping out of it in eighteen languages. Scared green, too. The Whitman kid, lying on her face. A nut. A kook. Harold Page half-up, sagged to rest on the arm of the chair. Edie Thompson standing there. "Sit down, Edith," Tyler said, in a normal voice that was not unkind.

She said, "Thank you."

"When I take over at midnight," Conrad was eager to show his mettle, "Carlson tells me that the old lady is in, and her . . ." Conrad flipped a finger toward Edie, "and Mr. Whitman, he'd come in, the middle of the evening. Now, the young lady on the couch, there —she and the boyfriend—they came in just about then. I saw myself that he didn't stay but a couple of minutes."

Granny said, in the loud voice of the totally deaf, breaking in without regard to anyone's thoughts but her own, "Are all of you deaf? I believe that I requested a glass of water."

Ronnie Mungo said smoothly, "May I fetch Mrs. Whitman her drink, sir?"

"Go ahead," said Tyler. (And if you run, boy, then I've got you.)

Mungo went edging along to the dining room door. Something was on his mind, all right. "And pretty soon," the guard was continuing, "comes the last one in, the housekeeper or whatever she is. And that's it, sir. And *nobody* got out."

"Where is Mrs. Beck, now?" said Tyler, in a tone that was unusually light for him.

He had better find out!

He sent the cop into the east wing. (The other cop was out in the car, stirring up inquiries about Mungo.) When Ted Whitman began to sputter, Tyler sent him along to "show the man." Ted was like a poorly trained small child; you had to give him something to do, to stop his nuisance.

Conrad said he knew the house, so Tyler sent him to the kitchen wing. As he went, Mungo returned with a glass of water. Mungo asked no questions. Tyler stopped himself from thinking that this was odd. It might or might not be. Tyler had to remember to compensate for his own prejudice.

The ambulance boys were enough to take over here, so Tyler gave them the nod, to look after Page and keep the peace. He himself went up the stairs.

The turret room was a weird place. He glanced into its bath, the closet, amused to think that the whole dark prisonlike area was probably thick with Page's fingerprints. That Edith was a spunky one, though. Young, and a little ignorant, as the young are bound to be. But a doer. The Chief rather fancied a doer. He could forgive a lot in a person who did things. Oh, she had a down on her cousin Wendy, that was for sure, and wasn't going to let Wendy Whitman get away with a thing. If *she* could help it. Which she can't probably, thought Tyler. He himself felt almost convinced that Wendy had been the one to battle Myra on Wednesday night. Senseless violence. That was from kooks. And she was a kook, of the purest ray serene. But where had Mungo been at the time? Tyler wanted to know *that*. And would.

Meantime, what about this housekeeper? A funny one.

He came out of the turret and climbed to the upper balcony. He glanced down into the deep room where Edie and one of the white coats were bending over Harold Page. Wendy Whitman, on the sofa, looked like a squashed fly from here.

Tyler knew he couldn't sweep *her* up and tidy *her* away to his jail because she had broken the law. No proof. No evidence. But the family doctor was coming, and Tyler thought that Wendy would be swept up, privately, into some expensive joint and be out of the way for a while, at least. It would be the best that could be done. A female. A rich one. A young one. Even if he had the proof, had the evidence, he thought bitterly.

But Wendy had not been the murderer. He couldn't pin that on her, even in his imagination. Not her style. Nor did he doubt *her* alibi. Oh, she had put Myra into the hospital in the first place. Probably. Into the coma. Somebody hadn't wanted Myra to come out of it. Who? Mungo? Or the housekeeper, maybe?

He wanted that one.

He pushed at a door. Wendy's room. Quite a layout. Bath enormous. Built-in wardrobes. Even a kind of private sunroom overlooking the town.

He looked over his town. Funny, you could see the whole town from here; yet you didn't really see it. It lay there like a . . . well, like a skeleton. You saw where the bones were connected with the bones. But the throbbing flesh, the moving changing blood of it, you could not sense from here.

Not that these people even try, he brooded. They don't notice that they are a part of a world. Go through their lives, getting what they get. How am *I?* That is the question. The hell with what's down there, or out there, or over there—unless and until it begins to bother me.

Many lived like that. Many, rich and poor.

Oh, he conceded that there were loners, natural loners, people who didn't trespass but didn't duck in a crisis, either. They were fine. Some of *them* were fine.

But there are some others—and Charles Tyler, for his sins or his fate, was one of them—who can't help seeing all around, how things flow, how causes affect, and effects cause, and currents cross, and tendencies rise and fall. Can't help trying to *do* something that will improve the whole body. Even if it is only to sweep one town, like a good housekeeper, every day, and in spite of the dust that would settle back, still keep the place at least from being buried under its own filth and rotting entirely.

Now, now, it wasn't a bad little town. *He* watched it. He knew quite a lot that went on under those roof lids—in all-priced houses. But he kept the streets fairly safe and clean, enforcing the laws.

That was his job. He believed in it. You had to have law and the law had to be enforced. That might be the best that you could do, and not quite good enough, but that much *had* to be done.

He could see the Whitman gates from here. A bit of a crowd accumulated? Oh, sure. He wouldn't be sitting on this nest of snakes all by himself for much longer.

Well, put the boy in the hospital—for his own protection, if for nothing else. And apprehend the murderer. He sighed, turned.

Guest room. Bare. Hall closet. Nothing. He started down.

Harold Page was having a vision. He felt pretty groggy. They said he was running a pretty good fever. He guessed he must be. Sunk in the chair . . . would it be forever? . . . he kept seeing the common room at the hospital, his hospital, and the people in it. It was a pattern and not a pattern. You'd think, at first, that it was just an ordinary bunch of people.

But the difference was, each person there was a bead, sliding on its own string. It might look as if the threads were crossing, the beads touching, clustering, attracted or repelled. But it wasn't so. (Like a boy and girl could get married and all, and yet not really touch.) Well, those poor people at the hospital, each was a separate bead, sliding on his own thread, and each was very lonely and frightened.

Until the doctor came. And then the doctor, who was trained and who would know how . . . then it was as if the beads would melt and give a little. Or, the poor people would awaken to where they were and who else was there. So the pattern made a little something.

He sure hoped that he could get to be a doctor. He wondered whether he ever would. He would *like* it, very much.

Nobody moved here. Nobody spoke. Nobody connected.

Except Edie, who was trying to smile cheer and comfort to him. Harold smiled at her.

Conrad said, "No housekeeper anywhere out this way, sir." Tyler had met him in the dining room.

"You check with your man on the back, whether she left the house?"

"Thought of that." Conrad appreciated Tyler's competence. "Malone *was* on the dining room corner, all right—only you sent him down to the gates."

"Then she could have gone out the back way."

"Could have. Probably did. But . . ."

"Take a look in the cellar," said Tyler practically. "Try the outside cellar door. Maybe they heard her getting out that way." But why? he wondered.

"Right, sir. But there's something I got to thinking . . . Excuse me. The truth is, the Page kid hasn't got a perfect alibi."

"That so?"

"I don't think so. Not if it could have happened, at the hospital, around midnight? Not much later?"

"That's close. Go on."

"Well, right about then, was when I heard this dame screaming, inside. So I come in. It was only the Whitman girl, blowing her top. But see, *then* is when I searched the round room, the one halfway up. And there was nobody to see the front door, except the—what's her name, Edith?—the one who's on Page's side all the time."

"How long were you off guard?" Tyler was quick.

"Five minutes, anyhow. That's time for him to slip in the front door. Murray, on the other corner, mightn't have seen. Fact, see . . . he wasn't supposed to cover the front door. I was. So I just thought . . ."

"Uh huh," said Tyler.

(Yep, that kind of case. Timetables. And one hell of a lot of psychology, he thought gloomily.)

"What was she blowing her top about?" he asked. "The Whitman kid?"

"Well, I . . . uh . . . was a little late getting in. So I dunno." Conrad looked earnest. "I wasn't too sure what Mr. Whitman would want me to do."

Tyler didn't condemn him for being a hired hand, which he was.

Conrad was enjoying himself. He liked making reports. He liked not having the responsibility. But sounding sharp. It didn't cross his mind that he had forgotten something.

In the big room, nobody moved. Nobody spoke. And it could not hold. Edie had a gone feeling, as if she'd had a tip that something terrible was going to happen, very soon.

Then Granny, with a languid motion of her arm, held up the empty glass and Ronnie Mungo, for his manners, moved helpfully and took it from her. He put it on the table at the end of the sofa. It clicked on the wood. And Wendy convulsed. She bounced to sit up. Her hair was a great tangle. Her eyes looked hot. Immediately, there was a force loose, and what it would do, no one could know. She sent one wild look around.

Granny could *see*, and her pale hand came up and her chin up, and it was an order. So Ronnie Mungo—who had constituted himself Granny's aide-de-camp, somehow—with a closed obedient look on his face, bent over and touched Wendy on her nape.

Wendy was on her feet, like a rocket. "Who touched me?" she screamed. "Who touched me?"

Chapter Sixteen

Mrs. Beck was roused from stupor to alarm at the piercing sound of Wendy's voice.

Oh, no, no! No, no! She knew that note. What could she do? How could she stop it? She twisted, and lifted, and pain was brutal, but her hand got all the way up to the knob.

Ronnie moved to take hold of Wendy but she went whirling. She whirled back. "Ronnie . . ." A high shrill hysteria. "Let's *go. Why* can't we go?"

But now Granny had her ears turned on. "Wendy, you absolutely cannot elope. It would *not* do, at a time like this. Will someone kindly give that child a pill or a shot or something? Where is Dr. Brewster? I called him hours ago. Where is Mrs. Beck, for pity's sakes? We *pay* the woman. Teddy . . . ?"

Ted had come out of the east wing, blinking.

"We couldn't find Mrs. Beck, Mother," he said, querulously, and then, "Charles?"

Wendy whirled. Tyler was there. Conrad, behind him, was poised, watching, with his hand on the knob of the cellar door.

Wendy spun. She threw out her right arm, taut, to its fullest extension. "Look! It's the *madman!* He's *inside*, Daddy! Don't let him hurt me anymore?"

She ran. In panic. Her small feet were quick in her ridiculous little shoes. She ran straight on, toward Harold. She veered. She ran toward the two men in white coats, who waited respectfully at the bottom of the foyer steps. She veered, reversed, and ran up the stairs.

Ronnie had been drawn after her. He called up, standing under the balcony, "Oh, come off it, Wendy," like a man who had had enough, and more.

Wendy shrilled down. "You all don't think he's dangerous? Well, you are *stupid! All* of you!"

Wendy ran on upward, a flash of bright blue, vanishing like a brilliant bird in flight.

Or a bright bead, sliding . . .

And Granny screamed.

The light was bright enough to hurt, when the man opened the door and Mrs. Beck slumped forward. There was a commotion. Seemed like a lot of men. Her arm, her whole side, hurt like sixty. Two of the men were like doctors. She didn't quite pass out under their ministrations. She knew she'd better not. Oh, it didn't hurt to play as weak as she liked, until she saw a chance. Or saw whether she *had* a chance—as she thought she might. After all. After all. If you're lucky—and if you are shrewd, of course, besides.

Then they were trying to put her on a stretcher, but she fought that. She didn't want to be lying down, flat. She wanted to *see*. So they finally had her on her feet, the two of them practically carrying her. One of them had done something, so her arm wasn't quite so draggy on the pain.

She tried to look, to see what was what. Wendy wasn't here. She knew that. Which was good, probably. It was Wendy who mattered. Mrs. Beck could handle all the rest of them. Easily, she thought, with contempt.

Now, she could see the madman, over there. He had his eyes shut. So they had him. The old lady had screamed; now she just sat and trembled. Let her. She didn't matter much. Mr. Whitman was there, looking as if he didn't know enough to come in out of the rain, which he didn't, in her opinion. *He* didn't count. There was Edith, and Edith said, "Mrs. Beck, it was Wendy who fought Myra. Wasn't it? *Please,* say so."

Then Myra's brother yelled, "I'm in charge here."

Mrs. Beck thought, *They don't know a thing.*

"We'll get you to the hospital and you'll be looked after, right away," the Chief of Police was saying, in a stern, but respectful manner. "But do you think you could answer a question or two?"

Mrs. Beck had had her clue and wanted nothing better. "I can answer," she said stolidly. (After all, there was only one thing to say.)

Tyler said, "Did you fall, Mrs. Beck?"

"I was pushed," she said.

"How did it happen?"

"I thought I heard something." (She'd keep Wendy all the way out.) "So I went to see. But I made a mistake." (That's right, she had—but all was not lost yet.) "The madman was in the house, all right. But he was behind me."

"*He* pushed you?"

"That's right, sir."

(Mrs. Beck saw Edith sit down on the ottoman with a kind of funny smile on her face. Well, pooh to her, thought the housekeeper.)

The other man (one of the guards, she remembered) said, "That cellar door was locked, sir. Unlocked it myself, with Mr. Whitman's key. She couldn't . . ."

"Lock it from the outside," said Tyler. "Right." He began to clear a way, until Mrs. Beck could plainly see the madman, who opened his eyes and looked up at her with a funny expression. Kind of a steady, sad look.

"Do you know this man?" barked Tyler.

"Yes, sir. That's him. That's Harold Page." And the madman tipped his head, like he was listening hard for something she wasn't saying.

The guard said, "Excuse me. Mr. Whitman's gun is down there. Cellar floor."

"Why is that?" Tyler said.

(But this was easy.) "Well, sir, *I* took it, because we all knew how dangerous he was. But he got at me from behind. Tried to kill me, I guess." She played fading out weakly. (But I don't kill so easy as some, she thought to herself.)

"All right. Now, we'll get you taken care of."

Tyler was in charge. The men wanted her on the stretcher. So Mr. Mungo and the guard fellow were holding it. Mrs. Beck let herself be tilted and lifted up. All right, she was hurt. Let them make a fuss over her.

Oh, Mrs. Beck knew she was riding on the wind. It all depended on whether Wendy would keep her mouth shut. But one thing, for sure, they were both in it, and if one told, the other had something to tell, too. Mrs. Beck was not consciously a philosopher, but a principle that she believed appeared (although not as such) in her mind. Everybody looked out for himself first. Naturally. So that was what *Wendy* would do. Barring one of her fits, that is. But Mrs. Beck had hope that all would be well. She would get back as soon as she could. Who knows? Maybe right away, with a cast on. The old lady never listened to anybody. Mr. Whitman never *did* anything. They'd probably dope Wendy up, or get the doctor to do it. It would be all right. She was feeling lucky.

She saw one thing, as she was sinking down. The madman was looking sorry for her. Well, he better be sorry for himself, she thought. And put him out of her mind. He was mad. He didn't count. Nobody would listen to him.

But when she saw Mr. Mungo's face, right close, she couldn't help murmuring to him, "Tell Miss Wendy not to be afraid. Be *sure?* Becky will be back to take care . . . Tell her? Poor lamb."

Mr. Mungo ducked away and said to the men, like the gentleman he was, "Easy. Easy. Here, let me open the door for you."

Mrs. Beck lay back, cozy to the pain.

Edie watched them go, without having said a word.

She had just heard an enormous lie. She knew, of her own sure knowledge, that Harold hadn't pushed the housekeeper down the cellar stairs. She, herself, had left Mrs. Beck in the kitchen and gone to him.

She guessed she knew who *had* done it. (Screaming and shaking and crying that somebody was in the tree!) Wendy must have done it. Just then. No wonder, that shaking! But why Wendy had tried to kill her slave and worshiper, Edie could not imagine.

She had given up any more screaming—for herself. She felt stunned by the weight of the truth of this house, that must fall. Must fall.

She realized that Tyler had his eye on her. He said crisply, "I've got to do what I've got to do."

"I know." She knew. Another accusation against Harold Page. Enough and more, to hold him. She would give her testimony later, in due course, in good time, and proper order. It would still be her word against Mrs. Beck's. No proof. Her word and Harold's, if his could only count.

Tyler seemed to flush. Did he *want* her to fight, now? "I'm holding him for Myra, too," he said. "Suspicion of murder. There's a hole in his alibi."

"No," she said, wonderingly.

"*You* proved he was inside, all right," Tyler said, almost angrily, "in time to have a go at Mrs. Beck. But last night, the guard came off the front door and searched your room. Did you let Page in then? After he'd been busy in the hospital?"

(Damn it, thought Tyler, *I'm* playing the game. The timetables, the loopholes, the ins-and-outs of opportunities. And it's flimsy. The truth is, and always was, *some people wouldn't do some things.* Which is not evidence.)

Edie said, "No, sir, I did not."

Her passivity annoyed him. He said, "We'll take a chance and let the patrol car get Page where he's going."

"That's okay," said Harold Page, almost eagerly.

But Tyler went to the mantel and stared at the water glass. He snapped at the other uniformed man, who had reappeared from the east wing at last. "Go get Jansen. Then take Page. And I want Edith Thompson down at the station for further interrogation. Now. And I want Mungo, too."

"Yes, sir."

Tyler turned and snarled at Edie. "No more questions?"

"Well, there's one," said Edie, almost listlessly. "May Harold please have his shoes on? Cousin Ted, you know where his shoes are." She saw Tyler blink surprise.

"Shoes?" said Cousin Ted. "Oh. Yes. Certainly." He wiggled to his feet. "Oh dear, I forgot, Charles. Found them in the turret room. And that's how we knew . . . er, something. I—I forget. But I do know exactly where I put them. Yes. I'm sure I do."

Cousin Ted went off to his own quarters. Granny, outraged by all these indignities, had obviously turned off her hearing aid again and was stony in her chair.

"I'll get my things?" said Edie to the Chief, half-question, half-announcement.

He nodded, gloomily. As she started up the stairs, she saw him turn and stare again at the water glass.

Doesn't mean a thing, Edie conceded. Not now, when they have discovered a time when Harold could have come in, and then put his prints on the glass, or anywhere else, at any time between midnight and morning.

She didn't get it, Tyler was thinking. She missed that one. She missed two points about the shoes. One, *we* searched, after Myra was found, and they sure weren't here then. Two . . . *Augh!* He shook his big head. Order, he had to have. And would. Order and reason he would have and reason would go to work.

He supposed he'd take the glass. He didn't need it.

He thought, A glass of cold water she gave a hot and thirsty boy, on a hot day—because it figures. There are some things that some people *will* do. And you *know* it, but it's not evidence.

Well, get on with it. Better tell the old lady what's up. He crossed swiftly.

Edie saw him cross and heard Granny say, "I will not listen, Charles. I cannot and I will not budge, either."

I guess you can't, thought Edie sadly.

She went into the turret room to get her things. What things? Couldn't think. Purse? Wrap? Toothbrush? Nightwear? Anyway, she was leaving.

It was sad, in a way. These people were the only ones of her blood in the world. But she had put herself against them and there she would always be, even when the truth came out.

Oh, it would come out. In questions and answers. In long ordeal. The newspapers. The time it would take. The torment. The tarnish. And now another charge. Edie's word and Harold's word against Mrs. Beck's, now. Against the victim's word? Who *protected* Wendy?

Wendy was scared? No law for her? *She* could push a woman down stone stairs and the woman would protect her? The family would protect her. The money would protect her. Her youth, her looks, her childish will. Her very callousness would protect her.

No, no. Not forever. Sooner or later, in a courtroom if need be—somewhere—the law must be for Wendy, too. *Some* law.

She rummaged in her dresser drawers. What did you take when you didn't know where you were going, for how long? In fact, she snatched up her purse and took her light coat off its hanger.

When she stepped out upon the balcony and closed the wooden door softly behind her, she knew that Granny was still haughtily deaf, and silent in the chair. Cousin Ted not there at all, and no cop in uniform, either. Harold waiting, slumped on the chair-arm heavy of head. Tyler was standing at the steps to the foyer, with his back to the stairs.

But all of them faded from her attention.

Wendy was poised, halfway down the lower flight. And in the heaviness of the silent air, Wendy said, in the wheedling, little-girl's voice she knew how to use when she wanted it, "Who was that, Uncle Charles?"

Edie saw Tyler turn, with a swift defensive motion, to look at her. He did not speak. (He was no uncle of hers, thank God!)

Edie had said nothing and made no noise but Wendy suddenly turned her head far around and looked up at her.

Little Wendy. Her grown body, handsome in the bright blue. Her hand, tight on the iron rail. Her dark hair swirling. Her face, her pretty, vicious face, and her lost and terrible eyes . . .

Tyler was thinking, in quick flashes. *This* kook knew what was down cellar. Jumpy as a cat! Did Mungo know, too? Didn't he take the trouble to give me his *alibi* for this pushing? But the point is . . . my point . . . did Mungo or the housekeeper do it to Myra? *One of them* wasn't going to have Myra telling the truth about Wendy Whitman. Now, why not? And which one? I have to hold the Page kid. In the face of what I've got, I have to do that. But this Wendy could tell me what I want to know.

Will I get at her? Using an assault charge, say? Nope. Let me take one step . . . and psychiatrists, three deep. Prominent family. They can afford it. The best "understanding" that money can buy. Oh, the headshrinkers may wrap it up some day and give it to me for a lollipop. I don't want to wait. What's to be done?

Then Wendy said, "Why won't you tell me it was Becky? I saw her. On a stretcher. What's the matter, Uncle Charles? Please?"

Tyler kept looking up at her, now very intent and concentrated. Intuitive in spite of himself, he had the inspiration to say nothing.

So Wendy twisted. Edie looked down into those eyes, calm and intent. There was a sudden bond between her and the big policeman, as strong as iron. He had not spoken. Neither would Edie speak. *There was a law.*

Wendy twitched, twisted to look down again. She was pinned in beams of silent deep attention. She drew a nervous breath. "Harold?" she said on a rising whine.

But it was too late. The boy was half-unconscious. She couldn't reach him. Not anymore.

And heavy must fall.

Wendy pulled herself into a pouting chiding mood. "Oh, Uncle Charles, you're not believing what *she* said? Why, she's just lying!" Tyler did not move an eyelash. "*Becky* is."

Now Wendy fluttered down toward him, and he watched with a cold heart. Sex-kittying will get you nowhere, either, he thought, but it felt sad.

"*I* didn't push her," cried Wendy, hitting his sad silence like a wall. "Whyever would I push Becky down the cellar stairs?"

Chapter Seventeen

SHE WAS the destroyer. Now, they watched her destroy.

Wendy went whirling on the carpet to her grandmother. "Granny, *you're* not going to believe what some stupid servant says about me?"

But Granny had one little hand curved to shade her eyes. She made no response. She hadn't heard a word.

"But she's a murderess!" shrieked Wendy. "You can't believe *her*."

Cousin Ted came out of the east wing, with Harold's shoes in his right hand. He stopped in his tracks.

"Daddy!" cried Wendy. "She is. She is. She is. She told me."

Ted Whitman, in the limbo of total incomprehension, giggled. It was a terrible sound. Wendy reeled.

But Granny had seen her, now, and leaned forward. "Go upstairs to your room," she said commandingly. "The doctor is coming to see to you."

"But she told me," wailed Wendy, drifting, pleading. "How she got into the hospital, with her white uniform and everything. *Becky* did."

Tyler was pulled a few steps toward the middle of the room. But then he stopped and simply stood and listened. His face accepted nothing. His instinct knew. Edie was frozen on the balcony.

"She even made a nurse's cap," said Wendy, "to fool them. And she did something to Myra. She *told* me. *I* didn't know she was going to do it."

Out in the driveway, Dr. Brewster's car had pulled up. He was in the ambulance where he had taken over and was expertly attending to Mrs. Beck's arm and shoulder. Ronnie Mungo stood by, as if to be helpful.

Inside, Wendy Whitman was attending to herself.

"*I* didn't push her. *He* did. Harold did. He was in the house. Edie let him in, so it's *her* fault."

Now the girl, in her bright blue, with her hair flying, was turning and turning in the middle of the floor, turning to each person in succession and none of them spoke to her.

(Harold Page was in a nightmare, he thought, probably.)

"But Becky didn't *know* he was in the house, you see? And that's why she thought it must be me. That's why she said that."

The housekeeper had not said "that."

"What's the matter?" screeched Wendy at all the silent faces. "I tell you she is lying! She's a common murderess!"

Her eyes began to roll. She seemed to grow sly. "Oh, you don't know, but she was going to *kill* him. Kill him, too." Wendy was pointing at Harold Page. "She took Daddy's gun. And she was going to kill him. She said, 'Put it on the madman.' She said 'Put it on the . . .'"

Tyler seemed to sigh. She glanced at him, the wheels whizzed in her pretty head, behind her sick and evil eyes.

"I didn't want her," Wendy said, like the old Wendy, willful and petulant. "I didn't feel like taking *her*. What would be the use of going away, if *she* came, too?" Then her prancing feet were still and she began to shake her head from side to side, and her hair flew. "Oh, she shouldn't have done that to Myra," said Wendy with grave disapproval. "*I* didn't say she should."

She looked up at Edie and stamped her foot. "Don't you understand? Becky just wants to get *out* of this whole *mess!*" cried Wendy. "That's all she wants. She doesn't care *what* she says!"

It was a nice description of Wendy's own behavior. But nobody spoke.

"Look," the lost girl said, suddenly woeful, "how she beats me. Becky is so mean. You don't know." Her right hand went to her left forearm and began to twist at the flesh through the thin blue fabric. "She often beats me. Look at the marks." The hand clawed under the chin. "See what she does? Daddy, please don't let her beat me anymore?"

Harold was closing his ears to echoes, his heart upon the pain he thought he dreamed again.

Edie thought, Oh no, no more! But was still. It held.

Until Ronnie Mungo came dashing in; Tyler turned. Ron said, "Excuse me. Dr. Brewster is out there with Mrs.—"

"Ronnie?" said Wendy. Her voice became gruesomely gay. Her body became seductive. She sidled toward him. Tyler stepped out of the way. (The big man looked ill.) "Ronnie, there you are, darling.

Why don't we just go, now? It's perfectly all right. Nobody believes what Becky says. She is just a crazy old fool. So we can go to Mexico and be married and go to Paris—and everything?"

Ronnie Mungo's foot went back and groped for the step to the foyer.

"I told you I didn't care," said Wendy, walking toward him with her hips swaying. "If you and Myra were shacking up once, why should I care about that? *She* cared. Myra didn't want me to have you." Wendy giggled. "She was stupid."

Ronnie was looking down at her as if he saw a serpent. Cousin Ted plopped into a chair. Fallen.

"But she's dead, now," said Wendy gaily.

Then Wendy seemed to know that this world was not going to be with her. That she was all alone, in some other. "I didn't mean . . ." She looked around in terror. "I didn't mean . . ." Her arms flew up. "I-never-did-mean-anything," said Wendy, in a different voice, with a great deadening. And with a seeping out of all her false, bright, desperate force, she began to fall.

Ronnie caught her. He said, over her head to Tyler, "What shall I do with her?" as if she were rubbish.

Harold Page had lifted his head. His skin was tight to the bone and of the bone's color. But he made no sound.

The doctor came into the house. They took Wendy to the foyer, as if these men, not members of the family—the doctor, the policeman, and even Ronnie Mungo—knew that the sight and sound of her, now, was better hidden.

Edie went quietly back into the turret room. She hunted in the folds of her peignoir and found what she was after.

When she came out, the doctor was consulting with Granny. He was a middle-aged man with a soothing manner and a nervous, realistic eye. "Can't handle it here. You really should not try, Mrs. Whitman. I don't advise it. You must think of yourself."

"This place you speak of," said Granny briskly, "is it respectable? We can afford what it costs, of course."

Edie went down the lower flight and up into the foyer and around the corner of the wall. They had put Wendy on a silly little Victorian settee. Edie did not look at her. She looked at Tyler, whose eyes met hers with patient courage. She held out to him the paper napkin, folded and pinned, to make a boat or a hat. Or a nurse's cap.

"This is for you," she said gravely.

Tyler took it. Understood. Nodded. Did not smile. Went swiftly out the front door to where the ambulance waited, on his orders, for him to come.

Edie heard Wendy's little-girl's voice saying to the young cop, whose back was stiff to his duty and whose face was not telling how he felt, "I was always pretty." She sounded like a child, a real one, beaten and miserable, hunting for one tiny grain of assurance, some one little good thing, from which to take a taste of pleasure, a bit of the nourishment of pride.

Edie stumbled back into the big room, passing the doctor, who was hustling out of it. Cousin Ted had not moved. He lay in the chair as he had fallen, looking like the frog-footman. Edie went to him and gently took from his unresisting hand the shoes. Her brain began to move with a jolt. Harold's shoes. Well! She would hardly have been letting him in at the front door at the very moment that his shoes were being found in her room. But his alibi didn't matter anymore.

She knelt before Harold, with the shoes. He bent and took them from her. He fumbled at the laces. Edie guessed that he would like to hide his face, so she rose and walked apart.

Outside, Tyler had made short work of Mrs. Beck. He had the paper hat. He had the news that Wendy was talking, which the woman had feared, and therefore quickly believed. She agreed, vindictively, that *Wendy* had pushed her down the stairs. (Tyler had not doubted it.)

Wendy was out of his hands, but off his streets. He hadn't much fear that Wendy would be back. Soon or ever. It seemed to him that it was very late, too late, for her. And she hadn't killed his sister. Now he bent his skills upon the one who had, and Mrs. Beck soon began to boast about her method. He was able to refrain from touching her. He told the men to take her away. He had "gotten" enough to arrest her. He would get more, much more. He would "get" her, solidly, beyond the shadow of a doubt. He didn't think that Mrs. Beck would go to the chair. But *she* would be off the streets, he vowed. Forever. That was his job, wasn't it? To enforce the law, and protect the innocent, as early as he could.

Then he said to Mungo, who was hanging around, "All right. Let's get down to it. Did Myra threaten you?"

Mungo was trying to look blank, but Tyler wasn't having any of that. "Did she threaten to tell about your affair and bust up your impending marriage?"

"No, sir, she did not," Mungo said, his tanned face switching over to earnest honesty, now that he knew that Tyler knew.

"She was there Wednesday night. You spoke to Myra."

"Yes, sir. I've said so." Under Tyler's icy eye, Ronnie went on. "The fact is, Myra tried to . . . er . . . convince me that it wasn't a good idea to marry Wendy Whitman. She was right, I think." Ronnie flew one eyebrow.

"And . . . ?" Tyler used his terrible patience.

"Well, sir, Wendy didn't much like that. You see"—now there would be the confidence, man to man—"that's why *I* was so sure that Page hadn't got in, as they thought. Wendy was spoiling for some kind of battle when they . . . er . . . put me out."

"And you went?"

"Yes, sir." Mungo tried on his charming grin, carefully seasoned with a touch of rue.

"So nothing was said about your past association with my sister? How did Wendy know it?"

"Well, in fact, it was Wendy who did say something. On Wednesday. She seemed to know all about it, and said she *had* known for a long time . . . and couldn't care less. You . . . er . . . heard her."

"How did she know?"

"I can't say, sir. Wendy was wild at Myra for being what she called a 'hypocrite.'" Then Mungo added, with a touch of noble sternness, "But she was wrong. Myra was a good friend of mine, I think. And I'm sorry."

"But you didn't think fit to tell me your strong suspicion? Who had knocked your good friend down."

Mungo had an odd look. As if to say, "Come now, really!"

"Because you had to marry the money, eh?" snapped Tyler. "You couldn't offend it. You needed the money bad, from what I hear."

"I did and I do," said Ronnie and shrugged. He looked bleak.

"Why did you stick your neck out, trying that fool stunt of getting Page out of here? You don't seem the type to stick out a lot of neck—to me."

Ronnie said rapidly, "As soon as I heard that Myra was dead . . . and *I* thought it was from the injuries that Wendy had . . . er . . . probably caused . . . Well, I knew it was going to blow. *Wendy* was going to blow, I mean."

Tyler thought he was being somewhat honest, at the moment.

"So there was this kid Page. *I* knew he was just unlucky. In fact, I knew all about what they had done to him before. So, when a damsel in distress appealed to me . . ." Ronnie began to look uncomfortable. "That's about all I can say, sir. If I said I felt like being the Good Samaritan, on an impulse, you wouldn't believe it. Call it a challenge. I didn't . . . think it through."

"I'll call it," said Tyler dryly. "Let me see. The Whitman money. Myra wasn't going to get it—being dead. Wendy wasn't going to get it, or her mother's money, either—being nuts. Ted will have to be a kind of ward of the estate when old Mrs. Whitman goes. He'll never be in charge. The one (you thought?) who will get all of it . . . (and this came to you like an uncontrollable impulse, eh?) . . . that one is Miss Edith Thompson. And there she was. In distress, too. Why let her get disinherited? Recoup your losses. Right?"

But Edith is too smart for *him,* thought Tyler confidently.

Ronnie said hastily, "But old Mrs. Whitman wasn't—"

"Dead," snapped Tyler, "and isn't, yet. Also, it slipped your mind there's a baby who is an heir. Forgot? Oh, you didn't think it *through*—I guess."

Tyler half turned away. He had better not touch this fellow. But then swiftly, he turned back and pounced. "Now, you tell me how *you* knew what they had done to Page before. You mean at the time of the divorce? This beating? Nothing got around. I didn't hear it."

"No, sir, it was a simple divorce action on the grounds of 'mental cruelty.' Not that detail—the way it worked out. But they clobbered him with it, just the same. He had no chance. Wendy lied when she said he beat her, and Mrs. Beck lied herself blue to back that up. The Whitmans . . . er . . . chose to believe them. Page had to go quietly."

"But you knew all about it? Who told you?"

"Oh . . ." Ronnie blinked. "Why, Myra told me."

"When?"

"Why, at the time." Ronnie saw nothing amiss.

"I see," said Charles Tyler heavily. At the time, Myra had been engaged to the Whitman money. Hadn't offended it with the truth. Her brother's bitter sorrow came out in anger. "You also knew that Beck was down cellar, maybe hurt. Didn't you?" he roared.

"No, sir. No, sir."

"Come on."

"I thought I heard something. I didn't *know*."

"You need a little practice in Samaritanism, wouldn't you say?" said Tyler, with bitter contempt.

"Sorry," said Mungo, slipping out from under, the voice light, the eyes curious. (Why do you care, hurt or not? Especially when now you know she killed your sister. The foxy eyes were wondering.)

"What a specimen you are," said Tyler. "Get in there. Tell Page he is free to do what he wants, will you? So long as I get his statement tomorrow. And Edith, too."

"I'll be very glad to, sir," said Ronnie Mungo smoothly.

Charles Tyler thought, He's one of those. He isn't glad. He isn't sorry. Doesn't judge, of course—not he. Wouldn't get that much involved. Laissez-faire. Wouldn't help the wronged—without profit in sight. Or the suffering. Doesn't dream of stopping the wicked. Wouldn't have the word in his vocabulary. One of those.

And so had his sister Myra been . . . one of those.

He reached, in pain, for charity. Perhaps not totally. She hadn't cared what happened to Harold Page. But maybe she *had* been a good friend of Mungo's. Maybe, for him, she had made one try. He didn't know. There might have been that one flash of concern for another living person. At *some* risk to herself. She had died of it. Tyler had doubt, but he would give her the benefit. She was dead.

Deliver us? he said, beneath his breath. Then . . . went about his business.

Chapter Eighteen

In the big room, Granny was saying, "Dreadful woman, putting such nonsense into little Wendy's head. Such *vulgar* lies about poor Myra. Well, she's gone. We have arrangements to make, Ted. Will you speak to Charles about the funeral, or shall I?"

Ted stirred. His mother had told him what to think and gratefully he began to think it. "Lies. Dreadful. Poor sensitive little Wendy. No wonder she was upset! Did I?"—Ted seemed to lose his grip entirely for a moment—"tell you that Myra is dead? Oh. Well.

Yes." His mother had also told him what to do. "We must, of course, make the arrangements. Don't worry, Mother. I'll see to everything."

He was like a balloon that had partially collapsed but now received new air. He got up and trotted toward the foyer. Wendy wasn't there now. They had taken her outside.

"Ted?" called Granny after him. "Teddy? It would be best not to speak to any newsmen."

Ted turned on the steps. He touched his eyebrows with an arched hand. "Oh, Mother . . . I am not *absolutely* stupid."

Poor man, thought Edie, I rather hope that he is.

When Ted was gone, Granny got up with spry energy. "A great deal to attend to," she muttered. *She,* of course, would see that somebody saw to everything.

"Can I help you?" said Edie, without thinking about it.

"I think not, Edith," said Granny, with a frosty look. "I shall go to my room. As soon as my lawyer arrives, I shall be able to manage. After all, I retain him."

She started toward the east wing. Nothing could be given her. She hired what she wanted.

Harold was still bent over, one shoe on, his fingers awkward on the laces. Granny halted to look down at him. A frown creased her pale forehead. "I have always been generous," she said. "No one can say . . ."

For a moment, Edith thought the old lady would break under the weight, but Granny did not. "*I* am paying for that child's special education," said Granny briskly. "Later on, I suppose there are persons who can be employed to look after him."

Oh no, you can't! You can't, thought Edie. Oh, you poor old woman, you can't do that!

Ronnie Mungo came bounding in. "The doctor thinks it best to take Wendy along, right now, Mrs. Whitman, while she—er—isn't minding what they do. I am sorry. Very sorry, ma'am."

The old lady was looking at him in her old way, her eyes shifting.

"About Myra and me," said Ron, softly, "I can't imagine where poor disturbed Wendy got such an idea. It is just . . . not true, you know."

"It makes no difference," said old Mrs. Whitman with great conviction and authority, "whether it is true or false, as long as you don't mention it."

She swept away. Her creed, thought Edie, and seemed to have a revelation. Lila Whitman was the source of the evil in this house. Cruel and lazy. Supping with the devil, by a spoon not long enough.

But she was gone and Ronnie Mungo turned to the two of them who were left, with a resumption of jaunty good cheer. "Mrs. Beck broke down, all right. Tyler was too much for *her*. So Tyler says to tell you"—now, he addressed Harold—"that he'll want your statement tomorrow. But you are free."

"Oh yes. Oh yes. Oh yes." Harold rammed his swollen foot into the other shoe at last, and the pain was fine. It seemed to clear his head. "Thank you," he said.

Edie began to feel fiercely practical. "Will you help me?" she said to Ronnie, demandingly. "I must get him to a doctor and maybe find a place for him to stay."

"You must?" The voice was light, the gaze curious, as if he were examining a species he had not often encountered.

"Will you take us, in your car? And please, catch that Dr. Brewster. Is he still here? Ask him where to go."

Ron was still gazing at her.

Are you weighing, thought Edie, whether it is necessary or advisable, or any special "kick," to help me? "Will you *do* it," she cried, "for *no* reason?"

He said, lightly, "Of course, fair damsel," grinned his mischievous, mocking grin, saluted and started for the foyer.

Then you can run along and play, she said to herself. As if he had heard, Ron glanced back over his shoulder. She felt the curtain falling. He went on.

Edie ran up to the turret room to throw her things into her suitcases. She worked very fast.

Now she could mourn. Myra is dead, who shouldn't have died. And I'm sorry. I'm sorry. I didn't know her, but I do know she shouldn't have been cut down, just cut down by those two. People come in all kinds. But what shall we do with the destroyers? Call them unfortunate? Which they are.

My father labored all his life trying to help the unfortunate. But I am seeing too much destruction, too many unfortunates, rich or poor, who carelessly destroy. How shall we stop them before the compassionate are all their servants, as well as their victims?

Oh, I am not where I want to be, not in the front lines. I want to count, to make a difference, a better difference. I'm doing too little, patching and mending, and failing too often, because it's too late— and too late for too many. Study, then? Find out how? Begin sooner? Work with the new ones, the littlest ones, the ones not lost yet . . . where the chances are? Shall I learn to work with children?

Oh, for that I'll need more patience. I've got the energy, I'm boiling with it, but it needs harnessing. It needs to go where it can feel it matters. That's *my* harnessing. I'm not my long-suffering father and not my patient, easygoing mother, either. I am me . . . and I must do what I can. I wish . . .

I wish I had a man like Charles Tyler. Not he . . . but like him. That is not absurd. Not absurd at all. Not at all.

She came, thoughtfully, out on the balcony with her bags, the big one and the small. Harold Page was waiting down there, all alone.

You didn't get destroyed, thought Edie. Maybe, once, when you were very small, somebody gave you an everlasting clue?

She went down to him. "There's one thing," she heard herself saying. "You'll get to raise your little son, Harold. I'm sure of it. You can win. Could you think about *that?*" She was wishing to lift his spirits, now.

"Yes," the boy said, "I will think about that. In a minute." He looked exhausted. "You don't hate her now, either. Do you, Edie?"

"No," she burst, "but I hate *something*. I hate the rotten misery of spoiled lives. Human beings are not *supposed* to grow up to be such monsters—such dangerous, unhappy monsters."

"Do you think," said Harold as if he hadn't heard her, "they'll figure out what it was that Wendy wanted?"

Edie felt impatient with him. You survived. You have things to do. Get on with it. It was only your bad luck, that Wendy took a notion to run away with you—for fun. But Mrs. Beck "couldn't approve"—so . . .

Then the whole story of Wendy flashed clear into her mind. A baby, here. A little new one. The only child, with a pair of silly parents, in a cold old house dominated by a grandmother who bought everything. Who had hired a woman to raise the child. Who couldn't be bothered, hadn't even noticed, how the servant had become the master, how Mrs. Beck had twisted her own solitary meaningless life around Wendy's, like a strangling poisonous vine.

Oh, pity, thought Edie, to have been born into this. To have been ever indulged, from the beginning, to have escaped justice, to have been denied it, to have lacked it. And then to be forever told, by that powerful, sick hired woman, that nothing so difficult, or so sweet, as a struggling life was for you.

She no longer thought that Wendy had run away with Harold Page for fun, or money. But instinctively, for her own salvation. And had not made it. Wendy had been going to marry Ronnie Mungo, not for love nor money, but for her own last chance. He would have married the money. Wendy would have got away. *Anywhere*. To shuck off the past? To go somewhere else, looking for the turning-around place? Too late. Too late. She hadn't made it. Had followed bad with worse, spiraling downward. How could she have made it—all alone—never having had a clue?

"What Wendy wanted?" said Edie aloud. "I think she told us."

The boy was all right. He could take it.

"What she wanted," said Edie, slowly, "was only human. Only human. Wendy wanted to mean something. But she . . . was a prisoner in a tower. Don't you think so?"